PENGUIN CLASSICS

TALES OF THE MARVELLOUS
AND
NEWS OF THE STRANGE

MALCOLM C. LYONS is also the translator of the Penguin Classics edition of the complete *Arabian Nights*. He was Sir Thomas Adams's Professor of Arabic at Cambridge University and is a life fellow of Pembroke College, Cambridge. He is one of the world's leading experts on classical Arabic literature.

ROBERT IRWIN's books include *For Lust of Knowing: The Orientalists and Their Enemies*, *The Middle East in the Middle Ages*, *The Arabian Nights: A Companion* and (as editor) *The Penguin Anthology of Classical Arabian Literature*. He also introduced and edited the Penguin Classics *Arabian Nights*.

Tales of the Marvellous
and
News of the Strange

Translated by
MALCOLM C. LYONS
and with an Introduction by
ROBERT IRWIN

PENGUIN BOOKS

PENGUIN CLASSICS

UK | USA | Canada | Ireland | Australia
India | New Zealand | South Africa

Penguin Books is part of the Penguin Random House group of companies
whose addresses can be found at global.penguinrandomhouse.com.

This translation first published in Penguin Classics 2014
This edition published in Penguin Classics 2015
001

Translation copyright © Malcolm C. Lyons, 2014
Introduction, Further Reading and Glossary copyright © Robert Irwin, 2014
All rights reserved

Set in 9.35/12.49 pt Adobe Sabon
Typeset by Jouve (UK), Milton Keynes
Printed in Great Britain by Clays Ltd, St Ives plc

ISBN: 978-0-141-39504-3

www.greenpenguin.co.uk

Contents

TALES OF THE MARVELLOUS
AND
NEWS OF THE STRANGE

Introduction

Wonders

Here are wonders and mysteries indeed. The first mystery is the name of this book. The medieval Arabic manuscript which contains *Tales of the Marvellous* has lost its first page, and consequently the title of this story collection is not known for certain. But the opening lines of its page of contents, after praising Allah and the Prophet and his Companions, boasts that this book contains 'tales of the marvellous and news of the strange' ('al-hikayat al-'ajiba wa'l-akhbar al-ghariba'). *'Ajiba* is an adjective which means 'marvellous' or 'amazing', and its cognate plural noun *'aja'ib*, or marvels, is the term used to designate an important genre of medieval Arabic literature that dealt with all manner of marvels that challenged human understanding, including magic, the realms of the *jinn*, marvels of the sea, strange fauna and flora, great monuments of the past, automata, hidden treasures, grotesqueries and uncanny coincidences.

There are many instances of the marvellous and the supernatural in the Qur'an. For example, in the Sura of the Cave (18) the story of the Men of the Cave is cryptically alluded to:

> Or dost thou think the Men of the Cave
> And Er-Rakeem were among Our signs a wonder?

The Men of the Cave are usually identified with the Seven Sleepers of Ephesus, Christians who took refuge in a cave from persecution at the hands of the Emperor Decius and awoke many years later. (Er-Rakeem is perhaps the name of the dog who accompanied them.) More generally the Qur'an repeatedly called upon believers to marvel at what God had created – as in these lines from the Sura of the All Merciful (55):

He let forth the two seas that meet together,
Between them a barrier they do not overpass.
O which of your Lord's bounties will you and you deny?
From them come forth the pearl and the coral.
O which of your Lord's bounties will you and you deny?
His too are the ships that run, raised up in the sea like landmarks.
O which of your Lord's bounties will you and you deny?

Creation is filled with clear signs for 'those who will reflect'. And, of course, the Qur'an itself is one of God's marvels. Extraordinary things were signs of God's creative power. To marvel at God's creation was then a pious act.

Marvels featured prominently in both medieval non-fiction and fiction; the literature of the marvels of the sea constituted an important sub-genre of 'aja'ib. For example, the late tenth-century 'Aja'ib al-Hind (Marvels of India), attributed to the sea captain Burzug ibn Shahriyar, presented alleged facts about the Sea of Fire, whales, mermaids, cannibals, cattle-eating snakes, ritual suicides and so forth. In practice, the wonders of the sea also encompassed the wonders of India. Tall stories from the Persian Gulf, Indian Ocean, the Indian subcontinent and the Spice Islands provided entertainment, as well as occasions for pious reflection. Later whole encyclopedias of marvels were to be compiled from shorter works on the subject. The most famous of these was 'Aja'ib al-makhluqat wa gharaib al-mawjudat (Marvellous Things of Creation and Wondrous Things of Existence) by Zakariyya al-Qazwini (d.1283). Such purportedly factual reports were to furnish the basis for the adventures of Sindbad the Sailor and other fictions. The first page of Tales of the Marvellous, in praising God, stated:

His miracles have spread everywhere, his marvellous works on land and by sea, the marvels of his perfect works in every direction and every country, all these attest that the blessed and most high God is One, Eternal, Unique, and Master of All. Consider that, then, ye who know how to see.

'Sa'id Son of Hatim al-Bahili' explicitly begins as a marvels-of-the-sea story, as the Umaiyad caliph tells his vizier: 'I want you to bring me an Arab seafarer who can tell me about the wonders and the perils of the sea and to do it now. It may be that this will cure my sleeplessness.' (But this story soon changes into quite a different yet still marvellous narrative.) In the third of the Quest stories, the narrator who had left his own country in search of marvels ends up in Serendib, where he encounters an idol worshipper who tells him: 'I am a man who searches for wonders and marvels just as you do.' The Talisman Mountain, which features in the story of that name in this collection, is a variant on the fateful Magnetic Mountain that appears in mariners' yarns and in *The Thousand and One Nights* as the 'Story of the Third Dervish'.

In the Sindbad stories (which Antoine Galland translated from a separate Arabic manuscript but which he probably also knew from a seventeenth-century Turkish manuscript of *The Thousand and One Nights* and which he added to his French translation of the Arabic manuscript of *The Thousand and One Nights*) it is not only the monsters that are marvellous in Sindbad's travels, but also the trees and plants, and the amazing natural wealth of the islands and littorals of the Indian Ocean. 'O which of your Lord's bounties will you and you deny?' There is perhaps a further latent sense in all this. Just as Sindbad felt moved to admire the handiwork of God who created him, so the storyteller's audience were being called upon to admire the inventiveness of the world conjured up by Sindbad's real creator, the storyteller. Marvels were, of course, the stock-in-trade of *The Thousand and One Nights*, and most of the marvels related therein, such as the lady in the casket, the *jinni* in the bottle or the flying horse, were pure fictions. Yet some of them were based on what purported to be fact. For example, the story of the expedition to the City of Brass and the account of how the Abbasid caliph al-Ma'mun tried to pull down the pyramids of Egypt are found not only in the *Nights*, but also in serious works of non-fiction, such as al-Mas'udi's tenth-century chronicle *Muruj al-Dhahab* (*The Meadows of Gold*). We should also bear in mind that the boundaries between fact and fiction were not as clearly drawn then as now. It was common in the medieval Arab literary world to present fantasy as fact. Even in modern times there are those who have been reluctant to recognize fantasy stories as fictions. In 1962 the American novelist Paul Bowles got to know Larbi Layachi, a watchman in Tangier. When Bowles explained how the plots of films were usually made up, Layachi was particularly struck by the fact that it was not forbidden to lie when making a film. Then something else struck him:

'And books, like the books you write,' he pursued. 'They are all lies too?'

'They're stories, like *The Thousand and One Nights*. You don't call them lies, do you?'

'No, because they're true. They happened long ago when the world was different from the way it is now, that's all.'

I did not pursue the point.'[1]

What the Manuscript Is

The German Arabist Hellmut Ritter discovered the unique manuscript of the *Hikayat* in a library in Istanbul (MS Aya Sofia MS no. 3397) and publicized his discovery at a conference of Orientalists in 1933. The anonymous manuscript is not complete, for, besides the title page, the second half is missing.[2] Originally the collection should have contained forty-two tales 'from a well-known book'. It seems fairly clear from the internal evidence provided by the stories that this collection was first put together in the tenth century. But the manuscript itself is clearly of a later date and hitherto it has been dated by scholars to the fourteenth century on the basis of its calligraphy. Recently Jean-Claude Garçin has tentatively redated the manuscript to the sixteenth century. The name of the patron for whom the manuscript was copied is given at the bottom of the surviving volume. Unfortunately, that name is partly illegible, but it is obvious that the name is Arab rather than Turkish and that the exalted personage is addressed as '*al-muqam, al-karim, al-'ali, al-sami*, effectively 'your highness'. During the period of Mamluk Turkish and Circassian rule in Egypt and Syria (*c.*1250–1517) such entitulature would have been strictly reserved for high-ranking mamluk officers. Therefore Garçin believes that the manuscript should be dated to the sixteenth century, when protocols were looser and an Arab notable might be addressed in such a grand manner. But there can be no certainty about the dating. Internal evidence suggests that the manuscript was produced in Egypt or Syria.

According to the tenth-century book cataloguer Ibn al-Nadim, the writer al-Jahshiyari set out to compile an anthology of a thousand stories from all sorts of Arabic, Persian and Greek sources. But when he died his compilation only comprised 380 stories, and it was subsequently lost. The immensely prolific and learned Syrian literary scholar Salah al-Din al-Munajjid (1910–2010) sought to attribute the authorship of the *Tales of the Marvellous* to al-Jahshiyari, though not only did he not provide any evidence for this attribution, but some of the events cryptically alluded to by the prophetic hermit in 'Sa'id Son of Hatim al-Bahili' clearly postdate al-Jahshiyari's death in 942 or 943.

Poetry and Rhymed Prose

Some of the tales in *Tales of the Marvellous*, particularly those about the tribulations of lovers, carry a heavy freight of poetry. 'Budur and 'Umair Son of Jubair al-Shaibani', 'Sul and Shumul', 'Miqdad and Mayasa' and 'Sakhr and al-Khansa'' rely heavily on 'other men's flowers'. The poetry is there to adorn the story, or in some cases perhaps to delay the progress of the narrative. It never seems to advance the story. Though the poetry is not particularly distinguished, its presence in *Tales of the Marvellous* is one indication that the collection had pretensions to be something more literary than a collection of folktales. Additionally rhymed prose (*saj'*) is sometimes used in the stories for rhetorical effect, though this has not been registered in the English translation. (Richard Burton's attempt to render rhymed prose in his translation of the *Nights* has served as a sufficient deterrent here.)

Flaws and Narrative Incompetence

Though the *Tales of the Marvellous* are indeed astounding, they are not flawless. They are written in a vulgar style, and their Arabic is sometimes incorrect. The diacriticals that are used to distinguish some letters from others have often been omitted. Where the words are vowelled, the vowels are sometimes incorrect. Occasionally the scribe has not understood what he was transcribing, and often the odd sentence or two has been skipped. For example, in 'Talha, the Son of the Qadi of Fustat' there is no account of Tuhfa's departure from Cairo and her arrival in Damascus. In the same story, the marriage of Talha and Tuhfa happens at the beginning of the story and at its end. Similarly, in 'The Forty Girls', the prince sleeps with the sorceress on the first night and finds her to be a virgin. Then, after he has slept with the other thirty-nine girls, he encounters her as if for the first time and again finds her to be a virgin! In several stories there is an unheralded switch from third to first person. This occurs, for example, in the first and second of the treasure-hunting stories. In the First Quest, the emir listens to the treasure hunter's story, but towards the end the story has burst out of its frame, and he has become part of that story. Similar flaws can also be found in the *Nights*, for some of its stories lack both internal logic and plausible motivation.

In *Tales of the Marvellous* the leader of the Third Quest starts off as an idolater, but when in danger prays to Allah, but subsequently reverts to being an idolater. In 'Mahliya and Mauhub and the White-Footed Gazelle', Haifa', the princess, who was turned into a gazelle, is described as the daughter of King Jairun, but later she identifies herself as the daughter of King Mulahhab. And so on.

It is unfortunate that the first of the stories in the collection, 'The King of the Two Rivers', is so seriously damaged by narrative inconsistencies, gaps and indecipherable words in the manuscript that it has not proved possible to make complete sense of the tale. Right at the beginning the astrologer's prophecy is missing, even though we can guess from what follows that his words boded no good for Prince Kaukab. Also, we cannot know what the circumstances were that led to the evil chamberlain's dismissal from the territory of Jaihun. Nevertheless, the somewhat gruesome tale is worth persisting with.

'The King of the Two Rivers' and the tales that follow are full of surprises and proto-surrealist imagery. In this enchanted world the frontier between men and other creatures is more fluid than in the place we live in today, for in these tales a man might easily be transformed into a beast, a hideous *jinni* can take on a pleasing human form, and people are confronted by statues that walk and wield swords. With the text of *Tales of the Marvellous* we have something that is very old and yet is quite new to us. The stories are windows on to a world whose strangeness is heightened by the passage of the centuries. We are confronted by a past in which people did things very differently indeed and, in confronting this past, we should beware of what the social historian E. P. Thompson termed 'the enormous condescension of posterity'.[3] The variety of the stories – comedy, romance, derring-do and fantasy – is beguiling, and so is the energy of their telling and the unpredictability of their narrative pathways.

How Tales of the Marvellous Relates to The Thousand and One Nights

Tales of the Marvellous has many affinities with *The Thousand and One Nights*, and it is likely that close study of the two texts in the future may provide clues about their parallel histories. The oldest substantially surviving manuscript of *The Thousand and One Nights* dates from the late fifteenth century (and not from the fourteenth century as earlier scholars believed), and it was this manuscript which served (with the introduction of the Sindbad stories) as the basis of the first seven volumes of Antoine Galland's translation into French, which were published over the years 1704–17. It was his translation that rescued the *Nights* from the obscurity that it had fallen into in the Arab lands and assured its lasting reputation throughout the world. In 1949 an expert in papyrology, Nabia Abbott, published two fragmentary sheets of paper, dating from the ninth century, which carried the title *The Book of the Tale of the Thousand Nights* and then a few lines of the opening frame story of the *Nights* in which Dinazad asks Shirazad (sic) to tell her stories giving examples of various qualities and characteristics. It seems likely that the Arabic story collection had a Persian precursor and possible that the Persian book in turn might have had a Sanskrit precursor, though neither of these has survived. As for the Arabic *Thousand and One Nights*, stories continued to be added to the original core group of stories throughout the Mamluk and Ottoman periods (thirteenth through to nineteenth centuries).

The Thousand and One Nights does not contain 1,001 stories. The number of stories varies according to what one counts as story and which edition one is reading, but in Richard Burton's translation there are perhaps 468 stories, whereas in the Arabic manuscript that Galland used there are only thirty-five and a half stories. The tales are told night after night by Sheherazade to the Sultan Shahriyar in order to delay her beheading. Not only does Sheherazade's narration frame the stories, but one also finds within that narration stories within stories and sometimes stories within stories within stories. There are tales of love, magic and adventure. There are long, heroic epics, examples of wisdom literature, fables, as well as stories about exemplary piety, adultery, daring criminality, sorcery and cosmological fantasy. Despite the current popularity of abridged and bowdlerized versions, the *Nights* is not a children's book. Though it is reasonable to ask which story collection is older, no sensible answer can be given to that question, for both story collections evolved and changed over centuries. All this has been a necessary prelude to a discussion of the contents of the *Tales of the Marvellous*.

Tales of the Marvellous is probably the oldest surviving story collection with material in common with the *Nights*. (Indeed *Tales of the Marvellous* seems to be the oldest of all Arab story collections that have been discovered so far.) The following stories are found in both collections, though in slightly different forms: 'The Six Men', 'Budur and 'Umair', 'Abu Muhammad the Idle' and 'Julnar'. Moreover, 'The Forty Girls' in *Tales of the Marvellous* gives an extended version of the core of 'The Story of the Third Dervish' in the *Nights*. The motif of the lady kept in a casket by a *jinni* is common to both the frame story of the *Nights* and ''Arus al-'Ara'is' in *Tales of the Marvellous*. 'Talha, the Son of the Qadi of Fustat' is very similar to two stories in the *Nights* in which a feckless spendthrift is rescued by his resourceful slave girl: ''Ali Shar and Zumurrud' and ''Nur al-Din and Miriam the Sash-Maker'. Additionally, we know from the list of contents given in the opening pages of *Tales of the Marvellous* that the missing second part contained 'The Story of the Ebony Horse', and that too is also found in Galland's translation of the *Nights* and in Egyptian manuscripts which postdate Galland.

Setting aside the actual duplication of stories and story motifs in the two collections, there is a broader family resemblance, for *Tales of the Marvellous*, like the *Nights*, contains all sorts of tales that are drawn from a variety of sources, many of which are anonymous. But *Tales of the Marvellous* lacks the elaborate overall framing device that distinguishes the *Nights* and it does not offer anything to match the *mise en abîme* of story within story within story, in which Sheherazade's talking for her life frames the story of 'The Hunchback' and this in turn frames the stories of the stories of the Christian, the inspector, the Jewish doctor and the tailor, and then the tailor's story encompasses that of the barber, who relates the sad stories of his six brothers. But 'The Six Men' in *Tales of the Marvellous*, with its perfunctory opening frame, in which the king lies sleepless for lack of stories, may have furnished the basis of the more elaborately framed stories of the barber's six brothers in the *Nights*. Also 'Mahliya and Mauhub and the White-Footed Gazelle' contains boxed within it the story of the enchanted gazelle. As in the *Nights*, the Abbasid caliph Harun al-Rashid features in several stories, though usually as a witness rather than a protagonist: 'Muhammad the Foundling', 'Budur and 'Umair', 'Abu Muhammad the Idle', and 'Ashraf and Anjab'. More surprising is the appearance of Harun's cousin Muhammad ibn Sulaiman, the governor of Basra, in several stories: 'Budur and 'Umair', 'Ashraf and Anjab' and 'Abu Muhammad the Idle'.

Several of the tales in *Tales of the Marvellous* do have a rudimentary frame in which a ruler who is bored or depressed consequently needs to be told a story in order to rescue him from his mood. At the end of the narrative we are to understand the fact that the story did the job with the ruler and the storyteller was well rewarded is a guarantee of its merit. Exceptionally ''Arus al-'Ara'is' ('The Bride of Brides') contains an unusually complex set of framed stories, as, after a king's baby daughter dies, a blind man sets out to comfort him by telling the story of 'Arus al-'Ara'is, which will surely lead the king 'to hate scheming women and treacherous girls'. The blind man heard the story of 'Arus al-'Ara'is from his father, who heard it from his grandfather, a police chief, who heard about it from a man who was in prison for attacking women and who would rather stay there than re-encounter 'Arus al-'Ara'is. The prisoner then tells how, before he met 'Arus al-'Ara'is, he set out travelling as a merchant and after strange and supernatural adventures at sea he alone survived a shipwreck and came to be marooned on an island. After ten days a *jinni* arrived on the island with a lady in a glass chest. After spying on them and witnessing strange things, the merchant was eventually detected in his hiding place by the lady and he was forced to supply her with a ring, which she used to kill the *jinni*. A little later 'Arus al-'Ara'is tells the man the story of her birth, her subsequent adulterous and murderous career and how, after engineering many deaths, she was locked in a chest and pushed out to sea. Eventually the *jinni* rescued her from the wooden chest only to keep her captive in a glass chest. One of the stories she tells the merchant, purportedly to explain the making of the wooden chest she was cast out to sea in, is a story lifted from the Arabic *Alexander Romance*. In that story a king was trying to build a city on a coast, but night after night monsters came out of the sea to destroy it, until that king had talismanic images carved to repel the monsters, making it possible to complete the building of Alexandria. During her enforced sojourn with the *jinni* he told many stories of the wonders of the sea, and some of these she also relates to the marooned merchant. She also tells of how she got the *jinni* to use magic sand to destroy her home city and of her affair with another castaway and what happened to him after he raped a mermaid. Then she transmits the *jinni*'s story of how his father was killed by the monstrous *daran* and tells more about her time with her demonic captor and how she earlier tried to use the *daran* to kill him but failed. Finally, we are back in real time as, once her narrative has finished, the besotted merchant decides to stay with her and bring her to his home town. Though more sexual and homicidal adventures ensue, once they have left the island we have found our way out of the series of bizarrely boxed stories (though we never get back to the blind man who was relating all this to the bereaved king). The story describes itself as 'a long, remarkable and curious story', and it certainly is that.

Although there are many overlaps and similarities between *Tales of the Marvellous* and the *Nights*, there are also subtle and not so subtle differences. The stories in the *Nights* often pretend to have a didactic aim, and in some cases that is clearly actually the case. The exordium of the manuscript of the *Nights* used by Galland boasted (not very convincingly) of its instructional purpose: 'the purpose of writing this agreeable and entertaining book is the instruction of those who peruse it, for it abounds with highly edifying histories and excellent lessons for the people of distinction, and it provides them with the opportunity to learn the art of discourse, as well as what happened to kings from the beginnings of time'. *Tales of the Marvellous* makes no such claim, but only promises wonders and strangeness. Then, though both collections contain plenty of marvels and magic, arguably *Tales of the Marvellous* offers madder marvels, which come on thick and fast. There are other more incidental differences. The Umaiyad caliphs and their governors and generals feature more prominently in *Tales of the Marvellous* than in the *Nights*, and so do Christians. The fact that protagonists in *Tales of the Marvellous* frequently invoke the name of 'Ali, the cousin and son-in-law of the Prophet, as well as the fact that 'Ali is given a heroic role in two of the stories, might suggest that the compiler had Shi'i sympathies. On the other hand there is no sign of any particular hostility towards the Umaiyad caliphs, which one might have expected from a Shi'ite.

Relief after Grief

Besides belonging to the category of *'aja'ib*, many of the stories in *Tales of the Marvellous* can also be described as belonging to the genre of *faraj ba'd al-shidda*, or 'relief after grief'. In this kind of story the protagonist or protagonists undergo many hardships or tests before attaining success and happiness. The most famous collection of such stories was made by the Iraqi judge and anthologist al-Tanukhi (940–94). 'Relief after grief' can be seen as a quasi-religious genre in which the protagonists' patience and trust in God will ultimately be rewarded by Him. (It is easy for a modern, secularized reader to miss how the tales of marvels, magic, adventure and thwarted love in both *Tales of the Marvellous* and the *Nights* are suffused with an Islamic religiosity.) In *Tales of the Marvellous* the characters who suffer before attaining a happy end are often separated lovers. Examples of the tribulations endured by lovers and their ultimate happy reunion include 'The King of the Two Rivers', 'Talha, the Son of the Qadi of Fustat', 'Sul and Shumul', 'Miqdad and Mayasa' and 'Budur and 'Umair'. In the opening of this last story the restless and depressed caliph Harun al-Rashid demands to be told 'a story of infatuated lovers and of a happy outcome to affliction'. Of course, just as the protagonists in this kind of story must bear their hardships with patience (*sabr*), so too must those who read or listen to these tales. It is striking how anxious the compiler is to signal in the titles to the tales those stories which, after troubles, will end happily. The description 'relief after grief' occurs repeatedly in the titles of a majority of the stories (but this excessive repetition has not been reproduced on the English contents page).

Patience must be the correct response to a tale of suspense. In Beatrix Potter's *The Tale of Peter Rabbit*, the rabbit is told by his mother: 'You may go into the fields or down the lane, but don't go into Mr McGregor's garden.' The person who reads this does not want the rabbit to go into Mr McGregor's garden for he knows that if the rabbit does so something bad will happen to him, and yet at the same time he does want the rabbit to break the interdiction, for otherwise there will be no story. So it is with 'The Forty Girls' in *Tales of the Marvellous*, where the prince is told by the sorceress that he may explore every room but one. It is as if he is compelled by that very interdiction to go through the forbidden door. Prolepsis is a closely related way of generating narrative suspense. Thus, if at the beginning of a story an astrologer predicts some dreadful thing, the reader or listener waits and, as he waits, he wants and does not want the predicted disaster to happen.

Love

Delaying the climax is the stock-in-trade of the love stories. These tend towards the lachrymose, and verses mostly of a melancholy kind adorn these stories. Poetry was the language of love, for prose was seen as a poor vehicle for the expression of the emotions. Poetry both conveyed passion and served to instruct lovers on the etiquette of love. In medieval Arab storytelling love comes at first glance (a second glance would count as ogling and would therefore be sinful). It is even possible to fall in love by report as in 'Julnar', in which Badr falls in love with Jauhara as soon as he hears her described. Or one might fall in love through seeing a portrait, as with Mahliya, when she sees a painting of Mauhub. Regular dating and the slow growth of love over weeks, months or years was not envisaged by the storytellers. Although passion is celebrated, the sexual act is not lingered over. Customarily in these romances love is fated, as are the painful separation and ultimate blissful reunion.

The ninth-century lexicographer al-Asma'i,[4] who travelled among the Bedouin in order to clarify the meanings of Arabic words, reported that 'some of the Arabs say "'Ishq (passion) is a kind of madness"'. The Qanun, the famous medical textbook by the eleventh-century philosopher and physician Ibn Sina (Avicenna), discussed lovesickness as a delusionary form of madness akin to melancholia. The plight of several lovers in Tales of the Marvellous seems to bear out Ibn Sina's diagnosis. In 'Budur and 'Umair', we are introduced to the case of Budur, whose 'letter comes from one who spends her nights in tears and her days in torture. All day she is bewildered and all night she is sleepless. She takes no pleasure in food, cannot take refuge in sleep, does not listen to rebuke and cannot hear those who speak to her. Longing has mastered her . . .' For the most part, the exalted code of love was reserved for the nobly born; it was not for bakers, washerwomen, porters and seamstresses. In 'The Six Men' in Tales of the Marvellous there is nothing noble about the hunchback tailor's attempt to have sex with the merchant's deceitful wife, and he does not get to spout poetry, but is handed over by the merchant to the police chief so that he can be flogged. Similarly, the paralytic's desire for a beautiful young woman results in him ending up with dyed eyebrows, shaven and naked in the street, an object of mockery.

'Aja'ib could have an aesthetic resonance for, if a person or an artefact was perceived of as being beautiful, the common response was not jamil! (beautiful!), but 'ajib! (amazing!). The compelling power of physical beauty looms large in these stories. In Tales of the Marvellous, as in the Nights, people are loved for their physical appearance rather than their character. The moon features frequently as a simile for beauty (and indeed Budur's name means 'moons'). Beautiful women are conventionally compared to gazelles. It was more common to evoke beauty through metaphor and simile than by close physical description. Beauty was a blessing from God, and according to the eleventh-century scholar and Sufi al-Ghazali God had worked as an artist to design the human form. Yusuf, or Joseph, was the exemplar of male physical beauty in Islamic lore. The Sura of Joseph in the Qur'an describes how a governor of Egypt's wife, who passionately desired Joseph, accused him of rape, but was found out. Then:

> Certain women that were in the city said,
> 'The governor's wife has been soliciting her page; he smote her heart
>   with love; we see her in manifest error.'
> When she heard their sly whispers, she sent to them and made ready
>   for them a repast,
> Then she gave to each one of them a knife.
> 'Come forth, attend to them,' she said.
> And when they saw him, they so admired him
> That they cut their hands, saying 'God save us!
> This is no mortal; he is no other but a noble angel.'

In *Tales of the Marvellous*, the tale of 'Muhammad the Foundling' is calqued on that of the Qur'anic Joseph, for the devastatingly handsome Muhammad is, like Joseph, falsely accused of rape, though the fact that his shirt is torn at the back, not the front, suggests that he is innocent. Though handsomeness in a man is a sign of nobility and virtue, a woman's beauty is a much less reliable guide to her inner qualities. The beauty of 'Arus al-'Ara' is lures men to their deaths. Similarly, in 'The Six Men', the hunchback weaver sees 'a woman rising like a full moon on a balcony' and he recollects that 'she was so very lovely that . . . my heart took fire', but that vision of loveliness will lure him to his doom and, in the stories that follow, the paralytic and the glass seller with the severed ear will similarly be betrayed by female beauties. In Arabic *fitna* means sedition or civil discord, but it also means seduction, temptation or distraction from the service of God.

Heightened Pleasures and Pains

In *The Waning of the Middle Ages* the Dutch historian Jan Huizinga wrote of the medieval sensibility as follows: 'the outlines of all things seemed more clearly marked than to us. The contrast between suffering and joy, between adversity and happiness, appeared more striking. All experience had yet to the minds of men the directness and absoluteness of the pleasure and pain of child-life.'[5] So it is with the characters in *Tales of the Marvellous*. Tuhfa faints from longing for Talha, while Talha, for his part, rubs his cheeks in the dust when he learns that she has been sold to another man, and then his grief becomes so extreme that he is taken for mad and is locked up in an asylum. 'Umair, on hearing verses that speak so strongly of his own emotional state and his love for Budur, gives a loud cry and tears his clothes before collapsing unconscious. People beat their cheeks from despair. They faint from surprise. They tear their clothes from heightened passion. They also fall off their chairs from laughing.

Misfortune breeds misfortune. The authors of the tales in *Tales of the Marvellous* delighted in being cruel to their characters, and Schadenfreude is definitely one of the dark literary pleasures provided by this collection. Hands and feet are lopped off, eyeballs plucked out, lips cut away, penises slit off, people burned alive, women raped, cripples and blind men mocked and robbed, and the ugly have their deformities seized upon and exaggerated. Here political incorrectness has gone mad, and there is 'Laughter in the Dark'. In fact, as in fiction, public executions were popular entertainments. But the good suffer almost as much the bad in these ruthless stories. Read what Kaukab, Ashraf and the various lovers of 'Arus al-'Ara'is have to undergo. Thomas Hardy would have approved, for he wrote: 'Cruelty is the law pervading all nature and society; and we can't get out of it if we would.'

Misogyny and Rape

As a character in A. S. Byatt's long short story 'The Djinn in the Nightingale's Eye' observes,

> It has to be admitted . . . that misogyny is a driving force of pre-modern story collections . . . from Katha Sarit Sagara, The Ocean of Story, to *The Thousand and One Nights*, Alf Layla wa-Layla. Why this should be so has not, as far as I know, been fully explained, though there are reasons that could be put forward from social structures to depth psychology – the sad fact remains that women in these stories for the most part are portrayed as deceitful, unreliable, greedy, inordinate in their desires, unprincipled and simply dangerous, operating powerfully (apart from sorceresses and female ghouls and ogres) through structures of powerlessness.[6]

In 'Julnar' the sorceress Queen Lab's voracious sexual desire leads her to sleep with one man after another, before turning them into animals (perhaps metaphorically as well as literally). Yet even her passion pales beside that of 'Arus al-'Ara'is.

The depiction of women as man-eaters is one side of misogynistic fantasy; the other is their portrayal as the victims of rape. In the story 'Sakhr and al-Khansa'', Miqdam, the chieftain of one tribe, steals into another tribe's encampment and 'seeing al-Khansa' alone and defenceless, he lusted after her, and although she defended herself she had not the power to stop him from raping her'. But all is square when Sakhr, the brother of al-Khansa', rapes Haifa', the sister of Miqdam. Rape also features prominently in 'The Talisman Mountain' and in ''Arus al-'Ara'is'. (The latter story includes the rape of a mermaid.)

Deceitful Women

As already noted, women are frequently portrayed as deceitful. In the tale of the tailor, included in 'The Six Men', a female customer lures the tailor to her house with the promise of sex, but there he suffers an evil fate. Similarly, in the tale of the paralytic man, he encounters ultimate humiliation in a house full of beautiful women. The story of the lustful and treacherous 'Arus al-'Ara'is, a medieval Arab Medea, would seem to be the misogynistic story par excellence, and yet this unusually complex narrative has its ambiguities. For example, after killing the *jinni*, she seems to repent: 'Alas for all scheming and treacherous women, who keep no covenant of love or pact of faithfulness and who neither abide by nor show loyalty to their lovers.' At times she uses sex as a lethal weapon, yet at other times she genuinely desires to be loved. It is also conceded that she is the prisoner of fate's decree, for, almost from the first, we are to understand that she has been born under an evil conjunction of stars. Hers is a grief-after-grief story, as she becomes by turns a villainess and a victim of villainy.

The storyteller or storytellers show a particular hostility to scheming and deceitful old women. Thus it is an aged bawd who sets up the paralytic man with his ill-fated assignation. Similarly, it is an old woman who sees the glass seller being given a large sum of money and who promises to set him up with her beautiful unmarried daughter, and of course no good will come of that.

More bizarrely, in 'Mahliya and Mauhub and the White-Footed Gazelle' the queen of the *jinn* crows has responsibility for engineering the parting of couples. The same story features an aged sorceress who tricks the lion and successively cuts off his tail, ears, nose and whiskers. 'The Talisman Mountain' features an evil-omened old woman with a face like a vulture.

Medieval Arab fiction had no kind of monopoly on misogyny. There are at least as many examples in medieval European poetry and stories. To take just examples from English literature, according to the twelfth-century *Valerius's Dissuasion Against Marriage* by Walter Map, 'no matter what they intend, with a woman the result is always the same. When she wants to do him harm – and that is nearly always the case – she never fails. If by chance she should want to do good, she still succeeds in doing harm.'[7] Geoffrey Chaucer, in 'The Merchant's Tale' in *The Canterbury Tales*, cited Ecclesiastes as the authority for Solomon finding one good man among a thousand, but out of all women not a single one. And from 'The Wife of Bath's Prologue' in the same book we learn how the wife in question saw off five husbands. Towards the end of the fourteenth-century English poem *Sir Gawain and the Green Knight* Gawain sums up the case against women:

> Who with their wanton wiles have thus waylaid their knight.
> But it is no marvel for a foolish man to be maddened thus
> And saddled with sorrow by the sleights of women.
> For here on earth was Adam taken in by one,
> And Solomon by many such, and Samson likewise;
> Delilah dealt him his doom; and David later still,
> Was blinded by Bathsheba, and badly suffered for it.[8]

Racism

As is the case with many of the stories in the *Nights*, blacks are presented as violent and often stupid as well. In 'The King of the Two Rivers', the king's son is taken captive by ten villainous Magian blacks, but he succeeds in slitting all their throats while they are asleep. In 'Muhammad the Foundling and Harun al-Rashid' it turns out that it is a black furnace-man who is guilty of deflowering Miriam. But racism is most outrageously to the fore in 'Ashraf and Anjab', in which the sadistically villainous Anjab is described by Harun al-Rashid as follows: 'This man is black as a negro . . . with red eyes, a nose like a clay pot and lips like kidneys', and his mother is no better looking for she 'was black as pitch with a snub nose, red eyes and an unpleasant smell'. In 'Sa'id Son of Hatim' the monk Simeon predicts that the shrine of the Ka'ba will be destroyed by drunken and singing blacks. As Bernard Lewis's *Race and Slavery in the Middle East* put it when discussing the role of blacks in *The Thousand and One Nights*, it 'reveals a familiar pattern of sexual fantasy, social and occupational discrimination, and an unthinking identification of lighter with better and darker with worse'.[9] But, exceptionally, Masrur, who features in both the *Nights* and *Tales of the Marvellous* as the caliph Harun al-Rashid's black headsman and faithful companion, is presented in a favourable light.

In 'Anjab and Ashraf' and other tales ugliness is a shorthand way for the storyteller to indicate a villain. One finds the same kind of thing in the novels of Sax Rohmer, Dennis Wheatley and Ian Fleming (and their villains often have the double misfortune of being foreign). Names may also provide clues for readers who want to know which side they should be on. In 'Mahliya and Mauhub and the White-Footed Gazelle', Mukhadi', the name assumed by Mahliya when she is pretending to be her vizier, means 'impostor'. Dickens indulged the same kind of signalling with, for example, Gradgrind in *Hard Times* and Wackford Squeers and Lord Verrisoft in *Nicholas Nickleby*.

More on Wonders: Jinn and Magic

The wonders on offer in *Tales of the Marvellous* somewhat resemble those found in *Ripley's Believe It or Not*, a cartoon feature that ran in the *New York Evening Post* in the 1920s and 30s and which compiled bizarre events and items of information so strange as to seem incredible. In *Tales of the Marvellous* the *jinn* are the chief engineers of the bizarre. *Jinn* is the collective plural of *jinni*, and a female *jinni* is a *jinniya*. *'Ifrit* and *marid* appear to be synonyms for *jinni*, though there may be an implication that they are exceptionally powerful *jinn* (*'ifrit* and *marid* are each mentioned just once in the Qur'an). According to the Qur'an, the *jinn* were created from smokeless flame. Since *jinn* were referred to several times in the Qur'an there could be no question for the believing Muslim but that they really existed. They can fly through the air and travel at great speed. They can conjure things out of nothing and they are shape-shifters. (As a young man visiting a Sufi shrine in Algeria, I once encountered a *jinni* in the form of a cat.) For some reason the shape that a *jinni* chooses to shift into is often hideous – as in 'The Talisman Mountain', in which the queen summons up three *jinn*, 'each eleven feet tall, with ugly shapes, eyes set lengthwise, hooves like those of cattle and talons like those of wild beasts'.

Some *jinn* are believing Muslims, and there is one such in the story of 'Abu Muhammad the Idle'. Good believing *jinn* feature in 'Mahliya and Mauhub and the White-Footed Gazelle'. The *jinni* in ''Arus al-'Ara'is' is fairly virtuous until, corrupted by 'Arus al-'Ara'is, he is persuaded to destroy a city (like many *jinn*, he is not that bright). 'Sul and Shumul' not only features *jinn*, but even presents a remarkably mild and benign Iblis (the Devil), something that is without parallel elsewhere in medieval Arab fiction. According to some authorities, Iblis was a fallen angel, but according to others he was to be numbered among the *jinn*.

As the story of ''Arus al-'Ara'is' suggests, sex between humans and *jinn* was possible and indeed, in non-fiction, both medieval legal texts and guides to the etiquette of love envisaged this possibility. Under Muslim law *jinn* could own property and men and women could marry them (as Sul does in one of the tales in *Tales of the Marvellous*). The fictional expert on the *Nights* in 'The Djinn in the Nightingale's Eye', commenting on the interventions of the *jinn* in the *Nights* story of 'Qamar al-Zaman and Budur', had this to say: 'It is as though our dreams were watching us and directing our lives with external vigour whilst we simply enact their pleasures passively in a swoon. Except that the djinns are more solid than dreams . . .'[10]

Transformations

In 'Julnar' Badr is turned into a stork and later he succeeds in turning Queen Lab into a mule. In 'The Forty Girls' the prince encounters the sister of the sorceress who has been turned into a horse. The scrawny ape in 'Abu Muhammad the Idle' turns out to be a *jinni* under enchantment. In 'Mahliya and al-Mauhub and the White-Footed Gazelle' a princess in love allows herself to be transformed into a gazelle. Towards the very end of the same story Mauhub is turned into a crocodile.

Therianthropy, the transformation of a human into an animal, is usually presented by storytellers as a form of imprisonment. Rescue usually comes from anagnorisis (recognition), as when a king's daughter divines Badr's humanity beneath his appearance as a stork.

Sea People

Medieval Arabs seem to have been fascinated by the people who lived in the sea. Captain Burzug ibn Shahriyar's *Book of the Wonders of India* had this to say on the subject: 'Someone who had been to Zaila and the land of the Ethiopians told me that in the Ethiopian Sea there is a fish just like a human being, in body, hands and feet.' Lonely fishermen 'hold congress with the females. From them are born beings that look like men, and live in the water and in the atmosphere.'[11] The story of ''Abdallah the Fisherman and Abdallah the Merman' is found in the *Nights*. 'The Story of Julnar' is found in both the *Nights* and in *Tales of the Marvellous*. Vengeful mermaids feature in ''Arus al-'Ara'is'. On the other hand, the crew on the Second Quest for treasure enjoy pleasant sex with scaly-skinned but friendly mermaids. More generally, those on the Second and Third Quests for treasure encounter many wonders of the sea, including strange fishes, a boiling sea and an island white as camphor.

''Arus al-'Ara'is' also has a marvels of the sea prelude, and later the *jinni* who holds her captive likes to entertain her by telling her of the marvels that he has encountered.

> While I was staying with the *jinni*, one day when he was sitting and telling me about the marvels of the sea and its islands, he told me about a bird like a swift whose excrement if applied to the eyes would produce instant blindness, while on another island was a tree whose fruit if eaten by a woman would cause her to give birth to a son. He told me of herbs that would harm men and others that would help against every illness, of a type of kohl that would clear the sight and another that would blind it . . .

The sea also acts as a kind of roulette wheel, its chance operations giving men good fortune or ruining them. Carefully accumulated treasures are lost to the stormy deep, and powerful tides carry men who are close to drowning to strange islands and new fortunes.

Treasure Hunting

The fictional treatment of treasure hunting evolved in parallel with non-fictional treatises devoted to the same subject. *Matalib*, the purported science of treasure hunting, was an established genre of writing, and in medieval Egypt professional treasure hunters had set themselves up as a guild. The fourteenth-century North African philosopher and historian Ibn Khaldun had this to say on the subject:

> It should be known that many weak-minded persons in cities hope to discover property under the surface of the earth and to make some profit from it. They believe that all the property of the nations of the past was stored underground and sealed with magic talismans. These seals, they believe, can be broken only by those who chance upon the necessary knowledge and can offer the proper incense, prayers, and sacrifices to break them.[12]

In the course of a sceptical and coruscating account of treasure hunting, Ibn Khaldun wondered 'why should anyone who hoards his money and seals it with magical operations, thus making extraordinary efforts to keep it concealed, set up hints and clues as to how it may be found by anyone who cares to?'[13] Many of the 'professional' treasure hunters were really con men who preyed upon the gullible, and Jawbari's thirteenth-century manual on rogues' tricks, the *Kashf al-Asrar* (*Unveiling of Secrets*), described them as 'masters of a thousand and one dodges'.[14] Additionally, many treasure-hunting manuals are so full of wondrous accounts of magical spells, death-dealing automata and stories about ill-fated earlier seekers after treasure that they should really be reassigned to the category of entertaining fiction.

In fiction, as in purported fact, one needed more than a good map and a shovel in order to unearth ancient treasures, for the treasure hunter might expect to encounter guardian monsters, killer statues and magical traps, and that is indeed what the participants in the Quests included in *Tales of the Marvellous* do encounter. As the leader of the First Quest asserts, 'He who dares wins.' Their perilous adventures can be compared to those of Indiana Jones, though the supernatural features more prominently in the medieval stories. The treasure-hunting stories bear witness to the awe experienced by the medieval Arabs when they contemplated the wonders of antiquity and they asked themselves what had happened to the fabulous wealth of the ancient Greeks and Romans, as well as of the Pharaohs and Persian emperors – and besides material treasures there was also thought to be a lost knowledge that could only be acquired at a price. The ancients were believed to have anticipated global catastrophes and taken steps to preserve their secrets in some form that would survive fire and water. The pyramids were commonly thought to be storehouses of esoteric wisdom, but in 'Sa'id Son of Hatim' we learn how Adam, foreseeing the Deluge, had his secret knowledge written down on baked clay tablets, which were then sealed in a cave.

As the stories of dangerous automata suggest, medieval storytellers envisaged advanced technology not as something that would be achieved in the future, but rather as something whose secrets were lost in the distant past. The statue of Memmon, king of Ethiopia, near Thebes in Egypt was reported to sing when struck by the sun's rays at dawn. It was said that the Greek artificer Daedalus constructed moving statues that were animated by quicksilver and which walked in front of the Labyrinth that he had also constructed. In *Tales of the Marvellous* death-dealing automata guarded the treasures sought by the protagonists of the Quest stories. Unusually, in 'Julnar' the sorceress Queen Lab is mistress of a group of singing automata. Statues were dangerous. They hardly ever featured as objects of art in medieval Arab literature. Instead, some were characterized as evil-averting talismans or guardians of treasure, while others were human beings or animals who had been turned to stone. In several of the tales in *Tales of the Marvellous* demons enter the statues and speak through them. Stone monks guard treasure in the first of the four treasure-hunting stories. A statue on the Talisman Mountain has the power to immobilize ships. Such things, neither alive nor dead, are intrinsically uncanny.

Treasure-hunting stories are full of marvels and excitement, but, as with the *Nights* story 'The City of Brass', they also carry a lot of moralizing about the transience of worldly wealth and the vanity of earthly power. For example, the treasure seekers on the First Quest enter a gallery in which there is a sarcophagus in which:

there was a dead man surrounded by piles of dinars with a golden tablet by his head. This had an inscription: 'Whoever wishes this rubbish, doomed as it is to perish, let him take what he wants of it, for he will leave it behind as I have done and die as I have died, while his actions will be hung around his neck.'

Then again, those on the Second Quest encounter a shrouded corpse with a tablet of green topaz at its head, on which was the following inscription:

'I am Shaddad the Great. I conquered a thousand cities; a thousand white elephants were collected for me; I lived for a thousand years and my kingdom covered both east and west, but when death came to me nothing of all that I had gathered was of any avail. You who see me, take heed for Time is not to be trusted.'

In the fourth story, that of the golden tube, the message in the tube runs as follows:

'In the Name of God Almighty – This world is transient while the next world is eternal. Our actions are tied around our necks; disasters are arrows; people set themselves goals; our livelihood is apportioned to us, and our appointed time is decreed. The world is filled with hope, and good deeds are the best treasures for a man to store up. Toleration is an adornment and hastiness is a disgrace . . . A man's wife is the sweet flower of his life and finds acceptance as many such flowers do.'

A treasure hunter might hope to end up rich: he should certainly end up conventionally pious.

In Sura 89 of the Qur'an, Muslims and unbelievers are admonished:

Hast thou not seen how thy Lord did with Ad,
Iram of the pillars,
the like of which was never created in the land,
and Thamood, who hollowed the rocks in the valley,
and Pharaoh, he of the tent-pegs,
who were all insolent in the land
and worked much corruption therein?
Thy Lord unloosed on them a scourge of chastisement;
surely thy Lord is ever on the watch.

So also in *Tales of the Marvellous* a good Muslim should take warning from what befell the great kings in the pagan past.

The golden tube also contains a promise: 'Whoever wishes to see a wonder should go to the Scented Mountain.' One gets the sense that the treasure hunters are not so much seeking tangible treasures but really they are on a quest for adventure and strangeness. The story of a quest for treasure turns out to be the story of the quest for a story. As the man on the Third Quest says, when the centaur tries to bribe him not to see the magical crown, 'We only want to look at marvels and to see what we have never seen before, and if we see the crown we can put it back in its place.' (The plot of the Third Quest has a faint but eerie resemblance to Kipling's story 'The Man Who Would Be King').

The Pagan Past

The history of medieval Egypt took place in the shadow of the pyramids. Shepherds took their flocks through the outlying rubble of Karnak, and women washed clothes in the shade of the ruins of Philae. Since knowledge of hieroglyphs and the real history of Egypt had been lost, a fantasy history was constructed. The scale of the ruins, far beyond the ability of any medieval sultan to match, suggested the supernatural power and fabulous wealth of the bygone dynasties of pre-Islamic times. One of the glories of Egypt was the number of marvels it contained. At the beginning of 'Mahliya and al-Mauhub and the White-Footed Gazelle' the Arab general 'Amr ibn al-'As marvels at a great ruin at Heliopolis in Egypt. He 'saw a huge old building bigger than any he had ever seen, surrounded by remarkable remains'. This leads him on to ask the hermit Matrun for its story. According to Muslim lore Ikhmim in Upper Egypt was the capital of the country's sorcerers (though in the story of Mahliya this pre-eminent role has been usurped by Samannud). The sheer wild inventiveness of this story, with its jumbling of Muslim, Christian and pagan beliefs and rituals, cannot pass without comment. Here we have a mechanical vulture, visionary dreams, conversation with a pagan god, magical transformations, thrones of wrath and of mercy, an enchanted gazelle, a herder of giant ostriches, lustful *jinn*, speaking idols, a queen of the crows, a weeping lion, a fortress guarded by talismans, a crocodile with pearls in its ears, the sacrifice of virgins to the Nile and much else. The narrative is one long carnival of extravagant fantasy. (Al-Maqrizi and other Arab historians told the story of how every year a virgin was sacrificed to the Nile in order to ensure its flooding, until the Arabs conquered Egypt and 'Amr ibn al-'As put a stop to the practice. But the story is probably an anti-Coptic libel.)

Prophecy

One of the conventions of medieval Arab storytelling is that if an astrologer makes a prophecy, it invariably becomes true. One cannot beat fate. Unusually, the astrologer's prophecy in the opening of 'The King of the Two Rivers' does not in the end come true, though it serves to get the story moving. Also the prince's prediction that he will attack his father with a great army is never fulfilled, though it serves to explain why he was sent out in the desert. 'Abu Disa' sends up astrology mercilessly. The message of that story is perhaps that as long as one trusts in God everything will work out all right. In one of the more bizarre scenes in 'Mahliya and Mauhub and the White-Footed Gazelle', set in a church in Baalbek (in what is now Lebanon), the pagan god Baal addresses Mauhub with the following words:

> Great king and leader, you will meet sorrows, difficulties and dangers, grave matters, the revelation of hidden secrets, heavy cares and troubles following one after the other. All this will be thanks to a beautiful gazelle acting as a lover wounded at heart. Take your time in dealing with this affair, Mauhub, and now, farewell, great king.

Here prophecy serves as prolepsis, since it promises ordeals and adventures to come.

According to Ulrich Marzolph, who has made a close study of these tales, 'Sa'id Son of Hatim al-Bahili' 'is the most remarkable story in the collection'.[15] It certainly is rather strange, and I believe that it has no other close parallel in Arab literature. A narrative to comfort a sleepless caliph, it starts off as a fairly conventional tale about the wonders of the sea and the conquest of part of India but then turns into something quite different, for the Muslim expeditionary force encounters an incredibly ancient hermit, Simeon, who declares himself to be the disciple and former companion of the biblical prophet Daniel. However, while Daniel is long dead, Simeon has succeeded in living on into Islamic times.

Setting the meeting with Simeon aside for a moment, it should be noted that in the Old Testament and the Apocrypha Daniel was noted for his prophecies. He retained this reputation in medieval Islamic times, and all sorts of prophetic treatises were spuriously attributed to him. According to Islamic tradition, Daniel acquired his knowledge of the future in a place known as the Cave of Treasures. Several of the prophetic treatises attributed to Daniel attach their predictions to astrological and meteorological phenomena such as eclipses, thunderstorms, rainbows and oddly shaped clouds. But the prophecies of Daniel that Simeon preserves in his story have little or nothing in common with this sort of divination. His prophecies can be classified as *malahim*.

In Arabic *malahim* literally means 'slaughterings', and its singular form is *malhama*. The term is used to designate prophecies that treat of such grand matters as the rise and fall of dynasties, future wars with Christians, the Muslim conquest of Constantinople and Rome, the coming invasion of Gog and Magog, the Last Battle and the End of the World. These treatises drew widely on Jewish and Christian material and they were often attributed to monks. For example, *The Vision of the Monk Bahira*, which seems to have been produced in the eighth century, was very popular. There was a proliferation of apocalypses in the late Umaiyad period (early eighth century). In general, things were predicted to get worse before they got better. Armand Abel, who made a special study of *malahim* prophecies, remarked that these popular fantasies were really more interesting than 'the bourgeois Arabian Nights'.

Simeon's prophecies are a bit of a dog's dinner, as they seem to be drawn from a variety of ill-assorted sources and times. Some of the events 'predicted' had already happened at the time this story was put together, while others have yet to happen (and probably never will). The prophecies are obscurely and allusively pitched in a manner that anticipates those of the sixteenth-century French astrologer Nostradamus. But Simeon's predictions are moralistic, since the dreadful things that are to come are divine punishment for the decline of Muslim piety and practice.

At times Simeon seems to be prophesying events during the Arab–Byzantine wars of the tenth century. The Qarmatians sacked Mecca in 930 and stole the Black Stone from the shrine in Mecca. Dailam is a mountainous region in northern Iran, south of the Caspian Sea. Although the Abbasid caliphs sent several expeditions there, it was never really under their control. Then in 945 Dailamite Buyid warlords established a protectorate over the Abbasid caliphs. Simeon foresees four rival caliphates existing simultaneously. From the tenth to late twelfth centuries there were three competing caliphates: the Abbasid caliphate in Bagdad, the Fatimid caliphate in Cairo and the Umaiyad caliphate in Cordova. But it is hard to think of a fourth caliphate. Hajaj ibn Yusuf never killed an Abbasid ruler in Mecca. Though the Church of the Holy Sepulchre was demolished by the Fatimid caliph al-Hakim in 1009, it was not actually burned down.

Other 'predictions' seem to refer to events in the thirteenth century, while yet others cannot be confidently attached to any real events. In 1236 Cordova fell to the army of Ferdinand III of Castile, although the Christian Reconquista of Spain was not completed until 1492. The 'Persian' invasion is predicted to happen more than 600 years after the death of the Prophet. So that would place it in the mid to late thirteenth century and therefore what might be being 'prophesied' was the Mongol invasion of Iraq, their killing of the last Abbasid caliph in Bagdad and then their invasion of Syria, which was launched from Persia. Ghadanfar is the name of a fictional character in the popular chivalrous romance of 'Antar, which is set in the period just before and during the rise of Islam. In 'Antar, he is the son of the heroic Arab warrior 'Antar by a Christian princess, and for much of the epic he fought as a crusader against the Muslims. But Simeon calls him 'al-Farisi' (the Persian), and that makes no sense at all.

Earlier in the story of 'Sa'id Son of Hatim al-Bahili' the infidel king told his people not to fight the Muslim expeditionary force. 'For five hundred years,' he told them, 'their empire has been advancing victoriously, so make peace with them and do not resist them or they will conquer you.' What kind of chronological sense is that? The Muslim conquests began in the early seventh century. So are we to understand that the Muslim encounter with the infidel king and with Simeon took place in the twelfth century? If so, how could the story of the expedition have been told to Hisham ibn 'Abd al-Malik, who was Umaiyad caliph from 724 to 743?

Coincidence and Fate

In 'Talha, the Son of the Qadi of Fustat' what was the chance of Salih (Tuhfa's former protector in Damascus) ending up begging at her husband's house in Cairo? Or in 'Muhammad the Foundling and Harun al-Rashid' the chance of the caliph happening to go to the very bathhouse where Khultukh happened to be working? Fate guides Badr and Jauhara to the same island. The broad comedy of the bogus astrologer 'Usfur depends heavily on a ludicrous sequence of coincidences. But perhaps the message is that 'Usfur's aggressively nagging wife is right, for if you trust in God everything will be well. And as the king observes towards the end of the story, 'When God grants good fortune to one of his servants, He makes all things serve him, and when fortune comes, it acts as teacher to a man.' Of course coincidences (*ittifaqat*) made the storyteller's work easier, but there was a pious subtext, as medieval Muslims were inclined to detect the hand of God behind such occurrences. Abu Mansur 'Abd al-Malik al-Tha'alibi's tenth-century treatise, the *Lata'if al-ma'arif* (*The Book of Curious and Entertaining Information*) included chapters 'Concerning curious coincidences and patterns in names and patronymics' and 'Concerning interesting and entertaining pieces of information about various unusual happenings and strange coincidences'. Coincidences were indications of a divinely ordained destiny at work. As the film-maker Pier Paolo Pasolini remarked of the *Nights*, 'The chief character is in fact destiny itself.'[16] It is fate that turns men's lives into stories.

The article devoted to 'Religion' in *The Arabian Nights Encyclopedia* touches on fate and remarks that 'religious belief in the stories appears as the belief in fate. Although fate rules the hero's life, there is no story in which God intervenes directly to steer the course of the narrative. Fate acts as God's representative.'[17] But this is one respect in which *Tales of the Marvellous* does differ from the *Nights*, for God intervenes directly in 'The King of the Two Rivers' by restoring Kaukab's hands and feet. In 'Abu Muhammad the Idle' He responds to the princess's prayer and saves her from rape by the *jinni*. In 'Miqdad and Mayasa' He sends the archangel Gabriel to instruct 'Ali ibn Abi Talib to free Miqdad from captivity. A *deus ex machina* indeed!

Dreams of Opulence

An obsession with fabulous wealth pervades these stories. When the lost prince entered the castle of the forty girls, 'he found that it had a huge door with plates and ornamental patterns of gold and silver. It was covered with hangings and in the entrance hall there were various types of singing birds.' The story goes on to list the extravagant accessories – the gold, silver, crystal ware, silks, aloes wood, ambergris and so on – as well as the rich food. In the Third of the Four Quests, a man describes how he acquired seventy of the *al-andaran* stones: 'each of which was worth a *qintar* of gold. In the crown that they formed were set three hundred pearls, rubies and emeralds, worth *qintars* of gold, and various types of chrysolite, pearls and gold from the best mines were picked out for it.' Though we cannot be sure of the exact composition of the readership of *Tales of the Marvellous*, it is a fair guess that evocations of extravagant decors and costumes were as much to be marvelled at by those readers, who surely did not dine in marble halls, as the monstrous beasts that the storyteller had conjured up from the sea.

Christianity

As already mentioned, another respect in which *Tales of the Marvellous* differs from the *Nights* is that Christian themes feature prominently in the former. Christians appear in the *Nights*, but as the authors of *The Arabian Nights Encyclopedia* note, there 'Christians and their roles serve as a negative stereotype'.[18] This is not the case in *Tales of the Marvellous*, and although its compilers appear to have been Muslim, they were thoroughly familiar with Christian doctrines and practices, and these feature prominently in 'Sul and Shumul', 'Sa'id Son of Hatim al-Bahili' and 'Mahliya and Mauhub and the White-Footed Gazelle'. (It is a little strange that in the last story Mauhub, a Christian, should be receptive to a prophecy delivered by the pagan deity Baal.) 'Sul and Shumul' also survives in a manuscript in Tübingen dating from the four-teenth century and it was probably composed in Syria. Part of the Tübingen manuscript has been broken up into nights, evidently in prep-aration for the insertion of the story into *The Thousand and One Nights*, though it never reached its intended destination. (*sul* is Arabic for 'question', and *shumul* means 'reunion'). In 'Sul and Shumul' and in several of the other stories Christian monks and hermits feature as con-veyors of knowledge and wisdom. The man who went on the First Quest was a Christian who was recruited to the treasure hunt in a church, and only after the Quest was over did he convert to Islam. In general, these stories betray no hostility to Christianity, except that in 'Sa'id Son of Hatim', the monk Simeon denounces the Jews and Christians for having corrupted and altered their scriptures, in particular by removing all references to the future coming of Muhammad and the truth of his message. (This alleged tampering with the Torah and the Gospels has been and continues to be a common feature of Muslim polemic against Christians and Jews.) Because the Jews and Christians had corrupted the divine revelation, 'the Great and Glorious God afflicted them with wars and discords, bringing ruin and destruction on them, forcing them to pay tribute as subjects'. Under Muslim rule Christians were protected and free to practise their religion as 'People of the Book' (*ahl al-kitab*), but they did indeed pay a special tribute known as *jizya*. Simeon's status in this story is a curious one, for he was a Christian monk and former disciple of Jesus 'on whom be peace', who, having lived to witness the mission of the Prophet, has become a Muslim hermit.

The Rewards of Idleness

The first of the four treasure hunters makes this confession:

> As a young man I enjoyed myself, squandering my goods and my wealth and consorting with kings while for me the eye of Time slept. But Time then woke to betray me, destroying what I had and after I had spent three days at home without food, I left to escape the gloating pleasure of my enemies, without any notion of where to go.

In 'Talha, the Son of the Qadi of Fustat', the young man swiftly squanders his inheritance and has to be rescued by his faithful and far more competent slave girl. In 'Abu Muhammad the Idle' the protagonist's comically extreme idleness makes Ivan Goncharov's Oblomov seem like a go-getter, but, of course, everything works out fine for him after he gets someone else to spend a few coins on his behalf. The young idler who squanders his inheritance but who wins through to a fortune that is not really deserved makes several appearances in the *Nights*, and indeed 'Abu Muhammad the Idle' is included in the *Nights*. The latent message may be that man proposes, but destiny decrees. Or perhaps it is that feckless men will always find capable women to look after them. The prince in 'The Forty Girls' would have achieved nothing without the continuous guidance and prompting of the sorceress disguised as a horse.

Bedouin Stories

Two Bedouin stories, 'Miqdad and Mayasa' and 'Sakhr and al-Khansa'', are included in *Tales of the Marvellous*. Miqdad is known to history. Since Miqdad grew up in *jahili*, or pre-Islamic times, but lived on into the Islamic era, he is counted among the *mukhadram*, those people, especially poets, whose lifespans extended across both eras. The word *mukhadram* derives from the verb *khadrama*, 'to cut the ear of one's camel'. God knows why. Miqdad was one of the earliest to convert to Islam and he died in 653 or 654. In the fiction of 'Miqdad and Mayasa' he is portrayed engaging in single-handed combat against preposterous odds. Though he shows a remarkable ability to chant poetry as he fights, it is a matter of record that in early Arabian tribal conflicts warriors did chant poetry as they went into battle. Al-Khansa' ('Snub Nose'), together with her beloved brother Sakhr, are also known to history. She was a seventh-century poet who specialized in laments for the dead. She converted to Islam and died after 644. Sakhr really was one of her brothers, whom she commemorated in elegies after he was killed in tribal warfare, but of course the details given by the story are fiction and improbable fiction at that. The *Nights* similarly contains tales of Bedouin derring-do and love, such as 'The Lovers of the Banu Tayy' and 'The Lovers of Banu 'Udhra'. These fantasies evolved out of the well-established genre of the *ayyam al-'Arab*, or 'the [battle] days of the Bedouin Arabs', stories which, in a mixture of verse and prose, celebrated the wars and skirmishes of the pre-Islamic tribes. A third story, 'Sul and Shumul', starts off as a Bedouin tale but then mutates into something quite different. The youth of the two lovers should be noted, for Sul and Shumul are only fourteen.

Most of the tales contained in *Tales of the Marvellous* should not be classed as folklore. Moreover, they do not have the appearance of stories that first circulated orally before being written down, and neither are there indications that they were part of the professional storytellers' repertoire and were told in the market place or on street corners. Instead the tales, which display creative ingenuity and even at times erudition, must be classed as literature. Perhaps we should regard them as very early and impressive examples of pulp fiction.

Notes

1 Paul Bowles's introduction to his translation of Larbi Layachi's, *A Life Full of Holes* (London: Weidenfeld & Nicolson, 1964), published under Layachi's pseudonym Driss ben Hamed Charhadi, p. 10.

2 The titles of the stories in the missing second volume are as follows: 'Salma and al-Walid', 'The Thief of the Barmecides', 'Jamila the Bedouin', 'Sa'da and Hasan', 'Fawz and al-'Abbas', 'The Female Singer Hawza', 'The Drinker Ahmad', 'Ardashir Son of Mahan', 'The Golden Pigeon', 'Ahmad al-'Anbari', 'The Ebony Horse', 'Al-'Aquluqi (The Attendant)', 'Badr and the Vizier', 'Shams al-Qusur', 'Salman', 'The Island of Bamboo', 'The Island of Diamonds', 'The Confused King', 'King Shaizuran', 'Bayad and Riyad', 'Tahir Son of Khaqan', 'Abu'l-Faraj al-Isfahani', 'The Slave Girl Who Swallowed the Piece of Paper'.

In a minority of cases the stories that go with these titles can be identified. 'The Ebony Horse' is found in late manuscripts of the *Nights*. 'Badr and the Vizier' appears under the title 'The Story of King Badr al-Din Lulu and his Vizier Atamulk, Surnamed the Sad Vizier' in a compilation of stories put together by François Pétis de la Croix under the title *Les Mille et Un Jours*. First published in 1712, this collection, which drew on diverse sources, has been edited and republished by Paul Sebag (Paris: Phébus, 2003). 'The Golden Pigeon' features in at least two Arabic manuscripts. The love story of 'Bayad and Riyad' similarly survives in two manuscripts, in this case originating in Spain or Morocco.

3 E. P. Thompson, *The Making of the English Working Class*, 3rd edn (Harmondsworth: Pelican, 1980), p. 12.

4 Al-Asma'i, quoted in Michael Dols, *Majnun: The Madman in Medieval Islamic Society* (Oxford: Clarendon Press, 1992), p. 315.

5 J. Huizinga, *The Waning of the Middle Ages: A Study of the Forms of Life, Thought and Art in France and the Netherlands in the Fourteenth and Fifteenth Centuries*, trans. F. Hopman (Harmondsworth: Penguin, 1955), p. 9.

6 A. S. Byatt, *The Djinn in the Nightingale's Eye: Five Fairy Stories* (London: Chatto & Windus, 1994), pp. 123–4.

7 Walter Map, quoted in Carolly Erickson, *The Medieval Vision: Essays in History and Perception* (New York: Oxford University Press, 1976), pp. 198–9.

8 *Sir Gawain and the Green Knight*, trans. Brian Stone, 2nd edn (Harmondsworth: Penguin, 1974), p. 111.

9 Bernard Lewis, *Race and Slavery in the Middle East: An Historical Enquiry* (New York: Oxford University Press, 1990), p. 20.

10 Byatt, *The Djinn in the Nightingale's Eye*, pp. 134–5.

11 Captain Buzurg ibn Shahriyar, *The Book of the Wonders of India*, trans. G. S. P. Freeman-Grenville (London: East-West, 1981), p. 23.

12 Ibn Khaldun, *The Muqaddimah: An Introduction to History*, trans. Franz Rosenthal, 3 vols., 2nd edn (London: Routledge and Kegan Paul, 1967), vol. 2, p. 319.

13 Ibid., p. 324.

14 'Abd al-Rahmâne al-Djawbarî, *Le Voile arraché*, trans. René R. Khawam, 2 vols. (Paris: Phébus, 1979), vol. 1, p. 243.

15 *Das Buch der wundersamen Geschichten: Erzählungen aus der Welt von 1001 Nacht*, trans. Ulrich Marzolph (Munich: C. H. Beck, 1999), p. 654.

16 Paul Willemen, *Pier Paolo Pasolini* (London: British Film Institute, 1977), p. 74.

17 Ulrich Marzolph and Richard van Leeuwen (eds.), *The Arabian Nights Encyclopedia*, 2 vols. (Santa Barbara, CA, and Oxford: ABC Clio, 2004), vol. 2, p. 688.

18 Ibid., p. 523.

Further Reading

There is very little to read on *Tales of the Marvellous* in English, apart from a page in Robert Irwin, *Arabian Nights: A Companion* (London: Allen Lane, 1984), and a short article in Ulrich Marzolph and Richard van Leeuwen (eds.), *The Arabian Nights Encyclopedia* (Santa Barbara, CA, and Oxford: ABC-CLIO, 2004). There is an article by Ulrich Marzolph, 'As Woman Can Be: The Gendered Subversiveness of an Arabic Folktale Heroine', *Edebiyât*, 10 (1999), pp. 199–218 (on 'Arus al-'Ara'is); see also Ulrich Marzolph, 'Narrative Strategies in Popular Literature: Ideology and Ethics in Tales from the Arabian Nights and Other Collections', *Middle Eastern Literatures*, 7 (2004), pp. 171–82 (mostly on 'Abu Muhammad the Idle'), and Geert Jan Van Gelder, 'Slave-Girl Lost and Regained: Transformations of a Story', *Marvels and Tales*, 18 (2004), pp. 201–17 (on 'Talha, the Son of the Qadi of Fustat'). Those interested in the various motifs and tale types in *Tales of the Marvellous* and how they feature in other Arab stories should consult Hasan M. El-Shamy, *Folk Traditions of the Arab World: A Guide to Motif Classification*, 2 vols. (Bloomington and Indianapolis: Indiana University Press, 1995).

There is an extensive secondary literature on *Tales of the Marvellous* in German. Hans Wehr published the edited Arabic text as *Das Buch der Wunderbaren Erzählungen und Seltsamen Geschichten* (Wiesbaden: F. Steiner, 1956). This edition formed the basis of the translation by Hans Wehr, Otto Spies, Max Weisweiler and Sophia Grotzfeld, edited by Ulrich Marzolph and published as *Das Buch der wundersamen Geschichten: Erzählungen aus der Welt von 1001 Nacht* (Munich: C. H. Beck, 1999). Those who seek more detailed information on the stories and, in particular, the classification of the story elements according to tale types must consult this book. Also the relationship between *Tales of the Marvellous* and the *Nights* is discussed in the appendix to the sixth volume of Enno Littmann's translation of the *Nights*, *Die Erzählungen aus den Tausendundein Nächten*, 2nd edn (Berlin: Deutsche Buch-Gemeinschaft, 1953), and in Heinz and Sophia Grotzfeld's *Die Erzählungen aus 'Tausendundeiner Nächt'* (Darmstadt: Wissenschaftliche Buchgesellschaft, 1984). The two Bedouin stories and 'Sul and Shumul' have been discussed by Sophia Schwab in an unpublished PhD. thesis, 'Drei arabische Erzählungen aus dem Beduinenleben untersucht und übersetzt' (Munster, 1965). In French the classification of the stories is discussed in Aboubakr Chraibi's *Les Mille et Une Nuits: Histoire du texte et classification des contes* (Paris: L'Harmattan, 2008). Jean-Claude Garçin has argued for a late date for the manuscript of *Tales of the Marvellous* in *Pour une lecture historique des Mille et Une Nuits: Essai sur l'édition de Bulaq (1835)* (Arles: Sindbad/Actes Sud, 2013).

The thematic articles in volume 2 of Ulrich Marzolph and Richard van Leeuwen (eds.), *The Arabian Nights Encyclopedia* (Santa Barbara, CA, and Oxford: ABC Clio, 2004) will also be found useful in providing a social and cultural background to the tales in *Tales of the Marvellous*. Hugh Kennedy, *The Court of the Caliphs: The Rise and Fall of Islam's Greatest Dynasty* (London: Weidenfeld and Nicolson, 2004) provides a very readable account of the history and culture of the Islamic heartlands in the eighth and ninth centuries. On 'Aja'ib, see Mohammed Arkoun, Jacques le Goff, Tawfiq Fahd and Maxime Rodinson, *L'Étrange et le merveilleux dans l'Islam médiéval* (Paris: Editions J. A., 1978), the Louvre exhibition catalogue *L'Étrange et le merveilleux en terres d'Islam* (Paris: Réunion des musées nationaux, 2001) and Roy Mottahedeh, ''Aja'ib in *The Thousand and One Nights*', in Richard Hovannisian and Georges Sabbagh (eds.), *The Thousand and One Nights in Arabic Literature and Society* (Cambridge: Cambridge University Press, 1997), pp. 29–39. Captain Buzurg ibn Shahriyar's treatise on the wonders of the sea has been translated by G. S. P. Freeman-Grenville as *The Book of the Wonders of India: Mainland, Sea and Islands* (London: East-West, 1981).

On the occult, see Emilie Savage-Smith (ed.), *Magic and Divination in Early Islam* (Aldershot: Ashgate, 2004); Marina Warner, *Stranger Magic: Charmed States and the Arabian Nights* (London: Chatto & Windus, 2011); Amira El-Zein, *Islam, Arabs, and the Intelligent World of the Jinn* (Syracuse, NY: Syracuse University Press, 2009). On prophecy, see Toufic Fahd, *La Divination arabe: Études religieuses, sociologiques et folkloriques sur le milieu natif de l'Islam* (Paris: Sindbad, 1987). So far there is very little secondary literature on Arab treasure hunting, but see Irwin, *The Arabian Nights: A Companion*, chapter 8.

On sex, see Abdelwahab Bouhdiba, *Sexuality in Islam*, translated by Alan Sheridan (London: Routledge and Kegan Paul, 1985); Afaf Lutfi al-Sayyid Marsot (ed.), *Society and the Sexes in Medieval Islam* (Malibu, CA: Undena Publications, 1987).

Acknowledgements

I gratefully acknowledge the advice and corrections of Ruth Bottigheimer, Aboubakr Chraibi, Malcolm Lyons and especially Ulrich Marzolph. I am also grateful to Hugh Kennedy for providing me with access to the Arabic text of *Tales of the Marvellous*.

Tales of the Marvellous

and

News of the Strange

Tale One

The Story of the King of the Two Rivers, Saihun and Jaihun, His Son Kaukab and His Experience with the Chamberlain Ghasb. An Astonishing Tale.

Of the stories presented in this text, this is the most seriously affected by lacunae. These cover the introduction of Prince Kaukab, who is the son of King Fulk, king of both Saihun and Jaihun, while his unnamed mother has had an important if unrecorded role to play in causing the exile from Saihun of the villain. This man, 'the chamberlain', is found in the service of Farah, whom Fulk appointed as ruler of Jaihun and who is generally referred to as 'the king'. Yaquta is Farah's daughter, once wrongly described as his sister.

They say – and God knows better and is more glorious and nobler – that amongst the stories of ancient times and past peoples is one that is suited to the intelligence of men of understanding who both ask and give. There was a great, powerful and distinguished king named Fulk, who commanded the obedience of his subjects, whom he treated with generosity. He was strong and powerful and could seize wild beasts with his bare hands. His reputation spread, and he humbled lions in their thickets and abashed powerful kings. He had a servant named Farah, whom his father had brought up with him and of whom he thought so highly that, when his territories increased, he handed over half of them for Farah to rule, exercising authority over their peoples. Fulk ruled what was known as Saihun while Farah ruled Jaihun and its surroundings.

Life was easy for the inhabitants of these lands; there was no enemy for them to fear and no bloodshed, and so they enjoyed a life of ease, eating and drinking untroubled by sadness. Fulk himself was a generous man, prodigal with gifts, a distributor of robes of honour. One day as he was riding outside his city with his men a messenger approached him, and at the sight the escort drew up in two lines watching him. The man dismounted and approached the king on foot.

[lac.] When the king heard this he said: 'How did this dog get on to the mainland?' [lac.] The vizier said: 'That is the way to the left of town,' but the king said: 'He is safe and, by the Lord of the Ka'ba, no one will reach him.' He then concealed what he was thinking from the vizier, and the vizier did not return to the subject. They had pigeons with them and wherever they arrived the vizier would release them, and so the king would know what nobody else knew.

As for the commander of the citadel, when they reached it he came down, kissed the ground and sent out provisions, as well as stores of all kinds. [Kaukab] gave generous gifts and camped beneath the citadel in order to hunt, he being a great and generous prince. Pigeons were carried in cages behind the hunters and sent off every morning so that the king might enjoy hearing what his son was doing. [lac.] The king and the prince's mother were relieved as the time mentioned by the astrologer had passed.

The prince told his companions to take provisions for three days and form a great circle within which to hunt. Afterwards they could go back to strike camp and return home, this being a long distance away. He told the vizier that there was no need for him to come with them and he could stay as last man in the camp. He himself rode out lightly equipped with the commander of the citadel, and after two days they came to a depression shaped like the palm of a hand in which there were so many beasts that they crowded against each other.

He called for the mare that was mentioned earlier, tightened the girths around its flanks and mounted. He then struck in his spurs and dropped the reins, at which the mare bounded off like a lightning flash up a high hill and down the other side, where it galloped across open country. The prince, who thought that his men were following him, reached a place where there was water, which he spurred the mare to cross. It pricked up its ears, blew out its nostrils and reared up so as to show the hollows behind the top of its legs. The prince hit it on the rump with his whip but then saw that it was confronted by a lion. He drew his sword, made for the lion and struck it on the forehead, from which the blade emerged gleaming through its blood.

He rode on until sunset, when he dismounted on a mountain and said: 'My father and the astrologer were right in what they said as there can be no doubt that I am facing death.' He was distressingly tired and felt regret when this was no longer of any use. He released the mare, which began to circle round him before coming back to graze, going on doing this until late evening, while the prince neither slept nor ate nor drank. The mare, whose girths had been loosened, came up to him and nudged his feet with its head while blowing through its nose, while for his part he rubbed its face.

When he mounted and rode on, he came across a narrow worn track, which he followed until he came to a mountain in which there was a defile, along which he rode for the rest of the day and all through the night until morning. In the distance could be seen an obscure, dark and stinking lake, and when he got there he dismounted gloomily and, taking some filth from it, he put it over his heart. He unbridled the mare in a show of sympathy, but although it started to graze, what it cropped tasted too foul to be ingested. As the prince had been suffering from sleeplessness he closed his eyes and lost consciousness.

Just then at the edge of the lake a boat appeared, and from it ten black men, as big as buffaloes, emerged and pounced on him before he could resist. When they had seized him the mare shied away and galloped off like a wild beast up into the mountains, but as it had never been there before it lost its way.

So much for the prince, but as for his escort, they were at a loss to know what had happened to him and went around searching for him unsuccessfully throughout the desert. When they had despaired because of his lengthy absence the vizier said: 'I told him, but he did not accept what I said, and now what is past is past.' He sent word to the king and insisted that he would stay where he was until God granted him relief from his sorrows by allowing him a sight of the prince.

He did this, while the king, on hearing the news, was reduced to helplessness and had the horses' tails clipped in sorrow for the loss of his son. He filled the night watches with his cries, while the boy's mother almost killed herself with grief and cut off her hair, as did her maids. The citizens wore black mourning and all the king's men were filled with grief.

The king built a tomb for his son in his palace and stayed beside it, mourning and lamenting like a mother bereaved of her child and as restless as a grain of corn in a frying pan. The prince's mother and her maids were shrieking and, with the spread of the news, the king lost all powers of endurance.

He sent everywhere to look for information, and word reached the servant of what had happened to the prince after he had been sent as a messenger. The chamberlain to whom he had gone had made him his doorkeeper and put him in charge of his affairs, allowing him to do what he wanted. When he heard of what had happened to the prince and that the secret had come out he made a show of grief in front of the son of the king's servant. So much for the king.

The vizier and his men stayed where they were for eighteen days after the prince had gone missing. Meanwhile the mare had gone up the mountains and over the hills, facing fearful perils, until God brought it to the right path, which it began to follow. It had become emaciated through lack of fodder but when it reached the vizier's camp it caught sight of the other horses and approached them snuffling. There were people all around it, but it went on until it reached its stall, where it fell down dead. This was an even greater blow to the escort than the absence of the prince, and the vizier shed bitter tears as he stripped it of its trappings and buried it in a shroud out of respect for the king and the prince. He then gave orders for the party to move and he rode on with them until he had reached home. The day of their arrival was one of great solemnity as the only one missing from their ranks was the young Kaukab, for whom they turned their saddles upside down and lowered their banners.

So much for them, but as for the prince, when the black men had seized him he remained tied up for the rest of the day until nightfall. His captors then went to a narrow gulf whose fresh water was whiter than milk and sweeter than honey. They followed this until late evening, when they went ashore and collected wood for a fire. When it had blazed up they brought up the prince and threw him down, still tied up, and looked at one another. One of them told them that he should be given food lest he die, but they did not accept the suggestion.

Kaukab went up to them, behaving as though he was one of them. He had heard that the king's chamberlain was of Magian stock and amongst them was a brother of his. And when they saw what he was doing they asked him what his religion was. 'It is that of my father Ghasab, the king's chamberlain.' On hearing this, they went up to him and kissed the ground in front of him, exclaiming: 'He is the brother of our leader! We have a gift for him, and tomorrow we shall be on the Saihun.'

They gave Kaukab something to eat and, after eating it, he sat until nightfall when they spread bedding for him in an attractive place, making him welcome. He slept until morning, when he sat looking at the water until afternoon. What he could see was a large stretch of water with clashing waves into whose stinking waters our [sic] gulf entered. This led to the open sea and was the way home for the blacks.

They went to a spot where, after taking their evening meal, they spent the night and they went on like this for ten days, after which they were in sight of castles, fields and estates. When the owner of one of these was approached with a request for food he produced enough for a whole month together with wines of various types and he extended a welcome to Kaukab.

After three days the company left and moved to a large and splendid island with many trees and fruits of many kinds, carpeted with saffron, where they stretched their legs after having moored their boat to a stake.

Kaukab decided to keep nothing back from them and when they asked him for his story he said: 'We were out hunting and I followed a gazelle, but when I failed to catch it I became confused and didn't know how to get back to my companions.'

The blacks believed his story and, after eating and drinking peacefully, they drank wine as the breeze blew and the water flowed while the trees rustled gently in the moonlight. They went on like this until dawn, by which time they fell into a drunken sleep to make up for their sleepless night. While they were unconscious Kaukab got up, exclaiming: 'God is greater!', and cut their throats before dragging them to the river, into which they sank like stones.

Kaukab then removed the stake to which the boat was moored, and it set off as fast as lightning. It was only a short time before he came in sight of land, where people were swarming like locusts. Porters came and removed the boat's cargo, taking it to an inn and leaving the boat moored to the shore. Kaukab himself put on magnificent clothes and started to go around the city inspecting its shops.

So much for him, but as for the drowned bodies of the blacks, when they floated to the surface, people cried out that their throats had been cut, and word of this reached the chamberlain. He and the sultan came with three others and when they had looked at the faces, the sultan said: 'Let them go to hell.' One of them, however, whose name was 'Umar, was recognized, and the chamberlain sent his servant to the citadel, where the doorkeeper was given the news. He went to the black slave, who had taken the food to the boat and who was mortally afraid of him, and asked him about those who had been on board. He named them one by one and added that with them had been a young boy with a moon-like face who said that he was your eldest son. On hearing this, the chamberlain told him to go off and to say nothing if anyone questioned him.

The chamberlain thought over the details of his plan and asked those around him whether anyone had come ashore from the boat. An old man with jug-like ears and a rope tied round his waist came up to him and said respectfully: 'Master, I saw someone wearing a face veil followed by two porters who were carrying all his bedding and belongings.' The chamberlain called for the head porter and consulted him privately, after which the man left briefly before coming back to speak to him and the chamberlain then, surrounded by men, went to the door of the inn.

Before Kaukab knew what was happening, when he looked up there was the chamberlain and a crowd of people around him. The chamberlain sent a mamluk to tell him to come to his house, which he quickly did, going in and sitting with the mamluk as he was instructed. The chamberlain dismounted and ordered him to be brought to him. 'Kaukab!' he exclaimed on seeing him, and when Kaukab answered, he asked what he was doing there. 'This is something decreed by God,' Kaukab replied, and when the chamberlain asked where his mother was he said that she was in the city with his father. 'Whoever suffers does not forget,' said the chamberlain, 'and the man who was responsible for this exile of mine will have to put up with this misfortune as the Lord of mankind has put you into my hands.'

On the chamberlain's orders Kaukab was tied up, thrown down on the ground and beaten until he fainted, after which a heavy brick was tied to his feet and he was left at the side of the house. He stayed like that for ten days in accordance with the will of God and to fulfil the destiny He had decreed, but when the king returned to the city the chamberlain became afraid that someone who had a connection with Kaukab or could recognize him might catch sight of him, and so he removed him by night and put him in a dungeon amongst the thieves. He then went early in the morning to present his services to the king, who greeted him and called him forward to take the seat that he enjoyed thanks to his privileged position. He then told him to order a general release of prisoners in the hope that God might restore him to health after a long illness that had been getting worse since the disappearance of Kaukab – 'and I wish that I may be his ransom,' he added.

On hearing this, the chamberlain said: 'News has come that he has reappeared and entered the city, filling it with his moon-like radiance.' 'Chamberlain,' exclaimed the king when he heard this, 'for this news you deserve a jewelled robe of honour.' He produced one as valuable as Caesar's kingdom and publicly invested him with it. When it had been put on, all who were present offered their services, saying: 'This man has enjoyed such good fortune with the king as has never been known at any time at all.'

The chamberlain rode off, followed by the people, who only dispersed when he had reached the door of his house and gone in. He then sat down to think out a subtle scheme, asking himself how he could kill Kaukab if people had seen him. He did not sleep until night had passed and light had returned. When the crowds at the gate saw him coming out they called down blessings on him, surging around him until he reached the royal palace and approached to present his services to the king before taking his seat.

The king did not know what was going on as his mind had been affected and he had been unable to ride out thanks to his illness. He had signed over power to the chamberlain to distribute gifts in his name as though he was his father, and he knew no more than the common people about what was happening, and what information he received was wrong. The chamberlain said: 'O king who rules over the length and breadth of the land, may I be allowed to speak?' 'Say what you want,' the king told him, 'and I shall listen and follow your council and advice.' The chamberlain then said: 'Things are going easily, and two-thirds of the people support the ruler, but any ruler who does not act decisively is no more than a servant. This is a big country with a large population amongst whom there are many mischief-makers, thieves and wrong-doers. If the damage that they do is not checked, no one will be left at ease and people will be robbed in broad daylight by armed force. Travellers who come and go will spread word that yours is an inferior country in which wives of respectable men can be seized at sword point.' 'What do you advise me to do, then?' asked the king, and the chamberlain replied: 'Cut off the hands of those who deserve it and hang those who deserve to be hanged, while those who owe a blood debt but have no legal opponents should be set free.'

He went on talking nonsense until the king turned to him, raised his hand and put it on his neck, saying: 'I have no responsibility for this; it is you who will be held to account for what is done to the citizens, so act in a way that will ensure your salvation in the world to come when you stand before the Giver of life. I shall not be accountable for any crime committed by a *dhimmi*, a Christian or a Muslim, and it is you who will have to answer for them in the presence of God, Who knows all hidden secrets.'

When the chamberlain heard this he showed his teeth in a smile and rode off from the palace to his house, where he dismounted. He told himself that before putting Prince Kaukab to death he should kill a number of others and when it came to the point he should not execute him alone. He then told his officers to inspect the prisoners he was holding, and, when they did, the number came to six hundred. Of these he publicly freed one hundred and fifty to general commotion, as people called down blessings on him. On the following day he brought out a hundred and had their heads cut off, while he crucified thirty, leaving the citizens frightened to death. On the third day he executed another hundred and on the fourth day he entered the dungeon himself and had the young Kaukab almost beaten to death. When the beating stopped Kaukab asked what he was going to do with him and he said: 'I am going to put you to shame so that you can see for yourself your disgrace.' 'What did I do to you?' asked Kaukab, and the chamberlain replied: 'What dog are you to do anything to me? I want to see your mother suffer for your loss, as you and she were responsible for my being driven out and exiled from my own land. She took a hundred thousand dinars that were owed to me and spent a year casting stones at me.' 'Listen,' said Kaukab, 'I swear that I will give this back to you.' 'You worthless fellow,' replied the chamberlain, 'who can be safe from your schemes? But now it is clear that you are helpless.'

When Kaukab heard this he felt humiliated and was moved by fear to point to the debt that the chamberlain owed thanks to the favours done him by the king his father. 'If your father stood on his head until he lost his senses, that would not make up for what I did with him and the kingdom that I gave him,' replied the chamberlain. Kaukab told him: 'What you do with me, Almighty God will continue to do with you in the next world, and while this world is transitory the next is everlasting.' 'Are you sitting there threatening me?' exclaimed the chamberlain. 'Take him away.'

He was taken out with his hands tied and a rope around his neck, but the watching crowd were so struck by his beauty that they wanted to free him from the chamberlain, and one of them raised a cry that the chamberlain should be stoned. He told himself that the crowd were going to rise against him and that even if the sultan and his troops were with someone whom they attacked, these would not be able to help him. So he gestured with his hand to hush them and removed the rope from Kaukab's neck. He ordered that he be given a seat, and when this was done servants surrounded Kaukab, keeping him from the people. The chamberlain told one of them to cut off his hands and feet without cauterizing the wounds, so that he would die quickly and the crowd would not be able to save him.

The servant did as he was ordered, and the crowd raised a shout against the chamberlain, and had they been able to get to him they would have struck him down with the stones they were throwing. They did reach the young Kaukab and, using their kerchiefs, they cauterized his hands and feet, cutting up their own clothes to use as bandages. They brought sherbet and rose-water for him to drink, sprinkling some over him and wiping his face before fetching a gown in which they placed him and carried him underneath the royal palace. The king's sister, who was mentioned earlier, was sitting looking out from her balcony with his wife and when she saw the crowd hurrying below she told Sawab, the servant who had brought her up, to find out what was happening and why the crowd had collected. The servant went down and stood watching until he saw the young Kaukab being carried past, unrecognizable because of the loss of blood and his change of colour. At this sight the servant told the people to put him down as his mistress might take pity on him. Kaukab himself had lost consciousness and no longer looked like himself.

Sawab went up to the princess, Yaquta, and told her the story, at which she came down to look for herself, and when she saw the handsome shape of the man whom they had put down and his delicate beauties she felt pity for him in her heart, as God Almighty had intended. She went back and, after having taken her usual seat, she told Sawab to place Kaukab in the mosque opposite the palace and to lock the door in order to keep the people away from him. When he had done that she summoned him by name and on his arrival she said: 'You know that you brought me up and when you washed me in the bath I uncovered my whole body for you and you carried me on your shoulder. Now there is something that I need from you.' 'If you tell me what you want, I shall do it for you,' he said, and she told him: 'I feel pity in my heart for this boy and I want you to bring him to me.'

Sawab waited until nightfall, when everyone was asleep, and he then opened the postern door, lowering a curtain over it. He went up to Kaukab and carried him over his shoulder up to the palace, where he stopped and locked the doors before putting him down in front of princess Yaquta. She put him in a chamber with a fine lattice window of iron looking out over the Jaihun, through which he could watch everything and see the emirs and the troops passing in front of him. The floor was carpeted, and he was given a raised seat. She told him that he could relax happily for he was the apple of her eye; because of the wrong that had been done to him she felt pity for him in her heart, and he had no further cause for fear. She introduced him to her housekeeper and put Sawab in charge of the palace so that he should not be with her. She continued to supply Kaukab with sherbet and spread *sultani* herbs over his wounds to ease the pain as God in His majesty had decreed that he should triumph over his enemies.

So much for him, but as for the chamberlain, he went that night with twenty servants to where Kaukab had been but, finding no trace of him, they remained in a state of perplexity. A number of people had seen him on his way, and they followed him and told him that Kaukab had been lucky and that, after being left there, he had been carried off. The chamberlain went back with his men in a state of deep, unremitting gloom that did not allow him to sleep.

As for Kaukab's parents, his father sent messengers with letters to the city where the chamberlain was and where they questioned the general signs of mourning that they saw. The chamberlain made a display of sorrow and presented them with gifts and robes of honour. They then went back to the king but could not tell him what had happened to Kaukab. Sorrow for him continued, with many expressions of grief as well as a general feeling of gloom, while his parents raised their tearful laments to Almighty God.

Kaukab remained in hiding with Yaquta, who looked after him herself. She did not tell her mother, and the only person who knew the secret was the housekeeper, while ten times a day she would fetch Kaukab all kinds of good and tasty food. As for the chamberlain, he admitted to being perplexed about the affair but said that he did not think that Kaukab could be in the palace. He ordered a pretty ten-year-old girl to be brought to him as his attendants watched and he told her: 'I intend to give you to the princess so that you can find out what she is doing and then tell this servant.'

He sent the servant with her together with a present of clothes, and the princess admired her when she arrived, telling herself that she could be entrusted with her heart's secrets, while the servant was to stay outside the door. She expressed her gratitude to the chamberlain. Five years passed, during which she was impressed by the girl's cultivated intelligence, her skill, her mastery of Arabic poetry and her fondness for the unusual. Taking her as a close companion, she told her about Kaukab and when a month later she was alone with the chamberlain's servant she told him the story and he in turn passed it on to his master.

[lac.] He found the king happy that his illness had been cured and told him that he had something to say to him that he wanted to tell him in secret as he could not speak before all those who were present in the court. When the king heard this he had the court cleared and then told the man to produce what he had to say, at which he began: 'Know, great king, that there have been many strangers gathering in the city, and cultured men have been talking. Were you to hear that your sister Yaquta had fallen in love with a man whom she kept in her palace, what would you say about it?' 'What are you saying?' exclaimed the king, and the chamberlain went on: 'You heard what I said, but don't be hasty so that you can get what you want, fearful as this may be.'

A servant was standing by the king's head and when he heard what had been said he went to the maid and told her what had happened. They were proposing to move Kaukab to another safe place when they were confronted by the king with the chamberlain looking on and the maids standing behind them. Looking at the servant, the chamberlain exclaimed: 'Black dog, did you take it on yourself to tell them so that they could hide him somewhere else?' He drew his sword and advanced on him before delivering a blow that struck off his head. This terrified the maid and her companions, and the king told the chamberlain that he could do what he wanted with them. He took them to his house and beat them so savagely that he tore away their flesh. He then returned to the king, who asked him what he had done. 'I questioned them,' he said, 'and they told me that Yaquta had been made pregnant by her lover.'

The king struck one hand against the other and exclaimed: 'There is no power and no might except with the Almighty God! By God, when my master hears this he will attack me and take my lands away from me, and what can I say to him?' He repeated this angrily, saying that his master would be furious, and he then told the chamberlain to cut off Yaquta's head. The chamberlain, however, told him that he would wait until midday on Saturday, when he alone would drown her and her lover in view of all the sailors, 'so that they can talk of what you did and everyone who hears can call down blessings on you'. 'Do what you want,' said the king.

A proclamation was made, and news of what had happened spread amongst the people, amongst whom no one talked of anything else. Sawab heard of this and when Saturday came he went to his mother in a state of confusion and asked her: 'Who told the chamberlain about this and how did it happen?' 'See what clever plan you can make,' she told him, 'and send word at night to the boat owners that they are not to leave any boats on the river.' Sawab did this, and only one small boat was left out, in the bottom of which were two black sacks and two thin stone pillars that would take three men to lift.

He went in to stand in front of the king, whom he saw to be broken-hearted because of his sister [sic] Yaquta and unable to speak.

Just then in came the chamberlain, who was dragging her beside him by the hand. When Sawab saw her, looking as she did like the full moon, he shouted in front of the king to the chamberlain and, taking her from him, he struck her on the head with the palm of his hand and struck Kaukab with a blow to the face that almost blinded him. When the chamberlain saw what he had done to them he told him to take charge of them. 'I shall do whatever you want,' Sawab said, and he wrapped them up and took them out as the people watched before placing them in a small boat. There was unrest amongst the spectators, and the king stood up before going up to a balcony to look over the river, which stretched as far across as the eye could see.

Sawab and his porters took them, wrapped up as they were, and threw them into the boat, with the sacks in front of them. There was increasing disturbance as girls shrieked, and the king, shedding tears, went back to the city. Sawab took the boat below the city and moored it until nightfall, and at midnight he put out and sailed back below the royal palace. It was then that he removed Kaukab and Yaquta and produced a hiding place in which they stayed.

News reached the boy's father of what had happened to his sister, and he said to her: 'This is a good ruler, so come with me and let us enjoy going to see him, for I have heard him praised both as a good man and an effective leader.' When she heard this, she said: 'Your Majesty, how can I enjoy this? Sorrow has penetrated my inmost self of which my son is a part.' 'What you say is true,' the king replied, 'but we should have a brief respite from our sorrows or else we shall die, and after that the lands will face destruction.' She did not disagree, and the king left the vizier in his place to look after his subjects while he himself moved off with his tents and his troops. No banners were unfurled and no drums beaten, while only one small bugle sounded, as there was only a small force with the king.

So much for the king, but as for Yaquta's mother, she summoned Sawab to a consultation. 'This is a strange affair,' she told him, 'and a lesson for those who can learn. Do you know who this boy is whose hands and feet have been cut off?' 'No, by God,' replied Sawab, and she then told him that this was Kaukab, the son of King Fulk. He had told her his story from beginning to end, including what the chamberlain had done thanks to his enmity towards his mother. 'He suggests that you should go to his father Fulk and tell him what happened to him and Yaquta, for otherwise that damned man will arrange for us all to be destroyed even if we hide beneath the edge of the world. As he has no hands or feet, put him in a carrying couch like a split oyster and leave with your men. I myself shall not stay behind but will follow you. Make a forced march across the dangerous country and pass through my husband's land. Then send a Bedouin to Fulk to tell him what has happened and don't stay here lest you suffer the vengeance of this creature who is no man and who will not see the face of the Merciful God in the next world.'

When Sawab heard this he went out and told his companions what had happened. They mounted and, taking with them camels and mules, they left the city and when they were at some distance from it they made for one of his garrison castles, a strong place and so high that its top was almost out of sight. Sawab told his party to go up, for they could stay there even if they were besieged until the Day of Resurrection. Kaukab, however, said: 'Carry me to my father so that he can see me and satisfy his longing as well as avenging me if he can for what has been done to me.' 'Do what you want, master,' said Sawab, 'for we are your servants.' They then stored all their baggage and that evening Sawab set out, leaving the castle and pressing on towards the gate of Saihun, unafraid because the castle walls were as high as a star in the sky.

When the chamberlain was unable to find Sawab and his men, he gave a hundred dinars to a Bedouin, asking him to find out where they had gone and promising him a robe of honour and a horse. The man agreed, mounted his dromedary and rode off in pursuit of Sawab's men, whom he joined and accompanied to the castle. He then started back to the city with people staring at his white dromedary, which was moving like the wind and leaving a trail of pebbles scattered by the soles of its feet. Its rider had no need to lash its flanks, as it was like a gust of wind or a pigeon in flight.

So much for the Bedouin, but in the city was a sailor who had been given a thousand dinars by Sawab's people, who had told him that he could live on this for the rest of his life as long as no one knew about him. The possession of the money drove him out of his wits, as he had no idea what it was worth. He bought clothes for his daughter, his other children and his wife, as well as a new boat for himself, and he appeared in clothes that he used only to wear at the 'Id. His neighbour, another sailor, went at night to the chamberlain and told him about this, at which the chamberlain summoned the man and questioned him. Because of his fear he gave away his secret and was imprisoned. Next morning he was taken before the king, who asked him for his story, and when he had heard it he told the chamberlain: 'This is a poor fellow. Don't talk to him but let him go.'

The man was released, and the king ordered his men to pursue Sawab to his castle and lay siege to it. When the Bedouin learned that the king had come, he tethered his dromedary by its reins, went into his presence, greeted him, kissed his hand and told him what had happened, at which the king ordered his men to set off in pursuit of Sawab. They followed him for a whole month before catching up with him under a mountain soaring up into the air. When Sawab saw how many men were there he and his followers took refuge on the lower slopes of the mountain. He fought until nightfall but was defeated by numbers and had to take refuge on the peak, although the water was at the mountain's foot.

Young Kaukab, despairing of life, crawled off to perform his prayers, and Sawab told his mistress that they were lost. 'Things are in the hands of God,' she told him, 'for the enemy have the water, while none of us have more than to wet our lips as our beasts die.' On hearing this, Yaquta said: 'It may be that God will bring us speedy relief, answer our payers and help us to avoid destruction, while pitying our exile.'

Next morning clamour and shouts were raised from all sides with the chamberlain telling his men not to stop until they had cut down their enemies with their swords. The water was under their control, and Sawab's men drank what they had, with some giving theirs to others, while Kaukab took none, offering his sacrifice to Almighty God. In the evening their enemies patrolled around them and lit fires in front of them. Kaukab crawled away from his friends, but Yaquta caught sight of him and asked him what he was doing. 'There is something I need to do,' he told her, 'and I raise it as a complaint to God. So sleep, secure in His protection.' She was afraid that he might try to commit suicide, and both she and her mother kept him in view, with tears falling over their cheeks.

As for Kaukab, he looked up to heaven, bare-headed and tearful, and stretching out his arms he said: 'My God, has my mother not entrusted me to You? Did she not shed tears and bare her head before You, saying that she gave me to You? If this is something You have already decreed and written down as my destiny, look down on me. My Lord, to whom should I go for refuge when it is You Who have led me safely along my way? How am I to reach You, on Whom I depend for my livelihood? Grant me Your gracious pity and forgiveness and do not allow this unbeliever to slake his hatred on me. My God, if Iblis helps him, help me, for You are the best of helpers. My God, You know that I have no one to aid me, come to my aid and take my part. My God, I am thrown down at Your door, unable to stand, so do not drive me away. My Lord, I can no longer endure mankind, take my soul and release me, for You are the only Master to Whom I turn in all humility, so do not forget me. Look on me with Your eye that never sleeps, for here I am before You, and You can hear me. I have put my hopes on You, so do not disappoint me. Lord, You know what is hidden in secret.' He wept and struck his head on a stone, adding tears and groans. The tears were followed by an effusion of blood as he threw himself down on the ground, which was stained by blood from his face.

Yaquta and her mother both bared their heads and joined him in his supplications. Yaquta said: 'My Lord, You know our state so show us Your mercy, most merciful God.' She then recited these lines:

Lord, You Who see and are not seen,
You see our cheeks that lie in dust,
Our heads uncovered before all,
And how the tears drop from our eyes.
You see our dwellings which are desolate,
So look at us, You Who decree our fate.
Be gentle, You Who see and are not seen.

She tore her hair, which was carried off by the wind, but just then a heavenly voice called out: 'Cover your heads so that the angels of the Lord may visit you.' Yaquta and her mother did this, and suddenly there was a blaze of light like a lightning flash, and the voice said: 'Young man, turn on your back and stretch out your hands and feet, for these have been granted to you by God Who provides you with nourishment in the darkness of your intestines.' At that a hand joined one of his wrists and another the other. Kaukab exclaimed: 'By God, I feel the veins joining up, with the blood flowing and the flesh becoming firm under a covering of skin! Looking at the gift God has granted me, I kiss the ground in gratitude to Him.'

He then got up like a moon emerging from cloud, praising God the Omniscient for having ended his pain. He stood and walked as though this was his first day, his heart filled with happiness at God's gift. Next morning he put on his breastplate, strapped on his Indian sword and fastened his jewelled waist-belt. He then came down from the mountain peak and rode off alone [lac.] The king said that no one was to shoot at him as he might be a messenger whose rights would have to be respected. 'Why shouldn't we kill him and burn his body so that he doesn't try to get something from us?' asked the chamberlain, but on hearing this the king told him: 'Wait! Don't talk like this or rush to harm him before we find out why he has come. Then if he deserves to be hanged, we can hang him.'

When Kaukab had come close he dismounted and began to walk through the ranks of the king's men, who parted for him and sheathed their swords. On seeing the king, he threw himself on him and embraced him, experiencing a feeling of passionate love for him in his heart, for which he could not account. He then said: 'King of Jaihun, have you no fear of the Lord of destiny, He Who says to something: "Be", and it is. Has the life of this world deceived you, and its victims are cheated in their bargain. Why do you not inquire into the condition of the people? [lac.] You have been entrusted with their affairs but have not acted as a ruler should; you have been raised above them, but have not shown justice. I do not think that you have your wits about you when you send away a man like me and associate yourself with this chamberlain. The whole world watches him in silence for the power is in his hands, and he and they are like two moons – blessed be God, the best of Creators!'

Just then the chamberlain came up to him and said: 'You fellow with the fiery hot eyes, what dog are you to stand before the king and make this speech at him?' 'Don't you recognize me?' asked Kaukab on hearing this; 'Open your eyes and look at me. I am the man who had two hands given me by God, and it was God Who restored them to my wrists, as He restored my feet to my legs. That was through the power of the Creator of heaven and earth, and I am the noble hero who owes obedience to this king and have no blame to attach to him. As for you, I shall strike off your head in his presence and use your blood to gain his favour, for I am Kaukab, the son of Fulk, the lord of the two rivers, Saihun and Jaihun.'

Kaukab then told his story to the king, explaining what the chamberlain had done to him, leaving the king to exclaim: 'By the Lord of the sacred Ka'ba, Zamzam and the Maqam, Fulk is my master!' Then he went on: 'Strike this pimp, the chamberlain, with your spear points,' and his men rushed at him with their spears, drawing their swords. The first to strike him on the head and cut him in two with his sword was Prince Kaukab. His soul left his body – may God show him no mercy but turn him away! May He moisten no ground for him but curse him! A number of soldiers went on striking him with their swords and thrusting at him with their spears until he had been cut to pieces and God had delivered the people from him.

At that moment Sawab came down from the mountain with the king's sister, his mother and all his men, and it was just then that Fulk arrived with his men as the cavalry horses whinnied and the earth shook with the numbers and the trampling of hooves. He and King Kaukab [sic] dismounted and kissed the ground in front of Fulk, who, when he saw his son Kaukak, fell to the ground in a faint. Kaukab then embraced him and he gave thanks to God for having restored his son to him.

When his mother heard, she came and embraced him, before saying: 'My son, tell me your story. We have been filled with concern for you, so tell me what happened.' Kaukab told the whole tale from beginning to end and, on hearing it, Fulk's delight at the safety of his son was matched by his furious anger at what the chamberlain, God curse him, had done. 'Praise be to God Who has granted me the gift of your hands and feet!' he exclaimed. He then clothed Kaukab in a splendid robe of honour and entered the city in which was the son of his servant. There he gave his instructions to the qadi and the witnesses and drew up a marriage contract between his son Kaukab and Yaquta, the daughter of his servant. He provided them with a splendid banquet attended by high and low alike and he presented them with an abundance of wealth as well as gifts and treasures. Kaukab lay with Yaquta and was delighted to find her a virgin.

He stayed for three days with her brother and then went back with his father to the kingdom of Saihun, which was transferred to him, and he stayed there with his father until the latter died.

This is the full story – Glory be to the One God and blessings be on the best of His creation, Muhammad, his family and his companions.

Tale Two

The Story of Talha, the Son of the Qadi of Fustat, and What Happened to Him with His Slave Girl Tuhfa and How She Was Taken Away from Him and What Hardships Befell Until There Was Relief After Grief.

In the Name of God, the Compassionate, the Merciful

They say – and God knows better – that there is a story dating from past times which tells of a qadi in Fustat, one of the leading men of the city, who lived in luxury with possessions, property and estates. To his great joy God granted him a son, the most beautiful child ever seen, whom he called Talha. He gathered everyone, high and low alike, to a magnificent banquet, after which he handed the boy over to nurses, who continued to suckle him and look after him carefully until, by the time he was six years old, he had grown into a big child. His father then chose a teacher to instruct him at home and bought him a servant and a maid of the same age as himself. The maid's name was Tuhfa, and the teacher was told to let her learn everything that he taught Talha. As a result Talha learned nothing that she did not.

Talha's fondness for the girl turned to love, and for her part Tuhfa was so enamoured of him that she could not bear to be parted from him for the blink of an eye. They were still in love when they grew up, and by then they had mastered every branch of learning and culture. The qadi was pleased to hear of this. He gave orders that Tuhfa's position should be regularized and he gave her in marriage to Talha in a fine wedding on which he spent a huge amount of money. He held a banquet to mark the wedding attended by all Egyptians, high and low, men and women, and the love felt by each of the pair for the other increased.

After the marriage had been consummated, Talha gave orders that Tuhfa be taught all the skills needed by slave girls, such as singing to the accompaniment of musical instruments. This was done without his father's knowledge, and Tuhfa became the most accomplished of all in this art.

The qadi lived for some time after Talha's marriage but then died, and after his death Talha began on a career of reckless extravagance. He disposed of all the properties that his father had bequeathed him until he was reduced to poverty, having nothing left and nothing to fall back on. At this point, when it did no good, he began to feel regret, and things went on like this until for three days he and Tuhfa had nothing at all to eat. As they sat opposite each other in tears, Tuhfa said that if things went on like that they were bound to die, but she had a plan, difficult as it would be for her. 'What is it?' Talha asked. 'Tell me.'

'Master,' she said, 'if we stay like this without eating for another day we shall very certainly die. What I think is that you should take me out to the market and sell me, for girls like me are in demand. You will be able to live off what you get for me, and I shall be able to live with whoever buys me, and this will mean that neither of us will die. By God, master, whatever I have to eat or drink I shall share with you.'

When Talha heard this he almost went mad and with tears raining down his cheeks he asked: 'Tuhfa, can you do without me?' 'By God, master,' she said, 'I didn't say this because I was tired of you or because I hated you, but because I am sorry for you and pity you and don't want to be responsible for your death. But the decision is yours, so do what you want, as you think fit.'

For a time Talha bowed his head in silence, thinking over her suggestion and finding it good. 'Tuhfa,' he said, 'since things are as you have described, and you're not doing this out of boredom or dislike, I shall do what you advise, but for three days the sale will be conditional, and if I find that I can endure this and enjoy life after parting from you, I shall finalize it, but if not, I shall take you back, and we shall have to endure whatever the Glorious God decrees for us.' 'Do as you want, master,' she told him.

Talha got up straight away and went to one of his friends whom he asked if he knew a slave-dealer in Fustat who could sell valuable slaves. The friend sent for one, whom Talha went to greet. On seeing him, the man recognized him from his description and asked him how he was and what he wanted. 'Sir,' said Talha, 'I have a slave girl who was brought up with me and of whom I am fond. I want to sell her conditionally for three days, and then take her back if I find that I cannot do without her.'

The dealer agreed to do this for him, and he went back to tell this to Tuhfa, before taking her by the hand and going out with her. Both were sad and miserable at the prospect of parting, but Talha went on until he handed her over to the dealer, taking a tearful farewell of her as she too wept. This went on so long that people were crowding around them, and so he left her and went away.

The dealer was astonished to see how beautiful and perfectly formed Tuhfa was and he exclaimed: 'By God, I never thought that beauty and loveliness could be combined in a single person!' He asked her for her name, and when she said 'Tuhfa' [rare gift] he said: 'Whoever gave you this name was right for, by God, you live up to your name.' He then cleared a space in his auction house that was suitable for a lovely girl like her and brought out a carpet and such utensils as would suit her. He then produced food and drink, which she enjoyed, but she spent the night shedding sorrowful tears because of her parting from her master.

Next day a prosperous and wealthy Syrian from Damascus came to the house. He was acting as an agent for a Damascene merchant who had described the kind of slave girl he wanted his friend to buy for him when he went to Fustat, a description whose match was scarcely to be found anywhere in the world. Every day that the man had come there he had been shown girls, but none of them fitted the description he had been given. That had been going on for so long that he had despaired of finding the one he had been asked for. Tuhfa, however, was ten times better.

When the Syrian came in next day the dealer hurried up to tell him of Tuhfa, saying: 'Sir, I have got just the girl you want or even better.' 'Bring her out so that I can see what you have brought me,' the man said, and the dealer took him by the hand and led him to the sale room. After having seated him he fetched Tuhfa to show to him. She was gorgeously dressed with the most splendid ornaments, and when the man saw her beauty and her perfect figure he was filled with astonishment. 'By God,' he exclaimed, 'this is what I was looking for, and many, many times better. If in addition to her beauty she possesses culture and learning, that would add perfection.'

'By God,' said the dealer, 'I know of no one in all Fustat who knows more than she does, as she has a perfect mastery of all branches of learning and culture.' The Syrian then questioned her, asking her what she knew and at what she was proficient. She said: 'I know the Qur'an by heart and can recite its various readings; I have a knowledge of the stars and of arithmetic; I can play chess and backgammon and I can accompany my singing on a variety of instruments. I am familiar with all of this.' The Syrian told her to recite a passage from the Qur'an and she started with the *fatiha*, reciting it in so heart-rending a voice that he almost fainted through humility. The dealer swore that nowhere in the east or the west could he hear a better reading.

Tuhfa then took a lute in her lap and, after striking a number of different modes, she produced these lines:

Our dwellings may be far apart,
So that I cannot visit you,
But still this love of mine remains the same,
And God forbid that it should ever change.

When the Syrian heard this he again almost fainted with joy and delight at the sweetness of her singing. 'By God,' he exclaimed to the dealer, 'this girl is invaluable, and nowhere in the market is there anyone like her.' He then asked the dealer to name a price, to which he answered: 'Eight thousand dinars, and she is worth more than that.' On hearing this the man realized that it was true and he was sure that his friend would buy her on sight for five thousand dinars and think it cheap, for he knew that her real worth was ten thousand. 'I'll take her from you for a thousand dinars,' he said, paying him a hundred dinars for himself.

So delighted was the dealer that he forgot that Talha, her master, had specified a conditional sale for a period of three days. The buyer joyfully took Tuhfa off straight away, as he was afraid that she might be removed from him by force or someone might hear of her whom he could not turn away.

[Wehr, the editor of the Arabic text, notes an obvious lacuna in the text covering the journey from Fustat to Damascus and her transfer to her new master.] He hired a place for her, thinking in his heart that she would soon forget the past, and he set aside for her the best and cleanest apartment in the house, to which he fetched a carpet and such utensils as would suit her. He brought her fine clothes, ornaments and expensive jewels and he gave her a number of maid-servants, before leaving her for a time to recover from the tiredness caused by the journey.

It was then that he called for her and when she came he questioned her to discover what she knew. He was filled with admiration at the abundance of culture and outstanding learning that he saw in her and he presented her with a magnificent robe of honour and a great amount of money. He told her to go back to her room, where he would spend the night with her, an announcement which she greeted with tears and sobs. He was surprised to be told of this and said that she was bound to forget, not knowing that this was an expression of her great love for her master Talha.

That night her new master came joyfully to her room, filled with desire for her, and she greeted him with the best of welcomes, making a show of patience. When he had sat down he ordered food to be brought and when they had both eaten he followed this with wine to make her feel at ease. After he had drunk to her lovely face and perfect beauty, he asked her to sing. At first she refused and made excuses but when he pressed her politely she agreed. Taking the lute, she put it in her lap, then tuned it and began to sing so beautifully as to rob the Damascene of his wits:

> I feel love's pain on every side;
> It changes me and robs me of my youth.
> My love for Talha drowns me in its sea,
> And it is this that brings me deep distress.
> Never shall I forget him – this I swear –
> Until my corpse lies shrouded in the earth.

When she had finished, she gave a great cry and fainted. The sight of this disturbed and distressed her master, who went up to comfort her, but she wept so bitterly that she fainted again. He felt sorry for her and asked her to tell him her story and who had been her master and who it was she loved. She said: 'I was brought up from childhood with my master, whose father was Malik, the qadi of Fustat. It was he who had bought me when I was a child and he reared me with his son Talha until neither of us could bear to be parted from the other even for the blink of an eye.'

She went on to tell him about herself and Talha from beginning to end, how he had gone from riches to poverty, how he had squandered all his goods, how the two of them had spent three days without eating and how she had advised him to sell her, thinking that she would be bought by someone from Fustat, who would not take her away. She would have been able to look at Talha and hear about him at all times, but God, the Great and Glorious, had decreed that they should be parted. 'By God,' she said, 'you will find no use in me nor will anyone else after Talha, and I know of no one who suffers a worse fate than mine during his life.'

She shed more tears, and when the Damascene had heard about her and Talha he felt pity for them and sympathized with her in her grief. 'Tuhfa,' he said, 'if this is the case and you have shown such loyalty to your master, I call on God and His angels to witness that I give you back

to him as a present. Do not suppose that I am merely saying this to comfort and calm you for, by God, I have never gone back on my word.'

On hearing his promise, Tuhfa jumped up, kissed his hands and his feet,
giving him the most heartfelt thanks and saying: 'Master, how good and
generous you have been! I am your slave, and so do with us what befits a
man like you.' He told her that she could be happy, as God had decreed
that she should be reunited with her master and that, if He so willed it, he
would soon be with her. She took heart, believing in his promise, and, after
they had drunk, she took up the lute and went on singing to him as he
drank and poured wine for her until he had made her drunk. He then took
his leave and left her in her room while he went off to his bed.

For Tuhfa the pain of love and longing for her master was partially
relieved as she was sure that she was going to meet him, and this calmed
her dismay. After that the Damascene used to come to her room every
night and drink with her while listening to her singing, choosing the
songs and leaving after he had had enough to drink. That went on until
he had made all necessary preparations for a journey to Egypt, as she
kept on reminding him of his promise and he kept on comforting her.

So much for Tuhfa, but as for Talha, for the three days that he had
stipulated he stayed tearful and distressed, trying but failing to endure,
and finding himself unable to forget her. He then went to the slave-dealer
to ask what he had done with her, and the man produced a purse with
the thousand dinars that was the purchase price. 'I did my best for you
on this,' he told Talha, 'as I owe you a favour, God bless you.' 'What is
this?' asked Talha, looking at the purse. 'The price for the girl,' said the
dealer, and Talha, who had almost fainted, said: 'Give her back to me,'
but the man said: 'When I sold her I forgot you had made a condition.'

Talha now slapped his face, rubbed his cheeks in the dust and cried
out at the top of his voice while people gathered around. He almost died
and was losing his wits, but the dealer told him not to take it so hard. 'I
forgot about the condition when I sold her,' he said, 'and it was only
afterwards that I remembered, but the buyer had gone.' When Talha
learned that Tuhfa had been sold and taken away, he realized that the
condition would no longer be valid and after what had happened there
was no way in which he could get her back. He fell to the ground in a
faint and when he recovered he struck at his head and his cheeks.

A crowd gathered around, expressing pity for him but blaming him
for what he was doing. They then turned against the slave-dealer, crowding in and turning their blame on him. He was afraid that he might find

himself in difficulties with the sultan and when an opportunity came he made off. Talha for his part kept asking where the merchant who had bought Tuhfa had gone, hoping to enlist his sympathy to get her back from her new master in pity for what he had done to himself. When he asked the slave-dealer about the merchant he was told that the man had taken her off immediately after the sale. The dealer himself was then told that this man had not bought her for himself but for a Damascene named Muhammad son of Salih, a most generous man, full of good deeds. He went back and passed on his news to Talha, who was not in his right mind and who tore his tattered clothes and poured dust on his head. He left the money with the dealer and in his grief he started to wander through the streets, sobbing and weeping. Some people pitied him, but others were scornful and kept asking him what was wrong and abusing him. This went on so long, with children following him and shouting abuse again and again, until he was taken to the hospital as a certifiable lunatic and put in chains.

For six months he stayed there in this wretched state until one day the qadi of Fustat happened to pass the hospital. People complained to him that the man in charge was not looking after the patients or the lunatics properly and was taking its money for himself. The qadi, intending to investigate, dismounted and went in to see what things were like. His eyes fell on Talha, whom he recognized and addressed by name, at first getting no answer from him. The qadi had been one of his father's greatest friends and he asked Talha what had brought him to this. At that point Talha said: 'Master, the common people mistreated and afflicted me, taking me and throwing me in here six months ago.'

The qadi shed tears of pity and ordered him to be taken to the baths, sending him one of his own robes of honour and his riding beast. When he had been cleaned up in the baths, he came out, put on the robe, mounted the beast and went to the qadi's house. He was taken in and brought up to the qadi, who gave him food and drink until he recovered, forgetting his distress and sufferings. It was then that the qadi asked him for his story, saying: 'How did you lose what your father left you, and what happened to your slave girl Tuhfa, for I knew that you were very fond of her?' On hearing Tuhfa's name Talha was choked by tears, but, after having wept and sobbed noisily, he started to tell his story to the qadi from beginning to end.

The qadi wept out of pity for him and summoned the slave-dealer, whom he reproached for what he had done and from whom he took the gold. He then said to Talha: 'Would you like to hear how I think that, God willing, you may be reunited with Tuhfa?' Talha asked about this, and the qadi said: 'I shall give you some of my own money over and above what you have yourself, and I shall use it all to buy goods that you can take to Damascus. I shall then write you a letter addressed to the *'udul* and the leading men of the city, asking them to help you buy back your slave girl. I hope that you may succeed and, if you do, come back here and I shall appoint you to a suitable post. I shall be there to help you, and you will also have what I hope will be a profit from your trading.'

Talha thanked the qadi, who then spent fifteen hundred dinars on buying goods suitable for Damascus, and he wrote a letter to its qadi and the *'udul*, asking them to look after him and help him. He also got for him a letter from 'Abd al-'Aziz, the ruler of Egypt, to his brother 'Abd al-Malik son of Marwan. Talha was then sent off to Tanis, where he loaded his goods on a ship that was due to sail in the direction of Damascus. Two days off Tyre, however, it was wrecked, leaving Talha naked, penniless and sadder than before. He decided to make for Damascus, hoping to find employment as a servant so that he might be able to buy back Tuhfa.

When he got there he was a changed man, in the grip of misery and care, but when he saw the city from the outside it filled him with wonder and he sat down to rest before going in. He had with him some pieces of dry bread, salt and groats that someone had given him and he took these out as he sat by a stream in the shade of a tree. He broke the bread and left it on a stone as he crushed what salt he had and sprinkled it on top. He was about to eat when up came a rider on an Arab mare, dressed as a king and galloping in pursuit of a gazelle. After he had hunted it down he made for the shade of Talha's tree as he was tired. He dismounted, took off his boots and gaiters and, after washing his hands, feet and face, he was about to stretch out on his back in the shade when Talha, who was embarrassed, called out: 'Come here, master, the food is ready!' at which the rider turned to look at him.

This turned out to be 'Abd al-Malik son of Marwan, and Talha's invitation prompted his admiration. He said to himself: 'This man apparently comes from a good background, and courtesy demands that I should not treat him with haughtiness, for if I don't accept, that will seem to be mockery and a show of pride on my part.' He got up and sat with Talha, accepting some of the bread and salt, while Talha talked animatedly to him. He then asked Talha where he came from and when Talha had told him he was from Egypt he went on to ask for his name. When Talha told him, 'Abd al-Malik asked if he was the son of the qadi. 'I am,' said Talha, at which 'Abd al-Malik asked: 'How can you be Talha son of Malik when you are dressed like this?' 'A proper question,' said Talha, 'but things happen as God decrees and wills.' 'What has brought you to so wretched a state?' 'Abd al-Malik went on and when Talha burst into tears he pitied him and urged him to show endurance before repeating the question.

Talha now told him the whole story from start to finish, how he lost his money, approached the slave-dealer and sold Tuhfa. 'So she is the only reason that you came here,' said 'Abd al-Malik, adding: 'and who was it who bought her?' 'It was a Damascus merchant who bought her for another Damascene named Muhammad son of Salih,' said Talha. 'Abd al-Malik knew the man, and he told Talha to finish his remarkable story. Talha said: 'When I knew that Tuhfa had been passed to someone else and there was no way in which I could get to her, I lost my wits and became mad. I was thrown into hospital and stayed there for six months, suffering the bitterness of a wretched life. Then, in accordance with the will of God, the Great and Glorious, it happened that the qadi of Fustat wanted to inspect the hospital and when he caught sight of me he recognized me and brought me out. He was good to me and gave me a large amount of money as well as advising me to come here and writing a letter for me to the qadi and the *'uduls*. He also got me a letter from the emir to the caliph, may God prolong his life, asking for help with Muhammad son of Salih, in the hope that he might restore Tuhfa to me. Then my ship was wrecked at sea, and I lost all my goods. I emerged in the state that you see and made for Damascus, hoping to make the acquaintance of Tuhfa's new master and be accepted by him as a servant. Were I to be taken on as a groom I might catch sight of her some day and hear about her before I give up the ghost. This is the true account of what happened.'

At this point he was choked by tears, as he heaved deep sighs and wept. 'Abd al-Malik was filled with pity, but just then chamberlains rode up, dismounted in front of him and greeted him, while the emirs presented their respects. Talha realized that this must be 'Abd al-Malik himself and he jumped to his feet and started to present excuses for having invited him to eat. 'There was nothing wrong with that,' 'Abd al-Malik assured him. 'I listened to your story and I gladly acknowledge that I am in your debt for the salt of yours that I ate. I swear by Almighty God to see that you get back both your slave girl and your riches. This I guarantee.'

'Abd al-Malik ordered Talha to be taken to the baths, and one of his chief officials took him off, bringing with him a bundle of clothes suitable for a man of his rank. He mounted him on a sturdy beast and provided him with a fine house. 'Abd al-Malik left him to recover from his tiredness and then summoned him together with the court officials. He sent for Muhammad son of Salih, only to be saddened by the news from his family that he had left for Egypt.

At his court there was a bitter enemy of Muhammad's who was intensely jealous of him. This man said: 'Commander of the Faithful, this is an impossible lie on his part, and he must have told his family to turn away your messenger so that he should not be summoned to your court. I saw him a few days ago, and no one has left for Egypt in this period. I can produce a witness who saw him leaving the baths.' When he heard this 'Abd al-Malik was furiously angry with Muhammad and gave immediate orders for his house to be plundered and for all the women there to be brought before Talha so that he could take back his slave girl Tuhfa as he had been promised, with the caliph's guarantee.

Five hundred servants were sent to the house, but by the time they had got to the street in which it was, news that the caliph had ordered it to be plundered had preceded them. All the women and servants were frightened as they did not know what this was all about and so they rushed out and hid with neighbours. Tuhfa, seeing this, was terrified and went up to the roof of the house, over the boundary wall and then down into the next-door house. This belonged to a weaver, from whom she asked help and who hid her. Muhammad's house was plundered with everything in it being seized, and all the women taken to the caliph. He ordered them to be shown to Talha so that if he saw Tuhfa he could take her, but amongst all of them Tuhfa was not to be found.

'Abd al-Malik was saddened and he regretted having had Muhammad's house plundered but said: 'Nothing can counter the actions of Fate.' He then told Talha: 'You know what we have done and how we have brought down disaster on Muhhamad son of Salih in order to put your affairs in order and to reunite you with your slave girl. Now we shall present you with ten virgins in order to make up for her.' 'Commander of the Faithful,' he replied, 'I have no need of any other girl but my own,' and he burst into tears. 'So what do you want me to do with you?' the caliph asked, and Talha replied: 'Send me back home and give me some suitable employment.' The caliph offered him the post of qadi that his father had held, but he declined out of respect for the current holder, who had treated him so well. He was then offered a post in the administration, which he accepted, and he was handed a letter of appointment as overseer of Egyptian taxes and sent off to Egypt with a large gift of money. He was met by the emir, 'Abd al-'Aziz son of Marwan, the qadi and the leading citizens and, on entering the city, he dismounted at a house that had been prepared for him. The qadi asked him about his journey and what had happened to him after they had parted, to which Talha replied with the full story from start to finish. This astonished the qadi, who praised God for having brought it to a happy ending. For a month Talha acted as overseer of the tax-gatherers of Egypt.

As for Tuhfa, after she had stayed for a long time with the weaver, she told him that she would prefer to go home to Egypt in the hope of finding her beloved master Talha and discovering what had happened to him after she left. She went to Muhammad's treasure chamber and was happy to find in it a large sum of money as well as jewellery. She then asked the weaver if he would do her a favour in return for fifty dinars. 'What do you want from me?' he asked, and she said: 'I want you to take me to Egypt and look after me on the way.' He agreed, and she gave him money with which to buy food for the journey and pay for places in the caravan for them both. When they got there she told him to take her to the mosque of Malik, and when he asked about this he was shown the way.

The mosque was near the house of her master Talha, and she was distressed to see that its door was shut and it was abandoned. She paid the weaver what she had promised him, and he left for Damascus. For her part, she saw in the mosque a tailor who lived in a house next door to it, in whose hallway was the tomb of its former owner. She hired the house from the tailor and moved everything that she needed into it. Then she gave the tailor some money and said: 'I am a stranger here on my own with no one to run errands for me. If I were to give you a dirham a day, would you find it acceptable to do this for me?' He said: 'Lady, even if you spent the whole time giving me orders, I would do whatever you wanted with the greatest willingness.' She told him to buy the necessary food and drink for them both and she gave him a dirham, after which he left.

She spent the night there and very early next morning he came back to ask how she was and whether she wanted anything done for her. She said: 'I have decided that I want you to buy me a slave girl to keep me company and act as my servant.' The tailor agreed and fetched her a number of girls from one of the sale rooms, of whom she picked one.

The tailor bought her, and Tuhfa weighed out the money, after which she told him to buy her clothes. She treated the girl well and when she wanted something she would tell her to go to the mosque and speak to the tailor, telling him what to do.

The tailor had a witty way of talking and whenever the girl came to him on one of her mistress's errands he would play around with her, flirting and joking and making her laugh at his elegant insults. One day Talha passed by his father's mosque. He dismounted and went in before invoking God's mercy on his father and on those who were praying there. This coincided with the arrival of Tuhfa's girl on an errand from her mistress. She went to the tailor, flirting and joking with him and laughing as he insulted her. Talha heard and disapproved of this, cutting short his prayers and turning angrily to the tailor. 'Damn you,' he said; 'when you are in a house of God, you must respect it and what you are doing is not permissible in a place like this.' The tailor did not recognize him and said: 'Sir, this girl is a trial to me.' Talha asked if she was his slave girl, and he replied: 'No, by God! She belongs to a lady who has so overwhelmed me with kindness that I cannot cause her any distress or find fault with anything that her slave girl does.' 'Who is this lady?' Talha asked, and the tailor told him: 'Sir, she came from Damascus and is prosperous, high-minded and open-hearted and she says that she was brought up in this street. I have never seen anyone lovelier or more generous.'

When Talha heard this, he wondered whether the lady could be Tuhfa. 'Does she show herself to you?' he asked the tailor. 'Yes indeed,' the man replied; 'I run errands for her, and she provides me with my daily bread.' 'Describe her to me so I can have a picture of her,' Talha told him, and he began to describe Tuhfa. Talha was convinced that this must be his slave girl, for he told himself that the description matched. 'Is there any way for me to see her?' he asked, and the tailor replied: 'I think that you want to marry her and, by God, she will suit no one else.' 'Well, how can I see her?' Talha repeated. 'What would you give me to ask her in marriage for you?' said the tailor, and Talha told him: 'If you arrange for me to marry this woman whom you have described for me, I shall let you have a thousand dirhams from my own money.' The tailor said: 'Stay where you are until I come back.'

The tailor hurried to Tuhfa, who was on friendly terms with him, and said, after greeting her: 'Lady, I have come to you on a matter which will bring advantages to both of us.' When she asked him what this was he said: 'I want to arrange for you to marry a young man like the rising moon. No one has ever seen anyone more handsome and, by God, he is the only fitting husband in the world for you and for him you are the only fitting wife.' She gave a surprised laugh, thinking that this was a joke on his part, and said: 'I shall not disobey you, Abu'l-'Abbas, so do what you think right.' The tailor went joyfully to Talha and told him: 'She said "yes" to me, so make up your mind, with God's blessing and His help.' Talha did not trust this but said to himself: 'I think I know that this woman must be Tuhfa but first I have to put it to the test and clear it up. If she is, then this is the fulfilment of my hopes, but if not, I shall not spend much on her dowry and I shall part from her straight away.'

He went off that day, having agreed with the tailor to come back next day because of their arrangement. So he went to the mosque next morning with ten of the city's leading shaikhs, and the tailor got up to meet him, kissed his hands and welcomed the shaikhs. 'Here I am,' said Talha, 'so what is your plan?' 'This is in God's hands,' the tailor replied, and when Talha asked who was to give the bride away, he said that he would do it himself. Talha pointed out that two people would have to listen and testify to the fact that she had given her approval. The tailor took two of the shaikhs who were in the mosque and brought them to the hallway of Tuhfa's house, where he sat them down. Then he lifted the curtain and went to Tuhfa, who welcomed him after he had greeted her. She then came out to the door of her room and stood there in sight of the two shaikhs, whom she did not recognize and who were dazzled by what they could see of her beauty.

The tailor talked to her, and amongst the things he said was a reminder that on the day before he had suggested that she should marry, putting him in charge of this so as to see that it was done with her approval. 'What have you got to say about this?' he asked. She smiled in surprise at his intelligence, being sure that everything he said was a joke to make her laugh. 'Abu'l-'Abbas,' she told him, 'I am content that you should be in charge. I entrust my affair to you, so do what you think right.'

None of this was serious. She thought that she was fooling him, not knowing the real position or what he had done. For his part he told the witnesses to give their testimony about what they had heard and seen, and, while Tuhfa laughed, this is what they did. The tailor left her quickly and said to them: 'You have seen this woman and heard what she said.' They testified to what she had said and that she was content to put the tailor in charge of things, at which he took their hands and brought them out to Talha, to whom they repeated this. He paid out thirty dinars for a dowry and had a marriage contract drawn up with the shaikhs acting as witnesses. Talha paid the tailor what he had promised and he went to Tuhfa with both dowry and contract.

When she saw that this was serious she told him that she had taken all of this to be a joke. 'I never took any of this seriously,' she told him, 'and everything that I said to you was intended as a joke.' 'How can one joke about something like this?' he exclaimed, adding: 'You are far too important to me to allow me to play a joke on you in a matter like this. God Almighty has decreed that this is a lawful marriage.' She felt ashamed and looked down in silence, at which he went off to Talha and said: 'She has thought better of it, so get someone to watch the house door lest she leave.' He posted a man there to stop anyone coming out and, when she realized that, she was filled with care and sorrow.

Talha sent into the house all that was needed in the way of furnishings, utensils, food, drink and fruit and distressed Tuhfa by leaving word that he would come in the evening. When night fell he came in without drawing attention to himself, but she noticed and rushed to the hall where the tomb was and sat sobbing tearfully over it. Talha asked about her and on being told that she was weeping he said: 'Let her be.' He then ordered food to be brought to her, but she was too distracted to eat.

While she was in that state she heard a knock on the door and a beggar calling out to the inhabitants: 'Give me some of what was left over from the food that God had provided for you as for three days I have tasted nothing.' Tuhfa felt pity for him and hurried to open the door, telling him to come in. He entered the hall, and she brought him the food that Talha had sent her, at which he sat down and ate like a starving man. Talha, who had been told of this, said: 'Let her do what she wants,' and he ordered more food to be brought.

On seeing the beggar's wretched state, Tuhfa asked him where he came from. He told her: 'I am a stranger from Syria, a Damascene.' He was then choked by tears and he cried and sobbed aloud. 'What makes you weep?' Tuhfa asked, and he said: 'Why should I not weep when the favours that God had showered on me were snatched away because of an Egyptian slave girl who had been bought for me. It was thanks to her that my house was plundered and I was driven from my own land, a poor man bereft of fortune.' 'Who did this to you?' Tuhfa asked, and he said: 'It was 'Abd al-Malik son of Marwan, who wanted to take my slave girl from me by force, and it was he who ordered my house to be plundered with all my goods being taken with everything else I had and whatever I had acquired throughout my life. I have been reduced to poverty as you can see. I am a stranger here; there is no way in which I can restore my fortune, and I cannot go back home for fear of death.'

When Tuhfa heard this, she was certain that the man must be her Damascene master, Muhammad son of Salih, and she now recognized him, although distress and poverty had altered his appearance. When she was sure of that she jumped up and, clutching on to him, she wept and sobbed loudly. 'Master, by God, I find what has happened to you terrible. You may not have recognized me, but I am the Egyptian slave girl you mentioned.' When Muhammad heard the tone of her voice, he shouted as loud as he could: 'By God, lady, you most certainly are!'

Talha heard their raised voices and was told by the slave girls that their mistress was clinging to the beggar, weeping and telling him that he was her master from Damascus, while he was doing the same thing, obviously believing what she said. When Talha heard this he rushed to the hall, his heart fluttering, in order to clear the matter up. His eyes rested on Tuhfa, and in his amazement he almost lost his senses and shook with excitement. Such was his joy and delight that he thought that he was seeing all this in a dream. He gave a great cry and clasped Tuhfa to him, while she, alarmed by the cry that he gave as he grasped her, turned round and when she saw his face she recognized him and fell down in a faint.

The slave girls came up and sprinkled water on her face until she recovered. She started to sigh as she stared at Talha and said: 'Was it you who married me and I did not know?' 'Yes,' he said, 'it is true that you didn't know, and I for my part was not certain of it.' Then he asked her if she knew the beggar. 'How should I not know him,' she answered, 'when he is my Damascene master for whom I was bought from Fustat and it is thanks to me that he has been reduced to this state by disaster and poverty?' On hearing this, Talha came up and embraced Muhammad as they both wept. Talha said: 'Brother, don't grieve for anything you have lost, for I swear by God that I shall not eat my fill on any day on which you are hungry as long as I have life in my body. So take heart and be comforted.'

Muhammad thanked him for this and praised him, after which Talha told him that it was not by his choice or wish that 'Abd al-Malik had taken any of his goods. 'By Almighty God,' he swore, 'I was distressed by that, but it had been decreed by Fate.' He took his hand and that of Tuhfa and led them both into the house, after which he gave Muhammad the robe that he was wearing and they sat talking. 'You should know,' Tuhfa said, 'that I have never seen a more generous or noble-minded man than this master of mine, for when I told him what I felt for you and how I had advised you to sell me when we were in difficulties, he was full of regret and wanted to see you, calling God to witness that even before this he would give me back to you. I can tell you that it was only to find you that he went to Egypt, intending to take you back with him and bring you to Damascus so we could meet in his own country and his own house. As God had decreed, however, 'Abd al-Malik had sent for him, not knowing that he left some time earlier and it was when he heard of this that he ordered his house to be plundered and his women seized. I wanted to flee but did not see how I could do it success-fully, so I took some of my master's money and climbed to the roof. From there I went down into the house of a weaver who sheltered me and kept me hidden. When the search for me had finished and I was in despair, I asked the weaver to take me to Egypt.'

She told them her story from beginning to end, and Talha told of what had happened to him on his way and of how he had not wanted to marry anyone else except her, but the tailor's description of her had stirred a craving, as he recognized it and hoped that this would be Tuhfa. 'Praise be to God Who has made this come true,' he said, 'but you can-not marry me while you are still this man's slave.' 'I have heard what you both have said,' Muhammad told them, 'and, by God, Talha, it was only because of you that I came here and you can see what happened to me. I gave Tuhfa to you and I shall not take back my gift, may God give you His blessing with her.' 'If that is so,' Talha said, 'God has given me huge riches and vast bounty, and I call Him to witness that I shall share this with you and I shall write to tell the Commander of the Faithful that you are not guilty of what you were accused and that you were not in Damascus at the time.' 'This is up to you,' Muhammad said.

Talha did as he had promised, and the caliph restored to Muhammad much more than he had taken from him and he arrested those who had lied about him. Muhammad went back safely to Damascus, while Talha stayed in Fustat with Tuhfa his wife, leading the pleasantest, most com-fortable and prosperous of lives until death overtook them.

This is the complete story, and we take refuge with God from any additions or subtractions. Praise be to the One God and blessings be on the best of His creation, our master Muhammad and his family.

Tale Three

The Story of the Six Men:
The Hunchbacked, the One-Eyed,
the Blind, the Crippled, the
Man Whose Lips Had Been
Cut Off and the Seller of Glassware.

In the name of God, the Compassionate, the Merciful

They say – and God knows better – that there was in the past a king who ruled every region whether on land or in the sea and who commanded the obedience of all their citizens. He was a man of intelligence and understanding, piety, modesty and chastity; he was just in the treatment of his subjects, behaving well and acting as an excellent administrator. He was very fond of stories, studying books and histories, and anyone who had something remarkable to pass on in the way of news, proverbs or tales would tell it to him.

The gatekeepers of his city had instructions to let no one through without asking him to tell them about himself, what he wanted and from where he came. The king had agents who would let him know what they had picked up, and when strangers entered the city they would be asked for news and the details of their journey, as a result of which information would be gathered from them of other lands and rulers, which would be passed on to the king.

This went on for some time until one day the king found himself worried although he could not think why, and when this had lasted all day until nightfall the worry increased, and he was distressed and wakeful. When this had gone on for too long, he summoned a housekeeper of his and told her to fetch him someone to entertain him with conversation to dispel his cares that night. When the woman asked where she should go, he said: 'to the lodgings of the strangers', and when she did as he told her she found a large group of blind men, as well as others suffering from various handicaps, together with beggars. She went up to them and asked them all who would go with her to the king to tell him the most remarkable thing that had happened to him in his life, and so enrich himself for the rest of his life.

Before she had finished speaking she was approached by six men, one blind, another one-eyed, a third a hunchback, a fourth a paralytic, a fifth whose lips had been cut off and a sixth who was a glass worker. 'We want to go to the king,' they told her, 'and each one of us has a fine and remarkable story of the misfortunes that we have suffered.' When the housekeeper heard this and looked at them she laughed at them and said: 'Come on, may God Almighty give you His blessing.' They followed her and stopped when they reached the palace door, while she went to the king and told him that she had brought six people, each with a strange story to tell. The king told her to admit them so that he could look at them, and when they came in they greeted him and called down blessings on him. He laughed when he saw them and told them to tell him their stories, promising to reward anyone who had something wonderful to tell.

He told one of them to start and asked him for his name and his occupation. 'May God aid Your Majesty,' the man said, 'do you want the name that I was given at birth?' 'The name by which you are best known,' the king told him, at which he said: 'Abu'l-Ghusn.' 'God grant you long life, Abu'l-Ghusn,' said the king, 'and what is your occupation?' Abu'l-Ghusn said that he was a weaver, and the king told him to begin his story.

'You must know, Your Majesty,' the man said, 'that I used to be a tailor in such-and-such a city in a shop that I had hired from a prosperous and wealthy man. This was in a large house at the bottom of which was a mill, while the owner lived upstairs. One day when I was weaving in my shop I looked up to see a woman like a rising full moon on the balcony of the merchant's house, looking out at the people. She was so very lovely that when I saw her my heart took fire and for the whole day I did no work as I was looking up at the balcony, peering at where she had been. When I had found this a long business and evening had come, I despaired of seeing her and went away so full of sorrow that my feelings would not allow me to eat, drink or sleep and I blamed myself because of this.

'That continued until morning, when I hurried to my shop and sat in the same place, looking out to catch a glimpse of her. I sent away anyone who brought me something to weave lest this distract me from keeping watch. This went on until she came out as she had done before, and when I saw her my heart fluttered and my senses left me as I fell unconscious. After a time I got up and left the shop, in the worst of states.

Next day I sat there thinking with my hand under my cheek, and my eyes turned towards her. When she came to her seat she saw me staring fixedly at her and returned my love, laughing in my face as I laughed in hers and greeting me with a gesture, which I returned.

'She then went away but sent her maid with a number of fine clothes wrapped in a bundle. "My mistress greets you," she said, "and asks you to use these clothes to cut out a tunic for her and tailor it as well as you can." "To hear is to obey," I said, "and praise be to God Who has revived me, now that she has seen that she needs me." I cut out her tunic as she sat in front, watching me with my head bent over my work, and whenever I wanted to take a rest she would beg me not to put it down. In my longing for her I was happy with what she said, and by evening I had finished the gown and handed it over to her.

'Early next morning the maid came back and said: "My mistress sends you a special greeting and asks how you passed the night. She herself was unable to sleep because her heart was filled with thoughts of you and, had she not feared slanderers, she would have wasted no time in coming to you. She asks you to cut out and sew elegant harem trousers that she can wear with her tunic." I agreed, and after cutting the material, I concentrated on the sewing until she came to the balcony and gave me an encouraging greeting as I sewed. She did not let me stop until I had finished.

'I then went home in a state of perplexity, not knowing how I was to feed myself, but before I knew it, as I was sitting there, the maid came to me and said: "My master sends you his greetings." I was alarmed to hear her mention her master, fearing that he might have found out about me, but she said: "Don't be afraid; there is nothing but good here. My mistress brought you to his notice with subtlety and things are going as you would wish." I went happily to the man, and we exchanged greetings, after which he welcomed me and asked kindly about how I was. He then called for some chests, from which he removed clothes of *dabiqi* linen, from which he told me to cut him out some good shirts. I cut twenty from the linen and the same number from byssus and again from Marwaz cotton, and I went on working until it was dark without breaking my fast or tasting any food.

'"How much do I owe you for your work?" the man asked me, and when I made no reply he said: "Tell me and don't be shy." I then said that I would take nothing, and when he said: "You must," I said: "Twenty dirhams." Then behind him came the lady who seemed angry with me and said: "How is it that you are going to take dirhams?" When I understood this, I told the man that I would take nothing that night, and I went off and applied myself to the work, although I had absolutely no money at all. For three days all I had to eat was two ounces of bread and nothing more, and I was dying of hunger. Then, when the work was finished, the maid came and asked me what I had done with the material, and I told her that it was finished. She said: "Take it and go up." So I took it and went with her to the lady's husband and when I handed it over to him he wanted to pay me, but I swore that I would not take anything, and said: "What is this work worth? The days are long and here am I in front of you and at your service." He thanked me, and I went back home but I could not sleep that night thanks to hunger and the evil state that I was in. My livelihood had vanished because of the work that I had done for the lady and her husband.

'Next morning I went to my shop, but before I had finished opening it a messenger came from the husband and I went to him. "Abu'l-Ghusn," he said, "you have been kind enough to make those clothes, and I'm sorry that you have taken no payment. I have decided that I want some *jubbahs* cut out for me and I want you to take charge of the work and do it well. This time I shall pay you and take no refusal, so cut me out five *jubbahs*." I did this and went away in the worst of states, dying of hunger. Every day I had to think carefully of what I could spend, but when I thought over the lady's beauty I set no store by my sufferings, telling myself that one kiss from her would wash them all away, and if I took possession of that lovely face I would not care how much I had to endure. So I sewed the linings and brought them to the man, who approved of my work and thanked me profusely. "May God grant you a good reward, Abu'l-Ghusn," he said, "and I want you to accept payment for all your work." He called for a purse in order to weigh out the amount, and I was wanting as little as possible and that only because I was so poor. Then, when I was thinking of taking it, his wife gestured to me from a distance that I should take nothing, implying that if I took a single dirham she would be angry with me. This alarmed me, and I said to the man: "Don't be in a hurry, sir. There is plenty of time, and nothing that you have is going to be lost, nor am I so poor that I need it now." I went on insisting until he removed the money and thanked me.

'I left him not knowing what to do now that I had lost the money, but my heart was inflamed by my love for the girl. So I went back home suffering from a combination of love, poverty, hunger, nakedness and exhaustion, but I encouraged myself with the promise that I would get what I wanted.

'The woman had told her husband of my feelings for her and that I was trying to make advances to her. The two of them had decided to amuse themselves at my expense by using me, unwittingly, to make their clothes. When I had finished all the work she had given me she began to watch and when she saw her husband weighing out the money she sent her maid, who said: "My mistress greets you and asks you to lend her money at such-and-such a time." I could not say no, and so the girl began to take every dirham of mine that could be found. I was left with little or nothing to live on but most deeply in love. The lady would make me promises and quieten me by telling me not to spoil what I had done and she would contrive something that would very soon lead to my advantage.

'One day when I was sitting with my eyes fixed on the balcony I was joined by an old teacher of mine. He saw the girl and understood what was happening to me. He jumped up and went off to his house and came back later with three large pieces of cloth. "Abu'l-Ghusn," he said, "I know the magic of the stars and am an expert in spells. You know that I am fond of you. I have investigated your star and have discovered that you are deeply in love with a girl who is in love with you, but you need the help of incense, spells and a charm which has to be written for you when your lucky star is in the ascendant. When this is fastened on your arm and she sets eyes on you, she will not be able to restrain herself from throwing herself on you and looking for union with you. You will then get what you want."

'I was delighted by this, hoping that he would bring me relief and that with the help of his magic I might achieve my desire. I told him that I was in difficulties and began to complain to him of what I suffered thanks to my love. He said that he would get me to my goal and asked me to quickly sew up what he had brought as clothes. He added that I would need drugs and perfumes, saying that, were he not a friend, he would ask money for this. Perfumes had to be got to use as incense in the place where he was going to write the charm, and for these and the censer he would need many dirhams and he suggested that I should weigh out the necessary cash. 'I shall write out the charm myself in friendship and solidarity with you,' he promised. I got up immediately and borrowed money, which I passed over to him, and he got a large quantity of perfume and incense. I told him that I would sew his clothes as quickly as I could and urged him not to fail to satisfy my wants.

'I began to sew and went on night and day until in two days' time I had finished. I brought the clothes to him, telling myself that, as he had volunteered to do what I needed, I should give him a present. So I sold a garment of mine and bought a gift, which I presented to him. He refused to accept it until I had pressed him, after which I waited expectantly. Five days later he brought me a small amulet tied up and told me: "I have done what you wanted, so take this amulet and fasten it on yourself in this hour and you will see that what I told you was true."

'I took the amulet and fastened it on some time before the girl made her appearance. I went forward laughing and saying to myself: "I wish you knew that I had enchanted you so that I can take possession of you whether you like it or not." Her maid then came up and, after passing on her greetings, said: "My lady says that a happy ending is near at hand for you in spite of her husband, who has gone out on business to one of his estates, where he will stay for some days and then you can get what you want." I thanked her and told myself how expert the teacher was in magic and spells, and I spent a happy night, not believing that dawn would ever come. Although I did not know it, the woman had told her husband about me.

'In the morning the maid came to me and said: "My mistress sends you her greetings. She is overcome with longing for you and says that her husband is intending to leave this coming night, so stay where you are." I could not believe that evening would come until I saw her husband ride away dressed in travelling clothes. I then realized that I had got what I wanted, and when it was dark the maid came and told me to get up, which I did, not believing in my happiness.

'When I entered the house the lady met me and said, after welcoming me: "My heart's blood and its fruit, I could not rest or settle down until my husband left. Praise be to God Who has united the two of us in perfect happiness." She called for food, which was put in front of us, and I enjoyed a kiss from her. Then, when we had finished eating and washed our hands, I said to her: "Lady, give me a kiss to bring back my life, for I am dying." "Silly fellow," she said, "what is the hurry? The whole night is before us in which you can get what you want."

'Before she had finished speaking I heard a violent knocking on the door. "What is that?" I asked, and she said: "By God, my husband has come and is at the door." "Oh, oh! What are you saying?" I exclaimed. "You heard," she said, and when I asked what I should do, she said: "By God, I don't know," and I stayed in a state of bewilderment. Then she said: "Get up, and I shall fasten you to the millstone in place of the mule. When my husband comes and falls into a weary sleep we can go back to eating and drinking." "Hurry!" I told her, and she quickly untied the mule and put me in its place, snuffing out the candle. "Don't stop going round, God help you," she told me, and then she left me and went off to open the door for her husband, who came in and sat down for a time.

'I was going round in circles and when I stopped for a rest I heard him say: "What's wrong with that wretched mule? He's not moving normally tonight, and we have a lot of grain to be milled, so when is it going to be finished?" He got up and went to the mill, where he poured grain in the hopper before coming to me with a whip with which he kept on striking my legs as I ran while shouting at me in the darkness as the grain was being ground. He kept pretending not to know me until it was almost dawn, and whenever I wanted to rest he would come up and strike me painfully, saying: "Miserable beast, what's wrong with you tonight that you can't go round?"'

'When dawn broke he went back up to his own quarters, and I stopped like a dead man, still fastened to the ropes and the wooden pole. The maid then came, exclaiming how sorry she was for what had happened to me. "Neither I nor my mistress could sleep last night because we were so worried about you," she told me, but I couldn't make any reply. So I left, half-dead with exhaustion and my beating, and when I got home I found that my teacher who had written the charm was there. He greeted me, blessed me and said: "I can read happiness, coquetry, kisses and embraces in your face." I cursed him for a liar and a cuckold and told him that I had spent the night grinding grain in the place of a mule and being beaten until morning. "Tell me your story," he said, and when I did he told me: "Your star does not accord with hers, but if you want I shall alter the charm." I told him that there was another piece of his material in the house which he wanted me to tailor for him, and I then went to the shop, where I sat waiting for someone to bring me some work that might help me out of my difficulties.

'While I was sitting there the maid came. "How are you, sir?" she asked. "My mistress sends you a special greeting as her heart is consumed by fire. But don't be sad as the way is open for you." I told her to go away as all the grain must have been milled. "Glory to God," she exclaimed, "it looks as though you suspected my mistress of being responsible for this!" "Leave me," I told her, "for God may send me someone for whom I can do some work and so earn some spending money. I don't want to speak to your mistress or to have her speak to me."

'The maid went off and told the lady what I had said and before I knew it she came out on the balcony with her hand on her cheek pretending to weep and saying: "Delight of my eyes, how are you?" I made no reply but when she came up swearing a great oath that she had had nothing to do with what happened to me, when I looked at her lovely face, I enjoyed this so much that I forgot the pain of my beating and accepted her excuse, telling myself: "No lie can come from a face as beautiful as this." So we exchanged greetings and talked for a long time, after which I went on working for her without pay.

'Some days later the maid came back and said: "My mistress greets you and says that my master intends to spend the night with a missing friend. She says that when she knows that he has got there, she will get you to come to her house and when the entrances are locked she will bring you out and you can enjoy the best of nights in exchange for your earlier sufferings, and you will receive in full all that you missed."

'In fact, her husband had said: "The hunchback has regretted his friendship with you," to which she had replied: "Let me play one more trick on him that will make him notorious throughout the city without my knowing anything about it." In the evening the maid came and brought me into the house and concealed me there until the entrances were locked and there were no passers-by. Then I was taken out, and when the lady saw me she welcomed me and exclaimed: "God knows what love I have for you in my heart. By God, I really long for you and tonight you will get all that you missed and be freed from grief." She had food brought in, but I told her to give me a quick kiss as she was dearer to me than life itself. Before I had finished speaking out came her husband from one of the rooms. He caught hold of me and said: "You vicious fellow, is this how you reward me? I introduced you into my house and chose you over all the others and now you have come to betray and disgrace me. By God, I'm not going to let you go until I've taken you before the police chief."

'In the morning I was taken out and given a hundred lashes, after which I was paraded round the town on the back of a camel, while a man shouted out: "This is a criminal who assaults men's wives." I was then driven out of the city and went off not knowing where to go until I found these fellow sufferers and joined them.'

The king laughed so heartily at this story that he almost fainted and he then placed the hunchback on one side. This is his tale.

The Story of the One-eyed Man

The king then summoned the one-eyed man, and this was his tale. After calling down God's blessing on the king he said: 'The story that I have to tell is wonderful and strange. I was a butcher in my town selling meat and raising rams, which I fattened up before slaughtering them. My customers were important and wealthy men who vied with one another for my meat because of its excellence, so that I became very rich and acquired houses and estates. This went on for a time, but one day when I was in my shop selling meat an old man with a huge beard stopped and pushed money towards me, telling me to give him some of it. I was happy to do this and when I had given him good meat I looked at his coins and found that they were beautifully engraved and almost translucently white. I put them aside but when I opened their box, wanting to bring them out and use them to buy sheep, all that I found in it was bits of paper shaped to look like dirhams. I slapped my face and began to laugh until a crowd collected and I surprised them by telling them what had happened.

'Then I went on with my business and slaughtered a large ram, which I hung up within my shop, while I took out slices of meat from it and fastened them by the shop door, saying to myself that I hoped that the old man would come. Shortly afterwards he did, and I took hold of him and called the people to come and listen to my story, describing him as a shameless rogue. When he heard this, the man said: "Which would you prefer, to let me go or to have me disgrace you?" "How could you do that, you rogue?" I asked, to which he replied: "You sell human flesh and say that it comes from a ram." "That's a lie, damn you," I retorted, but he then claimed that hung up in the shop was a human corpse. "If what you say is true," I told him, "the sultan can have my blood and my wealth." He then called to the people that if they wanted to check that he was telling the truth they should go into the shop. They rushed in and found that the ram that I had slaughtered had turned into a man and was hanging there.

'They shouted at me and, taking hold of me, they began to beat me and slap me, while the old man struck out my eye. Then they took the corpse to the chief of police, and the old man accused me of slaughtering people and passing off their flesh as mutton. "We have brought him to you, so punish him as God's justice requires." I tried to speak, but the police chief would not listen, and he immediately ordered that I be tied to the whipping post and given three hundred lashes. My flesh was lacerated by the whip, and I fainted. Then all that I owned was seized, and I spent a long time in prison. When I was released I was expelled from the city and wandered off until I came to a large city, where, as I was a skilful cobbler, I opened a shop and started working to earn a livelihood.

'One day I went out on some errand and heard behind me the sound of horsemen and footmen, with others clearing the way for them. I went off the road and asked some people who these were. "The emir is going hunting," they told me, and I started to look at how handsome and well dressed he was. Our eyes met, and he then looked down, saying: "I take refuge with God from the ill fortune of this day!" He turned his horse and rode back with all his men but not before he had given orders to one of his servants, who seized me, threw me down and gave me a hundred blows, almost killing me.

'I didn't know the reason for this, and when I had made my painful way back home I treated my injuries until I was able to sit up. Then I struggled step by small step to a friend of mine, who was one of the emir's entourage. When he saw me he asked me what had happened, and I told him of my encounter with the emir. He laughed so heartily that he fell over backwards and I said furiously: "By God, you are laughing at what has caused me the greatest pain." "Brother," he said, "the emir cannot bear to look at a one-eyed man as he thinks that this is an evil omen, particularly if it is the right eye that has been lost, and he can only content himself by doing what he did." I thought about how much I was earning through my work and I moved away to another part of the city where there was no one that I feared.

'After a time I had put my affairs to rights and had made money. Then one day I heard the sound of hooves behind me and, after crying out in alarm, I looked for a hiding place. The horses had almost caught up with me, and I didn't know what to do, but then I saw a closed door. I gave it a violent push, and it fell open, showing a long hall, which I entered to let the riders go by. Then, before I knew what was happening, two men jumped out and took hold of me. "Praise be to God Who has put you in our power!" they exclaimed, adding: "for these last three nights you have allowed us no sleep or rest, enemy of God, and we have tasted the pains of death." I asked them what this was all about, and they said: "You abuse us and try to kill the owner of the house, and isn't it enough for you that you and your friends have reduced him to poverty? Show us the knife with which you have been threatening us every night." They searched my waist and discovered a large knife that I had been carrying for fear of people I might meet. I cried out to God and told them that mine was a strange story, but when I started to tell it to them they would not listen but gave me a painful beating and tore my clothes. They could then see the scars of my earlier beating and exclaimed: "Enemy of God, these marks have been left by a whip, and you can only have been beaten because you are a habitual thief."

'They took me to the police chief, and I said to myself: "My sins have brought me down, and it is only the Almighty God Who can save me." The police chief said: "Evil man, what has led you to enter people's houses, steal their goods and threaten to kill them?" I implored him in God's name not to act hastily but to listen to my story. "Are you going to listen to the tale of a thief who has reduced people to poverty and who bears the scars of his punishment on his back?" my captors said, and when the man saw the scars he said: "It must have been because of a great crime that this was done to you." On his orders I was tied to the whipping post and given a hundred lashes. Then I was mounted on a camel with a proclamation being made: "This is a criminal who breaks into people's houses."

'I was expelled from the city and wandered aimlessly until I met these people and joined them. If the king wants to strike me and give me a hundred lashes, let him do so, for this is what I get from kings.' The king laughed and ordered him to be given a reward and a robe of honour.

The Story of the Blind Man

The king then summoned the blind man and asked him what story he had to tell. The man said: 'Your Majesty, you must know that one day I went out to beg as usual, and fate led me to a large house on whose door I knocked, hoping to speak to its owner and beg something from him. The owner said: "Who is at the door?" and when I didn't answer I could hear him coming down the stairs and repeating the question in a loud voice. I still said nothing and I heard him coming to the door, and when he asked who was there and I said nothing he opened the door and said: "What do you want?" I asked for some of the remains of the food that Almighty God had given him. "Blind man," he said, and when I answered he told me to hold out my hand. I did this, thinking that he was going to put something into it, but instead he took it and brought me into the house.

'He led me up a series of stairs to the top of the house, and I was sure that he was going to give me something, but when he stopped, he repeated: "What do you want, blind man?" "I want you to give me some food," I told him, but all he said was: "May God make things easy for you." "Why didn't you say that when I was at the door?" I asked, to which he answered: "Why didn't you answer the first time I asked who was there?" "What are you going to do now?" I said, at which he told me that he was not going to give me anything. "Take me down the stairs," I said, and he merely said: "The way is in front of you."

'I started going down as best I could but when I was about twenty steps from the bottom my foot slipped and I fell on my face, breaking open my head. I left the house in a daze and met a companion of mine, who asked me what I had got that day. "Leave me," I said, "for I met a swine who did me down today, making me climb up three storeys. I fell on the way down and am in great pain."

'I had some money of my own and I wanted to take some of it and spend it on myself. The damned fellow who owned the house was following me and listening to what I was saying to my companion without my knowing it, and when I got to my lodging he came in behind me. I waited for my companions, and when they had all come in I told them to shut and lock the door and then to check the rooms in case there were any strangers there. When my man heard this, he took hold of a rope that was hanging from the roof without our noticing. One of my companions checked the rooms while the others started striking the walls with their sticks, and they went on doing this without coming across anything.

'When they then came up to me I told them that I needed a share of what we had got, and each of them brought out what he had in his pocket. When it was all in front of us we weighed it out and found that it came to ten thousand dirhams. We left this in a corner and, after taking what we needed, we scattered earth on what was left. We brought out something to eat, and when we had all gathered round I heard beside me the sound of a stranger chewing. "By God, there is a stranger here!"

I told the others, and I stretched out my hand and took hold of his. There followed a fight which lasted for some time as I held on to the stranger, but later he called out: "People, a thief has come in wanting to play a trick on us and steal our money." A large crowd gathered and he came up and attached himself to us as we had done to him and accused us as we had accused him, pretending to be blind like us lest he be suspected.

'He then called out that the sultan should advise on the matter, and before we knew it we had been surrounded by the police chief and his men, who took us all off to the sultan's office. He asked for the story, and the man who could see called down blessings on him and said that he thought that it was only by torture that things would become clear. He volunteered to be the first, and they tied him to the whipping post and gave him three hundred lashes. In pain he opened one of his eyes and when he was given another three hundred he opened the other. "What is this, damn you?" said the police chief. "Master," he said, "give me a token of immunity so that I may tell you about what we do."

'When he had been given this he said: "There are four of us, and we pretend to be blind, although we can all see. We go into people's houses to look at the women there and do what we can to harm their relations and their husbands. This has got us a total of ten thousand dirhams. I asked them for my share, but they refused and after beating me they took all I had. I ask help from God and from you, as you have a better right to this money. If you want to know the truth of this, give each of them a hundred lashes until he opens an eye, and this will be clear to you."

'The police chief ordered us to be whipped, and I was the first to be tied up. He said: "You evil rascals, do you deny God's grace and claim that you are blind?" "God, God!" I exclaimed, "not one of us can see," but I was given a hundred lashes and lost consciousness. The man told the chief to wait until I had recovered and then have me beaten again. Meanwhile each of my friends received a hundred strokes as the chief told them: "Open your eyes or else I'll beat you again." The man said: "Sir, send someone with me to take the money, as these people are too afraid of disgrace to open their eyes." The chief did this and after giving the man two thousand dirhams he took the rest and expelled us, saying that if we came back again he would have us killed. I walked off until I joined up with these others, and this is my story.' The king laughed at him and marvelled at his tale.

The Story of the Paralytic

The king then summoned the paralytic and asked him for his name and his story. He said: 'I am generally called Abu'l-Sha'sha' and this is my story. One day when I was going on some errand of mine an old woman asked me to stop briefly as she had a proposal to make to me which, if I liked, I could then carry through. I stopped beside her and she said: "I shall tell you something and then direct you to a pleasant place, but don't say too much." "Go on," I told her, and she said: "What would you say about a fine house with a flowery orchard, gushing streams and ripe fruits? There is clear wine, camphor-scented candles and the lovely face of one whom, after some hardship, you can embrace if you succeed in carrying out what I tell you."

' "Lady," I asked, when I heard this, "is all this in this world?" "Yes, it is for you if you want to act," she replied. I asked her what she had seen in me to make her choose me rather than some immoral man, but she said: "Didn't I tell you not to talk too much? Keep quiet and come with me." She went off, and I followed her, lured by what she had described, and she then said: "The girl to whom I am taking you likes those who agree with her and dislikes those who don't. If you obey and do what she tells you, she will become your slave." I said that I would not refuse anything I was told to do and I went with the old woman into a large and lofty house where there were many servants and retainers. When they saw me they said: "What are you doing here?" "Don't talk to him," the old woman said, "for he is a craftsman whom we need."

'I went into a large courtyard, in the centre of which was the most beautiful orchard that had ever been seen. She sat me on an elegant bench with a covering of heavy brocade. Before I had waited long I heard a great commotion and saw girls coming towards me surrounding one who had been favoured by God with perfect beauty. I got to my feet when I saw her, and she took her seat while I remained standing in front of her. After welcoming me, she told me to sit down and then came and asked if all was well with me. "Very well indeed," I told her, after which she had an ample meal brought in. We ate, but she could not stop laughing, although when I looked at her she turned to one of her maids as though she was laughing at her. All the while she was treating me affectionately and joking with me. Longing for her overcame me, and I had no doubt that she was in love with me, sharing my feelings, and that she would grant me my wish.

'When I had finished eating, trays of gold and silver were produced on which were glasses of fine crystal containing wine of indescribable excellence. Ten girls lovely as the moon then came up carrying lutes and they began to sing heart-rending melodies with delightful voices. I had never seen anyone more beautiful. When my hostess then drank a *ratl* of wine I stood up, but although she told me to sit down again, I drank what she had been drinking standing up, and she started to pelt me with soft cushions. I didn't like that and became very angry, but the old woman standing there winked at me so I held back and said nothing. That did not stop my hostess, who told the girls to join in pelting me, and this almost got me to fall on my face, while she was telling the old woman: "Mother, I have never seen a shrewder young man, nor one with a sweeter disposition or more charm. I shall give him what he will love to achieve from me."

'When this had been going on for what seemed to me to be a long time she went off to do something, and the old woman came up to me and congratulated me on getting what I wanted. "Lady," I said, "how long do I have to put up with being slapped by her and her girls?" She said: "When she gets drunk you can have what you want, but take care not to move or to scowl or else you will lose everything." "When will that be?" I asked. "At midnight," she replied and I said: "By the glory of God, I shall go blind, and if this goes on until midnight I shall be dead." "Pull yourself together," she told me "and put up with this for an hour, for if you take it lightly you will get what you want."

'The lady came back and told the girls to leave, which they did. She then told me to sit down, and when I had done so, another girl came up and smeared me with aloes juice and *nadd* by way of perfume. Then the lady said: "Have you not come into my house and agreed to accept my conditions? Whoever disobeys me I expel and whoever puts up with my jokes gets what he wants." "My lady," I told her, "I am your slave and will bear with whatever you do." Then she said: "Almighty God has inspired me with a love of amusement and novelties. As you can see, I spend each day in pleasure and enjoyment, and I allow those who accept this behaviour of mine to have what they want and to reach their goal, but those who disobey me I slap until they become blind." I told her that I would obey her and follow her instructions, and she said: "If you are telling the truth, then don't disobey me at all."

'When I said that I would not she told the girls to sing and dance, which they did. Then she told one of them: "Take my darling, the light of my eyes, dye his eyebrows and then pluck off his moustaches and bring them to me." Using terms of endearment, she told me to go off with the girl, which I did in a state of perplexity, not knowing what she was going to do with me. The old woman was standing outside the door, and I asked her about this, but she told me that all would be well as the girl would only dye my eyebrows and remove my moustaches. "Dye on the eyebrows can be washed off," I said, "but to pluck out the hairs of my moustache would be very painful." She repeated: "Take care not to disobey her for you have what you want from her in that she is in love with you and her heart is yours. You will spend the rest of your life with her in the happiest of states with the most perfect pleasure."

'The girl sat down to dye my eyebrows but when she started to pluck my moustache I began to cry. "By your life," the old woman conjured me, "you should be happy today for by showing endurance you will get what no one else has got." I put up with it, and when the girl had finished she went off, leaving me in the charge of the old woman. The girl told her mistress that she had done what she had been told to do and asked if she wanted anything else. "Yes," said the lady, "I want you to shave off his beard so that he becomes smooth-chinned, to keep me from being hurt by his rough hairs." "My God, my God!" I exclaimed to the old woman. "I'm afraid that I shall be disgraced, and how am I going to be able to go out amongst people?" "This is good news for you," the old woman replied, "for she only said this because she wants you not to leave her until your moustaches and your beard have grown again. This is because she loves you and can't find any other way of stopping you leaving. So be patient, for you have got what you want."

'I let the girl shave me, and she brought me back to her mistress with dyed eyebrows, moustaches that had been plucked out, a shaven beard and red face and cheeks. When the lady saw me she laughed so much that she fell over on her back and said: "You have won me by your good nature." She then told her girls to strike up all their instruments and to sing, and she urged me to get up and dance. When I did this she used all the cushions that were there in order to hit me as well as pelting me with all the oranges and lemons she could find. This went on until weariness and the blows made me fall down in a faint.

'When I had recovered the old woman said: "She never allows anyone to take her until he has removed all his clothes and is completely naked.

She will do the same until only her harem trousers are left and then she will run from her lover as though she is trying to escape from him. He will follow her from room to room until he is fully aroused, when she will stop and give herself to him. So now take off your clothes." I did so, and the lady stripped down to her trousers and said: "If there is anything you want, catch me." I began to run after her as she went in and out of room after room, and I was so overpowered by lust that I was like a madman. When she got to a big room I ran in after her, crazed by lust, but I trod on a thin board which gave way beneath me, and before I knew what was happening I found myself in the middle of the tanners' market, where the traders were with their hides.

'When they saw me they ran after me, shouting and striking me with their hides, and they went on doing that until I collapsed unconscious. Later they put me on a donkey, naked as I was with dyed eyebrows, plucked moustaches and a shaven chin, and they took me to the city gate, where my arrival coincided with that of the police chief. When he asked what this was he was told that I had fallen the night before from the house of so-and-so the vizier in this condition. He ordered that I be taken to prison, and next day I was given a hundred lashes, mounted backwards on a donkey and expelled from the city. I made off, hiding away from people, until I met these who are now my companions. This is my story.' The king laughed in astonishment at what he had heard.

The Story of the Man Whose Lips Had Been Cut Off

The king then summoned the man whose lips and penis had been cut off and asked him for his story. The man said: 'May God bring the king good fortune! I used to be one of the strongest of men, enjoying a life of ample prosperity until I lost all this and found myself relying on what I could get from others. One day I was out begging for something that would ward off my hunger when I came across a fine-looking house with a large entrance hall and a raised gate, with eunuchs and servants and a great throng of people. This was obviously a seat of authority, and I asked one of the bystanders who its owner was. The man told me that it belonged to one of the rich Barmecides, so I went up to the gatekeepers and asked them for alms. "Go in," they said, "and the owner will give you what you want."

'I entered the hall and walked along it until I came to broad steps leading to a large building, in the centre of which was the most beautiful garden that I had ever seen. The floors were covered with carpets, and curtains were hanging there. I stopped, bewildered, not knowing where to go as I couldn't see anyone to talk to. I made my way towards a bench and discovered a large salon spread with embroidered brocade, at the top of which was a handsome man with a fine beard. I went towards him, and when he saw me he welcomed me and asked me about myself. I told him of my sorry state and said that I needed what he could give me as it was three days since I had last eaten.

'When he heard this he showed concern and tore his clothes, saying: "Are you to starve in a city in which I live? I cannot bear that." He made me fair promises, thanking God for having brought me to him, and telling me that I must now share his food. I told him that I could not wait as I was in desperate need of something to eat, and he called to a servant to bring a small bowl and water so that we could wash our hands, but I could see neither servant nor bowl. Then he said: "Brother, join me in washing your hands in this bowl," and he gestured with his hand as though he was washing. Then he said: "Bring the table of food," but there was no one and no table to be seen. He told me not to be shy and pretended to be eating. "Eat up," he kept on telling me, "for I know how hungry you must be. Look at this beautiful white bread," but I couldn't see anything. I told myself that this was a man who liked to make fun of people and I said: "Yes, sir, I have never seen the like." He told me that it had been baked by a slave girl whom he had bought for five hundred dinars. "That was cheap," I told him, "for such a girl is beyond price."

'He then called out to a servant to bring the first course, a pie, telling him to put a lot of butter on it. "Brother," he said, "have you ever seen anything more delicious than this pie with all the butter? Don't be ashamed to eat." Next it was stew made from fatted duck that he wanted, and he repeated his call to me to eat up without embarrassment as he knew how much I needed food. I started fiddling with my hands and moving my jaws, wondering how long this was going to go on. He kept on calling for dish after dish and earnestly urging me to eat, as he went on describing the various types of food, until he got to the roast kid, urging me to eat some of it. "I have never seen anything like it," he explained, calling my attention to how fat it was and saying that it had been cooked with saffron. "God bless the cook who roasted it," I said. He then called for soup made from fatted chickens, explaining that they had been reared on pistachios. "Try it," he told me, "for you have never tasted anything like it in your life," and I agreed.

'He kept on encouraging me and gesturing with his hand as though he was putting food in my mouth but as he described the various dishes I was getting hungrier and hungrier and would have been happy with a loaf of barley bread. "Bring up the mixed fries," he called, saying that he had never found anything tastier than the spices that flavoured them or than the marvellous *burani* mixture. When I told him that this was enough, he called for the sweet, urging me to taste the excellent fresh almond cakes and to take one of the sweetmeats that he was holding before the sesame oil ran down from it. I thanked him and moved my mouth and my jaws as though I was chewing, and he then urged me to go on to another sweetmeat made from almonds, but I said that I had had enough and could not eat another thing.

'He ordered the table to be taken away and told me to wash my hands, and although I said no he insisted and I made a pretence of washing although I was desperately hungry. I thought about this and said to myself: "By God, I shall do something to make him sorry so that he never does it again." "Taste this glass of wine and tell me if you like it," my host said, and I told him: "It has a good colour and a pleasant bouquet, but I'm only in the habit of drinking old wine." He called for a ten-year-old wine and told me to taste it but warned me that it was so strong that nobody could drink a full tankard of it. I said that I would like a *ratl*, and he ordered it to be brought. "This is what I enjoy," I told him, and I pretended to be drinking. "Cheers," he said and joined in the pretence of drinking. I then asked for another to drink and when I had "drunk" it, I pretended to be drunk. He swore that I should drink yet another, and when I told him that I couldn't, he insisted. I made a show of drinking the next and then, pretending not to know what I was doing, I lifted my arm high enough to show my armpit and struck the middle of his head, knocking him down on his face, and I then followed this up with two more blows. "What's this, you scum?" he exclaimed and I told him: "Sir, I am your servant and your guest. You invited me into your house and gave me food as well as old wine to drink, but I got drunk and became quarrelsome. You should put up with this and forgive me." At this he laughed so loudly that he fell over on his back. Then he said:

"Man, I have been playing this joke on people for a long time, and you are the only one amongst them whom I have found with enough intelligence and wit to enter into it. I forgive you for what you did, and now you will become my real drinking companion and never leave me."

'A number of servants and pages appeared at his command, all differently dressed, and he told them to bring out a real table with all sorts of hot and cold foods, and then all the dishes that he had described were produced and we ate our fill, before washing our hands when he said. After this we moved to an elegant room, where we ate from the fine fruits that were set out there. A number of girls wearing ornaments of all kinds appeared and began to sing, and we stayed enjoying ourselves to the full until we fell under the influence of drink. He became very friendly, and I answered all his questions, discovering him to have great affection for me. He presented me with robes of honour and gifts until we became inseparable.

'I spent the night in his house, and next day we enjoyed ourselves in the same way again. When that had been going on for ten days, he put me in charge of all his affairs, and everything was at my disposal. Things went on like that for twenty years, but on his death the sultan took over all his wealth and mine as well, reducing me to poverty. Hardship and distress made me flee from the city, carrying with me everything that I had left, but Bedouin ambushed me on the way. They took me captive and after seizing all I had they tied me up and brought me to their camp.

'My captor would come and beat me every day, telling me that unless I ransomed myself he would cut me in bits. I began to weep and cry out, and after leaving me for two days he came back on the third and repeated his demand for a ransom. I told him that I had no money with me and I could not fetch a single dirham. "I am your captive," I told him, "so do what you want." He took out a knife and cut off my lips, and there was no trick that I could play. I did not know what to do as he pressed his demand, saying: "By God, if you don't pay, I'll kill you."

This Bedouin had a pretty wife, and every day when he went out she would make advances to me and try to seduce me, although I did not yield. One day he came in unexpectedly when I was weakening and she was sitting on my lap. When he saw this he went up to her and struck her a painful blow. To me he said: "You damned man, did you want to get your own back for what I did to you through my wife?" and, taking out his knife, he cut off my penis. I collapsed unconscious, and he then put me on a camel and threw me down at the foot of a mountain. When

I came to my senses I saw that I was near to death, so I started to walk a few steps at a time until I came across these people, whom I joined. This is my story.'

The king was amazed by these stories and wondered how they had come together and what the bond between them could be, to which they said: 'Deformity, exile and poverty.'' At that he gave them robes of honour and provided them with generous bounty before sending them off happy at what they had received from him.

The Story of the Glass-seller

The king called for the man with the severed ear and saw on his face and head marks of a beating. On being asked about this the man called down a blessing on the king and said: 'Your Majesty, I was a poor man and lived off what I could get by begging. My old father fell ill and died leaving a hundred dirhams and nothing else. This perplexed me as I didn't know what to do with the money, but as I was thinking it over it occurred to me to use it all to buy various kinds of glass, sell them and take advantage of the profit they would bring me. So I bought the glass and put the items on a large tray and sat down in a place where I could sell them. Next to me was a tailor who had a balustrade by his shop door, against which I leaned.

'I sat there plunged in thought, telling myself that the capital I had invested in the glass was a hundred dinars. I would sell it for two hundred and then use this to buy more, which I would sell for four hundred, and carry on like this until I had four thousand dirhams. I would continue trading and move my goods to such-and-such a spot, where I would sell them for eight thousand dirhams, which I would use to buy and sell until I had ten thousand. With this I would buy perfume and all kinds of jewels and make a huge profit. Then I would buy a splendid house as well as mamluks and other fine houses as well as riding beasts with trappings of gold, and I would indulge myself in eating, drinking and amusing myself. I would send messages to every singing girl in the city and have my way with them. Whenever I needed something I would sell some of my jewels and spend the money and I would use the rest to go on trading until my capital reached a hundred thousand dinars. Then I would send marriage brokers to look for princesses and the daughters of viziers.

'I would ask for the hand of the daughter of the vizier of my city as I had heard that she was perfect in all respects as well as being strikingly beautiful. I would offer a dowry of a thousand dinars and if they were not satisfied with this I would take her from them by force in spite of her father and mother. When she came to my house I would buy ten young eunuchs and have various different clothes and girdles made for them. I would have a heavy saddle made of gold and stud it with gems and then ride round the city with people greeting me and calling down blessings on me. When I came into the presence of the vizier with servants to the right and left of me, he would get up for me and after he had come forward to greet me, I would sit in his seat and he would sit below me, as I was his son-in-law. Two of my servants would carry two purses containing the thousand-dinar dowry I had got ready and I would add another two thousand to show my generosity as well as how little attention I paid to things of this world.

'I would then return home and if a messenger came to me from my wife I would present him with a gift and a robe of honour, while if he brought a gift for me I would not accept it but return it to him and I would leave my bride where she was. She would be decked out and when this was done she would be brought to me. My house would be put in order, and when the time had come for me to be left alone with her I would put on my finest clothes and take my seat on a dais covered with regal brocade, looking neither left nor right to show the soundness of my intelligence and my high-mindedness. My bride would be standing like a full moon in all her finery, but my self-esteem and pride would not allow me to glance at her. Everyone there would say: "Master, favour your wife and your servant with a glance as she stands before you, for to stand like this does her harm." When they had kissed the ground a number of times I would raise my head and give her a single glance and then lower my head again.

'As her attendants took her off I would get up and change my clothes for something finer, and when she was brought back for the second time I would not look at her until they had asked me many times, when I would spare her a brief glance and then look down. I would go on doing this until the ceremony of unveiling was complete. Then I would tell one of the eunuchs to bring a purse of five hundred dinars, which I would give to the bride's attendants, telling them to leave me alone with her.

' "When I am alone with her I shall [not] show her any respect or affection and when sleeping with her in the same bed I shall treat her with contempt and not approach her. Her mother will come and kiss my hands and feet, saying: 'Master, look at your maid-servant, for she is longing for you to approach her. Stretch out your hand to her.' I shall make no reply, and on seeing that she will get up and kiss my foot, saying: 'Master, my daughter is a girl who has never seen a man, and if she finds you holding back like this she will be heartbroken. So turn to her, speak to her and console her.' She will then give her daughter a goblet of wine, telling her to urge me to drink it. When she comes to me I shall leave her standing in front of me and not look up at her until she feels humiliated and realizes that I am a mighty sultan of great power. She will implore me for God's sake not to reject what she is handing me, as she is my servant and my slave. When I say nothing, she will press me, and I shall shake my fist in her face."

'I then did shake my fist, and it came down on the tray with the glasses, which I had put up above me. It fell to the ground and everything on it was smashed. "This is all your fault thanks to your pride and stupidity about your glass," the tailor called out to me, "and were it up to me, I would give you a hundred lashes and have you paraded around the city." I began to weep and to slap myself. People were on their way to Friday prayer and while some were sorry for me others did not care. As for me I had lost both profit and capital.

'I had stayed there for a time in tears, when a beautiful woman passed by. She was mounted on a fine donkey with a heavy saddle, and she exuded a scent of musk as she went on her way to Friday prayer. When she saw me slapping my face and weeping she felt sorry for me and asked me what was wrong. People told her: "This man was sitting there with a tray of glasses from which he hoped to make a living as it was the only thing he had, but it fell down, and all the glasses were smashed. That is the reason for this display of grief." The woman then called to one of her servants and told him to give me what he had with him, and this turned out to be a purse containing five hundred dinars.

'When I took this, I almost died of joy. I called down blessings on her and went back home enriched by what she had given me. Before I knew it there was a knock on the door, and this was an old woman who had followed me after having seen me being given the money. When I heard the knock I asked who was there, and she said: "Brother, I want a word with you." I got up to see who she was and when I opened the door I saw an old woman whom I didn't recognize. She said: "Little son, it is the time for prayer but I am not ritually clean and I would like you to let me use your house to get ready to pray." I willingly agreed and went back inside, telling her to follow, which she did, and I then gave her a bowl of water and showed her where she could wash, after which I sat turning over the coins and putting them in a waistband purse.

'When the old woman had finished doing what she wanted she came to where I was sitting and prayed with two *rak'as* before calling down blessings on me. I thanked her before reaching out to the dinars and giving her two of them, telling myself that this act of charity might cause God to save me from trouble. She said: "Glory to God, what are you thinking of? Because I blessed you and prayed for you to be rewarded, do you think that this makes me a beggar, to whom you have to give alms? Take your money and give it to someone who needs it, for I don't want it, thanks be to God." This gave me a high opinion of her, and I made my excuses to her. She then asked if all was well with me, and I said that, God willing, it was very well indeed. She said: "I saw you receiving charity and I would like through you to win a good reward." When I asked what she wanted she said: "I must tell you, my son, that I have a daughter, the loveliest and most perfect girl that eyes have ever seen, who is also rich and prosperous. She is unmarried but wants a husband and one of her own choosing, and this has put me into difficulties, as every Friday she goes out and tells me to look for a man to bring her, saying that he should be pleasant, handsome and rich. Every Friday I bring her one, and she sits with him to eat and drink and then sends him away, saying that he does not appeal to her. You have all the qualities that she describes, so come and it may be that you will make an impression on her and so live with her, enjoying the most prosperous of lives in possession of all her wealth, and becoming the richest man of your age."

'When I listened to this and heard what she said about the girl I was swayed and felt strongly attracted to her, telling myself that God might help me to obtain what I had wanted to get from my glass. I asked the old woman how I should approach the girl, and she told me that she liked a man who was well off, and so I should take with me all that I had, and when I met her I should be as polite and flattering as I could. In this way I would get all I wanted both of her beauty and her wealth.

'I collected all my money and set off with her, scarcely believing in my happiness. She walked ahead, and I followed her until she brought me to the door of a large house. When she knocked, a Rumi maid-servant came and opened it, and my guide entered and told me to come in, which I did, finding the place both spacious and handsome. The old woman took me to a big room, furnished with carpets and hanging curtains. I sat down with the dinars in front of me and then, taking off my turban, I put it down beside me.

'Before I knew what was happening out came a girl more splendid and more beautifully dressed than had ever been seen, with the most attractive scent. At the sight of such beauty I rose to my feet, and when she saw me she laughed. I was delighted, and she ordered the door to be closed before coming up to me and taking me by the hand to a separate room strewn with soft cushions, which we entered. We sat together, and for a time she laughed and joked with me before getting up and leaving after saying: "Don't go before I come back."

'As I sat there a huge, savage-looking black slave came in with a drawn sword. "Damn you," he said, "what are you doing here?" and the sight of him robbed me of speech. "Get up!" he said, seizing me by the arm, and when I did he took all the money I had with me, stripped me of my clothes and struck me with his sword, these being the scars that you can see, Your Majesty. He kept on doing this until I collapsed, being sure that he had finished me. I heard him call out at the top of his voice: "Where is the girl with the salt?" and a servant girl wearing an apron came up to him carrying a silver plate on which were grains of salt. He kept on stuffing these into my wounds, and I stayed motionless, as I was afraid that if they realized that I was still alive they would kill me.

'When the girl left, the black man called for the cellar keeper, and it was the old woman who had brought me who came. She dragged me by the feet and opened an underground cellar into which she threw me so that I landed on a number of others who had suffered the same fate. I stayed there for three days but thanks to God's grace it was the salt that kept me alive by stopping me from losing too much blood. When I found myself capable of movement I got up and sat on the pile of corpses, after which I got to the trap door and lifted it up. I went through into the house itself and by God's grace I found strength enough to walk a little to the entrance hall, where I hid myself until dawn.

'Next morning the damned old woman came out to hunt down another victim like me, and I followed her without her knowledge. I went on doing my best to treat myself for a month until my wounds healed and my strength returned. I had not lost track of the old woman and kept watching her as she picked man after man and took them to the house, without my saying anything. Then, when I had recovered, I got a strip of cloth and sewed it up as a waistband purse. I filled this with glass and fastened it on my waist, disguising myself and wearing a face veil so that I could not be recognized, and dressing as a Persian. Beneath my clothes I concealed a sharp sword.

'When I saw the old woman I asked her in Persian whether she had scales that could weigh five hundred dinars, in which case I would give her something to spend on herself. I explained that I wanted to buy a slave girl if she could produce one for me. She told me that she knew a banker who had scales of all kinds and I should go with her before he went off to his shop, so that he could weigh the coins for me.

'I followed her to the door, and when she knocked the very same girl came to open it. The old woman greeted her with a smile and said: "I've brought you a fat titbit today." The girl took me by the hand and brought me into the same room, where she sat chatting with me for a while before jumping up and telling me not to go until she came back. As soon as she had gone the black man came in, holding a drawn sword. "Get up, you damned fellow," he said, but as he walked in front of me, without his knowledge I removed my own sword that I had under my clothes and with it I cut through his legs so that he fell on his face. Then I jumped up to his head and cut it from his body, after which I dragged him to the cellar into which I and the others had been thrown. "Where is the salt girl?" I called, and it was the old woman who came. "Do you recognize me, damn you?" I said. "No, by God, master," she answered. "It was my house in which you prayed before throwing me in here," I told her, at which she called on God and begged me for mercy. I paid no attention to what she said but cut off her hands, first one and then the other, and I went on tormenting her until she died.

'I then went to look for the girl, who was startled to see me and asked me to spare her. I agreed to this but asked her how it was that she came to be here with the black man. She said: "I was a slave belonging to a merchant who had bought me for a thousand dinars. That old woman – may God have no mercy on her – often used to visit me and we became friends. One day she told me that there was going to be a wedding of exceptional splendour in her neighbourhood with musical instruments, songs of all kinds, feasting and various sorts of remarkable things. She said that she would like me to see it, and I got up quickly and put on my best clothes and ornaments, taking with me a purse of a hundred dinars. She then led me to this house, where, thanks to the trick the damned woman played on me, I have been for three years. Every day she has been bringing a man, taking his money and killing him in the cellar."

"Has she got money?" I asked, and the girl said: "Yes, if you can carry it, so ask God for help."

'I walked off with her, and she opened rooms into which purses had been thrown, but I remained in a state of perplexity, unsure what I should do. Shortly afterwards, however, I went out and hired ten mules but when I came back to knock on the door I found it open and when I went in I discovered that the girl had gone, as had most of the purses. I realized that she had cheated me and so I took what money I could find and I opened the cupboards to remove clothes, materials and furniture. I left nothing there but removed everything to my own house, where I spent the night.

'Next morning I was suddenly confronted by ten men, who took hold of me and said that I was wanted by the chief of police, to whom they took me. When he saw me he asked me where I had got the materials that were in my house. I asked for a guarantee of immunity, and when he had promised me this, I told him the story of my dealings with the old woman from beginning to end, including how the girl had run off. "Sir," I said, "take what you want of the stuff that is in my house but leave me enough to live on." He sent a number of his assistants with me, and they took the best of what there was, leaving me only what was valueless. The chief then became afraid that word of this might reach the sultan and so he summoned me again and told me that he wanted me to leave the city and stay somewhere else until the affair had been forgotten. I agreed and set off to where I could remain for a time before returning, but when I halted robbers attacked me and took everything that I had with me, leaving me naked and with no idea of where I should go. It was then that I met these people and joined them, as we were united by the ties of misfortune. This is my story.'

The king was astonished by all these tales and by the lack of intelligence shown by the last of them, the glass-seller, in what he did to his glass. He ordered all of them to be rewarded and given fine clothes. This is the story of their dealings with the king.

Tale Four

The Story of the Four Hidden
Treasures and the Strange Things That
Occurred. The First Quest.
The Story of the Second Quest and the
Marvellous Things Encountered.
The Story of the Quest for the Crown
and It Is the Third.
The Story of the Quest for the Golden
Tube and It Is the Fourth.

In the Name of God the Compassionate, the Merciful

Al-Fadl son of Muhammad told us that, when he was with the emir 'Abd al-Wahhab on a very hot day, with ambergris diffusing scent, the emir said to him that he wanted him to tell him a story of marvels.

Al-Fadl said: 'I told him: "Emir, in your prison is this foreigner who has written me notes asking me to bring him before you. I hear that he is a cultured and witty man, and if you order it, I shall fetch him here." The emir did so, and when the man was brought, he questioned him and, finding him eloquent, he ordered him to be looked after and his clothes changed. The servants took him to the baths, gave him clean clothes and provided him with food and water, after which they brought him to the emir.

'When he stood before him, the emir said: "I hear that you are witty and cultured and I should like to have a friendly conversation with you, so tell me what you have to say." The man said: "I shall tell you a story, part of which you know." "Go on," said the emir, and the man said: "You must know, emir, may God exalt you, that I have seen marvels and wonders in the world and have experienced hardships and terrors. As a young man I enjoyed myself, squandering my goods and my wealth and consorting with kings, while for me the eye of Time slept. But Time then woke to betray me, destroying what I had, and after I had spent three days at home without food, I left to escape the gloating pleasure of my enemies, without any notion of where to go.

' "During my wanderings I reached Kharshana and entered the church, where I sat with the poor, eating the bread that was distributed as alms. I stayed there for three days until on the fourth a very handsome man came in wearing a robe of yellow brocade and followed by a servant. He studied our faces and then greeted me and said: 'I hope that my reading of your face will not prove wrong. If you come with me, God willing you will prosper.'

' "I got up and accompanied him, happy at what he had said, and when we got to his house he went in and told me to follow him, which I did. The rags I was wearing were removed, and after I had bathed, he supplied me with the finest clothes and for some days I stayed eating and drinking with him.

' "He then told his servant to summon his companions, and in came ten men who took their seats after greeting us, and the wine cups were passed around amongst us. That went on for ten days, after which he told them to leave, taking with them whatever they wanted, and adding: 'We shall start, God willing, on such and such a day.' They went off and he turned and said to me: 'My reading of your face was right. I shall let you into my secret, and if you help me this will be thanks to your own kindness, while you will not be blamed if you refuse.' I said: 'Say what you want for I am at your service and will do whatever you tell me, thanks to the great kindness with which you have over-whelmed me.'

' "He said: 'My father left me books in which I discovered the way to the king's monastery with a description of its wonders.' 'I too would like to see it,' I told him and he said: 'Praise be to God that we are agreed.'

' "He started to get ready the mules and whatever else we would need. The ten men came to the rendezvous and each was provided with two mules, one to ride and one to lead. We armed ourselves, but after seven days of travel we had run out of water and there was only a little food left. We were losing our wits, and the mules were weakening, while one of us had lost his way in the darkness.

' "In the morning we found ourselves at the foot of a mountain. 'Stay here until I come back to you,' our leader said, and after looking he climbed up the mountain, followed by me. 'Where are you going?' he asked me and I told him: 'I shall stay with you to help you in difficulties as you helped me when times were easy.' He thanked me, saying that this was how he had thought I would act.

' "When we reached the summit we looked down at a broad meadow, and he told me to look right and left to see whether I could see anything. I looked and then told him that in the distance I could see the figure of a man. 'That's what we want,' he said, and we went off in that direction, to discover when we got there that this was a statue carved from black rock with a white cloak. On its feet were sandals of emerald green and on its head a cap of yellow stone like gold. Its eyes revolved in its head, and it was standing on a rock in the middle of the meadow.

' "'Go and fetch the others,' my companion told me and when I had done this he got them to dig. They set to work with picks and axes and we unearthed a channel full of cold water, from which we drank our fill. He told them to go on digging and we passed the night there.

' "At dawn he told us to leave with him, and we filled our water-skins and after three more days of travel we came in sight of a mountain green as an emerald. In delight he exclaimed: 'God is greater!' and explained: 'This is the mountain we are making for.' We slept there and next morning we found running streams, intertwined trees, fruits and flowers, and we could see the monastery gleaming like a bright star. We climbed up towards it and there, close to it, was a cave where we put our baggage and rested for three days.

' "When we then approached the monastery we found that its walls were forty cubits high with no gate, but at each of its four corners was a hermitage with four doors in each of which was a statue with a weapon in its hand, while between each two battlements was a statue of a monk holding a huge stone.

' "We were struck with amazement and told our leader: 'This wasn't what we had hoped to find, and how is it that you have endangered both us and yourself?' 'Tomorrow, God willing,' he replied, 'you shall see what I am going to do.' Next morning he collected all the ropes that we had and told us to dig in a certain place. We spent all night doing this and in the morning we came on a door which, when we had uncovered it, turned out to be of iron plated with gold to protect it from corrosion, with a great golden lock.

' "One of us went up to break it but our leader told him not to do that, and, lifting up a stone that he had put beside him, he hurled it at the lock and ran back. When it struck the lock a huge statue appeared from behind the coverings with a great rock in its hand. It moved over the ground, crying out in a loud voice. It shattered the stone and then returned to its place. 'This is what I was afraid of,' the man said.

' "'What is behind the door?' we asked, and he said: 'This is the gate of the fortress.' When we asked if there was any way to open it, he told us that we could do this by removing the stones. When a second stone was thrown at the lock, out came the statue and did what it had done before, but we kept on throwing stones until it did not appear. Then we went up and broke the lock and fastened one end of our ropes to the door ring and the other round the necks of the mules, whipping them to make them move. The door opened, and a cloud of vapour emerged.

'"We had to wait for three days until this had totally cleared and when we did go in we discovered a huge well. We tied ropes around the waist of one of our men and were alarmed to find that we could lower him for three hundred cubits. When he got to the bottom we left him there for some time before pulling him up and asking him what he had seen. 'A wonder,' he said, 'so go down yourselves.'

'"We went down in fear and dread and when we had got halfway we came on a huge stone bench on which were bronze statues with weapons in their hands. We stopped to look at them, and our leader told us to remove the flagstone. When we did we could see below it [lac.] of five cubits, in which there was the statue of a seated man holding a chain of brass. 'Pull it,' our leader said, and when we did he went on: 'A bronze ship will now come out to you, so throw these ropes on its prow and take care that it doesn't get past you.'

'"We tugged hard at the chain the statue was holding and then we heard a thunderous noise, and a ship came sailing up. We threw the ropes on to its prow and pulled it towards us before jumping on board. 'Bring the food and the baggage,' he told us, and when we had secured all this and re-embarked, he told us to cast off.

'"After this the ship took us at great speed in pitch darkness five hundred cubits under the mountain, where nothing could be heard except for the sound of the water. It then came to a halt at an iron net, on either side of which the water flowed, and our leader told us to strike a light. With this we lit the candles and when we looked around we saw an iron ladder at the top of which was a bronze statue with a sword in its hand. 'Who is going to come up?' it asked. [the question appears to be put by the statue and answered by the leader, but this is not specified in the text] He said: 'I am.' 'Don't you see what is at the top?' it asked, and he said: 'Glory brings an inheritance of riches. If you look for a beautiful bride, pay out a large dowry. Glory is a possession that lasts for ever and brings long-lasting wealth. He who dares wins, and this is a place of glory. I shall be the first to take the chance and risk my life, for what the writer of this book said is true.'

'"'We shall follow you, whatever you do,' we said, but suddenly there then appeared a serpent with an open mouth and teeth of steel.

Our leader said: 'Whoever throws himself into the jaws of this serpent and escapes will be safe.' 'No one can do that,' we said, but he laughed and took a bow, strung it, notched an arrow and tied a thin rope to its end. He then looked up to the roof, where there was a huge ring. He shot his arrow through the middle of it and then pulled on the end that he had before tying a thick rope to the other end and fixing it to the ring. 'Tie it to my waist,' he told us, 'and when I get up to the ring, lower me very gently to the back of the serpent, for the writer of the book says that there are steps there.'

' "We agreed to do this and pulled him up before lowering him on to the serpent's back. He went to the steps and told us to follow his example. When we did we found a flight of about a hundred steps up which we climbed to a roof that lay behind the serpent, praising Almighty God.

' " 'There are no terrors left,' the leader said, 'but take care in case there is something that the writer of the book failed to notice.' We walked along the roof to a large door, and when we opened it and went in we found ourselves in a hall that led to the courtyard of a huge palace built of various types of coloured marble with bands of gold. In the middle was a pool [lac.] long with a circumference of thirty cubits covered with a golden net. There was a gallery with open doors in each of which stood a statue. Our leader said: 'Each one of these rooms contains God knows how much wealth. The statues may be able to do us some harm – I am not sure – but I shall go to what I know to be there.'

' "When he entered the gallery he came on a sarcophagus of red gold and when he opened it, there was a dead man surrounded by piles of dinars with a golden tablet by this head. This had an inscription: 'Whoever wishes this rubbish, doomed as it is to perish, let him take what he wants of it, for he will leave it behind as I have done and die as I have died, while his actions will be hung around his neck. If he has sent good ahead of him, he will find good, but if he has done evil, it is himself that he will have harmed, for everything will perish except the Lord of heaven and earth.'

' " 'Carry this off,' our leader told us, and we took as much as we could. Then he said: 'Is there anyone here?' and when I had told him that there was not, he lifted the head of the dead man and took from beneath it a golden box, a ring and a knife. 'This is what I was looking for and what I wanted,' he said, before fainting with pleasure. 'How great a goal have we reached, if only this would stay!' he exclaimed, and I said: 'God will preserve you, for you are young and I hope that you will enjoy a long life.'

' "We left, locking the doors and replacing the soil as it was before. We loaded our beasts and after taking stores of fruit we went back to the statue, from where we took enough water for our needs. When we were within a short distance of habitation we found ourselves in a large jungle filled with trees in which we sheltered as the land had been abandoned for fear of the Muslims.

' "Suddenly a stray gazelle came in amongst our beasts. It was being pursued by a young horseman followed by other riders. When they stopped by us our leader took the golden box, the knife and the ring and buried them at the foot of a tree. The riders then took us to their emir, who removed all the money we had with us and ordered us to be put in chains. I saw that what we had got was better than what we could have hoped for in the land of Rum, but after the glory I had seen I have remained in prison until now and what distress is greater than ours and what tale stranger?"

'The emir said: "I have never come across anything stranger or more wonderful than this story of yours," and he gave orders for my companions to be brought out, released from their fetters and well treated. He then asked me to go with a messenger of his and fetch the box, the ring and the knife, promising that he would treat me with his accustomed generosity. I told him that I would make no conditions but would leave this to his own sense of honour and his liberality.

'He sent four thousand riders with us, and when we got to the place I unearthed the three things. It turned out that the box contained two *ratls'* weight of alchemical material, a hundred rubies and a hundred large pearls. I and my young companion were each given an ounce of the *ratls*, while every one of our companions was given a *mithqal*, while a great quantity of money was shared out amongst us. The emir told us that it would be better for us if we accepted Islam. I and my companion did this, while the others would not change their religion and were allowed to go by the emir, while the young man and I stayed and were accepted as his intimates.'

The Story of the Second Quest, with Its Marvels and Terrors

In the Name of God the Compassionate, the Merciful

The narrator of this story said: 'One day when Chosroe was seated, his chamberlain entered and told him that at his door was a man who claimed to have some advice to give him. Chosroe gave permission, and when the man had come in and greeted him Chosroe asked him who he was, what was his name and what was his advice.

'The man said: "I am Saʿada, son of al-Malik al-Akhdar, one of the descendants of ʿAbd al-Malik al-Akbar. I passed by an island in the Indian Ocean, where I came across a cave belonging to the great Shaddad, who ruled the East and the West. I was not able to open it up and remove its contents as I am a poor man without wealth or helpers. So I have brought the matter to you, and should you want to have the cave investigated, let me know and help me to open it up so that you may add to your wealth."

'Chosroe agreed to give him a hundred skilled men and ordered that he be provided with suitable picks, axes and other tools and he then sent him off with his workmen. They sailed from Ubulla with a fair wind and after just over three months they reached the island. The wind then strengthened against them and, fearing disaster, they anchored and disembarked, after which they helped themselves to water and fruit.

'As they were wandering around the island, admiring the quantity of its trees, its fine fruits and the sweetness of its waters, they suddenly heard a loud noise. When they looked up they saw a huge bird with a body bigger than that of an elephant whose wings obscured the horizon.

[First person narrative of one of Chosroe's men]

' "It swooped down on us and snatched up two of us with its talons before soaring off with them into the sky. We never saw them again. I told the others to hurry back to the ship before the bird destroyed us, but they said that they would spend the night there as it would not come back and they could go to the ship early next morning.

' "Before an hour had passed, that night we heard a noise of clapping coming from the sea and a mixture of voices. Mermaids came out of the sea and, on reaching the island, they approached us and smiled in our faces. They showed no sign of fear when we got up to go to them nor did they run away. Each one of us took one of them and we spent the most delightful and pleasant of nights, discovering that the only difference between them and our own women was that their skins had the roughness of small shells.

' "Dawn disturbed them and we could not hold them back as they rushed to the sea and dived in. 'Let us take the opportunity to save ourselves,' one of us then said, 'as we cannot be sure that the bird will not come back.' So we took what water and fruits we could and, running before the wind, we sailed for a month on a sea that was boiling like a cauldron and which contained creatures any one of which could smash our ship if it touched it with the edge of its wing. So whenever any of them came near we would beat drums and blow on trumpets, at which they would turn away.

' "We went on like that until Sa'ada asked us if we could see anything ahead of us. 'There is something white like the light of the sun,' we said, at which he prostrated himself in thankfulness to Almighty God, exclaiming: 'This is our goal!' We sailed on until we reached a huge island white as camphor, where we anchored and disembarked. I asked Sa'ada whether there was anything there for us to fear, and he said: 'No, you can safely go wherever you want.' So we went around without seeing anything dangerous but finding completely unknown trees and fruits the like of which we had never seen before, softer than butter and sweeter than honey.

' "Because the paths were so narrow and the trees so thickly interwoven Sa'ada lost his way to the cave and went to and fro bewildered and distressed. We went with him through trackless thickets, wandering around and looking for the cave until suddenly he came across it and prostrated himself in thankfulness to Almighty God. He told us to pitch camp and rest for the remainder of the day, which we did.

' "Next day we brought out the picks and axes and he told us to clear all around a rock, where we dug for a number of days. We then fastened ropes and chains around the rock and encouraged one another with shouts until we had moved it away from the cave entrance. 'Come on, boys!' Sa'ada said to us. 'We shall draw lots and whoever wins can go in, look around and tell us whether there is anything unpleasant or dangerous.'

' "We all took part in this, and the lot fell to a young man who was one of the bravest and most steadfast of our company. When he had got to the entrance of the cave and was standing on the threshold, a brazen statue of a lion with steel teeth sprang out and attacked him violently, carrying him off. We heard a single scream and the lion then dropped him and went back to its place, while we heard the noise of a body falling into a well. 'Damn you!' we said to Sa'ada. 'What made you risk your own life and that of your man?' 'Don't judge me hastily,' he replied, 'for anyone who is serious in pursuit of a great quest must take risks and enter dangerous places, but there is a way to put this talisman out of action at least for a time.'

' "From his sleeve he took out a book and, after looking through its pages, he told us to come out with him. He measured the distance from where the lion was to the entrance of the cave and then did the same thing along the ground in reverse. 'Dig here,' he told us, and when we did we got to the edge of the well. We used our axes to break it down and at this point we heard the lion falling into the opening that lay in front of it.

' "We then returned to the entrance of the cave. He told us to fetch planks, and we laid these from the entrance to the edge of the well. 'You can now enter safely,' he told us, and after we had done this all we could see was darkness. 'We daren't risk our lives by going in here without knowing what to expect,' we told him, but he said: 'I am with you,' and he went on ahead of us. We could see him calling us to follow, and as we walked along a dark passage he kept telling us that there was nothing there to fear.

' "He led us out into a wide space where there was an iron door with a lock. He took a club and struck the lock with a blow that shattered it before opening the door. 'Good news!' he told us. 'The end of the task is near, so draw lots for one of you to go in and tell us what he sees.' We did this and the winner entered and saw a flight of stairs at the bottom of which was a statue lying on its face. When he put his foot on the first step the statue moved and sat up; when he stood on the second step it took up a sword that was lying beside it. He reached the third step and it stood up and when he got to the fourth step it turned on a spiral spring and struck him a blow that cut him in half.

' " 'Don't be afraid at what you see,' our leader told us, 'for if a man's time is up he will die on his bed, and whoever does not come will not get enough to live on. There is nothing left for you to fear, so get me a large piece of wood from one of the trees.' One of us did that, and when he brought it back the leader told us that he would save us the trouble and run the risk for us. He then took the piece of wood in his hand and started to go down one step after another. The statue moved as it had done before, and when he got to the fourth step it turned and struck with its sword. The man met it with the wood, in which the sword stuck, leaving the statue motionless. 'You can come in safely,' our leader told us, 'as there is no trick left that you have to fear.'

' "Following him, we came to an open space with fine trees in leaf and water gushing from the mouths of lions and birds' beaks into a pool lined with gold, whose radiance dazzled the eyes. From the statues came tuneful sounds that captivated the heart. Standing over this was a huge palace by a great river, with a door of red gold studded with pearls and other gems. At the upper end was a silver couch on which lay a shrouded corpse with a tablet of green topaz at its head on which was the following inscription: 'I am Shaddad the Great. I conquered a thousand cities; a thousand white elephants were collected for me; I lived for a thousand years and my kingdom covered both east and west, but when death came to me nothing of all that I had gathered was of any avail. You who see me, take heed, for Time is not to be trusted. I stored all the wealth and the jewels that I collected in three caves, of which this is one. Its contents lie on the other side of my couch through a door which I constructed through my knowledge of astrology. No man can open it until the lucky stars are in the right place and this is due to happen on one day a year. Let no one who comes to it wear himself out for he will not get through to it until the stars give him the opportunity.'

' "Sa'ada said: 'What is written here is true, so be careful of what food you have and store it away, only eating enough to keep you alive, although there are also fruits on the island. We have to wait until the door opens, for if all the people in the world used every means that they could think of to hurry it on, they would not be able to get through.'

' "We stayed like that for four months, but then there was a great earth tremor, and we rushed in a panic to the door, which we found open. 'We don't know how long it will stay open,' Sa'ada told us, 'so look after yourselves and fetch timbers to set between the two halves of the door until you get what you want.'

' "We did that and went through to a room filled with jewels, gold and silver, from which we took all that we could and loaded our ship until there was no room for more. We removed the wood that we had put up as props so that anyone else who came would have the same trouble that we did and would have to wait as we had waited. We then took the topaz tablet with its description of the door and, after going back up, we replaced the stone that had covered the door and left.

' "We sailed off for some distance with a fair wind and we then experienced more of the perils and the marvels of the sea with its various types of beasts than we had seen on our way out. When we reached Hilla we gave thanks to Almighty God and wrote to the king to tell him what had happened and to say that we were in fear of Bedouin robbers on our way back. He sent us a thousand horsemen as well as many camels and mules. We loaded them with all we had and brought them to the king, who thanked God for what He had granted him. 'You have not fallen short!' he told us and he gave each of us enough to make him wealthy. We were all then numbered amongst his intimates until death separated us." '

The Story of the Third Quest, for the Crown

The story is told that Aban son of al-'As came on an errand to 'Abd al-Malik son of Marwan, but was kept waiting at his door for some days without being allowed in. He was followed by al-Sha'bi, who stopped at the door but was then admitted. Aban had told him that he had not been able to get in and had asked him to tell this to the caliph. Al-Sha'bi had willingly agreed, and when the caliph sent for him that night he went in, greeted him and was told to sit.

After a general conversation 'Abd al-Malik told him that he would like to hear something of the sea and its marvels, for he was passionately interested in this. Al-Sha'bi said: 'Caliph, at your door is Aban son of Sa'id son of al-'As, who has sailed the seas, seen their wonders and heard their stories, and who is, besides this, a pleasant and genial companion.' 'Abd al-Malik told his chamberlain to fetch in Aban, and he went out and did so.

Aban entered and saluted the caliph with the appropriate greeting, after which he was allowed to sit. When he was seated 'Abd al-Malik asked him whether he knew something of the wonders of the sea that would help pass the night. 'Yes indeed, Commander of the Faithful,' said Aban, 'and would you like me to begin with what I have seen or what I have heard?' [lac.]

'Mu'awiya son of Abi Sufyan supplied me with a hundred thousand dirhams, and I went to Kufa, where I spent ninety thousand, leaving me with only ten thousand. "This is all that there is between me and poverty," I told myself, "but I shall travel somewhere else and it may be that I will bring back a profit."

'In my mind I reviewed the various lands, but God prompted me to go to India. I went to Kufa and bought trade goods before boarding a Persian ship called *Al-Zarin*. We sailed off with a favourable wind, but the journey took so long that I was filled with regret for what I had done. I saw that I needed friendship and I told myself that I should talk to those who were on the ship with me and make friends with them. We went on talking together until we had all become brothers, and this continued until we reached Serendib, which seemed to me to be a land of great importance.

'When we had disembarked I hired a fine house. I began to go around the place and find out about it until I came to an idol temple. When I went in and looked around I saw in a corner a man busy with prostrations and *rak'as*. He had a censer in his hand from which was coming the scent of aloes and ambergris. He was eating from a plate, but I did not know what was on it. I asked someone there what he was doing and was told: "This is a man who is looking for something, asking about it and wanting a reply, but although he has been here for a year he has not got one."

'I was perplexed and astonished at a man who was prostrating himself to an idol and asking it for something. Then some days later I heard the sound of drums, trumpets and cymbals, and there was the man, surrounded by people, riding on an elephant. I followed him to his house and when he entered it I went in with the crowd. He took his seat, and after the people had congratulated him they went off, leaving me sitting there.

' "Is there something you want?" he asked me, and when I told him there was, he said: "Tell me." I said: "I saw you seeking for something in front of an idol and, as I now see that you are happy and pleased, I wonder if your prayer was answered and your request granted." He said that it had been, and I told him that I was glad and asked whether he would be good enough to tell me what it was that he had asked for and what had been the reply. I had left my own country in search of marvels and I didn't think that I could hear anything more marvellous than his story. He laughed and told me to stay with him. He then had food produced and after we had eaten he brought out wine and we drank.

'When the wine had had its effect on him he asked me where I had come from and when I had told him that this was Kufa he asked me for my name, which I said was Aban son of Sa'id. "God preserve you," he said, adding: "By God, I shall tell you the most wonderful thing. I am a man who searches for wonders and marvels just as you do. One day I came across a sheet of paper and I discovered on reading it that it described a quest for one of the crowns of the ancients. The man who wrote it grudged the crown to his successors and so had left it in a place that he described."

' "He said: 'I sent men to China, who brought back from it a stone known as *al-andaran*, which gleams at night as brightly as the dawn. It is risky and extremely difficult for the Chinese to find, and they say that they have to take it from the mouths of sea-serpents, which they kill but which sometimes swallow them. My men brought me seventy of these stones, each of which was worth a *qintar* of gold. In the crown that they formed were set three hundred pearls, rubies and emeralds, worth *qintars* of gold, and various types of chrysolite, pearls and gold from the best mines were picked out for it. At its right edge was set what was known as the Stone of Victory, which would rout any army to whom it was shown. Between the stones was one whose effect was to baffle the sight of any bastard so that he could see nothing, while in the centre was a stone which caused anyone who saw it to fall on his face out of reverence and respect. In attendance on it were seventy sages and seventy Magian priests, venerating and glorifying it.' The writer intended to explain the story of the crown and how it could be reached but his text broke off.

' "I remained perplexed and baffled and I asked every wise man whom I knew, but they could tell me nothing and I could find no information. When I was at the end of my resources I turned to that idol, asking questions and making inquiries, and for a whole year I stayed in front of it. Then yesterday I saw it move, and it called to me. I got up and prostrated myself before it. 'Raise your head,' it told me, and when I did so it told me that it had taken pity on me and it described how to get to the crown, which I memorized. Then it said: 'Someone else will share in this quest with you,' after which it fell silent, and I prostrated myself again in gratitude. I think that it is you who it meant would be my partner, so you can be happy to learn that you will come with me." "I'm not your man," I said. "Have you given up risking your life?" he asked, and I told him: "Our doctrine tells us that the time of our death and our daily bread are predetermined, and in matters like this there can be no fear."

"That is sensible," he replied, "and someone like you will make a suitable companion and, the day being what it is, I have already got money for you and you need not bring provisions or anything else."

'I left him and, after having deposited my money, I dressed in travelling clothes and strapped on a sword and a dagger, after which I went back to him. He was delighted to see me and, after having said: "This is what we need for the journey," he mounted an elephant and put me on another. When each of us was properly settled we set off and when night fell we sheltered in a cave, leaving the elephants to graze, and we slept until dawn. Then when day broke we mounted and rode off and we went on like this for twenty days, passing valleys and hills until we reached a huge mountain.

'We made our way to a cave in it, where we halted and left the elephants to look for food. My companion then removed from his baggage a light tent, which we set up in the middle of a meadow beside a stream, and in it he spread out fine bedding. "Cook me some food in the cave and bring it to me here in the tent at the noon prayer every day until I have finished what I need to do," he told me. I agreed and went back to the cave. I would then bring him his food every day at the time of the prayer and I would find him stretched out at the door of his tent like a drunken man. I would leave the food and the drink and go off until next day.

'We went on like this for a whole month. At the end of that time he told me: "Don't bring me anything tomorrow, and if you come and don't find me, then get on one of the elephants and go off under the protection and guardianship of God. Don't look for the crown, as there will be no way to find it."

'I was filled with sadness for him as I left him because of my fondness for him and because I had fixed my hopes on finding out about the crown. I passed a long night and in the morning I went up to the elephants and loaded them with my baggage before mounting. When I came to my companion's camp I could see that his tent was ablaze and filled with thick smoke. In my astonishment I stopped to look, bewildered and not knowing what to do.

'As I was standing there I heard a great crash coming from the mountain followed by another, and then came a strange voice which I could make out was telling me to go back. I returned to where I had come from and then on to where I had heard the voice coming from, but there was no one to be seen.

'I spent that day waiting to see what would happen and then on the following day I saw my companion coming towards me. I embraced him and exclaimed: "God knows what sorrow and distress I have suffered because of you, but praise be to Him that He has brought you back to me in safety and allowed us to meet. So tell me your news." "Bring me that saddlebag," he told me and when I did he took out a splendid robe, which he put on, and scented himself profusely. "Be happy and content," he told me, "as with God's help and His favour we have got what we wanted."

'He then started up the mountain and told me: "When my messenger comes to you, don't delay but put on clean clothes and perfume yourself." He went off and in the afternoon a handsome young man came up, greeted me and told me to get up. I did so, putting on clean clothes and perfuming myself as I had been told. The young man climbed up the mountain with me and brought me to a great cave, where I found a horse saddled and bridled. He mounted me on this and led the way out to a great palace in the middle of a flowery meadow filled with plants.

'He went in with me, and there I found my companion sitting on a raised seat with another by its side. We ate food that was brought to us, and I drank a *ratl* of wine that was passed to me. Lovely girls like moons, decorated with ornaments, arrived, sat down and sang most beautifully. For three days we stayed there in pleasure and enjoyment, and on the fourth I said to my companion: "May I be your ransom! Tell me your news."

'He said: "The crown had been entrusted to a group of *jinn, marids*, devils and sorcerers. When I had gone to my tent and begun on what I knew I had to do, they all collected around, intending to kill me, and, as you saw, they set fire to my tent and took me off to do this. In my despair I addressed entreaties to the Lord of Heaven, imploring Him to save me as I was His servant. Then, just as they were about to kill me, a huge cloud filled with flames overshadowed them, and the fire came down and burned them up together with their dwellings. I fled from there as fast as I could and when I came the people here welcomed me warmly, treating me with the greatest generosity and promising me help so that I might succeed in my quest. They sent off the man who fetched you, and you can be pleased and content, as tomorrow we can begin to open up the place we have been looking for and take the crown, if God Almighty so wills it."

'Early next morning we went to the place and began to dig. When we had been doing this for twelve days we came to a huge black rock covered with writing and remarkable pictures. When my companion started to read he showed signs of astonishment and when I asked why this was he told me: "Of course I am astonished, as the man who wrote this says that he will return again, take the crown and rule over the world as he did before. If this is true, then we shall not reach it." "Man," I told him, "what these people say is not true. Start to work, for I hope that the crown has been allotted to you by God."

'On his instructions I fetched ropes, which we tied to the rock, fastening the other end to the elephants, which we then struck. They dragged it clear, and under it could be seen an iron door overlaid with gold. After much effort we managed to open it and then we saw an underground creature which went before us as we followed it. It had lit a torch, and after we had gone for about three miles underground we reached a huge statue in the shape of a horse, but when we got near it we collapsed unconscious.

'For two days and nights we stayed in that state, but then I heard soft footsteps and saw a man with legs like those of a riding beast and a human face. He looked at us and then left, coming back shortly afterwards with a yellow herb, which he put on our faces. When we had recovered and stood up, he went off quickly with us behind him until he brought us out at our camp.

'While we ate and drank our rescuer stayed at some distance from us, but he approached when we called to him to come. We pointed to the food and drink, and he helped himself and then, becoming friendly, he spoke to us in the language of Sind, which my companion knew. He asked what my companion was looking for, and on being told, he said: "My brother, this crown was not left here unprotected. There are many black spells and astrological talismans as well as earthly marvels, and I think that you will face great difficulties." "I can put up with difficulty," my companion told him, "and I think that I shall get it." He said: "I have become fond of you and I shall help you and pledge to do all that I can, and when it comes to what I cannot do, I shall give you the friendly warning of one who hopes for your safety. Tell me what you want done with the crown after your death if you get it, for however long you live someone unworthy of it may take it and you will be like a man who came and killed a virtuous ascetic. You know what should happen to someone like that, and it would be better for you to leave the crown alone. I can show you a place where there are piles of gold and silver as well as gems of all kinds which you can take to your advantage without having to meddle with the crown."

'My companion was about to agree to this but he asked my advice, and I said: "We only want to look at marvels and to see what we have never seen before, and if we see the crown we can put it back in its place." "This man's advice will lead to your death," the centaur said, "so fear God and save yourself." "I must have the crown," my companion told him, and he said: "Then I shall do what you want and choose." He went on: "The first piece of advice I have for you is that you collect a large amount of this herb, without which you will not be able to pass the idols. Make sure that, if you are at a loss, you call 'Mubashshir,' three times, and I shall quickly come to you. But now I am going to leave you."

'He went off, and I said to my companion: "May I be your ransom! Never have I seen anything like him before." He told me: "On this mountain and in these valleys there are many like him. They are wise creatures and they date from when an Indian king came to hunt here and one night when he was drunk he copulated with his mare, which was tethered to the pole of his tent, impregnating it. When he sobered up and remembered what he had done, he went off immediately, leaving the mare behind and forbidding anyone to hunt there. The mare gave birth to twins shaped like this, male and female, and they multiplied, as you can see, filling these mountains." This was a great wonder.

'Next morning we got up and collected a great quantity of the herb, after which we entered the cave, and when we got to the statue it did us no harm. We went past it and continued for about a mile until we got to another statue, which had outstretched arms and on whose breast was a huge pearl gleaming like a lamp. When we caught sight of it we could no longer see in front of us and were blinded. When we went back from it we recovered our sight but if we looked at it again the same thing happened. So we took a piece of clay and made it into pellets, which we started to shoot from a bow at the pearl until we had extinguished its brightness.

'We walked forward, but when we got near the statue brazen hands emerged from the earth and took hold of our feet so that we could not move. I asked my companion whether there was anything he could do and when he said no, I told him to call "Mubashshir" three times. In next to no time the centaur emerged and asked us what was wrong. When we told him he laughed and said: 'If you can't cope with this small matter, you won't be able to deal with anything else.' We told him to do something to help us, and after leaving us for a time he came back with what looked like a whetstone and by rubbing this over the hands he cut through them and freed us from them.

'He told us to keep the stone in case we needed it again. We went back and spent the night eating and drinking until, when morning came, we entered the tunnel and, on reaching the statue, we pulled out the jewel that was on its chest and moved on. We were then confronted by a gate of red gold with its key in the lock. It was covered in mysterious writings, and in front of it was a lump of gold. As we came near, the lump stirred and moved, with the ugliest face that I had ever seen appearing from it. This addressed us in a tongue that I could not understand and from its foot spurted a huge stream. As we turned in flight the face gave a great cry and came out to the side of the stream, while more and more water flooded out until it reached the top of the tunnel.

'We were in despair and told ourselves that the water would never let us get to the crown. We thought of going back, but I told my companion to summon Mubashshir, as he might be able to find a way through. My companion called three times, and after only a short delay he came and asked what had happened to us. We told him about the water, and, after having looked at it, he led us to a spot near where we had first dug and told us to dig there. We did this until we had got down to a cubit's distance from the first hole and there we found a flagstone. "Remove it," he told us, and when we did we discovered an underground stream, for which we made an opening into which it poured.

'We waited for some days until there was no more water left and then went back into the tunnel. When we got to the statue and the golden gate we saw behind it a large square space, in the middle of which was a golden chest, on top of which was perched an eagle with outstretched wings. Lamps were hanging there, and there was a huge sapphire. We entered and went up to the chest, but when my companion touched it his arm from shoulder to hand was covered in blisters. 'This is yet another ordeal,' he said.

'In the upper part of the room I saw a golden container, and when we hurried to open it, in it we discovered green earth, which we thought must be alchemical material. My companion called three times on the centaur, and when he came and asked what the matter was we told him about this. He said: "Take the earth that is in the vessel and mix it with sap from a tree that I shall bring you. Then smear this on your hands and go up to the sarcophagus, for if God Almighty wills, you will reach your goal."

'We went out and, taking the sap, we mixed it with some of the earth from the container, smeared it on our hands and went up and opened the chest. There inside it was the crown wrapped in gold leaf. I was going to remove this from it when my companion shouted to me not to do that, and he lifted it out in its wrapping, before fainting with joy. He then called thrice on the centaur and, on seeing him come, he thanked him and kissed his hand. "I owe you a debt that I can never repay," he told him, "and I shall never be able to thank you enough. Now tell me how to put it on, for it contains a jewel that no one can look at without being blinded, but its wearer will want to control it." The centaur said: "I shall give you something to hold in your hand so as to counter what you fear. Now take what you want from here and go out, leaving the place as it was. I shall then fetch you what you want."

'We took the container and a quantity of gems as well as some of the golden lamps together with the great pearl, before putting everything else back as it had been. Then my companion said to the centaur: "Tell me what you have to say," and the centaur replied: "Take the gall of an eagle and safflower and use that to make the image of a gazelle." We made a net and used it to catch an eagle. We then took its gall and collected the safflower, from which we made a gazelle as we had been told, leaving it to dry and then carrying it in a box. Taking with us a large quantity of safflower, we mounted the elephants and went off by a different way from that by which we had come. I told my companion that he was going wrong, but he said: "I want to show you what I am going to do, so come with me and I shall bring you back to your people and give you these stones that I have with me, and you will keep me company." I had no choice but to find out what he was going to do, and, when I had agreed to accompany him, he said: "Come with the blessing of God Almighty."

'We went on until we reached a large orchard, in whose centre was a lofty dome towering into the sky. It had iron doors, and round it was a great river with a bridge with iron gates, opposite which was a huge palace whose door was locked. We came to a place near this amongst the trees where we dug up a tent of brocade, which my companion erected, spreading out fine furnishings. "I want your help in what I am trying to do," he told me, and I promised to follow his instructions. "In three days' time," he said, "all the kings of India will come to this orchard and lodge in this palace, and you will then see a marvel. I want you to take this incense and this herb and continue to use it to spread perfume before me without allowing anything to distract you."

'I promised to do that and got up to burn a great amount of charcoal. Two days later he took the bigger of the two elephants and ornamented it with various decorations. He then took out royal robes and a jewelled corselet, which he put on, taking the gazelle in his hand. He then produced a delicate gold image, set with gems, which he placed on the back of the elephant, with the crown still covered over in front of him, and he told me to spread the perfume when he gave the word.

'On the third day I saw that the palace had been opened up, and the Indians came out with their banners, which they set up by the orchard gate, and they decorated the dome beautifully. Soon afterwards a large dust cloud appeared, and there were the kings' elephants and their troops. When they came up it could be seen that the kings were riding on white elephants and dressed in the most splendid of robes. They came towards where we were in the orchard, and when they were near my companion told me to spread the incense with no slackening. I did as he told me, and when it rose in the air he uncovered the crown and set it on his head.

'When they saw it all the kings threw themselves on the ground before him, removing their own crowns and rubbing their faces in the earth as they prostrated themselves to him. For a long time he said nothing but then he told them to raise their heads, and, as they did, he was moving on out of the reach of the incense. He advanced to the orchard, where all the Indians prostrated themselves before him. Then he dismounted from his elephant, and we went to the dome in the orchard, which was draped with coverings of brocade and where there were golden chairs on which shaikhs were seated. When they saw him they prostrated themselves, uncovered their heads and removed the coverings from their idol. My companion went in and prostrated himself before it, after which he came out and took his seat on a throne with the kings standing before him. He then commanded what they thought was not right and forbade what they thought should not be forbidden, following in the path of previous kings.

'He ordered the people to disperse and came out and rode to the palace, where he declared the slave girls and women common property. The kings came out and sat down by the door while I stood in front of them. My companion summoned a man, to whom he whispered something before telling me to go with him to see what he had to say. The man took my hand and led me out, before saying: "What have you done to make him want you killed?" "He told you to kill me?" I exclaimed. "Yes," said the man. "There is something I want you to do for me," I told him, and when he asked what this was, I said that it was for him to take me to the kings, as I had something to say to them that would release them from their plight. He was filled with delight and, taking me to them, he told them about this. They all got up for me and said: "If you can free us we shall share our wealth with you and do anything for you that you want." I asked them why they had prostrated themselves to my companion, and they told me: "Our books tell us that our great king, whose crown this is, will appear, put it on and come out to us. We shall have no choice but to obey him, as we are sure that no one but him can win the crown. When we saw the changes that he was introducing and that he was behaving in a way contrary to what is in our books we realized that this could not be he."

'I told them to come up to a high place and, when they did, I called three times to Mubashshir at the top of my voice. The centaur came quickly and asked what was wrong. I said: "Was this what I deserved from my companion? I helped him to take the crown, and when he got it he ordered me to be killed." The centaur replied: "I knew that he would kill you," so I then asked him to save me from him. "Ride on me," he told me," "so that I can take you safely back home," but I said that I wanted him to show me how to disgrace and destroy my former companion and repay him for what he had done to me. He told me to take the gall of a kite, mix it with the safflower that I had and make the shape of a ferret to give to one of the kings. He was to take it to my companion while he was wearing the crown and it would then fall off. The great king, he said, would never act like this and would not appear until this was finished.

'I set a snare and caught a kite, whose gall I took and mixed with safflower, from which I then shaped a ferret, as I had been told. I gave this to one of the kings and told him to go to my companion without fear. When he did so the crown fell from his head, and the king rushed up and killed him with his sword. The others gathered round and burned his corpse, after which they gave me everything that he had with him. As for the crown, they wrapped it again in its gold leaf and, after reverencing it, they rode back with me to the place from where it had been taken.

'They treated me with all possible generosity, but I told them that I wanted to return to my children. I took with me a large quantity of wealth and left the rest there. I then put to sea but came naked to Jedda, and I have come to visit the Commander of the Faithful in the hope that I may be enabled to go back to collect what I left there, as this was enough to make me and my descendants wealthy.'

'Abd al-Malik was filled with astonishment at this tale and provided the narrator with fifty thousand dirhams. This is his story and what happened to him, and God knows better.

The Story of the Fourth Quest, for the Golden Tube

Al-Fadl son of al-Rabi' son of Hisham said: 'There was in Malatiya an old Rumi wall that the people there used to call the Wall of the Mother of Daughters. One day there came torrential rain followed by a severe earthquake, causing many stones to fall, some of which struck that wall. Next morning people went out to see what had fallen and they saw a golden tube. They went up to it and, after having demolished what was round it, they brought it down. On one side of it they discovered a golden lock and on the other a golden ring. They weighed it and discovered its weight to be twenty *ratls*.

'The emir took it and offered it for sale unopened. A first bid of a thousand dinars was raised to two, then to three and finally to four. It was handed over to the last bidder, who ordered it to be broken open. In it was found a golden book with strange writing that nobody could read. The emir sent to a monk with a reputation for learning and a knowledge of old scripts. When he looked at the book he laughed and said: "Emir, did you find this in a golden tube in a wall?" and when the emir said "Yes," he asked: "Did you break through to it or did it fall out thanks to an earthquake?" "It was an earthquake that did this," the emir told him, and he said: "Had you broken through the wall it would have caused the destruction of your city, whereas if the earthquake did it, it is the lands of your enemy that will be destroyed, and you will get the contents."

[lac.] 'The emir told him to read what was written, but he said that he would only do this if he were given a satisfactory reward. The emir ordered him to be given ten thousand dinars and asked if he were satis-fied. "Yes," he said, "and less would have been enough." The emir then told him to read out what was written, and he began: "In the Name of God Almighty, this world is transient while the next world is eternal. Our actions are tied around our necks; disasters are arrows; people set themselves goals; our livelihood is apportioned to us, and our appointed time is decreed. The world is filled with hope, and good deeds are the best treasures for a man to store up. Toleration is an adornment, and hastiness is a disgrace. [lac.] A man's wife is the sweet flower of his life and finds acceptance, as many such flowers do. Whoever wishes to see a wonder should go to the Scented Mountain." "Stop! That is enough," the emir said and when the people had dispersed and had all left his audience hall he asked the monk: "Do you know of any way to get to this place?" When the monk said that he did, the emir released from his prison those who deserved execution and set off for the mountain in company with the monk.

'When he got there he halted at its foot and asked the monk where they should go. The monk told him that what they were looking for was in a cave in one of the gullies, and the emir told his men to scatter and look for it. They spent the day investigating the mountain but when they came back they said: "We saw nothing but a lot of gullies, all of which looked alike." "Is there a sign that marks this gully out from the others?" the emir asked the monk. "Yes," he said, "for opposite it is a huge stone snake with a frog in its mouth and a scorpion on its head." "That's what you must look for," the emir told his men, and after three days of search-ing they found it in a large wadi, with the gully lying opposite the statue. When they looked they could see a great stone. There was writing over the door of the cave, and on the summit of the mountain was a huge statue on which birds were perching. There were rings with iron chains attached to a place on the mountain.

'The emir marvelled at the statue and told the monk to pull on the chains. When he did the secret place opened up, and a flight of steps could be seen leading to it. "Go up," the emir said, "for through the help of God we have got to where we wanted." We went on up to the stairs and after climbing some two hundred steps we came out at a fine square room with three open doors, near each of which was a closed door. In the middle stood a giant statue of gilded brass with what looked like a covered bowl on its head, which it was holding with its hands.

'When we got to the middle of the room and approached the statue, the monk told one of the emir's servants to go up to the closed door and strike it with a pick. He obeyed and struck a great blow, using all his strength, but at that the statue threw the bowl down from its head, revealing a pipe from which water flowed. We were in great danger, and the monk began to go round the room until he caught sight of a barred window. When he opened it the statue fell on its knees with its mouth open, and the water started flowing into this until it had all gone from the room.

'We gave thanks to Almighty God for this, and the monk told us that there was nothing else that the statue could do. He ordered the servants to break the locks on the doors, and when they did we opened them and went into the rooms behind them. In them was more wealth than had ever been seen and an indescribable quantity of jewels. We almost died of joy, but the monk told us: "Take care that no one takes the cover from the bowl and looks in it or he will die." Some of the servants rushed up to it, each thinking greedily that none but he would remove the lid. The one who did looked inside and dropped down dead, after which the cover went back on the bowl as it had been before. The monk implored us if we valued our lives to leave it undisturbed or we would all die.

'He then told us to carry off the wealth and the jewels, which we did, loading them on our riding beasts, and, after leaving everything as we had found it, we went off to Malatiya. The emir presented the monk with a large quantity of money, and he gave each of the prisoners many dinars, while freeing the slaves and giving them gifts as well as clothes.

This is the complete story.'

Tale Five

The Story of the Forty
Girls and What Happened to
Them with the Prince.

It is said – and God knows better and is wiser, greater, more powerful, more splendid, nobler, more kind and more merciful – that in times past there was a great and important Persian king who had three sons. He continued to lead a life of comfort until one day, when he had reached the age of eighty, he thought about who should succeed him on the throne.

He summoned his eldest son, whose name was Bahram, and told him: 'I dreamed last night that I was riding on a black horse with a sheathed sword, wearing a black turban and a robe of black brocade. I went through a barren waste where there was neither water nor pasturage until I came to a stormy sea. So afraid was I of that land that I plunged just as I was into the sea on my horse and crossed over to the far side. How do you interpret this dream, my son?'

Bahram said: 'Father, the horse is glory, and the sword power. The blackness is the many years you will live, and the sea means that you will live for more than a hundred years of unbroken rule and constant glory.' This interpretation pleased the king and he told Bahram that he would be pleased to learn that as crown prince he would succeed to the throne.

After Bahram had left, the king called for his second son and told him what he had told Bahram about his dream. This son said: 'Father, you will rule with great power over a huge kingdom extending from this land of yours to the Sea of Darkness, and it may be that you will penetrate for a day's journey or more into the darkness itself because you rode into that black sea.' This delighted the king, who said: 'My son, you are my partner in my kingdom and the inheritor of my prosperity.'

When the prince had left, the king called for his youngest son and told him what he had told his brothers about his dream. When the young man heard, he turned pale and exclaimed: 'God forbid that this dream come true! The blackness is great grief, and it may be that you will find yourself attacked by a king whom you cannot drive off. He may be of your own blood and this will be I.'

The narrator continued: On hearing this the king became furious and exclaimed: 'You have belittled and disparaged me by daring to talk to me like this.' He gave orders for the prince to be beheaded, but his viziers and ministers all joined together to intercede for him, an intercession that the king accepted on condition that they cast the prince away in a desert, where he would die of hunger and thirst.

They followed the king's orders and took him to the middle of the desert and were on the point of returning when the vizier gave him a jug of water and a little food, putting it in his clothes. 'My son,' he said, 'this food will last you for three days, and after that Almighty God will bring you relief.' Then, after taking his leave, he and his servants went away.

For three days the young prince wandered through the desert, not knowing where he was going. On the fourth day he had no food left and fear of death made his heart tremble. His strength was exhausted, and he was near his end. A hot wind was blowing as he shed tears and looked up to heaven, saying: 'I call on You Who bring speedy relief and save the drowning man from the sea.' He had looked right and left in search of someone who might help him when he saw something indistinct in the distance and, although he had been on the point of giving up the ghost, he set off towards it.

The sun was directly overhead, and he was confused and parched with thirst, when what he was aiming for became clearer and turned out to be a lofty and spacious castle towering into the sky. He remembered his father's castle and his city, as well as his own friends and companions, and as he thought of how he had been isolated and separated from them tears flooded down his cheeks.

When he went up to the castle he found that it had a huge door with plates and ornamental patterns of gold and silver. It was covered with hangings, and in the entrance hall there were various types of singing birds. The door stood open, and the prince went in, convinced that it was death that faced him.

In the halls was a series of mats, and felt coverings were fixed to the walls. The prince came to an elaborately decorated door leading to a marbled space in which were forty raised thrones with jugs set beside them, together with all kinds of elegant accessories. Leading out of this were forty rooms, each containing a bed with splendid coverings of varied colours. The doors of these faced one another, and whoever entered could pass by the whole forty, starting from the beginning. In them were gold and beautifully coloured paintings as well as various types of mattresses and coverings suitable for the daughters of great kings. At the upper end of the hall was a table of red gold, on which were set forty plates of white silver, around which were placed forty loaves of white bread.

The young prince could not restrain himself from going up to the food and eating one mouthful from each plate. When he had had enough he went back and searched for water. After looking around, he discovered beside the hall a drinking room with forty regal seats, and at the upper end one seat of particular splendour. By each seat was a golden tray with a crystal flask containing a drink scented more pungently than musk, with on the one side vegetables and on the other fruit. In the middle were flowers and scented herbs together with censers burning aloes wood and ambergris, continuously spreading their perfume. Each part of the room had its seat.

After the prince had taken a mouthful from each flask he started to look out of the windows, and there beneath them he saw a large wadi and a broad meadow, at the upper part of which was an orchard with two fruits of every kind, planted with trees producing both fruits of all sorts and blooms. From the tops of them bird song conveyed its own secret message.

The narrator continued: The prince looked up and as the wine had gone to his head and he was enjoying himself he stayed unconcernedly until the end of the day, when all of a sudden he heard the noise of horses' hooves. He looked out of the window and saw forty riders approaching, fully armed and prepared for war. Their leader was wearing a cloak of red brocade with a green turban, riding a horse black as a raven with a white blaze on its forehead.

When the riders reached the palace door they dismounted and put their horses away in their stables beside the palace, tethering them to their mangers, while on seeing this the prince hid away in a corner of the building. The riders came into the hall, disarmed and removed their riding gear, revealing themselves as women more beautiful than the houris of Paradise.

The prince was watching them from where he could not be seen as they went to the dining room. He was astonished by their beauty and their clothes but he did not know what they were. When they sat down they were annoyed to notice that a mouthful had been taken from each of their loaves and they started to look at those of their neighbours. Then they turned to the lady who was sitting in the place of honour and who had been riding on the black horse. 'Lady,' they said, 'this is something that we have never experienced before and what *jinni* or man has dared to do it?' 'Patience,' the lady replied; 'don't be in a hurry for I shall look into it, and whoever did it is bound to come back.'

They ate their fill and washed their hands, as the prince watched, and they then moved to the drinking room, swaying like branches, with their lovely faces, recalling the lines of the poet:

With slender waists and murderous coquetry
They aim at us with their wide eyes,
Lovely dark eyes that have no need of kohl.
They came up robed in beauty, stealing away my wits,
And when they tried to move forward a pace,
It was as though their feet were stuck in mud.

The narrator went on: They continued to relax with their wine, reciting poetry and telling stories until the night was past and day had arrived. Then each of them put on armour, equipped herself with a long spear and fastened on a sharp sword, after which they mounted and left through the castle gate.

Their leader was one of the great sorceresses, and thanks to her skill it was she who produced the food, drink, fruits and vegetables. She parted from her companions after telling them to go off as usual while she hid in order to discover who it was who had violated the sanctity of their castle. She then went back to a hide of hers at the side of the castle.

The young prince stayed where he was until the sun was high, and he then came out and approached the table, stretching out his hand to take a morsel from it. As he was about to put it in his mouth the sorceress came out and went up to him. At the sight of her he trembled with fear, letting the morsel drop from his hand. She looked at him and, seeing how handsome and how frightened he was, she went nearer and smiled at him, before sitting beside him and beginning a friendly conversation with him. When he complained of his plight to her she embraced him and kissed him, before asking him whether he was mortal or from the *jinn*. 'I am a mortal,' he told her, 'and the son of a king who has been betrayed by Time, which has parted me from my family and my friends.' 'How was that?' she asked, 'and what was it that brought you here?'

At that he told her the story of his dealings with his father, explaining what had happened. When she heard this and saw what a handsome and cultured young man he was, love for him took possession of her heart. She told him: 'Relax and be joyful, for I have fallen in love with you and will conceal your secret from all my cousins and companions.' She then ate with him before taking him to the drinking room, where she joined him in drinking pure wine. She then called him closer, and he jumped on her and deflowered her, discovering her to be a virgin. They went on like that until evening, when the girls were due to return, and it was then that the lady told him to go back to the hiding place that he had used the night before.

When the girls got back they entered the castle and took off their armour, putting on their female clothes before taking their places at the table. The girl who had been leading them saw the changes that had been made to the food and said to the sorceress, who had hidden away to find out who had been responsible for this the day before: 'Sister, who has done this?' 'I don't know,' replied the lady and although the other accused her of lying she concealed the affair and let no one in on her secret.

They all ate their fill, washed their hands and went on to drink wine as usual until dawn. Another girl was ordered to take the place of the first in the castle to see and then to tell who it was who had tampered with the food. The others then mounted and rode off, leaving behind the one who hid nobody knew where.

When the prince was certain that they had gone and that no one was left he came out from his hiding place and went to the dining room, where he approached the table and stretched out his hand to the food. At that point out came the girl, who was struck by his handsomeness and the perfection of his shape. When he saw her he was alarmed and terrified, not knowing what to do. 'Darling,' she said, 'don't be frightened but tell me about yourself, what you are and what has brought you here.' This calmed him, and his fear diminished thanks to her beauty and the sweetness of her words. He told her what had happened to him with his father, and she sat down beside him, telling him that no harm would come to him.

After she had eaten with him they went to the drinking room, where they drank wine, and when they were in a state of happiness she invited him to take her, and he discovered her to be a virgin, as God had created her. Love for him took hold of her heart and occupied her mind, and so they remained enjoying themselves until evening.

When the other girls returned the prince went back to his hiding place. They disarmed and after putting on their female clothes they went to sit at the table, where their leader noticed that the food had been tampered with. She asked the girl who had been left behind how this had come about, to which she replied: 'Lady, I saw nothing, and nobody ate anything apart from me.'

The lady kept on selecting a new girl each day until the prince had come to the last of them. Each one of them had conceived, and as the days passed their pregnancies became visible, although no one of them had found out the secret of any of the others. None of this, however, was hidden from their mistress, and on the forty-first day, when she ordered them to ride out as usual, it was she herself who stayed behind, saying that none but she would uncover the affair, and she chose an undiscoverable hiding place.

When the prince thought that the palace was empty he came out as usual and went to sit at the table. The lady saw how handsome he was and trembled with uncontrollable love and, coming out, she threw herself before him. At the sight of her the prince quaked, and the mouthful he was holding dropped from his hand, while what he saw of her beauty bewildered him. She realized this and sat down beside him, addressing him in friendly tones and telling him that no harm would come to him. 'I am the leader of these girls,' she told him, 'and I am yours and at your service.'

While she sat to eat with him she used her hand to put food in his mouth until he had had enough. They then washed their hands, after which they went to the drinking room, where she drank and poured him wine until he became dizzy. Then she said: 'My darling, tell me your story. Let me know about you and how it was that you came here.'

He told her the whole tale from beginning to end, telling her about his father's dream, his anger and how he had ordered him to be left in the desert. He explained how, after having been on the point of death, he had reached the castle and what had happened to him with the girls and what he had done with them.

When she had understood all this, she repeated: 'No harm will come to you, my boy, for these are my maids and they are a gift from me to you. I saw that they were pregnant. You may get children from them, and God may bring you relief and happiness. I myself am lovelier than them, and from this day on you will be my friend and lover, so after this don't approach any of them, for I am here at your disposal. If you do go to any of them, I shall imprison you, torture you and load you with iron chains.'

He accepted this, and they went on drinking. The lady kissed him and recited:

His visit took me by surprise and he delighted me;
As a visitor who brings me comfort I would ransom him.
In his appearance he is like the sun,
Or like a moon mounted upon a branch.
May God decree that we should never part,
Until we lie enshrouded in the grave.

She clasped him to her breast and invited him to take her. He deflowered her and found her to be a virgin whom no husband had known and no man had touched. He was delighted and filled with love for her, while her love for him was twice as great.

They stayed enjoying their delights until the girls came back from hunting, disarmed, put on their female clothes and greeted their mistress before sitting down at table and eating.

It was then that she went up to them and said: 'Damn you! You didn't tell me what happened to you.' They looked at her in astonishment, realizing that she must have seen the prince and that denial would do no good. So they told her what had happened and said: 'Lady, we did not dare tell you about this, and none of us knew that the others were pregnant. Here we are before you, so do with us what you want.' 'I myself have taken him as a lover,' she told them, 'and none of you is to approach him. Meanwhile look after yourselves until you give birth.'

The narrator went on: The prince continued for a long time to enjoy the most luxurious of lives with the lady who conceived his child and who loved him devotedly. Then one day she told him: 'Darling, I am going to leave you for a single day, and if you are distressed by my absence, open the store chambers and look at what is in them, all except for this one, which you are not to approach or open.' 'To hear is to obey,' he replied, after which she gave him the keys and rode off with all her girls.

The prince, left on his own, was heavy-hearted as he thought over his position. He went to the store chambers and began to open them, one after the other, looking at the wealth and precious treasures they contained, the jewels of various kinds, the arms and armour and the other valuables, such as no king on earth could match.

He went on doing this until he came to the last of them, apart from the one that he had been told not to enter. He found himself tempted, thinking that unless it contained the most splendid of all the lady's possessions she would not have forbidden him to look at it. He went up to the door and looked inside through a chink in it. What he saw was a most beautiful horse, which addressed him eloquently and said: 'Open the door for me, young man, and remove the fetters from my hooves so that I may take you to a pleasant land and a great kingdom which will be more attractive to you than having to live here alone with this damned shameless and wily sorceress.'

The prince, astonished by this, opened the door, removed the fetters and saddled and bridled the horse. He was about to mount when up came the lady, whose instinct had warned her of what was happening. He trembled at the sight of her, but the horse told him: 'Don't be afraid but mount me, for she will not be able to catch up with me.' At that the prince mounted, and the horse flew up with him into the air. 'Damn you, you have done it, you bastard!' the lady shrieked and the horse replied: 'Yes, he did it, and God released me at his hands.'

It flew away with him across the land, passing over desert wastes, rough country and plains, pursued by the lady until she found that she could not catch up, and the prince drew away from her. He went on until he reached an enormous city, passing all description, and here the horse told him to dismount. Night had fallen, and when he dismounted the horse told him: 'Have no fear but sit down so that I may tell you my story.' The prince sat and asked it for this, at which it began: 'You should know that I am the sister of the lady with whom you were, the mistress of those girls. We have another sister in this city, the most beautiful of all God's creation. I and my sister with whom you stayed studied sorcery until we became adepts. She ran away from her father, taking the girls with her, and isolated herself in that castle. After I had mastered another branch of sorcery I went to join her and stayed with her. One day I angered her by finding some fault with her, and she put a spell on me, turning me into a horse and imprisoning me in that store room, as you saw. I had been there for thirteen months before God sent you to me and I was freed at your hands. I have vowed to put myself in your hands and to carry you over every desert waste. I should tell you that my younger sister has a huge castle on the far side of a great river, where she has girls to wait on her. My father produced the river to cut her off from people, and whoever crosses it can marry her. Many princes have sought for her but none of them has been able to cross the river thanks to the strength of the current and the violence of the waves. Mount me tomorrow morning and go into the city to the king's palace in order to see him. If you are given permission, enter his presence and ask him for my sister's hand. When he asks you whether you know the condition that you must cross the river, tell him that you do. Then, when you get to the bank and cross over, you will obtain one who is unique in her age, of unmatched beauty, and this city and its surroundings will be yours.'

The prince was delighted and expressed his profuse thanks. He scarcely believed that dawn was coming before he mounted and rode off gladly and happily. When he entered the city the people there were amazed at how handsome he looked and as he rode on through the streets to the gate of the royal palace they were still admiring him.

Permission was asked for him to enter, and when this had been granted he went in and saw a huge palace in wide grounds, a seat of sovereignty over which only God, the Omniscient Listener, had power. When he came before the king he greeted him eloquently and called down God's mercy on him. The king, who was struck by his appearance, told him to be seated and started to talk to him, putting friendly questions to him before asking him what it was he wanted. 'Your Majesty,' the prince replied, 'I am here as a suitor, so do not send me away disappointed.'

'My son,' said the king, 'have you heard of the condition that you must cross the river?' 'Yes, Your Majesty,' the prince said, 'but I am anxious to have you as a father-in-law, and if I escape death this will be thanks to my good fortune and if I die I shall be like those who died before me.' The king said: 'My son, this is a serious matter on which you are embarking, fraught with perils that would whiten the hair of a child.' 'There is no might and no power except in the hands of God, the Almighty and Omnipotent,' the prince said, after which the king told him to spend the night in the palace and then next morning to do what he wanted. The prince agreed and passed the night there in the greatest comfort.

Next morning the king ordered his men to mount, which they quickly did, and he himself rode out, accompanied by the prince on his enchanted horse. The whole troop, prince and all, rode on until they reached a huge river, where the king and his men halted. They were saddened by the fact that so handsome a young man was facing death. For his part the sight of the size of the river and of the castle on its far side amazed and perplexed him, and he repeated to himself those words whose reciter is never forsaken: 'There is no might and no power except in the hands of God, the Almighty and Omnipotent.' He then took his leave of the king and shouted to his horse, which bounded beneath him like an arrow seeking its mark and plunged into the river. The king and his men watched as it took its rider through the waves and across the river, which was as broad as a sea, until he reached the far side and then came back to halt in front of the king.

The king was delighted to see him and presented him with a robe of honour, calling to the leaders of his state that if they loved him they should do the same. They loaded him with robes, and the king then returned to his palace with the prince at his side. He summoned the qadi and the necessary witnesses and married the prince to his daughter before sending him off to her by ship and arranging a great wedding.

At the end of this the bride was brought to the groom, and when he was alone with her he saw that she was more dazzling than the sun and lovelier than the moon. Love for her entered his heart, while she fell more deeply in love with him. She asked him about himself, and he explained all that had happened to him with his father, how he had got to the castle and of his dealings with her elder sister. He then told her about her middle sister and how she was the horse which had taken him to her. This astonished her, and she went off to discover her sister in the shape of a horse. 'Are you my sister Shah Zanan?' she said, going up to her. 'Yes, Badr al-Zaman,' replied the other, 'and your sister has brought grief on the kings of Khurasan. She did this to me, bewitching me and turning me into the shape that you can see, but the Great and Glorious God granted me this young man.' Badr al-Zaman kissed her between the eyes and asked her to resume her proper shape, but she said: 'By God, I shall not do that, as I have given myself to him and am content to stay like this. I have picked him out for you as he deserves someone like you and you deserve someone like him.' Badr al-Zaman thanked her and treated her with the greatest respect.

The narrator continued: After the prince had stayed with Badr al-Zaman for five years his father Bahram fell gravely ill, and when he was on the point of death he sent for the prince and named him as his heir. A few days later he died and joined his Lord, while the prince sat on his throne, ruling over all his lands and his followers with beneficence and generosity. Badr al-Zaman gave birth to three boys, who were taught all that princes need to know, writing, archery, riding and polo.

One day their father was riding with them to the polo ground. They were handsome boys like branches of a tree and, surrounded by their mamluks, they shone like stars, wearing differently coloured clothes. Just then a cloud of dust rose up, blocking the horizon, and when the prince asked his men what it was, they said that they did not know. He was riding on his horse at the time, and the horse said: 'Master, you should know that this is my elder sister and her girls. She has come to you with all her followers as she knows that you have taken over this great kingdom. She has taken with her all the gold, silver and jewels that were in her castle and has brought it all to you. Every one of the girls whom you impregnated gave birth to a boy fairer than the moon, and they are all mounted on Arab horses. She herself gave birth to a son more beautiful than the sun, and it is he who commands the forty others.'

When he heard this, the prince dismounted and gave thanks to Almighty God before remounting and riding out, surrounded by his three sons, with his mamluks at his rear and followed by the rest of his troops. When he got near to the newcomers he was overjoyed to see what his horse had described for him and gave thanks and praise to the Almighty. The girls dismounted in front of him and approached while the princess went up and kissed him. He welcomed her warmly and joyfully, and she told him to receive his sons, saying: 'I have brought them up in all the branches of culture fit for kings. You may have broken your covenant with me, but I have kept it and I have come to you myself together with all that I own.' At that the prince prostrated himself to God and prayed that she be granted a good return. 'This is your father,' she told her son and his brothers, 'and these three are your brothers. Go to him and present your services, for God has brought you together.' At that he went back to the city, escorted by his forty sons and their mothers, leaving the citizens astonished by the remarkable nature of this strange tale.

The king's eldest daughter was installed in a fine palace beside that of the prince, and he provided her with an allowance sufficient for her needs and for her maids, as well as granting her so many estates and villages that it would tire the tongue to describe them. This was because he feared her powers of sorcery and the evil that she might do to her middle sister. She realized this and told him one day that she wanted to meet her sister, but he refused to allow this, saying that he was afraid of her sorcerous wiles. 'I repent at your hands of the practice of magic for the rest of my life,' she said, 'and I only left my own castle after having turned in repentance to the Great and Glorious God.'

The prince was relieved on hearing this and made her give him a sacred covenant that she would not revert to sorcery. He arranged for her to meet her sister, after having consulted his horse about that. The horse told him that he could set his mind at rest since even if she did use sorcery, as she might, it would be able to counter the spells. In fact she did not use any magic, and the horse kept its shape in spite of the fact that her sisters kept coming to her and asking her to resume her human form, which she refused to do.

The narrator continued: One day the prince remembered what his father had done to him by exposing him in the desert and he prayed God to bring them together so that his father might see him and the kingdom, wealth and sons with which Almighty God had provided him. God answered his prayer, and one day, as he was riding his horse, which knew the wish that he had made to God, it asked whether he would like to be reunited with his father to show him what he had been given. 'How can I meet him?' he asked, and the horse said: 'Don't disturb yourself. It was only for this that I have stayed in this horse shape and I shall get you what you want.' 'I would like my father to see what God has given me,' he acknowledged. 'You are welcome,' she said before speaking words that he could not understand. At that a huge, black *'ifrit* named Qudah appeared in front of them, and she said: 'Qudah, you know what this young man has done with me. He wants to see his father to show him all that God has given him.' 'Tell me how he wants to appear, in a good light or a bad?' Qudah said, and she told him: 'On his regal throne in the place of his glory.' 'Then ask him whether he wants to go to his father or have his father come to him,' Qudah went on, and she said: 'He should go to his father with all his troops, his horsemen and his sons.' 'When do you want that to happen?' he asked, and the prince said: 'Tomorrow night.' 'To hear is to obey,' answered Qudah.

Qudah then left the horse and collected all the various troops of *jinn marids*. He told them: 'Know that the princess has asked me to do her a favour, and this is something I am obliged to do. I want you all to come tomorrow night and for each of you to carry one or two of the prince's riders so that by morning his whole army may have reached the gate of his father's city with their tents pitched and their spears fixed in the ground.' 'To hear is to obey,' they replied. The horse then told the prince to bring out his men with their equipment, weapons and all they needed for a journey. He did that, and by evening all of them had come out as ordered. The prince then dressed his sons in splendid clothes and mounted them on Arab horses, fetching out with them his money, stores and material. Every one of his men came out fully equipped and provisioned, and this went on all that day. When night fell, the *'ifrit* arrived with all his companions and followers, and God sent sleep on them so that they slept. While they were asleep the *'ifrits* came and took man after man with their equipment and their horses and set them down, asleep and unconscious, by the gate of the king's city before pitching all their tents.

When morning came the king looked at those men in astonishment and amazement. The prince ordered the nakers to be beaten and the trumpets blown, as banners were unfurled and shouts raised. The sight of all this dismayed the king, and after he had had the city gates closed he sent a messenger to discover what was happening. The man charged with this task was his vizier, the man who had taken the young prince out to the desert. On his arrival at the prince's pavilion he asked leave to enter, and when this had been granted he went in and delivered a courteous greeting, calling down God's mercy on the prince.

After returning the greeting, the prince said: 'You are the king's vizier who took me out to the desert and gave me food and water, although my father had wanted me to die. My Lord had mercy on me and preserved me, giving me this kingdom, as well as wealth and sons, praise be to Him. I have not come to make war on my father but to show him what the Almighty has granted me.'

On hearing this, the vizier prostrated himself to God in amazement at what Fate had produced. The prince said: 'I am content and happy with what God has given me, so go back to my father and tell him that, assuring him that both he and his kingdom are safe.' When the vizier did that the king was delighted and he came out to meet his son, embracing him happily and asking him to tell him about himself.

The prince told his father all that had happened to him and said: 'Father, I rule over lands such as eyes have not seen nor ears heard of. I shall stay here until I have satisfied my longing for you and for my brothers and then after a few days I shall go back home.' He summoned his brothers and gave them a warm greeting, after which he assigned to each of them a town and a large village. Then he went back to the horse and said: 'Lady, my needs have been fulfilled, and I should like you to resume your proper shape so that I might enjoy having you in my service.' 'Is this what you want?' she asked, and when he said: 'Yes, may God give you a good reward,' she went off for a while and came back in a shape whose loveliness would put the sun to shame.

He was captivated by what he saw and immediately summoned the qadi and the witnesses and drew up the contract of marriage. He scattered dinars and produced a wedding feast for her the like of which had never been heard of in any land. When his bride was brought to him he was delighted to discover her to be a pure virgin, as her Lord had sealed her. She occupied a great place in his heart, and he assigned her one of the beautiful palaces of her sisters.

He then proposed to return home and he took leave of his father, but his father said: 'My son, I should like you not to leave me until you lay me in my grave, when you can rule over your brothers after my death.' 'Father,' said the prince, 'this is the interpretation of your dream which God has fulfilled.'

The king's life ended, and he went to join his Lord. The prince's brothers were grateful to him for the favours that he bestowed on him, and Time helped him to fulfil his desires. He continued to lead the best, most pleasant and untroubled of lives until his death.

Tale Six

The Story of Julnar of the Sea and the Marvels of the Sea Encountered by Her.

They say – and God knows better – that amongst the stories of past peoples is one that deals with the land of Khurasan, where there was a great and powerful ruler called Shahriyar. He had a hundred concubines, but none of them had given him a son. He had sent agents round various lands and cities to inspect and buy slave girls, but whether he stayed with one of them for a day, a night or a year she would not conceive. The wide world shrank in his eyes as, whatever greatness he had achieved, he had no son.

One day when he was seated with his vizier a servant came in to tell him that at the door was a man with that day's girl, who was asking leave to enter so that he might present her to him. Shahriyar told him to bring the man in, and when he came he kissed the ground respectfully and said: 'Master, I have brought you this girl who has no match on the face of the earth for beauty, perfection and splendour.' Shahriyar lifted his head and looked at the girl, whom he saw to be so wrapped up in Venetian cloth that nothing of her could be seen. She was acting with composure and when on Shahriyar's instructions the man brought her forwards she took refuge behind him. He unveiled her, allowing Shahriyar to see the most beautiful face reflecting youthful charm that he had ever encountered, with seven plaits like horses' tails that swept down to her anklets.

The astonished king asked the man for her price, and he said: 'May God exalt Your Majesty, I bought her from Bahr al-Mulk Qamar for a thousand dinars. I have been exactly two years on the road, during which I have spent about five hundred dinars on her, but I present her to you, Your Majesty, as a gift.' Shahriyar accepted her and left her with his slave girls, telling them to look after her and give her a room of her own, supplying her with everything she might need. He entertained the man for three days and presented him with three thousand dinars together with robes of honour, providing him with one of his own special horses to ride. The man went off filled with gratitude.

The king ruled a coastal city known as White City, which overlooked the sea. In the dark of night he got up and entered the room that had been prepared for the girl and found her looking out over the sea. When she noticed him she paid him no attention or proper respect, while when he looked at her he saw that she had been suitably arrayed and was more splendid than the sun. It was as though Almighty God had given her more beauty, perfection and splendour than he had granted to any other of his creatures. 'Praise be to God, Who created you from a vile drop in a secure place!' he exclaimed, and then he went up to her, clasped her to his breast and kissed her between the eyes. He then sat down and had a gold table set with pearls and sapphires brought before him on which were such foods as no other king could have produced. The two of them ate, but the girl remained silent and although he did his best to get her to say even a single word she said nothing, and the astonished king exclaimed: 'Praise be to God, Who created your beauty but made you dumb. Perfection is His alone, Great and Glorious is He!'

The table was then removed and glasses of wine brought in together with fruits and scented herbs, while the slave girls fetched all their various musical instruments. She watched them, but neither smiled nor spoke. The king then got up and, taking her by the hand, he brought her to his own room, where he lay with her, finding her to his delight to be a virgin. She came to occupy a prime place in his heart, and he devoted his entire attention to her, abandoning all his concubines and taking her to be all that he wanted from the world.

He stayed with her for a whole year but was saddened to hear no single word from her. One day he came in to find her seated with her face more radiant than the sun. He kissed it and said: 'Heart's desire, my kingdom is not worth a single speck of dust to me in comparison with the joy my heart has experienced since you have been here. Day and night I have been praying Almighty God to grant that you bear me a son and that I may live to see him assume authority and rule the kingdom. The lack of an heir is my only grief in this world, and I would be content to die if a son were born.' When the girl heard this she looked down at the ground for a time and then raised her head and said: 'Peace be on you, O king!' Shahriyar was ecstatic with joy and replied: 'Peace be on you, together with the mercy and blessing of God. By God, this is a blessed day!' 'Almighty God has answered all your requests,' she told him, 'as I must tell you that I am carrying your child, and I have spoken to you although I had never intended to do so, since you should know of my pregnancy, although I don't know whether it will result in a boy or a girl.'

In his delight the king distributed ten thousand dinars as alms to the poor and that night he went to the girl and said: 'Desire of my heart, why was it that you did not talk to me for a year? How could you keep yourself from speaking, and what was it that stopped you?' She replied: 'The king should know, may God prolong his glory, that I am one of the daughters of the sea, with a brother and parents. One day, after a quarrel with my brother, I went to an island in what is known as the Sea of the Moon. There an old man seized me and took me to his house. I disliked him and when he laid hands on me I struck him an almost fatal blow. He took me out and sold me to the man who brought me to you. Had I not liked you and wanted to stay with you, I would simply have dived into the sea and gone back to my family, but I fell in love with you. If I wanted to spend three years without saying a single word [I could have done so].'

Shahriyar was astonished by this and asked the girl what her name was in the sea. She told him that it was 'Julnar of the Sea', and added that it was her heartfelt wish that her brother might see the luxury in which she lived, he being one of the kings of the sea. Shahriyar asked: 'By God, Julnar, how do you walk in the sea?' She told him: 'We make a talisman with the names that were on the seal of Solomon son of David, on whom be peace, and we either construct this as a ring or as an amulet to be worn on the shoulder and then when we walk in the paths of the sea the water cannot reach us, and whether we are on land or under water, it is the same for us. The sea acts as a roof for us, and it is so light that we can see the stars, the sun and the moon above it, as well as what is below the level of the land. More creatures live there than on land.' This astonished Shahriyar.

Nights and days passed until it was nearly time for Julnar to give birth and, after telling this to Shahriyar, she said that she wanted to send word to her parents so that they, and no earth dwellers, could be there with her. He told her to do what she wanted, and she removed from her shoulder an amulet containing a talisman. Out of this she took something black and, bringing out a golden censer, she filled it with charcoal and blew at it until this became burning coals. She then told Shahriyar: 'Get up, master, and hide away with one of the girls so you can see my parents and my brother as they come to me.' When Shahriyar had done this she put some of the drug that she had with her on the fire and whistled thrice. At that the sea parted and out came a handsome man with green hair and beard, looking like the moon, accompanied by an old woman who herself had green hair, together with five maids, like moons. They swam up to the palace window, and the young man called out to his sister, who replied: 'Here I am, brother.' 'What do you want?' he asked, and she told him to come closer. He came out of the water and approached the window, at which she got up and embraced him as he kissed her head. He then turned to the old lady and said something to her that Shahriyar could not understand. She too came up to the window with her five maids. 'My daughter, by the Lord of the Ka'ba!' she exclaimed and, clasping Julnar to her, she kissed her between the eyes and said: 'Neither I nor your brother or your cousins could enjoy a tranquil life while we did not know where you were. We went round all the seas in the world but caught no sight and heard no news of you. Who are you with? We shall rescue you even if his armies are as many as the sands.' She then breathed out flames that came out from her mouth and the sockets of her eyes and told Julnar: 'Come home, for I have been longing for you for a long time.'

Shahriyar said: 'I almost died from fear of the old woman, and for her part Julnar took her hand and kissed it, as well as kissing her cousins, the girls who were with her, who had shed tears of longing for her. She said: "Mother, you should know that I have fallen into the hands of a king who has no superior on the face of the earth or any who is nobler, with larger armies or more wealth. For him the world lies between my eyes. I am pregnant by him, and he has abandoned the whole world, leaving all his slave girls and his concubines; it is because I am enough for him that he has abandoned his kingdom, and I am all that he wants here. Were I not pregnant I would come with you, and no one could stop me, for as you know I can cross from east to west in the blink of an eye."

'When her mother heard what she said, her anger subsided, and she calmed down. Julnar herself turned to her brother and asked him why he was not saying anything. "What can I say?" he asked. "You know that neither on land nor sea is there anyone that I love more than you, Julnar, and it is only through you that I want what the world offers. If you are happy with this king, then that is what I look for." Julnar got up and kissed his hand and his head and when they were all happy she ordered tables of gold and silver to be brought in covered with foods of all kinds. Her mother then called to her and when Julnar answered she asked: "Should not the master of all this, the great king, be here?" ' Julnar got up and went to Shahriyar, who was some way off, shaking like a palm leaf. He said: 'By God, Julnar, I know that you love me but I am afraid of this old woman, and had I known that things were like this, I would never have been able to enjoy sleep.' 'Master, no harm will come to you,' she said, 'for as long as I am with you, you need fear nothing that lives on land or sea.'

Shahriyar got up and joined the company, who stood up to greet him, kissing the ground before him. They said: 'Master, take and keep this unique pearl, who has no equal on the face of the earth. No one who sees her can look at her enough. All the kings of the sea have asked for her hand, but she did not find any of them acceptable, so praise be to God, Who has made you attractive to her and subjugated her to you.' Shahriyar thanked them and told them that Julnar was all that he wanted from the world, after which they put their hands in the food and started to eat. They then washed their hands, and china plates filled with sweetmeats were produced. When these had been eaten they sat down to talk, enjoying each other's company.

Julnar's brother then brought out a chest of red gold, which he opened before removing three hundred sapphires, turquoises, emeralds and jacinths, as well as five hundred snow-white pearls, each weighing two *mithqals*, that shone like stars. He presented these to the king, who was asked to accept them and who won the favour of his guests by doing so. Looking at what he had been given, he exclaimed to Julnar: 'What is this that your brother has given me? Were I to give him all that I own and twice as much besides, you would still be more generous than me.' Julnar turned to her brother and said: 'Brother, the king presents his excuses to you and says that he does not know what to do for you or how to make you an honourable return as even if he took all he owns and much more he would not consider this a suitable present for you.' Her brother laughed and said: 'Your Majesty, all this is of no importance in our eyes and, God willing, every time that I visit you I shall bring more than this with me.'

They passed the most pleasant of nights, and then Julnar fell into labour, and when her pains increased her cousins and her mother went to her while Shahriyar went to an adjoining room, where there was a window near the roof from which he could look at the room without anyone knowing. He sat there and looked out of this window, which was only as big as the palm of a hand, and he could only use one side of his face. When Julnar was in difficulties her mother got up and took out a medicine bag, with which she perfumed herself and whistled. At this ten girls and an old woman appeared, whom she went up to and greeted. The old woman then removed her clothes and sat there to act as a mid-wife. Soon afterwards Julnar gave birth to a boy like a rising sun. Cries of joy were raised, and when the mother was asked what the child was to be called she said 'Badr.' They looked after him but spoke no single word, and no one, great or small, came to them from the king's palace. They anointed him with a white substance and perfumed him with something strange.

His uncle, Salih, then took Badr in his arms as Shahriyar watched, saying to himself that perhaps he was going to bring him the baby, but instead he went to the window and jumped into the sea. For a time both he and the baby were under the water but then they emerged with the baby wearing a necklace of pearls as big as pigeon's eggs, with a chain of rubies gleaming like the sun and worth a huge sum hanging over his chest above the swaddling-clothes. Her brother restored the child to his mother, who thanked him for what he had done. She then got up and put the child in a golden bowl studded with gems and, going to Shahriyar, she put the bowl down before him, saying: 'May God delight you, Your Majesty, with the sight of this great king, the fierce lion, and may He grant you good fortune and illumine your guiding star.' Shahriyar uttered a prayer of thankfulness and congratulated Julnar on her safe delivery. He then kissed the child and opened the doors for the servants, male and female, to come in, and there was rejoicing throughout the palace.

The citizens heard the noise, and the king distributed ten thousand dinars as bounty and sacrificed beasts, while, as the news spread, the people came to the palace. Julnar's mother and brother stayed with her for a time and then went back to the sea and left her. Every ten days, however, her brother would return to visit her, bringing a gift of jewels, and he would take the child and go down into the sea with him for a time. She told Shahriyar that there was no need for him to worry as, even if the boy spent a month underwater, he would come to no harm or fall into any difficulty since he belonged to the sea people. She added that, if Shahriyar wanted, she would tell her brother not to take Badr off again, as he had achieved his purpose. When Badr was five years old and Salih brought him back, she told him what Shahriyar had said, and he laughed and asked: 'Is a king like you afraid for this boy? Our object has been achieved, and I shall not take him away again so as not to distress you.' He then took his leave of Shahriyar and left.

Time passed, and the boy grew up. At the age of ten he was taught writing, the Qur'an and the art of horsemanship, which he practised until, by the time he was fifteen, he was an invincible rider and a dangerous fighter. One day Shahriyar went out to hunt and when he came back at the end of the day and entered his palace he found Badr seated on the throne, exercising authority with force and commanding greater reverence than that shown to him. He prostrated himself in gratitude to God and then went in tears to Julnar. She asked him why he was weeping and added: 'May God not lead you to weep as He has given you what you asked of Him.' 'That is true,' replied Shahriyar, 'but the poet says:

When something is completed, its decline begins;
Say: "It is finished" and it starts to fade.

There is no doubt that the end for which I asked God is near at hand. He has granted me [lac.] God willing, tomorrow morning I shall resign power and pass it to my son so that he may not be hurt by any change after my death.'

Next day he took his seat and summoned the viziers, emirs and officers of state, as well as his seventy subordinate kings. When they were all present he got to his feet and said: 'Kings and emirs, I call you to witness that I have appointed my son Badr to be your king in place of me.' They all accepted this, and he got them to swear an oath of allegiance. Some days later he died, and this was followed by deep mourning.

Afterwards Julnar told Salih that she wanted a wife for Badr. She must be his match in beauty so as to be his equal as a queen, for like to be joined to like. She went on: 'The girl must be a sea princess, and I know them well, having seen all of them.' Salih started to list the princesses, but even after he had named about two hundred, Julnar found not one of them suitable. Salih then said: 'Is your son asleep? There is one girl left whom I have not mentioned. If he is asleep, I'll tell you her name, but if not, I'll wait until he is, as were he to hear her described he might fall in love with her, and that might cause his heart to ache.' Julnar told him to speak out, as Badr was asleep, and he said: 'Sister, the girl is Jauhara the daughter of Samandal, the supreme king of the sea. She has no match on land or sea for beauty, radiance and perfection. Almighty God created beauty in ninety parts and granted her eighty-nine.'

Julnar said: 'I have seen her. Her beauty is unsurpassed, and I want no other bride for my son, God help me, for on Him do I rely.' Salih said: 'You do know that there can be no one more stupid than her father, a violent man, so don't tell your son about this until tomorrow morning.' She agreed, and next morning Badr got up, having heard all that had passed, including what his uncle had said. He had fallen violently in love with Jauhara and when he left the baths he went to his mother, and the two of them, together with Salih, ate the breakfast that was brought to them, after which they washed their hands.

Salih now got up and took his leave of his sister, intending to go off. When Badr got up with him he asked where he was going. Badr said: 'I am going to the shore to say goodbye to you,' at which Salih went off and on reaching the shore dived into the water. Badr dismounted and dived after him. When he had caught up, Salih again asked where he was going, and this time Badr said: 'Take me with you and marry me to the girl whom you described, as it may be that God, praise be to Him, will bring about our union. Otherwise there is nothing but death for me here, so deeply am I in love with her.' His uncle struck one hand against the other and pronounced the words that ensure that those who repeat them will never be disappointed: 'There is no might and no power except with God the Omnipotent.' Then he told Badr to go home while he himself went to Samandal and arranged things for him. Badr, however, said: 'Don't say this for, by God, my heart is consumed by a fire that can only be quenched if I go to Jauhara. I must come with you so that I may either achieve my wish or else die first.'

Salih asked if he was sure that he had to go with him and when Badr said that he was Salih told him to do what he wanted. He then produced a ring inscribed with all the names found on the signet of Solomon son of David, on whom be peace, and passed it to him, telling him to put it on his finger. Badr took it and put it on, and Salih told him that he was now safe from the violence of the sea or of anything else. He then took him by the hand and dived down for some time until they both emerged at his palace. 'Stay with me,' he told Badr, 'until I arrange things. I shall go to King Samandal and when I meet him I shall offer him a great amount of money for his daughter's hand. If he accepts, I shall thank him, but if he refuses I shall give him a harsh reply on the spot and collect my kinsmen and meet him in battle, with God giving victory to whichever of us He pleases. I shall then take the girl by force of arms.' 'May God give you a good reward on my behalf,' Badr told him.

They spent the night there and next morning Salih went to open the treasuries of his palace, from which he took a hundred chests of sapphires and other gems before going on to the palace of Samandal. When he entered, Samandal replied with cordiality to his greeting and welcomed him, saying: 'I see that you have brought me a present.' Salih explained: 'I have come to ask for the hand of your noble daughter, and one good deed should be repaid by another. Do you share the wishes of her suitor and will you accept his request?' Samandal laughed scornfully and asked: 'Salih, how has this occurred to you? I never realized that you were so short of sense that you should ask for my daughter's hand, when she is the unique queen of the age. If anyone but you had done this I would have cut off his head.' He then shouted to his troops, and Salih had to make his escape to an island.

He then collected all his men and launched a major attack on Samandal, shattering his army and capturing his palace. He seized Samandal himself and put him in chains, after which he looked for his daughter, but got no news of her, while similarly he could not find Badr. Badr meanwhile had escaped to an island, where he hid in a tree, while Jauhara had also escaped with fifty maid-servants.

Salih was distressed and exclaimed: 'Cousins, nothing that we have done, small or great, can make up for this loss.' They said that they would search throughout the sea and were bound to succeed, but he told them: 'My only fear is that the damned Jauhara may have fallen in with Badr, and I cannot return to my sister until I have news of her son.' He sent out search parties and took his seat on Samandal's throne.

So much for them, but as for Jauhara, she ended up in the island where Badr was, as he knew she would, since this was her only place of safety. As fate would have it she came and sat down beneath the tree in which he was hiding. At the sight of her he lost all self-control and exclaimed: 'Glory to God Who created this girl! By God, she is so lovely that I have never seen anyone to match her in beauty!' He kept on staring at her until she looked up and said: 'Who is in this tree?' When her girls said that they did not know she told one of them to put down what she was holding and go to investigate. The girl saw Badr, and after greeting him she told him to come down and talk to the princess.

Badr came down and when Jauhara saw him and asked who he was he told her that he was Badr, the son of Julnar. She went up to him and pulled him close so that his muscles trembled and she put water in her mouth before spitting it out over him and saying: 'Leave this shape and become a white bird with red legs and beak.' She then told one of her girls: 'Take him and have no fear of his family. They will be looking for him, and otherwise I would have killed him and been quit of him, for his entry into the sea and his arrival at our court were inauspicious in the extreme.' Then she ordered the girl to take him to the Waterless Island, let him go there and come back quickly.

The girl took Badr, transformed as he was by magic into a bird, and brought him to the Waterless Island. She had proposed to leave him there but felt unhappy, thinking of retribution and fearing that this would lead to his death. So she took him to another island filled with fruits and other good things and there she released him. She then went back to her mistress to tell her the news.

So much for Badr, but as for his mother, she waited for a time, but when word was slow in coming she got up without telling anyone and, after diving into the sea, she went to the palace of her brother Salih. On her arrival the maids came out to present their services and told her the story from beginning to end. She then went in to find her brother seated on his royal throne, and he rose out of respect for her and then, weeping bitterly, he repeated the whole story. She slapped her face and said: 'Brother, look for my son and do not forget about him. If I stay with you, the army will be tempted to take over our kingdom and so I shall have to go back to govern it, but if I despair of Badr, I shall give it up and return to you. Then I shall construct a tomb and sit by it, saying: "This is Badr's grave." So don't slacken in your search for him.' 'To hear is to obey,' Salih replied, and she then went back to her palace and acted as ruler of the kingdom. The search for Badr continued, but no news of him was found.

So much for Julnar, but as for Badr, he stayed in the island, not knowing where to go until in the distance he caught sight of pigeons and flew off towards them. When he reached them he told himself: 'By God, these birds will show me the way,' but the birds flew down to a hunter's net, and Badr went with them. Humans, however, do not eat bird food, and so, when the pigeons began to eat, the hunter spread his net, catching them and then killing them. He was intending to kill Badr, but on looking at his white body and his red legs like corals he told himself that he would not have the heart to kill him and so he went off with him to a pleasant and populous island ruled by an important king. One of the king's servants saw him passing by and admired the bird's mixture of colours. He called to the hunter, and when the man answered, he asked whether the bird was for sale. 'Yes, master,' the man said, and the servant pulled out five dirhams and said: 'Take this as its price.' He then took the bird and handed it over to the king, leaving it with him.

The king was impressed by the bird's beauty and asked the servant, Jauhar, how much he had bought it for and when Jauhar told him that this was five dirhams he brought out five dirhams and added ten dinars. He then took the bird and put it in a cage, providing it with food and drink, but the bird neither ate nor drank. This distressed the king, who told his servant to bring it to him. When this had been done it was let out of its cage and it then hopped down and perched on the king's thigh. A tray was brought before the king on which was what is to be found on kings' tables. The bird jumped up to settle on a roast chicken, which it ate, and to the king's surprise it went on to eat everything else that was on the table. The tray was removed, and drinking glasses and jugs were brought in. Girls with musical instruments entered, and the room was adorned with scented herbs and flowers, as well as the glasses. The king took up one of these and was about to drink when the bird hopped up, sat on his hand and then, putting its head in the glass, drained it. The king laughed, and the girls cried out and joined in the laughter. The queen heard the noise and asked what was happening. She was told that the king's bird had eaten everything that had been set before the king and that, sitting on his hand, it had drunk up the glass of wine that he was holding. She got up and went to him and when she had examined the bird she concealed her face from it. 'Damn it, are you hiding away from a bird?' he asked, but she told him: 'Your Majesty, this bird is Badr, the son of Julnar of the Sea, who has been enchanted by the daughter of Samandal, the supreme king of the sea.'

The king was astonished and asked her: 'By my life, tell me if you can release him from this spell.' 'I can,' she told him, 'but I have a compact with the girl who bewitched him that she would not break any spell of mine and I would not free anyone whom she had bewitched.' 'I ask you in God's name to turn him back to his proper shape, as I am sorry for him,' the king said. His wife agreed and went back to her palace and returned some time later with a red shawl with which she covered the bird. She lit a fire which produced vapours and, taking some water, she sprinkled this over the bird and wrapped it in the shawl, beneath which it trembled. Then she threw off the shawl and Badr stood up, looking like a full moon.

The delighted king sat him on his throne, addressing him by name. In reply Badr said: 'Your Majesty, may God give you a good reward on my behalf and enable me to recompense the two of you!' The king then asked him for his story, which he told from beginning to end. 'What do you intend to do?' the king asked, and Badr said: 'I want you to be good enough to prepare a ship for me and send enough of your men with me to take me to my kingdom. I don't know what happened after I left, and every day without me must have seemed like a month for my people and every month an age. If – and God forbid – my mother has died, I shall go back to serve whoever is king and become one of his retainers.'

The king agreed to this and prepared a ship for him, in which he placed everything that would be needed. Badr took his leave and went on board, after which the sail was hoisted, and for ten days the ship sailed on with a favourable breeze. On the eleventh day, however, the wind got up and dashed it against a mountain, where it broke up. Badr climbed on to a plank of teak, which was tossed to and fro by the waves for three days until on the fourth his feet touched ground.

When morning came he saw a lofty city, white as a dove, and by the shore were ten thousand camels, horses, mules and cows. When he got out of the water they all advanced and began kicking him to stop him climbing up. He went back into the water and swam along until he landed behind them as dawn was breaking. He made for the city gate and went in, seeing nobody on his way. He then entered the market, where a greengrocer was cooking some beans. After an exchange of glances the man called to him, and Badr replied: 'Here I am, master.' The man told him to come closer and when he did the man asked: 'Have you met anyone in the city?' 'No, master,' said Badr, and the man told him to come up to his shop, and when he did he was told to go to the upper end, where he entered a room and sat until the sun was fully risen.

At that point the greengrocer came back with food of various kinds, which he put in front of Badr and ate with him. They addressed each other, and the greengrocer asked Badr what had brought him there. After telling his story, Badr went on: 'I wanted to come up to the island from the sea but horses, cows and camels – more than ten thousand of them – stopped me.' The man said: 'My son, this is a city of magicians with a tyrannical queen. The horses, mules, cows and camels that you saw were all men like you until that impious woman transformed them. Whoever wants to ride on a horse, a camel or anything else can take his pick of them, for they are all being punished, and it was because they pitied you that they tried to stop you from climbing up on shore, fearing

that she would enchant you and you would become like them. Now get
up and look at the city to see how many people are there.' 'I'm afraid of
them, Father,' said Badr, but the man told him there was no need for
that as all of them would fear him.

Badr said: 'I got up and sat on the shop bench, from which I saw such
huge numbers of people that only God could number them. When they
saw me they asked: "Shaikh 'Abdallah, is this a captive of yours?" "No,
by God," the man answered, "he is my nephew, and I sent for him
because I am old and living alone with no son and no family." That
silenced them, and they made no reply. I stayed with him for ten days
but then, while we were sitting on the bench, up came a thousand servants holding clubs of gold and silver, followed by a thousand Turkish
mamluks, and after them rode a thousand maid-servants, in the middle
of whom was the young queen.

'When she came past 'Abdallah's shop she looked at me and stopped
in front of me, while 'Abdallah got up to kiss the ground respectfully.
She asked him whether I was a captive of his, and he repeated that I was
his nephew for whom he had sent because he was old and lonely. "Shaikh
'Abdallah," she said, "by the Fire and the Light, I am struck by his
appearance and I want you to hand him over to me." "On one condition," 'Abdallah said, and when she asked what this was, he went on:
"Swear to me that you will do him no harm." "Yes, I swear it," she
answered, and he told her: "I am satisfied and I shall hand him over to
you, for no one on the face of the earth can injure him, as I am with him
and you know me best of all." "I am content," she said, and he promised to hand me over next day when she came back from the *maidan*.
She thanked him and left.

'Abdallah called to me and when I answered he said: "This woman is
a tyrannical evil-doer called Lab, which means Royal Sun. When she
finds someone whom she admires, she takes him and enjoys him for
forty days before transforming him into the shape of some animal. She
then sends him off to the shore and looks for someone else, may God
curse her and remove all trace of her." "Father," I told him, "I am afraid
of her," but he said: "No harm will come to you, as she will not dare to
lift a hand against you while I am alive, as she thinks that you are my
nephew, whom I regard as a son."

'I thanked him, and we spent the night. Next morning she came back,
looking more radiant than the sun, and she greeted 'Abdallah, who
kissed the ground before her, as did I. "Get up," she said, and 'Abdallah

rose and took me by the hand, saying: "Take him, lady, and send him back when you have had enough of him." She agreed, and I was given a horse with a golden saddle. I rode beside her as people admired my physique and my handsome face, feeling sorry that I was going to be put under a harmful spell.

'When we reached the royal palace we went in and, after passing through a series of halls, we halted. Taking me by the hand, she led me into a house the like of which I had never seen. It was like paradise, with walls plated with gold, and around it and them were statues of women each holding a musical instrument. It was furnished with all sorts of silk brocade, and at its upper end was a dais on which was a throne of red gold inlaid with various types of gems, sapphires, *balkash* rubies and emeralds.

'The queen mounted the dais and took her seat on the throne, taking me up with her and seating me by her side, with her thigh over mine. For a time she issued commands and prohibitions, but then she called up a golden table encrusted with pearls and other gems, to which forty bowls of gold and silver were brought, containing various types of foods. As we ate she put spoonfuls in my mouth, and I kissed her hand until we had had enough. The table was removed, and we washed our hands, after which golden trays were brought in, on which were dishes of china and crystal containing sweetmeats of all kinds, dry, moist and pressed. More inlaid trays were brought with scents, and then came girls carrying musical instruments, each of whom went up to one of the statues, with the girl carrying a lute sitting beneath the statue of a lute girl, the girl with a flute sitting beneath a flautist and the one with cymbals sitting under a cymbal player, each one underneath the appropriate statue. They all began to sing in unison until I thought that the palace was rocking with me as I looked at the splendour of this luxury.

'We kept on drinking until it became dark, when candles were brought out on gold and silver candlesticks made of wax scented with camphor and amber. The queen was cheerful, and, as she became drunk, so did I. She turned to one of the girls, who was holding a lute in her hand, and said: "Get up! Your voice has changed, and it is killing me." "By God, lady," I objected, "she was singing well." When I had reproved her, she said: "Let her go down and fetch the carved instrument from the wall under which the lute player is sitting." This girl then sang in a voice such as I had never heard from any of them and played the lute in a way that I had never seen. The queen turned to me and said: "Darling, which of them is the sweetest singer?" "That one," I said, "for I have never heard a voice like this, and it has filled me with delight, as has her artistry." The queen said: "These perform at night, and the others by day." She called to the girls, who all got up and left, while the statues on the wall all came down and sat in their places and sang most beautifully and delightfully with the most entrancing of voices.

'We sat until midnight when the queen got up and took me by the hand to a lovely chamber, in which there was a niche lined with gold, with cushions of brocade, rugs and mattresses of satin. We went up there, and the queen took off her clothes and got into bed, clasping me to her chest and kissing my face as I kissed hers. I enjoyed her until morning, when she sat up and put on her clothes. I had followed her example when her maids came in to take her to the baths. I got up with them, and they took me to the palace baths, after which I was provided with a robe of honour worth a thousand dinars.

'I stayed like this for a month and then one day I got up and went out to the palace courtyard, where there was running water, in the middle of which were two birds, one white and one black, while on the palace battlements were birds of various colours, more in number than the drops of water. The black bird was going up and pulling feathers from their heads. I was astonished and I asked the queen to allow me to visit Shaikh 'Abdallah and then return to her. "Yes, on condition that you don't stay," she said, and I agreed.

'I left her and went to the shaikh, who welcomed me and asked how I was and how I passed my nights. I told him about the birds, and he told me that they had been enchanted by the queen. I told him that I had seen her doing this at midnight, and he said: "If you have seen her casting spells, she has taken against you. Sleep until midnight and then see what type of magic she is performing and then come back and tell me what it is so that I can counter it and, for God's sake, don't be too slow or that will be the end of you." When I went back to the queen I found her waiting for me at the table. "Welcome, darling," she said; "where have you been? May the world not exist after you have gone! Sit down." I sat with her, and we ate, but my head was drooping, and she addressed me endearingly and asked me if I had been watching magic. "Yes, lady," I said, and we sat until nightfall, when I went up to bed. She stayed with me until midnight, when she slowly got up. I opened my eyes and saw her open a chest, from which she took five containers, and from each of these she took red sand, which she scattered around, muttering a spell over it. When it was opposite the couch a stream flowed through it, and then from a small box she removed barley, which she sowed there, and it immediately sprouted up and ripened. She took it, ground it up and made porridge, which she put in a bowl. She then swept up the sand and put it back in the box where it had been, and after all this she came back and lay down to sleep beside me.

'Next morning she got up and went to the baths, while I went to Shaikh 'Abdallah to tell him what I had seen. "God damn her!" he exclaimed, and he told me to sit there for a while, while he went to his room. He came back some time later, bringing with him two *ratls* of porridge. He called to me, and when I answered he said: "Take this gruel and go back to the queen. When she asks where you have been, tell her that you have been with a friend. She will say that she has porridge as good as yours, but you should tell her: 'One good added to another is an increase of good. Let us eat them both.' Then take a dish, put the porridge on it, moisten it with water and eat it, as it will do you no harm. When there are only two spoonfuls left, steal away one of them and leave it in your sleeve. She will fetch her own porridge, moisten it and tell you to eat. Pretend to be doing this but instead eat what you put in your sleeve. When she sees that you have eaten it she will say: 'Leave this human shape of yours and assume the shape that I name.' Nothing will happen to you, and at that she will show confusion and say that she was only playing with you. Do you then tell her to eat some of your porridge and when she is eating take some water in your hand and dash it in her face, saying: 'Leave this human shape of yours, for another that I want.' She will be transformed instantly, and be damned to her."'

Badr said: 'I blessed him and thanked him, after which I took the porridge and went back to the queen in her palace. She greeted me fondly and asked where I had been, at which I told her that I had been with a friend. She said: "We have some porridge," and I suggested that we should eat both hers and mine. I then took a dish and, after having moistened my porridge, I ate it, but hid away a spoonful in my sleeve. When there was none left she said: "Darling, try my porridge to see which is better, yours or mine." After this she took her porridge, moistened it and told me to eat it. I pretended to do this, and she saw me chewing. She said: "What am I going to do with you?" Then she took a handful of water and threw it in my face, saying: "Change from this shape to that of an ugly, grimy mule." When nothing happened to me she got up, and I could see that she had changed colour. She said:

"Darling, don't hold this against me, for I was playing a joke on you," but I took some water in my own hand, threw it in her face and said: "Change your shape to that of a dark black mule." She threw herself on the ground and turned into a mule, with tears pouring down her cheeks. She rubbed her cheeks against my leg, and I tried but failed to bridle her.

'I left her and went to the shaikh, who asked me what I had done, and I told him the whole story of how I had turned the queen into a mule. He got up and fetched a bridle from his shop, telling me to take it back to her, as when she saw that I had it she would become docile and I could then bridle her and ride her wherever I wanted to go. He added: "You cannot stay anywhere on this island as that would be fatal for you. I would not be able to save you and I want to protect myself."

'I thanked him and left with his bridle. When the mule saw it she stretched out her head towards me, and I saddled and bridled her before mounting her and riding out of the city. When I had been travelling for three days I came within sight of a city more beautiful than that of the queen. When I entered it I was met by a handsome man, who greeted me and asked me where I had come from. When I told him that this was the Sorcerers' City he welcomed me and asked me to go home with him. When he had taken me there he told me to dismount. Shaikh 'Abdallah had told me that when I did that I was not to let the bridle out of my hand for the blink of an eye, but when my host told me to dismount he shouted to a servant to take the mule to the stable and tie it up there, treating it well. I said: "Sir I cannot be parted from this mule for a single instant, and if you can't let it into the house with me, then allow me to go on my way." "If the mule is lost, I'll give you a thousand dinars as its price," he said.

'As he went on talking an old woman came up and stood beside us. "There is no god but God," she said, adding: "Master, this mule resembles one belonging to my son which died and he still grieves for it. Would you sell it for whatever price you want? I'll give you a thousand dinars if you ask so that I may content him if only for an hour." I asked myself: "How can this old woman get a thousand dinars?" and I told her to produce the money and I would sell it to her. At that she produced from beneath her clothes a purse with a thousand dinars and told me to hand over the mule. "I'm not going to sell it," I told her but my host said: "Don't do that. You agreed to the sale so take the gold. In this city of ours we don't recognize lies and only accept fair dealing. You sold the mule and you cannot take back what you said."

'I took the purse with the gold and handed over the mule. I took the gold to the mosque and poured it out on my lap, only to discover that these were rounded bits of pottery made to look like gold. I struck myself on the face until blood flowed from my nose and I then left the city only to find three people, including the old woman to whom I had sold the mule and the queen. On seeing me, the queen snorted and said: "Welcome, by God!" The old woman was her mother and had broken the spell, so the queen seized my hand and whistled thrice on three different notes. Immediately an 'ifrit the size of a huge mountain appeared and set me on his shoulder, and within the blink of an eye we were back in her palace.

'When she had taken her seat on her throne her maids congratulated her on her safe return. They would have liked to kill me, but the queen stopped them, while I was like a brick tossed down in the middle of them. The queen then got out something white and recited spells over it for some time before putting it in water and sprinkling it over me. Then she said: 'Leave your human shape and take that of the ugliest of all birds.' I fell to the ground and turned into an ugly bird, which she put on a shelf in the palace.

'Just then the black bird appeared together with a white bird, with which it mated. When the white bird got up and spread its feathers the black bird flew away. The queen washed and took some of the water, which she put in a bowl on my shelf, telling me to drink it, as this was all she was going to give me. For three days I did not drink, but then one of the maids felt sorry for me and was impelled to bring me water and attend to my needs.' She then went to Shaikh 'Abdallah and told him what had happened. 'There is no might and no power except with God the Omnipotent!' he exclaimed, adding: 'By God, the boy is dead, but you have achieved something, so finish it off by doing your best to take word to his mother.' The girl asked who this was, and 'Abdallah said: 'She is Julnar of the Sea, the most skilful sorceress on the face of the earth, while in particular her mother is the greatest of calamities and disasters. You may be sure that the Almighty will single you out for reward, while Julnar will enrich you, and this will lead you to marriage, and you will be queen of the city.' After he had encouraged her with these hopes, she agreed and promised to go that night to Julnar.

When it grew dark the girl whistled and recited a spell, which instantly produced a female devil, who said: 'Give me your command.' 'I want you to carry me to Julnar in the White Island, for I have some business with her,' the girl said. 'Lady,' the devil told her, 'I have been there, and Julnar is in the worst of states because of her son Badr. They have captured Jauhara, the daughter of Samandal, the supreme king of the sea, as well as Samandal himself, and are holding both as prisoners.' 'Take me there immediately, Maimuna,' the girl said, and when Maimuna told her to mount she got on her back. After a mere blink of an eye the flight ended on the roof of Julnar's palace, and the girl dismounted.

When she saw Julnar she recognized her as a sorceress and greeted her respectfully, saying: 'Good news, lady! Your son is with Queen Lab, but he has been transformed into the ugliest of shapes, so help him while there is still time.' The news spread, and Julnar and her brother raised the *jinn* clans and flew off with the girl, who was telling them the whole story from beginning to end, including the role played by Shaikh 'Abdallah and how he had helped Badr.

Almost immediately the palace was taken by surprise, and the queen and everyone else in it were seized. The Badr bird was brought to his mother, who spat over him and recited a spell. A shudder ran through him, and he emerged as beautiful as the moon, although hunger and thirst had emaciated him until he was like an old water-skin.

Queen Lab was produced, and she, her mother and everyone in the palace, male and female, were put to death. Julnar then sent for Shaikh 'Abdallah and when he came she jumped up and kissed the ground in front of him, as did Badr, and after kissing him between the eyes she said: 'My son, had it not been for this man, you would have died.' She presented him with a robe of honour and married him to the girl he had sent to tell her about Badr.

With Badr, her brother and her mother she went back to the White City, of which Badr was now king. The citizens stood up for him and came to kiss the ground before him and congratulate him on his safe return. For some days he sat on the throne and then he followed his uncle and told him that he wanted to see Samandal and to marry his daughter. 'He is eager for that, my son,' his uncle told him, and when Samandal was produced he welcomed Badr, rising for him and seating him on the royal throne. The qadi was summoned together with Princess Jauhara, Samandal's daughter. A marriage contract was drawn up as well as an arrangement for the disposition of property, and this was followed by a wedding of unprecedented splendour.

Badr returned half of the kingdom to Samandal and went back himself to Julnar, with everything restored to its proper order. They all lived the best, most pleasant, comfortable and untroubled of lives until they were parted by the Destroyer of Delights and the Separator of Companions.

This is the story. Praise be to God Alone, and blessings and peace be on Muhammad, his family and his companions!

Tale Seven

The Story of 'Arus al-'Ara'is and Her Deceit, As Well As the Wonders of the Seas and Islands.

In the Name of God, the Compassionate, the Merciful

Amongst the tales of past times it is recorded that there was once a great and powerful king who had no son. He prayed that Almighty God might grant him one to whom he could leave his throne after his death. Then one night when he lay with his wife she conceived through God's will, and after nine months of pregnancy she gave birth to the most beautiful girl that had ever been seen. The baby was handed over to nurses, and her father continued to distribute alms and he would come every day to kiss her between the eyes.

This went on until one day the baby fell sick and, although the king collected wise doctors and men of learning and supplied them with whatever they wanted, she died, as God Almighty had willed. The king was broken by grief and spent a month mourning for his daughter and keeping away from his viziers, chamberlains and friends, staying alone with his sorrow.

Amongst his closest associates was a vizier distinguished for excellence of both life and doctrine, a man of generosity who showed sympathy to the poor, the weak and the widows. Many lived off the alms he distributed, and to them he acted as a father. When the king had suffered the loss of his daughter this man was so distressed that he no longer concerned himself with alms, as those who relied on him for food found out.

One day when he was seated by the king's door a blind man to whom he had been used to showing charity came up and called down blessings on him, before asking why he had interrupted his gifts, adding: 'I used to live thanks to your grace and that of Almighty God, and the fact that you have stopped has harmed me.' 'Don't you see the sorrow and distress from which we are suffering?' asked the vizier, adding: 'By God, this has distracted us from ourselves and from our own children, let alone from anyone else.'

When the blind man asked the cause of this grief, praying that God might distract his heart and remove the pain, the vizier told him that the king had suffered the loss of his fifteen-year-old [sic] daughter and was sunk in mourning. 'This has had its effect on us,' the vizier went on, 'as he is shut up alone, shedding constant tears, while we are left as sheep without a shepherd.' The blind man said: 'Almighty God has a way to remove this grief from the vizier, the king and all his subjects, both high and low.' 'How is that?' the vizier asked. The man said: 'Put me where the king can hear what I say and I shall tell him something to cure his heart and remove his sorrow. If he summons me I shall tell him a story both fine and strange that will make him hate women and girls and make him glad that his daughter died.' 'If you manage to do that,' said the vizier, 'I shall shower you with bounty and give you whatever you want in the world.'

On the orders of the vizier he was taken away; his matted hair was combed and everything was done to make him respectable. Next day the vizier rode out with him and, accompanied by servants, he went up to the curtain that separated him from the king. He placed the man there, telling him where the king was and to say what he wanted, as the king would hear.

The blind man began by greeting the king, calling down blessings on him and expressing eloquent and effective admonishment. As the king listened he relaxed, and some of his sorrow left him. He ordered the man to be brought before him and told him of the effect his words had had on him, asking him for more, as this had struck a chord in his heart.

The blind man said: 'I have an excellent tale that will console the king and lead him to hate scheming and treacherous women and girls. It is a long, remarkable and curious story containing a lesson for men of intelligence.' 'I like long stories,' the king said, 'as I want to get through the night, filled as I am with grief.' In order to hear it, he brought the blind man close to him and told him to start.

'May God bring you fortune,' the man said, and he then started on his story, which his father had told him on the authority of his grandfather, who had once been the police chief of a city. One day this man had been sitting at the prison door, inspecting criminals whom he might pardon and release, so hoping for a great reward from God. After many had been freed he was brought a one-eyed man, at the sight of whom he said: 'Damn you! Didn't I investigate your first crime when you plotted against the princess and were only saved from death by the death of her father from sorrow, after which you stayed in prison for a whole year? I then came across you again when you had attacked a woman in her own house and were seized by neighbours, who testified against you, after which you were beaten and imprisoned for another year. As for the third crime of yours that I looked into, this was when you tried to rape your own mother. I have freed you twice and I shall do so again today, but if you come back here again I shall cut off your head.'

'Return me to prison,' the man called out, 'for I would prefer to stay there rather than meet the evil woman who will kill me. For God's sake, spare me.' 'Who is this woman?' asked the police chief, and the man said: 'She is the one who got me imprisoned and pulled out my eye. It is a strange story.'

The police chief ordered him to be taken to his house, after which he called for him and said: 'Now tell me your tale. Don't conceal anything and tell the truth, for the best story is the truest. So tell me about the evil woman who did this to you.'

The man promised to tell the truth and gave his name, saying that he was a Bahraini merchant, who had been left a large fortune when his father had died. He went on: 'I started to sail in distant seas, making vast profits and coming back safely to Bahrain. One year I set out for China together with three hundred traders. When we put out to sea we had a fair wind and settled weather, and for six months we sailed safely and contentedly with nothing in sight except sky and water. Then one day a violent wind came that took hold of our ship, driving it on like an arrow, without us having any idea where it was taking us.

'This went on for seven days and nights until we came out into a sea that was dark as the blackest night. In the middle of it we saw a high mountain, at whose side was a great arch, through which the water poured. When we got near, the wind dropped, and we anchored by the foot of the mountain. We stayed there in a state of perplexity and we were disturbed to hear the crew whispering to each other.

'We had with us an old man, who had sailed the seas for a hundred years and knew their dangers. We gathered around him and asked him where we were. "You are in a difficult place," he said, "and there is no escape unless God wills it." This filled us with such fear and agitation that we spent the whole night tearfully imploring God to help.

'Next morning as the sun rose we saw something as big as a mountain coming towards us and we asked the old man what it was. "This is an abominable beast that snatches people," he said, "and whoever has reached the end of his allotted span is caught up by it and swallowed. The beast will then go away for the day, only to come back on the next and take another victim, and this will go on until God permits you to escape. If you try to fight it, it will smash the ship and destroy you all." "Damn you," we said; "who is going to want to throw himself overboard to be eaten?"

'The old man said: "Each of you should write down his name on a lot, and these should all be put together. Then blindfold someone and get him to pick one of them, and then you should give the beast the man whose name comes out, whether he wants it or not. It may be that God, the Great and Glorious, through His power, will enable us to escape." We did this, and the name was that of one of the merchants. Then the beast came close, and it was like the most enormous Bactrian camel, but greater and more terrifying. It had a frightening head and eyes and a wide mouth that could swallow a bale of cotton, while the repulsive smell that it gave off was unbearable. We were so frightened that most of us fell on our faces, swooning at the sight, but the rest went to the merchant and threw him to it in spite of his tears and cries for help. The beast swallowed him and then went away.

'We spent several days weeping and wailing, looking for God to save us, and we continued to pick lots daily and to throw the losers for the beast to swallow. This went on for a long time, but then we all went back to the old man and said: "Enemy of God, you have made up your mind to destroy us one by one so as to take our goods and our wealth. By God's truth, if the beast comes back, we will throw it you and you alone."

' "I was fair with you," he told us. "You draw lots, and if it is mine that comes out, then throw me in, but don't blame me." "We shall do that even without a lot," we said, and then we asked whether he had thought of any way of freeing us from the beast. When he said "no", we all agreed to do what we had said, and when it came at its usual time we tied him up and threw him to it, at which it swallowed him.

' "We've killed him now," we said, "but what are we going to do tomorrow?" Everyone decided that we should fight. Either we would kill the beast and free ourselves from it or else it would kill us, and this would be better than having to taste the pangs of death every day.

'We all agreed on this and next morning we armed ourselves with what we had and told each other that we had to hold together. Then, before we had noticed it, there the beast was. We cried out to God, hoping to scare it, but when it saw what we were doing it attacked the ship ferociously and broke it in pieces with a single blow. All our goods sank, and the beast started to gulp us down, one by one.

'I myself took hold of one of the ship's timbers and got on top of it. The winds started to drive me to and fro, lifting me up and then plunging me down, until they propelled me through the arch beneath the mountain to emerge into another sea whose vivid green waters were the clearest that I had ever seen.

'The waves then cast me up on what was beyond my experience, a beautiful island, well wooded and with many waters. I started to explore happily and I came to a spring of the purest water, sweeter than sugar and colder than snow. I drank my fill and then made for the biggest and tallest tree, where I sheltered at night, climbing down again when it was day.

'For ten days I stayed there, seeing no single creature, but on the tenth day, when I was about to come down, I saw something huge swimming in the sea and making for the island. When it was near enough I saw that it was a black creature, which was pushing something along the surface with its hands and chest.

'At this sight I retreated to my shelter in the tree and looked down to see what it was. It reached the island and came out of the water, and I could make out that it was the largest and blackest beast that I had ever seen, with thick lips like a camel but larger and more frightening. Its shape terrified me.

'What it had been pushing through the water was a closed glass chest, which it put down when it came to the spring, and out of it, when it was opened, came a girl. She was like a full moon, the most perfectly beautiful that had ever been seen, with jewels and magnificent robes, and the splendour of her beauty illumined all that was around her.

'The creature left her and went off to return later, leading a most enormous ram and carrying a huge fish as well as a large basket of fruits, the like of which I had never seen. From the bottom of the chest he produced a fire drill and lit a great fire with logs he had collected. He then skinned the ram, doused the fire and began to cut up the ram's flesh and throw it on to the embers. When it was cooked he ate and gave the girl her share, and they both went on eating until they had had enough.

'He then started to toy with the girl, getting closer and closer until he could lie with her, while she did the same thing with him, as he muttered to her using words that I could not understand. He then climbed on her as she lay still, allowing him to take her, which he did five times without any sound or resistance on her part. I was astonished at how she could endure it. When he got off her, he put his head on her thigh and fell asleep like a great bull, snoring and snorting in his sleep with a sound like rumbling thunder.

'When he was deeply asleep she eased his head gently from her thigh, got up and began to walk, swinging her hips and lighting the island with her radiant loveliness. On reaching the spring she undressed to bathe, and that beauty of hers robbed me of my wits until I could not look away.

'When she came out of the water she began to walk amongst the trees, shedding tears and lamenting her plight, saying: "Lord Whom we worship, Who frees slaves and relieves the distressed, I beg You for a quick release so that I may rest from my troubles."

'On hearing this, I felt pity for her. On my finger was a ring engraved with the greatest name of God, and I thought of speaking to her but supposed that she might not be human, as I had never seen anyone more lovely, and so I held back. As she was wandering through the trees and repeating her prayers she happened to look up to where I was. After staring at me for some time she asked: "Are you a *jinni* or a man?" I was too afraid of her to say anything and she asked: "Why don't you answer? Are you dumb and unable to speak or deaf and unable to hear? Say something and don't be afraid, for I am human and I think that you are too. The only way that you are going to get away from this wild and desolate spot is through my help."

'I remained dumbfounded and said nothing, and after a time, when she could see that I was staying silent and not answering, she got up and went off towards her companion. She woke him up and said: "Friend, I have just been asleep and I dreamed that you had become smaller and weaker. I would like to see whether you are still as strong as you used to be." He asked quickly what she wanted him to do, and she told him that she would like him to use all his strength to uproot a tree. "Say what you want," he said, and she led him towards me. Terror filled my heart and I had despaired of life as she looked at me, but then she pointed to a tree nearby, which was so big that ten men working together with spades and axes could not have uprooted it.

'Her companion rolled up his sleeves, tightened his belt and, with a shout, tugged so powerfully that the whole island shook beneath me. Up came the tree, roots and all, and was tossed aside as the girl laughed. The two of them went back, and she stretched out her thighs for him until he fell asleep, snoring as he had done before. She then put his head down on the ground and hurried over to me.

'"You saw what this monstrous evil-doer did," she said to me, "and you realize that, had I wanted to get you down from your tree, it would have been easy enough for me, and if I wanted to harm you I could. Don't be afraid but come down now, for I will do what you want." When I heard this, and after seeing what she had done, I climbed down to her, although I was still afraid. Without a word she came up to me and embraced me, holding me tightly. When my flesh met hers my lust was roused, and on noticing this she put herself at my disposal, and I lay with her, experiencing such delight as I had never known before.

'She had robbed me of my wits, and when I felt at ease with her I said: "My lady, I heard you ask God in your prayer how you might use one of His Great Names to escape from your plight. I have a ring on which is the Greatest Name." She showed delight, telling me to give it to her quickly, and when I did she took off an engraved silver ring set with a pearl such as I had never seen before. "Take this and put it on your finger in place of your own," she said, "and it will protect you against *jinn* and devils." When I took it from her she told me to go back to my place in the tree, which I did.

'She herself went quickly over to the black creature as he lay asleep and placed the ring on the parting of his hair before pressing down on it with all the strength she could muster. Then she took a knife and cut his throat from ear to ear, leaving a torrent of blood to pour out over the island, an act that filled me with alarm and terror as I watched.

'When she was sure that he was dead and could no longer feel anything or move, she sat beside him, sobbing and weeping, and I heard her say: "Alas for all scheming and treacherous women, who keep no covenant of love or pact of faithfulness and who neither abide by nor show loyalty to their lovers."

'I was astonished by what she said and what she had done, in that she had dared to cut his throat and then regretted killing him. She got up and came towards me, telling me to come down. When I did she asked: "Are you happy now that I have killed my lover?" "Yes I am," I said, "but tell me about this *jinni* and how you came across him, for I'm sure that this must be a strange tale." She agreed that it was but then stayed silent, and when I saw that she didn't want to talk about it I held back and didn't press her.

'I stayed with her for ten days, enjoying life on the island, forgetting my family, my son and my home land. For her part she gave me quantities of pearls, gems and corals, showing love for me, but then she came up to me and said: "I think that you have a wife and son and that you are longing for them. Take everything I have given you, as it will make you rich. Then go to the end of the island, jump into the sea and begin to swim, for it is not far to go. Don't be afraid of the waves, for if you hold out you will get to another island. When you are there, walk for twenty days towards the east and you will find enough fruits and fresh water sweeter than sugar, milk or butter, to eat and drink. After the twenty days you will come across a fisherman who is from an inhabited land. He will have a light boat and will be catching pearl oysters. Go up and complain of your plight to him, and he will take you back to civilization. So return to your family and your home land and leave me here for God to do with me as He wills."

' "Lady," I said to her, "as long as I live I shall never leave you, for to go with you is dearer to me than the world and everything in it." "Do you want me to go back to your country with you?" she asked. "Yes, by God, lady!" I said; "I cannot endure without you and your beauty and loveliness, for to part from you would be like losing the soul from my body. If you stay, I shall stay here with you, and if you leave the island, I shall go too."

' "I am now happy," she said, "and so sit down and listen to my story from beginning to end. If you are content, you can take me with you in the full knowledge of what I have done, and if you don't like it, you can go off by yourself." "Lady," I told her, "there is nothing I should like more than to hear what you have to say and listen to your fine speech and sweet words." "Listen, then, with your ears and your heart," she said to me, and I told her to tell me her story, as I would be her ransom.

'She said: "I am the daughter of kings. My father was lord of a coastal city that had nothing to match it on the face of the earth. It was the most wholesome and prosperous of places, and there was nowhere with more trees or sweeter fruits. It covered seven parasangs, and a river that ran right through the middle of it provided water for it and for its orchards. It had a fine city wall, and there were so many people there that only God could know their number. It was thanks to me that it and all those in it were destroyed, and I shall tell you about this from beginning to end.

' "My father was obeyed throughout the lands, and his undisputed and untroubled rule was of long standing. He had eighty wives and eighty concubines but he had no son to help him in his kingdom and no brother on whom he could lean. In his old age one of his fellow kings presented him with a slave girl of perfect and radiant beauty. When he set eyes on her he admired her and fell so deeply in love with her that he could not do without her. This was my mother. He preferred her to all his other women and when he lay with her she conceived instantly.

' "My father was delighted to hear the news. He took note of the date and the hour and gave alms to the poor and the wretched and continued to do so. After her nine months' pregnancy my mother went into labour and gave birth to me. I was the most beautiful of baby girls, and my father was overjoyed. On seeing me he thought that my beauty was a sign of blessing and he called me 'Arus al-'Ara'is [Bride of Brides].

' "With him were ten of the most learned astrologers of the age, to whom he had been in the habit of paying a salary as well as providing them with bounty and benefits. He got them together and said: 'I rely on you for I have saved you up for a time like this. Something happened in my palace yesterday which I want to use as a test for you, to find out what you foresee will be its consequences. You may investigate whatever you want, and I shall allow you three days for this.' He provided each of them with a chamber of his own and a servant to look after him as well as supplies of food and drink.

' "On the fourth night he sat on his royal throne and, having collected the leaders of his people, he called for the astrologers one after the other, telling them to produce their findings. The first of them took out his astrolabe and looked at what star was in the ascendant. He asked whether the king wanted to hear both the good and the bad news, and the king said that he did, telling the man not to hold back anything that he knew. The man began by pointing out that no force could overcome the fate decreed by Almighty God for His servants, and what was destined to happen would happen. He went on: 'What took place in your palace was that a girl was born to you at an unlucky time, this being when God cast out Adam, when Abel was killed, when Abraham the friend of God was thrown into the fire, and when the peoples of Lot, Thamud, 'Ad and Salih were destroyed. The girl born under these inauspicious signs is marked by misfortune. She will be wily and deceitful and more evil than any other of Adam's children. Through her both the king and his city will be destroyed.'

' "The king was furious at what the man had said and drove him away. He summoned another astrologer but when he put the same question to him the man gave him the same reply. He kept on calling for one after the other until he had questioned all ten of them, but all of them said the same thing, no more and no less, telling him that his daughter was the most unlucky girl born on earth. On hearing this, the king ordered their heads to be cut off and their bodies exposed on crosses; their houses were to be plundered and their women taken as booty. What happened to these men was the first instance of the misfortune that I bring.

' "I stayed with servants and nurses and by the time I was four I knew more about poetry and literature than anyone else. By the time I was seven I had studied various branches of knowledge, including grammar, and I had read stories, histories and accounts.

' "An uncle of mine who had ruled the city before my father until his death had two sons, al-Yasr and al-Yasar. Of these al-Yasr, the younger son, had helped my father take power, while al-Yasar, the elder, was kept in prison until he escaped and fled away for fear that my father would kill him. Al-Yasr, for his part, liked collecting money and continued to help my father. When I had reached puberty my father promised my hand to him, and I stayed at home for some years waiting to be married.

' "My father had given me a slave girl, who was on friendly terms with me and would never leave me. She used to tell me stories of lovers and their desperate passions and describe men to me. I was so fond of her that she stole away my wits. One day while she was sitting telling me stories and bemusing and enticing me with tales of all sorts, she said: 'By God, lady, you fit your name, 'Arus al-'Ara'is, but when I look at the beauty of your face and your loveliness, I feel sad at how all this passes without you knowing anything of the world and its delights and the pleasures of life. When a girl has reached maturity her only pleasure and delight is in a man. He should be handsome and attractive, well-spoken and intelligent and she could play with him and he could play with her.'

' "She kept on pressing this kind of point, and describing young men and those who were smitten by love in earlier generations until she had roused my longing. I told her that I was obsessed and distracted and I asked her to find a way to fetch me a handsome young man, after which she brought me one disguised as a woman. The reason why she had tried to seduce me was because she was jealous of my unique beauty, of the kindness and love that my father showed me and of the fact that he had put my mother in charge of all his women and slave girls.

' "The young man sat beside me on the same bed, and after the girl had anointed me with fragrant perfume and provided us with food and drink she went out, closing the doors and leaving us. The young man stretched out his hand to fondle me, and when he had got what he wanted, my heart was filled with love for him, and this attraction robbed me of my wits. After that he used to come to me in secret every day, entering and leaving without being noticed.

' "Soon after I had got to know him, my cousin al-Yasr asked my father to arrange our wedding, to which he agreed. Celebrations were held for six days in the city, to which everybody was invited. During this time no trading was done and in every market place and street people were eating, drinking, carousing and playing music. It was a great occasion, and people were beginning to say: 'There has never been a wedding like that of Princess 'Arus al-'Ara'is.'

' "On the day that I should have been brought to my bridegroom, my mother came to me in tears, having learned of my affair with the young man. 'My little daughter,' she said, 'tonight you will be taken to your cousin al-Yasr and you will be dishonoured and disgraced both before him and your father and everyone else. You have harmed yourself, as your cousin will find out that you are not a virgin, and your father will have to bow down his head in shame.'

' " 'Mother,' I told her, 'what happened to me was the result of a scheme planned by a woman like me who seduced me. She wanted to see me abandoned and so she tricked me and brought about my fall.' I then thought the matter over and sent an urgent message to my elegant young man. He came as usual and after we had eaten and drunk I said to him: 'You have to know that tomorrow I am going to be taken to my bridegroom and I'm afraid that you will never meet me again.' He wept and said: 'What can we do, lady?' 'I'll make a plan for you,' I told him.

' "I went to a chest and, after taking out a thousand dinars in a purse, I said: 'Go off and distribute this money straight away amongst a hundred young men in the city, friends of yours whom you can trust. Tell them to arm themselves and let them hide with drawn swords amongst all those many trees in the orchard. I will trick my father into seeing that we come at night in a big boat on the river opposite it, and with me will be all the daughters of the viziers, officers and leaders. We shall have all kinds of musical instruments with us but no men capable of fighting. When we get to you, you must all pull on the ship's ropes and draw it towards you before fastening it to a large tree. Then kill the servants on the ship so that each of you can take one of the girls and rape her. I myself will not resist you, and you can take me and make your escape wherever you want.'

' "This delighted the young man, who trusted what I had said. He took the money and went off to hand it over to his friends, who set out by night to hide themselves in the orchard. Next day my father came to me and, after having kissed me on the head, he embraced me and said: 'Light of my eyes and fruit of my heart, I have given the people cause for joy, providing them with huge banquets for your sake, and tonight I shall lead you to your bridegroom. Is there anything you need that I can do for you?'

' " 'Father,' I said, 'everyone is happy, eating and drinking, apart from me, your daughter. What I ask you to do is to order a boat to be prepared for me with wine on board. I shall then collect the daughters of the viziers, officers and leaders, choosing those who are suitable companions for me, all of them virgins. There will be food and drink and only two or three servants to see to the boat. Then have it proclaimed that nobody is to go on the river this night. We shall set off by moonlight with candles and our musical instruments and spend the whole night enjoying ourselves on the river, eating, drinking and taking our pleasures. When it is time for the dawn prayer we shall come back, and then I can be taken to my bridegroom while I am still drunk with wine.'

' "My father was delighted and agreed enthusiastically to do what I had asked. He gave the orders straight away and then at supper time he came to tell me that everything I had asked for was ready and that he had given instructions that every girl who had led a sheltered life should make sure to come.

' "I jumped up straight away and went to the boat where the girls were and when I boarded it I found the musical instruments. We started to eat and drink and enjoy ourselves, and this went on until we had got to the end of the river opposite the orchard. When we got there we moored, intending to land, but before we knew it, out came the hundred young men with swords and other weapons. They pulled the boat in with no one there to resist them, and each one of them took a girl, with my lover taking me, and we spent the rest of the night with them in the orchard.

' "Before I had gone on board I had said to my mother: 'At the end of the night go to my father weeping and shrieking. Tell him that one of the servants who had been with me had just come to you. He had been wounded and he told you that scoundrels had attacked the girls in the great orchard where they had been lying in ambush. When the girls had come opposite it, they had rushed out and taken them. Tell him to go to the rescue, as the men will be preoccupied with the girls, and he can have them seized and killed. As I shall have been amongst the girls, this will conceal my condition.'

' "When night ended she went to my father as I had told her, and when she told him all this he was upset and furious. He gave immediate orders for all his soldiers to mount and he himself left his palace and rode out, until they had all caught up with him, both horse and foot. Before we ourselves knew what was happening they had surrounded us and were attacking our ravishers, seizing them and killing them to the last man. They then took us all to the boat so that we could return home, and there was no leader, vizier or officer in the kingdom whose daughter had not lost her virginity.

' "This caused general sorrow and grief, and on my father's orders the fathers of the young men were arrested and imprisoned.

' "It was after this that the girl who had tricked me and introduced the young man to me had a private meeting with my cousin al-Yasr and my father and told them the whole story from start to finish. 'It was 'Arus al-'Ara'is,' she said, 'who planned the rape of the girls so as to remove suspicion from herself.' She explained that she had not told this to the king because she knew of his affection for me and had been reluctant to let him know something about his daughter that would displease him.

' "On hearing this my father and my cousin believed her and my father exclaimed: 'The astrologers were right!' and he regretted having killed them as well as the hundred young men. He ordered their fathers to be released from prison and given blood money for their sons, while provision was to be made for their women. He was filled with hatred for me and treated me harshly, refusing to meet me, to hear any talk of me or to mention me himself.

' "He had expelled me and my mother from the palace when I told my mother to go to al-Yasr to see how things were with him. It was clear that he was thinking about what the jealous girl had said, but my mother kept on talking to him until he asked my father for me. I was brought to him, and when he saw how beautiful I was he became totally infatuated with me and, concealing my condition, he said that he had found me to be a virgin whom no man had ever approached. My mother stayed with me in my husband's palace, but my father continued to treat me harshly.

' "It was only a short time before my husband began to hate me. This was because he had with him a pious old woman who made him afraid of me, warning him not to trust me. She told him of what the astrologers had said about the evil omens attached to me and reminded him of what I had done to the daughters of the viziers and the leaders. This led him to turn away and change his behaviour towards me.

' "When I saw this from him and from my father, I told my mother not to worry as I would arrange to have both of them killed. She knew where my elder cousin was and I told her to go and talk to him and to bring him to an empty house belonging to a servant girl of hers and to let me know me when he was there.

' "She did this and I went to him in disguise. He had never seen me before and asked who I was. When I told him that I was his cousin 'Arus al-'Ara'is, he asked why I had come, and I told him that I wanted to talk to him about something and that I would keep nothing back from him. He embraced me joyfully, staring at me without speaking.

' " 'Cousin,' I asked him, 'would you like to become king with me as your wife?' He wept and said: 'Lady, this is something that cannot happen, and I am a poor man.' 'That doesn't matter,' I told him, and when he said that this could only be achieved through wealth and power, I told him not to worry, for I would get my mother to take enough money to him little by little. When the contents of his brother's treasuries had been transferred to him he could recruit trusty helpers from amongst his father's subjects and pay them enough to satisfy them. 'I know that you have a just claim,' I said, 'as the kingdom belonged to your father, and your uncle got the better of him. People want money; they want you and will be ready to fight in a just cause, so that in this city you will find not merely ones and twos who want to fight but thousands. When you are firmly established with a thousand or two thousand followers, let me know, so that by a clever trick I can see that you get the kingdom without the need to fight a war.'

' "My cousin went back home and I returned to my palace, after which I started to send him money bit by bit, a thousand or two thousand dinars at a time. He followed my instructions and got large numbers of people to swear obedience to him. He kept this secret until he had collected two thousand men, all armed and equipped, waiting for my orders, and I was then delighted to get a secret message from him giving me the news.

' "At that point I pretended to be sick. I made it look as though I had despaired of life and was certain of death. I drank straw water, which turned me yellow and changed my appearance, and I sent word to my father that I was sick and sorrowful and that I was afraid that I might die without having seen him. When my mother had told him this, he immediately rode to visit me and said: 'Now that you are in such a state I can see that what the astrologers said was a lie.' He came close to me, but I pretended not to be able to speak, and, after staying with me for a time and shedding bitter tears, he left in sadness.

' "I stayed like that for some days before pretending to be getting better and showing gradual signs of recovery, until it appeared that I had been cured and had returned to health. I went to my husband, al-Yasr, and told him of this, saying: 'I vowed that, if I recovered, I would invite the whole court to a feast at which they could eat food of all kinds in my palace, led by you and my father, may God preserve you. I shall tie on an apron and carry a bowl from which I shall pour water for your hands and do all that I can to serve you.' He agreed enthusiastically that this was the right thing to do and ordered that all the invitations that I wanted should be sent out.

' "I gave instructions that all the state officials, including viziers and officers, were to come to my palace, while my husband invited my father. They sat by themselves, eating, drinking and enjoying themselves while I was standing to serve them, but I was also watching the guests. When everyone, including those two, was busy with their food and drink, I took the opportunity to remove the crown and the royal robes. I then covered my head with a turban and mounted a horse that I had kept ready. On this I rode to al-Yasar, to whom I gave the crown and the robe, telling him to mount, which he did. He shouted to his men, and I told them to make for the palace and kill everyone in it.

' "Al-Yasar started out immediately with more than two thousand sworn followers who had been waiting for his call. They made for the palace and started to put the banqueters to the sword, as my father's soldiers and his officers were unarmed. Most of them were killed, and this included everyone in the palace. The only ones to escape were al-Yasr and my father, who on hearing the shout had both fled from the bottom of the palace to the roof. As for my father, his heart was so filled with distress that he died there and then, but al-Yasr hid away, no one knew where.

' "Al-Yasar took his seat on the royal throne, and his companions took over the houses of those whom they had killed. A proclamation was then made to end the violence, and the city settled down. After this I was married to al-Yasar, who was delighted with me, recognizing my value. He was deeply in love with me, and my life was unclouded.

'"One day, however, my uncle's wife, the mother of al-Yasr and al-Yasar, went to see al-Yasar, weeping sadly, slapping her face and tearing her clothes, as she did not know whether her younger son was alive or dead. She began to warn al-Yasar about me, calling me a damned woman and saying: 'You know what she did to the leaders of your people, the viziers and the officers. She schemed against them and destroyed them, together with her own father and her husband, your brother. Beware of her, my son.'

'"What she said had its effect on al-Yasar, and he made me a lofty apartment in the middle of the palace. He filled it with everything that might be needed and provided a maid to serve me as well as a steward to attend to the door and a doorkeeper to guard me, both of whom he trusted and of whom he approved. He gave orders that no servant, male or female, and neither my mother nor anyone else, should be allowed in.

'"I stayed there on my own, only seeing al-Yasar once at the start of each month. I regretted what I had done for him and began to think of how I could escape from him. So I started to show signs of love to the steward, talking to him and smiling at him. At times I would uncover my head for him to see and at times my wrist, until love for me was firmly fixed in his heart, and little by little he lost his wits.

'"When I was sure of that, I enticed him in and provided him with food and drink, and when the wine had had its effect and I had dazzled him with my beauty as he drank, he stretched out his hand to me, wanting to sleep on the bed with me. I let him do this and afterwards I told him that I wanted to have the pleasure of seeing my mother. He agreed willingly, saying that he would not disobey me, whatever I told him to do.

'"When he called my mother she came in and embraced me, starting to complain of her longing for me and telling me that she could not bear to be parted from me. She said that al-Yasar had sworn that if he found her with me he would have her drowned in the sea. 'I am angry with him,' I told her; 'I only see him once a month and I regret what I did.' 'Where are your wiles and schemes that can rescue you from this?' she asked, and I told her that I would see to it straight away.

'"I gave her a thousand dinars and told her: 'Go round the whole city and look for some strong poison. Try it out on a dog or a cock, and if it has an instant effect bring it to me, for my release and my life depend on this.' She took the money and after she had been away for a while she came back with a small jug in which was a phial containing poison and yellow grease. 'I've brought you what you want,' she told me, and when I asked her what it was she said: 'I went on through the city until I was directed to a chemist to whom I gave the thousand dinars without telling him who I was and I went on flattering him until he gave me this ointment, which you must put on your hands and feet. The poison only works on the feet, but if you have smeared yourself with the grease it will do you no harm. Sprinkle it wherever you want, and if anyone treads in it bare-footed, it will get into his feet and he will die. So now do what you want.'

' "I was delighted and I sprinkled a little of the poison by the door of my room and on the carpet. I brought in the steward and made him sit on the king's bed, so that he would take his shoes off, and I began to eat and drink with him. I then told my mother to go to one of the king's servant girls and tell her that she had gone to ask about me. She had not found the steward but as the door was open she had suspected that something was not right. So she had kept herself out of sight in order to look in, and she had found him drinking on the bed with me. Filled with concern about this and, maddened by distress and anger, she had been at a loss for words and so had told this to the girl. I went on: 'If the girl asks you what she should do about the steward, tell her that you don't know. She envies and hates me and so she will go off and tell the king, and, if he comes, the trick I have planned against him will succeed.'

' "My mother went off and did what I had told her, after which the servant girl hurried to tell the king. He got up in a fit of jealous rage to run to my room bare-footed and tripping over the skirt of his robe, brandishing a drawn sword. When he reached the door and saw the steward sitting beside me, he believed what he had been told about me. He lost control of himself and told the steward to get up and leave. When the man did, his legs collapsed and immediately afterwards the king trod on the poison and collapsed without a word. My old mother had followed him to stop him from coming in to me and she too stepped in the poison and fell dead.

' "I had smeared on the ointment and I left in disguise, only to be met on the road by a coal-black slave who had been one of my father's servants and who knew me. He was living alone and he took me to his house, where I stayed in hiding. News that al-Yasar had been killed had spread through the city. He had been succeeded by his young son, who was twelve years old, but then suddenly my former husband, al-Yasr, had put in an appearance with a band of supporters. He had fought against the youngster whose father I had killed and after many had fallen he won control of the kingdom, taking his place on the throne. He then proclaimed a general pardon, and the city settled down, with the people content to obey his orders.

' "He then ordered it to be proclaimed that whoever brought me to him could have whatever he wanted, and he made an energetic search for me in many places. For my part, I stayed with the black man for ten days, during which he never left me, night or day. This vexed me; I lost patience and wanted to free myself from him. One day I left him sleeping and went around the house, where I found a rope. I took this and put it round his neck without him noticing it in his drunken sleep. I started to choke him and, sensing this, he woke and shouted for help, drumming his heels, while I tightened the noose until he died.

' "The neighbours had heard his cry and they burst in to find him dead, with me sitting weeping and wailing for him. 'By the Lord of the Ka'ba,' they exclaimed, 'this is 'Arus al-'Ara'is!' After this they took hold of me and, leaving the dead man where he was, they brought me to al-Yasr. When he saw me he prostrated himself to God, before smiling at me and saying: ''Arus al-'Ara'is, you are beautiful and desirable, but the blessings of this world are more attractive than you.'

' "He immediately summoned carpenters and told them to make him a big chest, which was to be lined inside and out with pitch. The townspeople knew about me and were eager to blame him, saying: 'O king, if you take 'Arus al-'Ara'is back into your palace, we shall no longer obey you, for since the day she was born we have seen no good from her but only trouble and care.' He told them not to worry, adding: 'I swore that if she fell into my hands I would not spare her life and I shall throw her into the sea. Whoever wants to watch can come to the shore.'

' "He brought out the chest, put me into it and locked it, after which he had me carried to the shore and every single person in the city came out to watch, setting up canopies to shield them from the heat. I was put on board a boat which sailed ten parasangs away from the city, after which the crew threw me into the sea and went back. I could not move in the box and the waves tossed it to and fro until they brought me to this green sea. It was there that the black *jinni* whom I killed came across it and he dragged it to the shore, without knowing what was in it.

' "When he had opened it he took me out and was astonished by my beauty. He muttered words that I could not understand, before leaving me and going off. Some time later he came back with a large quantity of delicious fruits of all kinds, the like of which I had never tasted or seen. There was also a fat ram which he slaughtered with a knife and whose flesh he cut up and cooked after starting a fire. He fed me and I ate until I was full and I drank water after which he started to dally and play with me until he fell on top of me and I let him take me.

' "For a time I stayed on the island with him, and then one day he brought this glass chest. He put me in it and fastened it shut, after which he threw me into the sea and started to take me round the seas and islands with him, showing me remarkable sights and wonders. I could understand what he said, as he spoke and acted like a human, and one day he sat telling me about the wonders of the sea and what was in the islands. He told me that on a certain island there was a huge quantity of red sand which, when the sun rose over it, turned to fire that would burn any creature that passed. When I heard this, it made me want to burn up my city and everyone in it.

' "For some days I changed my behaviour towards the *jinni* and scowled at him, although before that we had been on friendly terms and I had been in the habit of flirting with him and showing affection. He said: 'Light of my eyes, why is it that I see you frowning at me and acting differently? I have not been used to this, and if there is something that you want or need, tell me and don't hide it, for I shall get you whatever you want.'

' " 'I have been thinking of my cousin and how badly he treated me,' I told him, 'as well as how all the people of my city came together to have me thrown into the sea in the chest from which you rescued me. I want to pay them back for the evil that they did.' 'What do you want?' he said, and I told him: 'Fill this chest with the sand that you talked about and then shut it. You and I can climb to the top of the mountain beside the city and we can then scatter the sand over it all at night when the people are asleep. Next morning when the sun gets hot they will all be burned, and no single one of them will survive.'

' "He exclaimed disapprovingly: 'There will be good people amongst them as well as children and old men, together with beasts.' 'They are evil,' I told him, 'and this has to be done if I am ever going to love you again. There is no one there that I think about or worry about.' After a time he raised his head and told me that I could be happy again, as he would do it.

' "He left me for a time and then came back with the chest filled with sand. 'Get up, lady,' he said, 'for I have done what you wanted.' Together we went to the city, arriving there at night, and we scattered all the sand that we had over it, until we had done everything that we wanted. Next morning when the sun rose and it began to get hot the fire spread through the city and burned it all, as we sat watching on the mountain. 'Now I am happy and satisfied,' I said, and I came back here filled with joy and contentment.

' "The *jinni* was in the habit of leaving me on the island and going off around the seas and the other islands to tell me about them. When I had no one and nothing to see I would often become discontented and so I used to go for walks. One day, when the *jinni* had gone off and I was doing this, I came across a weeping man with torn clothes standing by the sea shore. He was young and handsome, and I went up to him and greeted him. 'What has happened to you?' I asked, 'and how do you come to be here? Tell me the truth and don't hide anything from me, for I am a human like you.'

' "When he heard this, his fears were calmed, and he said: 'Yesterday I was on board a ship which was carrying many merchants on their way from China. I fell asleep near the ship's side and this morning I found myself here. What happened or how I came here I don't know, and, as you can see, I am filled with dismay.' I told him to relax and have no fear, adding that I had a *jinni* friend with whom I lived, but I would not tell him about the castaway or where he was and I would try to find a place on the high ground where he and I could stay eating and drinking while the *jinni* was away, until God released us both.

' "He calmed down and was happy as I took him by the hand and showed him the spring, bringing him quantities of fruit and grilled fish. He ate and drank, after which he regained his spirits and asked me to lie with him, which, to his delight, I agreed to do. I hid him in a particular spot on the island, where I used to visit him.

' "Later when I was eating and drinking with the *jinni* and I was toying with him, I told him that I had a question for him, and when he asked what it was I said: 'A young servant of mine was sitting near the side of a ship at sea and one night he was snatched away. I don't know how this was or who did it, but after a time he came back safe and sound. Do you know of anyone who was carried off from a ship without knowing how?' 'Yes,' he said; 'he must have been taken by a bear-like creature called a *mibqar*, which comes up to ships when they are under way with their sails set. It swims alongside and, before anyone can detect it, it seizes any sleeping young man, putting its arms beneath his spine without his noticing. It then transfers him, sunk in sleep, to its back and takes him to an island. It goes to another beast like an ape, which comes to the man while he is still asleep and kills him as best it can, cutting his throat and drinking his blood. After eating his flesh it buries him in the sand. It must have been this beast that removed your servant, although he managed to escape.'

' "One day, when the *jinni* had gone off, I went to the young man and ate and drank with him, but while we were enjoying the greatest pleasure, I heard the sound of the *jinni* muttering as he came towards the place where I was, looking for me. I was afraid lest he come and disapprove of my being there so I told the young man to shelter in an overgrown spot that the *jinni* would find impenetrable. Then I went to the *jinni*, exclaiming: 'Oh my eyes!' and pretending to have just woken up. I was trembling with fear, as he didn't believe that I had been asleep there, and so he prowled around. He got to where the young man had taken shelter but when he found that he could not get in to search it he came back and walked around me for a time before leaving.

' "I felt sure in my heart that he had gone to fetch fire to set the place alight – as in fact he did – but meanwhile I had called to the young man, who had come out in a state of fright. I showed him the way that would take him to the furthest point of the island, telling him to hurry off and hide himself there before the *jinni* returned. Soon after he had gone the *jinni* came back holding something coloured like resin that I didn't recognize. When he set it alight it blazed up like sulphur, and, in spite of the fact that the thicket was damp, I was amazed at how in no time at all it had caught fire. 'What is this fire?' I asked, and he told me that he had become suspicious of me when he saw me sleeping here. 'I shall sleep with you by the spring,' I told him, and he kissed my head, my eye and my body, offering an excuse, which I accepted.

' "For some days I stayed with him but when he left I would go off to the young man and eat and drink with him. Then one day, when the *jinni* was away and I had gone to visit the young man, I found him lying under a tree at the end of the island. His face was black and his nose, lips, ears and penis had been cut off. He was weeping and wailing, and when I asked him what had happened he said: 'Lady, when you left me these last days I was lonely and felt sad. One night I climbed this tree and fell asleep until the moon rose and the stars came out. Just then out of the sea emerged the most beautiful girl. She was fair-complexioned with small eyes and ears that were almost invisible. She had no fingers and no buttocks while her hair was softer than silk. I stared at her in astonishment as she played on the shore, singing in a lovely voice words that I could not understand and dancing most beautifully. Then she came under my tree and threw herself down, stretching out to sleep. When she was quite still, I was overcome by a lustful urge to lie with her, so I climbed down and threw myself on top of her as she slept. She woke up and began to struggle violently, hissing in my face like a cat. So strongly did she struggle that I could not satisfy my lust, and she slipped from my hands like a fish from the hand of a fisherman, but in spite of this I had managed to take her by force before she finally escaped me and dived into the sea.

' " 'In the morning I was filled with passionate regret that she had managed to get away and I spent the day filled with sorrowful thoughts, finding no pleasure in food or drink. Yesterday, however, before I knew it, there she was again, doing what she had done on the first night and going to sleep under the tree. I told myself that if she had not liked what I had done before, she would not have come back, and I had no doubt that this night she would let me lie with her.

' " 'My lust increased, stirred up by Iblis, and I climbed down and approached her, only to have her seize hold of me and call out, at which some twenty others like her emerged from the sea. They surrounded me and began to beat me until I fainted. Then each of them started to bite me. One ate my right ear and another my left; the very first one ate my testicles and another my nose, after which they all dived into the sea and went off, leaving me here in the state you can see.'

' "I was furiously angry with him for having betrayed me by lusting for someone else, so I left him without a word and went back filled with evil thoughts. When the *jinni* returned I told him where the man was and incited him to kill him. 'Let me take him back to civilization and return him to his own country,' said the *jinni*, but I told him that he had tried to rape me. This infuriated the *jinni*, who went to him and, taking him by his feet and his clothes, hurled him into the sea.

' "While I was staying with the *jinni*, one day, when he was sitting and telling me about the marvels of the sea and its islands, he told me about a bird like a swift whose excrement if applied to the eyes would produce instant blindness, while on another island was a tree whose fruit, if eaten by a woman, would cause her to give birth to a son. He told me of herbs that would harm men and others that would help against every illness, of a type of kohl that would clear the sight and another that would blind it.

' "I was astonished by what I heard and I was impressed by what he told me. I wanted to see the island and its marvellous plants so that I could take them with me when I went back to civilized lands, but when I told him that I wanted him to take me there he exclaimed in horror, telling me that a *marid* who lived there was his enemy. He could not go to the *marid*'s island and neither could the *marid* come to his without his knowledge. 'Are you afraid?' I asked him, adding: 'I have almost given up faith in you.' I went on pestering him until he put me in the glass box and set off on the sea with me.

' "I asked him how the box was made and how it was that when it was shut no one knew how to open it. He agreed to tell me and said: 'There was a king called al-Hulaifi', the son of al-Munkadir, who had a profound knowledge of the wonders of magic. He wanted to build a coastal city for himself but, for all the time he spent on it, whatever he put up by day lay in ruins in the morning. He did not know what to do and was plunged in grief. Then, as he spent a night by the shore, he caught sight of variously coloured creatures, some with human faces and bodies like fish, some with heads like bulls and bodies like donkeys and some with heads like pigs and hands like men. Some resembled elephants with heads of snakes and others were like men but had only one leg and tails like sheep. When they ran, nothing could catch them. It was God alone who could count how many of these there were. The king saw them coming out of the sea and going round the buildings, removing stone after stone and throwing them into the sea until there was nothing left.

' " 'When he saw this he realized what was wrong and he remained keeping a cautious watch until he managed to catch a mermaid. He treated her gently and with courtesy, doing her no harm but asking her about the beasts he had seen and how he could get rid of them. She agreed to tell him how to do this in return for her freedom. The king, however, did not understand enough of her language and so he summoned a servant of his who had been sent to him as a present from the Indian islands. He asked the man whether he knew this type of creature and when the man said that he did, as there were many of them in his own country, the king asked if he understood what the mermaid was saying.

' " 'The man said: "She is telling you to make twenty glass chests, each containing the likeness of an owl. Put them in the sea, and when the creatures see them they will flee from them and not return." The king was surprised by this but he released the mermaid and when he had done what she said he never saw the creatures coming back again. He finished building his city, which is still there to this day and is known as Alexandria.' In the course of his wanderings amongst the seas and the islands my *jinni* found one of these boxes and removed the owl from it. This is it and he used to put me in it and take me round with him wherever he went.

' "One day he took me to the island of whose wonders he had told me. When we got there I saw that this was a verdant and well-wooded place with beautiful plants and strange birds with uncommon songs. When we got to the centre of it we could see something like a black mountain, the size of an elephant or bigger, with hair covering its face and eyes like blazing fire. It was coming towards us, and when my companion saw it he turned to me and said: 'Take this ring and put it on your finger.' Before he had finished speaking the *marid* came running towards me but when he saw me gesturing with the ring he turned from me to my companion, who closed with him, giving a great shout and muttering like the *marid*.

' "They began to exchange blows and kept on shouting, biting and tearing at each other with blood flowing from them both as the island shook thanks to the violence of their struggle. I had climbed a high tree, from which I watched them, and I had almost despaired of my companion and of my own life thanks to what I could see of the terrible *marid*. But then the *jinni* managed to take him by surprise and threw him down, not leaving him until he was dead.

' "I hurried down from the tree to see what had happened to the *jinni* and when I got near him, being unable to speak, he pointed to a nearby tree. I realized that he wanted something from it that he could eat and, as it had no fruit, I picked some of its leaves, which looked like those of a nettle. When I took them to him he started to eat, and then got up and stretched himself. I congratulated him on his safety, and he said: 'By God, had he not fallen because his foot slipped he would have killed me.'

' "I then asked him whether there was anything else there of which he was afraid. He told me that the only thing he feared and which could injure him was a rat-like creature known as a *daran*, which lived on one of the islands in a cave a mile away from the foot of a mountain. This was the bane of *jinn* and had killed others before him, including his own father.

' "I asked how he had done this and he told me: 'My father was an *'ifrit* who lived alone on this island. He had been in the habit of sinking passing ships until, when he had gone too far in his insolence, God used the *daran* to destroy him. They were miserably small things that people would think contemptible but they could destroy *jinn*. When they smelled a *jinni* they would jump on to him and attach themselves to his skin and they would go on nibbling at his flesh and sucking at the skin until they finished him off, even if he were the strongest and most nobly formed of his kind, leaving him no escape. There were hordes of them, outnumbering ants.

' " 'A ship with many merchants on board had come to the island, and they had landed to look for water or fruit. The *daran* hurried on board, looking for something to eat, and, although the sailors gathered to fight them with sticks and stones, the *daran* eventually got the better of them all and ate all that they had, including their provisions and even their clothes. They gnawed through the ropes, and with no ropes and no sails, all of which had been eaten, the ship was at the mercy of the sea, with those on board weeping and lamenting what had befallen them.

' " 'The ship happened to pass the island where I lived in my youth with my father. I was not with him at the time or else I would have been killed, for when he saw the ship pitching to and fro, he wanted to eat those on board. He went out to it and after pulling it towards him he attacked it in order to seize someone, but when the *daran* caught his scent, they swarmed over him, body, head and shoulders. He threw himself down and started rolling in the sand. It was just then that I arrived but when I saw him writhing there looking like a hedgehog thanks to the *daran* that were sticking to him I stayed at a distance watching. All the *daran* left the ship to come to him, and those on board were then free of them, but as all their ropes and their sails had been eaten they were tossed hither and thither by the waves. My father, who had been left lying on the sand, was so completely devoured that nothing was left of him at all.

' " 'The sight of this terrified me and as the *daran* spread over the island after finishing with my father I made off and came here. I realized that God had punished my father for his excesses, but since I met you I have begun to act as wickedly as he did by killing people and I'm afraid that God may punish me, since you made me destroy a city filled with people and animals.' I told him that, when his father had been attacked by the *daran*, had he thrown himself into the sea, no harm would have come to him, and they would have been drowned.

'"This was a mistake on my part, as I had never given good advice to anyone and had never told the *jinni* anything like this. 'By God, that is right,' he said, 'and had my father realized that, he would not have come to any harm but would still be alive and well.' I then left him for a time until he had forgotten what I had told him. I made a great collection of leaves and plants, which I have with me in bundles, and I cannot properly describe all that I saw on the island.

'"After that we both went back to our own island, where we stayed contentedly for some time. One day, when the *jinni* had gone off as usual, leaving me alone, I was walking there dejectedly under the trees, picking the best fruits, when suddenly I caught sight of ten armed men with water-skins and ropes coming through the trees. When I saw them I realized that their ship must have anchored off the island and that they had come ashore to look for water.

'"The sight of me alarmed them, but I was not frightened of them, as I realized that they were humans like me, whereas they thought that I was one of the *jinn*. They turned to run away, but I called out to them that nothing would harm them as I too was a human. I added that I had a strange tale to tell and explained that I had been on the island with a *jinni* for a number of years but that he had gone away the day before. I was unhappy with my lot and I asked them to take me with them wherever they were going.

'"When they heard this they came back to me and said: 'We have about three hundred merchants and a large number of other passengers on board and we have anchored off the coast here. Guide us to water so that we can fill our skins, and we will then take you with us and treat you well until we can bring you to your own country.' 'Come on, then, and I'll lead you to water,' I told them, saying to myself: 'How long am I going to stay with the *jinni*? He won't know what has happened to me, as there are so many lands in this sea, and it is time to go back to civilization.'

'"After looking at my beauty, they went off to talk to each other. 'Tell me what you're doing,' I said, at which they asked me my name. I told them, and they said: 'By God, 'Arus, you are beautiful, and each one of us is filled with desire for you. We are going to take you to a ship crowded with people where none of us will be able to get to you. We shall be full of regret and so we would like you to satisfy us now.' 'You could ask for nothing easier than that,' I told them when I heard this; 'Here I am, so do what you want with me.'

' "In their delight they began to kiss me, and I went off with them one after another, but while they were sitting with me my *jinni* appeared, towering over their heads. He took the man who was with me and tore him in half and although the others fled away he seized the leg of the dead man and used it to kill them all. Then he came back to me, frothing like a lion or a great angry camel, and he struck me on the thigh with a blow that removed some of my flesh. At this I despaired of my life, but I pretended to cry and said: 'It wasn't my fault. I'm a woman, and they were men. They forced me, and I could not resist.'

' "When the *jinni* heard this he believed me and took pity on me. He fetched me some dry leaves, telling me to put them on my wound, and when I did the blood stopped and the pain left me. He rushed towards the ship and when he was opposite it he shouted so loudly that both it and the island shook. He then struck it with his hand, plunging it into the sea and drowning everyone on board.

' "I stayed with him but I felt angry, while he excused himself and tried to conciliate me. I wanted to be shown the wonders of the sea and what God, Great and Glorious, had created in it, and so one day he took me by the hand and led me up the black mountain with the arch through which the water pours. When we had climbed the summit ridge I could see the world with its islands stretched out beneath me.

' "There was something there that baffled me, and I turned to the *jinni* and asked him what it was that I was looking at in the island. He told me that it was a river of sand beside the fire mountain, whose rocks would burn at night. We went to where we could see it pouring into the sea, huge, high and frightening, and we then went on for three parasangs until we came to a vast peninsula that lay beneath the mountain. In it were houses, huts and dwellings where I could see innumerable people coming and going. They had hairy ears like those of horses and they were making a great noise. The mountain on one side of it was so smooth that not even an ant could climb on it, while on the other side was the sea.

' "I was frightened at the sight of so many people. I had never seen anything like it before and although I had been with the *jinni* for about ten years he had never shown the place to me. I asked him whether the people there were humans or *jinn*. He told me that a *jinn* king had taken a mortal girl from the *zanj* and had brought her up until she reached maturity. It then became clear that she was pregnant, although he had never slept with her. This distressed him, as he realized that she must have betrayed him, and he exiled her to this spot, from which there is no way of out, and whoever sails past it drowns. The girl gave birth to twins, a boy and a girl, and she then lived like an animal, eating the fruits of these trees. When the boy grew up he lay with his sister and his mother. This was a long time ago, but it is from that girl that all these people are descended.

' "I asked him how they managed to live and what they ate. He said: 'God, the Great and Glorious, shows kindness to His servants and has created for them an immense and terrifying fish which He throws up for them every year and on which they live until the next year.

' " "When a ship is wrecked the waves throw up to them the drowned corpses from the arch through which you came. It was God Almighty Who brought you to this island, and had you gone on to them they would have eaten you. I have praised Him for having saved you and I remain full of wonder.'

' "I said to her: 'What happened to you after that?' She said: 'We went back to our island and I stayed thinking about how I could escape. I remembered the *daran* that the *jinni* had told me about and I said to myself that there was nothing else I could use and that he would have forgotten what I had said to him. So I went up to him flirtatiously one day and said: 'My friend, you have shown me every marvel, but there is one thing that I dearly want to see with my own eyes and that is the *daran*.' 'I can't go to that island,' he told me, 'for the *daran* are the only things I fear.' I went on flattering and pressing him and I asked if he could show them to me from a distance. At first he said he could not, but I went on urging him, saying that I wanted to see them flying at him, until he reluctantly agreed.

' "He put me in the chest and threw it into the sea, after which he took me round island after island until we reached one of enormous size, on to which we climbed. He had released me from the chest and he told me: 'Go on straight ahead by yourself and you will see the *daran* asleep. Take a look and then come back.' 'I daren't go on my own,' I said, and I started inciting and encouraging him and leading him on bit by bit until I could see a *daran*. It was a terrifying sight as it lay there asleep, looking like a rat with a long snout and saw-like teeth. When we were getting close, I kept talking to distract him, but at a distance of twenty paces the creature smelled him and darted at him faster than the blink of an eye.

'"It was only the *jinni* whom it attacked, and it didn't approach me. More and more of them kept coming and getting on to him, until he was almost completely covered. He threw himself on the ground and began rolling round in the sand, shrieking. When I saw this I thought that he was bound to die and so I went up to watch. When I had got close I shed tears in a pretence of grief, and the sight of me seemed to remind him of what I had told him, so he threw himself into the sea. By the time I came running up behind him he had disappeared underwater, and the *daran* came up to the surface and every last one of them dead.

'"I stayed alone on the island for three nights and days, going around, eating the fruits and drinking from the springs. I had given up hope for the *jinni*, but then on the fourth day I heard him calling to me. I went up and wept over him, saying: 'What happened to you, and where have you been these days? Tell me.' 'Damn you,' he said, 'didn't I tell you that these things were fatal to me? But for your advice to throw myself into the sea I would have been killed, but when I dived down they left me. I then went to my family and stayed with them for these last days until I came hurrying back to you lest you be distressed about me and say: "He has left me on my own."'

'"One day I asked whether there was anything he had to guard against, and he told me that the only thing he had to fear was something engraved with one of the Names of God, especially if this were applied to the parting of his hair, as it would kill him.

'"When I heard this I stored it away in my heart and when he was asleep or absent I used to cry out: 'My Lord, how am I to find one of your Names so that I can win free from this island and this *jinni*?' This went on until God brought you to me and you gave me your ring. I put it on the parting of his hair before cutting his throat while he slept, as you saw for yourself.

'"This is the whole of my story from beginning to end. I have told it to you so that if you take me it will be in full knowledge of my evil wiles and what I have done to others. Otherwise, you can go off alone and in safety, for there is a way for you to escape back to your own country, while these pearls will enrich both you and your children's children till the end of time. You can leave me here alone until God's judgement is fulfilled, for He is the best of judges."'

'When I had heard her story I stayed looking at her in amazement, thinking about what she had told me, but love and desire got the better of me, and I longed to take her with me. "How can I leave behind such unparalleled loveliness?" I asked myself. "I could never do this even if it means my death. She may have repented of her evil deeds, and if I am good to her it will put right what is wrong." But then I told myself: "Damn you! This is a woman formed by nature to do harm, with an inborn disposition for treachery, guile, evil-doing and wickedness. You heard what she told you and you know what the astrologers said about her to her father. It was all true; she admitted everything that she did; she showed no pity for her mother; she did not help her father, but she brought down great men and had virgins raped. After all this destructiveness, how can she suit you, who are neither the most manly nor the handsomest of men?" I told myself that she would not be right for me, nor I for her, and she would not look after me as a decent man should be looked after.

'I stayed silent for a time, looking down at the ground in perplexity, plunged in thought, but no one can escape his destiny, and love got the better of me. She stayed silent, looking at me, and I said: "Lady, I cannot bring myself to abandon you. God has given you to me, and it is through you that I shall win free and escape." I told her to take heart, repeating that I would never abandon her and telling her that if Almighty God brought me safely home, I would prefer her to all my family and treat her as well as she could wish, adding that she should put her trust in me.

'When she heard this 'Arus got up and collected all the useful things she had got ready for herself on the island. They filled more than ten bundles, each given a mark of its own, although I did not know what use they served, and she brought out pearls and jewels that I had never seen before. She then told me to walk behind her, and we went on until we had reached the coast. "Jump in after me," she said, "for there are places where you can wade and places where you can't. Take care not to stray."

'She took off her clothes and rolled them up in one of her bundles, which she held above the water, and she then started to wade, with me behind her, until we reached a huge island. When we got out of the water she put her clothes back on and sat waiting for me. We then started to walk along the coast, which we did every day from morning until evening, when we would stop for the night. We found plenty of trees and fruits on the way but we only came across water once every five days, more or less. When we reached a spring we would drink, bathe and relax for the rest of the day, and this went on for twenty days.

'On the twenty-first day we came on an old black man, who had moored a light boat while he wandered around the shore gathering oysters and pearls to store in the boat. When she was near, 'Arus jumped in and took her seat in it, telling me to be quick and join her. When I got in, she raised the anchor and put out to sea. The old man had been at a distance but when he saw us he came running up, shouting to us to take him with us, or else he would die of hunger and thirst.

''Arus did not look round as he was crying out for help, although I was asking her to take him with us, but she neither did this nor answered me. I went on insisting, as I was sorry for the man, but she said: "Keep quiet and don't interfere with me. This boat can only take one or two." We were quickly out of sight of him, but when we got to an inhabited coast I asked her to wait while I went back to pick him up, as we didn't want to kill him. "Damn you – meddle!" she told me."If he was the only man I had killed, I would be the happiest person on earth. Come with me and leave him, God damn him, for if you abandon me you shall never see me again."

'We went on by stages, passing cities and towns, until I got back home. I made for the house of my mother, who was a good old woman enjoying a prosperous life. I knocked at the door, and she came out and said: "Who are you?" "Your son," I told her. She embraced me, and I entered the house with 'Arus. My mother asked: "Who is this beautiful lady?" I said: "Mother, give thanks to God. This is my rescuer, and it is thanks to her that I am looking at you." I then told her the story, keeping back all 'Arus's misdeeds. My mother approved of her, recognizing her value and doing all she could for her.

'I then put on my own clothes and went to my own house in which was my wife with the son whom I had left when he was one year old. They had not noticed me before I knocked at the door, and my three-year-old son came out, and I embraced him joyfully. My wife gave me the best of welcomes, and when people heard, they started to come and greet me.

After ten days of rest, I wanted to do some business with the king of the city so that I might become one of his agents, as I had made up my mind never to put to sea again. I had decided to spend one day with my first wife and the next with 'Arus, whom I had married when I came back to my mother. In this way we passed five pleasant months.

'Then one night I thought about what 'Arus had told me and what she had done, and this made me feel disgust for her. As a result I began to avoid her, spending only one night in ten with her and turning to my first wife and my son. When 'Arus noticed this she went to my mother and told her that I was not keeping faith with her or repaying her for what she had done with me, and that she did not know why this was. My mother kept this to herself and did not tell me about it.

'As Providence had decreed, the only child of the king of my city was a beautiful girl of whom he was very fond. She was attacked by an illness which led her to eat the flesh of her own arms, as a result of which he kept her in chains. There was no doctor or sorcerer who did not visit her, but none of them knew how to cure her or could do her any good. He was so distressed that he kept away from all his subjects, both high and low, because of his concern for her, and I shared his sorrow.

'My mother came to see me one evening to cheer me by her conversation and she began to talk to me about 'Arus, blaming me for my behaviour and asking why I was not going to see her every day. She told me that this was having a bad effect on her and leading her to complain thanks to the love she felt for me. "Is this the way you reward her for the good that she did?" she asked.

'She went on talking about this until I told her that I had not given up going to her because of harshness or hatred, as she was still dear to me, but because I was preoccupied with the sorrows of the king. My mother repeated this to 'Arus, who told her to tell me that she had an instant cure for the princess and were she to visit her she could cure her, and the king would honour and promote me. I remembered the drugs that she had and I went to ask her whether what she had told my mother was true. "Yes," she said, "so take me to the palace and tell this to the king, for I will treat the princess and cure her at once."

'I went off filled with happiness and, after asking permission, I was allowed to speak to the king, whom I told that I had with me someone who could cure his daughter. He said that if this was true he would raise me to the highest rank and give me anything in the world that I wanted. He then told me to produce this doctor quickly, and I went back home and told 'Arus to dress and come with me.

'She did this, and I took her to the king, who went up to her and asked if what I had told him was true. "Yes, O king," she said, "and you can be happy to know that I will cure your daughter." He was delighted and told her to go to the princess, whose maids gave her the warmest of welcomes.

'For my part, I stayed with the king, but when 'Arus entered the palace I began to regret having brought her to the princess, asking myself: "Has this damned woman ever helped anyone that she should help me?" I began to tremble with fear, feeling in my heart that there was something wrong. I wanted to tell the king to remove her, but I was afraid that if I did he might be angry with me.

'A curtain separated the king's assembly room from the place where his daughter was, and we could hear all that was going on. We heard 'Arus chanting spells over the princess, using words that we did not know and could not understand, while the maids who were there with her were weeping. As soon as 'Arus had finished, the princess quietened down and then fell into a soundless sleep, although before that she had not been able to rest or to sleep for a single hour. All her attendants were delighted, as was the king when the good news reached him. He ordered that I be given a reward and presented me with a splendid robe of honour as well as a great quantity of money.

'When 'Arus was about to leave, she passed a sealed packet to the princess's mother and said: "Your daughter is asleep just now, and I shall come back tomorrow with another spell. Meanwhile, as she sleeps, anoint each of her eyes with a single touch of what is in this packet, and if you want to use it yourself, you will find it helpful."

'When I heard this from the other side of the curtain, I thought of the bird dung that she had with her which would produce blindness, and I swore to myself that this must be what she was going to do. I wanted to tell the king but I felt something stopping me and shutting my mouth. I tried to delude myself into thinking that this might be something else, as why should she do this when there was no hostility between the princess and her? I did not really think she would use the dung, but I still remained frightened.

'When 'Arus came out the king gave her a robe of honour and promised to reward her when his daughter had fully recovered. She left before me, as I stayed for a time with the king before returning home. I was met by my mother, who asked me about 'Arus. "Hasn't she come?" I said. "No, by God," said my mother. "I haven't seen her." I told her to go and look, as I was troubled, and her attention might have been distracted by looking at people on her way home. When I searched and still could not find her I passed a wretched night filled with concern.

'Next morning I went to my mother's apartment and asked her about 'Arus. "I've not set eyes on her since she left me yesterday," she said, and I told her that this disappearance meant no good. Then suddenly, while

I was there, twenty servants with clubs in their hands broke down the door and said: "The king wants you."

'My heart stood still; my wits deserted me, and I was sure that this was the end. I went with them like a dead man, despairing of life because 'Arus had gone. I then heard them whispering to each other and asking whether they had anything left of that ointment that produces blindness. When I heard this, I was sure that the princess and her mother had both been blinded.

'They brought me to the king, who was sitting on his throne with a drawn sword in one hand with the other held to his cheek. He and all those around him were weeping and showing obvious signs of distress. When I stood before him he looked at me, as I was trembling like a palm leaf on a stormy day. "Damn you!" he said to me; "what led you to bring me a woman whom you claimed would be able to cure my daughter? Thanks to her both my daughter and her mother have been blinded. Why did you do this when I had shown you no hostility for which you might have wanted to repay me?" "By God Almighty," I told him, "I only wanted the princess to be cured, and this is what the woman told me she could do." I wanted to tell him about 'Arus, but he would not let me speak and told me to fetch her immediately or he would have me killed and burned.

'He put ten of his men in charge of me, and for three days I went around the city without finding any trace of her. His men took me back to him and told him how eager I had been to get hold of her. He ordered my eyes to be plucked out, and when they started with my right eye I cried for help and told him the story of 'Arus from beginning to end. When they heard it his courtiers asked him to show me mercy, and he allowed me to keep my left eye but sent out to seize all the wealth and property that I owned, ordering me to leave the city at once.

'I left with my mother, my wife and my son, and we went through various towns begging until we got to a large and populous city, where we sheltered for the night in a mosque, hungry, tired and in a miserable condition. Next morning we went out to beg, and people helped us with alms until we were able to rent a house in which to live.

'One day my mother went on some errand to the market, where unexpectedly she came across the damned 'Arus, who was in the best and most prosperous of states. On seeing my mother she greeted her tearfully and started to kiss her hands, but my mother kept her distance and said: "Damn you, you repaid us by ruining us and reducing us to poverty." "I made a mistake with that drug," 'Arus said, "and I fled away for fear of the king, but I didn't do it on purpose. Tell me what happened to you after that and how your son escaped from the king. My only concern has been for him."

'My mother believed her and accepted her excuse. "The king had my son's right eye plucked out," she told her, "but the courtiers interceded for him, and the king let him go free, although he took all our wealth and exiled us. We have just arrived here without any worldly possessions at all." 'Arus slapped herself on the face, showing all the signs of sorrow, and she then took my mother to her own house, showing her goods, wealth and obvious signs of prosperity and telling her: "You can be happy as all this belongs to your son, so arrange for us to meet. You know how much I love him. What happened was decreed by Providence, and God will reward him and give him a greater return. I have more jewels and pearls than any king can collect and I shall spend all this on you."

'She provided food for my mother who ate, and she went on talking until my mother was reconciled with her and kissed her head. My mother then came to me and told me that she had been with 'Arus. "I met her," she said, "and she greeted me and treated me hospitably." "May God not give her life or bring her near me!" I exclaimed, but my mother said: "God has brought her near, and she did nothing wrong. She swore to me that the mistake she made with the drug was unintentional, and this is something natural to us all. She loves you and sorrows for you, while all the wealth that she has is at your disposal." "This is some new trick of hers," I said. "Leave her, mother, may God curse her, for I'm afraid of her evil wiles and her treachery." "Shame the devil; accept what I say and don't disobey me," she replied.

'She went on at me until I was made to turn to 'Arus. When she caught sight of me she got up and made a display of love and compassion, promising me all manner of good things, giving me splendid clothes and providing me with money. I stayed with her for a time, enjoying the most pleasant of lives.

'One night 'Arus approached my mother and said: "The king of this city is a prosperous man, and I hear that he has a daughter who is both beautiful and generous. He is so jealous of her reputation that he has given her a palace of her own, with nobody there but the maids who look after her. I think that you should take these pearls and ask her to accept them from you, as, if she likes them, she will give you many times more than they are worth. Things are not easy for us, as your son has no work, and we have expenses but no income."

'My mother was pleased by this and took ten pearls, which she asked one of the princess's ladies to take to her, saying that they had come as a gift. She continued to show such courtesy that she was taken to the princess, whom she told that she had seen no one else who deserved to have the pearls and asking her to accept them, which she did. My mother then stayed with her until the end of the day, amazing her with tales of the wonders of the seas. The princess told her to come back and visit her every day. My mother did this and would bring us back food and drink so that we lived well.

'Every day 'Arus would pass on a story to her, which she would tell to the princess as they talked in the evening. Then one day 'Arus asked my mother to let her go there herself, saying that the princess would be impressed by her stories and be even more generous to them. "Mention me to her," she said, and when my mother had done this the princess asked her to bring 'Arus. 'Arus then began to entertain her with tales of wonders and marvels, that were better than those my mother could tell, and these so captivated her that 'Arus would stay with her all through the day.

'One day the princess told her that as night was the pleasantest time for conversation she should spend it with her. 'Arus said: "Lady, I have a husband whom I love dearly and I cannot bear to be parted from him for a single hour. If you want me to spend the night with you, then let me bring him with me disguised as a woman and put him in a side room. Then I can sit and talk with you and when you go to sleep I can sleep with him."

'The princess agreed to let her do this, and she came to tell me to get up so that she could take me with her to pass the night in the palace. I could not disobey her, and so I went with her as she took me there, and after that I used to spend every night with her, and in the morning we would leave and go back home.

'One day, when she was eating with the princess, she crushed up over her food a drug that causes spontaneous pregnancy. The princess ate it, at which she conceived, and her belly became swollen. Her father was revolted by the sight and asked the servant who it was who visited his daughter. He was told that two women used to spend the evenings talking to her and going off by day. He told the man to let him and him alone know when they came, but 'Arus was too wily to allow anything to be kept from her and when she knew that the king had found out about his daughter's pregnancy she wanted to involve my mother and me and escape punishment herself. So she told my mother to take me with her to talk to the princess that evening, giving her a marvellous story to tell. "What's wrong with you tonight?" my mother asked, at which she said that she was not feeling well and if the two of us went she would join us in the morning.

'When my mother and I got to the palace the servant went to tell the king, who hurried up to us, sword in hand, and said to his daughter: "Damn you, who is with you?" She was startled and amazed, and the king went to the room, from which he brought out my mother and me. He saw that, while my mother was an old woman, I was a man. "Damn you," he said, "is it you who impregnated my daughter?"

'He went on striking his daughter with his sword until he had cut her in pieces. To me he said: "If I kill you that would not be enough to satisfy me but in the morning I shall see to your punishment." He had me taken away and thrown into prison. That night, however, he died of grief, and another man succeeded to his throne.

'At the end of the year I was freed, and I went off to look for my mother and my family, whom I found in the worst of states. I asked my mother about 'Arus, and she told me that she had not seen her for a year. She had hired a place in a quarter inhabited by people of blameless characters and she had placed a black servant at her door, giving out that she had no husband.

'One day, when I was sitting and thinking about my affairs, my mother came up to me. "I have seen 'Arus," she told me. "She said that she had made a mistake in the drug and she gave me money, for she wants to make it up with you." "Don't listen to what she says," I replied, "for she feels she must destroy me." But my mother insisted that 'Arus had excused herself and that I would have to be reconciled with her. She brought us together and produced food. We ate and drank, talking through the night until dawn, but when I got up to go, she clutched at me and called out to the neighbours that I had assaulted her.

'They came up and said: "Enemy of God, did you attack this woman?" After giving me a painful beating they handed me over to the police chief and testified to the assault, at which he punished me and threw me into prison. My mother went to 'Arus, whom she found in tears. When she asked her about me, 'Arus said: "He mentioned his wife to me and got up to go. I was seized with jealousy and so I took hold of him and cried out, at which the neighbours came in. They hurled abuse at him and took him off to prison, but don't be distressed. As long as he is there I shall give you all you want."

'I stayed in prison for a year and when I got out I went in search of my mother and my family. On my way I met a woman splendidly dressed and riding on a donkey, preceded by a black servant. When she saw me she told the man to be sure to bring me to her. He caught up with me and took me by the hand, saying: "My lady wants you." I thought that this might be someone who wanted to do me an act of charity that might bring her reward in the next world and so I went off with the servant, who took me to a villa. When I entered the hall and stood in front of the lady, she unveiled herself, and to my dismay she turned out to be 'Arus.

'"Do you recognize me?" she asked. "How could I not recognize you," I said, "when you are 'Arus, the king's daughter? What reward do I have from you?" "Don't talk so much," she said; "I cannot enjoy life when I see you walking around. Go back so that I can see that you stay in prison for the rest of your life. I shall look after you and your family, but be sure that if you leave prison I shall kill you or get you burned." "Damn you," I told her; "fear God and think of death and the Judgement," but she repeated that it would be better for me if I returned to prison. "How can I do this when I have spent a whole year there and have only just got out?" She said: "I'll go with you to the chief of police and tell him you're my son. If he asks you, agree that I am your mother and be very careful not to give me the lie, for you know my wiles and how I have the power to destroy you."

'When I had agreed, she dressed as an old Sufi woman and went with me until we stood before the emir, with whom were the shaikhs and the leaders of the people. She introduced me to him as her son, and when he asked me I confirmed this. He then asked her what she wanted from me, and she told him that I had approached her when she was asleep and tried to get from her what a man gets from his wife. Everyone there laughed at what she said but thought that this was something monstrous.

'I regretted what I had said and I told the emir that I hadn't known that she would tell this lie about me, but everyone there cursed me and asked God to clear them of any blood debt for me, saying: "This is a Magian, who deserves to be stoned to death." 'Arus said: "I don't want him killed, but let the emir order him to be imprisoned, for this is what he deserves."

'The emir ordered that I be given two hundred lashes, chained and put in prison, where I am now in my third year. When you wanted to free me just now I told you: "Have pity on me and send me back to prison so I may smell the scent of this world and enjoy living until death comes, as this is better for me than meeting the damned 'Arus, who will kill me." This is what she promised to do if she saw me out of prison and this is my story which I have unfolded for you, emir.'

The narrator continued: When the police chief heard the story of the one-eyed man and this damned woman he left a guard to watch over the man and rode off to the king's palace, where he repeated it from beginning to end. The astonished king ordered the man to be brought to him and when he came the king seated him near to him and told him to go over his story again in the presence of his courtiers and viziers. When he had done this everyone there was amazed and taken aback, and they called for 'Arus to be put to death. The king asked the man if he knew where 'Arus was living at the moment and when he said that he did, the police chief went off and, after having identified the house, he came back and said: 'She is in the house of a merchant with whom she is living as his wife.'

The king sent ten servants armed with clubs, who brought her to stand in front of him, and when she saw the one-eyed man there she realized what had happened. The king ordered her to unveil and when she did he was amazed by her loveliness, which exceeded the description he had been given. He asked her whether she was 'Arus al-'Ara'is and when she said she was he asked whether what the man had said about her was true. 'Yes,' she said, 'and there is much more that you have not been told.'

The king asked his courtiers what they thought should be done about her, and the vizier got up and said: 'My advice, Your Majesty, is that we should dig a ditch for her here, fill it with firewood, light it, wait till it is glowing and then throw her into it in front of you.' Everyone approved, agreeing that the vizier's advice was good.

The king gave the order, and all this was done, but as the servants came forward to seize 'Arus, she said: 'Wait a little, O king, and hear what I have to say.' 'Speak,' said the king, 'but I know that there cannot be anything good in what you say.' 'O king,' she said, 'I know for certain that I must suffer this punishment that you have prepared for me, but there are four things that I want you to do, one for me, one concerning you and two that are between me and this one-eyed man.'

'Tell me what you want,' the king said. 'Get someone to bring me a jug of water so that I can perform the ritual ablution before praying with two *rak'as*, and so ending my life and my work.' The king told a servant to give her what she wanted, and when he had brought her the water she went aside and began to perform the ablution. When she had finished she got up and gave the servant the jug with the remains of the water still in it. 'Keep the water,' she told him, 'and when you see that the king has had me thrown into the fire, pour it in after me.' The man, who didn't know what she had done with the water, promised to do this.

'Arus went back to the king, who asked her what she wanted from him. She said: 'The merchant from whose house you took me killed a cousin of his and buried him in its orchard. Put him to death for this and take his goods and his wealth for yourself.' The king laughed at what she had said about her husband as he was astonished at how eager she was to have people destroyed. He ordered the man to be brought to him and when this was done he asked him why he had killed his cousin. The man was so bewildered that he lost his wits and could not answer, at which the king ordered men to go to the orchard and if they found a buried corpse they were to tell him. They went off to dig there and when they came back they told him that they had found it.

The king ordered the man to be kept on one side until he had finished with the affair of 'Arus and the one-eyed man. This was done and he then asked 'Arus what were the two things between her and the man. She said: 'First ask him to absolve me of responsibility for what happened between us.' The king put the question to him, saying that it would not do her any good, and the man agreed to her request, while she in her turn absolved him. The king was astonished at how scrupulously she was treating him after the terrible things that she had done in her lifetime. He asked what the second thing was, and she said: 'King, I had a leaden ring that I passed to him long ago and I want you to ask him to give it back, while I myself have a ring of his inscribed with the name of the Great and Glorious God. Tell him to take it back from me, as it is better that he should make good use of it than that it should be burned with me.' 'You could not have asked for anything simpler,' the king replied.

He told the man to hand her her ring and take back his own. All the while the fire was burning in the pit, and when the man came near the edge 'Arus stretched out her hand as though to take the ring. She talked to him for a time but then gave him so violent a tug that he fell head first into the fire, after which she jumped in after him, and they were both burned up.

The king laughed so heartily that he fell over backwards in astonishment at what she had done with the poor man. 'By God,' he exclaimed, 'that damned woman did nothing to anyone that was more remarkable than how she treated this poor fellow. She kept her promise that she would have him burned, and if she had not thrown him in I would have done it myself because of the blindness of his heart and the fact that he followed her time after time, trusting her in spite of the fact that he knew what she was doing.'

He then called for her husband, the merchant, and asked him: 'Did this damned woman tell you any of her story?' When he said that she had, the king asked why he had not been on his guard against her and had then gone on to kill his cousin. When the man had nothing to say, the king told his servants to throw him into the fire with 'Arus, saying that he had shown himself to be more blind than the one-eyed man. When this had been done all the man's possessions were confiscated on his orders.

The assembly was about to break up when a servant came up and said: 'May God preserve the fortune of the king! This woman, 'Arus, asked your permission to purify herself before praying. You granted her this, and I gave her the water. When she had finished she gestured to me and said: "When you see me in the fire, scatter the water left over from my ablution after me." I did nothing that she told me without your leave, but she has now been burned, so what are your orders?'

The king was astonished and taken aback, and as he didn't know what to say or what 'Arus had meant by this, he asked the vizier what he should do. 'What can happen from this?' the vizier asked; 'Throw it in after her, may God and everyone else curse her.' 'Throw it into the pit as she told you,' said the king, 'so that we can see what she wanted.'

The servant went up and threw the water over the flames. 'Arus had put in it some of the resin that the *jinni* had been in the habit of collecting from green trees, which would instantly burn whatever it touched. As soon as the servant had poured it out, the fire blazed up and with lightning speed it reached the roof and the sides of the council chamber. The servant ran off in panic but he was caught by a tongue of fire which burned him to death. The bewildered king jumped up from his throne and he had only just reached safety when the roof fell on the vizier, who had advised him to burn 'Arus, leaving him buried beneath the debris.

'God damn you, 'Arus,' exclaimed the king, 'for both in your life and after your death you brought misfortune!'

Tale Eight

The Story of Budur and 'Umair Son of Jubair al-Shaibani with al-Khali' the Damascan, with News and Poetry about Them.

In the Name of God, the Compassionate, the Merciful, Who knows better, is Wiser, more Glorious and more Noble

They say that Harun al-Rashid was very restless one night and summoned Masrur, his executioner. When he arrived quickly the caliph told him that he could not sleep and wanted him to fetch someone to tell him a story that night which might fill the time and dispel his cares and worries. Masrur suggested that he should get up and enjoy a walk in his orchard, with its fine water-wheel, to which the words of the poet could apply:

> I have heard this wheel sighing like a girl
> Who sighs in grief for a lover who has gone.
> It stirs my longing with its memory,
> And from my eyes flow tears, themselves like eyes.

He said: 'Then you can look at the birds with their various colours and at the beauty of the roses, as the poet has said:

> Upon the beautiful blue sky
> Pictures of all kinds have been drawn.
> It is as though the moon that shines on us
> Is like a mirror that has been unwrapped.

We can pass by the Tigris with the sailors lying down in their boats and chanting their various ditties until we fall asleep or morning comes.'

Harun said that he was not inclined to anything like that, and Ja'far suggested that they should go up to the roof to look at the blue sky with its interwoven stars and the moon like a round shield of gold held by a negro, as the poet put it:

As though the rosy cheeks were overcast
When the lover took his leave and left.

He went on to point out that the palace contained three hundred girls, harpists, tambourine players, lutists, players on pipes and on rebabs, actresses and reciters. The caliph and his companions could sit in the assembly room; all the girls could come with their instruments and when well-strained wine had been brought in they could all sit eating, drinking and enjoying themselves. 'You might succumb to the wine,' he told Harun, 'or you might fall asleep and wake up next morning with your head still affected by the strength of the wine. This would be as the poet has described it:

Greetings, spring camp! May the rain fall on you,
And long may your traces enjoy blessings.
Within your dwellings flourish songstresses,
Coquettes who mingle charm with bashfulness.
[lac.] With cheeks of beauty and dark eyes.
Wine poured in glasses is like fire,
And as we sit these glasses seem like stars
That shine one following another in their course;
The noise made by its bottles seems to be
A burst of laughter, showing smiling teeth;
The colour of the candles imitates
The body of a lover whose loved one has gone,
And when the drums are beaten, they recall
The bells that call the caravan at dawn,
And when the flute repeats its melody
It seems that this is played by a whole group,
While from the *sarha* comes a different sound
Like that of frogs that croak in the moonlight,
And when its strings are touched the lute
Can tell us what it is they have to say.'

'I have no desire for any of that,' said Harun, at which Ja'far suggested that he might bring out chests of jewels and inspect their colours, looking at the reddish-green translucent emeralds. The poet said:

Five persons and an angel
Are the noblest of all beneath the sky.

Whoever loves them lives through them,
And all perish who have forgotten them.

There is turquoise blue, of which another said:

She kissed the blue stone in my ring,
Saying: 'Use this when you prepare my shroud.'
I said: 'When union with you is no more,
I shall kiss this with blood and flowing tears.'
If I wore mourning, I should be afraid
Of gossip, so my ring shall mourn for me.

Then there is black, as in the lines:

I swear by four who bear the name Muhammad,
And by another four, each named 'Ali,
By the two Hasans and by Ja'far
And Moses: help me, for I follow them.

There is the glowing red ruby, as in the lines:

My redness comes from my heart's blood;
Where is there any who lament?
I come from earth on which Husain was slain.

We can then inspect the stored treasures from Kush, Oman, Bahrain, Hind and Sind, as well as what comes from Persia, Yemen and Egypt, and we can look at materials from all the lands.'

When Harun told him that none of this attracted him, he said: 'Commander of the Faithful, there is only one thing left.' 'What is that?' Harun asked, and Ja'far told him: 'My master should cut off his servant Ja'far's head, as that might please him and relieve his depression.' Harun said: 'I am convinced that there is something that will relax me and remove my worries,' to which Ja'far replied that he was at a loss to know what this could be. Harun said: 'My relative, the Prophet of God, may God bless him and his family and give them peace, said: "The enjoyment of my people lies in three things: that a man should see something that he has never seen before, hear something he has never heard or go where he has never gone." In Baghdad, Ja'far, there is nowhere that I have not been and nothing comes to it that I have not seen. So you will have to go out and find someone amongst the guards who is spending the evening in talk and who can tell me a story of infatuated lovers and of a happy outcome to affliction, as this might have the effect I want, and either put me to sleep or pass the time until dawn.' 'Commander of the Faithful, to hear is to obey both God and you.'

Ja'far went out of the door and saw amongst the guards the shaikh Abu'l-Hasan al-Khali' of Damascus, the storyteller, and he went back and told Harun of this. Harun told him to fetch the man, which he did, and Abu'l-Hasan greeted him with respect and invoked God's mercy on him, saying: 'Peace be on the Commander of the Faithful, who protects the lands of religion and defends the descendants of Abu Talib. May God smooth your path, give you pleasing gifts and bring you at last to Paradise, while sending your enemies to Hell.'

He then recited these lines:

May you enjoy your glory
While dawn succeeds the night,
And may you prosper endlessly
As long as nights shall last.
Since you are heaven for all men on earth.

Harun replied: 'Peace be on those who follow right guidance, fear future destruction, obey the Omnipotent Lord and prefer the next world to this! Sit down, Abu'l-Hasan.' 'By God, Commander of the Faithful,' Abu'l-Hasan replied, 'I cannot do this until I am told whether I have been called here on this tranquil night for reward or punishment.' Harun said: 'You must know, Abu'l-Hasan, that I am suffering from sleeplessness and I want you to tell me a story tonight that I have never yet heard from you which may remove my cares and worries.' 'To hear is to obey, Commander of the Faithful,' said Abu'l-Hasan, adding: 'Do you want me to tell you of something that I have heard or something that I have seen?' 'News is not like sight and what the eye has seen has more truth than what the ear has heard,' said Harun, 'so if you have seen something novel, tell me about it.' 'On condition that you turn your whole attention, hearing and sight to me,' said Abu'l-Hasan, and Harun told him: 'I am both listening to you and looking at you, while my heart is your witness.' 'And you are not going to shout out in the room?' asked Abu'l-Hasan, to which Harun replied: 'As for that, the guards will not dare make a noise, as they are in awe of me.'

Abu'l-Hasan then began: 'The Commander of the Faithful, may God prolong his days, should know that I was in the habit of getting a grant from Muhammad son of Sulaiman al-Rub'i, the governor of Basra, the guarded city, at a fixed time. I would go to Basra and stay with him for a few days, reciting poetry and telling him stories before taking what he gave me and returning to the service of my master, the caliph.

'One year I went there as usual [lac.] and Muhammad instructed his officials and the prominent men to look after me, even telling the cook to give me only what I wanted. I felt a longing for fish and told the cook that this was what I wanted that day. "To hear is to obey," he said, and soon afterwards fish was brought to me, and I ate my fill. This was followed by a feeling of heaviness which could only be cured by walking or drinking, and I could not drink in Muhammad's house when he was not there.

'I had gone to Basra on a number of occasions, but this house was all that I knew in the city. Were a Baghdadi friend to ask me whether I had seen the place I would say "yes", but if he went on to ask if I knew such-and-such a street or such-and-such a square or district, I would have to say "no", and he would tell me that I was lying and that I had never seen the city in my life. So I told myself that I would commit myself to making a tour of Basra to help my digestion.

'I got up and started to walk round the city streets, but after a time I became terribly thirsty. I told myself that I could get a drink from a water-carrier, but then I thought that the jug of a water-carrier is used by lepers, paralytics and men with bad breath. [lac.] It might be that, if I were unlucky, someone like that might just have used it. So I went on along the road past houses and streets until I came to a small alley with five houses, one pair facing another and a fifth house in the middle. This last one was a sky-scraper with stone benches, mats from 'Abadan, a door with two teak leaves, a black curtain, an iron knocker and a long hall. When I looked at it I saw that over it were inscribed these lines of poetry:

> House, may no sorrow enter you
> And may Time not betray your lord.
> You are a welcoming house to every guest,
> When he can find no other place to stay.

I had told myself that I would go up to the door and ask for a jug of water when from within came a voice full of longing, coming from a sad heart. Someone was singing these words:

> By God, your Lord, my two companions, turn aside;
> If you reproach him, he may turn to me.

Tell him of me and ask him why he kills me by forsaking me.
Then put a gentle question if he smiles:
"What harm could come were you to grant union?"
But if he shows you anger, say to him
In a rough tone: "We do not recognize this man."

The voice that I heard was gentler than the breeze and more sorrowful than that of Ishaq your companion. It filled me with pleasure, and I told myself that if the singer was as beautiful as the voice, she would have everything. I went in to the house, moving from hall to hall until, when I came to the third, I could see behind it a girl with a perfect figure and swelling breasts, not too tall or too short, more beautiful than a statue and standing out more clearly than a way-mark. She was a well-brought-up Persian, as the poet described:

Created and perfected as she would have wished
Within the mould of beauty, neither tall nor short,
Round-breasted, like the sky, not too bright or too hot,
As though she was poured out from liquid pearls,
Showing a moon of beauty in each limb.

'The girl, however, was suffering from an illness and was lying on a bed of ivory plated with gleaming gold. With her were maid-servants, who lifted the curtain, allowing me to look at her. She said: "Old man, have you no shame before Almighty God? This brings disgrace on white hair." "Lady," I replied, "I know my hair is white, but what is the disgrace?" She said: "What disgrace is fouler than that you should force your way into a house that is not yours and look at strange women?" I replied: "Lady, I am a stranger and strangers are blind. I am dying of thirst but I didn't want to drink from the water-seller's jug, which has been used by people suffering from diseases. I asked for a drink when I was some way from your house and when no one answered me I told myself that the halls stretched over a distance and I happened to be coming through when the maid raised the curtain and you caught sight of me." "Is that so?" she said, and she then summoned a Turkish maid like a shining sun in a clear sky who, had she appeared to the people of the East, would have served them in place of sunrise. She was as the poet has described:

Is it your face I see or can it be the moon?
Are these your teeth or pearls set on a string?
Is this your figure stepping proudly, or a branch

Of the *ban* tree, or a *samhari* spear?
This slenderness has acted on my bones and waist
Until they are no thicker than a thread.
A lover may be killed by absence or closeness,
And I praise those who do not choose absence.
I thought that Babel was the home of magic,
Not knowing that it lives in Turkish eyes.

'The girl was carrying a silver tray with a jug of red clay covered with a napkin of brocade, on which was an amber apple. I drank from the jug when she offered it to me and then stood up. Her mistress said: "Old man, we did not blame you when you forced your way in and we gave you the water you asked for, so now leave or else we will have you thrown out." I said: "Lady, how can I go when I am as the poet has described:

Alas, my loneliness! As I stood at the door,
Its owner said: "Man, who are you?"
I am a stranger who has lost his way.
As I am helpless, will you be my guide?
"Go off, God guide you, this is not your way."
How can I leave when I have business here?

'The lady said: "Old man, what business do you have here and when did you see me so as to have business with me?" I told her: "Lady, I am an ignorant fellow, and it was thirst that forced me into your house, as even had I drunk no water for a month I could not bring myself to drink from the Tigris. I have no place of my own in Basra but when I happened to pass by the door of your house I heard a voice singing and I told myself that if the singer's shape matched her poetry, she would have everything. I went through the halls until I came to this door and caught sight of you, who are as the poet has said:

I thought what I had heard was overblown,
But when we met I found that it fell short.

When I heard your lines, your complaint moved me to sadness and heartfelt sympathy for your misfortune. Tell me about this, for I may be able to help you find relief." "Do you know these lines, old man?" she said, and when I asked what they were, she quoted:

When one man finds his secret hard to bear,
The one to whom he trusts it finds it harder still.

'I said: "Lady, have you not heard the lines:

> Bring your complaint before a trusty man,
> And he will soothe you, making you forget, or share your pain.

' "And have you heard these?" she asked, before reciting:

> Protect your secret from all questioners,
> For firm resolve consists of wariness.
> Your secret is your captive if you guard it well.
> But if you make it public, you are its.

'I said to her: "Lady, tell me, for it is difficult to find a cure when the disease is concealed, and it kills those who keep it hidden." "No," she answered, "I shall keep my secret to myself, for a poet has said:

> It is the trustworthy with whom secrets are safe
> And they are hidden by the best of men."

"Don't you know these other lines?" I asked:

> My secret is in a locked room with yours;
> The key is lost and the door is sealed shut.

By God, if you knew who I am you would tell me what you are keeping hidden and let me know your affair." She then asked who I was, and I told her that I was Abu'l-Hasan al-Khali' of Damascus, the intimate of the Commander of the Faithful, of the Barmecides and of Muhammad son of Sulaiman, the governor of Basra and of all the state officials and chiefs.

'At that she threw herself down at my feet and started to kiss them, saying: "I saw this in a dream but I never thought that it would really happen. People like you are depositories of secrets to whom things are told. You must know, Abu'l-Hasan, that I am in love." I said: "Someone of your culture and understanding could only love a man of intelligence, and I should like you to let me know who it is. If he is someone worthy of your love, I shall help you to get what you want, but if not, I shall tell you of the faithlessness and treachery of men with tales of those who have betrayed their lovers, using poetry, history and tales. It might then be that you would abandon your love for an unworthy man and concern yourself with someone else, as amongst men there are those who deserve everything and others who do not."

' "You are right, Abu'l-Hasan," she said, "and you should know that I am in love with 'Umair son of Jubair al-Shaibani." By God, Commander of the Faithful, there is no one more handsome, generous or brave than this 'Umair whom she mentioned, and I told her: "Lady, you have hit the mark, and this emir deserves to be loved. Did you and he talk together, were letters exchanged, did he see you in some fixed place or did you share a sign?" "Heedless man," she said, "he spent a year sleeping on my breast, breaking no covenant and untying no knot, and we slept chastely and virtuously, not indulging in disloyal fornication." "What led him to betray you and abandon you after that?" I asked, and she said: "Every day he was in the habit of riding out on a midday trip with his relations and companions, and he would stop here and have a cooked meal with strained wine, and he and I would sit and drink and amuse ourselves until one of us got drunk. He would go and sleep until morning, when he would ride off to see the sights. Then one day, when he had gone off as usual, I called one of my maids, as my hair had got ruffled when I was playing with my lover on the pillow, and I told her to comb it. She came and did this, and when she had finished I kissed her head. She kissed my hand and then the parting of my hair and my cheek, but my lover came upon her as she was doing this, and, turning on his heel, he left, reciting:

> If I should have a partner in my love,
> I would shun love itself even if I died of grief.
> So I have told my soul to die of love,
> As amongst lovers Qais died for Lubna.

He then left me and went off without a backward look.

' "I have begged the leading men of the city to get him to read a letter from me, hear what I had to say or listen to my complaint and give me an answer, but he has not done this, and, apart from God, I can only rely on you. Take a note to him, and if he sends a reply I shall give you five hundred dinars, while if does not read it and reply, you can have a hundred *amiri* dinars." "Lady, to hear is to obey," I said, "so write the note, and I shall go and do my best to bring you back an answer."

'She called for an inkwell and paper before writing: "In the Name of God, the Compassionate, the Merciful:

> It may be you forget the love we shared,
> But I remember you and your great qualities.
> I found that you surpassed all men in worth,
> For, while they all fall short, you are complete.

This letter comes from one who spends her nights in tears and her days in torture. All day she is bewildered and all night she is sleepless. She takes no pleasure in food, cannot take refuge in sleep, does not listen to rebuke and cannot hear those who speak to her. Longing has mastered her; separation has her in its grasp, and the fire of love controls her. She writes under duress, and her handwriting is mixed with tears and blood:

> When this complaint is made of my heart's love,
> It prompts both paper and the pen to weep.
> On each occasion when I want to rest,
> Estrangement calls: 'Get up and do not sleep.'

Were I to sit here writing a full account of the pains and agonies of separation and the burning longing, there would not be pages enough, but I beseech God the Creator, Who raised up the seven heavens, that, as He has decreed that we should part, so He may grant me a meeting with you.

> Should a day pass on which I do not see
> Your image or a messenger from you,
> The world shrinks for me and I seem to be
> A hand whose fingers have been cut away.
> By God, my ribs could not contain my heart
> Were it not sure that we would meet again;
> The pupil of my eye would drown in tears
> But for my promise it would see you soon.

I tell you that I suffer more than you, so give me back my mind. Your love is my delight and your abandonment of me my death. May God have mercy on the one who reads this letter and is moved by sympathy to answer it.

> This letter comes from one enslaved by love
> And in it she complains of love.
> Send a reply so it may let her rest.

Peace be upon you to match my longing for you, which is as long-lasting as the stranger's longing for his homeland and the dove's song on its bough. Peace."

'She then sealed the letter and gave it to me. I took it, Commander of the Faithful, and brought it to the door of 'Umair son of Jubair, where I found that he was out riding. I stood there for a time until he arrived with ten companions like frowning lions, while he was like the moon surrounded by stars. He had a dark moustache and the first traces of a red beard, while his face was like a moon. He had with him a sharp sword and was mounted on a sorrel horse of the stock of 'Antar's al-Abjar, which was worth more money than Caesar himself could produce. He was as the poet described:

> The garden rose blooms on your cheek
> And you stand like a shoot of the bamboo.
> Put down the sword that you are carrying,
> For your eyes cut more sharply than its edge.
> When you unsheathe it your sword blade is sharp,
> But the sword of your eyes cuts when still sheathed.
> Critics reproach me when they see my eyes
> Shed tears to rival the Euphrates' ebb and flow.
> This lover's tears grant union with no word of loss.
> I answered as the tears poured from my eyes
> Over my cheeks for fear lest we should part:
> "You who are bountiful to all but me,
> And who have not kept to your promises,
> Pay no attention to what slanderers say,
> For this is often the reverse of truth."

'When 'Umair caught sight of me he recognized me and threw himself down from his horse, embracing me and taking me by the hand to lead me into the house. After we had washed our hands in a copper bowl we were brought cups of sherbet and sat down after drinking them. A table made, legs and all, from *khalanj* wood was brought up, on which were creatures that walked, flew, were fetched up from the sea or bred in nests, sand grouse, quail, young pigeons, fatted chickens, breast of duck, suckling lambs and sugar sweets. 'Umair stretched out his hand and invited me to start eating, but I said: "By God, I shall eat nothing nor venture on your food until you do something for me." He asked me: "Did you pass by her door and hear her reciting such-and-such a poem and did you then go in and have such-and-such an encounter with her?" "By God, master, were you there?" I asked him. "No, I was not, and had I been, what need would there have been of the letter that you bring?" he replied. "Was one of your people with her?" I asked and he said: "It was better than that." "Did someone come from her to tell you the story?" I asked, and he said: "By God, no one from her would dare come near me." So I asked him who had told him, and he quoted a poet as saying:

> The eyes of lovers see what other eyes do not.

'As there was no reply that I could give him, Commander of the Faithful, I stretched out my hand and gave him the paper. When he had taken it in his hand he spat on it, threw it down and trampled it underfoot, making me very angry, and this did not escape his notice. He said: "Abu'l-Hasan, she promised you five hundred dinars if you brought back an answer and a hundred if you did not, didn't she?" I agreed that she had, and he said: "You and I will sit through the night eating, drinking, enjoying ourselves, listening to music and keeping each other company until morning, when I shall give you five hundred dinars, and you will not have lost anything." "By God, that is right," I told myself.

'We both began to eat and when we had had enough we went to the parlour, a room where the wine strainers wept and the wine flasks smiled, with herbs set out and flowers arranged. It was the time of the violet and the narcissus, Commander of the Faithful, with the flowers arranged in pairs. The poet has written of the narcissus:

> The violet has come, so drink clear wine,
> And pay no heed to those who talk of laws.
> When your companion brings this lovely flower,
> You think it must come from a peacock's tail.

Of the narcissus amongst violets he wrote:

> The fresh narcissus in its tender dress
> Is like an eye that has no eyelashes.
> It is a pearl set above chrysolite,
> White, but with gold that smiles amongst its leaves.

There was a winter rose in the room, of which the poet says:

> Do not forget to welcome this rose as your guest;
> Get up and drain your glass to honour it.
> This visitor brings life, so I should ransom it,
> For after only one month of the year it hides away.

When I looked again I saw a lily, as in the lines:

> You gave a lily to me as a gift,
> But when you gave this, you did not do well.

Half of its name means "evil", and you injured me;
I wish my eyes had never seen this flower.

Then there was a green apple, referred to in the lines:

The apple has undoubtedly the best of rights.
For it is like a pearl, a ruby or anemone.
It is enough that lovers send it to the ones they love.

'Umair filled a glass and drank and then filled another and gave it to me. I looked at what he had passed me and on it was written in gold wash:

The glass is heavy when it comes unfilled,
But when it is filled up with unmixed wine,
It can fly lightly off with the gazelles,
For it is spirits that make bodies light.

I drank, Commander of the Faithful, and for a time the drinking cups were passed around sportively. 'Umair then took a large cup and drained it, saying: "I am your servant," after which he refilled it and passed it to me. On this one I found inscribed:

Dawn calls out in the darkness: "Pour me wine,
Wine that turns the mild-tempered into fools."
It is so finely strained and clear, I cannot tell
If it is in the glass, or is the glass in it?
"Empty the glass!" my drinking partner says,
When it has something left that I desire.
I could not leave undrunk the wine you passed to me.

'We went on drinking all through the day until it became dark, and the young man then said to me: "Abu'l-Hasan, when the Commander of the Faithful drinks until evening, he says that to drink without listening to music is something a wine jug can do better." I agreed, and he clapped his hands, at which three swelling-breasted virgins came forwards looking like moons, one with a lute, another with a tambourine and a third with a flute. On the lute the following lines were inscribed:

Their music overburdens me, sounding before the dawn,
As they mix this with that of tambourines to my delight.
But then they set about retuning strings,
And, though they may succeed, they make me worse.

The tambourines had this inscription:

> I rise when summoned by its tuneful notes:
> "Get up, for dawn has chased the clouds away."
> I do, but drunkenness is still there at its height,
> And I can find nothing to cure my eyes.
> But she met me with wine clear as the sun,
> And so dawn smiled and night was driven off.

On the black ebony of the flute was written in letters of gold:

> In Dair Durta how many pleasures have I had,
> And how much food have I brought for its monks.
> For there there was a flautist who could play
> The sweetest notes to sound in the dark night.
> I say, though men may be dead drunk,
> Glory to God Who brings the dead to life.

The girls sat down, and after 'Umair had taken a glass of wine the one with the lute tuned her instrument and sang:

> Do you suppose a slip has made me tire my heart
> For you until it weakens more than can be thought?
> I swear by your face, like a rising moon,
> And by your black hair, which is a dark night,
> You are my heart's blood and through this I live,
> So how should it be this that angers me?
> With my own life I guard you from all harm;
> With you I am content and it is I who sinned.

"That is good, by God!" cried 'Umair, clapping his hands, but the tambourine player reacted with an exclamation, adding: "Do you sing a song like this in a room like this?" "How should I sing, sister?" asked the other, and the tambourine player began:

> You wretched ones reproaching their lovers,
> This is not something we deserve from you.
> Treat us with gentleness for we are weak;
> Masters of noble stock, do not kill us.
> I have outgrown all that I used to like,
> Except for listening to lovers' tales,
> For we have shared our feelings and our sufferings.

No noble man has been found to help me,
Although I am a helper of the sad.
Those who complain of love find that I share their pain,
And my sincere Amen follows their tears.

"Listen to this song, sister," said the lute player, and she started to sing these lines:

Love for you has me in its debt till death,
And passion for you rules my every move.
When you have gone my patience falls short and abandons me
To find my help in tears and lengthy cares.
When you are distant all my happiness has gone;
You leave, and so do all my happy joys.
The course of fate employs you against me,
And how can I oppose a hostile fate?

''Umair gave a loud cry and tore his clothes, before collapsing unconscious. One of the girls went up to him and then said to me: "My master is asleep so go and sleep yourself." I got up and went to a room which had been cleared for me and furnished with splendid bedding and perfumed with aloes wood, *nadd* and amber. I lay down with my feet being massaged until I was overcome by sleep. Then in the morning, when I got up to dress, I discovered beneath my clothes five hundred Umaiyad dinars. I took these and left, telling myself that there would be no harm in going to Budur to let her know that 'Umair had not read her letter or arranged to send a reply and get a hundred dinars from her to complete the deal.

'I went to her house and found her repeating these lines from behind the door:

Messenger from the beloved, tell me your news.
The watcher is not paying heed; use this and win my thanks.
Make my excuse gently to the beloved,
For this he might be willing to accept.
Then in humility ask him from me,
What wrong did I commit that he abandoned me?
You show a lack of justice in your love,
Matched by a lack of patience on my part.
From day to day I feared that we might part,
But now that fear extends from month to month.

When she saw me she said: "Shaikh, when you went you found that he was out riding and so you sat down to wait for him. When he came you met him and he welcomed you and took you with him into his villa. When you were inside, a table of food was produced, but you refused to eat until he had done what you had come for. He then told you to bring out my letter, which was in the folds of your turban, and when you handed it to him he took it and threw it away, treating it in such-and-such a way. You became angry and when he could see this in your face he told you to sit and drink, promising you the five hundred dinars which I was going to give you if you brought back a reply. You sat and ate, after which you moved to the parlour" – a room which she then described, together with the wine jugs and glasses – "and after you had drunk and night had fallen he told you that in similar circumstances the caliph Harun al-Rashid would say that to drink without listening to music is something a wine jug could do better. When you agreed he clapped his hands and three girls" – whom she described – "came in and each sang a song. When the first sang again he gave a cry, tore his clothes and fainted. The girls told you that he was drunk and you should go to bed, which you did. In the morning, when you came to put your turban on, you found beneath it a kerchief, in which were the five hundred dinars. You took these and came on to tell me." "Who told you this, lady?" I asked and she said: "Haven't you heard the line:

The eyes of lovers see what other eyes do not?

Take these hundred dinars, Abu'l-Hasan, and God be with you as you go off, for no single thing stays the same for one whole day and night."

'I left her and returned to the house of the emir Muhammad son of Sulaiman, who had come back from hunting. I stayed there for some days, spending the evenings talking with him, and then I took the grant that he made me and came back to present my services to the caliph.

'After a full year I went back as usual to Basra, where I told myself that I would not go to the emir Muhammad until I had met 'Umair and had the pleasure of looking at his face while spending a night drinking with him. When I came to his house I found that things had changed. The benches were ruined, and spiders had spun their webs over the door. I stood thinking of what time must have done to the man who lived there and I began to recite to myself:

This is the house, so let the riders halt.
Dismount, for both longing and memory have shaken me.
Here are the traces of loved ones, which sadden me;
Now they are absent, fire consumes my heart.
Alas for those friends whom I used to have;
It looks as though this never was their home.

'While I was reciting this a little servant came out of the house and said: "Who is this who is lamenting our house and weeping over its ruins? Don't we have enough worries without you coming to add to them?" "How can I not lament the owner of this house, who used to be my dearest friend?" "Who was that?" the boy asked, and I told him that it was 'Umair son of Jubair al-Shaibani. "This is his house," the boy said. "Is he still alive?" I asked, and the boy told me: "Yes, he is alive, but he would rather be dead." I asked what was wrong with him and he said: "He is on the point of death and wants to die but cannot and is alive but does not live." "Take me to him," I told him, and he asked: "Who shall I say?" I said tell him that Shaikh Abu'l-Hasan, the story-teller, is at the door. He went off to his master and then came back to invite me in. I went in and found 'Umair as ill as Budur had been when I first met her. There was a doctor standing over him, who was saying: "Sir, your pulse is normal; you have no internal disturbance; you are neither chilled nor feverishly hot and you are not suffering from palpitations. The only thing you complain of is sleeplessness and your floods of tears, and so it may be that you are under a spell," and he recited:

The doctor saw me and then told my folk:
"I swear that your young man has been bewitched."
I told him: You have come near to the truth,
But you should say "forsaken" not "bewitched".

I said: "Emir, may God Almighty not expose you to grief," and then I recited:

Seeing you sad and ill, I wished that I were dead.
When I heard you were sick, I could not sleep,
And I would rescue you from sickness and from pain.

I went on: "May God not expose you to misfortune! Why are you so emaciated?" He said: "Budur has abandoned me, and that is my only sickness, while to be united with her is my only cure." "The one who seeks is sought," I told him, adding: "Is it love for her that has brought you to this extreme?" "By God, it will take me further than this," he said, "and if you take a letter from me and bring back no reply, know that I shall certainly die."

'"When I left you last year," I told him, "I had found her dying of love for you, and whenever she sent you a message, you persisted in treating her harshly." He said: "Abu'l-Hasan, the love that she felt transferred itself to me, and my harshness went to her." "What is the reason for this change that I can see in you?" I asked and he said: "Some days after you left I felt the urge to drink on the Tigris and so I went on a barge with a number of girls. The lamps were lit with candles; herbs were set out together with beautiful flowers and I began to eat and drink. When I was in the middle of the Tigris I heard the sound of strings and when I looked I could see another barge throbbing with musical instruments and illumined by candles. There in the middle of it was Budur, who was living up to the full moon in her name. I looked at her and became as the poet has said:

> You took my inmost soul and then left me;
> May God preserve you, what was this you did?
> The young gazelle is jealous of her neck,
> And for a face she has a crescent moon.

Her maids were sitting in front of her with various musical instruments. When I set eyes on her I became unable to rest and lost my powers of endurance, but in my conceit I thought that she loved me. I tossed an orange towards her in order to attract her attention and she looked up and saw me. She said to her maids: "The twitching of my eye tells me that I can see the man who caused me distress. What has brought this boor here tonight to disturb us? Take me back to spend the rest of the night in the city." On her orders the sailors took her back and I felt as though the breath of life had left my body and I began to recite:

> What has the time of parting done to me,
> For it was parting that betrayed my hopes?
> Now the more beautiful that you become,
> The more I sorrowfully blame myself.

I went back and tried to compose myself, saying that tomorrow, when she was alone, I would send one of my servants to pass by her door. When she saw how magnificent he looked she would write to ask me to send her someone who could reconcile us. The night passed, and then the next day, and then a third, until I had to endure for ten days with no messenger or any news coming from her. She paid no attention to those I sent past her house to remind her of me, and when things had been going on for too long I got a number of people whom she knew to take her a letter. Then I sent her the emirs and leading citizens of Basra, asking her to read what I had written or to send me a letter of her own. All she did was to become harsher than ever, and I am left to rely on God and on you if you will take a letter to her for me. If you bring me a reply I shall give you a thousand dinars and if she does not answer I shall give you five hundred, and you will lose nothing. "Write your letter," I told him, "for I shall be glad to go."

''Umair took an ink-well and paper and wrote: "In the name of God the Compassionate, the Merciful:

> This letter comes to you from hope
> That lodges in my ribs and does not leave,
> From sleep, which now I seldom taste,
> And from a heart not occupied with blame.
> I am consumed with passion and with love,
> And one of these alone would leave me dead.
> By God, if passion could send messengers,
> These messengers would be my heartfelt sighs.

This letter comes from one who cannot rest and has no more endurance, who spends sleepless nights and days filled with cares. He is tearful and emaciated; harshness itself laments him; he can find no patience nor any place of refuge, for the world is too small for him. This letter is addressed to the moon of darkness and the sun of the forenoon, the mistress of the hearts of mankind, the most beautiful of all on earth or in heaven. Your slave kisses the ground before you and asks for the favour of your approval. Tears have exposed my secret, and, after God, it is to you that I complain, and the fire of passionate longing leads me to recite:

> I asked the paper to carry some of my feelings for me,
> But all it did was to add to my sleeplessness.
> It thundered in my hand and made me think
> That she whom I loved was in love herself.
> When it hears my complaint it bewails me

With pity, and would speak if I called it.
Were it to know the longing that my hands
Have written on it, it would be burned up.

Whenever critics blame me harshly for my love for you, I answer with a sorrowing heart and say: 'I know what you do not.'

' "Peace be on you. I long for you as much as a stranger longs for his homeland, as long as music sounds, the dove sings or the pigeon coos on the bough. May God show mercy to the reader of this letter, if she is disposed to answer it. I say:

From the despairing lover who has fallen sick.
To the full moon of beauty this is sent,
A letter from one whose love is sincere,
Unbroken, and whose covenants are kept.
Love's precious rights win the respect of noble men.
I do your bidding and am called your slave.
I cannot enjoy sleep till you remove your veil.
Promise your favour and grant me your love,
For every word of yours must be obeyed.
The moment when a lover has to part
Is longer than his union by a thousand years.
Peace be to you. Do not be miserly
In sending back this greeting to the one who loves."

He took the letter, sealed it and gave it to me. I took it but when I came to Budur's house and wanted to go in the doorkeeper stopped me and said: "Is this a khan? No one can go in without permission." I told him to go to his mistress and tell her that the shaikh Abu'l-Hasan was at the door. He went off and when he returned he invited me in. As I went in I could hear her reciting:

I must endure the outrages of time
Until you come back as a messenger.

Then she said: "Abu'l-Hasan, you went to the house of the emir 'Umair before me, but, while everything new is pleasant, everything old commands affection."

'Then she told her maids to spread out a mat for me at the edge of the hall. It was summer, and she and her maids were playing in the pool. She was wearing a short sleeveless tunic of satin, and when she took this off

I could see that underneath it she was wearing an embroidered garment of white *dabiqi* linen, on whose edge was written:

> She came out in a white chemise,
> Glancing through languorous lids.
> I said: "You passed by without greeting me,
> Though I would be content with a greeting.
> Blessed is He who clothed your cheeks in loveliness.
> Your shape is like the boughs of garden trees,
> While what I wear is like my fortune and my [lac.]
> White upon white on white."

'She washed and then [dried herself] with a towel of Rumi velvet [lac.] and round her waist was a green cloth with gold embroidery, on which was written:

> Clever and taught by cleverness itself,
> The rose gleams with her borrowed loveliness.
> She wore a green dress when she came,
> As leaves conceal the pomegranate blooms.
> I asked her what the dress was called,
> And she gave me a courteous reply:
> "I call it 'Heart-breaker,' for this is what it does."

It had a silk waist-band with a golden tassel, and written on it were the lines:

> I am the lock of a protected place,
> Which fingers have filled up with artistry,
> And when a heavy buttock lies within,
> I watch to see there is no treachery.

On her head she wore a blue cap with a white veil inscribed with the lines:

> Do you not see my lady's grace shown by her veil,
> And how it shines, a full moon in the dark.

'When she had finished dressing I handed her the letter, which she opened and read before throwing it away. "Don't do that, lady," I said. "Is there nothing left between the two of you but that I should go to him without a reply, which will certainly lead to his death?" I then played lightly on her feelings for some time until I noticed that she was softening, and I then swore to her that she should write a reply for me. She could not disobey me and so she called for an ink-stand and paper and wrote: "In the Name of God the Compassionate, the Merciful:

> You wrote complaining of the sorrows Fate has brought,
> And of your illnesses that find no end in time,
> Caused by your love and your abandonment,
> But harshness came from you and not from me.
> Pleasure and love accompanied your sleep,
> While my couch housed humility and tears.
> Were you prepared to help me for one day,
> The Day of Judgement will see me help you.
> So live in love and die of grief,
> For one soul is the payment for another."

"By God, lady," I said, "it would be better to abandon this letter. Have you no fear of God here?" "Are you a messenger or a busy-body?" she asked, and I told her: "Both, and I urge you for God's sake not to destroy that beautiful young man but to have pity on him." "What is all this, Abu'l-Hasan?" she asked. "By God," I said, "I can describe no more than a tenth of his sufferings." "Is this all for my sake?" she said, and when I said it was, she asked what had caused his harshness and hatred to change to love and humility. I told her: "Lady, Time suffers change, and whoever trusts in it is put to shame and no longer remains the same. Yesterday he was loved and then he became a lover, while the emir becomes a captive. You were gripped by love for him and now he suffers the pain of your harshness." "Abu'l-Hasan," she told me, "by the Great God, for every grain of longing you talk about, I have much more. While he was inflicting lengthy sufferings on me he became harsher and harsher, while I had to endure. Then I got the upper hand, but I swear that his situation hurts me, and I would ransom my darling with my life."

'Then she called for an ink-stand and paper and wrote: "In the Name of God the Compassionate, the Merciful:

> The letter came, and may I never be without the hands
> That played with it and filled it with their scent.
> I opened it and read it, and I found
> That it had come to cure my stricken heart,

As though Moses had come back to his own,
Or Joseph's robe had come to his father.

If this robe restored Jacob's sight, your message has revived one who
was on the brink of the grave. I took it in both hands and placed it over
my head and my eyes, kissing every letter in it a thousand times.

The letter came, brought by your messenger,
And I placed it in longing on my heart.
I opened it and read it and grasped what it said,
Remembering the days when my love had no cloud.
I'll hold it in my hand the whole day long,
And it will be beneath my pillow when I sleep.

The tents of union will be pitched, the banners of meeting unfurled, and
the breeze of gladness will blow as our dwellings are near. Cares have
melted me away; sleeplessness has consumed me, and I pray that the
One Whose hands hold the keys to our affairs may set in order the covenant of our union, and see to it that its mouth smiles. I say:

A letter came and had its breath passed by a tomb,
It would have brought to life the buried dead.
When I read it I saw that, thanks to this,
The people called down blessings on its memory."

She then shed tears and added these lines to her letter:

"I swear by God that if my heart were searched,
There would be nothing to find there except your love.
Respect the rights of our companionship,
And help me in my love, by God, by God.

My greetings to you equal my longing for you, and if God Almighty
wills it, I shall follow after my letter."

'She folded the letter and passed it to me, after which I took it to
'Umair. I heard him reciting:

Do you think love-letters between us have been banned,
Or that the price of paper has become too high?
You may have asked me how I was,
But separation has destroyed my power.
Although you are an enemy and not a friend,
Yet enemies show mercy on their foes.

'When I went in, as soon as he caught sight of me he rushed up to me and said: "Abu'l-Hasan, what are you bringing with you, wheat or barley?" "By God, it is wheat!" I told him and I gave him the letter. When he had opened it and read it he burst into tears and asked me whether Budur had written this with her own hand. I told him that she had, but he said: "No, Abu'l-Hasan, she would not be willing to write to me. You must have gone to a scribe and got him to write this because you were afraid that, if I didn't get a reply, I would die." When I insisted that she had written it herself, he said: "One of the maids who were attending on her when I was with her must have heard about my plight and have written this out of a feeling of pity for me lest I die." I repeated that she had written it, but he said: "I should say that iron is more likely to turn soft and rock to melt than that her heart should show any compassion for me."

'Again I said that she had written it, and as I was talking with him Budur herself came in reciting:

> I visit you with no reproach for your harshness,
> For noble persons visit after being asked.
> Although a house be distant, longing brings it near,
> And those who feel this passion do not think it far.

When he saw her he jumped up from under what was covering him and started to kiss her feet and her eyes, while she embraced him. They both began to weep, complaining of the pains of separation and what they had experienced of the bitterness of abandonment. I said to myself: "There is no god but God! These two are lovers who have not met for a year so I should leave them and go." But when I got up to leave, Budur turned and called to me. When I answered she asked where I was going, and when I said that I was leaving she said: "Sit down. I told you at the start that there was no question of fornication or debauchery between us."

'I sat down, and 'Umair had food brought for us, which we ate, after which we moved to the parlour, where we drank until midnight. I said to myself: "Kissing, yearning and the giving of oaths – I shall be in the way and so I should get up and leave them to sleep." "Aren't you going to stay with us until morning?" Budur asked, and I said: "It is for you to say, lady." She said: "By God, if you get up, you will have to pay for the room," so we sat and drank until morning. When it came she called to me and told me to go and fetch the qadi and the legal witnesses. When they came 'Umair brought out a white satin robe and the marriage contract was drawn up, after which he brought out a purse with a thousand dinars, some of which he gave to the qadi and the witnesses and the rest he passed on to me. I took it, and Budur withdrew, while 'Umair and I went on to spend eight days in eating, drinking and amusing ourselves, while she was putting her affairs in order.

'On the eighth night she was brought to him as a bride, and he retired alone with her, while I slept in a place that had been set aside for me. Early next morning, when he and I went from the baths to the house, his face was like the shining sun, and I began to recite:

> She was the only fitting bride for him,
> And he for her the only fitting groom.
> If any other man had wanted her,
> An earthquake would have swallowed up the earth.

I said to her: "The sparrow flies high and the hunter does nothing." "What do you mean?" she asked, and I said: "While you are happy, I am sad. Where is the covenant that was between us?" She asked 'Umair what he had promised me, and he said that he had promised me a thousand dinars if I brought him an answer. "My darling," she said, "it was I whom he brought, so give him a thousand dinars and another thousand from me." The two thousand dinars were produced, and after taking them I went off to present my services to the emir Muhammad son of Sulaiman. I stayed with him and took my grant, something I have continued to do until now.'

Al-Rashid was astonished by the story and presented Abu'l-Hasan with a splendid robe of honour as well as generous gifts.

This is the whole story. The blessings of God and His peace be on his Prophet, Muhammad our master, and on his family and his companions!

Tale Nine

The Story of Abu Disa, Nicknamed
the Bird, and the Marvels of His
Strange and Comical Story.

In the name of God, the Compassionate, the Merciful

A story is told that in Baghdad, the City of Peace, there was a weaver named Abu Disa, whom people called 'Usfur. He was a poor man with a wife and four daughters and every time he wove something for a customer he would steal some of the material. This went on until he had so much cotton that he wove it into a piece sixty cubits long, which he sold in the market for sixty dirhams.

Taking the money with him, he passed 'Arsat al-Hauz, where he saw a Persian astrologer surrounded by a crowd. The man was identifying names in the crowd and their lucky star and getting money from them. Abu Disa went home and told his wife about this. 'Become an astrologer yourself,' she said, 'and then we can live off a dinar a day without you having to leave us in misery.' 'By God, woman, you must be mad!' he exclaimed, pointing out that he was no good at reading, writing or arithmetic and could not speak well. 'How can I become an astrologer? Do you want people to slap me?' he asked. She said: 'Don't you see how well our neighbour the astrologer lives and how much he spends? If you don't become an astrologer, divorce me.'

Abu Disa loved his wife and so he asked her what to do. She said: 'Take some old notebooks and sit on a carpet in the road calling out: "The diviner, the foreign astrologer! Who wants his fortune told?" People will come swarming round you.' 'And if anyone asks me what's in the books, what am I to say, when I can't read a single word?' he asked. She said: 'If anyone asks you that, say: "I am not a writer; I am an astrologer and a diviner."' Then, when he asked where he was going to get the flowing robes, she told him that she would give him a shawl and a head cloth. She collected old notebooks for him and gave him an old carpet and a chair, saying: 'This is all you need.' 'For

God's sake, woman,' her husband said, 'don't make me try something I know nothing about so that people will laugh at me.' She told him: 'Don't crack, or else divorce me.' Because he loved her, he was forced to agree.

Next morning he took the carpet and the rest of the stuff and went to the highway where the astrologers sat and prayed with his hand on his heart: 'O Lord, Guide of the perplexed, guide me in my perplexity.' He was sitting on a road that led to a certain bathhouse and cried out: 'I am the astrologer, the diviner, the learned stranger!' On hearing this people rushed up from all sides. They saw how he was dressed and what he looked like, with his long beard hanging over his navel, which he had dyed with henna. He was wearing the shawl and the head cloth and looking like an old pimp.

Of those who gathered round him, one who knew him said: 'This pimp is 'Usfur the weaver, who has turned into an astrologer.' They were laughing at him as he was crying out and turning over his note-books, but just then the princess came out on her way to the baths, surrounded by her maids. She told one of them to find out what the shouting and commotion was about, and when the girl came back she told her that this was a new foreign astrologer, and the people round him were saying that no one like him had ever come to the city.

At the time the princess was pregnant and she told the girl to go to the man and say: 'My mistress wants you to look into the future for her. This dinar is a present for you, so look and see what her baby will be.' The girl went off and said this, and 'Usfur stretched out his hand and took the dinar, scarcely able to believe what was happening, as never in his life had he had a dinar in his hand or anything yellow apart from buckthorn berries. He exclaimed in gratitude and lifted the book up to his face before shaking his head and starting to turn over one page after another while biting his lip.

He stayed silent for a time, not saying a word, and then he shook his beard and said: 'This is a fortunate woman who will give birth to twins but not on earth or in the sky.'

The girl went off and told this to the princess. As it happened this was on the night that she was due to give birth and when she got back to the palace she began to walk in its orchard. She got to a tree-house where the gardener used to sit and she expressed a wish to climb up so as to sniff the air there. When she had done this and had sat there for a time she fell into labour and when the midwife reached her she had not enough strength to come down and so she gave birth to a boy and a girl, just as 'Usfur 'the astrologer' had said.

As the good news of the birth of the twins spread, alms were distributed and drums beaten. As for the princess, next morning she gave orders that 'Usfur was to be given a robe of honour, a mule and a thousand dinars. Her servants were told to find out where he lived and, after clothing him in the robe of honour and giving him the thousand dinars, they were to bring him to the gate of the palace so that she could see him.

'Usfur, with the dinar in his hand, had waited until the servant girl had gone and he then closed the notebooks and rolled up the carpet, which he put over his shoulder, and, carrying the books in front of him, he ran home as though in flight. When he got there he told his wife that he had got a dinar but added: 'I lied to the princess, and tomorrow they will come and hang me. This is the dinar, and if anyone comes looking for me say: "He's not here, so take your dinar and go." ' 'You're mad,' she told him, 'get out and shut up.' 'You're going to have your hand cut off for exposing me to this,' he said, 'for the first thing I shall tell them is that it was you who made me become an astrologer. Do you think I'm going to leave you safe and sound?'

He spent the night thinking of all the disasters that were on their way, and next morning there were slaves and eunuchs at the door, asking for the house of the new astrologer, for they had been told that this was it. 'Usfur shouted abuse at his wife, saying: 'You told me to be an astrologer, and I shall tell them that you taught me, so you will be the first to be slapped. Get up and tell them: "He's not here. He is a lunatic and doesn't know what he is saying." ' He then got up himself and went around looking for a place to hide and, as the only one that he could find was the oven, he lowered himself into it and pulled the lid shut.

As for his wife, when she heard the knock on the door she asked: 'Who is there?' A servant told her: 'The princess wants the astrologer,' to which she replied: 'Master, he is a poor, wretched lunatic who doesn't know what he is saying and here is the dinar.' The servant said: 'It's you who are mad. The princess has sent him a thousand dinars, a mule and a robe of honour. Let him come down or else we shall wreck the house.'

The woman went up screeching and looking for her husband, but when she found him in the oven the top of his hair was streaked and his face and body were covered with grime thanks to its dust. 'Get up!' she told him. 'What have you done to yourself?' 'Damn you,' he said; 'go away from me and don't let them come and see me.' She again told him to get up, saying: 'You're in luck. The princess has sent you a thousand dinars, a mule and a robe of honour.' 'Put the robe round your neck!' he exclaimed. 'I was warm here, but you wouldn't leave me.'

He got out of the oven, looking as though he had just come from a bath stove, and opened the door. When he went out one of the princess's men called to his friend: 'What's this?' and the man said: 'Look at the princess's astrologer! What do you think, boy? He hasn't washed his face for ten days.' As the people fled away from him the servants asked: 'What are you?' 'Usfur said: 'Yesterday I was with a number of *jinn* on the princess's business, making spells for her.' They took him to the baths and cleaned him up before bringing him out and dressing him in his robe of honour.

Then they tried to mount him on the mule, but he objected that it was too high for him and asked them to make it kneel down. They laughed at him and told him to put his foot in the stirrup, but he did this the wrong way round so that his face was pointing to its tail. As they laughed it farted, and he threw himself from its back, saying: 'There's a man under its tail!' The groom laughed and mounted from the stirrups, pricking the mule with his spurs so that it moved off to the head of the lane. Just then a black dog crossed its path, making it buck so that the groom fell off breaking both his hand and his foot. He screamed out, telling his friend what had happened and saying that this was because he had wronged the astrologer. 'Master,' he said to 'Usfur, 'I did wrong as people like me do, while people like you forgive.' 'You despise a man and then mount his mule!' said 'Usfur, and when he moved his lips the groom said: 'By 'Ali, every time he is at odds with someone he gets the mule to throw him.'

The servants then moved off, taking 'Usfur with them to the princess. She told him: 'You are now my astrologer and you will never again sit on the street or use your skill for anyone else. I shall give you a lump sum as well as enough pay to satisfy both you and your family.' 'Usfur said: 'Lady, do you think that I like sitting in the street? It was because of you that I was there since I saw in the stars that you were going to go past me on your way to the baths.' At that she gave him another robe of honour, and he left, riding on the mule, with servants escorting him to the door of his house. There he called 'Bsh, bsh!' to the mule, but it didn't stop, and he had to tell the servants to repeat this to it or else it would throw him. They halted it and got him down before going off.

He went up to his wife, who asked him what had happened to him.

'You plunge me into difficulties and then say: "What happened to you?" Get up and let's take all this and leave the city before they come around to hang me. You won't be safe yourself.' 'You faint-heart!' she exclaimed. 'Put your trust in God and keep quiet, for, by God, we're never going to leave this city.' 'You're only trying to get me killed,' he objected, 'but do you think that I'll leave you after me? By God, I'm going to tell them that it was you who told me to do this, saying: "Become an astrologer and laugh at the people." I'll let them hang you first before me.' Both of them then sat down to eat and drink.

Some days later, as had been fated, the king's treasury was burgled through a hole in the wall and purses containing ten thousand dinars were taken. A servant came to tell the king, who reacted with fury. 'Bring the astrologers and the sand diviners so that they can look and see who took them,' he ordered, for he had a great fondness for these people. He brought together twenty of them and told them that he wanted them to find the stolen money for him. They thought over the problem and made their calculations but could find no answer and were dismissed by the king. He was depressed, and when he went to his daughter she asked him why this was. He told her about the loss of the money and the failure of the astrologers. 'I don't know what to do,' he said, 'and my honour is affected.' 'What would you say if someone got the money back?' she asked, and he answered that he would give him a thousand dinars from it, as well as a robe of honour and a mule. She said: 'My foreign astrologer has no equal in the world and it was he who gave me the good news of my children's birth.' 'For God's sake, arrange for this quickly, little girl,' the king said, and his daughter agreed.

She sent off her servants to 'Usfur, and when they got there they knocked at the door. He looked down from a window and then withdrew his head. 'Bitch,' he said to his wife, 'the game is up. Here are the guards with their clubs ready to inflict punishment. Look and see what's there, seven hundred of them' – in fact, there were three – 'so what am I to do?' She got up and said: 'Who is at the door?' They said: 'Is the astrologer there?' 'Say I'm not,' 'Usfur told his wife, but she said: 'Yes, he's just coming.'

'Usfur cursed her, but he got up and put on his robe of honour and a grand turban before going down and saddling his mule. Then he went out and asked the servants what they wanted. They told him to come and speak to the king, and when he asked what the king wanted from him they told him of the robbery and that the princess had said that he would be able to find the money. He called on God's name and went with them. When he came into the king's presence, he greeted him and strode through the crowd to take his seat beside him. 'By God,' the king exclaimed, 'were this not the greatest sage of all time he would not have sat down beside me.' He then turned to 'Usfur and asked: 'Is it true what my daughter said about you?' 'Yes,' replied 'Usfur.

The king then said: 'I have lost ten thousand dinars from my treasury, and none of my astrologers have been able to find it. If you do, you can have a thousand dinars from it.' 'Usfur said: 'Your Majesty, I should like you to collect all these astrologers in front of you and get them to confess that they can't do it, and then, thanks to your own good fortune, I shall work things out.'

The king duly collected all the astrologers and when they were there he said: 'This is my daughter's astrologer, and he has told me that he will produce the ten thousand dinars. Acknowledge to him that you cannot, so that he may do it.' When they looked at 'Usfur the astrologer with his long beard they laughed and said: 'Since when has this lunatic been an astrologer? He is a weaver and what is he doing here, unlucky fellow? He is not going to be contented until we admit that this is beyond our powers?' But one of them said: 'What harm will there be in acknowledging this to him so that we can laugh at him, and the king can slap him until he sees stars?' So they made this admission to the king and added: 'If this sage can find the money, he will be our chief.' 'Usfur asked the king to give him ten days, to which the king agreed. He said to himself: 'I'll go and get my wife, and we can then leave this place. In ten days' time I'll be far away and free from this trouble, for where am I going to get ten thousand dinars from?' They then left the king's presence with the astrologers laughing at 'Usfur and saying: 'What is this unlucky fellow going to do?'

As for 'Usfur, he went to his wife and said: 'Get up, you bitch! Something has happened.' She asked him what was the matter, and he said: 'I have guaranteed to produce the ten thousand dinars that the king has lost within ten days. So get up and let's go. In ten days' time we'll be in a far-distant city, away from this trouble, with enough to live on for the rest of our lives.' 'By God,' she said, 'we're not going to leave here until our dying day.' 'You feeble woman,' he said, 'where am I going to get ten thousand dinars to give the king? You're trying to get me hanged, but I shan't let them do thus until they've hanged you first.' She told him: 'Over the next ten days there are a thousand chances of getting out of this.' 'Not even if the ten days were a whole year,' he said, to which she replied that something would turn up.

'Usfur felt relieved and told her that during this time he would not leave her but would stay sitting on the bench by the door, waiting to see what would happen. 'I want you to get me a jug,' he told her, 'and cover its mouth. Give me some date stones and with every day that passes I'll put one of them into the jug.' She agreed to this, and next day 'Usfur came down, spread out his carpet and sat by the door, with everything he had placed behind him.

So much for him, but as for the money, it had been taken from the royal treasury by ten thieves. Since then they had not been able to spend any of it or to find out what the king was doing, but then they heard that 'Usfur the astrologer had guaranteed to return it within ten days. This alarmed them, and they told themselves that he would not have done this unless he knew about them. They discussed what to do and decided that one of them should go to his house to find out what he was doing, and if 'Usfur recognized this one, he would know the others.

They were sheltering in a cave outside the city when they agreed on this plan, saying that, if 'Usfur recognized them, they should give him the money, asking him not to give them away. One of them volunteered to go and get news and when he came to 'Usfur's house he found him sitting reading from a book in front of him. He would glance at the book, then at the thief's face and then back at the book. 'By 'Ali,' the thief exclaimed to himself, 'he has recognized me!'

As it happened, near 'Usfur there were two men quarrelling. 'Usfur said to the thief: 'Do you know me?' and, looking at him, the thief thought that it was he who was abusing the other man. 'By the Lord of the Ka'ba, he knows me,' said the thief to himself, 'and his household know me too.' He then went to sit where he could hear 'Usfur without being seen. 'Usfur called to his wife by name and when she answered he said: 'This is one of the ten, and there are nine left to come' [referring to the date stones]. On hearing this, the thief ran off in fright without turning right or left until he reached his companions. When he told them what had happened they all said that it might be a coincidence, for how could he have known. 'By God, he knew me,' the thief insisted, 'and he said: "This is one of the ten".' They said: 'In that case someone else should go tomorrow, and if he is recognized we shall have to settle things with the astrologer.'

Next day another of the ten volunteered to go. He waited until the afternoon and when he went he found 'Usfur sitting by his door with the book in front of him, looking first at his face and then back at the book. The thief stood out of sight, where he could hear what he was saying. 'Usfur again called to his wife and when she answered he said: 'These are two out of the ten that have come.' When he heard this the thief exclaimed: 'By the Lord of the Ka'ba, that cuckold knows us!' and he fled back to his companions, his heart trembling with fear. His report was the same as that of the first thief, and he told them: 'If we wait any longer, we shall be killed.'

The leader of the gang said: 'Tomorrow no one is to go except me, and if it turns out that he knows us, I shall go in and arrange things with him.' Next day he waited until afternoon and then sneaked out to 'Usfur's house. 'Usfur was sitting at his door with the book in front of him, as a poet described:

He was looking at a book and then shaking his head,
And I can swear he did not know what it contained.

He kept on looking first at the book and then at the thief, to make him think that he was reading, something that he did when anyone went by. When the thief passed and 'Usfur kept staring at him, he became afraid and said: 'By God, this cuckold knows us!' He stood out of sight, listening, as 'Usfur called to his wife, and when she answered he said: 'By 'Ali, this is the pick of the ten and the finest of them.'

When he heard this, the leader told himself that there was no more doubt and he went back to the others and said: 'What are we going to do?' 'What's the news?' they asked. 'By God, he knows us,' their leader told them, 'and he has done us a favour by not giving us away! Come on, let's take him the gold and the silver and give it to him, together with a thousand dinars of our own, a hundred from each of us as a price for our heads. We can then ask him to be good to us and not tell anyone about us.' 'Do as you think best,' they told him, and at that they took all the stolen money as well as the extra thousand dinars and brought it to 'Usfur's door, where he and his wife were talking. They knocked, and 'Usfur's wife asked: 'Who is that?' 'We want to speak to the sage,' they said, at which 'Usfur came out, shaking his beard and spreading his fingers open. When they saw him they fell down at his feet, kissing them and clutching at the hem of his robe. 'We want you to do us a favour,' they told him. 'We know that you have known about us from the very first day, but you have not given us away. The ten of us took the king's gold, but we have been caught out and we have brought you a thousand dinars of our own so that you may oblige us by keeping this a secret. Here is the gold.' 'Usfur told them: 'God knows that I only asked the king for a ten-day delay to give you more time lest he kill you. For if I had told him about you he would have executed you all.' 'We know that, and that's why we are here,' they said, and 'Usfur promised: 'Now that you've done that, no harm will come to you.'

He took the gold into his house, and his wife asked him if he now saw what a blessing her advice had brought him. 'Bitch,' he said; 'you're never going to stop trailing after me until you get me crucified.' He then took the thousand dinars and sat eating with his wife and children until the ten days were up.

On the eleventh day the king sent ten servants to fetch him. When they came and knocked at the door, his wife asked who was there, and they said: 'Let the sage come and talk to the king.' She went in and told 'Usfur to do this and to give him the gold, pointing out that it was thanks to her advice that he had been successful. 'You bring luck, do you?' he asked. 'Had those feeble-witted fellows not come here, you and I would have been hanged today.' 'Get up,' she repeated, 'for relief comes between one moment and the next.'

'Usfur got up and put on the best robe that he had and walked on to the palace. There he found that permission for him to enter had already been given, so he went in and greeted the king, who stood up for him, as did all his courtiers, while the astrologers were forced to do the same. When he had sat down, the king said: 'Sage, we want the money.' 'Usfur politely agreed but said that the astrologers were to confess their powerlessness so that he could do what he wanted with them or else they should say what they did know. The king told them: 'You have heard what he says. Can any one of you produce the money?' 'No,' they answered and at that 'Usfur clapped his hands and said to the king: 'Come and get it.' 'Where is it?' asked the king and 'Usfur said: 'Buried in the square.' In fact, he had told the thieves to bury it there and they had done so.

When it was uncovered, shouts of jubilation arose, and the king said: 'Let all those who love me give this man a robe of honour,' at which they deluged him with robes. 'Usfur then said that he wanted the astrologers to be slapped all the way from the palace to his house. This was done on the king's orders, as 'Usfur rode on his mule with drums and trumpets going on ahead. When they got to the house the mistreated astrologers went off, and 'Usfur handed the bandsmen quantities of dinars. They then left gratefully.

'What happened to you?' his wife asked as he entered the house. He told her that he had had the astrologers slapped after admitting their powerlessness and he added: 'When they get back and slap me, I'll have made up for it in advance.' 'Cheer up,' she said, 'as nothing but good is going to happen.' He said: 'How often do you try to make me think that disasters are not so bad! Let's go somewhere else, for we've enough to last us till we die.' 'No,' she said, and he cursed her and told her that she would end on the gallows. He then stayed eating and drinking and going all the time to the princess and the king, who had told her that he had produced the money. 'There is no one like him in the whole world,' the princess repeated.

As fate had decreed, one day the king happened to eat out in the palace orchard, and when he had got up to wash his hands in the pool he forgot a ring he had been wearing on his finger which protected against poison. As he got up he left it by the side of the pool, and up came a lame duck that swallowed it in sight of a young eunuch. When the king remembered it, he could not find it, and to his distress no one could tell him anything about it, for, as the eunuch was intending to kill the duck and take the ring, he had said nothing at all.

The king ordered the astrologers to be fetched, as his emirs and viziers had interceded for them, reminding him that these were servants of his who had burned themselves out in his service. The king said: 'When I have allowed someone to make a wish, there is nothing for it but to let him have what he wants.' The courtiers were happy with this, and the king gave robes of honour to the astrologers and conciliated them. When they were all there he told them that he had lost a ring that he had had since his father's time and by which he set great store. He promised them a thousand dinars if they could find it. Some of them consulted the sand and others the stars but they could not track it down and when the king asked them what they had done they said: 'By God, Your Majesty, we are at a loss, and the ring has stayed hidden from us.'

The king then called out for the princess's sage, and his servants went off to 'Usfur, who was sitting at home. 'Something has happened,' he said to himself, and he got up and went out to ask who was there. 'Come and speak to the king,' they told him, and when he asked them what the king wanted, they told him of the loss of his old ring and that, as the astrologers couldn't find it, the king had sent for him to produce it. 'Usfur went to his wife and, after cursing her and wishing her ill, he said: 'What am I to do? Tell me.' 'What has happened?' she asked, and he told her about the loss of the king's ring and the fact that the astrologers hadn't been able to find it. 'The king has sent for me to produce it for him, so what am I to say? This is another case like that of the robbers, and this time the king will hang me, as he will say: "You are laughing at me, and it was you who slapped my astrologers."' She said: 'Go off and put your trust in the Great and Glorious God, for nothing but good will come of this.' 'You've got me ready for crucifixion,' he told her, 'so that you can sit until I alone become the victim, while you take the gold and go off, but, by God, nothing is going to happen to me before it happens to you first.'

He went out and rode to the palace on his mule. There he dismounted and took his seat by the door, waiting for permission to go in. Over the door was a silk screen covered with all kinds of pictures of ducks, doves, gazelles, hares and the like. 'Usfur sat looking at this and shaking his head. The eunuch came up to him, saying to himself: 'This sage has seen the duck on the screen and he knows that it took the ring. It won't take him long to realize that I saw it but said nothing and when he tells the king I shall be hanged.'

'Usfur shook his head at the eunuch, who told himself: 'By God, that pimp knows, and the king is going to have me killed today.' He held back 'Usfur in the hall and said: 'By God, wise man, take this hundred dinars from me as a sweetener and say nothing about me to the king, for I saw a lame duck swallow the ring by the pool in the orchard, where the king was washing his hands.' 'I knew that,' 'Usfur said, 'and had you not spoken to me I would have told the king to put you to death. Now go off and don't tell anyone or else I'll let him hang you.'

The eunuch left and went to the king, with whom, as he could see, the astrologers, viziers and a crowd of others were gathered. 'Usfur greeted them and took his seat, before asking the king what his orders were. 'What can you do for me?' said the king. 'I have lost a ring that was dearer to me than the whole of my kingdom and I don't know where it can have gone.' 'And these astrologers,' asked 'Usfur, 'how can this be concealed from them so that they don't produce it?' 'They can't do that,' the king told him, 'and I shall give a thousand dinars to anyone who can.' 'I can't do this until you tell me what I need to know,' 'Usfur said. The king agreed to this, and 'Usfur then asked him: 'Where were you when you lost the ring?' 'In the palace orchard,' the king told him.

'Take me there,' said 'Usfur, and the king and his courtiers got up and went off to it.

'Usfur took from his pocket a stick with a rope fastened to it and he lowered it into the water and left it for a time, causing one of the astrologers to exclaim that this was going to be a disaster. Then he lifted it and dragged it around, prompting another exclamation. Next he asked the king to get the eunuchs to see what wild creatures and the like, such as birds and beasts, were in the orchard and to show them all to him. The king ordered this to be done, and first of all he was shown the eunuchs, the servants young and old and every person who was in the orchard. They were followed by the wild animals, gazelles, hares and the like, and after them came the birds, geese, ostriches, chickens, falcons, sparrow hawks and so on. At the end came the ducks, and each one that the servants brought was made to pass in front of 'Usfur. When it was the turn of the lame duck, he stared at it wide-eyed, shook his head and spread open his fingers. The people there laughed at him, this being the duck that used to make the king laugh when he was angry. Now, when it passed, he laughed so much that he fell over on his back, but when 'Usfur saw it he gave so loud a shout that he startled his audience. 'Hold it,' he cried, 'for it was this that took the ring!' 'What?' exclaimed the king, and when 'Usfur swore that this was the thief the astrologers laughed at him, and the king told him that the duck had been there ever since his father's time. 'If you want the ring, take it from this duck,' insisted 'Usfur, and when the king asked what would happen if there was nothing there, 'Usfur promised that in that case he would replace the ring.

The king ordered the duck to be killed, although inwardly he was hoping that nothing would be found, but in fact there was the ring in its craw. When he saw it, he was delirious with joy and exclaimed to 'Usfur: 'By God, you have no match in the whole world!' He presented him with a robe of honour, a thousand dinars and food for three meals a day from the royal kitchens. The astrologers, cheated of their revenge, almost expired of anger and envy, and 'Usfur told the king that there was still one condition that he had not fulfilled. 'Tell me what you want,' said the king and 'Usfur told him that he wanted to drive the astrologers in front of him, slapping them from the palace to the door of his house. 'Spare them this,' said the king but when 'Usfur insisted he gave the order. 'Usfur mounted his mule, wearing his robe of honour, surrounded by servants, who were slapping the astrologers in front of him until they got to his house. The servants were presented with gold and dismissed, while the astrologers went off in the most wretched of states.

'Usfur went into his house and gave his wife the gold he had received as well as the robe of honour and told her what had happened. 'Didn't I tell you to go and trust in God?' she said. 'You ten thousand times harlot,' he exclaimed, 'you're always saying: "Go and trust in God," until a time comes when I go like a bird into a trap from which there is no escape. Get up and let's go to another town, for we have so much gold that if we ground it up and ate it we'd not reach the end of it.' 'By God, I shall never leave here except to go to my grave,' she said. 'Amen!' he exclaimed, 'and may God not bring you back from the dead but crush you.' He then sat back, praying to God for help.

For a time he enjoyed the pleasantest of lives, and the astrologers, filled with envy as they were, could find no way to harm him until one day they went to the king and said: 'Your Majesty, how is it that you have promoted over us a donkey who understands nothing but who beats us? This is unendurable, so either kill us all or let us have justice from him.' The king pointed out that 'Usfur had never failed to find what he was looking for, and they agreed but said that this was thanks to pure coincidence rather than knowledge. 'Fetch him to us,' they said, 'so that truth may be distinguished from falsehood.' 'I'll umpire this fairly,' the king told them, 'and so I'll hide something in the orchard. If you find it, I'll set you over him, but if he gets the better of you, don't try to hurt him again.'

When they had agreed to this, the king went to the orchard, where a bird was pursuing a locust. It swooped down, but the locust succeeded in getting beneath the skirt of the king's robe, pursued by the bird. The king took hold of them both, exclaiming on this remarkable coincidence, and keeping them hidden in his hand. He said that whoever could guess what he was holding would be set over his opponent and he told the astrologers to fetch 'Usfur, their enemy. When they called out to him he said: 'Well and good!' They told him that he was wanted by the king, and he told himself that this must be the decider. He got up and said goodbye to his children and his wife, to whom he said: 'You can be happy, you bitch. I shall be hanged, and they'll take the gold away from you.' 'Go off and rely on God,' she told him.

He went out to those who were waiting for him and then on to the king, greeting him as he entered and then taking his seat, looking at all the assembled astrologers. The king said: 'Sage, all these men have come here to say that you know nothing. I have argued with them about you and I'm going to decide between you. I have something in my hand, and whoever can guess what it is will be the winner.' One of the astrologers suggested that it was a gillyflower, another green leaves, another a water lily, yet another a narcissus, another a violet and another a lemon. Every one of them produced a guess, and every time the king said 'no'. At last only 'Usfur was left, and he was thinking about what had happened to him thanks to his wife, who had made him take up this art. The others said: 'Sage, why don't you speak? It's your turn.' 'Usfur said: 'Your Majesty, what can I say?' 'Go on,' the king told him, and he said: 'If it hadn't been for Jarad ['locust'] the bird ['Usfur] would not have fallen into the king's hand.' 'Very good, by God, very good!' the king exclaimed, and he took the locust and the bird from his hand. Everyone looked with astonishment at 'Usfur and exclaimed that there had never been anyone like him in the world. Jarada was the name of 'Usfur's wife, and what he had meant was that, but for her, he would not have fallen into that mess.

The king presented him with a robe of honour and, after giving him a hundred dinars, he asked him what he wanted. He said that he wanted the astrologers to be slapped as usual so that they wouldn't try anything against him again. The king gave the order and they left, while 'Usfur himself went back home and sat enjoying the pleasantest of lives. Word spread that this king had an astrologer who could find what was hidden, restore what had been stolen, and to whom every branch of knowledge was open.

The emperor of Rum had a learned astrologer unmatched in his age, and 'Usfur's reputation roused his envy. He told the emperor that he proposed to go off to hold a debate with him, saying that: 'If I win, we shall have got the better of the Muslims.' The emperor told him to get ready, and he took his servants, saddled up and set off, moving from stage to stage by night and day until he reached the king's city. He stayed outside it for three days, before his messenger asked permission to enter the king's presence.

When this was granted, the messenger entered and after presenting his services he said: 'Your August Majesty, the Emperor, Lord of 'Ammuriya, has a wise astrologer, the most learned of all those in Rum. It has come to his notice that you have a sage who has defeated all the men of excellence and learning and the astrologers. He has sent his own astrologer to you so that these two may hold a dispute in front of you, and whichever wins will be in the right.' The king sent a summons to

'Usfur that he should come and debate with the Rumi. When the servants reached his door and knocked on it, his wife said: 'Who is it?' They said: 'The king wants 'Usfur, as a Rumi sage has come from the emperor to debate with him, so that people can see which of them is the more learned. The winner will get robes of honour and gold, as well as being recognized as the wisest man of his age.'

'Usfur's wife went back to her husband and told him what the servants had said to her. He turned pale, and his appearance changed. 'Damn you, you bringer of "blessings",' he said, 'what am I going to do now? It only remains for this foreign astrologer to ask me something that I don't know in our dispute, and how am I going to answer?' 'Man, go off and put your trust in God,' she told him, 'for nothing but good will come of it.' He said: 'Every time you throw me on my head, and this time I'm going to be hanged. But, by God, I'm not going to let you get off with it when I'm gone. I'm going to say: "Master, it was she who got me to make fools of you by telling me to become an astrologer and laugh at people, though all I am is a weaver."'

He dressed and went out and, after reaching the palace and asking permission to enter, he went in, greeted the king and took his seat. The Rumi messenger was disturbed by the sight of his long beard and his wide eyes, but then the astrologer said: 'Your Majesty, I shall ask him three questions, and if he answers them he will have beaten me, and there will be no need for me to debate with him.' 'Are you happy with this?' the king asked 'Usfur, who said: 'Yes, and collect the people for me, so that they can act as witnesses.'

At that, the qadi, the *'udul*, the emirs and the leading citizens were brought in and told of the contest. When they had taken their seats, the Rumi astrologer pointed at 'Usfur, moved his hands gently and put them on the ground. At that, 'Usfur moved both his hands before lifting them up. 'Good, by God! Well done!' said the Rumi, adding: 'He has answered this question but there are two left, and if he gets them right he will have beaten me.' He then used his index finger to point at 'Usfur, who, widening his eyes, pointed at him with two fingers. 'By God and the truth of my religion,' exclaimed the Rumi, 'this is a learned man! He has got the better of me in two questions, but there is one left.' He then took out an egg from his pocket and pointed it at 'Usfur, who took a cheese from his own pocket and used this to point at the Rumi. On seeing this the Rumi exclaimed: 'By the truth of my religion, I used to think that I was the most learned of men and that I was in the right, but I have never seen anyone like this astrologer. Stretch out your hand, for I bear witness that there is no god but God and that Muhammad is the Apostle of God, may God bless him and give him peace.'

The king said: 'I didn't understand what the questions were or how they were put. Show me how he defeated you and what it was that you asked him first.' The Rumi said: 'I first asked him who it was who stretched out the earth and his answer was: "He Who raised up the heavens." Then I used my finger to ask if God had created Adam, and he used two fingers to say that He had created Eve as well. I brought out an egg and said that God created it between excrement and blood, and he produced a cheese to say that the same was true of it. In your presence, Your Majesty, I admit that he has defeated me and in front of you I accept conversion to Islam.'

The king now presented the Rumi with a robe of honour and a gift of five hundred dinars, and he gave the same to 'Usfur. 'Usfur asked him why he had given this to the Rumi when he had lost. 'Because he became a Muslim,' replied the king, at which 'Usfur said: 'I'll become a Muslim too, or a Christian, if you want.' The king and everyone there burst into laughter.

As the king was often told that 'Usfur was incomprehensible, he asked him: 'What did you say to him and what did he say to you?' 'When he moved both hands he meant that he was going to bury me, and I told him that I would lift him high up before dashing him to the ground and smashing his guts. He then told me: "You fool, I'm going to pluck out one of your eyes," and I said that I would take both of his. When he produced the egg he meant: "I'm going to eat this," and I said the same thing about my cheese.' The king [text 'vizier'] laughed and said: 'When God grants good fortune to one of his servants, He makes all things serve him, and when fortune comes it acts as teacher to a man.'

'Usfur's wife was in the habit of going and staying with the princess, who would give her robes of honour and money. 'Usfur approached her and said: 'You have sworn to me that you will never leave this city. Come on now. Tell the next lot who come for me that I died three days ago. That will be best, and for God's sake do what I ask so that we can get over this headache. If you don't, by God I'll kill myself.' 'I'll do it,' she told him.

For three days 'Usfur kept away from the king. The princess told servants to go to his wife, and when they did 'Usfur said that she had died. The princess was filled with grief and asked what had been wrong with her, saying: 'She was here the day before yesterday.' For his part the king asked about 'Usfur and was told that he had not been seen for three days. He sent off servants, who shouted for him, and when his wife asked who was there, they said: 'The king is asking for the sage.' His wife told them: 'He is dead.' They told the king, who asked when he had died. 'Two days ago, his wife said,' they told him, and he was very sorrowful and distressed. He went to his daughter to console her on the loss of her sage and found that she too was sad. She said: 'May God prolong your life in exchange for the astronomer's wife, a good woman who used to visit me.' He told her: 'I sent just now to ask for him, and his wife said that he was dead.' 'And I sent to ask for her just now, and he said that she was dead,' she replied.

The king kept saying: 'The astrologer is dead,' and his daughter kept saying: 'His wife is dead.' 'This must be one and the same affair,' the king decided. 'When night falls you and I will go with two eunuchs to find out who is really dead.' The princess agreed, and that night she, the king and two eunuchs went to 'Usfur's house and knocked on the door. No one answered, and they went on knocking until, as still there was no answer, they got impatient, and the king ordered the door to be broken down. This was done, and when they went up they found both 'Usfur and his wife dead. 'By God, the two of them are dead!' exclaimed the king. 'His wife must have died first,' his daughter said, which led the king to say: 'I'd give a thousand dinars to anyone who could tell me which it really was who died first.' At that 'Usfur gave a cry and sat up like a *jinni*, saying: 'I died first.' The king burst out laughing and said: 'Why did you do this?' 'Usfur told him: 'By God, your servant is no astrologer. It was my wife who made me do this.' The king laughed again and presented him with a robe of honour and the gift of a thousand dinars, taking him as one of his companions.

'Usfur stayed with the king, leading the most pleasant, enjoyable and trouble-free life until Death parted them. This is the whole story, and God knows better.

Tale Ten

The Story of Sul and Shumul with
Reports and Poetry, and
How Shumul Was Abducted,
As Well As What Ordeals
Her Cousin Sul Faced and How the
Two Were Reunited. It Is a
Marvellous Tale.

In the Name of God, the Compassionate, the Merciful

They say – and God knows better and is Greater and more Glorious –
that amongst the stories of past peoples is one of two brothers of the
Banu Sa'd known for their generosity, hospitality to guests and swords-
manship. One was called al-Khattaf, and the second al-Muhadhdhab.

The Banu Sa'd had made al-Khattaf their emir, entrusting their affairs
to him. He had a handsome son who surpassed all the other young men
in beauty, culture and understanding, who never hesitated to answer
questions and who stayed close to his father. His father named him Sul.
For his part al-Muhadhdhab had a daughter called Shumul, and both
children were of the same age. Shumul was the most beautiful and graceful girl of her time, surpassing the others in the splendour of her
loveliness, the shapeliness of her figure and her quick understanding.

Sul and Shumul were friends, and Shumul would join Sul to talk and
recite poetry, and they would then part with no suspicion of indecency
attaching to them. Day by day their love for each other increased.

One day they met as usual and, after talking for a long time and complaining of their love, Shumul asked Sul to recite some of the poetry he
had written about her. He produced these lines:

I swear by my parents there is an Arab girl
Who is without an equal in this world.
She is a full moon. My heart sickens with her love.
A slender virgin, dawn is on her brow,
Unchanging, she enslaves men with her loveliness,
And her face blunts and turns their glances back again.
She has dark eyes, the magic of whose lids
Comes from the languorous glances that they cast.

My longing for her will last all my life,
And I am bound in fetters of her love.
Shumul, you are my joy and the goal of my hope.
None other shall distract me till I die.
I swear this by the truth of the Almighty God,
To Whom we call, and to His Messenger,
Light of the Hashimis, who brought us the Qur'an.
This love of mine for you shall never fade
Until the pain of longing brings me death,
And my last journey takes me to my grave.
From there your love will raise me up to God.
If I am asked, then I shall say to Him:
'For Sul the fires of love are a just punishment,
And all mankind falls to Shumul's assault.'

'Well done, cousin!' exclaimed Shumul. 'Now give us more.' At that Sul
recited:

My heart is struck by love for a young girl,
A wild calf wearing anklets, love for whom
Has worn away my body. In her hand
Approval is a sword, and any man
Whom she took as a mate would scatter all his foes.
I shall meet death if I conceal her love,
But if I speak it, I cannot find words.

'Well done, cousin!' repeated Shumul, and again she called for more. At
that Sul recited:

Love for a girl has struck my heart,
Who charms her lovers with a smile,
A young wild calf who, when she bends,
Is like a branch kept fresh by rain,
Nineteen years old, a full moon in the night.
She has my heart's blood and my heart itself,
Thanks to the arrows that her eyes have shot.
These strike the lovers' hearts at which she aims.
When I ask her for union I am shown
The gross enormity of what I want.
How can I forget one who captured me
With a figure for which there is no like?

'Well done, cousin!' repeated Shumul, and she again called for more. At that Sul recited:

How am I to forget what fate has brought?
This is the only harvest for my eyes.
She dulls my senses when she turns to me.
I see how small she is, yet she is like a moon;
Her eyes are white and black; what would I give for them!
Her radiant beauty gives the moon its light.
I swear by God that she outshines that moon.
I cannot bear to be without Shumul,
And my endurance has come to an end.
In sadness I keep watch over the stars,
While my tears flood down from my eyes like rain.
My restless longing makes me watch those stars,
Until the light of dawn has filled the sky.
It is as though, thanks to my tears, these eyes
Are scratched by needles or are pricked by thorns.
I used to guard against this, fearing it,
But destiny has brought me what I feared.
Say to Shumul she can sleep quietly,
While sleeplessness and passion torment Sul.
Light of my eyes, my hearing and my sight,
You are all that I wish for from mankind,
My love for you is fixed within my heart,
And cannot be plucked from my inmost thoughts,
For it is closer to me than my eyes and ears.

'Well done, cousin!' repeated Shumul, and she again called for more. At that Sul recited:

I would give up my life for this gazelle
Who is at liberty to shed my blood.
I swear by pilgrims to God's Holy House,
Mecca, Mina, Zamzam and al-Safa,
That I love you. God knows this love of mine
For you outweighs the mountains and the hills.
It stays within my heart, between my flesh and bones;
It will remain there till my dying day,
Meeting no alteration when I die.

Then when I lie within my tomb alone,
I shall remember it till Judgement Day.
For at the Resurrection it will be with me,
Joined to me as my hand is to my arm.
Then when I look back at my death,
I shall see what is written in my book,
To destine me to heaven or to hell.
Shumul, here is a lover sick with love;
Show generosity to such a man!
Do not begrudge union to one like him,
And do not think it right to shed his blood.

'Well done, cousin! How eloquent you are!' exclaimed Shumul, adding: 'But dawn has broken and it is time to go.' At that Sul heaved a deep sigh and recited these lines:

Dawn is at hand and wrongly forces me to leave;
Would that I knew if I shall meet my love
Once more within an orchard to embrace,
And would that God had not created parting and its bitterness.
I pray that He may grant relief to me
From sufferings that other lovers share.
Light of my eyes, what do you want to do
With one whose heart has leaped out from his breast?
Grant me your love and so preserve my life;
Have pity on the length of my distress.

'Well done, cousin!' said Shumul. 'Now show patience, for patience is followed by relief.' She left and Sul went back to his family and spent some days without seeing her. He then talked to his nurse, Hamama, who had suckled him and raised him and who loved him as a mother loves her son. 'Nurse,' he said, 'thanks to Shumul I feel what is like the prick of a needle in my heart or like burning fire. As I have not seen her for days, would you go to her as my messenger?' 'My son, I would not grudge you my own life,' she told him, and he asked her to take Shumul these lines:

Though you are kept from me, yet in my heart
The coals of longing are stirred by your memory.
You torture me, and yet I long for you,
With longing felt by mothers for their sons.

Light of my eyes, my hearing and my sight,
Your love has made endurance play me false.
Do not go too far, you who torture me,
Whose memory is in my inmost heart.
I swear by the One, Everlasting God,
To seek Whose favour we come to His house,
My love for you will not cease while I live,
Until the breath of life has left my breast.
I hope for your forgiveness, stretching out my hand.
I ask that I may ever be with you,
For honey is less sweet to me than this.
I send my greeting to you every time a dove
Coos to lament a dear one it has lost.

He sprinkled musk with crushed saffron and camphor on the note, sealed it with amber and passed it to Hamama. She took it and went to Shumul, who realized as soon as she saw her that she was coming from him and winked at her, as her mother was present. Her mother and Hamama exchanged greetings, and Hamama sat there talking for a long time until everyone except Shumul's mother had left. She then stayed, sitting at her ease, until the mother had gone off about some business of her own.

At this point Shumul asked Hamama how she was, adding: 'And how is my beloved, the delight of my eyes, Sul?' The nurse was a cultured woman, one of the finest scions of a noble house. She said: 'Sul is infatuated with you and he longs to be close to you. This is his letter to you,' and, producing it, she passed it to Shumul, who kissed it and placed it over her eyes. She then broke the seal, opened the letter and studied its contents.

She broke into tears and said: 'By God, nurse, I was kept away from him for a reason, but I can find no comfort without him, and he is the one who knows of the love we shared in our youth.' 'My little daughter,' said Hamama, 'were you to let me ask your father and your brothers for your hand, God might bring comfort to the two of you by allowing you union, with you as his wife and him as your husband.' 'I'm afraid that my father would not allow that or consent to it,' Shumul replied.

She took a sheet of paper, scented it with musk and saffron, and wrote these lines:

The letter that I read from you brought me delight,
Serving my body as the breath of life,
And it was better than health to the sick.

Light of my eyes, my hearing and my sight,
You are my prop in this world and my life.
Within my body and my soul your love has pride of place.
I swear by the One God, for me you are unique.
You are my hope; I cannot turn away.

She scattered perfumes of all sorts on it before sealing it and handing it to Hamama, to whom she gave a sum of money, saying: 'Be patient, Hamama, and tell him that we shall meet after two nights.'

Hamama took the letter and brought it to Sul, who kissed it and placed it on his eyes before falling down in a faint. Hamama went to him, and some time later, after she had lifted his head on to her knees and given him perfume to sniff, he recovered and opened his eyes. He then sat up, took the letter, broke the seal and read it. When he had finished, he turned to Hamama and said: 'Nurse, what did the delight of my eyes say to you?' She told him that he could take heart and be happy and said: 'Shumul loves you more than you love her, and she promises to visit you after two nights.'

On hearing this, Sul sprang up delightedly, kissed her head and her eyes and gave her a large sum of money together with a fine robe of honour. Two days later Shumul sent him a message to say that she would meet him that night. He spent a long day waiting, and when night began to fall he went to the agreed spot. On seeing him she jumped up to greet him, and after they had exchanged lengthy embraces they both fell unconscious. Both Hamama and Shumul's maid sprinkled them with rose-water until they had recovered.

After they had sat talking for a long time, Shumul asked Sul what new poetry he had composed about her. He recited these lines:

I pledge my life to ransom a gazelle from Sa'd,
A sheltered Arab girl, whose love imprisons me.
She rises with the light of the full moon,
And it is like this that her splendour shines,
A tender girl, full-fleshed and innocent,
Who when she smiles shows teeth that shine like pearls.
Her lovely cheeks rob lovers of their wits,
Like perfumed roses; her mouth is a ring
Which her Lord has adorned with lovely teeth.
When she smiles sweetly, you would think that here

Were jewels hid away in oyster shells.
She is the mistress of all excellence,
As she deserves to be, and she holds me in thrall.
I long for her with every star that shines,
And with the moon illumining the dawn,
As long as God the Merciful is called by name,
And as long as men travel over land and sea.
I long for her whenever darkness falls,
When lightning flashes or when the dove coos.
I shall protect her while I live, and when I die
My love for her will cheer me in my tomb.
Then when the dead are raised it will be part of me,
Either to lead me on to Paradise,
Or else to take me to the fires of Hell.

'Well done, cousin!' repeated Shumul, and she again called for more. At that Sul recited:

The floods of tears bring wounds to my eyelids,
When they appear like rain upon my cheeks.
For long I had no burden on my heart
And I enjoyed my life amongst the chiefs.
The search for knowledge was my only care,
And to explore how God's verses came down.
I spent my time in ignorance of love,
And lived unwounded by the beautiful,
Until a swelling-breasted girl afflicted me,
Looking at me with magic in her eyes.
She was fourteen years old and her glance enticed men.
She was without a match in loveliness.
I ask for union, telling her to pity me,
But she has shown no pity for my tears,
Leaving me sunk in drunkenness of care.
I boasted over lovers and was false to them.
Do you have mercy on me in my wretchedness,
For in this you are now my only hope.
And rescue me from this fatal disease.
Either you grant your lover happiness,
Or, if you do not, I shall surely die.

'Well done, cousin!' repeated Shumul, and she again called for more. At that Sul recited:

> Who will secure me justice from a young girl of Sa'd,
> Bright as the moon, whose smile shows lovely teeth?
> When I saw her amongst the women, she was like
> A full moon shining in the dark of night,
> Gazelle, enchantress, her glance captures hearts,
> Hunting them down with magic as they melt with love.
> Within her languorous eyelids is a Yathrib sword.
> To you I hold my hand out, hoping for a gift.

'Well done, cousin!' repeated Shumul, and again she called for more. At that Sul recited:

> Shumul, dawn tells us we must part,
> And when it breaks, it adds love to my love.
> Would that the light of day would never gleam,
> And I might never have to leave my eyes' delight.
> Although I am your ransom, have I any hope
> From you or do you mean to leave me dead?
> I ask the King of Heaven for His grace,
> Which He grants to the pilgrims of His House.
> I ask mercy and favour from the One,
> Eternal God, for I swear by my love
> For you that cannot be undone,
> And has no bounds, that this wears me away.
> Shumul, do not reject or treat me with harshness,
> For you will kill me if you break with me.
> Now may the peace of God Almighty rest on you!

Sul left for home, and his mother said: 'I am afraid that this affair may endanger you, as before you people have been destroyed thanks to love, whose path no one can follow in safety. Tell your father, al-Khattaf, about it so that he may do his best to get his brother to give you the girl's hand, and she may be your wife and you her husband.' 'Mother,' he said, 'I would be ashamed to approach my father, as I hold him in awe and respect.'

He then recited these lines:

> My tears reveal the secrets of my heart
> When they pour down like floods of rain.

If you could only know my growing cares,
The burning pain of my abandonment,
Mother, you would bemoan my fated love.
Do me whatever good you can,
So that you may obtain goodwill from God.

After this he burst into violent tears, in which his mother joined out of pity for him. 'Be patient, my son,' she told him. 'It may be that God will bring this about through your father, so wait to see what answer he gives me.' Sul, however, continued to weep, and he recited:

How can I bear this when I have no patience left,
And in my heart burn raging fires of love?
I showed endurance but it drained away,
Thanks to the love that never gives me rest.
Mother, do quickly what you promised me,
In order to win mercy from Almighty God.

His mother agreed willingly and said: 'I shall speak to your father and then tell you what he says.' When al-Khattaf came she talked to him about this and told him that Sul was in a state of great distress, as Shumul was being kept away from him, and she feared for his life. 'Where is he?' his father asked and when she told him that it was only shyness that kept him from coming to him he said: 'I shall settle the affair for him, God willing.' His mother left joyfully and went to Sul, who was weeping. 'Take comfort and be happy,' she told him, 'for I spoke to your father, and, God willing, this affair of yours is settled.'

Sul recited these lines:

My flooding tears reveal my inmost thoughts.
If you knew, mother, how my heart is burned,
You would bemoan this wretched fate of mine.

He shed tears and his mother wept out of pity for him and swore to him that she would get him what he wanted even if it cost her everything she had.

When al-Khattaf had dismounted she provided him with food as usual. Sul was sitting at the table, and she told al-Khattaf to discuss the affair with him. 'What do you have to say, Sul?' he asked. 'Is it true what your mother says?' Sul felt too ashamed to lift his head and speak, but his father said: 'By God, my son, I have taken this to heart and I shall do it, for I can never abandon you. I swear that whatever you want you shall have and at this very moment I shall go about your affair.' Sul got up, kissed his hand and thanked him.

Al-Khattaf rose immediately, mounted and rode off in search of his brother, whom he found surrounded by many of his family. When they saw him they rose to their feet, presented their respects and helped him to dismount, before giving him a courteous welcome. His brother was pleased to see him and told him to come close, calling for food as soon as he was seated.

When the food came and al-Muhadhdhab had invoked the name of God everyone stretched out their hands to it with the exception of al-Khattaf. 'Why aren't you doing the same as the others?' asked his brother, at which al-Khattaf replied: 'I shall not eat any food of yours until you fulfil my need.' 'You can have anything you want from me, including my daughter Shumul,' al-Muhadhdhab told him. 'It is she whom I do want,' al-Khattaf said and he then stretched out his hand and began to eat.

'By God, brother,' said al-Muhadhdhab, 'it was not because I disliked him that I kept your son away but because I was afraid of disgrace. Why did he not come himself to ask for my daughter's hand? I don't know whether he wants this marriage or not.' At that al-Khattaf ordered Sul to be fetched, and when he came he gave profuse greetings to his uncle, who told him to approach. 'Sul,' he said, 'ask for what you want.' Sul said: 'I know that you are my uncle and that you brought me up. I want to join my wing to yours so that our close bonds may never be severed. I want you to marry me to my cousin, Shumul. Do not frustrate me or dash the hope that I have placed in you, for I have a better right to her than anyone else.'

He then recited these lines:

Join with me, uncle, for those who join are best,
And do not look to put another in my place.
You know how close I am to you, so strengthen this.
Those who join with their kin are shown mercy by God,
While those who break this tie act unjustly.
I place my hope in you, so join with me,
And do not let my expectations fail.

His uncle praised him and said that he was very dear to him. He then asked what dowry he would provide for his cousin. 'I myself, my wealth and my life are all yours, Uncle,' Sul assured him. 'As you say,' his uncle told him, 'but just now people want to hear what you are offering at this moment.' Sul then recited:

My Lord is great and generous beyond compare,
And He created every class of man to be unique;
He is the Lord of grace and generosity,
The Great and Glorious God, Pre-eminent.
He sent His prophets to reveal His truth,
And rescued us from error and ruin.
He gave us His pure Prophet, to adorn mankind.
Through him the unbelievers were destroyed,
And we were led to doing what was best.
I have asked for your daughter's hand; say what you want,
For in this matter I shall not delay.
Hear what I have to say, Uncle, and judge;
You can have all the silver that you want,
As well as every other type of wealth.
I shall give fifty servants for her, fifty slaves,
With fifty horses and as many mules,
Together with a thousand dinars on the spot.

'Take heart and be happy!' said his uncle when he heard this. 'Tomorrow, God willing, I shall get you what you want in the presence of your relatives and the tribesmen, and I shall marry you to Shumul on the terms that you have mentioned. I, my wealth and Shumul will be yours and at your service.'

The narrator continued: While this was happening Shumul was listening from inside the house and she was almost delirious with joy. Sul sent word to have camels, cows and sheep brought up to be slaughtered and he prepared a splendid feast, with butter and honey. Carpets were laid out and censers were used to spread perfume. The food was produced with plenty of wine; glasses and drinking bowls circulated as musical instruments and drums were played, while the guests began to eat, drink, dance and enjoy themselves.

It was then that al-Khattaf called to his son. 'This is your time, Sul,' he said. 'Get to your feet and kiss your uncle's head.' Sul stood up and gestured for silence, at which everyone obediently stopped talking. Then he said: 'Cousins, I want you to help me with the request that I am making to my uncle that he unite me to his daughter Shumul.' They shouted their approval calling on al-Muhadhdhab to add to their delight. He agreed and, rising to his feet, he shook Sul's hand again in the presence of them all. This added to their joy and, as the noise rose, people came up from all sides.

Sul left them to it and kissed the heads of his father and mother in gratitude for what they had done. He then told his mother that he wanted to go off on a journey. 'My son,' she said, 'what makes you think of going on a journey just now? Don't do it!' He insisted that he had to go to Iraq, and Shumul, on hearing of this, sent to him in distress appealing to him not to go. When he insisted that he would have to do this she said: 'Cousin, do not forget our covenant; guard against difficulties on the way and may God keep you safe.'

He took leave of his father, his cousins and everyone who was there but he was only away for a short time before he came back, bringing gifts, treasures, wealth, jewels with much else besides to the delight of his parents and his kin. He then produced a banquet even more magnificent than the first, providing food, drink, robes of honour and gifts. For seven days the people ate and drank, and on the eighth his uncle ordered the marriage to be consummated.

The people spent most of the night dancing, amusing themselves and enjoying their food. Then Shumul came out with bridesmaids attending to her needs, swaying between them in her delight like a branch of the *ban* tree or a thirsty gazelle. With her smooth cheeks, kohl-black eyes and heavy buttocks she was fascinating as she advanced and devastating as she retired.

She was as the poet has described:

Shaped like a *ban* tree she lives at her ease,
Covered with many lovely ornaments.
When she moves she is like the gleaming moon,
Shedding the light of beauty on all men.
Thanks to my Lord, she outshines all,
And is without an equal in the world.

While her companions played and she was walking happily towards her cousin Sul, all of a sudden an enormous snake appeared. Fire was coming from its nose; its teeth were like hooks and its mouth was like a well; it had a head like a cauldron and hair like horses' ears. It soared into the sky and in its full length it was like a huge mountain.

The sight of it terrified Shumul and robbed her of her senses. A dazzling ray spread from its back with a glare that reached the horizon, and it swooped down on her, snatching her away from her companions faster than the blink of an eye. She cried out to Sul; her companions shrieked, and in the tumult that followed many fainted at what they saw. The others questioned the witnesses, who told them what had happened to her. They struck themselves and poured dust over their heads, and in the commotion Sul came, striking his chest with a rock, slapping his face and gnawing at his fingers. He was about to kill himself when the others restrained him and he continued in this state until he lost consciousness, after which they sat by his head, weeping for him and grieving for Shumul.

Things went on like that for the rest of the night until morning. When the sun rose and the day became hot, Sul recovered but said nothing, and his movements were those of a dying man. He got up automatically without realizing the affliction that God had brought upon him and what it was that he, his family and all the others had seen. There was yet more wailing and lamentation as they all grieved and bewailed the disaster. Sul got up and drew his sword and he was again about to kill himself when his cousins held him back.

He threw away his sword and recited these lines:

How can I enjoy life now that she is gone,
My darling, whom disaster came to strike?
What happiness, what pleasure is in life?
My love has gone, so set, you crescent moon,
And as for you, sun, never shine again.
God pardon those who wish me a quick death,
For, with my darling lost, my life is black.

He wept bitterly until he fainted and he was so still and cold that they thought that he must be dead. He stayed like that for two or three days with the people weeping for him, for Shumul and over the disaster that had overtaken them. He then sat up, trembling, looking right and left and saying: 'I wish that I had been a ransom for you, Shumul.' His family were reproaching him, but he paid no attention to anyone or listened to what they said. He would neither eat nor drink in spite of advice from his mother that he should do this and show courage. 'Summon the astrologers and the sorcerers,' she told him, 'and ask them about your cousin. If she is still alive, go to look for her before you die of grief.' 'Mother,' he answered, 'I am never, never going to meet her again unless through the will of Almighty God.'

One night, when he was asleep, he saw Shumul in a dream. She was reproaching him and saying: 'When was it that you forgot me and sat back with your family?' She was sitting weeping in the cell of a monk as she said this. Sul started up in fear and alarm but then fainted. His parents, cousins and the rest of his family gathered around him and asked what he had seen in his dream. For a long time he gave no answer, but then, after another fit of fainting, he recovered and recited these lines:

> My darling's apparition came to me
> When the muezzin called in the dark night.
> She was in tears, and her reproach to me
> Was like that of a kinsman to his kin.
> 'Do you think of another and not me,'
> She said, 'although I am the best of all your friends?
> As a true lover, you should not forget.'
> Victims of Time are not like the carefree,
> And after her how can I enjoy life,
> Or sit again amongst the lovely girls?

When he had finished, they asked him how he was and what he had seen in his dream. He told them tearfully that he had seen Shumul in the cell of a monk and he swore by the only God that he would not rest or stay in any town but would travel around the regions, questioning travellers so as to hear news or find some trace of her.

He got up immediately and took a bag of Ta'if leather, into which he put everything that he would need on his journey. He had an ebony cane, set with silver, and on his head he wore a felt cap, while he also carried with him a number of books and spells. He took leave of his parents, his cousins and kin, who, after asking how he was, said: 'For God's sake, do not abandon your father and your mother to wander miserably through parts of the world that you do not know. There are plenty of girls here, so choose whom you want.'

With a deep sigh Sul exclaimed: 'I shall never, never do that! I must follow her wherever she may be or die for her.' 'Take any of us you want with you,' they said, but he swore that he would take no one. 'My son,' said his mother, 'by the breast that nurtured you I implore you to take me with you and do not let me die without you.' He replied: 'If I am unwilling to take a man, how should I take women?'

He then mounted his camel and rode to Rafiqa, where at a distance from the road was the cell of an anchorite. He halted beneath it and recited these lines:

By the Evangel and the Psalms, I call you, anchorite,
And by the well-wrought verses of your Lord,
By Simeon and Goliath, answer me.
By the Messiah and the bell you ring at dawn,
And by Mary, tell me if you have seen
A moon who serves me as my ears and eyes.
Answer me if you know, for I am lost in cares.
Tell me, and may the evils that you fear not fall on you.
I am afflicted and I cannot bear the loss
Of one I saw to be so beautiful.

When Sul had finished the anchorite opened the door of his cell and looked down at him. He was an old man with eyebrows that had sunk over his eyes and when he saw Sul he exchanged greetings with him and then answered his lines as follows:

Greetings to one who comes to me at dawn
And asks about the rising of the moon.
You ask, I see, about both sun and moon,
And this full moon of yours is a human.
But I have not seen it at night or in the dawn.
Tell me then who you are, so rain may give you drink.

Sul told his story, and the old man felt pity for him but told him reproachfully to go back to his family. Sul would not accept this but moved on towards Aleppo until he had come to another cell. Standing beneath it, he recited:

By the Evangel, anchorite, tell me,
And do not hide from me what you have seen.
I ask you by Nasut and by Jalut,
And by the lessons taught on Palm Sunday,
Tell me if you have seen a moon escaped from Paradise.
Tell me, and may the evils that you fear not fall on you.

A handsome anchorite looked down at him and replied to his lines:

> I swear by Simeon and the priest,
> I have not seen the girl whom you described.
> Tell me, what is this trial that Time has brought on you?

When Sul had told him his story, the man blamed him and asked him to return to his family. Sul would not listen and set off for Damascus, going on until he came to the pasture land known as al-Rauda in the territory of al-Qutaifa. There, standing beneath an anchorite's cell, he recited these lines:

> By the Evangel, I call on you, monk.
> May God avert from you the harm you fear.
> My love has been well known amongst all men;
> I am heartbroken, for we shared a love,
> And my beloved served me as my soul.
> I thought that I had won her, but then God
> Brought down on me what I could not ward off.
> An 'ifrit or a devil swooped down from the sky;
> Time robbed me of endurance and was false to me.
> I pray to God that He grant me relief.

The monk opened the door of his cell and called down praises on the Lord of angels and the Holy Spirit before answering Sul in these lines:

> Praise to the One Eternal God,
> Lord of all being. He is God alone.
> Tell me what happened to you, for your lines
> Have caused me pain, and I invoke
> Christ, Simeon and reciters of the Psalms.
> I have not seen the one of whom you spoke;
> Endure, for this is the best prop a man can have.

When Sul was asked for his story and had told it, the monk shed tears of pity and said: 'Young man, you are handsome but I can see no spices here.' Sul asked what he meant by spices, and the monk said: 'How can you leave your father and mother and go off on your travels because of a dream you saw? This was a nightmare, so be sensible and go back to your family.'

Sul left him and set off again for Damascus. When he came in sight of its trees and streams with their singing birds and when he saw the beauty of the buildings that surrounded it he recited these lines:

Would that I knew where the one is I look for in these lands.
Where is Shumul, whose memory tortures me?
Damascus was in bloom when I saw it,
As the scent of its flowers spread over me,
And birds upon its boughs exchanged their songs.
These boughs were intertwined and put out leaves and fruits;
Water gushed from the springs,
Spreading amongst the meadows and the trees.
I looked out on this loveliness, but cares
Rose to oppress me from my memories.
I took an oath which I shall never break
That I shall travel through the nights and days
Until I find the one I love, Shumul,
And so fulfil my hope through God Almighty's power,
Or die and then return to the great God.

He went on reciting these lines until he came to the city, may God guard it, and entered the mosque. He prayed with two *rak'as* and, having spent the night there, he left for Jerusalem, may God ennoble it. High above him he saw the cell of an anchorite, and, standing below it, he recited these lines:

Monk in your lofty cell, may the rain give you drink;
Live in tranquillity, free from the blows of Time.
Tell me if you have seen a moon that outshines all mankind.

When the monk heard this, he opened his cell door and looked at Sul, noting his handsomeness and his dignified appearance. He replied in the following lines:

Welcome to a full moon that comes at dawn,
To ask about a loved one he has lost,
A girl who has no match amongst mankind.
But I can swear by Jesus and by Simeon,
By priest and bishop, that I have not seen
This girl by night or in the light of dawn.

He asked Sul for his story and when he had been told of his grief he said: 'Young man, return to your family and, for God's sake, don't get yourself killed.' Sul left him and went on to Ramla and from there to al-Fustat, where he consulted sorcerers and wise men, none of whom could tell him anything. He then went to al-Qarafa, where there was a monastery overlooking the town, and he stood underneath this and started to recite:

> Monk living in your lofty cell,
> May God save you from any ills you fear!
> May you enjoy prolonged comfort and ease,
> Untroubled by disasters that Time brings!
> I call on you in Jesus' name and the clear verses of your books,
> Your monastery and your priest, to tell me
> If you have seen a moon that shows through clouds.
> My life and pleasure have gone with Shumul.

The monk, on hearing this, was moved by pity and opened the door of his cell to look out. He was a handsome and dignified grey-haired man and he said: 'Young man, you have distressed me,' and he replied to Sul's poem in these lines:

> Young man, you dismayed me by what you said,
> For Time brings with it its catastrophes.
> You have aroused my interest; tell me of your need,
> For you have called to mind the pleasures I enjoyed,
> And what God brought me with the passing nights,
> And what was written in the Book of Fate.
> As a young man I walked out cheerfully,
> While on my head the parting was still black.
> I loved a black-eyed girl like a full moon,
> But then Time came with sorrows and calamities.
> We were united but it parted us,
> Pouring my love a cup of death to drink,
> Leaving me wandering sadly through the world.

'I see that you are a sad man,' Sul told him. 'I am,' replied the monk, 'and if you come in I shall tell you my story.' Sul entered, and the monk shut the door before leading the way up to a room with high walls, white both inside and out, with lines of poetry inscribed around it. At the side of it was an orchard with all kinds of fruits and grazing gazelles.

At the sight of this Sul felt a sense of happiness, remembering how he had sat in gardens with Shumul and the pleasant times he had had with her. He began to recite these lines:

In an Egyptian monastery I thought of you,
And your love burns more fiercely in my heart.
The tears flowed from me as I mourned your loss,
And who would not shed tears for a lost love?
I shall scour east and west, desert and pasture, all my days.
It may be that the Lord will let us meet,
And bring us back to where we were before.
I send you greetings from a broken heart,
As long as the sun's light shines in the west,
And fishes in the depth give praise to God,
As long as the waves break upon the shore,
As long as turtle doves sing on the boughs,
And while the gleaming stars still shine.

When the monk heard this he exclaimed: 'By God, you are a remarkable man! You have stirred up old sorrows and disturbed me, for your story is like mine.' For all that, he felt great pleasure and produced food for Sul, telling him to eat. Sul told him that he had taken an oath that he would neither eat food nor drink wine until he was reunited with his darling Shumul. The monk urged him to eat and ate himself while offering wine to Sul, who still refused, and they sat talking until the monk said: 'By God, Sul, your tale is strange, but mine is stranger still.'

Sul asked him to tell him this, and the monk agreed and began: 'You must know, young man, that I suffered a greater misfortune than you. I come from a place called Barza in the territory of Damascus, and my father was a wealthy and prosperous man with an abundant livelihood. He had married a Damascene woman and moved out to Barza, where he stayed and where I was born. He was overjoyed by my birth, giving thanks to the Great and Glorious God, distributing alms, freeing slaves, giving gifts and holding a huge banquet. When I was five years old he sent me to school and had me taught all that boys should know.

'On the day of my birth a Damascene girl was born who lived in a house that my father owned and who was brought up with me. Neither of us could bear to be separated from the other for a single hour. From childhood on we were close to one another, as she loved me and I loved her, and I used to write poetry about her. Her name was Sukut while I am al-Mutayyam son of Tihan son of al-Sarir al-'Amiri.

'Amongst what I wrote about her are the following lines:

Love for a young girl breaks my heart;
With a flirtatious glance she steals my wits away.
My heart is filled up by my love for her;
The arrows of her eyes have pierced my vital parts.
She shares my own complaint and frets,
Thanks to the burning passion of our love.
"Be quick to come to me," she says, and I reply:
"I shall be quick, if you will do that too."

Sul, who had been listening, was delighted by his eloquence and the
beauty of his poetry, which served to increase his own passionate longing. 'Monk,' he asked, 'what happened then?' The monk replied: 'For a
long time we stayed in love like this, and I never did anything to harm
her. I then became anxious and unable to sleep as I thought over possible dangers to her. I composed a eulogy for the lord of Damascus, who
gave me a generous reward because he had known my father. I stayed
the night with him and told him my story, letting him know the love,
longing and passion from which I was suffering. I then asked him to
send to the girl's family to ask them to grant me her hand in marriage.

'When they agreed to this, he weighed out the dowry from his own
money, leaving me overjoyed. Some days later, however, Sukut fell gravely
ill. I stayed looking after her for a time, but she was gathered to the mercy
of Almighty God. This had a terrible effect on me, and I wanted to kill
myself but was prevented and for days I neither ate nor slept. In this cell
there was a Rumi who died at the age of one hundred and forty, and I
took his place, choosing seclusion and associating with no one, as after
the death of my beloved there was nothing that I wanted in the world. I
have stayed here until I met you, Sul, and this is the end of my story.'

Sul heaved a deep sigh and recited these lines:

Praise be to God Who has afflicted me
With love for one whose loss has caused me pain.
Praise be to our Creator, the Omniscient.
I ask Him of His mercy that He bring us close,
And reunite us after parting us,
So humbling the ill-omened envious,
And turning back our sorrow into joy.

The monk then reproached him and told him: 'Go back soon to your
family. You are a young man and you cannot endure toil nor do you

know where in the world your beloved is. So don't risk your life but return home.' 'By God,' said Sul, 'I shall wander through every single part of the world and either find what I hope for or die of grief.'

He stayed with the monk for three days but when he was intending to leave on the fourth a number of people arrived on a visit and came to al-Qarafa outside Fustat, near the monk's cell. The monk was glad to see them and said to Sul: 'You can be glad to know that you have got what you want. Shaikh Najah has come, and it is he who will lead you to your goal. He is a sorcerer, and all other sorcerers go to him for help, as he is their leader. He can summon devils and *marids* as he in possession of the Greatest Name of God which gives him mastery over all the others.'

The monk then brought Sul a donkey and took him down with him. When the shaikh saw him he got up to greet him, thanking him for coming and saying: 'We are not used to seeing you coming down from your cell, as it was we who were going to present our services to you.' The monk told him that there was something he needed and he told Sul's story from beginning to end, explaining how he had been parted from his cousin.

The shaikh looked at Sul and told him that he could be at ease. 'I was on my way to China,' he explained, 'on an errand for my father Iblis, God curse him, which only I could perform, and he had sent with me these flying devils. When I come here I usually stay no more than three days, but now that I have met you I see that yours is a remarkable case which can only be solved by Iblis Abu Murra himself. His authority extends over all the *jinn* and the devils, and none of them can conceal anything from him.'

When Sul heard this he burst into tears and recited these lines:

What can I say when fires of longing burn my heart,
And its anguish consumes my inmost parts?
I did not think Time would do this to me,
But perhaps you may pity me today.
Listen, God guide you; feel my sufferings,
So through your help I may find happiness.

When the shaikh heard this, he was pleased and impressed by Sul's eloquence and felt pity for him, realizing that he was sincere in what he said. He again told him that he could be at ease and that he felt compassion for him. Because of this and out of respect for the monk he would go back to Iblis, rescue Shumul and reunite her with Sul. 'You must know, Sul,' he said, 'that I am a man of authority, and all the *jinn*, in the sky or on the earth, obey me.' Sul was overjoyed when he heard this and recovered his senses.

For three days the shaikh stayed with the monk and on the fourth he ordered the emir of the *'ifrits* to carry Sul so they could fly with him, and he told Sul to hold his tongue and never mention the name of God. He then mounted him on the *'ifrit*'s back, and they all flew off through the night. At midnight they landed at the gate of a city, where the Shaikh told Sul his brothers lived and whose king was his friend. They waited until daybreak, but when it grew light the shaikh took Sul into the city with him. The gatekeepers came rushing out but when they saw Shaikh Najah they recognized him, kissed the ground in front of him and prostrated themselves before him.

When they told the king's guards of his arrival, the king himself with his officials and intimates came out to greet him. Najah went up and kissed the king's stirrup, while the king kissed his head by way of welcome before asking who the young man was he had with him. At this point Najah told him Sul's story from beginning to end, explaining what had happened to him and how he had lost his cousin, while adding an account of his eloquence and culture. 'This is as good as finished,' said the king and, turning to Sul, he told him to take comfort, saying: 'When Shaikh Najah comes here on any errand, the matter is settled quickly.'

This delighted Sul, who called down blessings on the king and then recited these lines:

A wretched lover greets the mighty king.
Greetings from Sul, of whom men talk all year.
Time has afflicted me, mighty and generous lord,
And I have come to you from the earth's end,
So as to ask you to fulfil my need.

On hearing these lines the king smiled admiringly and repeated his words of comfort, promising Sul that he would get what he wanted. They all left with the king, who was listening to the shaikh. Sul was frightened of the *jinn*, but the shaikh blew into his eye and said: 'All fear has left you. Look at the *jinn*, for I have cleared your sight and guarded you against any evil they can do and against the terror they inspire.'

The shaikh then turned to one of them and said: 'Go to such-and-such a spot and call to my servant to come quickly.' The *'ifrit* went off and did as he was told and soon afterwards he came back with the servant, and Shaikh Najah went with the king to his palace.

Sul said: 'Soon after that the two of them took me to sit in a beautiful, well-built house with high pillars, ninety-six spans long, made of onyx, yellow, red, white and green, with two stone benches and two facing halls. There was a pool with a fountain, seats facing each other and a network of seven pipes, with Taliqan matting and Samanian carpets. In it were birds of all kinds, ring-doves and pigeons, blackbirds, bulbuls and nightingales as well as peacocks, all of which were netted in so that they could not fly away.'

Sul was left there and he went on: 'We sat there to rest as maid-servants waited on us, bringing us splendid food and goblets of wine. We took off our clothes, and they washed us and fetched us fine clothes to replace our old ones. We put these on and sat for a time until the king's messenger arrived and told us that his master was calling for us. When we got to his palace we saw luxury that would stand the test of time and wealth that only Almighty God could count, with furnishings of all kinds and magnificent vessels. When we sat down we were brought food, which we ate, as well as wine in all sorts of containers of gold and silver, crystal and gems. Tables were brought in laden with splendid food of all descriptions, and when we had eaten our fill they fetched the wines. The glasses went around, and the king drank one and toasted Shaikh Najah with another. The shaikh drank this and refilled it and placed it in front of me, but I refused it. The king urged me to drink, but I insisted: "By God, I am not going to drink it until you unite me with my cousin." He told me to take comfort as he would see that I got what I wanted.'

After three days spent like this the king summoned Sul, who, when he came, kissed the ground before him and called blessings down on him. The king told him to sit and then summoned an 'ifrit named al-Sanduh, who on his arrival was told to take Sul immediately to Iblis, together with a letter. The 'ifrit placed Sul on his back, telling him to be strong and courageous, and he took the letter that the king had written in his own hand. Within the blink of an eye, there was Sul facing Iblis. After putting him down, the 'ifrit handed Iblis the king's letter and another from Shaikh Najah. When Iblis had opened and read them, grasping their contents, he looked at Sul, who was weeping for his cousin. 'Prostrate yourself to me, Sul,' he said, 'for if you agree to serve me I shall give you your cousin, Shumul, and more wealth that can be counted or described.'

Shedding bitter tears, Sul recited these lines:

Perpetual greetings to the mighty king
From wretched Sul, as long as the stars shine.
Lord, do as you think fit; desire has brought me here.
If you show me your bounty, I shall be
Your grateful servant till the end of Time.
Your grace and your eternal law encompass all mankind,
But God Alone is King Omnipotent.
I ask whoever caused my suffering
To bring it through His knowledge to an end.

Iblis was favourably impressed by Sul's lines and asked him how long ago it was that his cousin had been snatched away. 'A year and a half,' Sul told him, and he then asked who it was who had brought him here. 'Master,' said Sul, 'this was Shaikh Najah and the king,' and he went on to tell him his story from beginning to end with an account of the sufferings he had experienced during his search for Shumul. Iblis told him that he could take comfort as he himself would settle the affair and reunite them.

At this point Iblis summoned the *'ifrits* and told them to tell him about Shumul. They looked at each other and pointed to Abu 'l-Nahhada. Iblis told him to fetch his daughter immediately, and he went off and brought her. When she had come before him he told her to fetch Sul's cousin at once. 'Tell me what wrong had she done to make you burn up her cousin's heart and snatch her away,' he said. 'Master,' she replied, 'it was jealousy that made me do that.' 'Who is it that you love?' Iblis asked and she told him: 'I love Sul, and when he married this cousin of his, I was overcome by jealousy and produced this plot against him. I ask you, master, and I ask him, that we may marry in your presence.'

She then recited these lines:

The sight of you is my delight;
I see you both absent and here.
Each one whom Time has parted from his love
Finds in his sadness that death is more sweet.

Iblis told her that he wanted her to fetch him Shumul, which she did. Shumul was still dressed as she had been in the cave in which she had been put, and when she saw Sul she threw herself on him and they embraced tearfully, complaining of the pain of separation and the extent of their longing. Iblis ordered that they be given a fine house and he sent them such furnishings that had never been seen or heard of. He gave Shumul five human maids, swelling-breasted and moon-like virgins, and he ordered both her and Sul to go to the baths. The maids went with them and attended to their needs, and Iblis provided them with a bundle of regal clothes worth a thousand dinars, together with necklaces of gold, jewels and silver as well as ten thousand dinars' worth of other fine things.

He then called for Sul and said: 'Look at the wealth that I have given you, with other things as well. I want you now to bow down and worship me.' 'God forbid, master, that I should worship any but Him, Almighty is He. That can never be.' He then recited:

The Great and Glorious God is generous with His grace.
He is the One King, Who has no vizier,
And there is none to share His majesty.
It was He Who brought forth the classes of mankind,
And it was He Who gave me the true faith.
It is He Who is worshipped by us all,
And through the bounty of His grace I am enriched.
Master, may you remain in glory and at ease,
As long as birds are seen to perch upon the boughs.

Iblis admired the beauty of Sul's poetry and realized that he was a believer. He had him taken with Shumul to a house, where they shared their complaints with one another, Shumul accusing him of having forgotten her. 'God forbid that I should do that!' he exclaimed, and he went on to tell her how he had never stopped searching for her throughout the lands. For her part, she told him how good al-Nahhada had been to her, treating her with respect and showing her every kindness. She then told Sul that he would not be able to enjoy life with her if he did not marry al-Nahhada as well. 'I do not want anyone but you,' he told her, to which she replied: 'I know that, but she overwhelmed me with her kindness.' At this, he agreed and told Iblis.

Al-Nahhada's father was summoned and in the presence of Iblis he gave his daughter to Sul. The marriage contract was drawn up, and a wedding was held that neither men nor *jinn* could rival. The bride was given the most splendid adornments and after Sul had slept with her he stayed for three days, enjoying the most pleasant of lives. Al-Nahhada then presented him with robes, treasures and wealth such as had never been heard of or seen. He then asked permission from Iblis to return to his family. Iblis granted him this and instructed two *'ifrits* to carry the wealth, the maid-servants and all the possessions of Sul and Shumul back to the king and Shaikh Najah. 'To hear is to obey,' they said and they transported both Sul and Shumul as well as all their wealth, the maids and everything else that night, setting them down at midnight by the city gate.

Next morning they went to the king and the shaikh to present their respects. The shaikh asked how they had got on with Iblis, and Sul told him of the wealth, necklaces, jewels and maid-servants that he had given them and the good that he had done them, expressing his deepest gratitude. The king was delighted and he told the *'ifrits* to carry Sul, Shumul and all they had with them back to their families. 'To hear is to obey,' they said and they flew off at nightfall, arriving at dawn.

When Sul and Shumul saw their camp they were overcome by joy, and in the morning when the people there heard of their arrival they came out with drums, pipes and other instruments, splendidly decorated. Sul's father and his uncle were bewildered with joy and the tribe was turned upside down. Sul slept with Shumul in his family camp and was delighted to find her a virgin.

Al-Nahhada used to come, bringing them an indescribable quantity of gifts and staying for some days before going home. In fact, she would come every month whenever she felt a longing for Sul, and Shumul was deeply fond of her.

Sul and Shumul continued to enjoy the most pleasant and comfortable of lives and had both sons and daughters, while al-Nahhada had children by Sul. She built a palace in the lands of Sul's tribe, where she would stay whenever she came to visit him. They enjoyed their lives until death parted them.

This is the whole of their story. Praise be to the One God and may His blessing and peace rest on Muhammad and his family!

Tale Eleven

The Story of Abu Muhammad the Idle and the Marvels He Encountered with the Ape As Well As the Marvels of the Seas and Islands.

In the Name of God the Compassionate, the Merciful

They say – and God knows better, and is greater and more noble – that Harun al-Rashid was seated one day in the caliphal palace with Masrur, his servant, when Ja'far son of Yahya the Barmecide came in and greeted him. 'Peace be on you,' he replied, 'and on all who follow right guidance and fear the consequences of evil-doing.'

He went on to say that he was feeling depressed and wanted to walk around the markets of Baghdad dressed as a common person in the hope that he might find relief from worry and depression. 'I shall obey God and the Commander of the Faithful,' Ja'far told him, at which Harun removed his robes and put on the clothes of a commoner, tucking back his forelock and disguising himself so that he looked like an Arab merchant. Ja'far did the same, and the two of them left the palace and walked from place to place until they reached the bank of the Tigris.

Sailors were shouting invitations to would-be pleasure trippers, and Harun urged Ja'far to go on board with him so they might spend the rest of the day with them. Ja'far agreed, and Masrur called to the sailors to bring in the boat so they could board. They did this and when Harun's party were all on board they set off on their pleasure cruise.

While they were on their way and enjoying themselves to the full, ten small boats came into sight from the direction of Basra, laden with Andalusian copper. On the prows of each squadron of five of them were fifty men with nautical flags and Hijazi streamers, and in their waists were more men, hairless and beardless, holding Egyptian clubs and ornamented bucklers and wearing brocade with gilded turbans on their heads. They were holding crossbows and shooting at birds in the air, laughing if they hit one, cheering noisily and shouting: 'God is greater', and 'Praise be to the bringer of good news and the warner [Muhammad].'

Harun the caliph said: 'Ja'far, do you see how fine these ships are and the luxuries they have on board, the Chinese pepper, cinnamon, camphor, amber, pungent musk, aloes and splendid clothes?' Ja'far told Masrur to ask who owned the ships and all their cargoes, together with their crews. Masrur said: 'I went up and after greeting them I put this question to them, and they told me that the owner was a Basran merchant called Abu Muhammad the Idle, adding: "And how would it be if he were energetic!"'

Another man there said: 'Don't be surprised by this, master, as this is all a drop in the ocean for him.' Harun was very angry and he disembarked and told Ja'far to go back to the palace with him, as they had had enough of the pleasure cruise. When they got there he took his seat on his throne thoughtfully and filled with wonder. Just then a servant entered with a golden ring on his finger, wearing on his head a crown of red gold studded with pearls and other gems. He kissed the ground and, after calling down blessings on the caliph, he said: 'Master, your sister sends you her greetings and says that she made this crown for your son al-Mu'tasim, but it lacks one central jewel.'

Harun ordered chests of jewels to be produced and when they had been opened, he began to examine them one by one and was saddened when he failed to find one that would suit. An old man came up to him and told him that what he wanted could only be found with a Basran merchant called Abu Muhammad the Idle. This so angered Harun that he ordered a message to be sent immediately by pigeon to Basra, ordering that Abu Muhammad be sent to him.

When it was afternoon the emir Muhammad son of Sulaiman al-Rub'i was seated in his state room when the postmaster came in with the pigeon. 'God willing, it will be good news,' said the emir and he opened the message, read it and grasped its contents. He got up immediately and set off with his escort to the house of Abu Muhammad, whose servants jumped up and went to tell their master that the emir was at the door. Abu Muhammad looked out in alarm and, seeing the emir, he went down, kissed his hand and welcomed him. 'God willing, this will be a blessed day!' he exclaimed. 'There is nothing but good,' replied the emir, adding: 'you should know that the Commander of the Faithful has sent to ask for you.' 'I am at the command of God, the Commander of the Faithful and you,' said Abu Muhammad, 'but give me time to say goodbye to my children.' 'Impossible,' said the emir, 'for I have come out to look for you, and this is the caliph's letter, written in his own hand.' 'There is no might and no power except with the Great and Glorious God!' exclaimed Abu Muhammad, and no one who utters these words is ever left abandoned.

He then turned to a servant of his who was out of his mind with fear and said: 'Go to the shop and fetch me my kerchief.' The man hurried off and brought it, and Abu Muhammad put it in his sleeve. The emir sent him under escort to the river bank, where they put him in a boat that sailed to Wasit and from there to Baghdad, where they brought him to the caliph.

Permission was asked for him to enter, and when this had been granted he entered and kissed the ground before Harun, who welcomed him and told him to be seated. When he had taken his seat he said: 'Let the Commander of the Faithful ask whatever he wants.' And as he did so he put his hand in his sleeve, took out the kerchief and placed it in front of himself. He then presented a number of gifts, including a golden bird with eyes of rubies and feet of emeralds, which Harun admired, as there was nothing like it in his treasuries. 'There is something inside it that is finer than what is outside, master,' said Abu Muhammad. Harun ran his hand over the bird's back, which turned, and as it moved from a crack a weighty pearl fell out, gleaming like a star in the sky. Its beauty and radiant light illumined the room and it was followed by another. This went on until seven had come out, dazzling the eyes, each one worth the revenue of Baghdad.

'Fine, by God, fine!' exclaimed Harun and he then called for the crown that his sister had sent him and placed one of the pearls in it. To his great delight it filled the space as though it had been made for it, and he asked Abu Muhammad, who had told him that he needed such a gem. 'No one told me, Commander of the Faithful,' Abu Muhammad replied, 'and had the emir Muhammad allowed me to go back to my house, I would have brought a finer present than this.' 'By God,' said Harun, 'whoever named you "the Idle" made a mistake. How was it that you got all this wealth? Tell me your story.'

'To hear is to obey, Commander of the Faithful,' replied Abu Muhammad and he went on: 'Know, master, that my father was a wretchedly poor man who acted as a servant and who brought me up until I was ten years old. I would never move from where I was and I was so lazy that I would eat and drink lying on my side. Whenever people gave any food to my mother she would bring it to me and tell me to eat, but I was too lazy to do this, and my mother would feed me with her own hands. I found it hard to speak but I would say: "Chew it before giving it to me, mother," and she would chew the bread until it became smooth as broth before putting it in my mouth. All this was because I was too idle to move my jaws.'

This angered Harun, and he said: 'There could have been no other boy like you, but go on and tell me the rest of your story.' Abu Muhammad continued: 'We lived in a place without walls or a roof and we had nothing with which to build it up apart from straw and reeds, which we used as a shelter from the heat of the sun. My mother would go out to look for food for me, and I would sit without stirring from where I was. She would tell me to go out and play with the other children as, if I went off with them, I might lose some of my idleness. I would pay no attention, and she would bring some of them in to me, hoping that they might pull me out, but I would burst into tears and not stir from where I was, until she lost patience and dragged away my waist wrapper from under me. I would leave half my body to burn in the sun while the other half was in the shade and because I was so lazy I couldn't move into the shade, and I would stay like that until my mother came and, seeing the state I was in, she would feel sorry for me and move me out of the sun into the shade. She was bitterly distressed that I was too lazy to earn myself a living.' 'By God,' exclaimed the caliph, 'whoever called you Idle was quite right.'

Abu Muhammad went on: 'I stayed like that until one day my mother got hold of a genuine dirham. She brought it to me and said: "Get up, my son, and go out to look at what the people are doing. 'Abd Allah al-Basri has made a pious endowment in order to win a reward from God. He is about to set off for India, and the whole city and its people are in an uproar. Everyone, high and low alike, has gone out to look at the procession that he has ordered to move to the great square. There are many ships nearby, and the master of the procession is seated on an iron chair surrounded by servants, retainers and slaves."

'My mother kept pressing me to go and told me to take the dirham and go out to enjoy looking at the people. I got on my feet, thinking that the earth would not be able to support me. I was knocked, pushed and jostled but I didn't raise my head or speak to anyone. Mucus was dribbling down my face, and I was in the depth of misery, with people laughing at me as I cried. Eventually I got to 'Abd Allah al-Basri, surrounded as he was by people. I greeted him and said: "Master, take this dirham and buy me something that will do me some good, for I am a boy without a father." I was then overcome by tears and started back home. 'Abd Allah asked the people round him angrily whether they knew me. "Yes," they told him, "he is known as Abu Muhammad the Idle."

'The ships then put to sea, making for India and China. God decreed that they should have a safe voyage, and they were successful in their trading, while 'Abd Allah made a great profit on what he bought and sold. They had with them a quantity of dates, both dried and unripe, and these he presented to the ruler of China, who was ill and had been told by his doctors to eat Iraqi dates. He was delighted by 'Abd Allah's gift and presented him with a magnificent robe of honour as well as other gifts, including a huge quantity of money.

'The traders put back to sea and sailed for twenty days, but on the twenty-first the ships came to a halt and were unable to move in any direction. "There is no might and no power except with the Great and Glorious God!" exclaimed 'Abd Allah. Then he noticed a rag tied to the mast and remembered Abu Muhammad the Idle. He told the merchants that it was because of Abu Muhammad's dirham that the ships had halted, as he had been told to buy something that might be of use to him. The merchants asked him to take any of their goods that he wanted and give this to him, but 'Abd Allah said: "I can't take anything from any of you, even if you were to give me all the ships' cargoes, as I have to buy something he will find useful."

'The ships were lying close to one of the islands of the Zanj, and so 'Abd Allah boarded a small boat and left his ship with some of his slaves, taking the dirham with him. He came across a feeble old man who had with him a number of apes, amongst whom was one that was weak, ugly and sickly. "What are you asking for one of these apes?" 'Abd Allah asked him, and the man told him: "Ten dirhams." "I want a cheap one," 'Abd Allah told him, and the man said: "There is this sickly one." "How much is it?" asked 'Abd Allah. "Two dirhams," said the man. "We have only one," 'Abd Allah told him, "which is on deposit for a poor man, so sell it for him." The man took the dirham and handed over the ape, but said: "It will only eat a sweet made of sugar, with almonds and poppies, so don't feed it on anything else." 'Abd Allah's men agreed, and a slave took it and carried it on board.

'When this had been done, the ships moved off with the permission of Almighty God and sailed on until they reached Basra, but before they had got to the coast none of those on board had been able to eat a single mouthful without the ape on the rigging above them snatching some of it. Because it caused them such trouble they thought of throwing it overboard, but 'Abd Allah told them to let it be, saying: "It gives you amusement, and you laugh at it. God has nearly brought us home in safety thanks to the blessing of its orphan master." So they sailed on to Oman, where they saw men diving and bringing out jewels and pearls, all of which the merchants bought.'

The narrator continued: 'While they were doing this, the ape jumped up, removed its collar and jumped into the sea to the delight of the merchants, who said: "Now we've got rid of this destructive creature." They told 'Abd Allah about this and when he accused them of having thrown it in deliberately they denied it and said that they knew nothing about it. 'Abd Allah was saddened, but just then up came the ape with two oysters in its paws and another in its mouth. It took these to 'Abd Allah and then, quick as a flash, it dived again and after a time it came back with three more. It went on doing this until after ten dives it had brought out thirty oysters.

'Everyone on board was astonished at this, and when the ape jumped back to its place beneath the mast they began to covet the gems. 'Abd Allah opened the oysters and in each one of them to his astonishment and that of the others he found a pearl worth the revenue of Syria and Iraq. He took these into his keeping, and the merchants, who were amazed at what the ape had done and astonished by the pearls, asked him to sell them some of them. "I can't dispose of them," 'Abd Allah told them, "as they belong to the ape's owner."'

'They sailed on towards Basra, which God had decreed that they should reach in safety, and when word spread of their arrival the people flocked out joyfully to meet their relatives. My mother told me to get up to go to look at the ships and greet 'Abd Allah and ask him what Indian treasures he had bought with my dirham. All this brought out my energy. I got up, not wanting to stay where I was, and when I had gone to 'Abd Allah and exchanged greetings, I asked him what he had bought for me in the way of merchandise. "Here it is," he said, and he produced a small box from which he removed something wrapped up. Out of this he took the thirty pearls, each worth the revenues of Iraq.

'I was overjoyed, and my laziness left me. I got up full of energy, immeasurably happy and fortunate, as God had opened the door for me. 'What do you think of my advice?' my mother asked. 'Abd Allah told me about the ape and how it had dived into the sea, telling me to keep it and to be sure not to sell it. It was worth a hundred *qintars* of gold, he said, and was the cause of my fortune. He told me only to feed it on sweets made of sugar with almonds and poppies, and he advised me with the greatest earnestness not to neglect it. He sold some of the pearls for me to the merchants for fifty thousand dinars and handed the rest to me.

'I took them and went home with my mother, bringing the ape with us, and we called down blessings on 'Abd Allah. After we had repaired our own house we bought other houses, as well as property, orchards and slaves both male and female. I then went to a fine ship and sailed to Oman with the ape, accompanied by 'Abd Allah and other merchants. When we got there we found the divers at work, and I let the ape go. It dived down and came up with three oysters, one in its mouth and one in each paw. It did this twenty times and fetched sixty oysters. I sold them all and went back to Basra having made a hundred thousand dinars. I built a villa with a fine orchard next to it, watered by a number of streams, and I constructed baths and two mills, one for saffron and the other for wheat. I bought estates, orchards, khans and whole districts. I had slaves of both sexes; I became the wealthiest man in Basra; in a short time I had become proverbial and I was the master of men.

'One day I was sitting with the ape seated in front of me on a chair of red gold, studded with pearls and other gems, eating its fill of its sweets. When it had had enough it shook itself, got down from the chair and sat down before me. Then it spoke to me in eloquent Arabic and said: "Damn you, Abu Muhammad, how long am I going to act as your servant, getting money for you until I have made you the wealthiest man of your time?" When I heard it speak, I quaked with fear and said to myself: "By God, it would be a wonder if this ape were not a king of the *jinn*," and I asked it who it was. "I have been good to you," the ape replied, "so that you may relieve me of the pain of love and the distress of passion that has sickened and inflamed me." "Master," I repeated, "who are you? What do you want and whom do you love?"

'The ape said: "You should know that I am a *jinn* king and I love a Basran girl called Badr al-Sama', the daughter of Marhab al-Tamimi." "You can do things that I can't, master," I told it, but it said: "Things are not as you think. Had I power over her, I would not have served you and given you all this wealth, but she is kept from me by spells, magic books and formulae, sacred names and talismans which keep me away from her house, and love for her is killing me." "How can she be reached?" I asked, and it said: "If you do what I tell you, you will get to her, but if you disobey me, you will die." "Say on," I told him, "for I shall certainly never disobey."

'He told me: "Go off tomorrow, taking a purse with a thousand dinars in it. Go to the qadi, greet him and give him a hundred dinars and give another hundred to the official witnesses. Tell them to accompany you to her father and ask him for her hand, giving him whatever money he asks for, and I shall replace it for you." "To hear is to obey," I said.

'Next day I took the thousand dinars and went to greet the qadi. He got up to welcome me gladly, saying: "This is a blessed day." I gave him two hundred dinars and divided another two hundred amongst the witnesses, telling them that I wanted them to ask the hand of Badr al-Sama', the daughter of Marhab al-Tamimi, on my behalf. "To hear is to obey," they said, "for who has a better right to her than you who are today the wealthiest person of your time?"

'They went off with the qadi to a mosque by the door of Marhab's house. When we went in, Marhab came to us and, on seeing the qadi, he went up to greet him and kissed his hand. The qadi and the witnesses jumped up to greet him, and the qadi then led them in prayer. After that he went up to Marhab and, addressing him with respect, he said: "We have come to ask for the hand of the sheltered pearl, the guarded jewel, on behalf of this honourable man, Abu Muhammad. You know all about him, his reputation and his riches." He said that he would gladly accept but on condition that I hand over as dowry ten thousand dinars, ten satin robes, ten maid-servants, a thousand sheep, a hundred cows, ten thousand hens, a thousand *ratls* of sugar, ten *ratls* of saffron, ten of *qamari* aloes, ten of musk and a thousand of henna for the wedding. I told him that I had all that he wanted and more, so I could do this. He added: "and she is not going to leave my house," to which I said: "I agree to that."

'I then got up and went home, where I told the ape everything that Marhab had asked for, and it promised to produce it. It rose and went into the sitting room, where I didn't know what it was doing, as it was out of sight. When it did not appear I went into the room to see what was happening, but I could not find it and remained perplexed, saying to myself: "It has gone, and I don't think that it will come back." I then went out and sat for a time, when suddenly there it was coming up to me. "What are you doing sitting here?" it said. "Get up and come into the sitting room." "What am I supposed to do?" I asked, and it repeated: "Get up and come into the sitting room."

'When I did, I discovered ten trays of gold and ten of silver piled with dinars, as well as ten packages of satin. When I saw this I went out again and asked what I was to do with them. "Send Marhab what he asked from you," the ape said, "and add another thousand dinars." I got the boys, girls and servants to carry these on their heads and I saw to it that Marhab got all that he had asked for and a thousand dinars more. He was delighted and summoned the qadi and the witnesses, drew up the girl's marriage contract and went happily home.

'On the night of the wedding the ape came to sit in front of me and asked me what I intended to do. "Whatever you tell me," I replied, and he said: "Take care not to covet the girl, or I shall come back and burn you up and leave you as a lesson for those who can learn." I agreed to this and when evening came I found the world full of candles and torches burning in holders of gold and silver. There were servants and serving girls, and everyone who saw me congratulated me on my good fortune, as there was no girl on the face of the earth more beautiful than my bride.

'They then brought me to her house and sat me on a seat of honour, covered with silk and Rumi brocade. There was incense, ambergris and aloes, as well as singing, with drums and pipes, and everything was filled with splendour. Then ten maids, beautiful as moons, came in holding the train of the bride, who was like the moon at its full, more lovely than a statue and standing out more clearly than a banner, with hair dark as night. Above was the narrow path to Paradise; her eyebrows were curved like bows; magic lay in her eyes, and the Pleiades rose from her brow. Copies of the Qur'an were scattered round about her; she was wearing golden bracelets with pearls, together with necklaces and pendants of red gold, while the maids were shouting out praises to God and blessings on the Prophet, the bringer of good news and the warner.

'When I stole a glance at her I could see that she was indescribably beautiful, with a net of large pearls on her head. At the sight I looked down at the ground, not daring to stare at her again, and I said to myself: "By God, I have never seen and never will see a girl like this." I wished that she were mine, as she was worth the wealth of the whole world, and I remained regretful that I would have to part from her. People were telling me to look up and see what Almighty God had given me, but I was too frightened of the ape to do this. Then they pushed her towards me and went away, leaving her with me. I sat at the side of the hall and fell asleep without having approached her.

'Next morning I went out to the market, and people went in and asked her how the night had been. "He never looked up at me," she told them. Then, when it was afternoon, I went to my house, where the ape was sitting by the door. "Tell me what you did," it said, and I told it: "By God, I did not learn and do not know whether this was a man or a girl." "That's what I want," it said.

'It then left, and I was praying to God that he would not come back, but back it came at midnight with servants, both negroes and Indians, carrying on their heads trays of gold and silver, filled with dinars, pearls, gems, musk, aloes, incense and other things passing all description. I remained astonished and amazed at all these riches and I went up to the ape and asked it what it wanted me to do with them. It said: "When you get to the house tonight and see the girl asleep, I want you to go to the top of the room and remove the brocade that is covering an iron door. Open the door and you will see an iron couch with four legs inscribed with talismans. Over the door is a white crested cock; kill it; wrap it in the tablecloth and put the four poles from the couch over it and you will be protected from any harm that I or any other *jinni* could do you."

'On the second night my bride was brought to me, after which the servants left her and went away. She fell asleep, and, while she was sleeping, I killed the cock, wrapped it in the cloth and put the four poles from the couch over it. Suddenly there was a huge crash like a peal of thunder and a fiery *'ifrit* swooped on the girl. I fainted at the sight and when I recovered I heard a voice saying: "By the Lord of the Ka'ba, the girl has been carried off!" and there was a sound like the rustling of wind and bitter weeping. At this I shed tears, struck my head and was filled with regret when it was no longer of any use, for to me the whole world was worth no more than a bean.

'I fled from Basra, sad and tearful, with no idea where I was going, and I was reciting these lines:

The pain of parting makes me melt away,
As lovers do when those they love are harsh.
I wonder at the patience that I showed
When I had lost my love, for that was wonderful.
Beloved, do you know that since you left,
I have remained confused in misery.

I then heard a voice that said: "Damn you, have you no fear of Almighty God that you hand over a girl to an unbelieving *'ifrit*?" I walked for a time amongst the palm-trees until I caught sight of a person, whom I approached. When I asked him who he was he said: "I am one of the *jinn* who were converted to Islam at the hands of 'Ali ibn Abi Talib, may God ennoble him." "How can I get to my wife?" I asked him, and he said: "Wretched fellow, you had a bird which you allowed to fly away and now you want to fly after it." But he added: "Follow this road with God's blessing all night until dawn and then by the shore you will see a huge cave in which there is an idol made of white stone. You must drink of the water that there is coming out of the cave and smear your face with its mud. Stay there and a barge will pass you as you stand opposite the statue. Various different creatures will emerge, heads without bodies and bodies without heads, and they will prostrate themselves in adoration to the idol rather than to Almighty God. When you see that, embark on the barge and cross to the other bank and walk along it until sunset. On a high point you will see a castle built of bricks of gold and silver. That is where your *'ifrit* will be. I have now told you about this, so goodbye."

'I followed his instructions and reached the cave, where I saw that the creatures had arrived. I waited until they were busy worshipping the idol, and then I boarded the barge and crossed to the far shore, after which I walked along the bank all day until nightfall and I went on walking until the sun rose next morning. It was then that I looked down over a lofty, spacious and solidly constructed castle built of silver and gold. It had a door of aloes wood inset with ivory slabs studded with gleaming pearls and set in white silver with a golden knocker adorned with rubies. I went up, saying: "Where are the leaders? Where are the champions?" strengthening and encouraging myself, holding a deadly sword and telling myself that I would either rescue the girl or die fighting for her. When I entered, my heart was strong, but I was afraid of the ape.

'As I got to the middle of the place I saw rooms of red gold and a dome of pearls and other gems, with a door set with panels of silver and studded with jewels of all kinds. In the middle there was an inlaid ivory couch decorated with variously engraved panels. On this was seated the girl, who was reciting the Qur'an and praising and glorifying Almighty God. When she caught sight of me she exclaimed: "Abu Muhammad, there is something that we have to settle between us." "Lady," I said, "I excuse myself before Almighty God and before you." "Tyrant and evil-doer," she said, "did you have no fear of God when you handed me over to a vile *'ifrit*?" "Praise be to God that you are safe!" I exclaimed, and she said: "You abandoned me, but the Great and Glorious God came to my help and destroyed my enemy." "How did that happen?" I asked and she said: "When he snatched me up and flew off with me I fainted and when I recovered consciousness I was in this castle. I plucked up courage and when he was about to approach me I looked up to the heavens and cried: 'God Who aids those who call for help, Who answers the call of those who are in distress and Who fulfils the needs of those who pray, save me from the evil of this damned *marid* in accordance with Your will, most Merciful of the merciful. I call on You through the truth of Muhammad, the Seal of the prophets.' Before I had finished my prayer a meteor came down from the sky and burned him up, leaving him as a pile of ashes and protecting me from his evil." "Praise be to God that you were saved!" I exclaimed.

'I then got up, and the girl and I took all the precious jewels, wealth and treasures that were in the castle and went down to Basra. There we were met by her father and her relatives, who were delighted by what we had collected. Amongst that, Commander of the Faithful, was this jewel which I have brought you.'

Harun was amazed and delighted by this story and he rewarded Abu Muhammad generously, making him one of his boon companions. He was a constant visitor at court, and he and his wife led the most pleasant, delightful, luxurious and carefree of lives until they were visited by death, which none can avoid.

This is the story, and praise be to the One God, and blessings and peace be on our lord Muhammad, his family and his companions.

Tale Twelve

The Story of Miqdad and Mayasa,
Together with Poetry and Reports, and
the Conversion of Miqdad and
Mayasa at the Hand of
'Ali Son of Abi Talib, the
Exalted by God.

In the name of God the Compassionate, the Merciful, Who knows better, is Wiser, more Glorious and more Noble

Amongst the stories of the nations in past times it is related that there was an Arab king called Jabir son of al-Dahhak al-Kindi. God had provided him with a daughter more beautiful and a better rider than any on whom the sun had ever shone. Such was his delight in her that he had her instructed in all such arts as those of writing, providing nibs for pens, horse management and riding, as well as fighting against heroes. She emerged as a brave and skilful fighter and an admirable poetess. There was no one who did not wish to look at her or to have her as a wife.

Her reputation spread throughout the lands and reached Quraish. One day, as they were sitting and talking of brave men, amongst them was Abu Jahl son of Hisham. He said: 'You who are renowned for courage, is there amongst you anyone who would dare to ask for the hand of Mayasa, the daughter of al-Dahhak al-Kindi, the chief of the Banu Kinda?' They said: 'That man surpasses us in reputation and birth, but we shall all approach him, and each of us will ask Mayasa's hand for himself or for his son if he has one, and whoever can produce her dowry can marry her.' 'Let each of you take the chiefs and elders of his clan and set out,' said Abu Jahl.

They did as he said and collected their arms and equipment before riding off and eventually reaching the camp of Mayasa's father. He made them dismount and treated them as honoured guests. They stayed for three days, and on the fourth Abu Sufyan addressed them and said: 'People of Quraish, why do you not let your brother know what you have come to say and what is in your minds?' They said that they would like Jabir to be there with them, and when he came they praised and honoured him, before saying: 'Jabir, by al-Lat and al-'Uzza, we are filled

with joy that we are all here together in this auspicious gathering.'
'Cousins,' he asked them, 'what is it that you want? Tell me, and you
can have whatever it is.' They told him that they had come as suitors for
the hand of Mayasa so that whoever could pay her dowry might marry
her, amongst them being men of all ages and without equals.

Jabir stayed silent for a time and then replied: 'Chiefs who are
renowned for your bravery, you have heard of my daughter's beauty,
courage and skill. Because of my love for her I have allowed her to
decide that she would only accept as a husband a man who can defeat
her in combat.' They agreed to that but said that she herself should first
be consulted. Jabir accepted this and went to tell Mayasa what the
Quraish had said and that they had come to ask for her hand. 'Father,'
she told him, 'did I not promise myself that I would only marry a man
who can defeat me in battle? Go and tell them that whichever of them is
distinguished for his bravery should come out to challenge me, and
whoever defeats your daughter can marry her.'

Jabir left her and went to the Quraish, who asked him when he sat
down with them what had happened. When he told them what Mayasa
had said they armed and equipped themselves before mounting and riding out to the field. Mayasa put on her breast-plate and called for her
horse, which was of a famous Arab stock, with a long neck, broad chest
and widely parted ears and which could overtake whatever it chased,
while it itself could never be overtaken. It was as the poet has said:

A grey horse like a gleaming meteor,
Pampered, it grazes in lush fields.
My critics say it draws men to the fight;
It is dawn bridled with the Pleiades,
A lightning flash saddled with the new moon.

Mayasa in her armour settled herself on its back with a *khatti* spear fourteen spans long whose point was like a snake or a blazing fire and, equipped
with an Indian sword, she rode to the field. Amongst the clan had been a
man called al-Aswad al-Kindi, who had died, leaving a young son named
al-Miqdad. He had reached the age of fifteen and was in the care of his old
mother called Khallat al-Ghitrif. When he saw the brave heroes assembled
he went to her and asked who they were. 'My son,' she told him, 'these are
the Quraish, who have come to ask for the hand of your cousin Mayasa.'
The father of Mayasa was Miqdad's uncle, his father's brother who had
died leaving him nothing, and his mother had then taken charge of him.

'Why am I not with them?' he asked her and she repeated that they were Quraish, adding that he had no equipment or otherwise he could have gone out with them. 'Go to my aunt,' he said, 'and borrow a breast-plate from her, which I shall return to her when I come back.'

His mother went to his aunt and, after telling her the story, got what he needed and brought it back to him. He put on the breast-plate and went to tell his aunt that he still needed a horse to ride. She told him that if he went to the red tent he would find one which he could take. What he discovered there was a horse with lopped ears and a clipped tail, but he took this, mounted it and rode off reciting:

Why is it that my clan have gathered here,
Carrying their weapons in the early dawn?
A noble rider has come to meet you,
A chief who is accustomed to sword blows.
If you should want to challenge with your spears,
I shall leave you cast down upon the ground.

At the sight of him on his horse the others laughed at him in mockery, and one of them said: 'This fellow is riding a bull!' Miqdad found this hard to bear and he called out at the top of his voice:

I do not want to ride a crop-eared beast,
One from whose tail the hairs have been plucked out.
But though I do not want this, by al-Lat,
I hold in my right hand a flashing sword,
And you, Quraish, will see wonders from me.

When he saw the horsemen on the field he charged them with a terrible battle-cry, routing them in confusion. He then rode towards Mayasa, addressing her as 'the glory of the Arabs, lady of high birth', after which they charged each other. A long and confused battle followed, but however often he confronted her, he saw nothing but her eyes. He realized that she wanted to humiliate him before the Quraish, who were all craning their necks and staring at the fighters.

He then reversed his spear and struck her on the breast with its butt, unhorsing her and leaving her lying stretched out between the ranks of spectators to their astonishment. He then recited:

Have you yet seen prowess like this
So making you ignore my deeds?

I swear by al-Lat I am no coward,
But one who charges on the day of war.
Who is the lion of Kinda, their hero when it comes to war?
Know it is I, whose sword cuts off the coward's head.
I rode against Mayasa to teach her
That I am champion of both men and *jinn*.
I fought against her until she was left
To wear the garment of shame and disgrace.
The land of Mecca and all men should know,
I am fifteen years old and younger than my horse.
When I am twenty my face will be stern,
As I fight with my long and pliant spear,
Unhorsing foes to leave them prey for wolves.
Merit cannot be hidden, and my foes
Shall bear in mind that I am named Miqdad.

He continued to look at Mayasa until she recovered consciousness. She then looked up at him and said: 'Miqdad, by al-Lat and al-'Uzza, you have defeated me, and had it been a stranger who had done this I would have killed myself, but you are to be my husband, and I shall be your wife since, if you accept the conditions my father will lay down, I shall certainly marry you.' Then she removed the veil from her face and appeared as the moon on the night it becomes full. Miqdad kissed her three times and then left. Mayasa called out at the top of her voice: 'Quraish, whoever wants entertainment should stay here, but if any are looking for marriage, let him go off in peace, for I shall take none of you as a husband.' When they heard that, they lowered their spears, shook up their horses and returned home.

Mayasa then approached her father and asked him to marry her to the man who had defeated her, her cousin Miqdad. He said: 'My little daughter, the chiefs of the Quraish and the most distinguished leaders of the Arabs have asked me for your hand, but you have not wanted them, and do you want instead a penniless youngster, a vagrant of no account?' 'He is a hero of renown,' she told him, 'and I saw what he did to the Arab chieftains and men of rank. I swear by al-Lat and al-'Uzza that if you don't marry me to him he and I will leave in spite of you, and I shall bring disaster on both nomads and settled folk alike.'

Her father was angry and summoned the leaders of his clan to tell them what had happened. They gave him a mixed response, and in the morning he prepared a huge feast, to which he invited the whole clan, high and low alike. He then called for Miqdad and said: 'Nephew, I want to marry you to my daughter. Can you cope with her and supply the dowry that I shall ask from you.' 'Yes, Uncle,' Miqdad replied, 'so tell me what it is that you want.' Jabir asked for a hundred reddish camels with black eyes and long necks, five hundred sheep and twenty horses, twenty slaves, ten of each sex, a thousand *mithqals* of gold and another thousand of silver, a hundred ounces of pungent musk and another hundred of camphor as well as ten large green panniers. 'You are asking him for too much,' the clansmen told him; 'you know that he is penniless and yet you want all this.' For his part, however, Miqdad agreed willingly.

The entertainment lasted for three days, and on the fourth Miqdad told his uncle: 'Time is getting on and I have made up my mind to get what you asked for.' He mounted and rode to Mayasa's tent, where he recited:

> Do not abandon our fair love;
> For my hopes for our union will not fail.
> The leave I take is not from one who goes,
> But one who stays and seeks no cure for love.

Mayasa replied with these lines:

> The peace of God be on you every hour,
> Although you may be sorrowful and sad.
> Come quickly back so you may win
> The union that you hope for with your bride.
> They have allowed you seventy days for this,
> So hurry, noble rider, to your task.
> Do not seek wealth if it cannot be found,
> But come back quickly to your lover's call.

Miqdad took his leave of her and set off in haste. He saw three riders with a howdah and said to himself that this was the first part of Mayasa's dowry. He rode up to greet them and to ask them to what tribe they belonged. The leader said: 'I am al-'Abbas, and these are my brothers. What do you want, Miqdad?' Miqdad realized that he could get nothing from them and so he told them his story from beginning to end. Al-'Abbas felt sorry for him and told his servants to separate his camels from those of his brothers. There were thirty-three of these, carrying loads of linen, silk and other goods, and he told Miqdad: 'I pity you but at the moment this is all that I have, so take it as a gift to serve as part of what you are looking for.' Miqdad said: 'Sir, I swear by the God Who has exalted you above many that I shall take these as a deposit of yours until I return.' He began to recite:

Children of Hashim, best of men,
Whose grace has raised me up,
You give out wealth without being asked,
Dispensing no mean livelihood.
You feed the hungry and control your wrath,
Striking the heads of foes but favouring your friends.
I met your champion and he honoured me.
How generous a man is al-'Abbas!
He gave me everything he had,
Keeping back nothing for those he had left.

He rode on night and day across the desert wastes until he reached the city of Chosroe Anushirwan, where he halted in a wooded valley with streams and fruits known as the Valley of Flowers, as it had been a beautiful place in former times. He dismounted and let his horse with the plucked tail loose to graze, telling himself that he was unsure how Chosroe's men would treat him. After eating some of the fruit, he fell asleep with his arm beneath his head.

While he was asleep his horse whinnied and pawed the earth beside him. He woke to see a great cloud of dust and when he rode towards it he found a caravan. He told the men with it to abandon their goods and leave, but they said to one another: 'How stupid this boy is! There are three hundred of us, each more than a match for him, and he says this to us!' They started laughing in astonishment at him, but when he realized that they were making fun of him he charged them with so terrible a shout that the earth shook. He continued to slaughter them and when they attacked he defended himself. When he had killed more than a hundred and fifty of them, the rest took flight, amongst them being a shaikh mounted on a speedy horse, who had seen heads without bodies and bodies without heads. He went to the vizier, who, when he had heard that the caravan sent by Chosroe was coming, had ordered the shops to close, with no trading to be done until Chosroe's goods had been sold. It was not known that these had been seized by Miqdad.

While the vizier was sitting on his balcony he caught sight of the

shaikh, whose turban was round his neck and his feet out of the stirrups, while his tongue was hanging out. He supposed that the man must
have come with news of the caravan, and when he came into his presence he asked about this. 'I have escaped death,' the shaikh told him,
and when the vizier asked him who he was, he said that he had come
from the caravan sent by Chosroe. 'Where did you leave it?' asked the
vizier, to which he replied: 'With an *'ifrit* of the *jinn*.' 'Damn you, what
are you saying?' asked the vizier, and the man replied: 'Master, I am only
telling you what I saw with my own eyes after I had come near to death.'
He then told the vizier what Miqdad had done and how the caravan
guards had been killed.

The vizier told his men to look after the shaikh while he picked five
hundred of his soldiers. He then called for the shaikh to act as their
guide and to fetch Miqdad. The shaikh agreed and left with the men,
but when he was within a mile of the valley he began to tremble. 'Were
you not told to listen to what I tell you?' he asked. 'Yes,' they said, and
he went on: 'Look at that valley beside the hill. The young man must be
on the far side, so go off and fetch him while I wait for you.'

The riders spread out in search of Miqdad, and when he caught sight
of them he mounted and charged them, continuing to slaughter them
until he had killed all five hundred. The shaikh fled away towards the
city, and when the vizier first saw him he told his entourage: 'I think he
is bringing good news that the young man has been captured.' Then,
when the shaikh came before him sometime later, he greeted him and
asked where the soldiers were. When he was told that they had been
killed he was furiously angry and ordered the shaikh to go out with
another thousand.

The shaikh left with them, and when he had got to the critical spot he
told them that Miqdad was by the hill. They spread out over the length
and breadth of the valley, and Miqdad, on seeing them, attacked and
kept on killing them until his arms were covered in clotted blood, and
he would wrench an opponent from his saddle and kill him by dashing
him on the ground. This went on until most of them were dead and the
rest took flight to tell the vizier what had happened.

The vizier exclaimed in a fury: 'Is Chosroe to be told that for all our
numbers we were defeated by one man?' 'This is an indefatigable and
insatiable fighter,' the shaikh explained. 'Promise him safe conduct and
then you can lure him into the city and lay an ambush for him in the
lanes. Then you can take him, and he will be yours to judge.' The vizier

approved the plan and passed his signet ring to the shaikh, telling him to give it to Miqdad.

The shaikh left, and when Miqdad saw him and rode against him he said: 'Master, I am here as a messenger.' 'A messenger from whom?' Miqdad asked, to which he replied: 'From the vizier of Chosroe Anushirwan, and this is his ring of safe conduct. If there is anything that you need, he will provide it for you.' He then passed the ring to Miqdad, who believed in the promise and stored away in the valley the spoils he had taken from the caravan. He blocked its narrow entrance with a tall tree that he had cut down lest any of the goods be carried away, and he then set off with the shaikh, who entertained him with tales and humorous anecdotes until he reached the city gate.

The vizier had prepared the ambush, which Miqdad reached when they had come to the centre of the city. The shaikh told him: 'Master, we have gone the wrong way,' and he turned his horse around, at which the ambushers shouted on all sides. When Miqdad's horse heard the whinnies of other horses and the cries of the ambushers near at hand it reared up, and Miqdad gave so terrible a shout that the city shook with fear. He charged the attackers, who took to flight, and he rode on to the vizier's palace, where he dismounted.

The shaikh opened the gates and said to those around him: 'Wherever this man fights he defeats everyone and unless I do something fast, he will exterminate the lot of us.' So the vizier opened the door, kissed the ground before Miqdad and said: 'Things did not turn out like this because of anything that I said. We are now at your command, so give what orders you want.' Miqdad told him that he had come out to look for a dowry for his cousin and he told his story from beginning to end. The vizier was sorry for him, telling him that he could have all that his uncle had stipulated and entertaining him generously. He immediately wrote to Chosroe and told him about Miqdad.

When Chosroe read the letter he was filled with amazement and said: 'Nothing can be too much for a boy like this. I shall send him this ring of mine, and when he comes to me he can have whatever he wants from me.' His messenger brought the ring to the vizier, who summoned Miqdad. Miqdad rose respectfully, and the vizier said: 'You handsome man, this is the ring of King Chosroe, who promises you all that you want.' Miqdad took it, kissed it and placed it on his head before leaving instantly.

When he reached Chosroe he was given permission to enter and after coming before him he greeted him eloquently, calling down God's mercy on him. 'Boy,' said Chosroe, 'what led you to act as a highwayman, spreading fear on the roads?' 'Your Majesty,' Miqdad answered, 'I am not to be blamed for what I did but should be excused.' When Chosroe asked what his excuse was he explained that he had done this because of the dowry that his uncle Jabir had demanded for his daughter Mayasa. As this was beyond his means he had done what he did in the hope of coming before the king. 'Show me some of this bravery of yours which entitles you to this dowry. I have heard that you are a brave and a hardy fighter, but hearing is not like seeing.' Miqdad asked how many squadrons he had in his army and, when he was told that there were two hundred thousand, he told Chosroe to select ten thousand from these, and from them a thousand men, of whom five hundred of the strongest should meet him in battle. Chosroe promised whoever would bring him Miqdad's head a thousand dinars of red gold, ten robes of brocade and ten thoroughbred horses, with the same reward going to anyone who took him prisoner.

On hearing this, his men quickly saddled and bridled their horses, put on their breast-plates and mounted in order to ride out to the field. Miqdad approached Chosroe and asked for water, with which, when it was brought him, he washed his hands and feet. He then took off his turban and tore it in half, using one half to cover his head while the other he tied on the end of his spear, from which he had removed the point. He then dipped this in water and settled himself on his horse's back. 'You are mad,' Chosroe told him, but he replied: 'You will soon see what I can do.'

He then rode out of the city to the *maidan*, where Chosroe's brave champions attacked him with loud shouts, but he charged them and broke them. Chosroe was sitting where he could see and he watched the fight, looking at Miqdad as he skirmished on the right and the left, disrupting the ranks of his opponents and leaving the mark of his spear on them. Had he wanted to kill them all with his spear point he could have done it. Chosroe was amazed by this, but Miqdad told him to order them to make a concerted charge against him. Chosroe did this as he wanted to see if Miqdad could really resist. In fact, he reached down to his boot and took out a spear head, which he threw into the air and caught on the end of his spear before striking it on the ground and going on to charge his opponents. Whenever he had an opportunity for a thrust, he reversed his spear and unhorsed his man by striking him on the chest, and when thirty had fallen the rest fled.

Chosroe became more and more astonished, and Miqdad came before him and praised him in the following lines:

King who is crowned with awe, great lion of the woods,
Others may boast of generosity but you outreach them all.
I came to you in hopes of winning wealth;
Do not prolong my torment but grant this to me.
Give me what I desire. This is the only way
In which I may secure the one I love,
Or, best of patrons, give me some of it.

When Chosroe heard these lines he gave orders that Miqdad's mouth should be filled with pearls and other gems, that he should be given a thousand *mithqals* of gold and twenty robes of honour, at the same time presenting him with camels, horses and slave girls. Miqdad stayed with him for a hundred and twenty days and when at the end of that time he wanted to leave, Chosroe gave him twenty containers of amber and twenty panniers filled with pure camphor.

Miqdad was delighted to receive all this and he recited these lines:

O best of all who tread upon the earth,
Chieftain in war and lion of the woods,
You have freed me from harm, fulfilling all my hopes!
You are men's hope in trouble and to you
Persians and Arabs bow submissively.
Your generous deeds surpass all boastful kings,
So may you prosper while the lightning pierces clouds.
You gracious master who directs all things,
Amongst the Arabs your bounty has spread!

He then took his leave of Chosroe and set off for home, passing by the vizier, who presented him with a robe of honour and a splendid gift and with whom he stayed for three days.

He had been absent from his people for longer than the time stipulated by his uncle, Jabir. The clan of Sinbis were allies of Kinda, and amongst them was a powerful and headstrong man called Malik son of Riyah, who was known for his bounty and liberality. When the time had passed and there had been no news of Miqdad, Jabir asked people who had come from Syria about him, giving them his description. They said: 'We saw someone who looked like that near Tabuk. There were a number of Bedouin camping there, and when he tried to drive off some of their beasts one of them shot him with an arrow and killed him. We shrouded him and dug a grave, in which we buried him, but we don't know what happened after that.'

[lac. Jabir said to himself] 'Miqdad was led to that by his wish to collect money so that he might attain his desire. Now he is dead, and this is what I wanted, as the husband I would like for my daughter is Malik son of Riyah al-Sinbisi.' He agreed to this marriage and produced a banquet, at which the Arabs stayed eating and drinking for seven days, after which they dispersed to their own camps. Malik went home and sent his brother Mahir with seventy riders to escort Mayasa to his clan with her slaves, male and female. When Mahir and his men came to Mayasa they provided her with a howdah, in which she took her seat, and on their return they reached Wady'l-Jandal, a large meadow with flowing water. They were happy to travel by moonlight, but their arrival happened to coincide with that of Miqdad, who was on his way from Iraq.

As he was riding he detected a pleasant scent and asked himself from whom it came as it must be from in front, for had it come from behind it would have come from his camels. He was a man who gave full value to what he heard and spent his nights on guard. Mahir's men were happily travelling with Mayasa when Miqdad caught sight of them. He told his companions that this must be a bride being taken to her husband and that he would soon take over her caravan, while he wondered who the people were. He told his servants to stay with the camels, and he himself went up to Mayasa's escort and asked them from what tribe they were, who was in the howdah and who her father might be. 'Go on your way,' they told him, 'for whoever asks about what does not concern him will not enjoy the reply. We are the people of Sinbis, a noble and powerful clan, and in the howdah is a bride from Kinda, Mayasa, the daughter of Jabir son of al-Dahhak.' 'Where are you taking her?' he asked and when they said: 'To her husband,' he asked who this was. 'Malik son of Riyah, our chieftain,' they replied. 'Didn't her father promise her in marriage to Miqdad son of al-Aswad al-Kindi? He asked. 'Yes,' they told him, 'but he was killed by Bedouin in the lands of Tabuk on the Syrian border, and her father then chose Malik.'

Miqdad stayed for a time plunged in thought and when he was certain that this must be Mayasa he heaved a deep sigh and retired to dismount, check his bridle and tighten his girths. He then rode back and told the servants to let the camels go and remove their loads, after which he dropped his reins, couched his spear and charged into the middle of the escort, calling out: 'Damn you, abandon the howdah and save your-selves, for otherwise I shall leave your corpses on the ground. I am Miqdad.'

They laughed at him and said: 'Go away, Miqdad, and don't hope to get the girl, for by al-Lat, al-'Uzza and Hubal the great we were sure that we would meet you when we came out and we wanted to see you.' Miqdad shouted and charged them, striking one of them and killing him. When the others saw this they all attacked but he stood firm, strik-ing to the right and the left and overturning their ranks. When he had killed five and captured the rest he recited:

Through treachery they took my wife,
But I destroyed them with my cutting sword.
I killed five, leaving them as food for beasts.
Woe to the man who broke his covenant,
[lac.]
So I shall sever spines and necks with my sword edge,
Until to my great joy they turn in rout.

Mayasa recognized Miqdad's voice when she heard it and, raising the curtain of the howdah, she burst into tears out of longing for him, soak-ing her veil. Miqdad then recited:

Lady of the howdah, do you not see my grief
And what has happened to me during this long fight,
Against the Quraish's lordly lion cubs?
I am Miqdad, a man without a care;
I long for you, so listen to my words,
Then look as I do battle in the fray,
And you will see a lion that has fathered cubs.

On hearing this, Mayasa signalled to Miqdad that he should charge Mahir's men, and so he levelled his spear and rode against them. Mahir himself came out against him and called out: 'Miqdad, you are exposing yourself to death, but if you leave behind what you have with you, my men will let you go in safety.' He recited:

Leave all your wealth and baggage or meet death
At the hands of a tireless champion,
One who does not turn back but leaves ruin,
As he cuts through men's hopes and shortens lives.

As they charged each other Miqdad forestalled Mahir with a thrust to his chest, which brought the spear point out through his back, leaving him hurled to the ground weltering in his blood and twitching spasmodically. His men were distressed to see this, thinking that their chieftain, Malik, would accuse them of weakness. They charged, calling out: 'Miqdad, are you attacking us because of some old war that there has been between us?' When Miqdad said 'no', they told him that they were reluctant to fight him and when he asked what they intended to do they said that, while he wanted Mayasa for himself, they wanted her for their chief, Malik son of Riyah. 'We should let the girl choose between the two of you,' they suggested, 'and she can marry whichever of you she picks. She is listening to what we say and has watched the fight, and if she prefers to go with us you should go back and not stand in her way, while if she picks you we shall hand her over to you and leave. You should realize that it was only your personal pride that led you to fight us. No good will come of this, as pride is destructive; those who think they are going to win will lose, and whoever imagines himself to be invulnerable is mistaken.'

They then came up to Miqdad and repeated that the choice should be left to Mayasa and that they would accept it and hand her over to him if this was what she wanted. On hearing this, Miqdad agreed and swore by his father and mother that if she wanted Malik he would not oppose her or them. He then went up to the howdah and called to Mayasa: 'You hear what they say, for they have allowed you to choose between us.'

Then he recited:

Lady, the choice is yours, so tell us what you want.
I have forced them to choose humility
Leaving them in confusion and regret.
Go with them if you choose and leave me in distress,
But if you pick me, I shall scatter them.

He stood waiting for her reply but when she said nothing he recited:

I shall accept your answer, so reply,
For you are like my hearing and my sight.
Go if you wish and I shall still love you;
Union with you is life, while if you leave I die.
If you want me, you must know that my sword
Splits skulls and cuts through other blades.

You have already seen what one of us can do,
The haughty lion, charging to the fight.
Speak out and do not fear what enemies may say,
Since for me you are like my inmost heart.
Which, although tortured, lies in pledge to you.
Do not cut through what gives me the power to endure.

When Mayasa had heard his poetry, she said: 'Cousin, be on your guard with these people.' Then she said: 'People of Sinbis, will you accept my choice?' and when they said they would she told them: 'As you allow me the choice, I pick Miqdad, and you can leave either in safety or in confusion and regret. If Miqdad is too weak to fight you, I shall come down from my howdah, mount my horse and help him to victory.'

Her words left the escort staring down at the ground. Then they looked up and said to each other: 'Are you going to hand over this girl to Miqdad who is here alone and retire from him when you are the champion riders of the Arabs? This would be a disgrace, and if you all charge and attack him with your swords there will be no escape for him, and he will fall to your spears.' One of them, a man named 'Auf son of al-Sabbah, said: 'If you all charge him Mayasa will dismount from her howdah and help him fight. I think that you should let her go with him and go off yourselves to Malik your chief to tell him what Miqdad did to you.' His companions shouted: 'Shut up, damn you! Do you want the Arabs in their assemblies and the women over their spindles to talk about you and say that a boy from Kinda met seventy riders from Sinbis, scattered them with his sword and took off the bride they were escorting?' 'Auf said: 'I have given you good advice, and this is better than that the Arabs should tell of how one man killed seventy riders and only one escaped.' 'Who is that one going to be?' they asked, and 'Auf told them that he would climb to the hilltop and not fight but watch what was going to happen.

When 'Auf left them they all rode out against Miqdad. The first to challenge being a well-known champion, Sharrab al-Halak. He charged, reciting:

If we give up the bride, what are we then to say
Or tell our families when they meet us?
Abandon her, Miqdad, and leave here in safety,
Or else you will lie underneath the earth.
Go off and do not stand against us on our way,
Lest you be forced to drain the cup of death.

The two opponents charged each other, and after a long fight Miqdad forestalled Sharrab al-Halak, thrusting with a spear, whose point came out through his back, leaving him weltering in his blood. When they saw this the others shouted at Miqdad, but he struck right and left until he had killed them all. He then turned his reins, intending to attack 'Auf, but 'Auf called to him: 'Look after your bride! I gave them advice, but they would not accept it.'

Miqdad went back and halted opposite Mayasa, reciting:

Lady, have I an equal or a match amongst mankind?
I met the riders making to us with their spears.
It was my love for you that spurred me on to fight,
Exchanging thrusts on both the left and right.

When she heard this Mayasa smiled and said: 'Cousin, you have cleared away shame and taken your revenge, but there are many others like you, and every disaster is followed by a greater one.' Miqdad collected the weapons of the dead and took charge of their horses, their goods and their slaves, whom he ordered to fasten the loads to the camels. He then hurried off to the tents of his own clan, travelling through the night, and when dawn broke he was in sight of Ascalon. He could see the traces of a deserted camp with its dwellings and shelters. Remembering his experiences on his travels, he was moved by sorrow and longing to recite:

A star shone from the east. God grant a happy dawn!
Some dawns have led to bloodshed, others to success.
The lover who complains cannot be blamed
For looking for relief from sufferings.
When you turned from me you caused me to doubt,
And fires of passion shot their darts at me.
Would that I knew what you did to my life
When, before dawn, parting afflicted me.
I am a wretched lover with a wounded heart,
Moving from Syria to Raqqatan.
I crossed the mountains, leaving barren land,
Until I found myself on fertile ground.
I came to Chosroe's hall, where I collected wealth
And then I took my leave and travelled at my ease,
Making for my own clan, joyful and with success,
When suddenly I met a troop of men,

Like lions, riding fully armed with spears.
Amongst them was a camel decked with silk,
Carrying such beauty that obscured the dawn.
For on it was a howdah decked with pearls,
And in this was a lady beautifully dressed.
I asked who this might be who so delighted me.
They said: 'This is the noble bride,
Mayasa, who is going to her groom.'
I was amazed and shouted: 'Let her be,
And hurry off as quickly as you can.'
They scoffed at me and challenged me to fight.
So I poured for their heroes cups of death,
Spilling the blood of one after the other on the ground.
For with my spear I am the greatest champion.

Miqdad had scarcely finished before he caught sight of a rising dust cloud. When he saw this he ordered the servants to halt and made the camels kneel, removing their loads. As he looked at the dust it cleared away to show camels carrying howdahs followed by three formidable riders wearing chain mail. As they came into view Miqdad shouted at them and wanted to capture them. He asked them who they were, and one of them rode towards him and said: 'Not so fast, young man! I am the Meccan champion who uses his sword to fight in the holy war, Abu'l -Hasan 'Ali.'

When he heard this name Miqdad drew back to Mayasa, trembling and stammering. When she asked him why this was, he said: 'I swear by my father and mother that I have never set eyes on a rider like this one. When he shouted at me I thought that the sky had fallen down on the earth.' She said: 'Was it not you who asked whether there was anyone to match you amongst men, when I told you that every disaster is followed by a greater one? Make sure that you deal with him as you dealt with others before him.'

On hearing this Miqdad recited:

Mayasa, this is my goodbye, as my heart is on fire.
I never thought that I would find one to force my respect.
But even noble men are led to bow their heads to him,
Fearing to meet him, and how wonderful this is!
I am afraid he will soon capture me,
And I shed bitter tears at having to leave you.

Mayasa, on hearing these lines, urged him on to fight and recited:

> No man is noble who fails to defend
> His lady, and his friends will think him weak.
> But if you would prefer to do this, then leave me
> And I shall meet this man and conquer him.

She was about to get down from her howdah when Miqdad stopped her. He rode out with his spear levelled, dropping his reins, but 'Ali, upon whom be peace, gave his angry shout that the Arabs knew well and recited:

> I am 'Ali, who has destroyed the Arab champions.
> I have won fame in times of angry war,
> And my sharp sword cuts through the riders' heads.

He charged against Miqdad, pressed him hard and, allowing him no time to react, he seized the rings of his chain mail and plucked him from his saddle. He had lifted him up and was about to dash him down on the ground when his uncle, Hamza, called to him to spare him. He put him down softly and, on seeing this, Mayasa recited:

> You conqueror of riders, treat my friend gently.
> It was because of me that he met fearsome foes.
> And if you want to kill him, kill me first,
> For I could never bear to see him dead.
> You are a man of mercy; pardon him,
> For you are generous in what you do.

When 'Ali saw her, modesty kept him from addressing her, and, thinking that he had not accepted her intercession, she recited:

> Hero, be generous to me, you who are my support.
> Give him to me, you man of noble birth.
> I am a stranger here, so grant me your bounty,
> As in all matters you are my best hope.
> I disobeyed my parents for his sake,
> And his life is my wish and my delight.
> Free him for me so I may be near him,
> And take the weapons, howdah and camel.

When the imam 'Ali heard these lines he called to her: 'Say no more, girl. We are the people of the House of Mercy, who spare those who are in our power.' He went up to Miqdad and asked whether he knew the words of salvation that saved men from their trespasses, 'I bear witness that there is no god but God, and Muhammad is the Apostle of God, may God bless him and give him peace.' 'Say this and you will be one of ours and turn to us,' he told him. 'Master,' said Miqdad, 'stretch out your hand for I bear witness that there is no god but God and that Muhammad is the Apostle of God, may God bless him and his family and give them peace.' He proceeded to tell 'Ali of what had happened to him because of Mayasa. 'I want to take her back to her father and marry her,' he said, 'and then return with her to the Prophet.' He added: 'I would like something that would bring me near God and His Apostle,' and 'Ali taught him prayers that he could use, amongst them being the prayer of relief after hardship, telling him that when he was overtaken by any misfortune he should seek help from Almighty God through the medium of Muhammad, and God would remove it from him and bring him relief, if this was His will. 'Ali then left him and went off leaving Miqdad to return to the camp of his clan, joyfully and delightedly, thanks to his acceptance of Islam. He was praising God and reciting:

Praise be to God who led me after error to Islam;
I am content with God, my noble Lord, Who has no like.

He pressed on his way night and day, not turning aside for anything on his way to the camp, when he was met by his uncle Jabir with his clan and his cousins. They greeted him, congratulating him on his safe return and asking him about the men sent by Malik son of Riyah. 'Good news!' said Miqdad, 'I left them thrown down on the ground as a prey for the wild beasts.' Then he added: 'Are you not ashamed of having promised your daughter to me and then betraying me and giving her in marriage to someone else?' 'People came from Syria who told us that you had been killed,' they told him, 'but now it is clear that they were lying and you have a better right to her than anyone else.'

Jabir had in fact come in order to trick Miqdad. 'Auf son of al-Sabbah had ridden off when Miqdad had killed his companions and when he reached Kinda he went up to a high point and called at the top of his voice: 'Men of Kinda, quick, quick!' When they asked him about this he told them that the men of Sinbis had been killed and Mayasa taken by force. 'Who took her from you?' they asked, and when he told them that this was Miqdad they took it as a great affront, and Jabir went out with his best riders to meet and deceive Miqdad and his uncle Tarrad for having done this and to return Mayasa to Malik.

When he met Miqdad he pretended that he would take Mayasa, provide her with her bridal gear and then return her to him. Miqdad handed
her over together with all the wealth that he had with him as well as the
camels and the slaves, after which he left and went off. When Jabir dismounted he wrote to Malik to tell him that his men had been killed, in
revenge for whom he wanted to capture Miqdad and his uncle Tarrad
and hand them over for him to kill. On receiving the letter, Malik rushed
from his tent in a frenzy, mounted his horse and, armed with sword and
spear, he rode off immediately to Jabir, whom he found seated surrounded by his clansmen. They exchanged greetings, and while Malik
wept for his brother, Jabir tried to cheer him by saying that he had sent
to him so that he might avenge himself and take his bride. 'I shall take
Miqdad and his uncle by cunning and hand them over to you, as well as
bringing you Mayasa as a bride. You can then do what you want with
them.' On hearing this, Malik stopped weeping and told him to waste
no time.

After promising to go off to do this, Jabir immediately jumped up and
approached his brother Harith to ask for his help in the capture of Miqdad and Tarrad. Harith agreed, and the two of them went to ask the pair
to come with them so that they could consult on some matter. Miqdad
and his uncle agreed and were taken to a tent pitched at a distance from
the tribe. When they entered they were brought food and drink and
after they had eaten they kept on being given wine. When this had had
its effect on them Jabir and his brother approached them and tied them
up tightly. They then left them in the isolated tent and went to tell Malik
what they had done.

Jabir told the women to deck out Mayasa as a bride and lead her to
Malik, which they did. When Malik came in, Mayasa looked at him
and, disliking what she saw, she struck him on the chest, leaving him flat
on his back. She then went off to the tent of Miqdad's mother, whom she
told what Jabir had done to her son and her brother. Bursting into tears,
his mother left her tent and, mounting her camel, she called on God, the
Great and Glorious, to help her on her way and lead her to Muhammad,
may God bless him and give him peace. God answered her prayer and
folded up the desert for her so that she reached the Prophet in his mosque
in Medina, where he was surrounded by Muslims. He asked her about
herself and she told him that she was looking for help against those who
had wronged her with regard to her son. Looking at his face, she confirmed her acceptance of Islam and recited these lines:

The peace of God be on the best of men!
Muhammad, I am here to wish you peace,
Emaciated, sleepless, sick with sorrow as I am.
I have come here from the Wady'l-Na'am,
Riding a camel whose swift strides
Resemble lightning flashes in the dark.
For Time that hurts the noble has wronged me.
My husband left behind a little child,
A baby who was weak and not yet grown.
I left him in the charge of my brother,
But he wronged him as though he were a slave,
To pasture his horses [lac.]
Young men of Badr then arrived,
Belonging to the Quraish, lords of the sacred land,
To ask from our great shaikh a noble girl as bride.
She said that none of them would be her match
Unless they could inflict a wound on her,
So leaving her mail coat stained with her blood.
Riders from Sinbis, Nizar and Hisham
Wheeled round beneath the battle dust,
But in their ranks was only one great champion, my son.
She saw the blows that he struck in the fight
And he brought her down to the ground for all to see.
She called her father, and when he had come
She told him to give her in marriage to that man.
He did, but wrongly asked him for a huge dowry,
Putting him off for three months in his treachery.
My son then took his leave and went away,
Leaving my heart to be consumed by fire.
He travelled to Iraq and on to Chosroe's lands,
Confronting champions along the way.
The great king, Chosroe, satisfied his hopes,
With gold and silver and perfumes and robes.
But Jabir, thinking he had been too long,
Promised his daughter to the chief of Sinbis as a bride,
Sending her with an escort of proud men.
My son met them when they had reached Wady'l-Na'am.
He fought them, splitting skulls and cutting bones,
Until they were all left there in heaped graves,

Except for one man who escaped, the lion 'Auf,
Who made his way to Jabir in his camp.
Hearing the news, Jabir went to my son,
Planning to kill him, sheltered by the dark.
My son met 'Ali, your great son-in-law,
At whose hands he accepted Islam with his bride,
But she was taken off by treachery
In order to wed Malik, Riyah's son.
She would not break her covenant or betray her love,
And so on my swift camel I came here,
Surmounting hardships to appeal to you.
Now here I am, best guide of all mankind,
Hoping that in your bounty you may rescue me
From this distress, for you are my treasure.

When the Prophet had heard her lines he consoled and heartened her,
telling her that he would send someone to free her son. To his delight she
then recited the Confession of Faith and, after having accepted Islam,
she took her leave of the Prophet and hurried off homewards on her
camel.

As for Miqdad, when he recovered from his drunkenness and discovered that he and his uncle were tied up, he recited:

Jabir, free me and find how boldly I can fight,
Showing how my slim Indian sword can cut.

Looking at the state he was in, he recognized that he had been tricked
and deceived, but he remembered how the imam 'Ali had told him that
if he fell into difficulties and prayed to God for help, using Muhammad
and his family as intermediaries, help would come. He raised his eyes
heavenwards and called loudly for help, saying: 'My God, I ask for Your
aid, so aid me, and for Your protection, so protect me. I invoke Your
Prophet Muhammad, so rescue me and avenge me on the man who
wronged me. It is to You that men complain and it is You Who wards
off calamity. In Your compassion, trust me in what I say and do and rescue me from the toils of hardship. Relief from You is near at hand; do
not burden me with more than I can bear. You are my True God, Whose
proof is clear and Whose supports are firm. You are in every place;
guard me with Your eye that does not sleep and shelter me in Your
inviolable shelter. I call on You through Muhammad, the best of men,

the light that shines in the dark. Free and release me, Compassionate and Almighty God, for You know my needs and have power to fulfil them. Grant me this, Generous Lord in Your mercy, most Merciful of those who show mercy.'

Before he had finished his prayer, Gabriel, girt with light, came down to the Prophet and said: 'Muhammad, the most High God sends you His peace and chooses to honour you with His greeting. He orders you to send your cousin and son-in-law 'Ali son of Abi Talib to free Miqdad son of al-Aswad al-Kindi, who is tied up and who has just addressed his prayer to the God, Who is near at hand and Who hears the prayers of those who call on Him.'

The Prophet turned to his uncle Hamza and to 'Ali, ordering them to leave and telling them Miqdad's story and how his uncle had betrayed him and left him in bonds. 'To hear is to obey, Prophet of God,' they told him and they went to their homes, where they put on their armour and took up their weapons before leaving together. 'Ali then recited:

> Misguided unbelievers will soon learn,
> When they see blows that are hotter than fire,
> That those who disbelieve Muhammad, best of men,
> And disbelieve in God and in the resurrection,
> Will have to face me on the battlefield,
> As I come fully armed with sword and spear.

When 'Ali had finished these lines a voice was heard, although there was no one to be seen, and the voice was reciting:

> Ride on, you who are rightly guided! Go
> To unbelievers who deny their God.
> They have betrayed Miqdad the champion,
> While I am of the *jinn* of this wadi.
> I am here to proclaim Muhammad's name,
> Whom God has sent out as a guide to men.

'Ali and Hamza pressed on with their journey until they could look down at Jabir's camp. There were confused sounds of men to be heard, and 'Ali dismounted, tightened his belt and took up his sword and his shield. Leaving Hamza stationed there, he rode boldly towards the tent where Miqdad was being held and there he heard Miqdad calling out: 'My God, I beg You in the name of the pure family of Muhammad to free me from this torture, Omnipotent as you are.' Before he had finished speaking 'Ali lifted the curtain of the tent and said: 'Good news, Miqdad! Almighty God has listened to your cry and granted your request, sending you one to save you from your foes.' 'Who are you?' Miqdad asked him, and he replied: 'I am the imam 'Ali son of Abi Talib, God's crushing rock and His piercing arrow. I am the lion of war who clears away distress.'

'Ali then cut through Miqdad's bonds and those of his uncle Tarrad, who accepted Islam at his hands. He then took Miqdad by the hand, and they went to the tent of Malik son of Riyah, whom they tied up and left where Miqdad had been. Next morning, when the Kinda clansmen went to congratulate him and wish him a happy morning and continuing success, 'Ali charged them and drove them off. The camp was filled with shouts as warriors dashed out to seize Mayasa and to kill Miqdad led by Jabir, who was holding sword and shield. 'Ali attacked him, allowing him no chance to resist, and gave his angry shout that the Arabs knew so well. 'Damn you, clansmen of Kinda!' he cried. 'Are you looking to attack us, relying on your numbers? Do you know, you wretches, who it is you want to attack? I am the great champion, the fighting wolf. I am the husband of Fatima, the maiden and the cousin of the Apostle of God.'

When the people heard that this was the imam, they rushed to arm themselves, mounted their horses and charged him all together. He shouted at them and drove them back before breaking into the middle of their ranks and starting to deliver blows left and right, reciting:

I have grown old in battle, where I lead the charge;
I come of an exalted stock, surpassing all.
If any seek me out in war, I bruise his face,
And leave him to shed tears and to lament,
I am Muhammad's cousin, Fatima's husband.

He then shouted: 'Damn you, enemies of God, where can you flee when I am in pursuit?'

When they had been routed 'Ali went to Miqdad and told him to see to his wife, saying that he was going to hand over to him his enemy, Malik. He recited:

I am a man who kills his enemies in war,
Striking against both champions and slaves.
They do not see my blows but yield to sorrowful regret,

As owls and vultures haunt their ruined camps.
I am the son of Hashim, Fatima's husband,
And I can boast I am the best of men.

Miqdad collected the spoils of the dead, with their weapons, horses and camels, to Mayasa's delight. 'Ali then approached Malik and Jabir to ask them whether they would recite the words of salvation that saved men from their trespasses, 'I bear witness that there is no god but God alone, Who has no partner, and that my cousin Muhammad is the Apostle of God.' They refused ever to do this, and 'Ali told Miqdad to cut off their heads.

'Ali then left to return to the Prophet, who was delighted when he arrived with the new converts, whose faith was renewed at his hands. Miqdad became one of his companions and paladins and was the champion of the Muslims, sitting with him and fighting with him in the Holy War until his death. He then fought with 'Ali, the Commander of the Faithful.

This is the complete story. May God bless our master Muhammad, his family and his companions and give them peace.

Tale Thirteen

The Story of Sakhr and Al-Khansa'
and of Miqdam and Haifa'.
With Poetry and Prose.

In the Name of God, the Compassionate, the Merciful

They say – and God knows better – that in past times amongst the early stories of the peoples there is one which tells of a wealthy man named Malik, who had three sons and a daughter. The eldest son was named Khath'am, the middle one Shaddad, and the youngest Sakhr, while the daughter was al-Khansa'. Her father and her brothers were so jealous of her honour that they gave her a tent of her own, isolated from the clan, and when they went out to hunt they were in the habit of leaving slaves and servants to guard her, such being their concern for her.

One day they had left to hunt while the slaves and the servants were out with the pasturing beasts, leaving al-Khansa' alone in her tent. It happened that a man passed by, either having fallen from the sky or risen from the earth. Seeing al-Khansa' alone and defenceless, he lusted after her, and although she defended herself she had not the power to stop him from raping her. She instantly conceived, but she had taken the cap her attacker was wearing on his head and the stick he had been carrying in his right hand.

With the passage of time al-Khansa''s pregnancy became apparent, to the disapproval of her father. He summoned his eldest son and asked him whether he was responsible. 'God forbid, father!' he exclaimed. 'You are accusing me of something from which I would recoil in horror.' Malik put the same question to Shaddad, who gave the same reply and was dismissed when his father was convinced of his innocence. He then summoned Sakhr, his youngest son, and asked him whether he had lain with al-Khansa'. Sakhr realized that she had become pregnant and said: 'Yes, father. I approached her one night when I was drunk, not knowing what I was doing and thinking that she was one of the slave girls.' 'I

grant you both your lives,' his father said, 'but take her and leave me.'
'To hear is to obey both God and you,' Sakhr replied.

Sakhr then took his sister al-Khansa', put her on his mount and went off
with her into the desert. There he made her dismount and, drawing his
sword and seizing her by the hair, he said: 'No one has told me about you,
so tell me yourself. I know that you must have been raped, so tell me about
it and who was the rapist, or else I shall instantly use my sword to repay
you.' 'Put it away,' she told him, 'and give me time to recover. When you
went with my father to hunt and there was nobody left in the camp but
me, a rider came, from where I have no idea at all, and when he saw me on
my own with no one to protect me, lust prompted him to attack me, and,
as I couldn't defend myself, he raped me.' 'Would you recognize him if you
saw him?' Sakhr asked, and she said: 'How could I fail to recognize him
when I have a picture of him before my eyes and I took clear evidence from
him?' When Sakhr asked what this evidence was, she told him about the
cap she had taken from his head and the stick from his right hand.

When Sakhr heard this he put al-Khansa' on a camel, while he himself
mounted his horse and rode the whole night long. He then made her
dismount before reciting these lines:

> Do you imagine I can taste sweet sleep,
> When no star guides me as I struggle on,
> Thanks to the blow that has struck Malik's clan,
> Abasing heads that I used to protect?
> I look for revenge upon him who wronged me,
> Using my sword and the point of my spear.
> Even if I must reach up to the skies,
> I shall wreak vengeance on that wretched man.

He continued to travel around the Arab encampments with his sister,
hunting game on which to feed her. This went on for up to three months,
and he would take her into one camp after another so she could study
the faces of the men there. When her pregnancy had lasted for nine
months she told Sakhr that her time had come, and he brought her to a
tree in the desert. He then walked away as she grasped its roots and
called: 'Helper of those who seek for help, Protector of the fearful, come
to my rescue!' She gave birth to a child like a full moon whom Sakhr
named Taghlib, as its father had overpowered al-Khansa'. He wrapped
him in cloths and went off while she washed herself clean before he put
her back in her howdah and set out across the desert wastes with their

ruins and camps. Al-Khansa' kept examining the faces of all whom they met but without finding her rapist.

Sakhr had sworn not to omit a single tribe in his journey until he had taken his vengeance and cleared away his shame. The first that he entered with al-Khansa' were the clans of the Banu Wabra, Zurara, Hamdan, Sulaim, Tanukh, 'Amila, Tayy, Dhubyan, Qahtan, 'Adiy, Himyar, Khafaja, Sinbis, Fazara, 'Abs, Ghailan, Jubair, Ghassan, Kinana, Kulaib, Qais, 'Uqail, Lakhm, Dhadham, Sa'd, Damra and Murra. He left no single Arab tribe unvisited but in spite of staying for one, two or three months with each he failed to find his enemy, and this weighed heavily on him. He recited:

> Who will tell Malik that I long for him,
> And that I seek for vengeance and to meet my foe
> And strike him down, whatever obstacles there are,
> With my keen Indian sword that kills brave men?

This went on for seven years, by which time the young Taghlib was well grown, handsome, tall and well proportioned. Sakhr bought him a horse and taught him to ride it, while he and al-Khansa' continued to visit tribes until he reached that of Rabi'a. When he got there he made al-Khansa' dismount at the side of the camp, where he pitched a tent for her. While they were doing this a group passed, amongst whom was an extremely handsome young man, tall as a cliff, like the idol Hubal. He was wearing an 'Adani robe and a Yemeni *burda*, while on his head was a precious turban. His face was shining like the moon on the night it becomes full. When al-Khansa' saw him she told Sakhr: 'By God, brother, this is my enemy. There can be no doubt about it.' 'Take care that you are not just struck by his appearance so that you make me responsible for his blood.' She said: 'Have I not spent seven years going round the tribes with you and scrutinizing men's faces?' 'Yes,' he agreed, and she went on: 'And have I accused anyone?' 'No,' he said, and she repeated: 'There is absolutely no doubt whatsoever that this is my enemy, and if you have it in you to take your revenge and clear away your shame, this is the man who attacked me.'

Sakhr made his camel kneel and took out his tent, which he pitched and into which he sent his sister. He thought about how he could kill the man and he recited:

> My case is strange. My hot breath robs me of sweet sleep
> Thanks to the great misfortune that struck me,
> Crushing my strength and lowering my head.

Unless I kindle blazing war, I shall take no more pleasure in my wine,
Or ever ride a horse or trim a bow.
The shame that I have suffered brings despair.
Tell Malik from me that I am a champion;
I shall not live unless I kindle war
And let death gorge its fill on the base man.
For death comes both to the care-worn
And to those who enjoy their glass of wine.

He walked around until he came across a black slave, whom he asked to
identify a man fitting the description that al-Khansa' had given of her
attacker. The slave told him that this was a formidable fighter of high
status and great reputation, the excellent emir al-Miqdam, whom all the
clan of Rabi'a, with its four thousand horse and foot, obeyed and who
was a champion feared by all the tribes.

Sakhr left the slave and went off thoughtfully. As he was walking
amongst the tents he noticed one that was isolated from the others, with
a few people patrolling the space between. He found a woman to ask
whose was the tent pitched on its own away from the tribe. 'Man with
the handsome face,' she replied, 'that is the tent of al-Haifa', the sister
of the emir al-Miqdam, the most beautiful of mortals with a lovely figure, sweet speech, a pearly smile, laughter loving, devastatingly attractive
and without a flaw. She was created to fascinate men and to be looked
at with wonder by both high and low, as in the poet's lines:

She is most beautiful to look at, with her smile,
Her splendour and her perfect loveliness.
She tempts men through the beauty of her form,
Her cheeks, and the new moon within her glance.
She is a marvel, unmatched in her coquetry.
If she looked at an anchorite, it would divert his prayer.
She has no match in beauty, even beauty's self.

She can only be a fit mate for you with your handsome face and the
splendour of your appearance.'

Sakhr asked her why the tent was set apart from the others, and the
woman told him that her brother was so jealous for her honour that he
wanted no news of her to spread. 'You see that the sand round it has
been levelled by the camels,' she went on, 'and she is guarded by sixty
fine riders, all of whom would lose their heads if so much as an ant

approached her tent.' Sakhr dismissed her courteously and went back to
the tent of al-Khansa' reciting:

> I must make fires blaze to burn my foes,
> Leaving brave men as food for beasts and birds.
> I shall take the revenge for which I wish,
> And give the beasts their fill of flesh and blood.
> For I shall shatter skulls and empty veins
> As I charge through the noble horses' ranks.
> Miqdam was unaware I am the lion,
> The skull-splitter who does not flinch in war.
> He brought me shame and he must feel regret.
> I taste no sleep and show no smiling face
> Because of the great deed that I hope to achieve.
> He who opposes me will know that I bring death
> To the mailed horsemen whom I face in fight.
> I do not rush my quest but bring repentance to my foe.
> I trail my cloak and I defend myself,
> But turn my eyes from women modestly.
> My sword is sharp, and my mail coat shines bright,
> While the fame of my valour never wanes.

Al-Khansa' said: 'May you achieve your wish and avoid death! I find you
reciting poetry in which you talk of your strength as though you had
already taken your revenge and cleared away our shame.' Then she recited:

> Sakhr, recite no poetry while you are still disgraced,
> Until you take the vengeance that you seek.
> Carry no sword nor strike, and do not boast,
> Until you clear away your shame by striking down your foe,
> And win your life or die and be excused.
> You should not laugh or smile until this shame has gone,
> So that the horsemen of the clans may know
> That what I say of you is proved by fate,
> And what you do will be unparalleled,
> As you are feared for striking off men's heads.

He replied to her in these lines:

> The horsemen of the clans will know
> That what I say is what I mean to say,

And not its opposite. I am a lion in the fight.
If I should meet my fate, all will be lost,
But otherwise there will be life that brings new birth.
I hope to go on till I reach my goal,
But if not, let no woman weep for me.

For a whole month Sakhr did not reveal to anyone what was in his mind. Then one night of rain and storm wind when the riders were on watch by the tent of Haifa' he took his sword and went out in darkness so intense that no one could see where he was putting his feet, until he reached the tent and discovered that there were no men there. He raised the flap and saw the girl sleeping on a bed of juniper wood set with red gold and studded with pearls and other gems. Over it was a covering of green silk, and below was a censer of Indian aloes wood and a lamp of red gold set with gems with burning *ban* wood. The girl was lying on her back with drops of sweat showing on her forehead like moist pearls. She was alerted by Sakhr's arrival and jumped up in fear, saying: 'Who are you, you vilest of the Arabs?' Sakhr drew his sword and said: 'I swear by the Ka'ba, the place of the Black Stone and the place of Abraham that if you utter a word I shall make you into a lesson to be talked of amongst all peoples breaking your joints and your bones.' The girl saw that he was handsome as well as eloquent; she weakened and looked down bashfully as he got into bed with her. He covered her and went on to rape her. She asked him in God's name to tell her who he was. 'You will soon hear,' he said, and then he recited:

Did Miqdam know when he brought Malik shame
With what a champion he had to deal?
Did he suppose that he could get his wish,
While Sakhr would be left in bitterness?
I swore that I would not be left to die in grief
Until my promised vengeance was fulfilled,
And so I shall take vengeance on his clan
And let my anger loose to pay him back.
For I am one who, when the war fires burn,
Visits destruction on his enemies.

He remained asleep until morning, but when he was close to being exposed Haifa' said: 'Get up, young man. Morning has come, and I'm

afraid that you will be killed.' He addressed her by name and recited the
following lines:

Haifa', the time has come for us to part,
But the fire in my heart cannot be quenched.
How can I bear tomorrow when it comes?
How am I to forget you, having reached my goal?
This death is fated for us; we cannot escape.
Some day I may fulfil my hopes,
For what I did last night cannot be hid.

He then clasped Haifa' to his breast, and she clasped him to hers,
until they were overcome by sleep, only waking after dawn. Miqdad
came to check on his sister and when he looked at her tent he saw
footprints going to it but none coming back. He followed them to the
tent and when he lifted the flap he saw a young man and Haifa' embracing, both fast asleep. This had a profound effect on him, striking him
as a monstrous crime, and he lifted his turban on the point of his spear,
a call to war amongst the Arabs at that time when they had met some
disaster.

His clansmen came rushing up from all sides to ask what was wrong,
and he said: 'Arabs, let everyone who knows what is due to my high
position and rank fetch a bundle of firewood.' They hurried up from all
directions, bringing enough wood to fill the space around the tent, and
Miqdam ordered the slaves to dig a trench and start a fire there, which
they did. As the flames blazed up and smoke rose to the sky al-Khansa'
heard the commotion and was unpleasantly alarmed by it and by what
she could see of the fire. She asked one of her maids whether she knew
what was going on, and the girl told her that Miqdam had found a
young champion with his sister. He had ordered firewood to be collected
and a ditch to be dug by the slaves. They had lit a fire there, as he
wanted to burn the lovers. 'I take refuge with God from the evil of this
day,' exclaimed al-Khansa', 'for by God, the Lord of the Ka'ba, this
must be my brother Sakhr.'

She called for her son Taghlib, who was then thirteen and, after comb-
ing his hair, she put on his head Miqdam's cap and gave him his stick.
She told him: 'Go to Miqdam, the emir of the Arab, the chief of this
clan, for he is your father. Present your respects and kiss his hand and
his mouth, then sit on his lap and say: "Father, do you remember when

you were at such-and-such a time in Wady'l-Siba in the desert? You passed by such-and-such a place, where there were tents, and on your way you came to a tent which you entered. In it you found a girl who was there alone. You raped her and you gave her this cap and this stick. She is my mother, and you are my father."'

Taghlib went off to look for al-Miqdam and he started to go through the ranks of people who were admiring the beauty of his appearance until he reached Miqdam. He took his hand, kissed it and put his arms around his neck, while Miqdam was astonished by how handsome he was. He felt a stirring of emotion and asked: 'Who are you?' at which Taghlib repeated what his mother had told him to say. Miqdam felt instinctively that this was his son and he turned to the boy and exclaimed: 'What a good uncle you have and what a good father!' He then recited:

> God has shown my son to me, and he is like
> The Pleiades above the other stars.
> He who wrongs me will meet wrong in return,
> And those who injure me will find I injure them.
> Those who use violence will meet it in return,
> While those who plant good seed will find the harvest good.

He repeated: 'What a good uncle you have, and how excellent is your father!' He then called out to tell his clansmen to return home, saying that no wrong had been done to their emir that day. With Taghlib in front of him he went to Haifa''s tent and when Sakhr saw him he jumped up to unsheathe his sword, reciting:

> Is Miqdam not acquainted with my might,
> And with the vengeance that I feared I could not take?
> Out of a sense of honour I held back,
> Planning to move with prudence and no haste.
> I then paid back the author of the crime
> With what was even worse than what he did.

He came forward, brandishing his sword and reciting:

> Tell Sakhr's clan of the grave dangers that he met,
> But I have cleared away their shame and mine,
> Searching through difficult and narrow ways.
> It was Miqdam who was at fault,
> But I surpassed all men in what I did,

Taking his sister in the dark of night,
Although no blame can be attached to her.

When Miqdam saw Sakhr with the drawn sword in his hand he called
out: 'Sakhr, do not bring harm on yourself, for you have done me no
wrong.' Taghlib then entered the tent and told his uncle to relax because
Miqdam, his father, had admitted what he did and had sent away the
clansmen whom he had collected. He added: 'He had wanted to burn
you to death, but I brought him the clues that he recognized.'

Miqdam then took Sakhr by the hand and led him from Haifa''s tent,
with Taghlib going on in front, and on reaching his own pavilion he
called for the qadi who was there in the camp. When he had gathered
the chieftains and leaders of his clan, he asked Sakhr for al-Khansa''s
hand, and Sakhr agreed to the marriage, after which Sakhr asked for the
hand of al-Haifa', which Miqdam granted to him. Everything was then
regularized. Miqdam provided banquets, and both couples remained
enjoying the pleasantest and most luxurious of lives.

After some years had passed Taghlib had become the most handsome
of young men, a champion rider who answered the calls of the distressed and the lost. His reputation spread. His mother al-Khansa'
collected a large amount of money, which she distributed amongst fighting men, winning them over to support her and her son, whose authority
they accepted and who all obeyed him. As a result the other Arab tribes
were in awe of them. She supplied her husband with wealth and won
support from her clansmen, with whom she shared dangers, while her
father and brothers joined her, and their original friendship was restored.
Sakhr was a generous provider of food and drink, and both high and
low from far and near collected around him.

After things had gone on like that for a long time Sakhr heard of a
horse in the tribe of Mazin, to whose owner he was prepared to offer a
thousand dinars of red gold. He took the money and went there to the
man, Dhu'aiba al-Mazini, who entertained him generously. Sakhr
handed over the purchase price, took the horse and started back to his
own people. When the leading men of Mazin heard of that they went to
Dhu'aiba and said: 'Were you not rich enough to allow you to do without selling a horse which used to protect us from the hostility of our
foes? In particular, it is a man from Rabi'a, our enemies, who has got it,
and this is something that we cannot agree that you should do.'

They continued trying to press him until he mounted a horse, put on his armour and, taking the money with him, he rode up to Sakhr, who had dismounted to rest by a brook. He told him that his clansmen had objected to the sale of the horse and he had had brought back the money. Sakhr was to take this in return for it, as this was causing a feud between him and his clan. Sakhr refused, saying that, although this would have been acceptable before the sale, the horse was now his, and the money belonged to Dhu'aiba. 'But I can easily return it to you in a different way,' he said, 'and if you come to my camp with me you can have all the money and the horse in the presence of my clan, whereas if I give it to you now everyone will think that I was overtaken by weakness, and you took it from me by force.' Dhu'aiba said: 'I cannot go with you, so take the gold and hand over the horse.' 'The horse is mine and you have the right to the gold. You are trying to wrong me, and I shall refuse to agree.' Dhu'aiba said: 'Whatever happens, you are not going to stop me from taking this horse.'

Sakhr said nothing but saddled and bridled his horse, put on his breast-plate and mounted, reciting these lines:

Dhu'aiba, you will find against what champion you come.
Will you wrong me and rob me of my fame?
My spear is long and with my Indian sword
I split men's skulls and cut their bodies through.
I could not then enjoy my life or take my share of wine.
On guard, Dhu'aiba, for before your goal
Gnawing disasters rise up in your way.
The sons of Malik have no equal amongst clans.
I swear that you will find no love from me,
For I think you the lowest of the low.
Will you insult me and take off my horse,
When I still hold my straight spear in my hand?
How shall I raise my head if you confront me with a frowning face?

On hearing this, Dhu'aiba became angry and said: 'Sakhr, had you said anything else, I would have gone back, but you have challenged me.' In reply to Sakhr's lines he recited:

Sakhr, you shall learn which of us will be
Cast down above a mound of sand.
When I am hunted by the fates of death
I press my enemy with a scorpion's sting.

Do you question the merits of my clan?
I swear that this is something very strange.
The leaders of my clan will hear of me
That I, Dhu'aiba, am a champion,
Although you are a stubborn warrior,
Yet, thanks to love, I am a grim lion,
They may hear otherwise that I have fallen prey to beasts.

Each charged the other, and, after a lengthy fight, in an exchange of blows, it was Sakhr who thrust first, with his spear striking Dhu'aiba's chest and coming out through his back, Dhu'aiba was hurled down and lay weltering in his blood. When he fell his horse strayed back to the Banu Mazin, and when it was seen coming back without a rider it was realized that Dhu'aiba must be dead. Voices were raised, and both men and women wept, while mothers and children raised cries of lamentation. All the clansmen mounted and rode out against Sakhr, whom they found resting by a stream.

When he saw them he knew that they must be looking for vengeance and jumped into his saddle, tightening his girths and putting on his breast-plate. Before he had finished he had been surrounded and he turned to ask the Mazinis what they wanted to do. For their part they asked him what had happened to Dhu'aiba. He told them: 'His folly got its own reward.' They said: 'Sakhr, after killing our chief, are you going to escape with your life? Far from it! We shall leave you as a hamstrung prisoner.'

'Fight fairly,' Sakhr told them, 'and come out against me one by one.' 'Damn you,' they said, 'will anything less than your blood be enough for us?' He then recited:

The scum of Mazin came out to trick me,
Saying that they had come to cut me down.
They did not know my sword was my defence,
Whose blows split skulls, and my Rudaini spear.
A foolish wretch of theirs had done me wrong
And, as he should have guessed, he is now buried in the earth.
Banu Mazin, do not come out to meet me in a fight;
For war's chances are varied. It may be
Before you reach me you will be destroyed.
For I am Sakhr, war's true father, and Malik,
My father, fought with you before my birth.
I shall pour death for anyone who comes.

Sakhr then charged a man called 'Ammar son of Salim with a terrifying shout, and after a confused fight they exchanged two blows. Sakhr's was the first to land, and it left 'Ammar hurled down and weltering in his blood. Sakhr rode off with his spoils and he recited:

Tell Rabi'a from me I stoke the fires of war,
And strike down foes with my sharp-pointed spear.
The clan of Mazin know that I shall kill them with my thrusts.
But who will tell my kin that I alone
Defend them from the spears of enemies?

He kept on killing or overthrowing his enemies one by one until they launched a concerted charge against him. He began to strike blows throughout their ranks, and when their attack failed he recited:

Banu Mazin, death has fled from the fight.
I am a son of Malik and I fear no blow.
With my Rudaini spear I am a champion.

Every challenger who came against him was killed until a Mazini rider, Waqqas son of Daghfal, came out reciting:

Sakhr, you face a spear thrust that will leave you on the ground.
It piles up corpses and wounds enemies.
No clan that insults me will live on at their ease.

Sakhr charged him, reciting a reply to his lines:

You will learn which one of us is the weakling
And on the field of battle who will be thrown down.
I am the finest fighter carried by a horse [lac.]
Mazin will find out where it is I stand,
And who is to be buried in the tomb.

Each rider then charged the other, and for a long time they circled round, cutting and thrusting, advancing and retreating, until Waqqas forestalled Sakhr in an exchange of blows and left him lifeless and weltering in his blood on the ground. The Mazinis surrounded him and carried off his corpse on their spear points, taking the horses and wealth that he had with him and making for their people.

When al-Khansa' heard the news she struck her face, tore her clothes and poured dust on her head, calling out at the top of her voice: 'Alas for Sakhr, lord and dearest brother!' In her display of mourning she was joined by the women of the tribe, who matched the loud cries of grief that she uttered. This was a great misfortune, and al-Khansa', in floods of tears, began to recite:

I ask God's pity, Who is merciful,
And I take refuge with Him from this awful news.
You might be happy when you go to sleep,
But before dawn disaster may have struck.
I slept only to be awakened by horsemen
Who came with news they brought me from the east.
They told me Sakhr had been killed, surrounded by his foes,
And he now lay beneath the stones and earth.
From God's judgements where is a man to flee,
For all men are ruled by His destiny?
I saw Sakhr on his lean sorrel horse,
Calling: 'Do you want to warn me?'
I saw Sakhr surrounded by his foes,
Like a way-mark, on top of which burns fire.
With horses, spears and swords surrounding him.
The Mazinis showed their hostility;
Death showed itself, but our clan were at home.
Sakhr served as the rock of our defence,
A shelter for us as the pigeons of the house.
But now this fort of ours has been destroyed,
And there is no strong tower or house now left us.
I weep for Sakhr as a dove laments,
Prompted by longing and its cares,
As long as the sun rises, followed by the moon.
My tears will never cease throughout all time,
As long as longing prompts the dove to mourn.
Sakhr, my brother, you had shared my grief,
And did not let my secret be revealed.
You were my helper, hidden in my heart.
May God show you His favour throughout time,
As long as the star of the morning shines.
I shall now slaughter all the Mazinis
And take their free-born women as my slaves.
I shall not let a rider of theirs live
Now that the lion Sakhr is no more.

She asked her husband: 'What do you think of the great disaster that has afflicted me?' He told her: 'You can do what you want, as the Arabs obey you; you have money to scatter and I am behind you.' At that, she opened her treasuries and dispersed her money, preparing equipment for war, distributing horses and sending out men. She then said to her son Taghlib:

'My son, how can you bear it now that your uncle is dead? I wish I knew what you feel.' Taghlib said: 'Endurance is ill-omened, but I keep this hidden within me. I shall launch an endless war, seizing riders and destroying champions.'

He sent word to his cousins, the Banu Malik, and they answered his call with three thousand riders, after which he raided the Mazinis. They met at a water-hole named al-Munhil and fought throughout a summer's day. The Mazinis had come close to winning when they were outnumbered by reinforcements of both horse and foot, whose approach strengthened the Malikis. Fighting continued until the two sides separated at nightfall, by which time the Banu Mazin had lost three hundred and the Banu Malik one hundred. Al-Khansa' sent after them a thousand riders from the Banu Ghallaq and the Banu Khalaf al-Radi. At the sight of them the Banu Mazin raised their war-cry and assembled to fight, being joined by the Banu Dhu'aiba, Jabir and Sulaim, and what followed was a battle of unparalleled ferocity.

Taghlib rode out between the ranks and called: 'Where is Waqqas son of Daghfal, the killer of Sakhr?' Waqqas shouted out a challenge and came out reciting:

I know Taghlib the spearsman will come out to die.
Although I take revenge on him a thousand fold,
That will not be enough till I destroy his tribe,
Champions and all, thanks to my cutting sword.

Taghlib startled him with a great shout and then killed him with a thrust, leaving him writhing and weltering in his blood. The Banu Malik and the Rabi'a, who followed them, charged the Banu Mazin, and fighting continued until night parted the two sides, by which time many of the Banu Mazin had been killed and the survivors routed. After having produced this slaughter, Taghlib and his clan went home.

Khath'am lamented Sakhr, his brother, in the following lines:

Eye, shed your tears, as I lament a great and noble man,
A champion, supporter of the law, a carrier of loads.

Eye, weep now he has gone, for such a loss
Stirs up my sorrows and anxieties.
This will go on until I see Mazin
Weakened and quivering on coals of fire.
I never thought Time would afflict me with such loss.
As I lament my fate, I pour my foes
A stream of words that flow from Sakhr's blood.
And I shall strike down Mazin in an empty waste.

Al-Khansa' heard the news of Mazin's defeat and of the return of her brothers and her son, Taghlib. She sent them these lines:

How splendid were those men who rode
Towards Buqai'a in Tamhadi lands,
To face the Banu Mazin. They achieved
Their goal and left their foes thrown on the ground.
Have you achieved your wish, Taghlib the good,
And you, my brothers, wreaking your revenge?
Stay where you are, for I shall come to you
And use these sons of scum to cure my heart.
No rider of theirs shall I leave alive
As long as horses carry me and camels can be led.

When these lines reached Taghlib and al-Khansa''s brothers, they dismounted and stayed where they were. Miqdam then sent a summons to the Banu Numair and the Banu Rabi'a, with whom he rode out together with al-Khansa' in her howdah to the lands of the Banu Mazin. When word reached the Mazinis, they fled away under cover of night and halted when they reached the Banu Shaiban. They were followed by al-Khansa' with her men, and a violent day-long battle ensued with swords at work and men falling until the Banu Shaiban and the Banu Mazin were on the point of victory. At that point al-Khansa' removed her veil and called out: 'Riders of Rabi'a, deal with these wretches!' Her men charged, but after furious fighting throughout the day victory again was almost in the hands of the Shaibanis when al-Khansa' mounted a horse, put on a coat of mail made by Da'ud, strapped on an Indian sword and, with a long lance, charged into the middle of her foes, striking down both Shaibanis and Mazinis. The sword was at work and blood flowed until in the evening the Shaibanis and their allies took to flight. Al-Khansa' and her men followed in pursuit, killing everyone they caught, on horse or on foot, and causing huge losses. As night fell al-Khansa' retired and stayed collecting men to fight the Banu Mazin, Murra and Shaiban and their allies.

As for the Banu Mazin, they consulted with each other about launching an attack on the Banu Malik and the Banu Rabi'a, in the hopes of winning a victory and killing enough of them to cool their ardour. They approached the Banu Darim, who agreed to support them, and they then moved out against al-Khansa', putting their ranks in order and seeing to their weapons. When they attacked, a cry was raised as riders mounted and charged each other. Al-Khansa' and her husband Miqdam rode out with their men, and the furious battle that followed brought quick destruction and defeat on the Banu Mazin, the Banu Darim and Tamim at the hands of the Banu Malik and Rabi'a, with only those mounted on swift horses managing to escape.

Al-Khansa' went back after having killed many men, so achieving her goal, and she recited these lines:

Time marked me with its bites and cuts;
The pressure of its blows has caused me pain.
Men died together whom it had destroyed,
And thanks to them my heart has been distressed.
They were the chiefs and ornaments of Malik's clan,
A source of pride and grandeur, who shunned fear,
Guarding their neighbours from all harm,
As pouncing lions when it came to war,
Striking and thrusting with their swords and spears.
Squadrons of horsemen charged beneath the dust.
We cut forelocks they thought could not be cut,
Striking their heads with spears as hawks strike geese.
We give the entertainment that is due,
Storing up treasures of praise and renown.
In battle we wear mail and in peace silk.
Whoever thinks that he will pass through war
Unscathed, displays in this his feebleness.

She determined to launch another attack on the Banu Mazin and went out with ten thousand riders. When the Mazinis heard of this they took up a position where the road passed between two mountains and before al-Khansa' knew it they had charged and killed a number of her men. Taghlib attacked with a shout, backed up by his men, and what followed was a great battle with furious fighting which lasted until nightfall. The champions of the Banu Mazin suffered badly and were defeated while their leaders were killed. This went on until it was dark, and they then made off with their followers to the Banu 'Abs, Ghailan and Darim. The Banu 'Abs told them: 'Banu Mazin, you did not share with the Banu Murad and Shaiban [lac.] with money and men. You began the evil by killing Sakhr and by Dhu'aiba's attempt to recover his horse after it had been sold to him. If you want us to treat you as neighbours, we will protect you from your enemies but you will have to stay with us and launch no raids.'

The Mazinis did stay there for a long time, and the Banu 'Abs sent the following lines to al-Khansa':

Khansa' has lorded over us
And spoken to us in a lofty tone.
She killed the Mazinis, bleaching their leaders' hair.
Tell her from us that we are rich and lofty men.
We shall protect the Mazinis from her
To see these good men suffer no distress.

When this message reached al-Khansa' she said: 'By God, I shall see to it that the 'Absian mothers lose their sons and I shall do what I want with them until they have no defenders left.' She collected all who were under her authority and set out to raid the Banu 'Abs. When they heard of that 'Amra said to them: 'Clansmen, you know that the Banu Rabi'a and the Banu Malik are swordsmen and fighters with a fire in their hearts that others do not have. In particular this woman has sworn that she will not remove her veil, use kohl on her eyes, wear a woman's dress or put on ornaments of gold until she cannot see any Mazini or hear that any one of them has been left alive. She has enjoyed victory in her battles with them and destroyed many clans. Many clans chose to support the Mazinis like Shaiban, Dhubyan and Murad, but she destroyed them all. What you should do if you want to be safe is to make peace with her and send away her enemies.' The 'Absians said: 'We shall give our lives in support of the Mazinis and whether in hardship or in ease we shall allow no one to take power over them.'

They all joined together and sent to Fazara, who came with the Banu Tamim and Darim, driving their beasts with them. They met al-Khansa' on the road between the twin mountains of al-Rahub and Wakif, and fighting broke out. Al-Khansa' told the 'Absians that she was not looking for vengeance upon them but upon the Banu Mazin, the killers of her brother, Sakhr. They said: 'Have you not already avenged yourself on them, al-Khansa', so what else do you want with them?' She replied: 'By God, I shall pursue them until there is no single rider of theirs left to be seen. I shall kill their men and leave their women as widows who can find no rest nor see any brothers as they caused me to lose my own brother, Sakhr.' 'You are far from achieving this and the process will be difficult.'

At that Khath'am, al-Khansa''s brother, attacked and killed an 'Absian leader, after which each side charged the other, and many were killed. While this was going on a dust cloud appeared, which cleared away to show ten thousand riders of the Banu Kilab led by Taghlib and his father Miqdam. Taghlib was reciting these lines:

> Does 'Abs not know we are good thrusters with Rudaini spears,
> And in battle [lac.] we strike with our right hands.

He and his men then charged, and the Banu 'Abs and Mazin were driven back. Taghlib's men caught up with them in the ravine, where there was furious fighting under the battle dust, in which many 'Absians and Mazinis fell. Al-Khansa' went back relieved and contented. Her opponents consulted about how to make peace, and they entrusted the negotiations to ten wise emirs.

These men came to the camp of al-Khansa' and called to her: 'Al-Khansa', you have been waging war for seven years. You have destroyed the Mazinis and their adherents and have taken many times more than your rightful vengeance. We are here to ask you to stop fighting them and to renew the ties of kinship and we would wish you to answer our request.' She replied: 'By God, I shall not make peace or accept this request until you bring me a thousand women who have lost their brothers as I lost Sakhr.'

At that Tirimmah son of Salim, who wanted the war to continue, recited:

> Should 'Abs continue, they will meet with death.
> Either they should return to noble acts
> And strive for peace before they are destroyed,
> Or they should treat their clients well,
> Protecting them in order to win fame.

Malik son of Sakhr added these lines:

'Absians, be sure it is not you we want to fight.
Our vengeance must be upon the Mazinis, not you.
Go back so that you may expect to find
Your reputation lifted up on high.
Abandon the Banu Mazin, for they
Are nothing more than cows, food for the sword.

The Banu 'Abs went back to the Mazinis and told them of the women that al-Khansa' was demanding, and they collected a thousand who had lost brothers in wars with her. When they went to her each was weeping and bewailing a dead brother, and al-Khansa' recited these lines:

Sakhr, my brother, never shall I forget you
Till I am laid to rest within my tomb,
And were it not for all these who lament
Their brothers round me, I would kill myself.
They do not weep for one like you, Sakhr,
But it is by their tears I am consoled.

She was then moved to sympathy for them and out of pity for them she granted their request for the lives of their menfolk. She had food brought for them and ate with them, and this sharing of salt served as a preparation for peace. She returned the wealth, arms, beasts and horses and whatever else she had taken from them in her raids on the Mazinis, the Banu Tamim, Shaiban, Dhubyan and 'Ajlan, leaving the women to go off filled with happiness. This was after al-Khansa' had consulted Taghlib, her son, her husband, Miqdam, and her father and brothers, none of whom disagreed with her.

For seven years after the death of Sakhr she had been killing large numbers of the Banu Mazin and their supporters. It was in the presence of the women that she agreed to peace, sparing their men, and this peaceful solution was accepted, praise God, thanks to His aid and the excellence of His design.

This is the end of the story, and God forbid that we should add to it or subtract from it. Praise be to the One God and His blessing and peace be on the best of men, our master Muhammad, his family and his companions!

Tale Fourteen

The Story of Sa'id Son of
Hatim al-Bahili and the Marvels
He Encountered at Sea and
with the Monk Simeon.

In the Name of God, the Compassionate, the Merciful

They say – and God knows better – that one night Hisham son of 'Abd al-Malik found himself unable to sleep and he told his vizier: 'I want you now to bring me an Arab seafarer who can tell me about the wonders and the perils of the sea. It may be that this will cure my sleeplessness.' 'The only man suitable for this is someone from Bahila whose name is Sa'id son of Hatim al-Bahili, the chief of his sept and his clan,' said the vizier. 'He has a remarkable story to tell, and if the Commander of the Faithful wants to have him brought so as to question him about where he has gone and what he has seen on his travels, let him do that.'

Hisham agreed, so the vizier immediately ordered Sa'id to be fetched, and it was not long before he arrived. Hisham was seated in a palace of his by the river Barada in Damascus. He had wine in front of him, and there were girls singing to a number of instruments. Sa'id addressed him with a greeting appropriate to a caliph, and Hisham looked up and returned the greeting before telling him to sit down.

His seat was brought close to the caliph, and when he had taken it the caliph passed him a goblet of white crystal containing ruby red wine which he had been holding. Sa'id refused it and said: 'I am an old man [lac.] and I have given up wine for two reasons, firstly because of religion, and secondly because we are chiefs and leaders of the Arabs, and wine robs a man of his wits. When this happens manliness goes, and faults, flaws and blemishes appear.'

When the caliph heard this he did not press him, realizing that here was an intelligent, excellent and religious man. He gave orders for the removal of the wine and the musical instruments from in front of him. He had formed a high impression of Sa'id, who impressed him with feelings of both love and awe. He said: 'Sa'id, may God grant you good fortune thanks to your obedience to Him and protect and preserve you. We ourselves love what you love and dislike what you dislike.' 'May God guard and keep you, Commander of the Faithful,' replied Sa'id.

Hisham then said: 'Sa'id, I hear that you are a seafarer and that you have seen the sea's terrors as well as its strange marvels.' 'Before you hear what I have to tell you,' Sa'id replied, 'I have brought you a gift, which I hope you will accept.' Hisham said: 'A gift from you will certainly be accepted and not rejected,' at which Sa'id produced a small silver box. When he opened it, he took from it a box of gold with two golden locks and from this he removed four different gemstones as large as hazelnuts, which spread radiance across the room. Hisham was amazed and told his slave girl: 'Take this box and its contents and be careful lest it blind you.' He then turned to Sa'id and asked him to tell him of the wonders that he had seen.

Sa'id said: 'God save our master. I was a young man in the caliphate of 'Uthman son of 'Affan, whose vizier was your grandfather Marwan. He had brought a number of Muslims to the province of Basra and its districts under the command of 'Amr son of al-'As, ordering him to put to sea and conduct a holy war against any who opposed Islam and refused to acknowledge the mission of the Prophet Muhammad, may God bless him and his family and give him peace. I was one of the men sent with him.

'We went to Basra and from there to Oman on the shore of the Islamic sea. The emir then set out with his entire force, making for the cities of Hind, Sind, China and inner China. We reached a large island, which was the nearest land to us and whose inhabitants were a tall Indian race of idolaters. They came out against us fully equipped and bristling with weapons and engaged us in a furious battle. Their king came to attack us mounted on a white elephant, and with him were a number of other elephants, who were sent forwards to fight with Indian swords attached to their trunks.

'They formed up by the shore, and we disembarked to meet them, confronting the elephant riders and showering them with arrows and stones. They turned back in flight, and we killed many of them, leaving only a few to take refuge in the city. We shouted: "God is greater, and there is no god but God, and Muhammad is the Prophet of God, may God bless him and his family and give them peace!"

'There were four thousand of us, horse and foot, and the city was in the middle of the island, having seven solid iron gates. We laid siege to it and continued to fight for ten days, as their king watched from the wall. He then came to us and told his interpreter to ask us what we wanted by besieging them. The man said: "Arab, what is it you want from us?" and 'Amr told him: "We want you to accept Islam and to acknowledge the One God, Who has no partner and Whose messenger is Muhammad. If you refuse we shall fight you until you pay us tribute as our inferiors." The king agreed to pay tribute and taxes, with fighting to cease on both sides, adding that if anyone from Sind accepted Islam they would do so too and obey us unreservedly.

'He asked 'Amr to tell us to stop fighting, and when we had done this we camped by the city and they brought us out food and fodder, as all the peace terms that we had made with them had been accepted. Some of us went in to look around the place and found it a vast city with a huge church of gigantic size, which shockingly enough contained more than ten thousand idols, one next to the other. When we asked them what these were they told us: "We found that our forefathers used to worship an idol for a thousand years before throwing it into a pit and worshipping another one. It was from there that all these were collected."

'Devils used to speak using the tongues of the idols, but when we mentioned the One God and recited the Qur'an the idols fell on their faces, and the devils left them, to the amazement of the people. We were delighted and went back, leaving the idols overthrown. We then went through the city, in which we saw a great quantity of trees. There were cloves, peppers, sandalwood, myrobalan, date palms and fruits. They claimed to us that their date palms and other trees would come into fruit twice a year, while thanks to the amount of water they had we saw many water mills there.

We stayed there for a month and then left the city on our way to Hind. The Indians had coastal fortresses as well as villages and cities each with its own ruler, no one of whom had any power or authority over any other. We went on from island to island, land to land and city to city, being received peacefully and given all that we needed as well as the tribute and taxes we wanted together with everything else that we asked for.

'When we had conquered Sind we put to sea, and after some days and nights of sailing we came to a sea of red blood. We asked the sailors who were with us what this was, and they said: "This is the Sea of Blood, and all the fish and other creatures in it are red-blooded."

'After sailing off we reached another sea on our way to China and inner China. We caught sight of a ship and after we had steered towards it we came to a huge city with six gates of solid iron. It was a populous place with more fighting men than could be counted by any but God, the Great and Glorious. Their king, who was a sensible man and a wise administrator, told his people not to fight us, as we would defeat them and every other nation. "For five hundred years," he told them, "their empire has been advancing victoriously, so make peace with them and do not resist them or they will conquer you. Wise men have said: 'Do not oppose a prosperous state or else the world and its people will be your enemies.' "

'The king sent our emir a gift, together with tribute and taxes, and our dealings with them were uniformly good. We stayed there for four months and I together with some others had begun to wander around the island when I found myself confronted by a hermitage made of iron in which was a very old monk whose eyebrows had sunk over his eyes thanks to his age. We called to him: "Monk, by the God Whom you worship, talk to us." He leaned out towards us from his hermitage and asked us who we were and from where had we come. We told him that we were followers of Muhammad, may God bless him and his family and give them peace. "The Hashimi prophet of Quraish?" he asked. "Yes," we said, and we then asked him: "By the God Whom you worship, who are you, what is your name and how do you know about the Prophet Muhammad?"

'He said: "I am one of those who worship the One God. My name is Simeon the monk, and I was a disciple of the prophet Daniel, upon whom be peace. I served with a number of prophets and martyrs and I was a disciple of Jesus, the son of Mary, upon both of whom be peace. I stayed with him until God caused him to ascend to Himself and I called on God, the Great and Glorious by His greatest Name, to guard me so I could live to see Muhammad, God bless him and his family and give them peace. God granted my request, but when I saw the Jews and Christians quarrel and fall apart in disagreement, burning the Torah and the Evangel and removing from them the name of Muhammad, I left them and came to this hermitage, where I have stayed for five hundred years, awaiting the people of Muhammad. I give thanks to God that the breath of life has not left my body before I have seen them and come on this blessed people and their descendants, the followers of the true religion, whom God has exalted over all others." [Qur'an 3.79]

'We said: "Monk, this is a verse from the Book of God, the Great and Glorious." "Yes, Muslims," he replied, "and it was to be found in the Torah and the Evangel and in the pages that God revealed to the prophets in which He described Muhammad, may God bless him and his family and give him peace. He was described in all the books, but the Jews and the Christians corrupted, altered and removed what was written from its context, so the Great and Glorious God afflicted them with wars and discords, bringing ruin and destruction on them, forcing them to pay tribute as subjects."

' "Simeon," we told him, "your learning is deeply rooted. Do you find that the books say that they will have an empire?" He replied: "Muslims, by Him Who sent Muhammad as a prophet to convey His truth, in the days of al-Asfar the Byzantine Christians will have an empire when al-Ghadanfar al-Farisi appears. When Constantine is killed they will be defeated [lac.] and the people of Syria will be trampled underfoot. Woe be to the inhabitants of Antioch, Aleppo and Caesarea as far as the land of cities, Homs and Baalbek! Their enemies will ravage up to Faqus and Damascus with its beauties for forty days, crushing their regions as one kneads the leather of Ta'if. I can see the Persians herding the daughters of the Muslims naked and barefooted to their own lands and castles." "When will this be, Simeon?" we asked and he told us: "Six hundred and more years after your Prophet, when heresies have made their appearance and you have changed and altered things, with the first of you reviling the last and the last the first. There will be treachery both in secret and in the open; you will abandon Friday prayer and wear brocades and silks, drinking wine to the sound of songs and music, with flutes and lutes. You will have no use for the Qur'an; you will dislike minarets and cause mosques to fall in ruins; you will openly practise adultery and no longer command what is good while forbidding what is evil. You will abandon the pilgrimage and the Holy War, being frugal in what is lawful and fond of what is unlawful. Men will content themselves with men and women with women; you will lie about what you own, swear false oaths, refuse to pay the zakat tax and abandon prayer. You will direct your oaths against God, squander what has been entrusted to you, show obvious faithlessness, treat generosity with ingratitude, and dress in the robes of falsehood. There will be one caliph in the east, another in the west, another in Yemen and another amongst the Rum. You will struggle with one another, and there will be strife in Iraq and Syria. Then the Persians and Turks will come, together with the apostates, until it will be as though you were living in Dailam. You will have as ruler a descendant of al-'Abbas, the Prophet's uncle, but they will overpower him and remove him as a prisoner from his empire, while you will be no more than the people of Khurasan and Hawazin. Al-Hajjaj son of Yusuf will then kill him in Mecca.

' "These people will take the Black Stone and the gutter pipe, as well as destroying the drapes of the Ka'ba, with all the coverings there. They will crush the Syrians, spreading destruction and death and committing detestable excesses. Barbarians will come who yell like barking dogs and howl like wolves. Woe to the people of Iraq, to the children of al-'Abbas, the uncle of your Prophet, and to the children of Hashim! I see that, after their grandeur, they will lose their empire and their lands, and others will have dominion over them. This is because of their own evil deeds, for your Lord does not wrong His servants."

'Simeon went on: "The Syrians will suffer at the hands of the Banu'l-Asfar and the lawless races of Turks, Khazars and barbarians, who will go through the lands, destroying them, for what God commands is brought about. I seem to see the Muslims barefooted and naked, their women ravished and their children herded in confusion to the lands of Rum. I can hear trumpets sounding in Jerusalem and from the top of the holy Ka'ba. The Church of the Holy Sepulchre will be burned down in war and siege. Muslims and Rumis will do battle over Jerusalem, and only two cities will remain to the Muslims: Damascus and 'Amman, the cities of peace. Woe to the inhabitants of Jerusalem and Palestine from the Rum!"

'He continued: "Woe will come to the people of Cairo, Mount Muqat-tam, lower Egypt and what lies between, at the hands of the Turks and after them the barbarians, and woes will come to the people of Andalus and Cordova, with their yellow banners and their geldings, at the hands of Turks and then barbarians and westerners, whose speech is like the twittering of birds. I see that they have crossed over the sea and sold the Egyptians as slaves are sold, because of their wrong-doing and their abandonment of the Holy War, the pilgrimage and the commandment to do good and to forbid evil. Their evil deeds were obvious throughout the land, and God does not wrong His servants."

'He then said: "Affliction will come to the Yemenis, the Hijazis and the people of al-Ta'if from the Abyssinians, the blacks and the various races of negroes, the children of Ham. They will be governed by slaves thanks to what they did and thanks to their heresies and wickedness and their abandonment of the Holy War and the pilgrimage. The last of them reviled the first, and they found fault with the companions of God's Prophet, may God bless him and his family and give him peace. They failed to do what He told them, that is to command the good and forbid what was evil, and God does not wrong His servants."

'He told us: "I see Abyssinians and blacks standing on the walls of the Ka'ba and removing stones so as to leave no trace of it. God, the Great and Glorious, gave them power over the people of Mecca, who had committed sinful excesses. It was because of what they had done that vengeance overtook them. I see the black Abyssinian drunken, with trailing robe and sleeves, singing in his own tongue and inciting his companions, Abyssinians, negroes and blacks, to tear down the Ka'ba and destroy the stone set there by Abraham the Friend of God, upon whom be peace. He is removing the foundations of the Sacred House and passing the stones with his own hand to the man next to him, who passes it to another and so on to the last of them until they are thrown into the sea. He himself stays in his place, going neither forwards nor backwards and moving not an inch. What can you do with people whose ranks stretch from Mecca to the shores of the sea with their army drawn up from Mount Abu Qubais to the shore of the Red Sea?"

'We said: "Monk, tell us how it was that you first began to acquire this knowledge." He replied: "I was a disciple of the prophet Daniel, upon whom be peace, and it was thanks to him that I studied and acquired knowledge of hidden secrets." "How was that?" we asked, and he told us: "I heard – and God knows better – that when He created Adam he conjured up his descendants before Him and fashioned them in the form of light, one generation, one people and one age after another, with one prophet and one messenger following another. Adam was the first of them and the last was your Prophet Muhammad, may God bless him and his family and give him peace."

'He went on: "When God expelled Adam from the Garden of Eden, He thought over how things should be done and laid down His plan. Adam was afraid that the knowledge of stored secrets might be lost, thinking of the Flood, in which God was to drown the people of Noah. He used the knowledge he had and transferred it on to white skins, before removing it from them and destroying them for fear lest they be ruined in the Flood and nothing be left. He transferred the knowledge from those skins to clay tablets that he had made with his own hands, baking them in fire. When this had been done the knowledge and the texts that contained the revealed words of God were kept stored in safety.

' "Adam then put all these on the mountain of Hind and called on God, the Great and Glorious, to preserve them, as He preserved those of His books that He revealed to the prophets whom He sent out. The cave in which they are preserved is sealed under the mountain and is only opened on one day in the year, that of 'Ashura, when it is brought up and remains open from the morning to the afternoon prayer. If anyone enters it on that day and busies himself in transcribing those tablets until the afternoon has passed, he stays there until he dies of hunger and thirst, whereas if he leaves earlier he will escape safely with the knowledge that he has written down. Many have perished, but many men of learning, wise philosophers, have escaped.

' "The prophet Daniel, upon whom be peace, was an Israelite who had heard of this and had learned that the cave was in Mount Manda-qid in India beside wadi Sarandib. He went from Jerusalem to India and climbed the mountain on the day of 'Ashura. He entered the cave which was hollowed out in white rock for as far as the eye could see, and the tablets were arranged all around its sides, containing every branch of secret knowledge. When we came we were split up, and Daniel told us to write down what was on the tablet he assigned us, from the beginning on. We transcribed what he wanted of the secret knowledge stored there and before afternoon came he told us to leave and took what we had written.

' "We gave great praise to God for what we had done and for our safety, while the prophet Daniel, upon whom be peace, took what had been written there, allowing him to know all he wanted, including the past and the future until the Day of Judgement, although God knows more. You must know that he wrote two books, one small and the other large."

'Simeon went on: "God created the seven heavens and the seven earths, the seven days of the week, the seven spheres and the seven climes. He created the world to last for fourteen thousand years, the first two thousand of which were to see Adam and his children, with Sheth and Idris in the next two thousand, Noah and his people, whom God destroyed in the third, Abraham the Friend of God and King Nimrod son of Kana'an in the fourth; Isma'il and his people, the Arabs, in the fifth, Isaac, Jacob and the Israeli tribes in the sixth, with Moses, Jesus, the disciples and the prophets who were with them, such as David,

Solomon, Job, Jonah, Zakariya and Yahya, up to the time of the Messiah, the Spirit and Word of God, in the thirteen thousands. He then despatched your Prophet, may God bless him and give him peace, the seal of the prophets and lord of the apostles, after three thousand six hundred years.

'"This is what we found in the book that the prophet Daniel, on whom be peace, wrote on the history of the prophets. We were with him in the cave, and this was what Adam had recorded of God's revelation passed by Michael from Israfil from the guarded tablet written by Almighty God in His own hand, for He is always at work. Glory be to Him Who does what He wishes and decrees what He wills!"

'We said: "Monk, we should like you to tell us dates so that we may learn from you and check the truth." He replied: "We found the dates in the Book of Battles and Strife, where Daniel wrote that from Adam to Noah was a period of 1,242 years; from Noah to Abraham was 570 years; from Moses who spoke with God to David was a thousand years; and from the Messiah to Muhammad, may God bless him and give him peace, was 624 years. These dates are found in the two books of Daniel, which I told you about when I started. You, the people of Muhammad, live in the last thousand years of the world, but knowledge is only in the hands of God, the Great and Glorious."

'We said: "Monk, the Great and Glorious God is alone without a partner, but the people of Sind and Hind have been worshipping idols for ten thousand years." "They tell lies in their arrogance," he said, "and thanks to their holy book they take Adam to be their god, claiming that he fled from the people of Sind to Iraq and the Hijaz and that he built the Kaʿba at Mecca before going back to Syria and dying in the Holy Land and being buried in Jerusalem. But it was Abraham, the Friend of God, on whom be peace, who built the Kaʿba."

'We wrote down all that we needed, Commander of the Faithful, and were taking our leave when he said: "I conjure you, followers of Muhammad, by the truth of your Prophet, to wait a while." When we did, he said: "On the Day of Judgement you will bear witness in respect of all peoples who have preceded you, for your religion is the best, your Prophet, Muhammad, is the best of prophets, may God bless him and give him peace, and his people are the best of peoples. So do you testify for me that I bear witness that there is no god but God and that Muhammad is the apostle of God."

'Simeon then raised his hand towards the sky and said: "People of

Muhammad, I should like you to repeat for me the prayer that I am about to make." When we had willingly agreed he went on: "My Lord, I invoke you by your Sacred Names, by Your perfect words and by the books that You have sent down to Your hundred and twenty-four thousand prophets, by the writings and books that You have revealed, by Your secret Name inscribed in the light of day, by Your secret Name inscribed on the gates of Hell, by Your secret Name inscribed on the gates of Paradise, by Your secret Name written on the seven lands, by Your secret Name written on the seven heavens, by Your secret Name written on the seven seas, by Your secret Name written on the seven hills, by the secret Name written on the foreheads of the angels who surround the Throne, by Your glory, which begins and ends with 'In the Name of God, the Compassionate, the Merciful' and by all Your Sacred Names. Grant us Your gracious protection and direct us to what is good."

'He went on: "My Lord, look on me with favour and not anger when You take me to Yourself. You are the most merciful of the merciful, Mighty, Gracious, Noble, Omniscient, Holy King, Faithful Master, Glorious in the richness of Your grace and power, God of grandeur set on high Who listens to our prayers, One, Alone, Unique and Everlasting, Generous in Your bounty from past eternity, All-Hearing, All-Wise in Your power and might, You know what is secret and have power over all things, and there is no power and no might except with the Exalted and Omnipotent God."

'When he ended his prayer we said: "Amen, amen, Lord of the worlds." Then, by God, he had scarcely finished speaking before he fell from his hermitage and was dead when he reached the ground, may God have mercy upon him. There was no crash or any sound at all, and it was as though he had been lowered to the ground on a rope, and his face was like a full moon, illumined by radiance. We went up to him, washed and embalmed him and buried him in his shroud beside his hermitage.

'We left him, and went back to our comrades, filled with wonder at what had happened. Then our emir gave us the order to leave. We embarked and sailed off but when we had got far out to sea we were met by a violent storm wind. The waves broke over our ship, and we were confronted by such perils that I cannot describe, with our ships being driven on like lightning bolts. They were scattered, and it was only a full year later that we all met in Oman.

'As for my own ship, Commander of the Faithful, it took us to the Chinese sea and from there to inner China. We reached an island in the sea of Yemen, containing a huge castle together with the abandoned well and the lofty palace [Quran 22.44]. The wind drove us on to a coast fringed by red dunes, green *arak* trees and the tree that drips blood on the grave of the prophet Hud, on whom be peace.

'From the Yemeni sea we reached the land of the Nisnas, and the wind took us on for three nights and days. We saw marvels such as people shaped like large men but with only one foot, one hand and one eye, who when they talked to each other sounded like saluki dogs or foxes. They had less intelligence than any other race of men, and when we took a number of them they started to laugh and cry like babies, and we laughed at them in amazement.

'We then left them in their own land and went on until we reached the abandoned well and the lofty palace. We looked at a huge, strongly built castle with a wall larger than any other whose like has not been seen. We measured one of its stones and found it was forty square cubits, using the old cubit measure. We discovered that the castle was filled with the dead, many lying on couches of juniper wood. They were tall, and below was an iron tablet with an inscription in red gold: "I am an example for kings to heed. I lived for a thousand years, ruled over a thousand cities and built a thousand castles. A thousand virgins were brought to me; I sent out a thousand armies and filled a thousand treasure chambers. A thousand kings submitted to me; I stored arms in a thousand chambers and gold and gems in another thousand. I had a thousand ships; I deflowered a thousand virgins and fathered a thousand sons. Then the prophet Hud, upon whom be peace, came to me and summoned me to worship the Great and Glorious God. I refused to believe him and drove him away, at which he called on God to curse me. God destroyed me, and here I lie cast down and brought low by the abandoned well and the lofty palace. Let whoever sees me take note, fear God and believe in His books and His Apostles. I have ordered this to be inscribed when I give up the ghost and my life ends, to serve as a warning to those who see it." '

Sa'id went on: 'We left the lofty palace and the abandoned well, which we found on looking at it was more than a thousand *maliki* cubits deep, cut into rock and black as purgatory, one of the wonders of the world. We left that land with the grave in the dune of blood-red sand and the trees that drip blood with a pungent scent of musk. Above it there is a stone slab with the following inscription: "This is the grave of the prophet Hud, upon whom be peace. Whoever comes to it should confess the unity of God, for there is no other god but Him, the One God with no partner, Whose servant and apostle is Hud. He should also acknowledge the Prophet, who will be sent at the end of time, the last of the prophets, whose name in heaven is Ahmad and on earth Abu'l-Qasim Muhammad, the possessor of every excellence and merit, whose mission is to all peoples. Whoever testifies to him will succeed and be safe whereas those who do not believe in him will be amongst the infidels who will be for ever lost and punished by the Lord of the worlds." '

Sa'id said: 'We raised our voices in the confession of faith and heard a voice echoing around us that said: "Happiness and blessing be yours, people of Muhammad! Would that I had been with you and that I may join you at the Resurrection through the intercession of your Prophet Muhammad, may God bless him and his family and grant him peace."

'We went back to the Valley of the Ants, where we were told that we would see wonders. When we asked what these were we were told that there was one valley ahead of us full of apes with another one beside it which contained huge ants as big as goats. This was the place where Solomon had gone, as had Dhu'l-Qarnain, Alexander the son of Philip the Rumi. We all agreed to go there and when we got to the Valley of the Apes we found that their old king had a golden tablet around his neck on which was inscribed: "In the Name of God the Compassionate, the Merciful: This is a covenant delivered by Solomon son of David, upon whom be peace, guaranteeing safety to all apes in their own lands and territories and at the edge of Yemen. Anyone, human or *jinn*, who comes to their land is to leave without harming them. You are those who believe in God and in His Apostle Solomon son of David, upon whom be peace." '

Sa'id said: 'We left them and went back to the Sea of Yemen, where a storm wind drove us like a lightning bolt to the China Sea, which is the sea of 'Iraq. From there we sailed back to our own country after an absence of seven years, rejoining our comrades and our emir, 'Amr son of al-'As. This, Commander of the Faithful, is what we saw in the way of marvels and terrors.'

Hisham son of 'Abd al-Malik was amazed by Sa'id's story and rewarded him with the greatest generosity. This is the full story, praise be to the One God and His blessings and peace be on the best of His creation, our master, the Prophet Muhammad, his family and his companions. We seek forgiveness from the Almighty God.

Tale Fifteen

The Story of
Muhammad the Foundling and
Harun al-Rashid.

In the Name of God, the Compassionate, the Merciful, I ask for Your help, Noble Lord

A tale is told that Harun al-Rashid went out as usual one day, accompanied by the vizier Ja'far the Barmecide, Yahya, al-Fadl son of al-Rabi', Khalid, al-Rabi' son of Yunus, Ishaq son of Ibrahim of Mosul, Ubada al-Mukhannath and the eunuch Masrur. He went on board his private barge and sailed down to a garden of his named al-Lu'lu'a, three parasangs below the city. There was no place on earth more beautiful, and it contained every single plant named by God. At its centre a dome had been set on four marble columns, with a pool containing a fountain, a silver pump and gold and silver statues through whose mouths water poured and whose eyes were rubies and sapphires. Nothing like it was to be found on earth.

Harun and his companions went up there, and as he took his seat in the dome surrounded by the others, Ishaq sang to them. Masrur the eunuch got up to take a walk in the garden and he heard a little baby crying. 'What is that?' he said and he followed the sound until he discovered beneath a tree a baby in swaddling-clothes of embroidered Antioch silk lying on a gold-embroidered mat. By its head was a purse containing a thousand dinars, and a note had been left on its breast. The baby itself was more radiant than the rising sun, and on its forehead was a circlet of pearls, each five carats in weight, gleaming like stars.

Masrur, exclaiming at the child's beauty, sat down and took him on his lap, saying to himself: 'Here is the son of the tree, but who do you suppose is his real father?' Then he noticed the purse and added: 'And he has enough gold to live on.' When he saw the note he found written in it: 'Whoever finds this child should treat him with respect for the sake of Almighty God, as he comes from the greatest of families. His mother died, and this world is the home of misery. The thousand dinars are for his upbringing, and whoever rears him can expect Paradise as a reward from the Great and Glorious God. He has been put for shelter into this splendid garden.'

Masrur took both the child and the note in his arms and set him down in front of al-Rashid. When al-Rashid saw him he glorified God and exclaimed at his beauty, saying: 'Praise be to Him Who created this child and formed him!' He then asked Masrur about the father, and Masrur told him that this was the son of a tree. 'Can a tree father a child?' said al-Rashid, at which Masrur told him the story and passed over the money and the note. When the tender-hearted al-Rashid had read it he shed bitter tears and told Ja'far to take the boy up to the palace and give him to his wife, Zubaida, together with the gold, which belonged to him and which would have to be kept safe for him. 'Get up quickly and don't delay in taking him to Zubaida lest he start to shriek, and this may affect his heart.'

Ja'far stood up, and a little eunuch carried the crying child on board the barge. When they reached the palace Ja'far went to Zubaida's apartments and asked permission to enter. When her servants told her that he was there with a eunuch she told them to let him in, and he then put the baby down in front of her. She exclaimed at its beauty, and in answer to her question he told her its story and passed over the note and the gold. 'Mistress,' he said, 'I have no need to tell you to take charge of this child, as the caliph took pity on him and told me to be sure to give him to you to look after.'

Zubaida sent at once for two wet nurses to take turns in looking after the child, one by night and the other by day. As for Ja'far, he went back to the caliph, and they spent three days enjoying the sights of the garden, before al-Rashid returned to his palace.

Nights and days, months and years passed until the child was ten years old and looked like the rising moon. He was sure that he was one of al-Rashid's own children, and to Zubaida he was as dear as if he were her son. She named him Muhammad the Foundling and had him taught to sing, until his voice and his artistry were unsurpassed. 'Do this well, my boy,' she used to say, 'so that you may be even better than Ishaq al-Mausili on the lute.' As for al-Rashid, he had forgotten him.

By the time he was fifteen Muhammad had reached maturity and had a face brighter than the sun. He used to ride with Muhammad al-Amin and al-Mu'tasim, and they would go to play polo on the *maidan* of the palace, where he would defeat them, as he was stronger, more vigorous and nobler.

Al-Rashid had had a new palace built with a dome and a garden and when the servants had cleaned it out he came and sat in its hall with a number of his courtiers, while Muhammad the Foundling was playing polo with his sons. Muhammad hit the ball so hard that it flew up from the *maidan*, which was at the back of the palace, and rebounded from the roof of the hall to strike the dome before coming back to ground. Al-Rashid exclaimed in alarm, thinking that the hall was collapsing, and he jumped up to run out, but when he wanted to know what had fallen his companions looked and saw the polo ball. Al-Rashid exploded with anger and told Masrur: 'Go to the *maidan* and see who is there. If this was one of the palace mamluks, cut him down with your sword, while if it was one of my sons, you can do what you like. But hurry.'

Masrur opened the gate to the *maidan* and went out to where they were playing. 'What is all this polo?' he demanded. 'Your ball bounced down from the roof in front of the caliph, and he is very angry indeed. Tell me who hit it.' 'What did we tell you, Muhammad?' the others said to him: 'The ball struck the roof of the new palace.' Masrur repeated: 'Tell me who hit it.' 'It was my brother Muhammad,' said al-Amin, passing on the blame. Masrur said: 'So you hit the ball in front of the caliph? Blessings on you, you dog!' Muhammad urged on his horse and said: 'You cupper, you dog, yes I struck it. Are you threatening me?' and he raised his mallet and cut open Masrur's head so that the blood poured down over his clothes. With an exclamation of distress he made for the door, while Muhammad rode away.

Masrur went off to the caliph and stood outside, indulging in the wildest fit of weeping and saying, with mucus dripping from his nose: 'How can I go in with this wound in my head?' Al-Rashid asked him what was wrong and why he was weeping like that. 'Come on and tell me what has happened to you,' he said, and then, when Masrur entered, he saw the blood on his clothes and asked: 'Who did this to you?' 'Your son struck me,' said Masrur. 'Al-Amin?' asked al-Rashid. 'No, by God,' said Masrur. 'Al-Mu'tasim, then?' 'No, Commander of the Faithful.' 'Al-Ma'mun?' 'No.' 'Damn you,' said al-Rashid, 'what other sons do I have?' 'That handsome one,' said Masrur, but when al-Rashid asked Ja'far who this was, Ja'far said that he did not understand. 'Go off and call for him,' ordered the caliph. 'By God, I am not going,' exclaimed Masrur, and at that the caliph told Ja'far to go and see who it was who had struck Masrur. 'Here is my ring,' he said; 'take it to him and bring him here.' Ja'far objected that it would be better if Masrur went, and the caliph agreed and swore: 'Masrur, you and you only are going to go. Any *jinni* would die at the sight of you, and are you going to run away from a boy? Off you go and bring him here quickly.'

The boys were still on the *maidan* when Masrur ran up. 'Are you back, black man?' said Muhammad, spurring his horse towards him. Masrur called out: 'This is the ring of our master, the Commander of the Faithful, and he wants you.' He threw it at him and it fell in front of his horse. Muhammad dismounted, took the ring and kissed it and then rode to the palace door before dismounting again and entering. Masrur had hidden his sword in a closet near the hall and he now told the caliph: 'He is coming.' The caliph bent over laughing, but his eyes were fixed on the door.

Muhammad came in, wearing a corselet of silver thread set with gold, a belt of brocade round his waist and on his head a brocaded cap secured by a wrap of white brocade. He shone more brightly than the rising sun, and when al-Rashid saw him he exclaimed: 'There is no god but God. Praise be to the One Who created and formed you! Who are you?' Muhammad kissed the ground before him and greeted him as caliph. Al-Rashid replied by calling down God's blessing and mercy on him, but repeated his question. 'I am your son, Commander of the Faithful, may God allow Islam and the Muslims to enjoy your long life.' 'Who was your mother?' asked al-Rashid, and Muhammad told him that this was Zubaida. 'I have never set eyes on you,' said al-Rashid.

Masrur was saying that when he had talked to him Muhammad had given him no reply, but al-Rashid shouted to him to stay in his closet, and he remained silent. Al-Rashid then told Muhammad to come up to him, which he did before kissing his hand. He was told to sit, and when he had done so al-Rashid said: 'So Zubaida is your mother?' 'Yes, Commander of the Faithful,' Muhammad told him. 'I cannot rest until this problem is solved,' said al-Rashid and at that he got up and, taking Ja'far with him, he went to Zubaida's room and sat down with Ja'far in front of him. He then called to a eunuch to fetch his mistress, and when the eunuch had entered and passed on the message she came out and took her seat behind the curtain. 'Is this boy your son?' al-Rashid asked her and when she said 'yes' he then asked who the father was. 'Ja'far the vizier,' she said, at which Ja'far trembled and turned pale. 'My Lady,' he exclaimed, 'one should not joke in a place like this. Don't do it, for you have drained me of blood. Now divorce me.' She laughed, but al-Rashid said: 'This is no place for laughter.' 'Have you forgotten the boy?' she asked him, and she produced the note, which he took and read. 'Yes, by God, I remember!' al-Rashid exclaimed, and he passed the note to Ja'far, who said: 'By God, it is the foundling.' 'What was wrong with you?' Zubaida asked Ja'far, who replied: 'A man bitten by a snake will die unless he gets medicine from Iraq. By God, it will take a month before I come back to life.'

Al-Rashid then asked Zubaida what she had taught the boy, and she told him: 'By your life, Commander of the Faithful, I swear that nowhere on earth does he have a match for skill on the lute or for his singing. Up till now he has not known that he is a foundling and he thinks that he is my son by you.' 'He can be glad,' said al-Rashid, 'for we take him as our son,' and he ordered him to be given a robe of honour worth a thousand dinars. Muhammad was delighted and asked to be given a lute, which was brought to him. He took it, clasped it to his breast and, after touching the strings, he sang these words with a voice finer than almond paste and sweeter than the water of the Euphrates:

As the girls walk they sway their tender limbs
As the south wind stirs the branches of Jabrin,
Or as Rudaini spears are shaken by men's hands,
Thanks to the supple shafts that make them bend.

Al-Rashid exclaimed in wonder and delight and said: 'From this day on you are not to leave me. Do not distress yourself for you are like a son to us, and a son of choice is better than a real one.' Muhammad kissed the ground, and he now became one of the caliph's intimates from whom he could not bear to be parted for a single hour and who had to be present whenever he ate. He was dearer to al-Rashid than his own sons and he was given an apartment off the hallway of his own private quarters in the palace so that he could be at hand to come quickly when called.

As it happened, al-Rashid had been given a Rumi virgin as a slave girl whom no one on the face of the earth surpassed in beauty. He had left her in his palace, promising himself that he would save her for later. Whenever Muhammad passed her room she would cling on to him and say: 'I love you! Come and spend the night with me, for I am yours.' He would reply by cursing her and saying: 'Is someone like me to repay the caliph's kindness by acting viciously in his palace? God forbid that I should do any such thing!' When she kept on at him and disturbed him he said: 'Listen to me! Do not hope for this and stop talking about it. Am I to commit a sin like this in the house of one who has brought me up and showered me with benefits?' 'So you are not going to do what I want now?' she said and he replied: 'Do you think that I am going to give you any other answer? Listen and understand, for I am not going to bring shame on the man in whose house I have been brought up.' 'Worthless fellow,' she said; 'so you're not going to accept what I offer? If I don't have your head cut off, I am not Miriam.' 'Be sensible and don't make silly boasts,' he told her and, removing his hand from her, he went to his room.

Miriam went to her own room, feeling diminished, but saying to herself: 'He doesn't mean it and he will come and spend the night with me.' She left him for three days and then called for a black slave who acted as furnace-man for the caliph's private baths. She took him by the hand and told him to come in. He was astonished and asked her what she wanted. 'By God,' she told him, 'I love you and I want you to spend every night with me.' 'Lady,' he replied, 'I am afraid of our master.' 'He will never know,' she said and she gave herself to him, and he deflowered her. She then shrieked: 'What have you done, you dog?' and he got up in terror and ran out of the palace. She waited for a time until Muhammad came past, wearing a shirt of Antioch silk and a gilded linen headband. He had been drinking with al-Rashid and was drunk. Dawn was about to break, and he was on his way to his room when she came out and took hold of him, pulling him to her bosom and dragging him by force into her room. She then turned over on her back, leaving him lying on her breasts and then crying out for help. Three eunuchs rushed in and, at the sight, they raised a cry. This disturbed al-Rashid, who was still drunk, and he asked what the noise was, telling Masrur to go and find out.

Masrur went towards the source of the noise and saw the eunuchs, who hurried up to him and told what Muhammad had done. Masrur exclaimed and said: 'This is the end for the young man.' He went to the caliph and said: 'Master, all is well, and there is nothing to alarm you.' 'Give me the news or I shall have your head cut off,' said al-Rashid and at that Masrur told him: 'Master, Muhammad the Foundling went to Miriam the Rumi and raped her.' 'What do you mean, raped?' said al-Rashid, who was a jealous man. He then bowed his head in silent thought before raising it and saying: 'Masrur, who am I?' Masrur replied: 'Master, you are al-Rashid bi-llah, son of al-Mahdi, the son of al-Hadi, the son of Mansur, the son of Muhammad, the son of 'Ali, the son of 'Abbas, the uncle of the Apostle of God, may God bless him and give him peace.' 'That is so,' said al-Rashid; 'now go at once, take Muhammad, cut off his head and bring it to me. Throw his body into the river. Go at once and be quick.'

Masrur left, shedding tears for the young Muhammad and saying: 'By God, he did nothing and the Rumi bitch has lied to hurt him.' In spite of that he took Muhammad and tied his hands while the headband fell from his head. He recovered from his drunkenness and turned pale. 'Masrur my friend,' he pleaded, 'have mercy on me! By God, I never did anything, and I know nothing of what she said. She pulled me down on top of her and then shrieked'. 'By God, that is true!' Masrur exclaimed. 'I know that you are not guilty of what she said you did, but what has happened has happened.' 'I ask for help from God,' said Muhammad.

Masrur then took him and put him on a barge together with two eunuchs. He was in tears, and they were weeping for his youthful beauty, while the sailors were shedding tears of sadness for him. They took the barge into the middle of the stream and across to the far bank, where they took out Muhammad and brought him up the bank. The weeping sailors told Masrur: 'For God's sake, wait! Pity this handsome man and don't deprive him of the breath of life.' 'Will you swear not to say anything?' he asked them, and when they said 'yes' he made them take an oath by the Qur'an and promise to divorce their wives if they broke their word. He made the eunuchs take the same oath, but then said: 'What am I to do? The caliph is now going to ask for his head.'

While he was talking a man appeared, going along the bank, and Masrur's followers took hold of him and brought him up. It turned out that he was the black furnace-man who had deflowered Miriam. 'Where are you running off to?' Masrur asked him, and he said: 'By God, master, the girl took hold of me and threw me on top of her, telling me she loved me, and I couldn't say "no".' 'Fine,' said Masrur. 'By doing what you did you have destroyed prosperous houses and brought this young man into sudden danger. Come up here so that we can settle things.' The two of them went up the bank, and Masrur cut off the man's head, which he took. Then, after throwing the body into the river, he said to Muhammad: 'Off you go. Keep a good look out and stay away for a year.'

Muhammad kissed his hand and made off to the desert in the direction of al-Mada'in, wandering in bewilderment until morning. His feet became swollen, and his Antioch shirt gave no protection against the sun's heat. As dawn broke he reached a village, where he sat by a stream to rest and wash his face. As he was thinking over what had happened to him through no fault of his own, the village shaikh came riding up on a mare, together with his two sons. When he saw Muhammad sitting there dressed as he was, he said to his sons: 'Look at this youngster. By God, he must be a fugitive, and I have never seen a more handsome face.'

He went up to Muhammad and said: 'My son, why are you here in the desert dressed like this? You are soon going to feel the heat, and it will kill you.' 'Uncle,' Muhammad said, 'what am I to do? I have done no wrong but I am a fugitive who has been wronged. I have come hoping to find someone to shelter me for a time in exchange for recompense from me and reward from God, thanks to the injustice done me. When the pursuit has stopped send me away to go down to Basra, and I shall not come back anywhere near Baghdad.' 'You have got your wish, my boy,' said the shaikh, 'as I and my sons will help you. I swear by Muhammad, the chosen Prophet, that were you to want to stay with me for a hundred years no one would interfere with you or set eyes on you.'

He called to his son and, when the boy answered, he said: 'Sulaiman, this is going to be your brother, so take him and hide him in your room, letting nobody see him. Then treat him well until I come.' Sulaiman agreed and went back with Muhammad to the village, where he took him to his pleasant room and brought everything he might need before going back to find his father.

Masrur meanwhile returned to al-Rashid, whom he found sitting with a bowed head, still under the influence of drink. Al-Rashid called to him and when he answered he said: 'Where have you been?' 'Master,' replied Masrur, 'didn't you send me to kill Muhammad the Foundling?' 'Yes,' said al-Rashid, 'and so where is his head?' 'Here in my hand,' Masrur told him and he held it up for him to see. In the dim light he did not check it but told him to throw it into the river. Masrur could scarcely believe this and left the caliph, still deeply drunk, to sleep where he was. He was sure that next day he would ask him for Muhammad and he said to himself: 'This was a great mistake. Why didn't I hide him away until he was asked for?' He spent an unhappy night.

Next day al-Rashid came from his room to the baths, after which he went to his court as his courtiers together with Ja'far the vizier came up while the eunuchs stood around the throne. Al-Rashid raised his head and said: 'Muhammad the Foundling is absent. Go to his room, Masrur, and tell him he is wanted.' Masrur stood there embarrassed, shaking like a leaf, and when al-Rashid asked what the matter was he said: 'Master, don't say this to me but have mercy on me.' Al-Rashid repeated his question, and Masrur replied: 'Master, didn't you order me to kill him and throw him into the river, and are you now asking me for him, when yesterday evening I brought you his head?'

On hearing this, al-Rashid exclaimed: 'There is no might and no power except with Almighty God! Did I really tell you to do that? You must be lying.' Masrur swore that it was true, and al-Rashid said: 'What had Muhammad done? Tell me and be brief.' When Masrur had told him what had happened, al-Rashid called for Miriam and broke into bitter tears. 'Alas for al-Rashid on the Day of Judgement!' he exclaimed. 'He will have to answer for having killed that handsome man.'

He kept on sobbing while Masrur wept until, when he had finished, he said to himself: 'Unless I tell the caliph that I did not kill Muhammad, I shall have cause for fear.' So he said: 'Listen, Commander of the Faithful. I did not kill him but left him alive in the desert. This was a mistake on my part, for I should have hidden him somewhere that I knew about, whereas now I don't know where in all the wide world he may be going.' 'Masrur,' said al-Rashid, 'you have brought me some consolation but now ride out this instant with a thousand mamluks and comb through the villages and the deserts as far as Wasit. I shall give a thousand dinars to any one of you who brings me Muhammad.'

The mamluks rode off, and the village shaikh, on seeing horsemen to the right and left, told his son that they must be looking for Muhammad, to which he agreed. Group after group of mamluks went out and then came back from Wasit without having found anyone who had seen or knew anything about Muhammad. Masrur told the caliph what the furnace-man had told him, after which he took Miriam, dressed her in a robe of wool and had her locked up in chains.

So much for them, but as for Muhammad, after fifteen days the shaikh smuggled him on board a barge on which he set off downstream to Basra. He had with him a sapphire ring, which he sold for twenty dinars, and with these he bought fine clothes and hired a house. He used to sit with a perfume seller, and rows of people would stand in front of him, calling on God to protect him. While he was there, up came a girl with a perfect figure and rounded breasts. She had joining eyebrows, dark eyes and breasts of marble; her face was brighter than the moon and the sun; she was wrapped in a gold-embroidered shawl, and there was a large crowd following her.

When she caught sight of Muhammad she stopped opposite him, and the breeze she felt came neither from north nor south but was known as longing, and she felt it four fingers' width below her navel. 'Look at this boy sitting here as we stand!' she exclaimed, and she took hold of him and tugged him into the booth, saying: 'By God, this is a beautiful face, and how ugly are the faces of the Basrans! You are my cousin, and I am from Baghdad.'

She took him into a lane, and the crowd was divided, with some following because they wanted to look at a young couple they loved while others were jeering at the girl and saying: 'A night with her costs five dinars.' She turned on them and said: 'It is God Who protects! I pass by here every day and put up with your jeers, but today you should apologize.' Most of the crowd told the scoffers to go away, saying: 'The sun and the moon have met.'

When they were left alone they walked on together, but Muhammad did not dare enter his house with a girl for fear that no good would come of it. For her part she said: 'Take me to your house so that we can drink through the night until breakfast. I am not going to leave you, as you are the lover I have been looking for.' He was embarrassed but was not bold enough to turn her away, although he had no idea where to take her. He went from one street to another, saying to himself: 'When I see a locked door, I shall tell her that this is my house but my servant has not come, and so I shall get her to go off.' He went into a street thinking that it was a thoroughfare and walked to the end of it, where facing him was a house which looked as though the decorators had just left. On the door was an iron ring and it had two teak leaves that looked like sandalwood, each with a brass ring that looked like gold and a Rumi lock weighing two *ratls*. He stopped and said: 'This is my house, but what has happened? May God cut off the hand of my servant! By God, I don't know where he has gone.' 'Is this your house?' the girl asked and when he said 'yes' she exclaimed: 'By God, what a beautiful house with its fine balcony up there. I have never seen anything like the leaves of its door, and it is as handsome as you. I shall unlock it.' She went forward and took a stick from the road, which she put into the lock, pressing it home so that the catches flew open. 'That's done it!' she exclaimed. 'Thanks to my good fortune I have got it open.' She pushed it open, and it closed behind them.

Muhammad said: 'I went in with her in a terrified state. We crossed a corridor to a curtain of brocade and when we lifted this up we came into the main building and found two arched passageways with one room facing another. The place was encrusted with gold and there was a rope there with ten satin tassels for the master of the house to use against moths. The house was washed clean as snow and adorned with lapis lazuli and gold. The girl went up to take her seat on the dais, where I followed her. She removed her shawl and said: "Do you suppose your servant has cooked anything?" She went into the room and found a door at the top of it, which she opened to discover there an oven and five stoves, each with a pot and a different kind of food, smelling like musk. There were five plates with sweetmeats and bread weighing a hundred *ratls*. "Cousin," she asked, "have you invited people?" "By God," I replied, "I don't know what my servant thought he was doing," adding to myself: "Fine, by God! There has never been any better preparation for a party, and the host must be a Turk or some respected man who will come and see us here in his house without his permission. We shall find that our day is over, but let us put our trust in God."

'The girl took a plate and five porcelain cups, dipping one into each of the pots. She put rice in a bowl and took a chicken and a bowl of sweetmeats and, after having covered the plate with fine bread, she came and put it in front of me. "Eat," she said, rolling up her sleeves, and I ate as though it was myself I was eating, since I did not know what I had got myself into. When we had both eaten and washed our hands she told me to strain the wine while she stood up and looked around. She opened cupboards, in one of which she found five tubs, each containing large jars full of ice-cold wine. "Fine!" she exclaimed. "He is trying to hide this from me although I love him." Taking a plate, she set three full jars on it and placed it in front of me. Then in another cupboard she found melons, fruit and scented flowers and these too she put before me. "Now we want some music," she said, but I told her that all we should do was to sit where we were lest the neighbours hear. At the top of the hall, however, she saw a closet and on opening it she discovered a lute, a harp and a tambourine. With an exclamation of pleasure she took the tambourine and beat it. I got up and took hold of her hand, saying: "We have an ascetic neighbour who will be here in a moment to tell us he disapproves. We don't want any tambourine playing." I removed it from her, and the wine cups passed between us.'

The house belonged to the attendant of Muhammad al-Zainabi, a man by the name of Khultukh. He had no wife and liked to drink with the Turks. It was he who had made all these preparations and had gone off to fetch these people. He arrived with them to find one leaf of the door open and the other shut. He exclaimed at what he thought the Turks had done to open the door, but they told him that it was like that when they found it. 'I don't know,' he said, and he told them to stay where they were until he went in to look around.

He entered slowly through the door and slowly raised a corner of the curtain. What he saw was a young man and a girl who looked like the rising sun. 'Good, by God!' he exclaimed for he was a good-natured man who loved company. He saw that no damage had been done to his house and he said to himself: 'God curse anyone who spoils their pleasure! Who can bear to part the sun and the moon?' He went back to the Turks, who asked if they could go in. 'No,' he told them, 'put it off until tomorrow and I will make it up to you.' They thanked him and went off, after which he stole back into the house. He took a flat loaf, drenched it on top of a pot and then opened a wine cellar, from which he took a jar which he opened. He sat there eating and drinking, taking a sip from a bowl, which was the only thing he had to drink from, every time that he saw the young couple drink. He saw that the young man was looking ill at ease and hoped that he would get up. As he was saying this Muhammad got up and as he went out to relieve himself he caught sight of Khultukh seated there with his wine.

Khultukh got up and went to him, saying: 'Don't speak and don't be afraid.' I am the attendant of Muhammad son of Sulaiman and whatever money I get I spend it on people. My house is yours, so don't be distressed but tell me your story.' Muhammad told him what the girl had done, and he said: 'Go down and drink and don't leave her. I shall tie a belt around my waist and when I come in, show anger and give me a light blow.' As Muhammad laughed he leaned over and kissed him on the mouth, taking possession of his whole heart.

Muhammad went down and told the girl to take the tambourine and sing. 'What about the ascetic?' she asked, but he said: 'We don't need to bother about him.' She took the tambourine and sang but then said: 'I don't think my singing was very good. Give me one of your *jubbahs* so I may do better.' Khultukh exclaimed in alarm but then said: 'Let him give it to her.' She stretched out her hand and took a *jubbah* of Coptic satin, elaborately marked, which, when she put it on, was too long for her. 'It's too long,' she said, before taking it and tearing off a strip from the bottom. 'Oh, Oh! She has ruined it,' exclaimed Khultukh, 'but let her be.' 'Why didn't you leave it till winter and then get it to fit you?' asked Muhammad, but the girl told him to mind his own business.

She asked him what he supposed had happened to his slave and he told her that he would have to beat him. 'What do you want from him?' she asked. 'He has done everything that you could want.' She went on to ask whether he had bought the house or built it. 'I bought it and it is mine,' Muhammad replied. 'And my *jubbah* as well,' said Khultukh to himself. 'What is the name of your slave?' the girl asked, and he told her that it was Khultukh. 'Was it you or your father who bought him?' she went on, and he said: 'It was my father who bought him and I inherited him.' 'God give you health!' exclaimed Khultukh, adding: 'Both I and this house have become this man's property, with the clothes thrown in as an extra. But he is a handsome fellow, may God be good to him!'

He rushed down, belted his waist and went out to the market with a basket, in which he put fresh fruit and newly picked flowers. He got a porter to carry this on his head before flinging open the door and interrupting the two as they were enjoying themselves. He left the basket in front of Muhammad. 'What kept you?' said Muhammad and, taking a whip, he struck him. 'Slowly!' exclaimed Khultukh. 'You hurt me.' The girl jumped up and interceded for him, saying: 'Don't beat him! Does he deserve this from you?' and she told Khultukh to come to her. He told her: 'This is a fine thing my master does! He sends me to check an account with his banker and bring his money and then he beats me.' From his sleeve he shook out two hundred dinars and when Muhammad told him to pick them up he produced a purse and left the gold in it.

Muhammad and the girl sat drinking until nightfall when they got up to sleep, with Khultukh spreading bedding in a fine gilded room, where the two of them slept until morning. The girl then got up and dressed, and Khultukh, who was standing there, recognized her and weighed out five dinars for her, saying: 'Lady, take this to the baths.' She said: 'Khultukh, I'm not going to take anything from this master of mine. Every night I spend with him I shall let him have the money to spend on us.' She then said goodbye to Muhammad and went out.

Khultukh went to Muhammad and said: 'Come to the baths.' Muhammad got up to go there and was dressed in a robe of Damiettan linen worth fifty dinars. Khultukh said to him: 'Listen and don't play games with me. I am your slave, and you must take over the house so that I can go to work. Here is the key so you can go out and come in. This is your house, and I am your mamluk.' Muhammad called down blessings on him and said: 'May Almighty God allow me to repay you.'

Muhammad spent a year in Basra, while al-Rashid was left in a state of great unrest. Then news came from his agents that the person he was looking for had been seen in Basra. He ordered Masrur to ride to Basra with a hundred men and have a proclamation made that anyone who sees a person fitting this description would receive three hundred dinars a year together with three meals a day. He would also be able to hope for a gift. 'To hear is to obey,' said Masrur and he rode off, making for Basra and pressing on until he got there. He then got a town crier to make a general proclamation that whoever saw a young man with long hair, a white face, hairless cheeks, joining eyebrows and a mole on his cheek would be given three hundred dinars a year and three meals a day, as well as being able to ask for what he wanted from the Commander of the Faithful.

Khultukh was buying bread when the crier came to his street and went to the market to make his proclamation. Khultukh climbed on a bench to see what this was, and he then said to himself: 'The young man he is talking about is the one who is with me. I'd better tell them, but, by God, I shall not do that until I have gone to him to see what he has to say.' He got down from the bench and ran to his house, where he called to Muhammad. When Muhammad answered he said: 'Masrur the eunuch has come with a town crier. They have given a description of you and said that whoever sees the man who fits the description will be handed the signet ring of the Commander of the Faithful and will be given such-and-such a reward if he leads the way to you.' 'It is for me that Masrur has come,' said Muhammad, 'so go and take the ring and tell him: "This man is with me." Then take whatever they give you.' 'If I say that, what will Masrur do with you?' 'He will take me and go off,' Muhammad told him, at which Khultukh said: 'They can keep their gold. I don't want you to go.' 'Khultukh,' Muhammad said, 'I want to do you some good and to bring you luck, so go and tell them.'

Khultukh left unwillingly and stood in front of Masrur, gesturing to him. Masrur ordered his men to hold him, and they rushed forward to do this. 'How rough you are!' Khultukh exclaimed, but Masrur asked what he wanted. 'The man you are looking for is with me,' Khultukh told him. 'What are you saying?' said Masrur, but Khultukh repeated: 'He is with me, so produce the caliph's ring, for this is going to please him.' 'It certainly will, by God!' Masrur exclaimed and he passed the ring to Khultukh, who took it and went to Muhammad with Masrur following him.

When Masrur saw Muhammad he kissed the ground in front of him and Muhammad went up and embraced him, saying: 'You have always been good to me although I blamed you.' 'Master,' said Masrur, 'the Commander of the Faithful has had no news of you.' 'But you told me to stay away,' Muhammad said. 'Get up now,' Masrur told him. 'What are you doing sitting here?' Khultukh asked him: 'And why have you come to take away my son?' Masrur laughed and said: 'This is the son of the Commander of the Faithful.'

When Muhammad told him what Khultukh had done with him, Masrur embraced him and said: 'May God produce more men like you!' He presented him with three thousand *riyals*, but Khultukh kissed them and put them back on his head, saying: 'God preserve the Commander of the Faithful! I take no reward for a good deed.' Masrur insisted: 'The caliph's bounty is not to be rejected!' and at that Khultukh accepted the money.

Muhammad mounted and said goodbye to Khultukh, who wept and kissed him. 'Don't be sad,' Muhammad told him, 'but come to us, as the caliph will welcome you.' Khultukh said goodbye and went back, while Masrur set off with Muhammad. When they got to Sarsar they were met by a mounted escort together with servants, and both groups went together to the caliph. He welcomed Muhammad and asked why he had hidden himself away. 'Out of fear of you, Commander of the Faithful,' Muhammad told him. 'If you fear the Great and Glorious God,' the caliph said, 'you need fear no one whom God created.'

He then ordered the Rumi slave girl to be produced, and she was brought in chains. 'She is an ignorant creature,' he said, 'and instead of having her killed, I shall sell her and give the money to the poor and needy.' Ja'far was present, and when Muhammad told him what had happened to him he exclaimed: 'By God, I have never heard of the like of this Khultukh!' 'Remind me to send him a robe of honour,' the caliph told him, 'and to give him an annual allowance of a thousand dinars from the state treasury of Basra.' 'To hear is to obey,' said Ja'far.

Two days later Muhammad fell seriously ill to the great distress of Zubaida, al-Rashid and the whole court, who uttered prayers of supplication to God. He was close to death, and his life was despaired of, leading al-Rashid to forget about Khultukh.

Khultukh himself had many friends, one of whom, an intimate of

Muhammad son of.Sulaiman, told him that he was about to be arrested, as a result of which he fled away with no more than five dinars. He went to Wasit, where he hired a mule to take him to Baghdad. There he tried to find someone to take a note from him to Muhammad the Foundling, but failed, as they were all concerned by the critical state of Muhammad's illness. Khultukh ate up all he had with him and then for two days he had no food at all. 'How false people are!' he exclaimed. 'I came here not wanting anything from anyone.' He went to work in the baths, where his good nature made him so popular that every day he earned two or three dirhams.

After a month Muhammad's illness subsided, prompting both al-Rashid and Zubaida to distribute alms. The doctor had recommended that he go to one of the public baths, where the smell would be good for him, and al-Rashid had ordered that he be taken there in secret without anybody knowing. As it happened, the baths to which they brought him were the ones where Khultukh worked. When he arrived with his escort and a servant carrying a candle, he was given a private room in which to sit. The baths were perfumed with ambergris and aloes, and he sat there like a golden branch.

Khultukh looked up and, recognizing Muhammad when he saw him, he exclaimed in distress: 'He must have been ill!' He poured hot water over him, saying to himself: 'Modesty prevents me from speaking. What do I have to distress me, now that I am making a regular living?' Muhammad asked what he was muttering and said that he had hurt him. 'How have I hurt you?' asked Khultukh, and at that Muhammad looked hard at him and recognized him. 'Khultukh, my father!' he exclaimed, and Khultukh replied: 'Yes, that is who I am. Come now. When you came here, did you not remember me?' Muhammad got up, greeted him with an embrace and said: 'Don't blame me, Father. I didn't recognize you. Excuse me, as I have just been ill for five months [sic].' 'I excuse you,' said Khultukh, 'and had I known that you were ill, I would have been deeply distressed.' 'I swear by al-Rashid's life that you must sit down and I shall wash you,' Muhammad told him. Khultukh took his seat, and the servant poured water over his head, while Muhammad rubbed his back.

When he was slow in returning, al-Rashid told Masrur to find out why this was. 'I hope nothing has happened to him,' he said, 'so go and hurry him up.' Masrur went off and when he came to the baths he went in and saw Muhammad. 'Master,' he said, 'what are you doing sitting there? You are a sick man. Don't let the bath-man impose on you.' 'Do you recognize this man whom I am washing?' Muhammad asked and when Masrur said 'no', he said: 'This is my father, Khultukh.' 'By God!' exclaimed Masrur and he then removed his clothes and said: 'It is I who should be serving him,' and he got up, embraced and kissed him, saying: 'By the life of al-Rashid, no one is going to rub him down except me.'

He had started to do this and was taking his time when al-Rashid said: 'Ja'far, I am worried. Go and see what is happening.' Ja'far got up and went that night to the baths, where he saw Muhammad pouring water over someone's head and Masrur washing him. 'Have you become bath attendants?' he exclaimed in surprise. 'Vizier,' said Muhammad, 'this is my father, Khultukh.' 'What, really?' asked Ja'far, and when Muhammad said 'yes', he too removed his clothes and poured water over him. When Khultukh kissed his hand he said: 'Khultukh, people should serve a man like you.'

When Ja'far was slow in returning, al-Rashid exclaimed at the lack of news and got up himself and went with two servants to the baths, where he saw them all acting as attendants. When he asked about this, Muhammad, Ja'far and the others laughed and said: 'Master, how can we not serve someone like this?' 'Who is he?' al-Rashid asked, and they told him it was Khultukh. 'By God!' exclaimed al-Rashid, and he stretched out his hand to take the bowl in order to pour water over Khultukh's head. Khultukh got up and, after kissing the ground, said: 'Spare me, master! Do you want me to be punished by my Lord?' 'Get up and put your clothes back on,' al-Rashid told his people, 'then come out, and tomorrow we shall interview Khultukh.' Khultukh kissed his hand, and they all left for al-Rashid's palace.

When Khultukh went to him, al-Rashid told him to come close and said: 'May God give you a good reward for the manly qualities you showed! My son, Muhammad, expressed his thanks to you so now tell me what happened to you.' 'Master,' replied Khultukh, 'I spent all my wealth and my life's savings and took flight from your cousin Muhammad the son of Sulaiman al-Zainabi. When I got here I could find no one to take a note for me or to let Muhammad the Foundling know where I was and so I went and acted as a servant in the baths until he came and I introduced myself.' 'Fetch me a robe of honour,' the caliph ordered, and when this had been brought he put it on Khultukh. Then he wrote immediately to summon his cousin Muhammad.

When this Muhammad arrived al-Rashid asked him how he dared treat a man like Khultukh as he had. 'Where is he, Commander of the

Faithful?' Muhammad asked, and al-Rashid said: 'He is here with me,' and went on to tell him what had happened to him. 'By God, Commander of the Faithful,' Muhammad said, 'I never intended to do anything to him, but he took fright and fled away from me. His money is untouched and his house is locked and sealed.' Khultukh came up, wearing the caliph's robe of honour, and kissed the hand of Muhammad, who presented his excuses and said: 'Come back with me to Basra.' 'I cannot leave the Commander of the Faithful and my master Muhammad,' Khultukh replied, and Muhammad replied: 'That is up to you.'

Khultukh then told him: 'I would like you to sell my house for me and send me what it fetches.' 'How much would you charge me for the whole thing?' asked Muhammad. 'If I bought it you would have no need to go there as you can certify to the sale here.' Khultukh named a price of three thousand dinars; Muhammad said: 'I shall send you five thousand,' at which Khultukh concluded the sale.

Muhammad went back to Basra and forwarded the five thousand dinars. After receiving them, Khultukh stayed with al-Rashid, and Muhammad the Foundling said: 'He is to live in my apartment, as, thanks to the huge debt I owe him, I have a greater right to serve him than anyone else.' This delighted Khultukh, who now did not have to ask permission before entering the caliph's presence, as he was accepted as one of his intimates.

This is the reward of good deeds, as a poet puts it:

Who acts well never goes without reward;
And kindness is not lost with God or man.

This is the end of the story. Praise be to the One God and blessings and peace be on the best of His creation, our lord Muhammad, his family and his companions.

Tale Sixteen

The Story of Ashraf and Anjab and the Marvellous Things That Happened to Them.

In the Name of God, the Compassionate, the Merciful

They say – and God knows better – that al-Rashid had appointed his cousin Muhammad son of Sulaiman al-Zainabi as governor of Basra. Every year Muhammad would collect the city's tribute, take it up to him in Baghdad and stay there for a month before going back to Basra.

One year he brought the tribute as usual and, on reaching Baghdad, he handed it over to al-Rashid. He then went to see Zubaida, his cousin and, after greeting her and presenting his services, he left and began to walk through Baghdad to look at the sights. On his way past al-Karkh he met an old man wearing white robes, with a linen turban and a belt around his waist. This man kissed the ground in front of him and said: 'Master, your servant is a slave-dealer who sells girls. I have one who would be suitable for the caliph al-Rashid. I should like you to do me the honour of coming to my house so that I may be set apart from all my fellows in this age. No one else deserves the girl.'

When he heard this, Muhammad went with him to his house and took his seat on a couch in his room. After the man had sold a girl, a mamluk and a eunuch, he got up and, after fastening a curtain of gold thread, he raised it to show a chair of Chinese iron, on which was seated a girl like a shining sun in a clear sky. Her face was veiled and he asked for and was given her permission to raise it, showing a face round as a moon with tresses that hung down to her anklets.

Muhammad exclaimed: 'By God, I have never seen anyone lovelier than this in the whole world. 'More than that,' said the trader, 'she can both read and write; she is versed in literature and is an artist on the lute.' He turned to her and said: 'Lady, I am told that you have a lovely voice,' at which she recited the opening *sura* of the Qur'an and other verses from it in a voice sweeter than the poetry of Ishaq al-Mausili. He told her to go on, and she turned to a girl behind her and took a lute that she was holding. After touching its strings and testing it she sang:

Our dwellings may be far apart,
So that I cannot visit you,
But still this love of mine remains constant,
And God forbid that it should ever change!

'By God,' exclaimed Muhammad, 'her beauty and her artistry fill me with wonder!' The dealer began the auction, and the bidding started at a thousand dinars, going up until it stopped at two thousand. 'Master,' said the dealer to Muhammad, 'you have made no bid for her.' 'Is no one going to go higher?' he asked, and the dealer told him that they had all stopped, and no one would bid more. 'How much is she worth?' Muhammad asked, and the dealer said: 'Three thousand dinars, and if you have the money, God bless you.' He shook hands with Muhammad, who asked for an ink-well and paper on which three thousand dinars was noted as a charge to be paid by the caliph with an extra hundred dinars for the dealer.

Muhammad then got up and so did the girl who put on a wrap of Dabiqi brocade. He took her hand and passed her to a servant, who brought her to al-Rashid's palace, where he himself asked al-Rashid's wife Zubaida to keep her while he went down to Basra, and then to send her after him. 'Cousin,' she said to him, 'you know of the caliph's reputation with women. It may be that he will see and admire this girl and then distress both you and me by taking her himself, as there is no one to match her in his palace. So take her and go off without saying anything about her to anyone who might tell the caliph, lest he remove her from you.' Muhammad realized that this was credible enough and so he took the girl away and put her on a barge, while he finished his business in two days, before taking his leave of the caliph.

He went down to Basra with the girl and installed her in his palace, showering her with favours and providing her with maids. He then married her and when he lay with her he discovered her to be a virgin and took the greatest delight in her. They remained like that for some time until one day she kissed his hand and, when he asked her about herself, she told him she was pregnant. 'Praise be to God!' he exclaimed, for he was a childless man, and he now distributed alms and gifts in his joy.

When the term of her pregnancy was completed she fell into labour, surrounded by midwives and nurses in the palace. The child to whom she gave birth was a boy like a rising sun, and the good news spread throughout the palace, with people going to congratulate Muhammad and to ask him what the baby should be called. 'Name him al-Ashraf,' said Muhammad, and in his joy he distributed alms and had Basra closed down to universal delight. Almighty God, however, did not allow the child to drink any milk, and Muhammad, sorrowful and distracted, was sure that he was going to die. 'See what you can do,' he told his people, and they told him that at the palace gate was a slave-dealer who had a girl with a one-year-old black baby. 'However this may be, bring the mother to me,' ordered Muhammad, and they fetched the mother, who was black as pitch with a snub nose, red eyes and an unpleasant smell.

When she was brought to al-Ashraf she took him on her lap and drew out her breast, which was like a sack of barley, while her teats were like black dung. She brought one up to the baby's mouth as God the Great and Glorious had willed and used her fingers to put it into his mouth. He drank his fill until the milk dribbled from the sides of it to the astonishment of Muhammad. 'By God,' he exclaimed, 'how strange it is that he drinks from this black girl and leaves untouched the milk of all the wet-nurses!'

The black girl then took charge of al-Ashraf and suckled him with her own son, al-Anjab, until both of them had grown, when Muhammad provided them with a teacher. They were taught to write, and they studied literature, grammar, Arabic and everything they might need, after which they learned to ride, to shoot and how to act courageously. They grew up well, and Muhammad loved them dearly and was struck by how fond they were of each other. Because of his treatment of the black boy, people thought he must be Muhammad's own son, and the boy himself used to call al-Ashraf 'my brother'. By the time they were twelve, he was like a tower and looked twenty years old, with enough pitch blackness for twenty bathhouses.

One day Muhammad was sitting with al-Ashraf's mother, 'Alam al-Husn, when he took a sheet of paper, dipped his pen in ink and wrote: 'In the name of God, the Compassionate, the Merciful; these are my instructions to whoever reads this note. I am Muhammad son of Sulaiman al-Zainabi. The only child of my body is my son al-Ashraf, the inheritor of my wealth and the perpetuator of my race. As for the black al-Anjab, I bought him and his mother for eighteen dinars. He is my son's slave, to be sold or freed as my son wishes, and no one is to suspect me of being his father.'

Muhammad wrote this in his own hand and then folded the paper and told 'Alam al-Husn that he entrusted it to her and she should keep it with her. 'Master,' she said, 'may good befall you! What is this?' He said: 'Take it and say nothing. No man can escape death, for this is a path that all must tread.' She took the paper, set it in an amulet and placed it amongst her books.

Three years after this Muhammad died, and Basra was handed over to his cousin Abu Ja'far. Al-Anjab, his mother and their maids remained in the palace, while al-Ashraf, who was of a generous disposition, started eating, drinking and making lavish gifts. This angered al-Anjab, who went to his black mother and asked her what she thought of his brother's behaviour. 'Are you mad,' she said. 'Do you think that al-Ashraf is your brother?' 'What?' he exclaimed, and she told him: 'My son, you are his slave and I am his slave girl, as his father bought us both for eighteen dinars. He can sell you or free you as he wants, for the authority is his. Your father was a negro herdsman and his was a noble 'Alid.' 'What am I if I am not his brother?' exclaimed al-Anjab, who found this hard to bear, and he asked her whether she was the only person who knew about this and when she said 'yes' he left her.

Ten days later he came back and told her that he wanted to spend the night with her, and she cordially agreed. When they both had eaten he got up to wash his hands, and she spread him out a bed. As he slept she slept nearby, but he got up in the night and, as she lay sleeping, he took hold of her throat like an *'ifrit*, squeezing it until he had killed her. He then laid out her corpse and covered it over before leaving her room that same night. Next morning her maids found her dead and went to her mistress, shrieking: 'Lady, al-Anjab's mother is dead.' This distressed the lady, and she had the corpse shrouded and buried.

Al-Anjab waited for some days after this before going to al-Ashraf, whom he greeted, before saying: 'Know, brother, that we held the sultanate, but I am not pleased that it has gone to our cousin, and this leaves me distressed.' 'Why is this?' asked al-Ashraf, 'for the earth belongs to Almighty God, and He bequeaths it to whichever of His servants He wishes.' Al-Anjab told him: 'After the deaths of our master and my mother, I can no longer stay in Basra.' 'What do you want?' asked al-Ashraf, and al-Anjab told him that he wanted to take what he had inherited from his father and to go to Baghdad while his uncle al-Rashid was still caliph. Al-Ashraf agreed and went to tell his mother what he had said. She exclaimed with an oath: 'Al-Anjab is no brother of yours! He is your slave who was bought by your father together with his mother for eighteen dinars, and if you wanted you could take him this instant to the slave-dealer and sell him.' 'Mother, what are you saying?' he exclaimed, and she said: 'Yes, my son. Now go, guard what is yours and say no more. Otherwise, if you don't want to tell him, then put him off.'

After remaining silent for a time al-Ashraf raised his head and said: 'Mother, I cannot break his heart.' 'If you don't,' she told him, 'this bastard will lose you your kingdom and your wealth.' He paid no attention to her but sent for the trustees as well as al-Anjab. He then produced all that his father had left him in the way of gold, silver, utensils and dinars and divided them in two, telling his father's trustees to give al-Anjab his share. They then divided the deeds covering properties and split these between themselves, but al-Anjab said: 'I am going to Baghdad, so what can I do with properties? Buy them from me.' When al-Ashraf had bought them for sixty thousand dinars, al-Anjab went up to Baghdad in a barge. On arrival he did not go into the city but went to the western side, where he bought a house with balconies overlooking the Tigris, together with mamluks and eunuchs.

One day he was sitting on his balcony drinking and listening to singers, when three boats belonging to al-Rashid's vizier came into view. The vizier heard the singers and asked whose house this was. 'It belongs to al-Anjab the son of Muhammad son of Sulaiman who was lord of Basra,' he was told. 'Praise be to God!' he exclaimed. 'Does the grandson of Sulaiman come to Baghdad, buy a house and live in it without us knowing that he has come or meeting him? This is wrong. Steersman, put in to the bank.' This was done, and the vizier and his chamberlain left the boat and went to knock on the door of al-Anjab's house. When a eunuch came out to ask who was there, they said: 'Go in and tell your master that the vizier is here.'

The eunuch went to al-Anjab and said: 'Master, the caliph's vizier has come and is at the door.' Al-Anjab got up, wearing a shirt of fine gold-embroidered linen and a headband set with gold and, quicker than lightning, he opened the door, saying: 'In God's Name.' The vizier entered with his chamberlain and, on looking, he saw a man black as pitch. 'Praise be to Almighty God the Creator!' he exclaimed. 'Muhammad the son of Sulaiman was a white man with a reddish-fair complexion, but God has given him this black son, and He creates what He wants.'

The vizier took his seat on the dais with al-Anjab sitting in front of him and he said: 'Sir, what is this wrong you have done us by coming to Baghdad and not telling us so we could come to meet you and present our services? That was not right.' Al-Anjab said respectfully: 'I did not want to burden you or the noble caliph by telling you that my brother al-Ashraf and I have parted because of our inheritance. He did not give me my proper share but only what he wanted, but I did not want a quarrel, which would have pleased our enemies and saddened our friends. So I took what I had and came here to live under the shadow of my master and cousin, al-Rashid, may God grant him long life.' 'In God's name,' said the vizier, 'come to my house so that we may finish drinking there.' Al-Anjab suggested leaving this to another time, but the vizier swore by al-Rashid that he must come that same day. He took al-Anjab by the hand, and the two of them embarked on the barge and sailed to the vizier's house, which overlooked the Tigris.

Al-Anjab sat on a balcony, while the vizier produced plates of food as well as fruits in vessels of gold and silver, together with singers. They drank for two days and two nights, and the vizier, who was drunk, took a pillow, put it under his head and fell asleep, leaving al-Anjab in a state of perplexity. Just then one of al-Rashid's eunuchs came in, carrying a note. Al-Anjab, whom he saw seated there like a mountain of pitch, asked him what he wanted, and he said: 'I have a note from our master al-Rashid for the vizier.' 'Hand it over,' al-Anjab told him, 'so I can give you a reply.' The eunuch did this, and when al-Anjab opened it he read: 'The vizier has caused us unease. Why has he stayed away, although he has been sent for, and people are calling for help? I have heard that my cousin al-Anjab, the son of Muhammad, has come to Baghdad without our knowledge. Come yourself and bring him with you so that we can find out why this was. Goodbye.'

Al-Anjab stretched out his hand and opened the ink-well, took a sheet of paper and wrote: 'From the servant al-Anjab son of Muhammad son of Sulaiman to the High Court. It was to you that I came. This vizier of yours to whom you have entrusted your affairs made me ashamed by sending me fifty letters telling me to come and saying: "This al-Rashid cannot do anything except through me. He is under my control, but I do not like him, as he is a treacherous man and is plainly planning a coup against me. I propose to forestall him and give the throne to you, as it is only you who are fit to hold the caliphate." Your servant is only here to tell you to be on guard against this vizier. Look into the matter, for yours is the supreme authority.'

He folded up the letter, sealed it and called for the eunuch, to whom he handed it, urging him with all vehemence to hand it only to al-Rashid. The eunuch did this, and, having opened it, al-Rashid handed it back to him to read out and when he did so al-Rashid trembled with rage, and the veins of his throat swelled up. He shouted for Masrur and when he came he said: 'Take your sword; go to the house of the vizier and cut off his head. Then get my cousin al-Anjab son of Muhammad; put him on a horse and bring him here quickly. Take care to show no pity or mercy and put someone in charge to guard the house.'

This pleased Masrur, who took a hundred eunuchs armed with swords and made for the vizier's house. When he broke in he found the vizier still asleep on his pillow and struck a blow that cut off his head. A cry of grief arose, but Masrur helped al-Anjab to mount and went with him into the presence of al-Rashid, who was with his wife Zubaida. When he showed her the letter she called on God to protect him and exclaimed on the far-sightedness of his cousin. Then, when he saw Masrur, he asked and was told that his orders had been carried out. He then asked where al-Anjab was and, on being told that he was at the door, he told Masrur to fetch him. Masrur went to tell him to enter, and when he did he kissed the ground respectfully, while al-Rashid looked and saw a man like a black camel.

When al-Anjab greeted him and kissed the ground before him for a second time, al-Rashid returned his greeting. He then turned to his wife Zubaida and said: 'Rest your eyes on this man. There is no doubt that he is your cousin for his nose, lips and eyes are those of Muhammad son of Sulaiman.' She was incredulous and asked: 'Have you a black son?' 'This man is black as a negro,' he told her, 'with red eyes, a nose like a clay pot and lips like kidneys.' He then turned and told al-Anjab to come forward, which he did. 'Master,' he said, 'your servant had not thought it proper to write to you, or else he would have told you about your vizier a year ago.' 'Take over his tasks,' al-Rashid told him, adding: 'his house, his wealth and everything he owned are yours as a gift.' He gave him a robe of honour and he left, calling down blessings on the caliph. Surrounded by servants and mamluks, with an advance guard of Turks, he made his way first to the *diwan* and then to what had been the vizier's house. News of him spread through both east and west, and people began to fear his power, almost dying of terror if he looked at them.

So much for him, but as for al-Ashraf, he deluged people with so many gifts that not the smallest thing was left him. He sold estates, property, orchards and their produce until, when he and his mother had not eaten for two days, she said to him: 'My son, if you go to your brother al-Anjab he will scarcely believe it when he sees you and he may give you a town or else five thousand dinars on which you can live, for I cannot think that in such a case he would be content to give you only a little.' 'Mother,' he told her, 'I have nothing that I can use to get food.' She said: 'I still have a golden armband whose weight makes it worth a hundred dinars. Take it and sell it when you get to Baghdad. Then buy a mule, a grand turban and a long gown, as well as a mamluk and a black slave to walk in front of you so as not to go to your brother in a miserable state.' He agreed to this, and she took out the bracelet and passed it to him, still with his father's note sealed inside it. He put it in a belt, which he fastened to his hand and then, after saying goodbye to his mother, he set off to walk to Baghdad.

There he looked with admiration at the river with its bridges and the balconies that faced each other before going into the market of the money-changers and selling his bracelet for ninety dinars. He took the money, fastened it to his waist and went out. There on the square he saw jugglers, storytellers and buffoons, but as he was staring at them with wonder a cut-purse came up behind him, pressed against him and slit away the gold. Al-Ashraf then felt hungry and made his way towards to a cook-shop in the market belonging to a man named 'Ubaid who had five cooking-pots standing over a fire. He told himself that he would go there and have something to eat before going on about his business.

'Ubaid had a fondness for the young, and al-Ashraf looked like a full moon, with a lock of hair hanging down to his trouser belt. When 'Ubaid saw him he greeted him and said: 'Please be so good as to come to your servant 'Ubaid, and do him the honour of taking a bite to eat in his shop.' 'Ubaid then came down to the bench outside the shop, kissed al-Ashraf's hand and helped him to take his seat on the bench. He then spooned out three portions of various types of food and, after putting this in front of him, together with a flat loaf of bread, he said: 'Eat, master.' When he had eaten, 'Ubaid brought him sweetmeats, and he ate these too.

Al-Ashraf said: 'I told myself to give him something and so I put my hand to my waist to produce a dinar, but there was nothing to be found. He saw me put my hand in and take it out empty and, thinking that I was making a fool of him, he slapped me and threw me down from the bench, making what I was wearing on my head fall off. I looked down with tears in my eyes, and when he saw that I had nothing to say he came back, picked me up and sat me down again on the bench. "Did I ask you for anything?" he said and I said: "No, but why did you hit me?" "I was angry with you," he told me, and I explained that a cut-purse had removed ninety dinars from my waist, and I showed him where the slit had been made. "That's true," he said, "and by God, master, I wronged you."

'He kissed my hand and asked me where I came from. I told him that I was from Basra and that I was coming to ask the vizier, my brother, to appoint me to some post or perhaps give me something that I could take back home. "Is the vizier your brother?" he said, and when I confirmed that he was, he asked me not to hold anything against him, saying that he had done wrong. "No harm will come to you," I told him, "for I don't hold this against you and would like you to join up with me and help me." "Yes, by God," he exclaimed, "with my money and my life!"

'When I had thanked him he asked me what I wanted, and I said: "An ink-well and paper so that I can write to my brother al-Anjab the vizier to tell him that I have come. When he knows he will send to fetch me and, God willing, I shall be able to help you and I shall be like a brother to you." 'Ubaid agreed and went off, coming back sometime later with five sheets of paper and an ink-well.

'I took a sheet and wrote: "From al-Ashraf to the vizier. This is to let you know of the arrival of your brother al-Ashraf. I had goods and money with me, but robbers attacked me and took everything that I had. I am at your gate but I am too dishevelled to go in to you and I should like you to be kind enough to send someone to fetch me without anyone knowing that I am your brother. I have no one to help me except God and you."'

Al-Ashraf then folded the paper and handed it to 'Ubaid, telling him to take it to al-Anjab. He agreed, saying: 'Everyone in the vizier's house knows me, and they are all friends of mine.' 'Ubaid's shop was opposite the vizier's house, and so he took the note and went in. The servants greeted him, calling him a rare bird, and he told them that he had a note which he wanted to deliver to the vizier. The vizier's private attendant said that he would do this and, taking it from him, he presented it to the vizier as he sat. When the vizier had read it he turned to him and said: 'Are you an attendant or a chamberlain?' 'I am only an attendant,' replied the man. 'Go and fetch the man who gave you this note,' the vizier said, and he then ordered a Turkish mamluk to go with him and when he saw the man who had written the note to cut off the head of the attendant.

A eunuch went to 'Ubaid and asked him: 'What was in that note that you gave to the attendant?' 'By God, I don't know,' said 'Ubaid. The eunuch told him that the attendant who had taken it to al-Anjab had had his head cut off. When al-Ashraf was told of this, he said that this must have been because of some personal quarrel between the two of them, and he wanted to write again. 'Ubaid told him to do that and when the letter had been written he took it and went to al-Anjab's door. This was guarded by one of his personal eunuchs, and when 'Ubaid, on being asked, said that he had come with a note for the vizier it was this man who told him to hand it over and he would give it to him. He did this, and when al-Anjab had read it he said: 'Are you a eunuch servant or a chamberlain? Why are you interfering in someone else's job?' and he ordered his head to be cut off.

This was done by a mamluk, and another eunuch went out and said: 'Save yourself, 'Ubaid, for the eunuch who took the note has been beheaded, and if things go on like this the vizier will have no one left.' Al-Ashraf insisted that his brother must have had some grudge against the two whom he had killed and that he wanted to write again. 'Write,' said 'Ubaid, adding, 'and may God cut off the vizier's right hand and let him be as angry as he likes.' Al-Ashraf wrote again, and 'Ubaid took the note and sat down by the vizier's house, where he came across a chamberlain who was carrying notes that people had written to him. 'Ubaid jumped up to greet him respectfully and asked him to take the letter to his master. The chamberlain took it and went to al-Anjab, with whom he left all the notes, including that sent by al-Ashraf.

When al-Anjab had read it he asked the chamberlain who had brought it. ''Ubaid the cook, who is at the door,' the man replied. 'Put him to the sword and plunder his shop this instant,' ordered al-Anjab. The chamberlain, who was one of 'Ubaid's friends, went out and told him to flee at once to save his life before he could be killed and his shop plundered. 'Ubaid ran off and went up to the shop roof to see what was going to happen. Meanwhile al-Anjab had told ten of his attendants: 'Go at once to 'Ubaid's shop, where you will find a beardless youth with long hair and a handsome face. Say: "Are you al-Ashraf?" and if he says "yes", beat him until the front of his face is indistinguishable from the back of his head. Then bring him to me.'

They went and plundered 'Ubaid's shop, breaking everything in it, while 'Ubaid was exclaiming in grief and saying: 'By God, no good has come to me!' Al-Ashraf was weeping for what the men had done to 'Ubaid's shop. They asked him if he was al-Ashraf and when he said 'yes,' he was beaten with clubs until he could no longer move while 'Ubaid was struck on the head until blood flowed from his nostrils. Al-Ashraf was taken to al-Anjab, and his face was uncovered so he could see. 'Brother, what have you done with me?' he said, and al-Anjab answered: 'You're still healthy, are you? Throw him down.' His men did this and then beat him unconscious with a hundred lashes, after which a smith was sent for, who made him an iron corselet, studded on the inside with what were like the heads of needles. Heavy fetters were put on his legs, and he was taken to the underground dungeon.

So much for al-Ashraf, but as for 'Ubaid the cook, he stayed where he was for a day and a night, and then was shattered to hear what had happened to al-Ashraf and that he was in al-Anjab's dungeon. He called to God for help and said: 'By God, the only thing left me is this silver ring which I can sell.' He took it from his finger and sold it for two carats, after which he went to knock on the gaoler's door. 'Who is there?' called out the gaoler. ''Ubaid the cook,' he replied, and the gaoler said: ''Ubaid, I feel for you. What did you do to get your shop plundered?' but instead of replying 'Ubaid asked him what had been done with the young al-Ashraf. 'By God, he is like a son to me,' said the gaoler,' and I am filled with pity because of the misery he is suffering. He has had no food for two days now, and though I used to hear him groaning there is no sound now and I'm not sure whether he is dead or alive.' 'Take these two carats,' 'Ubaid said, 'and open the door so I can talk to him.' The gaoler agreed and went to the top of the dungeon and opened it. 'Ubaid then called to al-Ashraf, who answered in a weak voice: 'Who is there?' 'Your servant 'Ubaid,' the cook replied. Al-Ashraf called down God's blessing on him and said: 'I am heartbroken because your shop was plundered, and it has all been thanks to me that your sufferings have been worse than mine.' 'I wish this had happened to me, not you,' replied 'Ubaid, 'and that none of it had affected you.'

'Stop all this useless talk,' said the gaoler; 'buy him something to eat and then think of some way of freeing him from this miserable plight of his. Take back these two carats and buy some food.' 'Ubaid took the money and went out to the market, where he bought a pomegranate, three flat loaves, some roast meat and a jug of water. He went into the prison and was shown to the dungeon where he saw al-Ashraf.

'I take refuge with Almighty God!' he exclaimed, adding that he was sure he would die, but that God would judge between him and the one who wronged him. Then, making al-Ashraf sit up, he rested him against his chest and fed him the pomegranate, as well as giving him water. When he felt stronger 'Ubaid asked: 'Is there anyone who can help you?' 'Yes,' said al-Ashraf, 'I have a mother in Basra and I should like her to know what is happening to me.' 'Whereabouts in Basra is she?' asked 'Ubaid, and al-Ashraf told him: 'Go to the river and ask for the house of Muhammad son of Sulaiman.'

'Ubaid willingly agreed, took his leave and left, but he said to himself: 'How are you going to get to Basra when you haven't got anything? I have only got my mother and I shall go to her and get something that will take me there.' It was a year since he had seen his mother, but he went to her little house in Baghdad, where he found her sitting at her spindle, saying: 'I would give my life to have 'Ubaid restored to me.' He went into the hall and knocked on the door but didn't answer when she asked who was there. 'Little wretches,' she exclaimed, 'you are always throwing stones at my door!' 'Ubaid went back and knocked again and this time when she asked he told her who he was. 'Welcome,' she cried and she jumped up, opened the door and embraced him in tears, saying: 'My son, have you only just remembered me? It is a year since I saw you.' 'Well, here I am,' he said. 'I had a dream that I was eating bread with a piece of meat and a jelly, but all I have is two carats and a *habba*.' She took these and a bit of cotton and went out.

He saw a wrap of hers, which he spread out in the middle of the room. He then took the bed cover, the pillow and the mattress, leaving the carpet, the lamp and the drinking bowl. He next took ten *ratls* of spinning wool, rolled them into a bundle and went out to the market, carrying them on his head. He put down the wrap and sold everything he had with him for twenty dinars. He went to the butcher and gave him a dinar and did the same with the baker, after which he went to knock on the prison door. When the gaoler asked who was there, he gave his name and said: 'Take this dinar and buy something for your household. I have left a dinar for al-Ashraf with So-and-So the baker, another with the butcher and another with the greengrocer. Get him every day a *ratl* of bread and of meat, together with vegetables and cook them or roast them, whichever you prefer. If he wants anything else, use your own money so that I can go to Basra and tell his mother how he is, before coming back with her.' The gaoler wished him success and sent him off.

'Ubaid first went to the dungeon and spoke to al-Ashraf: 'God be with you!' he said, 'I am going to your mother and I have paid in advance for you to have bread, meat, vegetables and anything else you want. The gaoler will fetch this for you.' 'May God reward you,' al-Ashraf replied, 'and may He allow me to repay you.' 'God be with you!' 'Ubaid repeated, and he took his leave and went off to hire a place on a barge.

After sailing downstream for some days, he reached Basra.

He asked about the river and was shown where to go. He saw a fine, large and handsome house, in the middle of which was a double door under a lofty arch, one leaf of which was open and the other closed. He went up to it and explained that he was a messenger from al-Ashraf. 'Don't make fun of us,' said 'Alam al-Husn, his mother. 'It is a long time since any messenger came here, and are you now at the door?' 'Yes,' 'Ubaid told her. 'What did al-Anjab give him?' she asked. 'By God, nothing but blows and humiliation,' said 'Ubaid. 'He put a collar round his neck, fetters on his feet and threw him down into a dungeon. I took his part and was distressed by what happened to him, for he had come to me and had eaten bread with me. He wrote two letters to al-Anjab, which I took to him, but as a result of what happened there my shop was plundered, and I was left penniless. I have an old mother whom I have not been in the habit of visiting. I went to her for the first time in a year and tricked her, removing her things without her knowledge and selling them. I then paid in advance so that al-Ashraf would get bread, meat and vegetables; I gave the gaoler a dinar and I bought my passage downriver to come and tell you what has happened to your son.'

When 'Alam al-Husn heard this, she slapped her face, drawing blood, until 'Ubaid told her: 'This does no good. Think of some plan to help him if you can.' She said: 'How can I talk to you, 'Ubaid, when I am unveiled, and my whole body is exposed?' 'Ubaid then removed his shirt and his waist-wrapper and gave them to her to wear, after which he went to the market and bought a dress, trousers, a veil and boots. On his return he called to her and when she answered he told her to take them, which she did. When she had put them on she called on God to reward him and asked him to be kind enough to take her to Baghdad. He told her to get up and then went to the river bank, where he hired a passage upstream for them both.

When they had reached Baghdad he suggested going to his mother to conciliate her and tell her what had happened. 'Alam al-Husn should come too so they could make some plan. When they had got to the house 'Ubaid told her to sit down behind the wall so that he could tell his mother and she could come out to her. 'Go on,' she told him and he went to his mother's door, where she was sitting in tears and saying: 'You have been away too long, 'Ubaid! I don't care that you took my things, but I want to see you.' He knocked, and when she came out she fell on his chest and told him to come in. When he did she kissed him and said: 'My son, you took everything that was in the house and left me with nothing.' 'Ubaid told her: 'I only spent it as Almighty God required. Listen to me. A noble young man came to me but got into trouble with the vizier' – and he told her the story from beginning to end, before adding: 'His mother is at the door, so go and bring her to sit with you.'

'Ubaid's mother got up, but 'Alam al-Husn had fainted because of her distress. 'Ubaid came and took her, finding that she had opened three wounds on her head by slapping herself. When he expostulated with her, she told him to stop, quoting a line of poetry:

Pain is at its bitterest when the loved one is near.

She then told him to take her to see her son. He agreed and went with her to the prison, where he knocked on the door. The gaoler asked who was there and when 'Ubaid said who he was the gaoler welcomed him and asked whether he had brought al-Ashraf's mother. 'I have,' said 'Ubaid, and the gaoler opened the door and took them to the dungeon, which he opened. When 'Alam al-Husn smelled the foul smell, she shrieked: 'My son!' 'Here I am, Mother,' he replied, and she was about to throw herself down when the gaoler took hold of her. 'What folly is this!' he exclaimed. 'If you do this you will die, and so will your son. Go out and get him freed quickly from the torment that he is suffering, for this will be best.'

She went out and said: 'I don't want to go to your mother's house, 'Ubaid.' When he asked where she did want to go, she said: 'Hire a shop and dig a sink hole in it for me. Then buy me a wash-tub and two water-pots and I shall become a washerwoman. Don't say no.' 'Ubaid did what she said and bought her all that she wanted. She herself was brighter than the sun with a body like camphor, and when she rolled up her sleeves her arms were like pillars of crystal, causing all those who saw them to call on God and say: 'Look at how this pimp 'Ubaid has made his slave girl into a washerwoman.' One would want his shirt washed by her and another his waist-wrapper, and they would use this excuse to try to flirt with her, while she would keep her head down and carry on washing.

Opposite her shop lived one of the personal eunuchs of the caliph, named Yanis, and he had a servant as well as a slave girl whom he had taken to the slave-dealer. He had told his servant that he wanted his dirty clothes washed, but not by him as he was not good at it. The man said: 'Master, you know 'Ubaid the cook?' 'Yes,' said Yanis, and the man went on: 'He has the most beautiful slave girl in the world, who can wash better than anyone.' 'Go and fetch her,' his master said, but the man said: 'Perhaps 'Ubaid won't let her go.' 'Then break his head,' said the eunuch.

The man went off and told 'Ubaid that Yanis, his master, wanted his clothes washed. 'Let your girl come and do this or else your head will be cut off.' 'Ubaid said: 'Sir, we are all at the command of the great man.' He then told 'Alam al-Husn to come quickly, for Yanis was one of al-Rashid's favourites. She got up and went with the servant to greet Yanis, and when he saw how beautiful she was he exclaimed: 'God damn you, 'Ubaid! Where did you get her from?' Then he told her to take his clothes and wash them, these being ten shirts from Dabqu and Damietta.

Next he told the servant to get twenty slices of meat, as well as vegetables and ten chickens and cook them in various ways. He was also to provide fruit, strain the wine and clean the house. 'Dear friends of mine are coming today,' he explained, 'so do the cooking well lest they make fun of you.' 'I shall,' said the servant.

Meanwhile 'Alam al-Husn had washed the clothes, folded them and pressed them flat like Coptic linen. The servant came back with the meat and the fruit, and he confessed that he was no good at cooking. She told him to leave what he had, and she then cooked the meat in various ways, together with the chickens, which she arranged on dishes with the rest of the food and the wine before cleaning the house and scenting it with incense until it was like Paradise. When Yanis came with his companions he noticed that this was not the usual scent and exclaimed with pleasure and when he went in there were the wine jars set out, together with scented flowers and fruits. The food was served, and when the guests ate they found a standard of cookery that was not to be equalled in the palace of al-Rashid. 'Well done, by God!' exclaimed Yanis to the servant; 'I have never seen you do so well as today.' 'Do you suppose that I did all this, master?' the man asked and when Yanis queried this he said that it had been done by 'Ubaid's slave girl. 'What?' said Yanis. 'Yes,' the servant replied, at which Yanis told him to go off and fetch 'Ubaid.

The man went to 'Ubaid and told him to come to the great man, who was calling out for him. He went to greet Yanis, who asked him whether this was his slave girl. 'She is a relative of mine,' he replied and Yanis said: 'Take six dinars to cover two months and leave her with me.' 'It is for you to command, sir,' 'Ubaid said, and the company continued to sit and drink. Yanis then said: 'Ask her if she is good at playing the lute,' and when 'Ubaid did this and she had said that she was he ordered a smooth and polished lute to be given her. She took it and, clasping it to her breast, she played a selection of airs that left the company ecstatic with joy.

Yanis jumped up, took her hand and kissed it, saying: 'Is there anyone in al-Rashid's palace who can play as well as this? This is superb artistry and, by God, were you a slave girl, you would be worth a huge amount of money!' He told his servant to give 'Ubaid ten dinars on condition that he did not ask for her again. 'Ubaid agreed to this and resigned his claims on her to Yanis. She stayed for a month with Yanis, who could scarcely believe his good fortune and handed over to her the house and all its contents.

One day, when it was his turn to wait on al-Rashid, he found that in front of him was a crystal cup, larger than a platter, made of red gold and worth a thousand dinars, in which were sweetmeats and two golden spoons. He and al-Fadl son of al-Rabi' were eating from it, and the eunuchs on duty were standing in front of al-Rashid as he ate. When he had finished, what was left over was to be removed by one of them. After he and al-Fadl had finished, he called to Yanis to take it away, but the eunuch in charge of the wine said: 'Leave it!' 'What do you mean, "leave it"?' al-Rashid said. 'It is his turn.' 'Master,' said the man, 'I wasn't talking about the food, but any dish that this man takes gets broken and is not returned.' In spite of this al-Rashid told Yanis: 'Take the cup and bring it back immediately after you have removed what is in it.' 'To hear is to obey,' Yanis said.

He took it and brought it home, where he told 'Alam al-Husn: 'Lady, take this and remove the sweetmeats. I have fallen out with the other eunuch in front of al-Rashid and I said that I would bring it back straight away.' He himself then went back and when al-Rashid looked up and saw him he asked: 'Where is the cup?' 'I am just washing it,' Yanis told him, but al-Rashid said: 'I don't want it washed. Go and get it at once.'

Yanis came home, where 'Alam al-Husn had lifted up the cup and washed it, but when she did it slipped from her hand like quicksilver, fell to the ground and smashed into a hundred pieces. At the sight of this she slapped herself until blood came from her nostrils. 'Let me die and rest from my misfortunes!' she exclaimed, and at that moment in came Yanis. Her hand was on her cheek and she was shedding tears as she looked at the disaster. 'Bring me the cup,' said Yanis, 'for our master al-Rashid is asking for it. I left it in a little bamboo basket.' She told him: 'Take it,' and when he asked where it was she said: 'In the basket.' 'How did you come to leave it in the basket?' he asked, and she said: 'I washed it, but it fell from my hands and broke.' 'Good God!' he exclaimed, slapping himself and shedding tears. He went to al-Rashid and stood behind the curtain. 'Who is it?' asked al-Rashid, and he answered: 'Master, it is Yanis the eunuch.' 'Come in,' al-Rashid said, and Yanis told him: 'Master, the cup is broken.' He went in weeping, with mucus dripping from his nose. Al-Rashid laughed and said: 'That is a wretchedly ugly face. How did this happen?' Yanis told him: 'It was thanks to a woman of mine.' 'Go and fetch her,' said al-Rashid.

Yanis went off faster than lightning and when he got home he told 'Alam al-Husn to come to face her punishment. She wrapped herself in a cloak and put on her *niqab* before leaving with Yanis, who took her to the palace and placed her behind the curtain. She told herself that she had never imagined that she would get there and that, God willing, relief might be at hand.

'Where is the person who broke the cup?' al-Rashid asked, and when Yanis said that she was behind the curtain, he told him to bring her in, which he did. When 'Alam al-Husn saw al-Rashid, she kissed the ground with due respect, threw aside her cloak, unveiled and began to recite these lines:

Master, best of all the Hashimites,
Imam of this age of the world,
Listen to the strange story that I tell,
A source of wonder to the unjust and the just.
I am the wife of Muhammad al-Zainabi,
And your vizier al-Anjab was his slave,
Who was brought up at one stage with my son.
But then my son fell into poverty
And made his way here to ask for relief.

Instead he fell a victim to this evil man,
And poor al-Ashraf is in his prison,
Drowning in floods of tears and chained.
He is not fasting but receives no food.
His father on his death left him his wealth.
As for the cup, I broke it, not Yanis.

'Who are you?' al-Rashid asked. 'I was the slave girl of your cousin Muhammad son of Sulaiman,' she told him, and he told Masrur to go to the prison and remove his cousin al-Ashraf from the dungeon and bring him just as he was. Masrur left at once and reappeared before al-Rashid with the young al-Ashraf looking like a worn-out water-skin in his iron corselet with fetters on his feet. 'May evil befall my father's son if I don't avenge him on this wicked slave!' exclaimed al-Rashid. He told Masrur to raid the house of the black al-Anjab immediately, to beat him until he lost his senses and to bring him with a turban around his neck.

Masrur took a hundred eunuchs with clubs to al-Anjab's house and attacked him, beating him until he was almost dead. His turban was left round his neck, and he was taken bare-headed before al-Rashid. 'Black dog,' said al-Rashid, 'what have you done to my cousin al-Ashraf?' 'I know nothing about him,' said al-Anjab. 'That is a lie, you dog,' Masrur told him, and he removed the curtain so al-Ashraf's state could be seen. Al-Rashid exclaimed: 'Evil slave, do you lay claim to nobility and kill my vizier unjustly?'

He then gave orders that al-Ashraf be taken to the baths and he presented him with a robe of honour from amongst his own clothes, telling him: 'Cousin, this man's house, his wealth, his possessions and goods with everything else that is there are yours. Now take this sword and strike off his head.' 'Master,' al-Ashraf said, 'I would not like to pay him back for what he did to me.' 'It is not for you to speak but for me,' al-Rashid told him, and he then ordered Masrur to behead al-Anjab, which he did, with his body being taken up and thrown into the Tigris.

Al-Rashid then wanted to learn the details of what had happened to al-Ashraf, who told him: 'A poor man did his best for me and, thanks to this, had his shop plundered. Had it not been for him I would have died. He spent his money on both me and my mother, and but for him she would have had nobody to bring her from Basra. May God grant him a good reward!' Al-Rashid asked his name and on being told that this was

'Ubaid the cook he ordered him to be fetched. It was not long before he came, and al-Rashid told him: 'You have planted a seedling here which has produced fruit, and it is for you to eat from it.' 'Master,' said 'Ubaid, 'will you grant me what I ask for?' 'Certainly,' al-Rashid told him, at which he said: 'Marry me to al-Ashraf's mother, for I am in love with her, and she has captivated me.' 'Yes, if you want,' said al-Rashid, 'but you may ask for anything at all that is within human power and I shall give it to you.' 'Ubaid, however, repeated that all he wanted was to marry 'Alam al-Husn. 'Do you hear what he says?' al-Rashid said to her, and she replied: 'Commander of the Faithful, I would not want him to be my servant. I can never repay him for the good that he did to me and to your cousin.' 'But do you accept his proposal?' he asked, and she told him that she would do whatever he told her. A contract was drawn up between the two of them, and the marriage was consummated to 'Ubaid's delight.

Al-Rashid provided him with lavish gifts, and his wife bore him children, both boys and girls. They lived the most pleasant, comfortable and splendid of lives, in constant enjoyment of al-Rashid's bounty. As for al-Ashraf, al-Rashid conferred on him the vizierate and the position of power that al-Anjab had enjoyed, and he stayed like this until he was visited by the Destroyer of Delights and the Divider of Unions.

This is the end of the story. Praise be to God, Lord of the Worlds, and blessings and peace be on Muhammad, his family and his companions.

Tale Seventeen

The Story of the Talisman Mountain and Its Marvels.

In the Name of God, the Compassionate, the Merciful

They say – and God knows better – that amongst the stories of ancient peoples is one of a Persian king who ruled his subjects with justice and was a man of intelligence and understanding. Thanks to the bounty of Almighty God he acted well and fairly and he was fond of buying mamluks and slave girls whom he would marry off to one another.

He had a thousand of each sex and amongst his special mamluks was one who, in spite of being the ugliest and most savage in appearance, was the best and bravest horseman of his time. Because of his courage and his skill the king was so attached to him that he could not bear to be parted from him. The king's vizier had a most lovely daughter, perfect in her beauty, admirably formed, with snowy teeth and black eyes. She was as the poet said:

> She enchants with the foliage of her hair,
> And goes far to avoid rebuke.
> Her hair wonders at what she does,
> And kisses her feet as she walks.

Praise be to God Who created her from the vile drop [Quran 77.20] and set her here in a fixed place to serve as a lesson for those who watch. Glory be to Him in His kingdom!

When she advanced she fascinated and when she turned back she destroyed.

Many kings had asked for her hand, but her father had refused to marry her to any of them as he hoped that thanks to her beauty and the excellence both of her characteristics and her actions she would marry his own master who, he knew, would undoubtedly ask for her hand when he heard of her.

One day the king turned to him as he was seated in front of him and asked him whether he would do something for him. The vizier bared his head and exclaimed: 'God, God, king of the age, by God I would do this even if it meant plucking my soul from my body!' The king told him: 'I have come to you as a suitor for your daughter's hand.' The vizier beamed with joy and said: 'Who could have a better claim on me? My daughter is your slave and the product of your grace.' 'But I don't want her for myself,' the king explained and the agitated vizier asked: 'Who is it you want her for, then?' 'For my savage-looking mamluk champion,' the king said. 'He was created from a coal of anger; he has never been seen to smile; he is uncouth and rough and because of these qualities and other base characteristics no one in the court is willing to look at him.'

When the vizier heard this, his heart contracted; his thoughts were scattered and all he knew was that he could not openly reject the king because of his earlier favours. He agreed to the marriage, saying: 'She is the maid-servant of the king,' but secretly he was planning to play an evil trick on him. The king ordered the qadi and the witnesses to be brought and a marriage contract to be drawn up between the vizier's daughter and the commander of his guard. When this had been done he produced a banquet of unparalleled splendour.

Although the vizier was overwhelmed by sorrow he made a show of gladness for the sake of the king. Word of the marriage spread through the city, leaving the people distressed thanks to the contrast between the beauty of the bride and the ugliness of the bridegroom.

The vizier went home to see to the preparations and the bride was decked out with the greatest splendour before being taken to her groom. What the spectators saw was indescribable beauty on her part and the greatest ugliness on his. On her father's instructions, she was first shown to him in a green robe, as the poet says:

> In her green dress she proudly swayed,
> And she was like a branch in leaf.
> Her glance was like a cutting sword,
> And her face like the rising moon.

She stole men's hearts and they were struck by renewed sorrow. She was then shown in a red robe, as the poet says:

> She came in a red gown like the blood of a gazelle,
> Causing the tears to flood down from my eyes.

When she was dressed in this I looked and saw
One pomegranate blossom set above another.
In my bewilderment I called to God:
Praise be to Him Who has joined snow to fire!

The attendants kept removing dresses and putting on others until this had been done seven times. Meanwhile the mamluk neither looked up nor turned towards her until they had left her with him. He then jumped on her and deflowered her roughly and crudely, leaving her with hatred in her heart, as virgins want flattering and gentle treatment, especially when they are in the bloom of youth.

When day broke the mamluk got up and rode off to serve the king, and the vizier, coming to visit his daughter, found her broken-hearted and in tears. When she saw him she jumped up and said: 'God will judge between you and me on a day when one of the heavens is removed and truth emerges to determine fate. Did you find any part of the house too restricted thanks to me or were you afraid of my food so that you afflicted me with this violent tyrant, no single vein in whose body fears Almighty God?' 'I did not command this or agree with it, my daughter,' the vizier said, 'but my hand was forced and the king ordered me. By God, I shall let this mamluk lord it over the king's women and take them as captives. I shall remove the kingdom from the king's grasp and hand over the best of it to the mamluk, as the king gave him the best of what I have. I shall let his enemies gloat over him as mine have gloated over me.'

He determined on this but kept his thoughts concealed. He used his property to buy mamluks, horses and arms and armour, all of which he handed over to the mamluk, while teaching him nobility and generosity. The emirs, soldiers and mamluks began to favour him; his power grew and he began to organize things bit by bit until it was he who controlled most of the state.

When this had been going on for some time the king fell gravely ill. He summoned the officials of his state, his friends and his viziers and made them take an oath of allegiance to his son, a handsome and good-hearted young man who had no knowledge of how he stood in the world. He then handed the reins of power to the ill-omened vizier, the father of the girl, after which he died and was buried.

After three days of mourning the prince rode out in a procession and when he had dismounted he took his seat on his father's throne. The vizier, with a firm grasp on power, started to play with him like a polo ball, tossing him from hand to hand, and, without his knowledge, his whole state inclined to the mamluk. When all the preparations they wanted had been made and nothing remained but to arrest the prince, they and their adherents armed themselves. They moved to the palace gate and sat down in the forecourt while the prince and his friends were seated drinking wine with no knowledge of what was about to happen to them. No single one of them came out without being seized by the vizier and his son-in-law, and after a time none of them were left with the prince.

A little servant boy passed through the forecourt, ignored by the vizier's men who did not interfere with him. When he got to the prince he said: 'Master, at the gate is the mamluk, your father's guard commander with the vizier. There are drawn swords, and everyone who went out has been arrested. I don't know what is behind this.' The prince thought this over and said: 'What harm did I or my father do to them? The poet has said:

You were brought up and nurtured in that house,
But were not told your father is a wolf.'

In spite of all this the vizier and his companions did not dare to attack him, not because of any weakness on their part, as they obviously had the upper hand, but because of the awe in which the kingship was held. The prince stayed there perplexed until he got up and opened his treasuries, in which he saw wealth and treasures, but when he came to one in the upper part of the palace he found it empty, with nothing in it except a carpet that was spread out. In his surprise he moved the carpet to discover a slab of veined marble with an iron ring. He pulled this and saw in front of him a flight of some twenty steps leading downwards. He went down and discovered a small room in which there were three men.

There is a remarkable story attached to this. The prince's father had been fond of drinking wine by the sea shore and every day when the sunlight reached that room it came to rest on a hidden door. If the king arrived in the light, well and good, but otherwise it remained motionless. The king did this without any of his officials knowing about it except for his vizier.

The prince was delighted at the sight. There were large ships there on parallel courses guarding the entrance to the sea against enemy attack. These were under the command of a very old shaikh who had a great knowledge of the sea, having made many foreign voyages, and this man had a great fondness for the king and his son. The prince told the servants in the room to call out to this shaikh on his galley. They went up towards him and before long he had disembarked and had come to kiss the ground before the prince. 'What is it that you want, O king?' he asked. 'Give me your orders.' 'Bring the great ship to the postern door,' the prince told him, and when this had been done the prince embarked and he ordered the young mamluks who still remained in his service to fetch all the wealth from the treasuries.

When this had been done, there was nothing left worth a single dinar, and the hundred-man crew saw to it that it was all taken on board. The prince then told one of the young mamluks to go to the forecourt and see if the servants were sitting there respectfully. In that case he was not to leave them, but otherwise he was to bring back word. He himself would be waiting for the boy's return by the harbour side.

Before he had finished speaking, there was a shout from inside the palace. The vizier's men had only been waiting for the king to be seized and allegiance sworn to a new man, with anyone who refused having his head cut off. This would ensure unity and leave no dangerous plots to be feared. Sword in hand, they made a rush to the king's throne room, only to find the place empty and the king gone. They put all the servants who were left in the palace, male and female, to the sword and collected all the stores they could find.

When the prince saw what was happening in his father's palace and realized that it was now in the hands of the vizier and his followers, he embarked and ordered the captain to tell his men to put out to sea. The sails were set and the ship sailed off like a storm wind or water spurting from a narrow pipe. Thinking about the prince's escape, the vizier realized that he could only have gone off by sea and he rushed up to the palace roof and looked out. From there he caught sight of a ship at sea and he shouted to the ones that were still left to overhaul it, promising gifts beyond count and promotion as commander of the fleet to whoever brought it in. To the prince he called: 'Where are you going? By God, if you leave I shall kill all the women and children in the palace, but if you come back you will be a ransom for them all.'

The prince paid no attention but sailed on, with the others in pursuit. It was sunset and for the ships there could be no overtaking at night. When dawn broke they could see each other and the captain, looking at his pursuers, called: 'Don't you realize that my crew are the pick of the sailors and that I know more than any of you about the sea? This prince has been wronged by his vizier, who has seized the throne from him.' This made them fearful, as they had not known about what the vizier had done. They wondered whether to go off with the prince but then they thought of their wives and children and told each other: 'You know that the captain's hundred men are stronger and better equipped than we are and he knows more about the sea. So let us all go back.'

They did this and when they got to the palace and the citadel they told the vizier: 'Master, we got no news of them and we don't know whether they went up into the sky or down into the earth.' The vizier bit his hand in regret at the escape of the prince. No one in the city knew what had happened but a rumour spread that he had been killed and that Qaraqush, the commander of the guard, had taken his place. This quietened the people and Qaraqush took over the throne, handing the keys of power to the vizier, who held authority while Qaraqush was the nominal sultan. Things were settled like that.

So much for them, but as for the prince, he and his companions sailed on, night and day, until they arrived at an island where they landed and rested for two or three days. They then embarked again with a supply of fresh water and sailed away. Things went on like that until, after three months of continuous sailing, the young prince was getting tired of it. He went to the captain and said: 'Uncle, are you going to take us to Mt Qaf? [at the world's end]' When the captain said 'no,' he went on: 'Do you want to confine us to the sea?' 'No,' said the captain, so the prince asked: 'Where do you want to take us then?' The captain ordered the look-out to climb the mast and to scan every quarter. It was then that in the distance the man saw a great black shape and told the captain.

The ship altered course towards it and after six days and nights of sailing they came in sight of a lofty mountain towering into the sky, filling the upper part of the horizon and blocking the lower. In the middle of it was a huge cave in whose entrance was an enormous brass statue with eyes of sapphires and a hand raised against the sea. What was in the cave could not be made out, but from it shone a radiant light.

The ship sailed on until, when it was opposite the hand of the statue in the mountain, it came to a standstill thanks to God's power, and could not move in any direction. The prince thought that they had stopped deliberately, but although the captain and the crew began to row, the ship still stayed fixed where it was. The captain then climbed to the masthead to look at the statue and the hand opposite him, and when he came down he searched through his belongings until he brought out a book that listed the perils and disasters of the sea. He had turned over twenty-one pages when he stood staring for a time. He then struck his head so that blood came from his nostrils and when the prince came up and asked him what was wrong, he said: 'Know my son, that this is a very deadly place. The statue that you see in the cave has a talisman in its raised hand. Any ship coming here from any direction goes on until it is opposite this and then it becomes motionless until all those on board die of hunger and thirst. Huge numbers have died here and however hard sailors have tried to row, their ships did not move and they starved to death. All we can do is to entrust our affairs to Almighty God and wait to see what happens.'

When the prince heard this, his countenance changed and he said to himself: 'We have escaped one form of death only to meet another and there is nothing we can do to help ourselves.' He got up, and telling himself that death was inevitable, he tucked the bottom of his robe securely into his belt and looked over the side, intending to jump into the sea, swim to the idol and remove it from its place. The captain took hold of him, saying: 'It was for your sake that we left our wives and our sons and do you now want to kill yourself? By God, that is not going to happen even if we ourselves all die! We shall sacrifice our lives for you.'

He went to the crew and asked: 'Which of you is going to go to that mountain, climb up to the cave and smash that idol? He can have as much wealth from me as he wants.' After he had encouraged them all with offers of money, one of them got up, jumped into the sea and swam off until he was near the side of the mountain. At first he could find nowhere to approach the cave but after going round very slowly he discovered a suitable place and climbed until he was close to it. Then suddenly, as he was on the final section, he fell head first into the sea and was killed. One man after another climbed after him until, when ten had been, no one else would go.

At this point the prince got up, tightened his belt, fastened his sword over his shoulder and then, without saying anything to the captain, he jumped into the sea and swam off. The captain shouted at him to come back but he paid no attention and climbed up until when he was close to the cave he saw unscalable rock which gleamed like a steel mirror and dazzled the eye with its brightness. He went back down to the shore and called to the captain to give him an axe or a hammer with which he could cut himself a stance, as no one could climb there thanks to the intensity of the light.

The captain gave him an axe and, taking this with him, he climbed to the smooth section in which he began to cut steps big enough for his feet, going on until he had reached the cave. What met his eyes was a remarkable sight, a wide cave buttressed with smooth stone, at whose upper end was a brass statue on a chair of Chinese steel, with sapphire eyes and a hand held up to face the sea. The prince made towards this and when he reached it he sat beneath its feet and dug away with his axe until, as had been destined, it collapsed on its face. In so doing it crushed the hand that held the talisman, which broke off and fell down into the sea.

As soon as it reached the water, the ship moved off like a lightning flash. The captain turned and said: 'Wait for your master's son,' but, try as they would, the crew could not control it and it sailed off like a cloud. The prince looked after them and exclaimed: 'They have left me and gone off, but, by God, this was not of their own choice, for it was only the statue that was holding back the ship.' He then fell on his knees, saying: 'There is no might and no power except with the Great God!'

He began to walk on the mountain and after a while he saw something dark in the distance and went on towards it. When he got near what he saw was a region full of trees and streams, with bulbuls and other birds. The trees were in leaf and the streams were fast flowing; the plants were scented with saffron and the soil with amber. He came down from the mountain and walked all that day until sunset, when he stayed where he was until dawn.

At daybreak he got up and walked on until he came to the first of these meadows, where he ate the fruit and drank from the water, looking around him with joy at what he could see. When evening came he slept in a tree, getting up and starting off again next morning. For three days he went on, walking through the thickets from dawn till dusk and then sleeping wherever he was. On the fourth day he said to himself: 'How long am I going to be here? I must press on until I get to the end of this wood.' After another full day's worth of walking, he had again slept where he was until dawn. This time when he set off and it was nearly noon, he emerged from the trees and looked out over open ground, at the top end of which was something dark in the distance, obscured by smoke.

He hurried on towards it, telling himself that there might be something there that he could buy to eat as he was tired of eating plants, and he arrived at sunset. What he found was a city with high towers and solid walls, teeming with inhabitants. He entered and had set off in search of a hostel when he came on an old man sitting on a bench. He went up to him and said: 'Sir, I should like you to direct me to a lodging.' 'To hear is to obey,' the man replied and he got to his feet, took the prince by the hand and led him to a house which he opened for him. When the prince went in he could see nothing there on which to sit and he asked the old man whether he had any mat. 'No, master,' said the man, at which the prince removed the ring from his finger and passed it to him, saying: 'Keep this till tomorrow in pledge for a mat.' At that the man spread out a mat for him and left him to pass the night there.

When dawn broke next day, the prince got up and called to the lodging keeper, telling him to go and sell his ring in the market. When the man got there he was told that this was a prince's ring, worth a hundred dinars. He sold it, but only passed on a fraction of the money to the prince, and as the prince was of noble stock and of an honourable nature he said nothing to him about it. After a few days he had spent the money and nothing was left to him from the sale of the ring. He then started to unpick the braiding of his belt, one piece each day, giving it to the lodging keeper to sell. The man would spend the purchase money exactly as he wanted, while the prince would get no more than two *qirats* for each dinar. He knew this well enough, but was prevented by shame from saying anything.

This went on until there was no more of the belt left, after which he broke off his sword ring and sold that, followed by the sword strap. At last all he had left were the clothes he was wearing; he had no money left to spend while the lodging keeper had made a sizeable profit. When the prince had become penniless the man came to him and asked: 'What spending money have you got for today?' 'I have nothing at all,' the prince told him, but the man said: 'Master, haven't you heard what the poet says:

Young men strip naked and they then are clothed;
Only base-born strip naked with regret.

You are wearing a new satin gown that is worth a lot and if you sell it I can buy you another coarser one, and the same is true of your turban band, your chest protector and everything else you have on.' 'Do what you think will be best,' the prince told him.

The man started to sell and spend, stealing half the price he got, until the prince was left with nothing at all. He stayed pounding the ground, with his face covered with dust. His shirt had lost its warp and weft, the patches that had been used to widen it, its sleeves, its collar and its lower section. The turban band had no cushioning, centre or edges, and the trousers were fixed to the waistband.

Knowing that he had no money left to spend and nothing to sell he approached the lodging keeper who said to him: 'Sir, you know that I run this lodging and I owe the sultan rent for it. Five days from tomorrow it will be a new month, and what are you going to give me?' 'By God, I have nothing at all left to give you,' the prince told him and he replied: 'You have five days left but after that you must leave me and go on your way.' The prince silently cursed, saying: 'He sold my clothes for whatever he wanted and I didn't hold him to account, but every man acts according to his own background.'

He got up and left his lodging, choked with tears, and wandering distractedly, not knowing where he was going. He told himself: 'If I sleep by a shop, it may be that ill luck will see that a hole is made in it and something is taken from it. Then people will say that this was taken by the stranger who is sleeping there.' He walked a little further and said: 'Shall I beg from the people? No, never!' He then recited these lines based on those of 'Ali son of Abi Talib, may God ennoble him:

> To carry piles of rocks and harvest thorns without a scythe,
> To plunge into the sea and weigh the sands,
> And put cooked wheat back into the ear of grain,
> To wear tight fetters and to gnaw leather,
> And drive away the lions from their cubs,
> All this is easier than to beg as a poor man.

By God, I shall never do that, even if I die miserably of hunger!'

He started to wander around until he came to an open mosque which he entered, thinking that he might pass the night there until morning, waiting for whatever God might decree. He had only been there for an hour when the muezzin came and asked who he was. 'A poor stranger,' the prince told him, 'but the lord of the poor is Muhammad, may God bless him and give him peace.' The muezzin refused to accept him and said: 'Get up and leave the house of the Great and Glorious God. Don't try to argue with me unless you can produce a tradition of the Prophet, and if you don't go, I'll break your head open with this wooden clog.'

The prince got up, his eyes brimming with tears, and said: 'My Lord, You have driven me from my kingdom and brought this fate on me.

Praise be to You for Your decree.' He walked on a little and came to the door of a furnace room, which he entered. A black man was sitting there stoking the furnace and the prince greeted him submissively and asked him whether he would allow him to spend the night there as he was a stranger. 'Sit down,' the man said, and when the prince had done this, he asked what his job was. 'Tell me, are you a con man, a flayer of the dead or a crooner?' 'By God, I know nothing about these things,' the prince told him. 'How do you get anything to eat, then?' the furnace man asked, and the prince told him that he had eaten nothing for two days. 'And what are you going to eat tomorrow?' 'I don't know.' 'What about working with me?' 'What would I have to do?' 'Fetch dry dung, wipe the sweat away from me, rake out the ashes, stir up the dung and buy us something from the market.'

The prince agreed to this and after passing the night there he started on his work, fetching the dung and removing the ashes. This went on for a whole year after which the furnace man said to him: 'What a dull fellow you are! After a year you still are no good at all with furnaces.' 'What do you want, sir?' the prince asked and the man told him: 'The brother of the senior con man has invited me to one of their feasts and I would not want to refuse, lest they accuse me of haughtiness and say: "He couldn't bring himself to come to our feast."' The prince told him to go and promised to look after the furnace for him. The man showed him what to do and went off, leaving him.

He sat stoking the furnace from dawn to dusk and on into the first third of the night. Just then he heard a loud commotion and there were four men with drawn swords standing behind him. One of them was about to strike off his head when another shouted: 'Don't kill him.' One of them then took the startled prince out of the furnace room while the other three threw on the fire something that looked like a chest made of willow. 'Are you the furnace man?' they asked the prince. 'No,' he said, 'but I am his servant.' 'Well, tonight your blood has been spared,' they said, 'but keep to what you have and don't quit. Stick to working with your furnace, for we know you but you don't know us.' After promising to give him some money next day they left him and went away.

The prince's heart was fluttering in fear at what he had seen but as he sat stoking, with his eyes on the furnace, he could see that the flames had no effect on the chest that had been thrown into it but merely encircled it. This was in spite of the fact that, had a mountain been put in there, it would have been dissolved. He got up and looked outside the furnace to right and left but there was no one to be seen. He went to the rake that he used for the ashes and putting it into the furnace he drew the chest out of the fire, looking as though it had never been in the flames at all.

He found it shut but opened it up to find clothes such as had never been seen, woven with gold and dazzling the furnace with their jewels. When he unwrapped them he discovered a most beautiful, shapely and deep-bosomed girl, straight as a spear, with a forehead bright as dawn, oval cheeks, dark eyes and heavy buttocks. Praise be to God Who created her from the vile drop, as the poet has said:

Created as she would have wished herself,
Well formed in beauty's mould,
Neither too tall nor yet too short.

She was drugged and unconscious and the prince said to himself: 'If I take the clothes and hide them, when she recovers I can say that the people who brought her here removed them.' He then took them, together with the ornaments and robes that she was wearing and dug a hole for them at the side of the furnace, before going back to his place and starting to stoke.

Not long afterwards, the girl came to her senses and called out the names of her servants, leaving the prince to think that she must be mad or deranged. He asked her what had happened, at which she opened her eyes and found herself in the furnace room. 'What is this?' she asked the prince. 'What brought me here and where are my clothes?' 'I didn't see any,' he said and he went on to tell her the whole story from start to finish, how she had been thrown into the fire and not burned and how he had pulled her out and lifted her up. 'That is true,' she acknowledged and she got to her feet. This was in the last third of the night and the girl was the queen of the city.

Next morning she told one of her servants to take one of the duty mules and go to such-and-such a furnace, taking the most splendid set of clothes from the store, and to bring back the furnace-man with all speed. The servant went to the furnace where the black furnace-man had returned and the prince had gone off on some errand. When the queen's servant came in he said: 'Sir, this is no proper place for you; you should not be doing this, so get up.' The furnace-man was startled and said: 'I'm not the man,' but the servant repeated 'get up,' and went out with him to where the mule was waiting. There was a robe of honour and other clothes and when the man had been dressed in these and mounted on the mule, the servant took him to the queen's palace and after asking permission he brought him to the queen.

When she caught sight of him she called out: 'What are you?' 'I am a son of Adam,' he told her, adding: 'and I said that I was not the man.' The servant agreed with this and the queen said: 'Wretched slave, where did you get this man from?' He told her: 'From such-and-such a furnace,' and she asked the man whether there was anyone there apart from him. 'Yes, my boy,' he told her, and she instructed her servant to go off with him and fetch her the boy, while she would not take back what she had given to the furnace-man.

The servant went off with this black man, who went ahead of him to the young prince, after he had come back from the market. He went up and slapped him, saying: 'How many times have I told you, you miserable fellow, to serve me until you prosper and I bring you wealth and make something of you, but all I hear is "no!" Get up now, get up and go.'

The prince did as he was told and mounted the mule, after which the servant took him to the baths, where he was cleaned up and put to rights, with his long hair being trimmed. When he left the baths he was dressed in a robe worth five hundred dinars and he rode off with the servant to the queen's palace where he dismounted from the mule. He was about to go in when behind him came the furnace-man. 'Damn you, where are you going?' the servant asked, to which the man replied: 'I'm going in with my boy.' The servant shouted at him and struck him, after which he went back and left the prince, who went on.

Permission was asked for him to enter the queen's presence and when this had been granted he went into a long hall crowded with retainers and servants. The luxury and wealth that he saw made him forget his father's realm as well as the shame and humiliation to which he had been reduced. The servant led him on until the curtain was removed and he saw what he had not seen the first time. It was as the poet says:

She came out from behind the curtains and I said:
To God be glory, Who created forms.
I used to think that the sun was unique,
Until I saw its sister amongst men.

He was robbed of his wits and reduced to confusion as the queen had taken over his whole heart.

She made him sit beside her and then called for food. When it had been brought she started to feed him with mouthfuls, jumping on to his knees and kissing him until they had both eaten enough. The food was then removed and wine produced, from which they drank until evening. The queen got up and went to a closet where she slept, while the prince slept where he was until morning.

For three days they went on like this, eating and drinking and enjoying friendly conversation. On the fourth she summoned him and said: 'You see what luxury you are experiencing but for my part I want my clothes.' 'I didn't see them,' the prince assured her, 'for when you were brought in, you were just as you saw yourself later.' 'Which would you prefer,' she asked, 'your present luxury and the fact that you can enjoy looking at me, or clothes worth five hundred dinars? If you bring them to me I shall present you with ten thousand dinars.' On hearing that he said: 'They are buried beside the furnace.' 'Go off,' she said, 'and bring them back quickly, after which you can have what I promised.'

The prince went to the furnace room and dug up the clothes. When he returned them to the queen, her face lit up with joy and she said: 'I knew that you had them because you had told me that the fire had had no effect on me when you took me out, for I realized that had I not been wearing them I would have been nothing more than a lump of black charcoal. You must know that in this pocket is a pearl that commands the services of a hundred *jinn* tribes and I shall show you some of what it can do.' She unfastened her collar and removed a small necklace from which she took a pearl on which were lines of writing. She put it on the ground and said: 'Servants of these Names, I conjure you by the Greatest Name of God, engraved on this pearl, to come here obediently.'

Immediately three *jinn* were standing there, each eleven cubits tall, with ugly shapes, eyes set lengthwise, hooves like those of cattle and talons like those of wild beasts. The prince was horrified and bitterly regretted that he had not known about the pearl. They asked the queen for her orders and she said: 'Go at once and bring me the four men who wanted to burn me, whether they are up in the sky or down in the earth.' The three *jinn* left for a time and then came back with four men chained and shackled in the worst of states. The queen looked at them and said: 'Damn you, what harm did I do to you to prompt you to repay me like that? Cut off their heads.' The prince saw the heads flying through the air and the queen ordered that the bodies should be carried away and thrown into the sea. When this had been done she dismissed the three.

The prince said: 'She turned to me and said: "I had taken these as boon companions, eating and drinking with them. They enjoyed my youth but all they wanted was vile fornication. I was a virgin, and had there not been four of them they would have got what they wanted, but they were jealous and schemed against each other until they all agreed to throw me into the furnace. God protected me from their evil thanks to the blessing of this pearl and the Greatest Name inscribed on it."

'She then looked at me and said: "My clothes are worth a thousand dinars", and she told her maid to fetch the money. Twenty purses were brought each containing a thousand dinars and she told me to take these and open a shop. I was to eat and drink with her and she said: "If you need a horse, all of them are yours and the house is handed over to you and is under your authority, but it is only occasionally that I will come back to drink with you."'

The prince said: 'Lady, no kingdom on the face of the earth is worth a single clipping from your nails. Am I to open a shop and not see your lovely face again?' 'I swear that I shall not cut you off from me,' she answered and, calling for a copy of the Qur'an, she was about to take an oath on this when he told her: 'This is on condition that you swear to let me stay with you for forty days, not leaving you and carrying on as we have been doing.' She agreed and, calling on God, she swore to his condition, before making him swear that he would not betray her as long as he was with her. They exchanged these oaths confidently, trusting one another, and then resumed the sportive pleasures that they had enjoyed before, coupled with wine drinking.

They continued to enjoy the most pleasant of lives until thirty-five of the forty days had passed, but the prince's heart was consumed by an unquenchable fire. Of the two reasons for this, one was the torment inflicted by his love for the queen, a love that he could not bring to its conclusion, while the second was her pearl. As he had only five days left, he began to think of some trick that he might play. He had a druggist friend with whom he sometimes used to sit when he left the queen, and he told her one day that he was going to go out and walk in the market. 'God be with you,' she said and he went to the man's shop and talked with him for a time. Then he said: 'Sir, there is something I want to tell you but I feel embarrassed.' 'What is it?' asked the man, 'and why are you embarrassed?' 'I have married a formidable-looking girl,' the prince said, 'and every time I come hoping to uncover her face she stops me and there is nothing I can do with her.' The druggist agreed to help and the prince took out two dinars and gave them to him. At the sight of the gold the man reached out for a small box from which he removed a number of things which he put in a twist of paper, saying: 'The dose is one *qirat* and no more, or else she won't wake up for three days.' The prince agreed to this and took the drug which he put down under his collar, after which he left and returned to his palace.

When he went in, he found the girl seated and she got up and seated him beside her on the couch. They started to eat and drink and went on until evening. He distracted her attention for a time pretending to be drunk. He filled a glass and gave it to her after which he filled another and drank it himself. Then, after having filled yet another, he pretended to scratch behind his ear. From this he removed a quarter of a dirham's weight of *banj* which he put in the glass and handed it to her. No sooner had it passed her lips than it went to her head. The prince took her in his arms and laid her on the bed, where he started to kiss her, using his hands to strip her clothes from her breast. He saw that her waistband was fastened with twenty knots and he started to untie them one after the other. When he had undone ten, he saw the pearl fastened in the eleventh but as he was about to undo it he received a blow on the back of his neck that knocked him down on to his face. Standing over his head was an old woman like a vulture, who was saying: 'You boor, what about the oath you took? You have betrayed it together with the covenants you made. Didn't you see how the four kidnappers lost their heads but not to a sword. Did you think that you would get off unscathed after uncovering her face?'

The prince tried to trick her, saying: 'Lady, I was carried away by drunkenness and love, and you know how love turns men over on their heads.' 'I forgive you,' she said, 'and so you can both sleep, embrace, and kiss, with me watching you.' 'God is not going to hide you away, you ill-omened old woman,' the prince said to himself, and he turned to the queen's clothes with no other thought than to free the pearl. When he had done this, he put it in his mouth and then got up and said: 'You ill-omened old woman, are you not going to let me uncover her face?' 'What are you saying, boor?' she said; 'has drunkenness got the better of you?' 'By God, lady,' he told her, 'I am only joking and tomorrow morning I want you to say nothing to the queen.' She swore to this and then took him to a bedroom and locked him in, after which she went to the girl and refastened the knots he had undone, before going off to her own room to sleep.

When the prince had settled down he remembered his own country, what had happened to his family and how he had been driven from his kingdom. He took out the pearl and told himself that he should try it to see whether it could help. He placed it on the ground and said: 'Servants of these Names, I conjure you by the Greatest Name of God, to take me this instant to my own palace.' Before he had stopped speaking he saw himself flying between earth and sky. [lac.] He found himself coming down from the roof to the centre of the palace where he saw the royal throne with his father's mamluk, Qaraqush, sleeping on it surrounded by young mamluks and servants, all of whom were asleep. He took a few steps forwards and kicked Qaraqush in the ribs so that he woke in alarm.

He was frightened by the sight of the prince and said to himself that he could not have attacked the palace unless his own officials had turned to him. Then, when he looked, he saw his own mamluks asleep while there was no one with the prince, who had neither sword nor armour. This raised his hopes for he thought that the prince must have hidden himself away in the palace. He got to his feet and said: 'Boor, do you think that those who whispered in your ear that you should take the kingdom from me were trying to do anything but destroy you?' He pounced on him and, taking hold of him, threw him to the ground, like a sparrow in the talons of a hawk. We have already mentioned his courage, skill and power, but the prince called: 'Servants of these Names, hold him.' The mamluk was advancing on him but was dismayed to find himself unable to move. He called to his own mamluks who jumped up, but then recognized the son of their former master. 'Damn you, take him!' shouted Qaraqush, but the prince told the servants of the Names to hold them, and they too were unable to stir. Qaraqush shouted at them again, but they told him that they were in the same state as he was.

The prince then told him: 'Don't hope to take the kingdom for yourself, for I have a Name that would allow me to destroy these mountains if I wanted.' 'What had I to do with this?' asked Qaraqush. 'It was the vizier's fault.' He then looked round and saw the vizier coming down from the roof and being put in front of him. 'What brought me here?' the vizier asked, and Qaraqush said: 'Look in front of you.' He saw the prince, surrounded by *jinn*, who asked him: 'What harm did my father do you that made you repay him like this?' 'He took the dearest thing I owned and gave it to this man, and so I took the dearest thing he owned and gave it to him too. After I had had my revenge I did not care whether things went well or badly.'

At that the prince told the *jinn* to imprison them, which they did, and he then ordered a proclamation to be made that the sultan had returned. His subjects were delighted and he proceeded to summon the senior officials who, on their arrival, asked for and were granted forgiveness. He then had the queen brought to him within an hour, and he astonished her by telling her his story from beginning to end. He went on to ask permission to marry her, which she granted. A marriage contract was drawn up and he proceeded to consummate the marriage, finding her to be a virgin untouched by man.

She occupied a major place in his affection, but when she asked him for the pearl he refused, saying that he had to keep it in case of an attack by a formidable foe. He ordered the vizier and Qaraqush to be nailed on crosses and tormented by hunger and thirst until they died. He and his wife remained enjoying the happiest and most pleasant of lives until death parted them.

Here our story ends. Praise be to God alone, and His blessings and peace be on Muhammad, his family and his companions.

Tale Eighteen

The Story of Mahliya and Mauhub and the White-Footed Gazelle. It Contains Strange and Marvellous Things.

In the Name of God, the Compassionate, the Merciful

It is said, and God knows better, that when 'Amr ibn al-'As entered Egypt and got as far as 'Ain al-Shams he saw a huge old building, bigger than any he had ever seen, surrounded by remarkable remains. Near it was a hermitage, and he gave orders that the hermit should be brought to him. His messengers hurried there and shouted to the hermit from all sides, at which he looked for the clothes that his ancestors had worn to bring them fortune when they went before a sultan or were faced with important affairs or great dangers. He put on a belt of red leather embroidered with crosses of yellow silk and fastened a band of white silk around his forehead, and from this he hung down a cross of red gold between his eyes and his neck.

Reciting a portion of the Evangel, he came to a picture of Jesus the son of Mary and prostrated himself to it, asking for help. He then took a number of wine cups and went out, carried on the shoulders of servants and guards. They mounted him on a piebald donkey with a white harness and set off after him, accompanied by the monks. When they came to 'Amr, the hermit greeted him courteously and spoke with eloquence. 'Amr allowed him to sit and, after returning his greeting, he occupied himself with someone else until the hermit had regained his composure and his wits. 'Amr asked his name and how old he was, to which the hermit replied that his name was Matrun and that he was a hundred and twenty years old. 'To what group do you belong?' asked 'Amr, and Matrun told him: 'My forefathers were amongst the disciples of Christ.'

'Amr then said: 'Please tell me about this building and why it was built, as well as about the trees planted here and the water channels that have been constructed, for what I see is wonderful.' Matrun replied:

'What you have asked me about is remarkable. It will take a long time to explain and it contains lessons for those who will learn and prompts thought.' I shall tell the emir – God help him – what I have heard about it and the stories that have reached me. I shall tell him about the huge old castle to which it was attached and why it was that its foundations were destroyed. I shall give the name of its queen and set out its story, so that he may have a clear view of it, if this is what God Almighty wills.

I must explain to the emir – may God grant him long life – that in the land of Zabaj there was a great king descended from Nebuchadnezzar named al-Shimrakh son of Janah. He treated his opponents with savage hostility and pride; he was an idolater with a passion for wine, dark-eyed girls and women, as well as for acts of violence. He had a huge arena constructed with walls of white marble and red onyx and two galleries topped with pure marble, each with a tree of red coral, on which were birds of gilded copper so constructed that when the wind blew through them they would produce delightful and remarkable songs. Their mouths were filled with pungent musk and their beaks and eyes were made of rubies and other gems. Over this was a dome of topaz and emerald, covered in rough brocade and surmounted with jewels, and in it there was a throne, to the right of which was a gazelle with two fawns under her made of red carnelian, stuffed with dinars and dirhams and inscribed with the name of Shimrakh in order to reveal his fortune and display his happiness.

On days when he was happy and content he would take his seat there and bring in those of his family and state officials whom he wanted. He would turn his head towards the throne covered by the dome, at which a vulture would give a shriek and, opening its beak, it would scatter on them the perfume that was in its belly. The gazelles would then utter melodious cries and pour out over them the dinars and dirhams with which they were filled. The king would reward those present with gifts and robes of honour and mount them on fine horses.

He had another throne for use when he was angry. This was made of yellow teak and placed under a dome of black and white ebony and covered in black silk, on top of which was an eagle made of split onyx and filled with globules of lead. To its right was a savage lion and to the left a fierce and hungry lioness suckling two cubs. When Shimrakh was angry or believed that someone was plotting against him he would sit on that throne snorting and cursing. The eagle would then turn and breathe out naphtha and smoke, while shooting leaden bullets, and the lion and the lioness would tear the object of his anger to pieces and eat him. The arena had twenty doors of juniper wood as well as ten of red gold marking the king's pleasure and ten of lead for his anger, so dividing the twenty between anger and gentleness. Fastened over them were a thousand coverings of goats' hair and purple cloth.

For all his arrogance and pride, Shimrakh was hospitable to guests; he gave justice to the wronged and provided food for the poor and the wretched, while wishing to do good. In his palace he had a thousand of the most beautiful girls of the age, for each of whom he provided a personal maid to serve her and rooms for her retinue of servants. When he wanted to sleep with one of them he would summon her, and she would come in all her finery, anointed with all kinds of perfume. He would then approach an idol that he had made of red gold, prostrate himself to it, glorify it and say: 'My God, I am going to lie with this girl in the hopes of having a son who will succeed to my throne, and any child of mine will be your servant.'

He would then lie with the girl who, if God so willed it, would conceive. When her pregnancy became obvious he would tell her: 'If you give birth to a girl, I shall cut you in pieces and make you suffer the force of my anger.' God, the Great and Glorious, decreed that the thousand gave birth to a thousand girls, wall-eyed, one-eyed or eyeless. When Shimrakh saw this he would sit on his Throne of Wrath and summon mother and daughter. When they came he would snort and curse and the eagle would turn and shoot lead bullets and the lions would spring at them and kill them. He would then put the dead mother's personal maid in her place, assigning to her her mistress's servants and her wealth. He continued to act like this over a period of time, with constant tyranny and continuous evil-doing, glorying in his long-standing rule.

One night he had been happily drunk and enjoying himself amongst his retainers, servants and companions. He then sank into a drunken sleep, only to wake up in terror and pull off his clothes, baring his breast before collapsing in a faint, which lasted for part of the day. When he recovered consciousness he held a general meeting of his people in his Hall of Pleasure and Contentment. This was attended by his intimates, his chamberlains and his viziers, who took their places according to their rank. One of the viziers asked: 'What was it that we saw happen to our lord the king and what was it that occurred to him in his sleep?' The king replied: 'I saw in a dream that the eagle that perches beside my Throne of Wrath flew up into the sky until it passed out of my sight, but then it came back, swollen in size until it was as large as a huge camel, and the sound of its shriek was loud as thunder. It seized me by my big toe and flew off with me into the sky, holding me upside down, until it had taken me beyond my own kingdom and beyond the whole world.

'I had despaired of life when it brought me to a gloomy and barren waste, both rough and savage, in which a huge fire was blazing with lofty flames. Fiery beasts as big as great elephants were there and they bared tusks like spears at me, shooting sparks and being about to tear me to pieces. I also saw snakes the size of tall palm-trees that were fast approaching me. The eagle was about to throw me down on my head amongst them, but when I had thought that there could be no escape a handsome and sweet-scented young man came flying on green wings between earth and sky. He rescued me from the eagle's talons and set me down on the ground before placing me on a green cushion. "Do you know me?" he asked, and when I said "no" he said: "I am the good that you did to wrong-doers and the justice that you gave to the weak against the strong. Had God, the Great and Glorious, not sent me to you, you would have perished in the fire thanks to what you did to your guests, your servants and your friends."

'I saw the mothers of my children sleeping on their backs in a green garden where there were fruit trees and flowing streams. They were wearing green clothes of silk brocade, and their children were rolling on top of them, while blood was still streaming from their throats. I could also see all the governors of the kings whom I had conquered during my reign propping themselves up on their elbows, talking and joking. I was ashamed, contrasting my sadness with their delight, and I said to the young man: "I repent." I promised him faithfully that I would abandon wrong-doing and aggression, that I would no longer slaughter my wives and children and that I would be true to my religion. "If you want a son," he told me, "dedicate him to the One, Eternal God." At that he vanished from my sight, and I woke up filled with terror at what I had seen and I have summoned you to ask for your advice that I may keep to the promise God took from me that I would abide by His covenant.' In reply, they all said: 'May God help you to reach His right guidance and confirm you in obedience to Him! We agree that what the king has decided will serve as an exhortation leading to his well-being and the completion of his happiness.'

Shimrakh ordered that his Throne of Wrath should be destroyed, the wild beasts killed and the eagle which he had used to punish his people broken and thrown into the sea. He had a proclamation made to all his governors that they should bring justice to those who had been wronged, abandon acts of sinful disobedience to God, and distribute the wealth of the mighty to the wretched poor.

This made him happy, and the vulture flew to his throne, scattering perfume, while the gazelles frisked round it, strewing dinars and dirhams. He then distributed splendid robes of honour, and those present left with the honours he had given them, while he himself went to an empty chamber and put on a coarse hair-shirt and prostrated himself to the Great and Glorious God. As he did so he prayed: 'My God, Lord of the heavens, Who causes water to flow and clears blindness from the hearts of men, You Who have saved me from punishment and affliction after showing me the supreme calamity, through Your magnanimity grant me a son to comfort me and fulfil my hopes as my successor. You listen to men's prayers and act in accordance with Your will.'

He left the chamber, removed the shirt and, after putting his clothes back on, he summoned the girl who was dearest to him and of whom he was particularly fond, and lay with her. By the permission of Almighty God, she immediately conceived, and he kept a note of the date and ordered everyone in the palace to obey her. When the months of her pregnancy came to an end, she gave birth to a boy like a full moon, whom his father named Mauhub. The mother died, and it was the other girls who tried to suckle the baby, but he would not accept their milk. To relieve his distress, Shimrakh went out to hunt and caught sight of a lioness with two cubs. He liked the look of the cubs and ordered that they should be caught, and they were taken unharmed and tied up. The lioness went with them to the palace and, after she had been calmed and become tame, the baby was put to her teat and accepted her milk.

Shimrakh was delighted and distributed money, while the lioness and her cubs were given the best food. She treated the baby tenderly and attended him constantly until, after having been suckled for two years, he weaned himself. As he grew up his father summoned teachers and astrologers, telling them to instruct and educate him. He learned all that was needed by a prince in a shorter time than any other, after which his father set him to mastering horsemanship, the use of arms and hunting, until by the time that he was fourteen he had reached the desired standard.

At that point his father summoned him and gave him the following advice: 'My son, in the case of our own great ancestors and every other king until now, when a son of theirs reached manhood his father would send him to the sacred church of Jerusalem to be given religious instruction by the bishops and to receive blessing from the patriarch and the archbishop. He would be baptized in the font with the Evangel being recited over him, so that he might return to the Eternal Lord, the great object of our worship. It is He Who will lead you in the right way to both righteousness and glory, since here is the completion of blessing and the fulfilment of what tradition demands. So now get ready to leave and may you enjoy success and happiness if God Almighty so wills.'

The narrators noted that it was recorded in the lives of the great kings that when one of them reached maturity and went to be baptized in the font of the church of Jerusalem splendid sacrifices would be made and bountiful alms distributed. The Evangel would be recited over him, and he would be taken to Bethlehem, where his picture would be placed on the walls of the church next to those of his ancestors with their names and dates. A record would be kept of when he came there, and the day would be kept as an official feast every year. A crystal candle fed with oil of jasmine would burn before the picture night and day, regardless of whether it was of a boy or a girl. The visitors would then return to Jerusalem. [lac.]

This is how Baalbek got its name, as Baal was a huge old statue – but there is no god but God Almighty, Who is great beyond compare and Whose Names are hallowed and besides Whom there is no other god. When visitors came there and prostrated themselves to the statue they would be entered by a devil sent by the sorcerers and divines who served the statue and spoke with its tongue. They were told what to do, and offerings and sacrifices were made to the idol in the presence of the deacons and monks, after which they would return to their own countries. Those who wished would marry, while others who were suited to the monastic life would become monks.

When Shimrakh told his son to set out, he gave him an armed escort together with equipment and money and sent with him monks and reputable shaikhs, choosing an auspicious day for his departure. When he reached Jerusalem he was met by the priests and monks assigned to the church, together with the patriarch and the archbishop. They provided him with food and barley and presented him with fine presents, as people came from all parts to look at him.

When he came to the church door, he put on the appropriate clothes together with a burnous and a woollen shawl. Golden crosses and golden censers were carried before him, and he was preceded by bishops and monks. After having approached the sacrificial altar, he went to the picture of Jesus son of Mary, on whom be peace, and after stroking this with his hand he immersed himself in the font. He drank wine as the Evangel was read out over him and he was provided with protective amulets, after which he took his seat on a regal throne of red gold. His picture was painted on one of the church walls, with name and date added. It was a speaking likeness, adorned with red gold, with topazes for eyes, and beside it was the picture of a lioness suckling him. A weighty covering of brocade was hung above it, and a crystal candle fed with oil of jasmine was lit before it to shed light on its beauty.

When all this had been finished Mauhub sacrificed beasts, gave away robes of honour and distributed largesse. This became an annual feast day for the people there. He then went to a mansion that had been furnished for him with the main body of the Christians preceding him and the deacons surrounding him. On his arrival he rested and showed himself to no one.

At that time the Egyptian princess Mahliya, daughter of al-Mutariq the son of Sabur, had arrived in Jerusalem. She was the same age as Mauhub and had been sent by her father to do what the other royal children did. It is said that her father had had thirty sons, but when they reached the age of ten, every one of them had died. Al-Mutariq had with him a number of sorcerers from Samannud and its districts, as well as from the temples of Sanawir and Ikhmim. When he saw what had happened to his sons, he summoned these men, together with the principal officers of his kingdom, and complained to them of his plight. They told him: 'O king whom we obey, you know that no diviner, sorcerer or astrologer can do anything about what the Creator in His foreknowledge has decreed. In the case of Moses's Pharaoh, He helped him choose an isolated cell, and when he was forced to abandon his great empire he could retreat there on his own when things became difficult and he was faced with a situation beyond his power, and not come out until he had succeeded in achieving what he wanted. Our advice is that you should follow his example and go off on your own. It may then be that this sorrow will clear away from you.' The king approved of this and rewarded his advisors.

He entered the cell and found it strewn with ashes. There was a gown of wool and iron fetters hanging on a chain from the roof. He put on the gown, fettered his hands and, after smearing himself with ashes, he implored God in all humility. 'My God, the God of Moses, Lord of Jesus, Who brings death to the living and life to the dead, remove this sorrow from me; grant me a child to comfort and help me.'

When he had left the cell, he summoned his favourite girl and lay with her. She conceived and gave birth to a daughter like a rising sun, for which he praised God, naming the child Mahliya. He summoned wet nurses to suckle her, and when she was older he brought in teachers, who taught her not only all that the children of kings needed to know but sorcery and divination as well, until she surpassed all her contemporaries in beauty and culture.

When she was fourteen, her father wanted to entrust her with the affairs of his state as he saw how admirably she could administer them. He sent her to Jerusalem, following the custom of his ancestors, providing her with a large armed escort as well as great sums of money. He also sent her mother with her, together with her nurses, personal friends and a thousand mamluks who were in her service. After having instructed her in what she would need to do, he accompanied her to see her off.

She arrived at the church at the same time that Mauhub entered it, and she followed the usual custom by taking the Eucharist and kissing the picture of Christ as well as the patriarch. After that she took her seat on the golden throne to have her portrait painted and it was then that she noticed the picture of Mauhub that had just been completed. The face was shining, and in front of it was the candle, while by its side was the lioness. She tried to distract herself by looking at other pictures, but her eyes always returned to this one until she could see no other.

For a time she stayed in a state of bewilderment, staring admiringly at it, plunged in thought, until the painter had completed her own portrait. She then dispensed alms and made sacrifices, but without being fully conscious of what she was doing. When that had been going on for a time, as the bystanders noticed, a senior priest went up to her and said: 'Great queen, now that you have done what you had to, why are you sitting looking at this picture, while the people are restless and sweating, and you must be tired after your journey?' She turned to him and said: 'Tell me, whose is this portrait and when was it painted, for I can see no other picture to match it amongst the others in this church?' The great patriarch told her: 'This is the portrait of Mauhub, the son of Shimrakh.' She then asked about the lioness beside it and was told that she had suckled him. 'She will have added courage to his heart and lent him strength,' said the queen, and she then asked when he had come to

Jerusalem. 'He is here now,' the patriarch told her, 'as he has not yet returned home.'

While the patriarch was talking to her, Iblis took possession of her heart. She went to the mansion prepared for her in which she was supposed to rest, but sorrows swept over her, marked by sigh upon sigh. She could enjoy neither food nor cool drinks, and so she called for her mother and said to her: 'Mother, they tell me that there is a great king here called Mauhub, the son of Shimrakh, and he is here for the same purpose that we are. When kings meet in any country it is their practice to exchange splendid gifts, and I should like to send him some Egyptian treasures and cloths, so that he may help me by talking about this later to other kings.'

When her mother had approved of this, she gave orders that splendid Egyptian cloth, fine jewels and lively riding beasts should be selected as gifts for Mauhub, together with handsome slaves, swift horses, soft goats' hair and old wine. From amongst all these she chose as gifts what surpassed all description, and this was loaded on to a hundred reddish camels to be sent off with the best of her viziers.

She wrote Mauhub a signed letter which ran: 'In the name of God, the Compassionate, the Merciful, Lord of the sky, Who makes waters flow, Who creates all things, Who brings the dead to life and death to the living: O king, strengthened by God, I am sending you this gift to complete part of my religious obligations and to fulfil my duty, as I have heard that you are enjoying a happy stay in this country. I present you with some of what I have brought with me from Egypt, although this is only a part of what Our Lord gives His servants. Let the king accept it if he sees fit, in accordance with the will of the Great and Glorious God, and may God exalt him and fulfil his resolves.' She then sealed the letter.

When the gift reached Mauhub and he had read the letter, it gave him a high opinion of Mahliya's intelligence, and he accepted the gift with approbation. After allowing her vizier to come into his presence, he made him approach and questioned him about Mahliya. When he had been told her name and those of her father and mother he realized her importance and was impressed by her description. He then wrote to her to tell her of the arrival of her gift and he sent her precious things from his own lands, Indian aloes, musk, amber and camphor, loaded on Bactrian camels, and he dictated the following letter to his vizier: 'In the name of Almighty God, the Eternal Lord, the Highest Witness: Supreme and fortunate queen, I should have been the first to send a gift to you, but in your noble-mindedness you took the lead and hurried to display your praiseworthy generosity. I have sent to you less than a single servant of yours would deserve, relying on your acceptance of my excuse. Should you agree to receive this, God willing, it would be the most excellent of favours.' He signed the letter as coming from 'The distressed servant, king Mauhub', addressed to 'The queen who must be obeyed, Mahliya.'

His gift made a deep impression on her, filling her with delight, and when she opened his letter she kissed it. Her passion for him increased and she remained in a state of perplexity, tearful, sad and restless for a number of days. Mauhub then gave orders for his tents to be pitched outside Jerusalem in preparation for a visit to Baal, and he went to the great church to celebrate a farewell Eucharist. When Mahliya heard of this she ordered her own tents to be pitched next to his and she took her place in the middle of her escort, muffled in a turban.

Mauhub took his leave of the church, distributing alms amongst the wretched poor. He then went to his tent, surrounded by his men and his personal servants. The gleaming radiance of his beauty was enhanced by his fresh moustache, the lines of down on his cheeks, his lustre and his widely set eyebrows, while its perfection was completed by his languid gaze. He wore robes of red brocade embroidered with gold and set with rubies and coloured pearls; on his head was a blue Yemeni turban, and he had an Indian sword strapped on with gold thread. He was mounted on a lofty sorrel horse and surrounding him were five hundred followers of the same age as himself holding maces of gold and silver in their hands, wearing gowns of brocade with gilt belts and coloured turbans.

When he rode past the tent of Mahliya and her escort, he stopped to look both at her and at the splendour of her tents, together with the numbers of her retinue and her escort. He asked to whom all this belonged and was told that they belonged to Mahliya, the daughter of al-Mutariq, the son of Sabur of Egypt. As he stood looking, it became clear to Mahliya what kind of a person he was. Love for him almost overmastered her and robbed her of endurance, but she managed to control herself and hurried back to her tent, where she collapsed in a faint. Her servants gathered around her in tears, not knowing what was wrong with her.

She remained unconscious for part of the day and when she had recovered her mother asked her what the matter had been. She said [lac.] 'I stood up, but weariness overcame me, and I fainted. He is the

THE STORY OF MAHLIYA AND MAUHUB

only man for me.' 'May God protect you!' exclaimed her mother, who then distributed alms on her behalf. When night fell she stayed tossing to and fro on her bed in her grief, alone in her sorrow, with tears flooding her cheeks like pearls falling over corals. She spent the whole night like that.

When morning came she ordered her tents to be struck and the beasts to be saddled. Then, wearing her most splendid clothes, she went out surrounded by her servants and her escort, preceded by a cross of red gold with a flashing ruby in its centre, carried on a long lance. Her route took her by Mauhub's tents, and she told her viziers that, if he asked who this was, they were to say: 'This is Mahliya's vizier, who is foremost in her regard.'

When Mauhub saw this splendour, he gave his greetings and asked about Mahliya. 'She has gone ahead with her escort,' he was told, at which he asked his informant for his name. 'I am Mukhadi', the queen's vizier,' the man told him, and Mauhub said: 'I can see that you are a man of wit and intelligence. Would you like to come hunting with me, for I am told that there are many wild beasts on our route?' 'I cannot refuse,' replied the vizier, 'for this is something that I would very much like.'

The two of them spent the night in light conversation, and in the morning Mauhub sent one of his personal attendants to Mahliya's tent to ask about her and the vizier Mukhadi'. The man was told that Mukhadi' was with the queen, dealing with some business of hers, and that he sent his greetings to the king. On hearing this, Mauhub gave the order to leave, being distressed at having missed the queen, while, for her part, she waited a day before moving off in order that love for her might take a firmer hold of Mauhub's heart.

In the evening she gave the order to move and throughout the night she travelled in the middle of her escort until, when morning came, she put on fresh clothes and joined up with Mauhub's men. She was riding a black horse with a gilded saddle and was surrounded by slaves and servants carrying batons of gold and silver. She halted at the tent of Mauhub and asked permission to enter. The chamberlain went in to tell his master that Mukhadi' had come. Mauhub was moved by joy and got up to receive 'him' with an embrace. 'What kept you from me?' he asked, adding: 'I sent to ask after you, but my messenger could not meet you.' At that Mahliya said: 'I was with the queen, who had some business to attend to.'

The two of them talked for a time, but then a letter arrived from

Mauhub's father Shimrakh, asking how he was and urging him to hurry back. Mahliya got up in order to ride off quickly, and Mauhub went to say goodbye. He asked her to sit with him for the rest of the day, but she refused and returned to her tent distressed and saddened by the extent of her suffering. Similarly Mauhub was greatly saddened and disquieted, for all that he thought his friendly conversation had been with Mahliya's vizier, Mukhadi'.

During the course of their journey, they exchanged gifts and letters, as well as meeting each other. Their hearts were filled with love and longing, but neither knew the other's feelings. When they reached the city of Baal, Mauhub entered in all humility and abasement, dressed as a monk. He prostrated himself to the statue, kissing it and lighting candles and lamps burning jasmine oil. He then took his seat on a chair amongst the deacons and monks to receive the Eucharist. When he had finished, Baal addressed him, expounding his religion, tracing his future, exhorting him with commands and prohibitions and ending: 'Great king and leader, you will meet sorrows, difficulties and dangers, grave matters, the revelation of hidden secrets, heavy cares and troubles following one after the other. All this will be thanks to a beautiful gazelle acting as a lover wounded at heart. Take your time in dealing with this affair, Mauhub, and now, farewell, great king.'

Mauhub could not understand this and was filled with surprise at what had been said to him, but awe restrained him from asking about what Baal had said. On that same morning Mahliya entered and, after following the religious observance, she took her seat in order to listen to Baal's instructions. After giving her orders and prohibitions he ended by saying: 'Queen, you will enjoy the most splendid of stations, and happiness will come to you as you rule over the kings of mankind.' [lac.] She could not understand what he said but she had an inner feeling that it concerned Mauhub. She said nothing in reply but made sacrifices and distributed alms.

Both she and Mauhub rode off, and her mare approached his horse, at which he swore that he would ride with her stirrup to stirrup. This was what she did, and on her arm she was carrying a Yemeni falcon, which was followed by hawks of other kinds, together with panthers and dogs. When they reached the hunting grounds they both turned aside and devoted the whole day to the chase with great success, leaving Mauhub delighted by the good fortune that 'the vizier' had brought.

When they returned to their tents she leaned across to say goodbye to him, and he said: 'Mukhadi', my brother, I would like you to come with me to my tent and take a meal there, so that we can spend the rest of this day in conversation.' She excused herself, saying: 'Sir, the queen is here and I must be in attendance on her. Otherwise I should quickly accept your offer.' Mauhub mounted her on one of his own horses and entrusted her with greetings to the queen, imagining all the time that his friendly conversation had been with Mukhadi', not knowing that this was the queen.

Mauhub took the game that they had caught to his tent, while Mahliya went off to hers, suffering from redoubled distress and sorrow, as was Mauhub. She spent the night full of sadness and grief, finding the dawn slow to break, with her sleep burdened by thoughts. A letter then arrived from her father, urging her to hurry home, and she got up perplexed, fearful and full of tears, only to collapse in a faint. When she recovered, she was visited by her mother, who asked her what the matter was. She said: 'I dreamed that I saw myself in a green garden with running streams whose trees were in leaf, but while I was looking at its beauty, suddenly an enormous lion filled the place with its roars and advanced on me and me alone. When it was in front of me, it crouched down and when I gestured to it, it abased itself to me. I grasped its mane and mounted on its back, at which it got up and set off with me at an even pace. I was filled with joy, but just then the messenger woke me with a letter from the king, and sorrow drained me of tears thanks to the loss of the pleasure that I had felt when riding through that well-watered place.' Her mother told her: 'Daughter, you have got your wish, as there is a good interpretation for this dream. The garden is a pleasant life, and the lion is the king of kings whom you will rule and who will submit to you.' This cleared away some of her sorrow, but her thoughts remained centred on Mauhub, and how both of them had just then been urged by their fathers to hurry home.

To her own father she sent the best of answers and went straight to Mauhub, splendidly dressed in her finest clothes, accompanied by her mamluks laden with gifts for him. Amongst these was a mirror, which, when he looked into it, would show her to him, wherever she was. If he spread out a rug and lay down on it, were he to look at the mirror it would seem that he was lying there with her. When she arrived he went out to meet her and said: 'Mukhadi', my brother, I am distressed at parting from you and feel great grief that you have to leave.' 'The queen has made up her mind to go off tomorrow, God willing,' she said, 'and so I have come to say goodbye and to give you her greetings and a message to say: "I have sent you a gift to remind you of me when you are alone, and cheer you in your sadness. If you need anything from our country, entrust the affair to me, so that it may turn out well."'

This only increased his sorrowful cares, but he accepted the gift and when Mahliya rose he was still convinced that she was the vizier Mukhdadi'. They took leave of one another, with Mauhub standing as Mahliya mounted. When she was in the saddle he said: 'Mukhadi', my brother, give my greetings to the queen and tell her to write to me if she needs anything, and she will get a favourable reply.' He then retired gloomily to his tent, weeping constantly and unable to sleep.

With him there was a beautiful gazelle that he had caught the first time he went hunting with Mahliya and which he had admired so much that he had kept it near him. When he was alone with his grief and his unbroken sorrows, the gazelle began to shed tears and moan, attracting his attention and astonishment. In the morning he sent for one of the priests of Baal and when the man came he said: 'Look at this gazelle. I have seen something that alarmed me, for when something happened to me last night that made me cry, I saw it shedding tears to match mine.' The priest said: 'This is a human woman who is under a spell. Hers is a remarkable story, and I see that she will bring you great joy. If Your Majesty orders me to release her so that he may learn what she knows, I shall do it.' 'I should like that,' said Mauhub, and the priest said something in a low voice, after which the gazelle shivered and became a lovely girl, whose beauty vied with the sun and put the moon to shame. Mauhub gave her something with which to cover herself and then started to ask her about herself and what had happened to her.

She said: 'Great King Mauhub, know that this a marvellous affair and that my story is long, remarkable and strange, and I shall tell it to you so that you may learn from it and take pleasure in it. I am a woman of the stock of the old kings of Persia. My name is Haifa', and I am the daughter of Jairun al-Mushawir, a king of Persia, handsome, a skilled horseman and a man both powerful and eloquent. I was his only child, and because of his love for me he built me a palace beside his own, filling it with furnishings and curtains. He made a garden for it in which he let loose various kinds of wild beasts and birds, causing streams to flow through it. He placed me there with a trustworthy nurse and he would send me all kinds of food and drink, but I would only see him once a year.

'When I reached maturity, I found myself inspired to act slyly and I was attracted to obscenity, as the power of destiny encircled me. I went to the castle wall on the garden side and removed a stone so that I could look out. I was amazed at what I saw of the gardens, because I had thought that I and my nurse were alone in the world. After a time while I was watching I caught sight of a most beautiful gazelle. I had never seen anything like it in the palace. It had dark eyes with golden pupils, white patches on its legs and coloured horns that were like branches. It stopped opposite me as I admired it, and while I kept looking I called to my nurse and showed it to her. She too admired it, and I asked her to find some way of catching it, and she went down, stopped it and then took hold of it and brought it to me. I held it joyfully and fed it on husked sesame seeds dipped in honey, and I mixed milk and wine for it. I devoted all my attention to it, and, while I never stopped looking at it, it never stopped looking at me.

'While I was sitting one day, the gazelle shivered violently and then appeared to me as a handsome young man. He looked at me, and I was startled and alarmed by his appearance, and he then came up speaking to me in pure, pleasant language that was sweeter than honey and softer than butter. "Don't be afraid, delight of my eyes and goal of my hopes," he said, "for you should know that I am a prince of the *jinn* who appear in the guise of gazelles, looking at this and that as we wander through desert wastes, and we enjoy ourselves in orchards and at the sight of lovely faces without arousing any suspicions. I have been living for some time in your garden and I saw you looking out like a branch of the *ban* tree or a shoot of sweet basil. I stayed bemused by love, looking at you again and again without your knowledge until love for you got the better of me and as my love-sickness increased I presented myself to you. I am known as the white-footed gazelle."

'He came forward, kissing my feet and sucking at them, and, by God, he made a great impression on my heart, attaching himself to it and taking over my hearing and my sight. I said: "Prince, I have fallen in love with you this instant, but my father is a giant who acts like a pharaoh, and I fear both for myself and for you." "Lady," he replied, "do not be sad but take comfort and consolation. I shall not ask you to do anything wrong, as my only concern is to look at you and enjoy your friendship. At night I shall be with you in my own shape but when morning comes I shall go back to being a gazelle. We can enjoy ourselves and play without anyone knowing."

'I set aside a pleasant room for him in my quarters and at nightfall I would go there with him and lock the door on us both. He would show himself to me in the most handsome of shapes, and we would eat and drink, enjoying recitations of poetry and marvellous conversation. He would tell me about pleasant things and sing *jinn* songs, before lying down on my bed. We would embrace each other and renew our covenant, swearing that neither of us would betray the other or take any substitute. We were swimming in an ocean of love and following one another in its pleasure and in the enjoyment of its sweetness, with no fear of hostile fate or of observant eyes. We were two matching branches or two shoots of sweet basil, doing nothing evil to arouse suspicion, and our love could not be crushed until treacherous Time put us to the test.

'One night after we had been drinking we lay down for a healthful sleep, exchanging embraces, anointed with crushed musk, and enjoying conversation. The prince's eyes then closed, and he fell asleep before me, to my great sorrow and distress. I was looking at his face and enjoying his beauty as though I was looking at a full moon or a sun appearing through the cloud, but just then my father suffered a painful seizure, which roused him from his bed. The maids and the servants shrieked, and the attendants and the children tore their clothes. I lost my wits and, being reluctant to disturb the prince from his sleep, I gradually removed his hand from me and got up. I opened the door of my palace and called to my nurse, whom I took with me to my father.

'I stayed with him until he had recovered consciousness, but when the prince woke and did not find me there he went round the palace and when he could not see me he thought what any lover would think of his beloved and remained in a state of perplexity, alarm and distress. When he looked at the palace door and found it open, he was confirmed in his suspicion and, thinking that I had betrayed him, he turned back to his gazelle shape and fled away to his own land, alone and sorrowful. When I left my father and came back to the garden in an agitated state I could not find him. I rushed out, slapping my face in my confusion, not knowing in the darkness where to head for or where I was going. I went on from land to land and place to place until I despaired and was sure that I was going to die.

'During the course of my travels I came on a valley full of grass and greenery with a stream of running water whiter than milk. There were many ostriches there, as big as elephants, which were grazing on the greenery and going back and forth to the river. With them was a man of dazzling beauty who appeared to be herding them with a palm branch in his hand. When he saw me he called out harshly and came up, speaking roughly in a voice like rumbling thunder. "Woman, where have you come from?" he asked, adding: "There is no way through for you here."

'I burst into tears at this reception and exclaimed: "Alas for my gazelle! Alas for my master!" He then asked: "Who are you looking for?" and I told him: "I am Haifa', the daughter of King Muhallab of Persia, and I have come in search of a gazelle with white feet or a man in a shirt." He said: "This mountain marks the end of the lands of the *jinn*, and as it hard, black and smooth, you must go back to where you might find a way to your beloved. Otherwise you can spend the night as my guest, for it might be that a *jinni* will pass by, and I could ask him about this, for I feel pity for you in my heart."

'I sat with him, and he brought me food. When night fell a large and noisy company of *jinn* arrived. When I looked I saw amongst them a huge one in human shape riding on a snake as big as a towering palm-tree with another great snake wound round his head as a turban. When he opened his mouth fire came from his throat, and everyone else in his company, who were smaller than him, were mounted on snakes. He was preceded by a man carrying a banner, with huge and terrible flames flashing from the top of his spear.

'He stopped beside my host, who greeted him and after welcoming him asked him whether in the course of his many wanderings he had come across my gazelle. He said in reply that this was the son of the king of his people and that between us was a distance of a two-year journey. "What do you want from him," he asked, "for his father is an oppressive tyrant?" The ostrich-herd replied: "I want to meet him, as there is something that I need, so tell me the way." The snake rider said: "If you want to get to him, mount one of these ostriches of yours, choosing one that is large and old, whose feathers have moulted away. It will take you the two-year journey in a single night and bring you to an old woman. When you see her, give her my name and make her swear by what she owes me. God willing, she will take you to the land of the gazelle." He and his company then went off like a breath of wind, leaving the ground scorched.

'My host told me that this was the king of the snakes, who journeys from east to west. He added: "I shall take you to the old woman he mentioned. She is the queen of the crows who part lovers, while I am king of the ostriches who unite hearts. It was I who was responsible for the love between you and the gazelle, for these servants of mine roam through the world promoting love amongst God's servants. When you get to her tell her that Hirmas, king of the ostriches, sends her his greetings and says: 'This is my ring and my messenger. I feel pity in my heart for Haifa' and I have entrusted her with this letter for you.'"

'He wrote a letter, which he passed to me before summoning an enormous ostrich, which had lost all its feathers, leaving its skin smooth. He told it: "Take this human to the land of the old queen of the crows. See that she has an easy ride and then come back quickly." I sat on its back, holding on to its neck as it flew between sky and earth, keeping my eyes shut. When dawn broke it told me to open them and get down, for this was the country of the old queen. I dismounted and found myself in a red land with interlacing trees, some of which were red with red leaves and green citrus-like fruit. There were flowing streams with fish to be seen in the clear water feeding on the green weeds, while on every tree there were as many as a thousand crows, both black and piebald.

'While I was in the shade of the trees, admiring their leaves and their fruit, I suddenly came on a great red dome set over an ebony couch on which sat a grim-faced and frowning old woman wearing dyed clothes, with ten jewelled bracelets on each arm, ten anklets on each foot and ten rings on each finger. She had a crown of red gold studded with jewels of all kinds. She held a sceptre of green emerald and flanking her on each side were two black 'ifrits with hooked iron clubs in their hands.

'When she saw me she gave orders to these two who took hold of me and brought me before her. She addressed me harshly, asking who I was, where I lived, where I had come from and who had brought me to a land in which she had never seen a human before. I was so frightened by her and her appearance that I could find nothing to say in reply. She laughed more and more and repeated: "Where do you come from and how did you get to my country?" This unlocked my tongue, and I said: "I am al-Haifa', the daughter of King Muhallab of Persia. I fell in love with a jinni known as 'the white-footed gazelle'", and I went on to tell her everything that had happened from beginning to end until tears overcame me and I could no longer control myself. I then handed her the letter from the king of the ostriches. She took it and, after reading it, she exclaimed: "Welcome to the letter and the one who wrote it!"

'She went on: "I am the old queen of the jinn crows who part lovers and companions. My nature is rude and rough, and I have never shown pity to anyone. It is through me that husbands are parted from their wives, companions from companions, and lovers from their beloveds, and in every land I am represented in this by an emir of the crows. Out of all these I feel pity for you and you alone, because you have come here and submitted to me obediently. I also owe a debt of honour to the writer of the letter, who has asked me to be kind to you and to bring you to what you want, satisfying your needs and doing what you tell me."

'She gestured to one of her two 'ifrits and told him to fetch her the emir of the crows in Persia, and in no time at all he was back with a crow flapping its wings on its head. He took the bird before the queen, to whom it prostrated itself. She asked it: "What did you do in Persia on such-and-such a night in such-and-such a month?" The bird said: "I parted two dear friends who were suffering from the pangs of love. They were like two branches or in their perfect beauty like two gazelles. For two whole years they had enjoyed the finest fruits of love." "You wronged a pair of pure and charming lovers," she told it. "You should not have parted them, for mankind is divided according to ranks and classes, and in a case like this, you should have asked my permission, and, had I not acted wrongly myself, I would have had you beaten. So now go and fetch me the messenger of love who cautions friends so that he may return this woman to her beloved and fulfil her wishes." "What was it that she lost and who is she?" asked the crow. "Look at her," the queen told him, and when he did he said: "This is the lover of the white-footed gazelle, and she is the daughter of the king of Persia." The queen said: "Tell me in God's name why did you separate this pair?" "I was jealous," the crow said, "and I made a mistake about her which I shall never repeat with anyone else." "Bring me the messenger to take her to her beloved," the queen repeated.'

The crow hurried off, and the queen gave Haifa' a fruit from the trees, telling her to eat it. She said: 'When I did, I found that it tasted sweeter than honey, and before I had finished eating the crow came back with a pleasant-looking bird like a parrot. When the old queen saw it she said to me: "When you get to the land of your gazelle, go around until you see a shaikh under a dome. Go to him submissively, tell him your name and ask him for what you want." She then told the bird to carry me there and to do it quickly. I thought that it was too small, but the old queen had not finished speaking before it snatched me up and flew off with me between the sky and the earth, going on for the rest of the day and the following night, until next morning we came to a fresh and verdant land, delighting the eyes with the beauty of its flowers and its freshness. There were vast trees with green leaves like silk brocade and huge boughs as long as spears. The foul smell of their fruit, of a violent red, would almost take the breath away. Between them were streams of running water and gushing springs whiter than milk.

'The bird put me down there and flew off. I wandered by the streams and through the trees until, all of a sudden, I came across a splendid-looking shaikh with a handsome face sitting on a bench of white marble under a marble dome covered with draperies of green brocade. In front of him were foxes, male and female, and rabbits wrestling and playing with each other. He was holding a staff of green emerald and using this to join in the play, although for all that he looked sad and gloomy. In front of him was a lofty palace built of silver bricks and bars of red gold.

'When he saw me coming towards him he asked me sharply: "Damn you, who has brought you into this land of mine?" I paid no attention to this but threw myself before him and rubbed my cheek on him as I started to kiss his feet. He said: "Where do you come from, as I feel pity for you in my heart?" I told him that I was Haifa', the daughter of King al-Muhallab of Persia, and that I had come out in search of the white-footed gazelle. I then told him my whole story from beginning to end.

'When the shaikh heard about the gazelle he shed such bitter tears that he collapsed in a faint. When he recovered he said: "This gazelle is my dear son, and you too are dear to me thanks to all your toil, for both of you have suffered misery. Since he left you he has been straying through the wastes without eating or drinking and he talks bitterly of how you betrayed him. I am myself a king of the *jinn*, and these deserts are mine. My son often used to wander around in the form of a gazelle. He left me for two years, during which I heard nothing of him and could find no trace of him, leading me to think that he must have been hunted down. Then, after my great sorrow and despair, he came back to me and told me of how he had suffered thanks to this affair of yours and he told me about you and your treachery, before fleeing away in tears. I built him this palace that you can see, intending to marry him to his cousin in it, but he refused and said: 'Haifa' has rights that I owe her as well as oaths and covenants, treacherous as she may be. By God, I shall never enter this palace except with her.'

' "I was at a loss to know what to do about this, but now God Almighty has given you to us both and I want you to fulfil this covenant of his and to clear away his suspicion of you." I swore to him with solemn oaths that I had never betrayed him and that never for a second had I wanted to forget him. He thought it right to treat me as a guest and he gave me a fruit from a tree a morsel of which satisfied my hunger, and he poured me a glass of incomparably tasty wine smelling of musk. He then provided me with clothes the like of which I had never seen in my father's kingdom.

'When I was quiet and rested I fell asleep, and when I woke up the tears of my gazelle were on my face, and when I opened my eyes I saw him leaning over me. I almost died of joy but I got up, and after a long embrace we both fell to the ground, fainting, and remained unconscious for the rest of the day. When we recovered we were carried into the new palace, and servants and slaves flocked to us. We took care to reproach one another in such a way as to add fire to our longing.

'We continued to enjoy a life of comfort, honour, pleasure and joy, in the greatest pleasure. For many years time was kind to us, but then there came a day when I felt a longing for the lands of men and I told this to my prince, saying that I wanted to see them again and after enjoying myself there to come back. At first he would not allow it but after I pressed him he said that, as he wanted to please me, he would let me do what I wanted. He would transform me into a gazelle and go with me in the gazelle shape in which I had first seen him. "If we are hunted down," he said, "only a sorcerer or a diviner will be able to free us from our shapes."

'When we had been transformed, we left for the lands of men, passing by many marvellous things and seeing countless wonders that I cannot stop to explain. Our most remarkable experience, however, was when on our way we came across a formidable lion. The beast had scraped itself a hole and was sitting there on its tail, shedding a constant stream of miserable tears that had filled the hole. It would not attack any prey that it saw and if any travellers came in sight it would not look at them.

'When it saw me it called to me and my companion in a melancholy voice with sighs and groans: "Dark-eyed gazelle with your face fair as the moon, your radiant brow, your diadem and red crown, I, the red lion, say that fear of doing evil has led me to endure sorrow and injury and if I did not hope that a meeting was destined I would abandon myself to gloomy fears." I had begun to look at him, marvelling at his grief and his flooding tears, when you caught me, O king, and Mahliya, the daughter of al-Mutariq of Egypt, caught the white-footed gazelle. Alas, I don't know what has happened to it.'

She shed tears, and Mauhub was amazed by her story. He then collected himself and asked: 'Was it Mahliya who caught the white-footed gazelle?' and Haifa' confirmed this, adding: 'We were united in our love, and how is it with one who deceives the beloved with something distasteful in this love of theirs? This must afflict the lover with great suffering and the taste of death.' 'Haifa',' he asked, 'who are you talking about in these terms?' 'Your friend Mahliya,' she told him, 'who promised herself to you and used cunning to meet you, calling herself Mukhadi' and tricking you into obedience to her.' 'By God, was Mahliya Mukhadi'?' Mauhub asked, and she said: 'Yes, and it was she who sent you the gifts that kindled the fire of love in your heart, leaving you with sleepless nights and care-filled days.' It disturbed Mauhub to learn that this was Mahliya. He was too preoccupied to set off and spent a wakeful night longing to find some way to let her know that he knew what she had done.

When the lioness that had suckled Mauhub heard of the eloquence of the miserable lion whom Haifa' had described, she said: 'This must be my companion and the father of my cubs, for whom I have been longing ever since your father Shimrakh caught me. I have been away from him for so long that I thought he must have been hunted down and killed, but I find from what she said that he has been going through the lands in search of me, grieving at my loss, and he must now have found for certain where I am. You, Mauhub, owe me a debt, as you have been a son to me and a friend to my cubs. This is one of the great lions, as we are their rulers with dauntless followers. I should like you to do me the favour of allowing us to meet here in your courtyard and under the protection of your rule, accepting him as a prince to help you as a vizier, for he is the finest of companions and the best of helpers.' Mauhub willingly agreed and set out at once with his followers and his slaves, carrying the lioness and her cubs in front of him. He also took Haifa' so that she could show him where he was in the wild.

When he got near he told his companions to do nothing to disturb the lion or injure it. It was as Haifa' had described, and close to it he released the lioness and her cubs, at the sight of whom it prostrated itself to him, and then, when it went up to them, they joined in their complaints. The lioness then said: 'Lord of the lions, King Mauhub, may God be his helper, has been as a son to me and he has graciously brought us together. I do not want to leave him and I have promised him on your behalf that you will be a good companion to him and act as his vizier, so go obediently in front of him.' The lion did this, and Mauhub returned to his camp.

After he had dismounted, he called for Haifa', the lion, the lioness and the cubs and asked: 'What do you think I should do about this deceptive and calamitous Mahliya?' They said: 'We think, Your Majesty, that you should use your search for the white-footed gazelle as an excuse to go to her, and you can tell her that you know how she deceived you before you left. You can then learn whether she feels in her heart what you feel or even more.'

Mauhub approved of this advice and rode out immediately, most splendidly dressed, to the entrance of her tent and asked leave to enter. When this was given him, he went in, and Mahliya sat him on a couch of red gold studded with splendid jewels, while she herself sat behind a curtain that had been hung between them. After giving him a flattering greeting, she asked what had brought him to her when it was she who should have gone to him. He said: 'Separation from you burned my heart and filled me with loneliness, so I wanted to come to you as a guest so that this might strengthen our friendship.' She replied: 'Welcome to the guest who follows right guidance and is a lord and chief. It was good and generous of you to come here first; you have done us a great favour, and we extend our welcome to you.'

On her orders animals were slaughtered and food was prepared, with no mark of respect being omitted. He stayed with her all that day, enjoying the greatest luxury and pleasure in the matter of food, drink, conversation and play. When his emotions had been stirred by wine and he was settled in a mood of delight, he told one of the slave girls there to give him her lute and when she had passed it to him he sang a song of separation and burst into tears. Mahliya moaned and joined in his tears and had she not been behind the curtain she would have been shamefully exposed.

When she recovered she told her close companions and her viziers to go, which they did, leaving Mauhub alone. He then fingered his lute again and sang a song, in which he spoke of Mahliya's cunning deception, weeping until he collapsed unconscious. When he had regained consciousness Mahliya said: 'One song of yours that I have heard was that of a lover consumed by love, and in the next you claimed to have been deceived. Who is it that you love, and by whom were you deceived?' Mauhub took the lute and sang in three modes clearing away all ambiguity from what he had said. Then, filled with emotion, he drank again. Mahliya gave him no answer but turned to the wine and drank her fill, after which they spent the whole night there.

Next morning, when the effects of the wine had worn off, she asked him who had told him that she was Mahliya after she had successfully tricked him, and he amazed her by telling her the story of Haifa' from start to finish. She then said that, thanks to repeated letters from her father, she had made up her mind to leave, although she was consumed by love and grieved at having to part from him. Mauhub shed tears at this and made her promise solemnly not to betray him, as he would not betray her, in words, the forming of friendships, or in joy and delight. They exchanged solemn oaths, and when they parted Mauhub asked her about the white-footed gazelle. She told him that she had sent it on ahead with the baggage and the servants, but that she would return it to him without delay.

He took leave of her in tears and went back to his tent, after she had presented him with ten horses and magnificent robes of honour, and when he got there he sent her many times more than she had given him. She left immediately, and he went at the same time, both complaining and in tears, and when they had settled back at home Mahliya wrote to him to congratulate him on his safe arrival and he replied to congratulate her in the most eloquent of terms.

When his messenger reached her she had him brought up to her and treated him with kindness, asking him how Mauhub was. He said: 'By God, lady, he cannot sleep at night or rest by day. The only friends with whom he talks are the lion, the lioness and Haifa', to whom he complains and with whom he weeps.' When Mahliya heard him mention Haifa' she told him to describe her, and he said: 'I cannot do this and can only say: "Glory to her Creator Who formed her!"' Mahliya thought about this and wrote a letter with no introduction or good wishes, which read: 'By God, Whom we recognize as Lord of mankind, we shall not meet again nor will you ever enjoy my love, as treachery is in your nature and you are an inventor of lies.' She sealed this with pitch and gave it to the messenger, telling him that if he brought back an answer she would inflict a painful punishment on him.

The messenger took the letter back to Mauhub who, on seeing that it was sealed with pitch, realized that Mahliya was breaking with him but did not know why. He opened it, noting what was in it, and in his bewilderment he took out the gifts that she had given him so that he might remember her. He was weeping and sobbing until he came to the mirror and the carpet and when he looked in the mirror he seemed to see her sitting with him, the only thing missing being the lady herself.

When the messenger had left Mahliya she sent an aggressive eagle with magical powers carrying a message under its wing which it was to drop on Mauhub. She told it to snatch the mirror and the carpet away from him and to hurry back, bringing no answer. In her letter she wrote: 'Being alone with Haifa' has taken your attention away from your solemn covenants, and your love for her has made you forget your other loves, you untrustworthy mine of treachery. It is not to be thought of that I should send you the white-footed gazelle or see you coming on foot beneath my stirrup. Goodbye.' The eagle flew off quickly and, having dropped the letter in Mauhub's room, it snatched up the mirror and the carpet from in front of him and soared away back to Mahliya.

Mauhub was sure that the disaster that had struck him was caused by Haifa', and he exiled her from his country. He stripped off his fine clothes, exchanging them for a gown of hair, and he neither ate nor drank. When his father heard of this he came and said to him: 'My son, I have gathered wealth and men only in order to protect you and bring you what you want. So what misfortune is it that has now struck you?' Mauhub was forced to tell him about the situation, and his father urged him to write a letter of excuse and to renew his oath, adding: 'No fault can be found with that, and it may be that she feels uncertain and will be inclined to accept your excuse.'

Mauhub wrote a letter shorn of the usual style of scribes, excusing himself and swearing that he had not betrayed Mahliya and would never deceive her. He sent this off with his original messenger, but when she learned that the man was near her land she sent someone to take the letter from him and she had him fastened to a cross for eleven days, before secretly letting him go. He fled as fast as he could back to Mauhub and told him what had happened, at which his sighs redoubled.

When he told his father how Mahliya had treated his messenger, his father said: 'My son, these treasuries are at your disposal. March against her with your men, or else spend all this money on her or tell me what you think.' Mauhub said: 'Father, I don't want to attack her before I have presented my excuse to her, especially as she is lodged firmly in my heart. I think that I should write to her to try to win her over, telling her of the state I am in and confirming my solemn covenant. If she gives a favourable reply, I shall go to her to ask for her hand in marriage, but if she intends evil, then it will be for me to act.' 'This is a matter for you,' his father replied.

The letter that Mauhub wrote was as follows: 'In the Name of the

Eternal God, the Generous Protector: Queen of rulers, clearer away of doubt, I read your letter, which came close to my heart and dispelled my cares, and I understood what it was you were talking about. Since I parted from you I have not tasted sleep, nor have I taken anyone to my heart, whether legally or against the law, nor have I felt inclined to listen to anyone's conversation. Because of you I have sat amongst the ashes and through grief for you I have dressed in mourning, depriving myself, thanks to you, of the company of God's servants. The lands have shrunk for me through grief, and my heart is obsessed by love for you. My mind is crippled because of you, and the sword of love has slain my body. You have dealt well with me [lac.] and if you turn to me in kindness, my weakness will leave me and my sickness will be cured. This letter is both an excuse and a warning, as I have not found anything that should be concealed. It is the last reproach that I will send you as before this I sent you solemn covenants, but you turned away from them to falsehoods and lies.'

He sealed the letter with musk and ambergris and looked for a messenger to carry it to Mahliya, but could find no one thanks to the distance to be covered and fear caused by her treatment of his first messenger. The mate of the lioness who had suckled him said that he would go and force Mauhub's words on her. Mauhub thanked him warmly and passed over the letter, after which he took his leave and left. The lioness said to him: 'Lion, I hold you very dear to me in my heart. You are going to Syria, where lions abound, and you will continue to look at other lionesses. I am afraid you may betray me during your journey, so swear an oath for me.'

After doing this the lion set off across the desert wastes and when he was within a three-day journey of Egypt Mahliya was told that he was coming from Mauhub. She sent an old sorceress to trick him and take away his letter. To meet him, she sat in a lovely meadow with trees and streams, facing a tomb surrounded by reeds, wearing mourning and weeping loudly. By her side was a jar of wine, with the body of a skinned beast, and there was a lighted fire and a cup filled with what appeared to be perfume of musk and ambergris. Beside the old woman was an image of a woman covered by a robe.

When the lion saw her he crouched down in front of her as he was both tired and ravenously hungry and he coveted the skinned beast. He was astonished by what he saw, and the old woman asked him: 'Lord lion, what are you looking at me for? I am a tearful old woman with a sorrowful heart.' 'Do not be alarmed,' he told her; 'I am a stranger from a distant land and when I saw you sobbing and weeping by this tomb with food and wine in front of you, I wondered what you were doing and sat down to rest in this meadow.' The old woman said: 'I see that you have a letter,' and the lion told her: 'I am a merchant's messenger carrying a bill of exchange to an Egyptian merchant so that he may get his money.' She told him to leave her and go about his business, but he swore that he would not go until she had told him who was buried there and what connection she had with him.

The old woman said: 'He was my son-in-law,' and she pointed to the image and the robe that covered it. 'He was a good husband and a good son-in-law,' she went on, 'and this daughter of mine was one of the most perfectly lovely ladies of her time, the best of wives and the truest companion, as well as being the most generous and graceful. No woman has mourned her husband as sorrowfully and tearfully as she has, but because of this sorrow and these tears she has just now been overcome by sleep.' The lion said: 'I have never seen anyone show greater sorrow for a son-in-law than you, may God reward you. But tell me what has this perfume and the skinned beast to do with your grief.' 'Lion,' she told him, 'my son-in-law who is buried here was himself a wild lion who could transform himself into the shape of the handsomest of men. The skinned beast is his food, and what is in the cup is his perfume, for when he was alone with my daughter he used to eat this meat, drink the wine and use this perfume, after which they would sleep, enjoying the happiest of lives. As you see, he then died, and we never forget him, night or day.'

The lion said: 'You should know, old woman, that I myself am in mourning for a lovely and graceful woman who preferred me to her mother and father, setting me on a pinnacle and recognizing my rightful position. She died, and I have remained in solitary loneliness with no resting place in any land. Most of my time I spend here wandering aimlessly in my grief. What I used to drink and the perfume that I used were what you have here and, by God, I am of kingly stock. Would you agree to marry me to your daughter, for I can see that you are the best of mothers-in-law, and I am sure that she would be the best of wives?'

'By God, my son,' replied the old woman, 'I can see no good in today's husbands, who frustrate and restrict their wives. If I were sure that you would treat her as well as her first husband, whose grave this is, I would agree to your marriage, although I am not sure that she would obey me, as I know that since his death her great grief has meant that she has had no interest in men.' 'Mother,' the lion told her, 'I would be the best of husbands and companions to her and I would make her forget her first husband. Further, I am a stranger with no kin, so make me your slave.' The old woman said: 'Give me your solemn oath so that both I and my daughter can have confidence in you.'

The lion did this and when the old woman was sure of him, she said: 'These covenants that you have made before God and that lie between you and me mean that you will work hard to give your wife a good life without restricting her or allowing her husband's family to gloat over her.' When the lion had agreed warmly she told him to come forward and share in their food and drink. On hearing this, he came up and ate until he was full, as well as drinking until he had become drunk, and in this state he fell asleep. The old woman then removed the image and, taking Mauhub's letter from the lion, she flew off with it to Mahliya.

When Mahliya had read it she wrote a reply, which the old woman took back to the lion, substituting it for Mauhub's letter. She then sat down, weeping and wailing, and she was doing this when the lion woke up. When he could not see the image he asked what was wrong with her and what had her daughter done. She said: 'When she woke up I told her we had agreed that she should marry you. She looked at you and said that you were suitably noble but she would refuse you because her first husband, unlike you, had a docked tail. She was afraid that she would be blamed for having too many husbands, and if you were like him she would marry you so that people would not notice what she had done.' 'If this is what you would advise, then please yourself by cutting off my tail,' the lion told her. The old woman passed him over to devils in human shape and told one of them to cut off the tail, which he did, and she then told him to cauterize the stump with the fire, which almost killed him.

She then said: 'My daughter has gone to her family so that they may deck her out as befits a bride. Meanwhile, fetch a ram and some wine so that we can prepare a feast for her family as you consummate the marriage.' 'By God,' replied the lion, 'I don't know where to find a ram or wine, or where I could look for something to live on, as I am a stranger with little knowledge of this land. Find me someone who will lend me money in return for a note of exchange, and I shall pay him back.' The old woman said: 'There is a merchant here who knows us and who has the meat and wine you need. He used to lend money to my first son-in-law, and if you want I will get you to meet him so that he can give you what you want.'

He told her to do that, and she told him to come so that she could arrange a meeting. The lion followed her, and she went to one of the devils, who was in the form of a merchant, and she told him: 'Give this son-in-law of mine what he wants and he will pay you back, as he is rich.' The devil gave him a ram and wine as well as whatever else he asked for, and the old woman slaughtered the ram and strained the wine. She then told the lion to sit until she brought him her daughter. She then went off and was away until nightfall, when she came back, saying that her daughter had a fever.

She kept on putting him off for some days, and he grew disturbed. Then one day when he was sleeping she came and shook him awake, causing him to start up in alarm and ask her what was wrong. 'The merchant has come to look for you,' she told him, 'and he said that he wanted me to take him to you so he could get his money back. I am here to tell you, for I'm afraid that, if you can't pay him now, he will put you in prison.' 'Can he do that?' the lion asked, and she said: 'Yes, by God, he did it to my first son-in-law until one of his eyes glazed over and he became so mangy and weak that he almost died.' 'How can we keep him away from me until I get married, as I am afraid that he might prevent me?' the lion asked. 'There is a way,' the old woman told him, 'for if I cut off your ears and nose and shave off your whiskers, when he comes he won't recognize you, and you will be able to consummate your marriage.' 'Do it,' the lion told her, and when she had done it all, she cut meat for him from the skinned beast, which he ate, and she poured him wine until he fell into a drunken sleep.

She then approached him with a hot iron, whose heat startled him awake. She told him: 'The suffering you must endure for this woman cannot compare with what her first husband endured.' 'And what was that?' he asked. She said: 'Queen Mahliya in Egypt suffers from a disease of the stomach that attacks her every year, and the pain can only be relieved by the liver of a lion. This is the time for her next attack, and she has sent out troops to find a lion. They are on their way here now.' 'What is to be done?' he asked, and she said: 'Go off with this bill of exchange of yours and when you have got the money for it come back after the lion hunt has finished and you can consummate your marriage. For this is what the queen did with my first son-in-law, who lies buried here. She had him caught and removed his liver, which she cut up in pieces, and we buried him here with us, as you see.'

The lion was very disturbed and told her: 'I'm afraid that I may meet her men on my way, so think of some trick that might rescue me from them.' She said: 'Go to that cup and smear your body and face with its perfume and then take this ring and fasten it on your neck, so that when they see you they will think that you are a fool.' The lion did all that and then fled away as fast as he could, hiding by day and travelling at night, until he reached Mauhub, altered and deformed.

'Noble lion,' Mauhub said, 'you are in any ugly state, so tell me what happened.' The lion told him the whole story from beginning to end, of his encounter with the old woman and how he had fled from Mahliya lest she kill him and cut out his liver. He added that he had not been able to give her the letter. Mauhub laughed at the story, astonished at the trick that had been played but furiously angry at the stupidity of the lion and how his passion for women had got the better of him. He then courteously asked him to pass over the letter, but when he saw Mahliya's writing he snorted and cursed before telling the lion: 'I didn't think that you would manage things as badly as this. Didn't you realize that this is the answer to my letter written in her own hand?' The lion wept at what had happened to him, and when the lioness who had suckled Mauhub heard what the old woman had done with him and how ugly he had become, she abandoned him and would not go near him.

Mauhub went to tell his father what had happened to the lion, and he opened Mahliya's letter to read to him. She had written: 'In the name of God, hidden in splendour, Lord of heaven and earth, Who makes the water flow: know, Mauhub, that whoever puts on the robes of contemptible treachery and deceives his dear ones loses all respect. How often does he want to reproach his friends for abandoning him? If he aims at glory, he is numbered amongst the miserable, and if he seeks, he will not reach his goal and will be close to injury on his return. If you are threatening me with the number of your warriors, you face defeat and have lost your wits. The likes of one who has a lion as his vizier is despicable. Come or go. As far as I am concerned you can do what you want, as it is all equal to me. Goodbye.'

When Mauhub had finished reading the letter his father said: 'My son, I advised you after the first letter that, before she could enlist help against you, you should go and take her by surprise. You refused and would not accept my advice. So now I think that you should go to her yourself with your troops and your servants and not rely on anyone else. When you get to her country you can take her by force, for you should not humble yourself before a weak woman with an insignificant kingdom, may God exalt you. Wealth is collected in this world to be spent in the pursuit of love, while men are recruited and equipment and weapons are acquired to give support.'

Mauhub told his father that he would follow his advice and he collected his people and those who knew the way to Egypt, asking them how he should go. They said that he should go by sea, as the land route was hard and difficult, and its lack of water and distance would not support armies. Accordingly Shimrakh ordered the launching of fifty ships, ten of which were filled with savage lions under the command of his own lions. Another ten carried wild elephants commanded by one of his viziers, as these were used in battle at that time, while thirty were filled with horses, men and weapons. Mauhub was on the finest and best of them with the most equipment.

His father, together with his countrymen, said goodbye to him as he set out and the ships put to sea with a favourable wind. They enjoyed a good and a safe voyage until they reached a place called Raya. Mahliya's father had died there, and the sorcerers together with the people of the country were unsettled. They knew about her affair with Mauhub and thought of deposing her, but she tricked them by providing herself with a strong castle in which she could be safe from them and alone with Mauhub.

The sorcerers, who had been in the service of the pharaoh, lived in Samannud and its districts. There was a division between two groups of them, each one of which said that the queen should live with them, and when this became clear, they collected wise counsellors and asked their advice as to where to build a fortress equidistant between the lands of the sorcerers and those of the ordinary citizens, to which everyone would have to go.

They could find no better or more extensive a place than the site of this fortress, whose stones were less numerous than its swarms of reptiles, snakes, scorpions and other wild creatures. It was a home of *jinn*, and the islands in the sea there were overrun by crocodiles. Mahliya was advised to build whatever kind of fortress she wanted there. Accordingly she summoned a chamberlain of hers called Nun and told him what to build, laying down limits and defining height, thickness and strength.

Nun hurried to obey, and the queen provided great rewards for her subjects who had been on the point of abandoning allegiance to her but whose services she now employed. To start with Nun found himself thwarted by the swarming reptiles who were the masters of the place, so he collected the sorcerers and asked them what he should do about this. They told him that reptiles and snakes would hide away if they heard the screech of an owl, and so he collected owls and let them loose in the danger spot. The reptiles dispersed, and the wild beasts were hunted down. When the site had been cleared of them, the stones were removed and the fortress was built. At their widest, its walls had room enough for twenty horses, and the fortress itself covered three square miles. At its corners were four towers, in each of which a thousand riders with their weapons could pass the night, and surmounting these were a thousand turrets around whose roofs a horseman could ride. In the centre of each was a great pit in which fires were kindled.

The west wall was set in the middle of the Nile, with two gates, one for the common people and the other for their superiors. The gates could only be reached by boat, and at that time there was no island there but only the stream which now flows behind the island. One branch of this was allowed to flow through the middle of the fortress and come out at its upper end. When the castle was destroyed, the present island was formed over its ruins, and the river was diverted away from where it had been. On the land side there was one gate used for hunting parties and excursions. These gates were made of gilded brass, and every one of them was topped with a huge dome of silver covered with various types of brocade, on which was placed a great bird that would whistle when the wind blew. It took forty men to open and shut each of them.

In the middle of this was a great palace, forty cubits high and forty square, supporting a golden dome, with four doors of sandalwood, juniper, teak, ebony and Indian aloes wood. The doors were covered with hangings and heavy brocade, and above each of them was placed a cleverly constructed brass falcon that turned and whistled with the wind. Mahliya would sit there as she could see whoever was coming by land or water over a distance of four miles.

The place was filled with lovely slave girls, and Nun moved all Mahliya's possessions there and beside it he built a church for her with a thousand steps to match the number of her viziers. When she went up to it, one of them would sit on each step until she came out after Mass. A thousand silver candles were hung there, fuelled with oil of jasmine, and there were pictures of prophets and saints, all this being looked after by a hundred Byzantine eunuchs. Ten other churches were built for the congregations of ordinary people. Around the fortress palm-trees were planted, seeds sown and canals constructed. When all this work had been done, it was surrounded by talismans to ward off snakes, wild beasts and all kinds of reptiles, as well as crocodiles, none of which ever came near it. Two beacons were placed there that could be seen from Bulaq. This is now called 'The Island', but originally it was the causeway leading to the garden of the fortress. It could only be used by those who had some wrong to complain of or some business to transact.

When there was nothing left to do, Nun went to greet Mahliya and tell her that her fortress had been completed, detailing what he had done and wishing her the fulfilment of her wishes and continued prosperity. She gave him robes of honour and rewarded him generously, but she kept the fortress shut, swearing that she would only enter it with Mauhub, whom she never forgot or ceased to mention, thanks to the pleasure she took in his name.

It was just when the fortress was completed that Mauhub arrived at Raya, which is two days' journey from Qulzum. He disembarked and held a meeting of his army leaders and his strategists. Before that he let his viziers know that he was proposing to advance on Egypt and attack Mahliya treacherously and without warning. 'A king like you,' they told him, 'should not use treachery. Your superiority to Mahliya means that you have no reason to attack her. Delay; move slowly and send her a letter of warning. This will give you the moral high ground, while another point is that we know nothing of this country and of its roads, and if we don't have to fight that will be our good fortune.'

Mauhub accordingly wrote to Mahliya, telling her that he had come to her country because of his yearning for her, his desire to be near her and other such remarks. He sent this off, but when the messenger got to Qulzum, its governor imprisoned him and wrote to Mahliya, telling him that Mauhub's ships had arrived, carrying a large and well-equipped force. He also forwarded Mauhub's letter, which she sent back unopened with its seal unbroken, saying that it should be returned to its writer.

When Mauhub got it back in this state he was furiously angry as well as saddened. In order to fight against his lions Mahliya had prepared four thousand buffaloes with their horns covered in iron and their necks protected by collars of Chinese steel, while against the elephants she prepared five thousand wildcats. She collected her men and organized her armies, supplying them with money and arms. All these were sent to Qulzum while Mahliya herself, without telling her people, went to a hermitage near Qulzum and stayed there.

When Mauhub's lion saw his master's anger, mixed as it was with passion for Mahliya, he went up to him and said: 'Know, O king, that I am the one who has suffered in body and been robbed of what I found sweet. I want you to send me out to start the fight so that I may settle her affair for you, destroy her armies and bring her to you.' Mauhub ordered him to attack, and Mahliya sent out her buffaloes. When they met she encouraged them to attack the lions, almost all of whom were killed within a day. There were only two wounded survivors, one of whom was Mauhub's lion, who was ashamed to go back to him and so went to the mountains of Qulzum, where he hid in a cave. The other went to Mauhub and told him what had happened, to his great grief.

He next sent out the elephants, telling their leader to make sure of victory in any attack. When they got to the land of Qulzum they were drawn up in ranks, with the cavalry behind them, and swords carried in their trunks, ready for what their leader was sure would be a successful attack. Before he knew it, however, the wild cats charged, fastening on to the trunks of the elephants and biting them, while seizing the men in their usual way. As a result both elephants and men were all killed except for their leader, who went back with the news to Mauhub.

Mauhub's spirit was broken and, realizing that he was beaten, he thought of returning home. His viziers and his closest advisors came to him and said: 'May God recompense the king for what has been lost, but his own survival and that of those who are with him is the most important thing. It was their lack of intelligence that caused the loss of the lions, for it is thanks to intelligence and organization that we see men conquer in war. We praise God, Victorious in battle, Who clears away sorrows. Stay where you are out of sight of the fighting and we shall settle the affair of Mahliya for you.'

It was then that Mahliya sent a beautiful bird under a spell to trick Mauhub. He was lying on his back, thinking things over, with his servants around him. The bird settled on the mast of his ship, and, for all that he was an experienced hunter, he had never seen a finer. It had a red beak with yellow eyes, green wings and a white body. He was so filled with admiration for its beauty that it took up the whole of his attention, diverting him from his problems. He took a cross-bow and shot a pellet at the bird, but missed. It flew off to the shore, where it sat on a palm-tree, and Mauhub called for a small boat, boarded it and, after landing, he shot at the bird but missed again. It flew to another tree, and Mauhub followed it. He was so eager to catch it that he followed it from tree to tree and place to place until his search had led him far out of sight of his fleet.

Mahliya sent clever sorcerers to the ships, whose anchor cables they cut, and they stirred up the sea against them, leaving them to stray, scatter and founder. At that the bird flew for safety high into the sky, and Mauhub, despairing of success, went back to his ships, but could find no trace of them or learn what had happened. He sat weeping in self-pity all day long, and as evening approached Mahliya sent out a fisherman, who was also a sorcerer, to bring him to her. As he sat by the shore shedding sad tears the fisherman approached with his net over his shoulder and halted opposite him. Every fish that he caught he would broil and eat.

Mauhub went up to him and, after greeting him, he asked: 'Where do you come from, for I have seen nobody else here?' The man told him: 'I am a hermit from one of Queen Mahliya's lands and I abandoned all my worldly goods to come and live here on my own, worshipping my Lord and living off the fish I catch. I go for shelter to the peak of that mountain there, where I pray. Before today I have never seen anyone here, so where do you come from?' Mauhub told him: 'I am a stranger from a distant land. I came here with some ships, but the wind wrecked them, and my companions have all been drowned, leaving me alone, and I don't know the way.' 'Had there been any good in you and had God wished it for you, you would have drowned with your companions. I think, however, that you must have disobeyed Him and you brought ill fortune on your companions so that they died and you remained to be put to the test in this world.'

Mauhub shed bitter tears and groaned loudly. He said: 'Fisherman, I am hungry and thirsty, so would you allow me to share some of this food with you?' The man replied: 'I have made a covenant with my Lord that I shall only catch enough to feed myself and I shall not help anyone who disobeys Him in any worldly matter. I am not going to break my word but, if you want, I shall lend you my net and teach you how to fish.' 'Do as you want,' said Mauhub, and the fisherman handed over the net and taught him how to cast it.

He spent the whole day making casts but caught not a single fish until in the evening, when he was both hungry and tired, a black fish swam into the net and was trapped. Mauhub took it and broiled it over the fisherman's fire. He then asked for water, and the man directed him to a spring at the foot of the mountain. He went there and drank, after which he came back to look for the fisherman, who was not to be found. He lamented his fate and shed more and more tears, spending the night miserable and lonely, unable to sleep.

In the morning the fisherman came back, and, after finishing his own fishing, he lent Mauhub his net. Things went on like this for some days until one day the fisherman handed over the net, saying: 'Take it and use it, for I want to go off on business of my own.' 'Brother,' said Mauhub, 'show me the way to some inhabited spot where I can put things right for myself by fishing.' The fisherman showed him the way to Qulzum and then left.

Mauhub set off, fishing along the way, until he came to Mahliya's hermitage, which was by the shore, and sat down wearily in its shade. His feet were swollen, and he had lost his colour and his good looks. The fishing bag was tied to his arm, and he put the net that was over his shoulder down in front of him before lying down on his side to rest, tired and full of sorrowful thoughts about himself.

Mahliya looked down from her hermitage, dressed as an anchorite in wool and black hairs, and when Mauhub caught sight of her radiant face he was so bemused and astonished that he almost lost his wits. He stared open-mouthed like one demented, and it never occurred to him that this was Mahliya. For her part, she looked away as though she did not want to see him again. Then, when she realized that love had overcome him and that he was in the grip of passion, she turned to look at him and said: 'You who are sheltering in the shade and staring at what is not allowed you, is there anything you need? I am a woman, and this is no place for men, but I shall give you what you need and you can then go.' Mauhub said: 'I am a stranger from a distant land. I came here with some ships, but the wind wrecked them, and my companions were all drowned. I was thrown up on the beach, and a fisherman whom I met gave me this net, with which I have been catching enough to eat until Almighty God brings me relief. It was the fisherman who told me how to get to the town that lies ahead so that I might make a living there, but when I felt weak I sat down in the shade of your hermitage. I am going to leave you, but show me mercy and kindness.'

Mahliya said: 'Young man, you may have sinned in the past and broken some covenants, so that your God has punished you and reduced you to this state.' Mauhub burst into a flood of miserable tears and moaned loudly as Mahliya asked why he was doing this. 'Is it all because of something your superior inflicted on you, or because of your sins or because you have been parted from your beloved?' she said. He told her: 'I weep for the kingdom I used to have, which I have exchanged for this misery, and your reproaches have doubled my sorrow.' She said: 'Don't you know that whoever defies his Lord, disobeying His commands and breaking His covenant, is humiliated and demeaned by Him and he should then revert to humiliating and blaming himself? I feel pity for you and had I not got to go to the city of Mahliya, where she is in the habit of meeting the monks, I would make you a room of palm leaves in this hermitage of mine, where you could shelter at night after spending the day fishing. But, God willing, I must go tomorrow morning.' 'Pure nun,' Mauhub replied, 'may I be your ransom for what you teach of intelligence, trust and religion. As I told you, I am a stranger here and I know nothing about these parts or where I should go from here. If you would think of taking me as a servant to stay with you and help you with your affairs, I would go wherever you want and come back when you do, serving you as long as I live.' Mahliya replied: 'Young man, you should know that people think of me as being modest, abstemious and trustworthy. My reputation is well known and my worth is established. If you have to stay with me in my service, then make a solemn pact that you will not seek to harm or injure me and you will not associate with anyone else apart from me. I see that there is some evil in your eye which indicates treachery.'

As she addressed him, the sweetness of her speech and its delightful tone added both to his sorrow and his love, and he gave her a solemn assurance that he would not betray her or play her false as long as he lived. She ended by saying that members of her religious order took no man as a servant without inscribing their names on his body, and that if he wanted to go with her he would have to follow the rules laid down by her predecessors. 'As you want,' he told her, and she said: 'Write these words on your arm: "The servant of his lord, the master of the monks".' He did that, and they spent the night talking to each other.

In the morning she came out from her hermitage with a tall Egyptian donkey, which was covered with a blue fur made of fine goat's hair. She mounted and told Mauhub to wait there until she came back from the queen in the Egyptian capital. 'By God, lady,' he told her, 'I should like to see the queen's lands as I have heard how splendid they are and I should like you to tell me to go either ahead of or behind your donkey.' She said: 'If you must do that, then take your net with you so you can be thought to be a fisherman, as I don't want anyone in the queen's city to know that you are my servant.' So Mauhub, with his net over his shoulder, followed at a distance behind the donkey until, when they got to a pool at 'Ain al-Shams, she told him to stay there, admiring the splendid crops until she came back. He did what he was told and cast his net into the pool, catching a number of fish.

As for Mahliya, when she entered her city she was met by the citizens and her viziers. She ordered a throne of red gold set with jewels and surmounted by a lofty dome covered with hangings of brocade to be placed in her orchard by the banks of the Nile. She then sat there, wearing her most splendid clothes and her finest ornaments, with the royal crown on her head and a garland around her forehead. There were golden crosses in front of her; to her right were a thousand Byzantine eunuchs of various races with belts of gold and silver, carrying clubs, while on her left were a thousand Nubian mamluks and a thousand slave girls of various races, carrying musical instruments. She collected her chamberlains and viziers, together with her nurses and her personal friends, and she ordered the citizens to assemble. She announced that the enemy had been defeated and that those of her subjects who had been wronged had received justice from the wrong-doer. She had animals slaughtered and gave away wealth, receiving the thanks of the people, who went away praying for her long life.

On one of the staircases of the palace she was playing with her royal ring and then claimed that it had fallen from her hand into the river, where it had been swallowed by a fish, and she claimed that she would recognize the fish if she saw it. The ring was a ruby the size of a goose egg and it had been an ancestral treasure passed on through generations for use on royal occasions and it was of inestimable value. Its loss disturbed her subjects, and she made a great show of grief before sending out a herald to announce to everyone that any fisherman or diver who found the queen's ring would be granted half her kingdom and would share the royal treasuries with her.

Fishermen were collected from every region, and when Mauhub was discovered fishing beside the lake of 'Ain al-Shams he was taken with the others to the queen. She told them all that the ring had slipped from her hand and described the fish that had swallowed it. The ring, she said, gave sanction to her rule and was her crowning glory, and it was because of this that she would share her wealth and kingdom with whoever caught the fish.

The fishermen stood before her and cast their nets, and servants took every fish that they caught and showed it to her, but she would say that it was not the one that had swallowed the ring. She started to look at Mauhub, who was amongst them shedding sorrowful tears, and she said: 'Ask this man why he is not casting his net and why he is hanging back so miserably.' Mauhub told her servant: 'I am a stranger of royal birth; I am not good at fishing and I don't have the courage to stand before the queen.'

When the servant passed this reply to the queen, she told him: 'Tell him to cast his net and he may find that this is his lucky day.' Mauhub made a cast, trembling with shame and fear, and he caught a big fish which the servants brought up to the queen, who exclaimed that this was the one, making a great display of joy that it had been caught. On her orders her attendants dispersed, as she said that no one was to take charge of removing the ring from it except the man who caught it.

On her orders Mauhub was brought to her, and she had a curtain lowered between the two of them. She then said: 'My ring was not lost, but I wanted to put the citizens to a test. This is the ring.' She threw it into his lap, and he kissed it and returned it to her in amazement. She then said: 'I want to ask you, fisherman, why you held back from fishing, why you were weeping and what it was you said about being of royal birth. Tell me the truth. If I find you telling a lie, I shall punish you, while if you tell the truth, you will get what you want.'

Mauhub said: 'I am Mauhub, son of al-Shimrakh, the king of Zabaj, whom you met in the church of Jerusalem, and you know what happened between us.' This made a great impression on her, and she wanted to investigate further. 'Did I not forbid you to lie, and yet you started with a lie?' 'What lie do you think I told?' he asked, and she said: 'Mauhub is a great, powerful and respected king, with a large army, attendants and slaves. There are rights that I owe him; I am bound to him by solemn covenants, and there are tokens that we share between us, whereas you are only a poor, wretched fisherman.' When she said that, Mauhub told her: 'High queen, I must tell you that haste in its various forms, the dominant power of love, distress and the disdain of kings have brought me to the state that you can see.' 'Prove it,' she told him, 'and give me a clear account of your circumstances.'

Mauhub told her what had happened to him since he left her up to when his ships were destroyed and the fisherman had given him his net, but he said nothing of his dealings with the 'nun'. She said: 'If you are telling the truth about being Mauhub, it was not hastiness or royal power that brought you down but your lustful glances, your treachery and fickleness, and the difference between what you say and what is concealed in your heart.' In reply he said: 'As for your hints about Haifa', don't you see that my feelings for her were linked to the fact that she was under a spell? By God, I never at any time betrayed you, and you were wrong to punish me, beginning by taking the mirror which brought me joy. In spite of that I never failed to keep my oath.' 'You wily traitor,' she said, 'even if I accept what you have said to excuse yourself about Haifa', what about the nun whom you agreed to obey, writing this on your arm? You are very far from being wronged in what happened to you, for this was only part of what you deserved. But now that you have tasted the punishment for treachery my thirst for revenge is satisfied, I can go back to showing you my generous nature, as love for you is mixed within my flesh and blood. I proclaimed to the people that you would be my associate in my rule, and this was a trick that I played on them. It was for you that I built a lofty palace, filling it with servants and slaves, and I swore that I would only enter it after you.'

She told him to sit in a corner of the orchard, which he did, and she then summoned an assembly of her people. At a private meeting with her viziers she said: 'I swore an oath before God that I would share my kingdom and my wealth with whoever recovered my royal treasure for me. God has decreed that this should be restored by the hand of a descendant of the mighty pharaohs, whom I have found to be a worthy equal. You know that this wealth cannot properly be shared except through joyful marriage, for I cannot break my word or fail in what I ordered.' They said: 'Do what you want, God bless you, for you do not need counsel from any of us.'

She collected the patriarchs, the deacons, the bishops and the monks to marry her to Mauhub. She slaughtered animals, dispersed money, distributed charitable gifts and gave away splendid robes of honour, making this a regular feast day. The vizier who had built the palace was instructed to renew the furnishings and the hangings. Women were brought in from every region; musicians were collected, and a message was sent to Mauhub's land to let his father know what had happened and how he had prospered. He was delighted and sent to Mahliya and to his son an indescribable quantity of gifts and wealth, together with Haifa' and the lioness with her two cubs.

Mahliya had a private meeting with Haifa' and asked for the whole story of her dealings with the white-footed gazelle. She then called for the sorcerers, and on her orders they released him from his gazelle shape and restored him to his proper form. When she asked for his story, he confirmed what Haifa' had said, and she promised to unite them when she had finished her banquet. She also called for the lioness and her cubs and sent to have her mate picked out from all the lions who were strangers to Egypt, and she arranged things between them.

When the vizier had finished setting the palace and its furnishings to rights, Mahliya had a general proclamation made that everyone was to come to the banquet, while anyone who did not would be punished. People flocked in from all parts, and the palace was given the most splendid and complete decorations. Mauhub mounted on a tall sorrel horse of good breed, with a jewelled belt around his robes, preceded by all the other kings and wearing the crown of Mahliya's father, which was a mark of royalty handed down from his ancestors. There were emirs around him and in front of him, while all the bishops, deacons and patriarchs were reciting the Gospel to him and invoking God's help and His blessing. So many candles were burning with incense and ambergris that their smoke filled the sky. When he entered the palace the slave girls there greeted him with their various musical instruments, and he was showered with musk.

Mahliya followed, riding in an ivory palanquin studded with sapphires and other gems and carried on the back of a huge Bactrian camel draped in green silk brocade. There were silken banners and surrounding her were her close associates and servants, and while the bishops, deacons and monks went in front with perfumed candles, behind her were the patriarchs. In the church she took her seat on a chair of fresh aloes wood, while Mauhub sat in front of her on a similar chair. The Gospel was recited over them and they received the Sacrament. Mahliya was displayed before Mauhub in thirty different dresses and on every day fresh food and wine was provided. Everyone sat at their tables and the rich were treated luxuriously while the palace was filled with crowds.

This went on for a full month until Mahliya gave presents to those who came before her in order of rank, after which she sent them back to their homes. Another banquet was then prepared for the white-footed gazelle and Haifa', who were given an apartment of their own, while the lion, the lioness and her cubs were given a district in the land of al-Samawa, where every lion now is a descendant of theirs, as before that there were none there at all. The vizier who had built the palace was given a special position amongst his colleagues. He was entrusted with the queen's secrets and was given a door to the palace that is known by his name.

Mahliya dispensed justice amongst her people and enjoyed a good reign. The death of Shimrakh was marked by universal mourning, and, on hearing the news, Mauhub was greatly grieved, but he had no wish to exchange kingdoms. He and his wife remained in the enjoyment of comfort and pleasure, guarding against all dangers.

The wedding had been attended by all the sorcerers, men and women alike, and the daughter of a sorceress, named Bahram, had fallen in love at the sight of Mauhub. She had never known or seen any man before, as she had been kept in seclusion in her mother's castle, and as her love grew, she found it unendurable. After the marriage Mahliya had instructed her learned men and the rest of her people that no single sorcerer, sorceress or soothsayer should enter any of the districts of Egypt. This was because, knowing the strength of their magic, she was afraid for Mauhub. As God, however, wished to fulfil His purpose, Mauhub told her that he wanted to look at the deserts of Upper Egypt and hunt game there. She allowed him to go where he wanted, sending with him the chiefs of her people and a number of servants with hawks, Indian falcons, dogs and hunting panthers, together with tents, horses, mules, camels and everything else that might be needed.

He set off on his hunting trip and when he got to the city of Ansina, the home of the sorceress al-Kharsa', he pitched his tents. When al-Kharsa' saw that he was camping in her land she sent him magnificent gifts as well as wealth. After a very successful hunt in the desert there, he came back highly pleased to his camp and, after eating and drinking, he spent the night there. While it was dark, Bahram, the daughter of al-Kharsa', came to see him and what she saw of his radiant beauty refreshed the love that she felt for him in her heart, and she fell under the control of Iblis. As she could not get to him because of the numbers of his men, she started to sob and weep until she collapsed in a faint. On seeing this, her mother told her not to hold anything back but to tell her why she was so sad.

Bahram said: 'When I went to the wedding of Mauhub and Mahliya, I was inflamed with love for Mauhub, but I have concealed it for all this time. When I saw him now this love was renewed. I am afraid that I shall die of it and I don't know what to do.' Her mother had pity on her and told her to console herself and not to despair. 'I shall trick him,' she said, 'and keep Mahliya away from him.' In fact, al-Kharsa' envied Mahliya her throne and opposed her rule, and so when Mauhub came back from hunting and rested in exhaustion, she sent him perfume in a golden chest and asked him to use it in place of any other, so that she might know that he valued her.

He replied, agreeing to this, but when he used some of the perfume he turned into a crocodile and slipped into the river. Next morning his companions looked for him in vain and when they asked about him they could find no trace of him or hear any news. They all returned to their mistress, weeping sorrowfully with torn clothes and loud lamentations. 'Damn you,' she said, 'what is this and what has happened to you?' They told her that they had lost their master, who had totally disappeared, and this so distressed her that she changed her clothes to white and black wool, making everyone in the palace do the same, and while she lamented she abandoned all food and drink.

She then sent a message to the leaders of the sorcerers, ordering them to search for Mauhub, and they scattered through the lands, populated and uninhabited, deserts, valleys and fertile plains, with no success whatsoever. Every day Mahliya's sorrow grew and worsened, and in her despair she recited elegies, amongst them being the lines:

> Are you far from me or near,
> Wounded, or dead, or carried off?
> I wish I was a cross hung around his neck,
> That I might taste the pleasure of his scent,
> Or that I was a doctor and might feel his tender hand.

She also recited:

> I wish that I might share his suffering,
> That I were blind, or in the grave with him.

Then she said:

> I wish that I might come to kiss his mouth,
> And feel the gaps between his teeth,
> Or would I were a cave for him to shelter in,
> A belt around his waist as token of his faith,
> A sacrifice, to mix with spittle in his mouth.

While she was weeping for him, Mauhub was with Bahram, the daughter of al-Kharsa', resting on the shore of the river under her castle walls in the shape of a crocodile. When night fell al-Kharsa' brought him out to her daughter, restoring him to his handsome shape, dressing him in fine clothes and anointing him with the finest perfume. She gave him a splendidly bedecked seat and strained the best wine for him. The two of them ate and drank in luxury, and when dawn broke she turned him back into a crocodile, and he stayed where he had been.

Things went on like this for seven successive years, but at the end of this time a boat on its way to Cairo with a merchant on board passed where the crocodile was. A wind got up, and as those on board feared to be wrecked they anchored by the crocodile. As they were looking at the disturbed waves of the Nile, it raised its head, and the merchant saw that it had yellow ears, in which were two huge pearls. In his amazement he went close to it but he told no one about this until he reached Cairo, where he sold his goods. When he told the story of the crocodile, Mahliya's agents disbelieved him, but they told their mistress, and when she heard of the crocodile with pearls in its ears she summoned the sorcerers and soothsayers and asked them whether they had ever heard of such a thing in their own lands, and they all agreed that they never had.

Mahliya ordered ships to be brought up, and she took with her on board her particular favourites from amongst the soothsayers, viziers and sorcerers, as well as the merchant who had seen the crocodile. She sailed to Ansina, and the merchant showed her where the crocodile had been, opposite which was the castle of al-Kharsa' and her daughter Bahram. She had an inner feeling that the crocodile must have been Mauhub and so she arrested Bahram and her mother, as well as all the sorcerers of Ansina, putting them to various tortures. One of Bahram's maids acknowledged what her mistress had done with Mauhub, as she herself was in love with him and was jealous of Bahram.

Bahram was tortured by Mahliya until she confessed and removed Mauhub from the shore of the Nile in his proper shape and his finery, releasing him from his spell. Mahliya embraced him, and they both indulged in protracted tears. Both Bahram and her mother were carried off in chains; their castle was demolished and their wealth plundered. When Mahliya returned to her own palace all the different classes of Cairenes asked to have the prisoners transferred to them so that they could charge themselves with their punishment and torture them. Mahliya thanked them, distributing alms and splendid robes of honour, and she gave thanks to God, Who had given her back Mauhub.

She crucified the sorceress al-Khansa' alive and had arrows shot at her until she died, and she had weights tied to Bahram and had her drowned in the Nile. It is said – and God knows better – that for a number of years before that the Nile flood had not reached its full height but in the year that Bahram was drowned it peaked at sixteen cubits. This led to the custom whereby a virgin decked in finery was drowned in the Nile every year until the caliphate of 'Umar b. al-Khattab, may God be pleased with him. He had a potsherd inscribed with the words: 'In the Name of God, the Compassionate, the Merciful: Nile, if it is thanks to the power and strength of the Great and Glorious God that you flow, then continue to do so, but if this is thanks to your own might, then we have no need of you. Farewell.' In fact, the power of God made it reach its peak, and up to this day the Egyptians have had no need to drown their daughters. God knows better what is hidden.

Mauhub enjoyed the most comfortable and carefree of lives for eighty years, during which Mahliya built him a palace called al-Nazar, in which she lived alone with him, and for all those years they enjoyed their life together, although no son was born to her. He died in his bed, and she lamented him long and deeply, burying him in the royal cemetery of the Pyramids. On her orders his palace was demolished and all its contents dispersed, while she herself lived for long in a hut made of palm branches, visiting his tomb and returning to her hut, where she lived off herbs. The government of the country was entrusted to her vizier. Haifa' and the white-footed gazelle died and were buried beside Mauhub.

There was a dispute amongst the soothsayers and sorcerers as to who should succeed her on the throne, and this quarrel led to a war, in which they all perished. The men of learning and the chiefs forbade further fighting and said that power should rest in the hands of a single person, lest they destroy themselves. Al-Munzara al-Sabiya was appointed ruler with authority over them, and hers was the castle which you have taken, emir. She built it on the foundations of a single tower of Mahliya's palace, and lived there. The ruined water channels were dug out and trees planted, while the place was entrusted to a companion of hers named al-Sukkar, an excellent old man, but the place, which still exists, is named after Mahliya's vizier.

This is the story of the castle, may God prosper the emir. All the lions throughout the districts of Egypt are descended from the lioness that suckled Mauhub, as the sorcerers used talismans to keep them from Mahliya's palace and its surrounds.

'Amr approved the story told him by Matrun the monk and rewarded him generously.

This is the story of Mahliya, Mauhub, Haifa', the white-footed gazelle, the lion and the lioness. Praise be to the One God, and blessings and peace rest on Muhammad, his family and his companions!

Glossary

Abbasid the dynasty of caliphs that succeeded the Umaiyads and which ruled from Baghdad over the heartlands of Islam from 750 to 1258.

'Abd al-'Aziz ibn Marwan (d.702). the son of the Umaiyad caliph Marwan, who made him governor of Egypt. Brother of 'Abd al-Malik ibn Marwan.

'Abd al-Malik ibn Marwan Umaiyad caliph 685–705.

'Abd al-Wahhab (ibn Ibrahim) a nephew of the Abbasid caliph al-Mansur (754–75).

Abu'l-Hasan 'Ali see 'Ali son of Abu Talib.

Abu Murra 'The Father of Bitterness', an epithet for Iblis, the Devil.

Abu Qubais a hill at Mecca.

Ahl al-kitab literally 'people of the book', the adherents of a revealed religion, that is to say, Christians and Jews.

'Ain al-Shams Heliopolis was originally an ancient Egyptian town (Iunu) but today is effectively a suburb of the much later foundation of Cairo.

'Aja'ib wondrous things, marvels.

'Ali son of Abu Talib (or 'Ali ibn Abi Talib) cousin and son-in-law of the Prophet, an early convert to Islam and caliph from 656 to 661. He introduces himself in the adventures of Miqdad as Abu'l-Hasan 'Ali.

al-Ma'mun Abbasid caliph who reigned from 813 to 833. The son of Harun al-Rashid, al-Amin was deposed after a fierce civil war and killed by his brother al-Ma'mun.

'Amiri dinars the name that the people gave to dinars minted by the last Abbasid caliphs in the early thirteenth century. So called because they bore the legend 'Amir al-Mu'minin (Commander of the Faithful).

'Ammuriya the Arabic version of Amorium, a Byzantine stronghold on the road from Constantinople which was taken by the Arabs in 838.

'Amr Son of al-'As (or 'Amr ibn al-'As) a general from the Quraish tribe who played a leading role in the Muslim conquest of Syria and Egypt.

Al-Andaran a shining stone which features in Persian traditions.

'Antar's al-Abjar 'Antar was a romance of Arab chivalry set in pre-Islamic and Islamic times. (The chronology is vague.) In the end, the faithful horse Abjar supported the corpse of 'Antar in the saddle so that he could continue to intimidate his enemies even when dead.

Antioch shirt according to the twelfth-century geographer al-Idrisi in Antioch excellent garments are made of a single weave. Though Antioch is in modern Turkey, in medieval times it was usually reckoned to be part of the province of Syria.

Arak tree or *Salvadora persica*, also known as the toothbrush tree, as Arabs used its twigs to clean their teeth.

'Arsat al-Hauz the Courtyard of the Pool. From context, a public space somewhere in Baghdad.

Ascalon a port on the coast of Palestine.

Al-Asfar 'the Yellow', an epithet conventionally applied to the Byzantines.

'Ashura a voluntary fast day on the tenth day of the month of Muharram. The anniversary of the martyrdom of Husain, the son of 'Ali son of Abu Talib, at Kerbela in 680.

Ayyam al-'Arab Battle Days (literally Days of the Arabs). The term designates the battles and skirmishes of the Arab tribes in pre-Islamic times and the stories told about those encounters.

Baal the most important god in Canaanite mythology. The word means 'lord' or 'master'. Baal features in Sura 37 of the Qur'an: 'Elias too was one of the envoys; when he said to his people, "Will you not be God-fearing? Do you call on Baal, and abandon the Best of creators?"' In Arabic the verb *ba'il* means 'to be lost in astonishment'.

Baalbek a small town in southern Lebanon, famous for its ancient ruins. The name of the place perhaps derives from the ancient god Baal.

Bahr al-Mulk Qamar The Sea of the Kingdom of the Moon.

Balkash rubies from a region in Kazakhstan.

Ban tree Oriental willow.

Banj frequently used as a generic term referring to a narcotic or knock-out drug, but sometimes the word specifically refers to henbane.

Barmecide a member of a powerful clan of Iranians who served the early Abbasid caliphs as viziers and secretaries.

Bulaq Cairo's port on the river Nile.

Burani mixture a dish composed of aubergine, lemon flavouring, tomatoes and pimento.

Burda outer garment.

Chinese iron or haematite, a valuable iron ore, often blood-red, with a red streak.

Chosroe pre-Islamic Persian emperor Kisra Anushirwan (531–79).

Dabiqi linen, Dabiqi brocade *dabiqi* is the adjective from Dabqu, a small town on the Nile Delta near Tinnis, specializing in textiles, which were sometimes embroidered with gold. Saladin collected a lot of money by taxing Dabiqi brocade.

Dailam a region of northern Iran, south of the Caspian Sea.

Dair Durta a large monastery a little to the west of Baghdad. Monasteries were conventionally celebrated in early Islamic poetry as places to get drunk in.

Damietta port on the Nile delta well known for its textile industry.

Daran a dangerous rat-like creature, unique to the story it appears in and presumably the invention of the author.

Dhimmi a Christian or a Jew under Muslim rule.

Dhu'l-Qarnain 'the Possessor of Two Horns'. The story of how he built a great wall to protect the rest of the world from the peoples of Gog and Magog, is told in the Sura of the Cave in the Qur'an. Dhu'l-Qarnain is traditionally identified with Alexander the Great, though it is not clear how he got that epithet.

Dinar a gold coin.

Dirham a silver coin of variable value, but approximately worth one twentieth of a dinar.

Diwan hall.

Fadl ibn Rabi' Harun al-Rashid's chamberlain and gaoler.

Faraj ba'd al-Shidda the genre of story devoted to the theme of 'joy after sorrow'. Such stories often have pious overtones.

Fatiha 'The Opening', the name of the first Sura of the Qur'an.

Fustat the old part of Cairo, founded by the Muslim conquerors of Egypt.

Gabriel the archangel and messenger of God, through whom the Qur'an was revealed to Muhammad.

Al-Ghadanfar al-Farisi the name Ghadanfar features in the chivalrous folk epic of 'Antar, in which Ghadanfar was the son of 'Antar by a sister of the King of Rome. Ghadanfar and his step-brother Jufran (who also had a Christian mother) fought as Crusaders. But Ghadanfar al-Farisi, Ghadanfar the Persian, makes no sense at all.

Habba a kind of food?

Al-Hajjaj ibn Yusuf (c.661–714) stern governor of Iraq for the Umaiyads.

Harun al-Rashid the Abbasid caliph who ruled from 786 to 809. He features in many of the stories of *The Thousand and One Nights*.

Hashim Hashim ibn 'Abd al-Manaf, the great-grandfather of the Prophet Muhammad. His descendants, the Banu Hashim, or the Hashimis, were one of the great Meccan families, and the Abbasids were among the Banu Hashim.

Hawazin a central Arabian tribe.

Hilla a town in Iraq founded by a Shi'ite Arab sheikh in 1102.

Hisham ibn 'Abd al-Malik the tenth Umaiyad caliph. He reigned from 724 to 743.

Hubal a pre-Islamic pagan god.

Hud a pre-Islamic prophet who features in the Qur'an. He was sent to the tribe of 'Ad to warn them to mend their ways, but they did not heed him and consequently were destroyed.

Iblis the Arabic name of the Devil. It is a matter of debate whether he should be considered as a *jinni* or an angel. In 'Sul and Shumul' he features in a bizarrely benign light.

'Id festival. There are two important festivals in the Muslim year, the 'Id al-Adha on the tenth of Dhu'l-Hijja, on which pilgrims to Mecca sacrifice animals, and the 'Id al-Fitr, the celebration that marks the end of Ramadan (the month of fasting).

'Ifrit a kind of *jinni*.

Ishaq the companion Ishaq al-Mausili (757–850), a cup companion of the caliph Harun al-Rashid, the greatest musician and composer of his age.

Israfil an archangel. Colossal in scale, he has four wings and his body is covered with hair, mouths and tongues. He holds a trumpet with which he will blow the Last Trump that will rouse men from their graves.

Ittifaqat coincidences.

Ja'far Harun's vizier. A member of the Barmecide clan, he features in several of the stories of *The Thousand and One Nights*.

Jahili of or pertaining to pre-Islamic times (literally 'ignorant').

Jaihun the Oxus or Amu Darya which flows into the Aral Sea.

Jedda a Red Sea port in the Hejaz province.

Jizya a poll tax on non-Muslims under Muslim rule.

Jubbah a long outer garment, open in the front, with wide sleeves.

Ka'ba the shrine housing the sacred black stone that is at the centre of the hajj or rituals of the pilgrimage in Mecca.

Al-Karkh a district of Baghdad where the main markets were. It became notorious for its turbulence.

Khalanj wood tree heath (Erica arborea), a hard kind of wood.

Al-Khansa' d. after 644. Khansa', or 'Snub-nose' was the nickname of Tumadir bint 'Amr, a celebrated elegiac poet, particularly famous for her laments for her brothers Sakhr and Mu'awiya, both of whom died as a result of tribal skirmishes. Very little is known about the real life of al-Khansa' and Sakhr.

Kharshana a town in the region of Malatya.

Khatti spear a spear sold in the Khatt coastal region of Bahrain and Oman. Such spears were famed for their excellence and were perhaps made in India.

Khurasan a region which in medieval times extended from eastern Persia through large parts of Afghanistan and Central Asia, as far as India.

Kinda a north Arabian tribe.

Kufa an Iraqi city founded by the Arab conquerors.

Al-Lat and al-'Uzza pre-Islamic pagan goddesses.

Mada'in or Ctesiphon, a town on the Tigris in what today is Iraq. It was the Persian capital prior to the Islamic conquest.

Magian the Iranian priestly caste in the service of Zoroaster. But often the term has the looser sense of pagan or Persian. Magians are usually villains.

Maidan an open space used as a parade ground or sports ground.

Malahim eschatological prophecies (literally 'slaughterings' or 'battlefields').

Malatiya or Melitene, a town in eastern Anatolia.

Mamluk usually a white slave soldier, often of Turkish origin. Exceptionally in 'Mahliya and Mauhub' Mahliya has Nubian mamluks in her service.

Maqam or Maqam Ibrahim, a small building near the Ka'ba in Mecca.

Marid a kind of *jinni*.

Marwaz cotton cotton from the region of Merv, an ancient city that was located in what is today Turkmenistan.

Masrur a black eunuch who was Harun al-Rashid's executioner and frequent companion in the caliph's adventures.

Mibqar a dangerous bear-like creature that swims in the sea, unique to the story it appears in and presumably the invention of the author.

Mikdad a historical figure, Mikdad ibn 'Amr was one of the first to convert to Islam. He was a Companion of the Prophet and he took part in the Battle of Badr and the conquest of Syria. But, of course, the story attached to his name in this collection is pure fiction.

Mithqal a weight approximately equal to four and a half grams.

Mu'awiya ibn Abi Sufyan the first of the Umaiyad dynasty of caliphs. He reigned from 661 to 682.

Mubashshir the name means 'messenger of good tidings'.

Muhammad ibn Sulaiman al-Hashimi an Abbasid prince who was a historical figure (d.789). A cousin of Harun al-Rashid, he was fabulously wealthy and based in Basra. But he is not known to have had a son called al-Ashraf (as in 'Ashraf and Anjab').

Mukhadram those people, especially poets, whose lifespans extended from the pre-Islamic era into the Islamic era.

Myrobalan the astringent fruit of an Indian mountain species.

Nadd incense of aloes wood, with ambergris, musk and frankincense.

Naker one of a pair of small medieval kettledrums.

Nasut and Jalut Nasut is a scribal misrendering of Talut. Jalut is the Arabic for 'Goliath' and he is referred to in Sura 2 of the Qur'an, whereas Talut was Saul's name in Islamic lore, according to which Saul led the army against Goliath, though David killed the giant.

Niqab veil.

Nisnas also *nasnas*, a half man, or a man split in two, of which only half is visible.

Parasang a Persian measure of length, something between three and four miles.

Pharaoh the personification of tyranny in the Qur'an and in Islamic folklore.

Qadi a Muslim judge.

Qaf a mountain at the end of the world.

Qais and Lubna Qais (*c*.626–89) was an early Islamic love poet whose beloved wife was unable to bear him a child. Therefore his parents forced him to divorce her. But he remained in love with her and eventually remarried her.

Qamari aloes this excellent type of aloes wood comes from India.

Al-Qarafa the cemetery area to the north and south of the Cairo Citadel. According to the twelfth-century traveller Ibn Jubayr, these cemeteries were popular with both robbers and ascetics.

Qintar a measure of weight, varying from region to region, but amounting to 100 *ratl*s.

Qirat a small weight, also a coin, one twenty-fourth of a gold *mithqal* and one sixteenth of a silver dirham.

Quraish one of the great Arabian tribes and the one to which Muhammad belonged.

Rafiqa the site of an Abbasid palace in Syria.

Rak'a in the Muslim prayer the bending of the torso from an upright position, followed by two prostrations.

Ratl a measure of weight, variable from region to region, between two and five kilograms.

Rebab a stringed instrument resembling the fiddle.

Riyal a silver coin.

Rum the Byzantine Empire.

Sabr patience or steadfastness.

Sa'id ibn al-'As an orphan who grew up in Syria under the protection of the early Umaiyads. Eventually he was appointed governor of Kufa which he administered harshly.

Saihun the Jaxartes or Darya, a central Asian river which flows into the Aral Sea.

Saj' rhymed prose.

Samannud, Sanawir and Ikhmim Towns in Egypt dating from Pharaonic times. Samannud is on the left bank of the Damietta branch of the Nile and contains the ruins of the temple of the god Onuris-Shu. Ikhmim, or Akhmim, in Upper Egypt had the reputation of being the home of Egypt's greatest sorcerers. There were a number of monasteries in its vicinity.

Samhari spear Samhar was a celebrated maker of lances which were esteemed for their elegance.

Sarha from context, a kind of musical instrument.

Serendib Sri Lanka.

Shabbara a kind of barge with an elevated cabin, used by princes and notables.

Al-Sha'bi a well-known expert on hadiths (sayings of the Prophet) who died in 723.

Shaddad legendary pre-Islamic king of the tribe of 'Ad, who in myth commanded the construction of the city of 'Iram of the Columns, intending it to rival Paradise; consequently he and his city were destroyed by God. A story of a Bedouin who rediscovered the city of 'Iram while looking for a stray camel was inserted in *The Thousand and One Nights*.

Sind the delta region of the Indus in the Indian subcontinent.

Sufi Muslim mystic.

Sultani herbs it has not proved possible to determine what kind of herbs these were.

Tabuk a station on the pilgrimage route to Mecca.

Ta'if an Arabian town in the vicinity of Mecca.

Ubulla a port on the Gulf.

'Ud lute.

'Udul plural of *'adl*, a juristic assistant assigned to a qadi.

Umaiyad the first Islamic dynasty of caliphs. It came to power in 660 after the first four 'Rightful Caliphs'. It was overthrown in 750 by the revolution that brought the Abbasids to power.

'Umar ibn al-Khattab (581–644). In 634 he became the second caliph after the Prophet. He is reckoned among the Rashidun, or 'Righteous' caliphs.

'Usfur bird.

'Uthman ibn 'Affan the third of the caliphs, he reigned from 644 to 656. Famous for his piety, he was one of the Rashidun, or 'Righteous' caliphs.

Wasit a town on the Tigris in what is today Iraq.

Yathrib the pre-Islamic name for Medina.

Zabaj Java or Sumatra.

Zakat alms tax.

Zamzam name of a well in Mecca.

Zanj black man or woman.

Zubaida the best-known of Harun al-Rashid's wives.

PENGUIN CLASSICS

THE ARABIAN NIGHTS: TALES OF 1001 NIGHTS GIFTSET
A NEW TRANSLATION BY
MALCOLM C. LYONS WITH URSULA LYONS

In a wonderful three-volume hardback slipcase, with an introduction by Robert Irwin

Every night for three years the vengeful King Shahriyar sleeps with a different virgin, executing her next morning. To end this brutal pattern and to save her own life, the vizier's daughter, Shahrazad, begins to tell the king tales of adventure, love, riches and wonder – tales of mystical lands peopled with princes and hunchbacks, the Angel of Death and magical spirits, tales of the voyages of Sindbad, of Ali Baba's outwitting a band of forty thieves and of *jinni*s trapped in rings and in lamps.

One of the best known and most influential works of literature ever written, this is the first complete translation into English of *The Arabian Nights* from the Arabic since the 1880s. It also includes new translations from eighteenth century French of the so-called 'orphan stories', for which no original Arabic text remains.

PENGUIN CLASSICS

FAIRY TALES
HANS CHRISTIAN ANDERSEN

Blending Danish folklore with magical storytelling, Hans Christian Andersen's unique fairy tales describe a world of beautiful princesses and sinister queens, rewarded virtue and unresolved desire. Rich with popular tales such as *The Ugly Duckling*, *The Emperor's New Clothes* and the darkly enchanting *The Snow Queen*, this revelatory new collection also contains many lesser-known but intriguing stories, such as the sinister *The Shadow*, in which a shadow slyly takes over the life of the man to whom it is bound.

'Truly scrumptious, a proper treasury … Read on with eyes as big as teacups'
Guardian

'With J. K. Rowling and Lemony Snicket bringing black magic to the top of today's children's literature, the moment seems ripe for a return to the original'
Newsweek

'Tiina Nunnally's wonderful new translations of Andersen are an invitation to open-ended, mind-engaging reading' Rachel Cusk

Translated by Tiina Nunnally

Edited by Jackie Wullschlager

PENGUIN CLASSICS

THE COMPLETE DEAD SEA SCROLLS IN ENGLISH
GEZA VERMES

'He will heal the wounded and revive the dead and bring good news to the poor'

The discovery of the Dead Sea Scrolls in the Judean desert between 1947 and 1956 was one of the greatest archaeological finds of all time. These extraordinary manuscripts appear to have been hidden in the caves at Qumran by the Essenes, a Jewish sect in existence before and during the time of Jesus. Written in Hebrew, Aramaic and Greek, the scrolls have transformed our understanding of the Hebrew Bible, early Judaism and the origins of Christianity.

This is a fully revised edition of the classic translation by Geza Vermes, the world's leading Dead Sea Scrolls scholar. It is now enhanced by much previously unpublished material and a new preface, and also contains a scroll catalogue and an index of Qumran texts.

'No translation of the Scrolls is either more readable or more authoritative than that of Vermes' *The Times Higher Education Supplement*

'Excellent, up-to-date ... will enable the general public to read the non-biblical scrolls and to judge for themselves their importance'
The New York Times Book Review

Translated and edited with an introduction by Geza Vermes

PENGUIN CLASSICS

THE BHAGAVAD GITA

> 'In death thy glory in heaven, in victory thy glory on earth.
> Arise therefore, Arjuna, with thy soul ready to fight'

The Bhagavad Gita is an intensely spiritual work that forms the cornerstone of the Hindu faith, and is also one of the masterpieces of Sanskrit poetry. It describes how, at the beginning of a mighty battle between the Pandava and Kaurava armies, the god Krishna gives spiritual enlightenment to the warrior Arjuna, who realizes that the true battle is for his own soul.

Juan Mascaró's translation of *The Bhagavad Gita* captures the extraordinary aural qualities of the original Sanskrit. This edition features a new introduction by Simon Brodbeck, which discusses concepts such as dehin, prakriti and Karma.

'The task of truly translating such a work is indeed formidable. The translator must at least possess three qualities. He must be an artist in words as well as a Sanskrit scholar, and above all, perhaps, he must be deeply sympathetic with the spirit of the original. Mascaró has succeeded so well because he possesses all these'
The Times Literary Supplement

Translated by Juan Mascaró with an introduction by Simon Brodbeck